# WHITE PROPHET

ৡ\*৶

Book 2 of the
Kestrel Harper Saga

ৡ\*৶

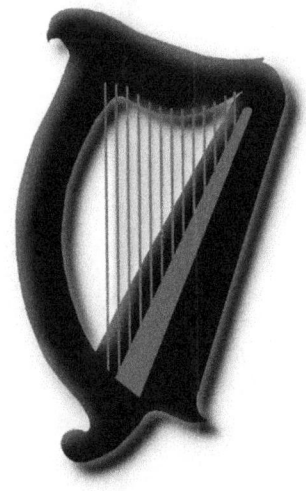

Tamara Brigham

≳*≲

*For Larry*

≳*≲

## ❧Prologue❦

S
he stood rigid against the side of the open door, under the rough-hewn tavern awning where he had been told she would be. He had only seen her one other time, the day they had met two months prior when she had freed him from his tormentors. It had been a simple misunderstanding, but one that had gotten him on the wrong side of a king and landed him in that swampy hole of a prison for more than ten years. Most did not live that long in such conditions, but he had been determined to survive, survive and escape. He did not know her, did not know why she had picked him for rescue, and had not seen her since that overcast, thundering night; she had been no more than a shadow then, and he had not expected to ever see her again. Whatever price she would extract from him would, he believed, be revealed through an intermediary, not in person. That assumption had been wrong.

He had moved on, barely giving her thought after that night. There was a lot of catching up to do, and survival had been his number one interest. When her messenger eventually caught up with him to request this meeting, he had been surprised. He could have ignored the summons, pretended he had not received her message, but he considered himself no idiot. She had paid his ransom and freed him; only a foolish man would ignore someone with as much influence and resources as she seemed to possess. He was curious to meet her, to find out why such an elegant woman had gone to the trouble of securing his liberty. She wanted something from him, and he was not going to learn what that might be if he refused to meet. There was no harm in a meeting. His instructions had brought him to this distant place, where he had expected to be kept waiting too long for her arrival. That she was here told him that whatever she wanted from him had to be important.

"So...what do you want with me?" he asked, a bit more snappishly than intended. He did not want her to think he was so easily manipulated as to jump to her beck and call. "You expect something for getting me out of that pit; what is it?"

Pushing her short dark hair behind her ear, she blinked as she stared at him, and he almost believed she had not heard him or did not understand his words. Her face was unresponsive and blank. Great. A foreigner who did not speak Trade. Everyone spoke Trade, didn't they? She blinked again, her hand still lingering at her ear. He started to speak but she cocked her head, waited a few more seconds, and then said, "There is a woman inside. Elyri. I want you to follow her."

He stared back. Of all the requests she could have made, that was it? Or was this some sort of test? He scowled, shook his head. "Simple enough...but why me? There are hundreds of people who would do that for a lot less than I'll ask of you." Smirking as he folded his arms over his chest, he added, "You might have sprung me, but I can't live off air. What does she have that you want? What has she done?"

His benefactor shook her head, seeming to match his smirk although her expression did not change, and then drew a pouch of coins from inside her worn leather vest. "My interest in her is not your concern. Your expenses will be covered, but know this...you are in no position to make demands...unless you wish to return to your last place of permanent residence."

That was a distasteful thought, but rather than show it, he merely shrugged and said, "I could simply refuse the job…go my own way…" He did no more than glance at the pouch of coins.

Her expression changed at last, the smile melting over it a disarming, seductive and vaguely menacing one that made his blood run cold. Very few people had that effect on him. "Yes…you could…but you won't." Her arm dropped to her side and the pouch slipped from her hand, clinking and jingling as it hit the dust at her feet. "I chose you because of your connections. You have access to what I want."

"And that is?" Something seemed to distract her, or she was bored; her narrow face turned and her gaze wandered away from him to fix upon some point further down the street, on something he could not see. Frustrated with her avoidance, he hissed, "Listen, lady…"

"I want the Káliel Serpents," she said softly.

Again, he stared. This woman was insane. The Serpents were of little value outside of Káliel. What could she possibly want with those brooches? "All of them?" She did not speak but bent to retrieve the bag of coins. He did not dare look away from her as she stuffed the pouch back inside her vest. Who knew what else she might carry under there. He was not interested in making any costly mistakes.

"One should not be a problem; I can get it easily enough. If this woman inside has another, no problem there either. I'll get them for you. The other will be trickier and it could take some time…maybe a year or more. If I do this…what is in it for me?"

"Your freedom," she replied with a bored yawn.

He snorted. "I've been free for two months. I may not want to go back there, but freedom isn't all it's touted to be. At least I had a guaranteed roof over my head and usually a daily meal." Truthfully, he managed to always have better than average shelter and filling meals when he wanted them, but he did not see the need to tell her that.

☙ ❧

"Come now…you hardly look to be in danger of starvation…and I know you are resourceful. I have been watching you; I know what you are capable of. But, if payment is what you desire, you shall have it. This, now," she brought the coin pouch back out, "and more to come. The Serpents are keys to the burial site of my…someone I must find. The treasure buried there is of little consequence. Bring me the Serpents and two-thirds of the treasure shall be yours. I warn you, however…" She pulled the offered purse away as he reached for it. "Fail to bring the Serpents to me, pursue the treasure on your own and it will mean your destruction."

Leaning against the tavern wall as a group of men staggered drunkenly out of the establishment and into the street, he considered her offer. A treasure? Obtained so easily? It might be a trap, or turn out to be a worthless treasure, but it was worth investigating. What more could a man just free from ten years' incarceration ask for? Expenses paid while he did the job, and, if he played his cards right, the chance to keep all of the treasure for himself. He was nothing if not greedy.

"I'll accept the job…on the terms you've offered. How do I reach you when I need more money? Where do I bring the Serpents when I have them?"

She waved a hand dismissively. "I will know when you have them…and I shall find you. Be thorough, be careful, and take as long as you need; I am in no hurry. Do not waste my money, however…and do not betray me."

"On my honor," he said, bowing, as she slid away, leaving the heavy purse in his hand. Fortunately, he thought, noting that she had not answered his question about money, honor is the one thing I lack.

# ❧Chapter 1❧

Lord High Justice Minos Cornell rolled over the woman's limp body, noting the pool of blood already becoming viscous from prolonged exposure to the air. The body was cold, though no longer stiff; she had been dead for a considerable amount of time. She appeared to be perhaps twenty years old, though he would never hazard a guess as to her actual age, and of enough wealth to afford the gown of blue velvet she wore, which was now tattered and stained. There was little unusual about her, she could have been any woman out of a thousand, except for one glaring detail. She was Elyri.

Beside the justice, the sheriff was relating how the woman was found in the merchant wagon an hour before the justice arrived. The wagon's owner was questioned but claimed no knowledge of the woman or how she had come to be there. The merchant arrived in Rhidam from Levonne four days ago and unloaded his wares upon his arrival. The wagon had been stored here ever since. Today, as he prepared to return to Levonne, he had discovered the corpse he believed had been haphazardly dumped into his wagon. He searched for signs of life and, finding none, sent immediately for the authorities. The sheriff would have dealt with the incident alone, as he normally did, if not for the fact that she was Elyri and bore an unusual triple-branched stab wound in her abdomen. He had never seen any weapon

❧ ✺❧

that could leave a wound like that and he felt it worth bringing to the attention of the justice.

The justice had never seen a wound like it either. As he studied it, drawing back the torn corners of fabric to inspect the area more closely, something gnawed at his gut, something he could not remember that should be able to explain this. Finding nothing more on her body, he examined the wagon bed where she had laid, and then the ground around the wagon, squatting, at last, to touch the scuff marks in the dirt and sawdust with his fingers. There was blood there too, and on the edge of the wagon bed, drops and smears that suggested more than was immediately obvious.

"Take her to Physician Sorvis to determine cause of death."

"She was stabbed, milord," the sheriff scoffed. "I think the cause is obvious."

Minos shook his head. "No, there's more to this, Harle. The wound is such that yes, she could have died from it, but you said yourself no one in the vicinity heard or saw anything. She made it here of her own volition, after being assaulted," he pointed to the blood in the wagon, "and climbed in on her own when no one would notice…probably during the night. There is blood on the ground, but not much…with all of the foot traffic, it's a wonder there's any. I do not know how far she could have walked with a wound like that, but I want everyone in the area questioned again about anything unusual they might have seen in the last few days…not just recently. Assume she traveled no more than a day with that injury and talk to everyone within that radius." He knew that included most of Rhidam and some of the outlying lands, but this was important. "I will bring this to the King and inquire how he wishes to proceed."

That pronouncement made the sheriff shift nervously. "Is it necessary to bring His Majesty into this?"

"There is something about this that does not present as a random, typical murder. She is Elyri; it has been many years since an Elyri was killed in Rhidam. She is still in possession of her valuables, or so it would seem; see…she still has her purse and it is full of coins." He thrust his hand inside and drew some of them out. He whistled. "Elyri bhelts at that. This was no robbery…"

"Maybe she escaped her attacker before he could take it, or he was interrupted," the sheriff offered. "Or perhaps the thief had no use for bhelts."

The justice shook his head as he put the coins back in the pouch and hung it from his belt. He was not about to leave that with the body. Someone would make off with it if he did. "Perhaps…but with the rate of exchange, I would think any thief looking for valuables would want them. This matter requires deeper investigation, and I need His Majesty's permission to assign more men to it. I will wait, however, until Physician Sorvis has a chance to look her over…and the King is free to meet. You have until then to see to this matter yourself."

Coin purse secured, Minos left the scene, brow furrowed in thought. They had yet to break the surface of this mystery, and he suspected that whatever they found beneath it would bode ill for many.

The light of the late afternoon sun filtered through the sparse growth of leaves on the ancient, gnarled oak, casting a kaleidoscope of patterns upon the damp carpet of fresh grass. In the boughs above, a pair of red-breasted blackbirds was building a sturdy nest to house the young birds to come. Spring had been slow in coming this year, but the newly budding leaves and the scatter of saffron and cream that dotted the meadow heralded its final arrival in Enesfel. A dozen peasants toiled in the field far to their right, cultivating the tender vermillion shoots that pushed through the moist soil in their search for nourishing sunlight. The first crop of the year. There had been heavy rain the week before, and though it had not rained in several days, the ground still held the water, and the morning air was thick with cool fog, making the task of finding a dry spot to rest, even beneath the midday sun, a difficult one.

The dampness had not hindered the nine individuals and horses sheltered near the immense oak. They had braved the day's discomforts for the chance of freedom in the open air, if only for a few hours. Four of the nine stood apart, were armed with bows, knives, and swords, and continuously scanned the horizon for any indication of danger. Their bearing and attire revealed their royal occupation, and their nearly identical expressions of calm menace foretold doom to anyone who cared to cross them.

Of the remaining five, four were children. Two wrestled in the wet grass several feet from the tree, emitting grunts of exertion, frustration, and occasional pain. The other two children rested quietly, one focused on the birds in the tree, the other more interested in the ninth individual watching over them. That man rested with his back against the tree trunk with a kestrel-shaped Cliáthan quarter-scale harp of glistening black wood resting tenderly upon his knees. The harper's white hands caressed the brass strings, producing a tinkling melodic song akin to that sung by the birds in the boughs above. His concentration was divided, however, as he kept his eyes trained upon the children wrestling nearby.

At the earliest sign of the queen's labor, he had done his best to occupy the children, eventually taking them out of the palace and out of the way of either their parents or the two court Healers. They had brought their noon meal with them and the children had slept briefly upon the thick wool blankets their guardian had brought. Now they were enjoying their afternoon of freedom. Such occasions were rare for the children of royalty. No doubt, the guards were less than pleased about spending their day attending children, but that was the duty they had been charged with and none of them would willingly defy the

King's order. Nor would they argue with the harper, although whether out of fear or respect, he did not know.

As for the white-skinned Elyri, he did not mind the duty. He had accepted the role of tutor for the royal children years ago when Muir Innis had reached a teachable age. The thirteen-year-old blonde prince reclined beside him, watching the birds, humming softly to himself, his handsome face creased with unvoiced concern. Nine-year-old Diona Cordelia also stayed beside the harper, resting her head of black curls on Muir's lap, her eyes never leaving the face of their tutor. Bertram Earl, better known as Bertie to his family, Diona's twin brother and the heir-apparent to the Lachlan throne, was soundly defeating his eight-year-old cousin Wilred Douglas Dugan in their wrestling bout. No doubt, sighed the harper, the royal women would be annoyed at the sorry state of their children's clothes, but he did not try to stop them yet. They were worried about the queen and the children needed their own ways to release that festering tension. He could think of no better way than the freedom of this outing and much needed physical activity, though Prince Bertram's tendency towards violence disturbed him.

With a victorious squeal, the larger of the two wrestling princes threw the other to the ground and kept him pinned, squirming, until he surrendered.

"Your turn, Muir," cried Prince Bertram, grinning triumphantly as Prince Wilred picked himself up out of the mud.

The thirteen-year-old shook his head and did not get up. "I do not want to wrestle with you, Bertie."

Prince Bertram wiped his muddy hands on his shirt as he came towards the tree. "You never want to wrestle with me. Afraid you will lose?" Near enough now, he hit Prince Muir in the shoulder with seeming playfulness, though with enough force to push the older prince back against the tree.

ॐ๙

"He is older and bigger than you are," Princess Diona snorted, sitting up and shoving her small fist into Prince Bertram's stomach. It looked far less playful than the blow he had given Prince Muir. Surprised by the power behind her unexpected punch, the heir stepped away from his sister with a scowl. "He is almost a man; you are still a child," she added. "You wouldn't win."

The back of his mud-smeared hand swiped across Prince Bertram's face. "You always say that," he whined, "but he never proves it."

"I do not have to prove anything to you," Prince Muir said with a shrug.

"Then prove it to yourself. I don't think you could beat me if you tried," the heir challenged.

Prince Muir looked at the man seated beside him. "What do you say, Lord Cliáth? Should I accept the challenge?"

Kavan Cliáth, their tutor, set his harp into its case. Princess Diona promptly climbed into his lap and snuggled against his chest. He put one arm around her as he looked from one prince to the other. "You do not need to wrestle if you do not desire to, my prince. It is your choice and your right to decline if you wish."

"You always take his side," Prince Wilred whined, shaking out his mud-encrusted blonde curls. He was annoyed that no one else took a pounding at the hands of the crown prince, but his annoyance never stopped him from engaging in those mock combats whenever the chance arose.

"Not a true prince…" Prince Bertram started, but he stopped when the bard's head snapped towards the east. "What is it, Lord Cliáth?" The children knew from experience that their Elyri tutor had an uncanny knack of knowing things before they happened. He was looking in the direction of home though they could see nothing around them except the guards, the peasants, and the meadow in which they rested.

Kavan paused, his eyes closed as he sorted the images in his head into some sort of logical order. The Sight did not always come in a linear fashion. When at last he opened them, he said, "We may return to the keep. Muir, Bertram, Diona…your brother has been born."

There was a faintly miserable flicker in Prince Muir's eyes but the eldest prince said nothing. Princess Diona clapped her hands, thrilled at the prospect of a new baby and not yet aware, or concerned with the fact that another male heir lowered her chance of ruling Enesfel. She was not old enough to understand or care about things such as that.

Prince Bertram yawned and shrugged. "It does not matter what it is, Lord Cliáth. I cannot wrestle with a baby. Why should I care?"

"A brother is a blessing I never knew," the Elyri replied, standing and motioning their escorts to the grazing horses. He tousled the princess's hair. "Nor, for that matter, have I ever had a sister. I would have been pleased with either. You should be honored and happy that he lives. Besides, he is nine years younger than you. It would not be proper for you to behave roughly with one that much younger until he is old enough to fend for himself. Now come; mount up. We shall return to the castle and welcome him. I do not want to hear any more discussion about Muir's family status, is that understood, Prince Bertram?"

The boy skewed his face, sighed, and then said, "Yes, sir."

Once he had helped the princess onto her horse, Kavan turned to Prince Wilred, who was too short to mount his new pony, and secured him in the saddle. There was a surprised squawk and the princess's cry behind him, and Kavan turned in time to see Prince Bertram drive Muir to the ground, pummeling him with small fists. Prince Wilred's enthusiastic shout of support was cut short by the bard's sharp gaze. One guard pulled Prince Bertram away, kicking and screaming, as Kavan knelt beside Prince Muir.

"He is not your brother! Diona is not your sister!" the young dark-haired prince shouted. "You are not a Lachlan, not a prince, not my brother! You are a coward and..." The guard holding him clamped one stout hand over the prince's mouth and tried to ignore the pain as the boy's teeth sunk into him.

Kavan helped Muir to his feet, noticing that the boy's nose was swelling and one eye was already beginning to discolor. He was limp and disoriented and seemed unable to stand on his own, and so the bard supported his weight. "Prince Bertram, Prince Wilred, enough. We will return to the keep at once. You too, my princess. No more of this; not another word. I will bring Muir."

With the help of one of the escorting soldiers, he mounted his white horse, took Prince Muir from the man's arms and followed the slow-moving horses of the other children. Prince Wilred was quietly chewing on his lip, and though no longer held by the stalwart guard, Prince Bertram too had grown subdued in response to the Elyri's tone of voice. The princess looked straight ahead, tears sliding down her cheeks. They loved their tutor dearly and knew he was displeased with their behavior; even if she had not actually done anything, she had been unable to stop her brother, and that was bad enough for her. They rode back to Rhidam in silence.

Harp strapped snuggly to his horse, Kavan steered the animal with his knees as his hands were preoccupied with brushing the mud from his charge's face. He did not speak and ignored, for now, the apologetic expressions of the other boys. He should apologize to the princess for snapping at her when she had been innocent of wrongdoing, but he did not feel that this was the time.

It was always the same, he thought with a weary sigh. He admitted to himself that Muir was his favorite of the royal children; Kavan had made peace with the boy's father when the man had been expelled from Enesfel in disgrace. Prince Muir was not responsible for the circumstances of his conception and birth, and it was Kavan's support and the queen's love for her son that allowed him any of the advantages the other children shared. Knowing firsthand how it felt to be without a parent's love, having seen the effect of similar circumstances on Muir's father, Kavan had been determined to be the boy's shelter and anchor as Ártur and Tíbhyan had been his.

When Prince Bertram had been younger, there had been fewer difficulties and Diona had been able to keep her twin under control. However, as he had grown older and understood that his brother was not a part of the family in the way Bertram and Diona were, the heir had become increasingly belligerent and cruel to his older brother. His continual taunting and bullying pushed Muir further away until the eldest prince no longer associated with most of the royal family, save for his mother and Princess Diona. Kavan knew that before long, when he was old enough to make such decisions for himself, Prince Muir would decide to leave home.

"Lord Cliáth?" the shallow voice coughed.

Kavan caressed the boy's forehead with his palm. "Rest, my prince. Do not talk."

Prince Muir shivered at the emotion in his tutor's nearly androgynous voice. Kavan normally kept his feelings hidden. To hear them now, to hear his sadness, disappointment, and fear, was heartbreaking. "My nose hurts."

The bard nodded. "Ártur will tend to it."

"I am sorry…"

"There is nothing for you to…"

The prince interrupted. "I provoked that. I said it would be good to have another boy in the family, one who would be nicer, even if he is not my brother…"

Kavan looked at him sternly. "This baby is your brother, Muir. You have the same mother. Words are no excuse for violence; a bully acts out of cowardice and fear. I will see that Bertram is dealt with appropriately."

"Father will not punish him." Prince Muir was resigned to it and knew from Kavan's failure to reply that the Elyri was too. "Do you think I am a coward?"

"Not wishing to fight does not make one a coward. I do not espouse violence…"

"Father always says you are the bravest man he knows. But…even Diona hits Bertie when he gets mean. I do not. He is a boy; I am nearly a man and I cannot defend…"

Kavan interrupted him with a serious shaking of his head. "You can. I have watched you train with Lord Cáner. I know you have the capability and skill. But you are also wise, Muir, and do not allow yourself to be goaded by Bertram's bullying. That can be difficult. It takes strength and courage to resist the temptation to give in to someone else taunts."

It sounded to the prince as though the harper had firsthand experience with bullies, but he saw no indication on Kavan's face that it was true. Surely the man's voice and his fair, unusual features would have brought some measure of torment, whether as a child or as a man. Muir relaxed, knowing better than to question his tutor about personal issues, and remained quiet for the remainder of the journey home.

They reached the castle gatehouse, still not speaking as they crossed the bridge into the courtyard, despite the greetings some of the palace staff offered. Though tempted to leave the other children in the hands of the attending guards and groomsmen who came for the horses, Kavan waited, helping steady Muir until each of them were assisted from their horses. They stood before him, heads bowed, waiting to be dismissed. "Clean yourselves, bathe and change your clothing before your parents see you. I will see to the queen's condition and let you know if you are permitted into her chambers."

"Will you tell Father about…?" Bertram's incorrigible demeanor had fallen away and he appeared to be the proper prince he was.

His sister growled and shot him a sour look. "Do you think he should not? You were told not to fight anymore."

Kavan interrupted her well-intentioned tirade in a calmer tone. "He will inquire how Muir's nose came to be broken, and I will not lie to him." Prince Bertram hung his head. "You owe Muir an apology."

Shuffling his feet, the prince shot his tutor an exasperated look but reluctantly muttered, "I apologize, Muir…"

"Sound like you mean it," started the princess, but she stopped upon seeing Kavan's perturbed expression. She wanted to get back in his good graces, but tattling on her twin was not the way to do it.

"I forgive you," Prince Muir responded, knowing as well as his sister, and Kavan, that she was correct. Bertram did what was asked of him, but without any true sincerity.

Sighing, Kavan said, "Go. Clean yourselves; I shall be with you shortly." He watched the three younger children head away at varying speeds, with Muir following behind them, dragging his feet though keeping his head high. Even in retreat, their personalities were evident to the bard and he wished again that he was not good at reading people.

He went to his room, intending to change into fresh clothing, and stopped inside the doorway before the great tapestry that hung upon his wall, taking a few moments to touch the ancient velvety softness of the cloth from which it was made. He had brought it with him from his home in Elyriá when he took up residence in Rhidam; it was one of the few treasures he owned. It had been a gift from bhydáni Tíbhyan and he could not imagine leaving it abandoned in his currently empty Bhryell house.

He was intimately familiar with the imagery now, the auburn-haired shepherd in the dusty gray cloak perched upon a boulder near a gnarled tree. His left foot was twisted under him awkwardly, his lameness obvious. He held a harp upon his lap and was surrounded by his flock as he gazed up at Dhágdhuán hovering before him with bleeding wrists and outstretched hands. There were gossamer záryph in the twilight sky, their wings of black, silver, and gold encircling the Intercessor. The color of their wings still disturbed Kavan; it was the sole depiction of those magical, mystical beings he had ever seen where their wings were not ivory in hue, though it was true to Kóráhm's description of the záryph that appeared to him. Knowing the identity of that shepherd was enough to comfort his uneasiness, however. It almost made him smile to look upon a face he had not seen in many years. The tranquility and joy he felt when studying this scene always threatened to pull him into it, a feeling he did not entirely object to any longer and that he often welcomed. Right now, however, he touched his fingers to his forehead, his heart, and then his lips before finding a clean robe to wear and leaving the room.

King Arlan's chamber was empty when Kavan reached it, but he could hear voices from the queen's adjoining room to the right. It was logical the King would be with his wife. Kavan wondered, as he stood before the window, how she and the new child were doing. Ártur MacLyr, Kavan's cousin and the court's lead healer, had warned her against bearing more children after the difficulties she had experienced during her previous pregnancies. She had come near to dying during the birth of Bertram and Diona, and her two consecutive children had been stillborn. Both of those labors had been extraordinarily difficult for the queen, and she had been weak and indisposed for many weeks afterward. Yet, despite all of the precautions taken, she had conceived again and had spent much of the nine months of her pregnancy in bed to lessen the chances of complications. Pulling the silver Kílyn Cross from beneath his robes, Kavan sat in the chair nearest the window, clasped his hands around it, and began to pray that both mother and child were healthy and safe.

Thankfully, the thirteen years since Arlan had wrested the throne from King Owain, had been peaceful and reasonably stable. The large number of deaths from the battles of that year, the cruelty and foolishness of Owain's immediate predecessors, and the plague of more than twenty years before had all taken their toll on the kingdom's productivity, resulting in near-famine conditions for the seven years following Arlan's ascension. Thanks to the hard work of the population and emergency assistance from the kingdoms of Hatu, Cordash, and Elyriá, Enesfel was strong again and on its way to full recovery.

"Welcome back, sínréc." The healer came from the other room, disheveled and tired looking, as though he carried a great weight upon his shoulders. "I suspected you would be here."

Kavan did not respond to that comment. "How are they?" he asked instead, preferring to focus on the queen and child rather than himself.

The healer started to wring his hands but let them drop limply to his sides. "The child is well. He is healthy and his chances of survival are excellent. I fear the queen's odds are not as good. It was an extremely difficult labor as before; she is feverish and has lost much blood. I have stopped the bleeding for now, but I fear it may not be enough to save her."

The bard's green eyes closed. "Does Arlan know?"

"He is with them," the healer replied. "I told him before he went in. We are searching for a wet nurse; the Lady will be unable to nurse the babe until her fever breaks, and perhaps not even then." He caught the pained expression that crossed his cousin's face as Kavan rose from the chair and faced the window. Guessing that his cousin had Seen something, though hoping he had not, he asked, "Kavan?" The younger man did not reply. "What is it? What do you See?"

"She will die, Ártur." The bard's voice was weak and small. There was a note of desperate finality to his words that Ártur did not like.

"She may pull through this. She has before; she can do it again. It is too early to make such conclusions…" Yet despite his hopeful protests, the healer knew his cousin would be correct. Kavan would not have spoken his thoughts aloud if he did not believe it.

"May the children see her?"

"It would be best if they do…if it is as you say…" A soft knock on the door interrupted and drew Ártur's attention away. "Prince Muir!" he exclaimed when he saw the condition of the prince's face. "What has happened?"

The prince entered and stopped before the healer. "It is nothing, Lord Healer, though I would appreciate it if you would attend to it."

Because Kavan did not turn, did not seem surprised by the prince's condition, Ártur presumed it had happened while they had been out of the castle. It was not difficult to deduce it was the likely result of an altercation with Prince Bertram. He laid one hand delicately over the boy's nose and eyes, and after several minutes of holding it there, his hand fell away.

"The damage is healed but the bruising will remain; you will have to endure that and the black eye for a few more days."

The prince bowed his head. "Thank you." After looking at the two men, he asked, "May I see my mother and the baby?"

After what had transpired earlier, it was difficult for Kavan not to notice that the prince did not refer to the new infant as his brother. He sighed, turned from the window as Ártur nodded in agreement, and motioned for the prince to follow him into the queen's chamber.

The room was dark save for the glow of a single candle burning beside the bed. Though the heavy velvet amber curtains were tied to the bedposts, the gauze was down on three sides, effectively shielding the queen from prying eyes. The prince came around the end of the bed and stopped, watching his mother caress the baby's red cheeks as the King's hand stroked her arm. The prince moved no further and Kavan stopped behind him with his hands protectively upon the boy's shoulders. They stood quietly for many moments until the queen looked up and met first Kavan's gaze and then Muir's.

"Muir…" she whispered, her voice weak and strained.

The whisper made the King start and turn. "Muir! What are you…?"

The prince cringed back against Kavan's body and the bard's hands tightened upon him. "Ártur says it is permissible for him to see his mother," Kavan began.

"I do not care what Ártur says; I do not want him to tire her."

The queen's free hand clasped her husband's wrist. "He may stay." The royal couple stared at each other, sharing well-practiced silent communication, and then the King got up with a huff. The woman smiled and held her hand to Muir. "Come. Meet your brother Hagan."

Cautiously eyeing the King, giving the man a wide berth, the prince did as she bid and went to the chair where the King had been sitting. Arlan pulled Kavan's arm and drew him aside, though not out of sight of his wife and child. "He should not be here," he hissed in a low voice. "He will upset her."

"The lady is not the one upset by his company, milord," Kavan pointed out.

The King glared at him, angry because he knew his friend was right. "She needs rest. She is not strong and could…"

"Which is precisely why Ártur believes the children should see her. She is their mother; it would be cruel to deny them this opportunity if they want it. And it appears she is pleased to see him."

Running one hand through his thick, short, black beard, the King closed his eyes with a heavy sigh. It did appear that Kavan was correct, and he knew, despite his own mixed feelings, that there was a strong bond between the mother and her oldest child. He could never really argue with Kavan; no matter what the topic of discussion, the Elyri was nearly always correct. And Kavan, like his wife, would defend Muir at all cost, though he could never fully grasp why.

"What happened to his nose and eye?"

"Bertram and he fought."

"About?"

"About whether Prince Hagan is Muir's brother."

"And Bertram did that?"

Kavan felt the amusement in the King's voice, though few others would have sensed it. The King was proud of his son's boldness, if not necessarily his behavior. The bard looked at his hands then towards the baby.

"He directly disobeyed me by bringing up the subject of Muir's position, and he bit the soldier who restrained him, hard enough to draw blood and likely require healing. Regardless of how you feel about what he did to his brother, Prince Bertram must learn obedience and respect, Milord. It is in his best interest to…"

The King coughed, effectively cutting short the lecture. He still became annoyed when Kavan presumed to tell him what he should do, largely because he knew the Elyri was usually right. "Well…I…" He cleared his throat. "Bertram will have to be punished, of course. He cannot behave this way with everyone who offends him. And you are right, he knows better than to bite anyone, or disobey you."

Both men knew the words were meant to appease Kavan's sensitivities, though it was unlikely that Bertram would ever be punished, or even spoken to regarding this incident. If he was, it would not be in a way that would teach the boy a lesson, and that saddened the bard. The King was setting up his son to be a less than effective monarch, and he would have no one to blame for such failures but himself. Rather than say it, however, Kavan bowed and joined Muir at the bedside to see the new child.

"He is a handsome boy, milady," Kavan said, placing one finger against the tiny hand. The infant clutched his finger and Kavan felt a brief, familiar, faint, tingling sensation. He glanced back at the King, and then at the queen, although what he saw was neither of them. He would share this revelation with her later, perhaps, but not now.

"He will be a man to be proud of," was all he chose to say.

She smiled, her haggard features brightening. "You think so?"

Kavan nodded and squeezed her hot hand with his, feeling her relax in response. He still wondered why his touch had that effect on many people. "I know he will." Her face tightened into a grimace and he frowned. "Milady?"

She shook her head to brush away his concern. "A twinge," she said. "Please, bring Bertram and Diona. Take Arlan with you. I wish to be alone with Muir." Kavan bowed and did as she asked, pulling the King out of the room despite the man's reluctance to leave. The babe in her arms had fallen asleep. "What happened to your nose?"

"Bertie and I fought."

"Why?"

He did not want to tell her, but Muir would not lie to his mother, any more than he would lie to his tutor. "He said Hagan is not my...when I said Hagan is my brother, Bertie hit me."

"Muir," she touched his cheek. "I am mother to all of you, you are kin, siblings. Hagan is your brother. Do not take Bertie's words to heart."

"I try not to," he snorted, "but he is not very nice. It is difficult not to take his words seriously when he makes his points with his fists. I don't like him."

The queen sighed. "I know, darling, but he is your brother and you must both try to get along..." She meant to say more, to not leave him with the impression that the success or failure of his relationship with Bertram was entirely up to him, but her face twisted painfully as she suppressed a cough and her hand clutched her belly.

"Mother? Are you well...?"

"It was a difficult birth, Muir...I may not live..." Perhaps she should have given him false hope, but she did not believe in lying to him either, even to spare his feelings.

"No!" He lurched to his feet, away from her hand. "Do not say it. You will live. You must live."

"Darling...you know this was not easy for me before...and that there was great danger in this pregnancy. Lord MacLyr is doing all he can; the rest is up to k'Ádhá. You must promise you will do your best to…"

Kavan had entered the room again and knocked on the bed frame, returning with the twins at his side. She did her best to smile and beckoned them to sit on the bed with her.

"You must promise that you will take care of Hagan." It had not been what she intended to say to Muir, but it was something she wanted all three of them to hear.

Princess Diona had already scooped up the infant and was rocking him gently. "Of course we will, mother," she said with sweet excitement.

"I will take care of my brother," Prince Bertram said pompously, stressing the 'I' and the 'my'. Muir looked at his feet.

"Bertie," the woman scolded, "Hagan is Muir's brother too. No more fighting." Bertram shrugged his shoulders. Knowing that it was going to take more than a single command to reach her middle son, the queen said, "Muir, I wish a moment with Bertram and Diona. You may come again later."

The eldest prince shuffled away, carrying the weight of perceived rejection. He looked back one last time and followed Kavan out of the room. Kavan's presence was support enough to keep his shoulders back and head up.

## ❧Chapter 2❧

The dusty dun horse slowed reluctantly and snorted and pawed at the rocky ground as its rider paused to stare at the stone walls of Rhidam's castle. The inner and outer gates were open, though it was approaching twilight, and there were people crossing the drawbridge, but the rider did not urge his horse to join them. His presence inside those walls would be unwelcome, and the business he had come to conduct would require more privacy then he could expect within. He shielded his sun-browned face, well-hidden within the hood of his cloak, and studied the few windows he could see. Which one did he want, he wondered. Where would he find the man he had come for?

He noticed two of the guards eyeing him suspiciously and kicked his horse forward, stopping again in front of them to ease their minds. He had to make it appear he was there for a better reason than staring at the walls and windows.

"Did you want something, mister?" asked the stockier of the guards, a large man with a ragged scar from his right cheek, across his nose, to above his left eye.

"Can...is there a man by the name of Caol Dugan within these walls?"

The other, younger guard uttered a guffaw. "Where have you been, sir? Of course Lord Dugan's here? He's married to the King's sister, after all; where else did you think he'd be? Do wish to see him? We can announce you if you wish?"

The rider was momentarily taken aback. He had heard about Dugan's marriage but had presumed it to be a rumor. How could someone like Dugan marry into royalty? Did that make his appointment as Lord High Inquisitor more than a rumor too? He had not expected to be welcomed inside the gates; the guards apparently had no reason to be suspicious of Dugan's acquaintances. That could be good and useful to know.

"Not now. I do not wish to disturb him this late in the day. But I do have business to conduct with him." He reached into his horse's bag, aware that the guards had their hands at once upon their sword hilts. When he pulled out a long, slender box and held it forth, not a weapon as they had feared, both guards relaxed. "If you will see that he receives this, I would be grateful." When one guard began to open the box, he continued, "Feel free, if you wish. It is a dagger I promised him, one that I am sure Lord Dugan will be pleased to receive at last."

Inside the box was indeed a blade, one of excellent workmanship, unlike anything they had ever seen. The writhing gargoyle gold handle, encrusted with ebony stones, did not inspire appreciation or awe of its design, but rather a sense of discomfort and loathing, but it was the tri-edged blade, gleaming an unusual blue-silver, that drew the most attention. The two men looked at one another. "Lord Dugan is expecting this?"

The stranger smiled under his hood. These men were not familiar with the legends then. How convenient. "Oh, by now I am sure he may have given up hope that he would ever see it, but yes, I am sure he is expecting it. I will be off; please tell him I will contact him soon." He turned his horse and departed before either of the guards could ask his name or where he could be reached. Shrugging, the smaller of the two guards took the box, motioned for someone in the gatehouse to replace him, and went into the castle.

⁊*⁊

The library always grew dark at this hour of the day, no matter the time of year, but Lord High Inquisitor Caol Dugan and Lord High Chancellor Bhríd Cáner always came here in the late afternoon to discuss military procedures, tactics, and sometimes matters of state. The Elyri chancellor had a wealth of knowledge that Caol was eager to obtain. Usually, Guthrie McHador was with them, and sometimes the King joined when he did not have other matters to attend to, but today the two were alone.

War strategy was the farthest thing from their minds at the moment. They had received word that the queen had given birth to a healthy son but was herself in grave condition. Their talk was muted, of birth, of life, of death. Prince Wilred scampered in but quickly departed when it was clear his father was in no mood for play. Caol looked out the window, grateful that Deidre had delivered normally and presented him with such a fine, healthy child.

A sharp knock came at the door. "Enter," Bhríd called. His command filled the room, though it seemed to Caol that the Elyri's voice barely rose above a whisper. He still had much to learn about the mysterious people called Elyri, but none of them were eager to answer the questions he had. Sometimes he wondered what they were trying to hide. How many of the stories about them were true?

The soldier who entered was a familiar face. "Hello, General Zarkosta."

"Greetings." The soldier bowed to the chancellor but when he spoke again it was to Caol. "A delivery for you, Lord Dugan." He presented the foot-long wooden box, plain and weathered with no exterior markings, to the inquisitor and waited for the man to take it.

A short glance produced hesitation as Caol reached for the box. He noted the insignia on the lid, the only mark of distinction it bore, before his hand touched it, and did not bother to open it once he had it. He gave no outward indication of the cold chill that overcame him. "Who gave this to you?"

"One of the sentries at the gatehouse. He said a gentleman on horseback left it with them. He did not leave his name, only told them to deliver this to you and to let you know he would like to meet with you at your convenience."

Caol ignored the cold sweat on the back of his neck. "Did he say where? When? What did he look like?"

The general shook his head. "Not that they reported to me, only that he would contact you. They said he wore a hooded cloak but they got the impression he expected you to know who he was."

Caol turned to the window, box clutched in one hand, unwilling to look at anyone. There was no way to see the man from here, if he was still there, but Caol made a pretense of looking anyhow. "Hard to know who someone is if they don't show their face or leave a name…but thank you, Yorick. If he returns, please have him brought to me at once, regardless of the hour."

That suggested that the man was important, or at least that his identity was important. The general and chancellor exchanged a glance before Yorick bowed and said, "Yes, milord," and left them.

The room was silent, and the inquisitor was aware that the chancellor was watching him. It made keeping calm and relaxed a more difficult than expected task. "What is in the box?" Bhríd finally asked.

Though he would prefer not to speak until he had the facts, he saw no reason to hide the truth; no one would likely believe it anyhow. Reluctantly he replied, "If I am correct, a Coryllien dagger."

"A Cor…" Bhríd straightened and slid to the edge of his seat. "I thought those were mythical. I have never seen one…or heard of anyone who has…"

Caol did not blame the Elyri for his excited interest. Real or mythical, the Coryllien daggers had played a key role in Elyri-Teren history. "There are very few in existence; I believe three or four."

"How did you gain possession of such an artifact?"

Caol shook his head. It was a long, often sordid, story, that he was not comfortable revealing. "I would rather not say. If he is who I think he is, the man was a business competitor of my father's who cannot be trusted. He is most definitely not a gentleman. This is likely counterfeit. I will not mention it to anyone until I have the chance to authenticate it, and I would appreciate it if you would do the same, Bhríd." He strode towards the door, adding, "I will be in my rooms should His Majesty have need of me."

The chancellor watched him go, wondering what Caol was concealing and why. He would not pursue the topic, however. A person's past was a private thing, and it was a wise man that did not pry too deeply without just cause. If Caol had come into possession of a Coryllien dagger, authentic or fake, it was not Bhríd's concern how or why. He was merely curious to see it. Alone in the room, he lit the nearest lamp with a sigh, picked up the book he had placed beside it sometime earlier, and chose to read until the evening meal was served. It might take his mind off that dagger…and off the weak queen.

❧*❧

Syl entered the King's chamber, followed by a slight wisp of a girl carrying a pudgy toddler. The girl looked uncomfortable, but Syl attributed her discomfort to being in the house of royalty for the first time in her life. The room was empty, but the lady healer knew her husband would be with the queen. She gestured for the girl to sit in a nearby chair and then went into the queen's darkened room alone. Her husband and the bedridden new mother looked up as she entered.

After a courtly bow, she began, "I have found a candidate for a wet nurse, milady. She has begun to wean her own child and has agreed to accept the task of tending the prince if you desire."

The queen pushed herself into a sitting position as Ártur adjusted the pillows to support her. "Please, send her to me. I should like to speak with her. Lord Healer, you may leave us."

Though he hated the idea, Ártur did as she asked and followed his wife out of the room. The waif that entered soon after was not the sort of woman the queen had expected. Somehow she had assumed a wet nurse would be older, more matronly, someone like the women who had attended Princess Deidre when they had been young girls. This petite thing could be little more than a child herself.

"Welcome to the House of Lachlan."

"I am honored to be here, milady," the girl stammered, nervous to be standing before the beautiful queen of Enesfel. "I am Cinda Maylor; this is my daughter Bianca."

"How old is she? Have you cared for any other children before your own?"

"Bianca is almost two. I am the eldest of seven children, milady, and had responsibility for the youngest three."

Almost two. The queen could not fathom this woman being any older than a child, and she felt compelled to ask, "How old are you?"

"Sixteen, milady…"

The queen stared at her. She looked younger than sixteen, smaller and less physically developed, but she was certainly old enough to be married and have a child of her own. Fourteen was a common age for marriage, particularly amongst the poorest of classes. "And your husband approves of you taking this employment?"

The young woman's face flushed. From her expression, the queen guessed that she had come by her child in a less than honorable fashion, through no fault of her own, much the way Brenna had conceived Muir. She had been lucky to find a husband in Prince Arlan. This poor thing might never marry. "My family needs the income," the girl began. "My father is not capable of providing for us, and our cousin, who once did, is no longer around. The chance to serve, to care for the prince, is a much more admirable and honorable profession than the ones my brothers would choose for me. I do not know the ways of court, but I will learn, and I will serve faithfully."

Such eagerness and nervous honesty won a smile from the queen. "Sit, Miss Maylor. Talk with me and we shall see."

In the King's room, with the door between open enough that the healers could hear if the queen needed them, Syl waited in the bedside chair, watching her husband with concern as he paced from the window to the queen's doorway and back again. He had changed little over the past thirteen years, though the lines at the corners of his eyes and mouth had begun to deepen. He did not share his cousin's lithe, well-toned build, nor did he have Kavan's finely chiseled, androgynous features. His hair was a little stiff and wiry, his smile a bit uneven, but Syl loved his face and the gentle hands that healed so many ills. In that one way, the cousins were very much alike, although Kavan would never be a true healer.

"Is it bad?" she asked in a whisper.

The man sighed and ran one hand through his reddish hair, pausing long enough to meet her gaze. "She is weak and cannot get out of bed still. I do not know what else to do. If she was not to move for another week, maybe two, she might recover, but even an attempt to roll to her side, or to sit, is enough to cause the bleeding to begin again…and I cannot find why. I did not want to assist her to sit, but I knew she wanted it. Thankfully, there was no bleeding. I heal her each time, but it does little good. I feel helpless."

She reached for his hands and stood to face him. He was a foot taller than she was but she barely noticed that any longer. "Ártur, there are some things we are not meant to stop. If k'Ádhá desires to take her to him, he will, and there is nothing you or I can do that will change it. I could not save Phaedr…it is the way life is. You know this." As an afterthought, knowing there was one possibility that could save the queen, she asked, "Has Kavan come?"

Ártur sighed and blinked away tears. "There was no miracle. He says she will…I am afraid we shall lose her within the next few days."

"k'Ádhá's will be done," she sighed, putting her arms around him, holding him tightly for mutual comfort, the thought as painful for her as for him. "That is all we can ask for, aeslag."

❧*❦

The pale glow of sunset through the window reflected off the blue-silver blade, giving it a vaguely pink gleam that brought a nauseous taste into the back of Caol's throat. He ran his finger absently along one sharp edge, not paying much heed to the paper-thin line of blood it brought forth. After popping the black stone from the edge of the dagger's hilt with gloved hands, he removed the glass vial enclosed there, careful not to spill any of the liquid it held. It was a fast acting, lethal poison, one with no known antidotes, and he had disposed of it, and the gloves, where no one would ever find them. He then thoroughly cleaned the blade with every agent he could think of that could break down such a poison, in case any had remained. What he did find on the blade had been the faint trace of blood.

The smirk that crossed his face as he replaced the stone in its setting could not be considered mirthful. If Halstatt expected him to forget the poison, he would be disappointed. Knowing Halstatt as he did, however, the man had merely covered all the bases in case Caol had grown careless with the passage of time. But he must be growing neglectful to leave the blood of his last victim on the blade he should have kept meticulously clean. The blood, while not fresh, was a recent acquisition. Caol wondered who the victim had been. Or perhaps the blood had been left there as a message, instead of by carelessness. Caol did not know if the messenger had been Halstatt, although he could not believe the man would entrust the dagger to anyone else for delivery, not even another kinsman.

Not if it was authentic. Which he knew it was.

Taking one last look at the monstrous face adorning the hilt, he replaced the dagger in its box and buried it safely in his chest of belongings. No one in the castle would find it there; he had the single key and it was the most personal property he claimed as his own. Until he found a more secure place to hide that blade, this was the safest place he could think of. But if Halstatt came looking for it, as Caol had no doubts he eventually would, Caol had to hide it somewhere else, somewhere away from his family.

He sighed, straightened, and returned to the bench by the window. Deidre would be coming to dress for the evening meal and he had not wanted her to see that dagger. The myths surrounding the Coryllien were not pleasant and nearly every child in the Five Sovereignties, at least those where Caol had grown up, had heard those stories. If she knew them too, he saw no reason to frighten her with the knowledge that the blades were not merely myths.

Some believed that the daggers had been created by the phae k'kairá, and left in the realm to wreak havoc and bring destruction upon the invaders that came after them. Since it had never been conclusively proven that the k'kairá existed, not many believed or repeated the tales, but Caol knew them all. Those of more recent prejudice believed the Elyri had made the daggers with the intention of using them to destroy the Teren. To Caol, that seemed preposterous. No matter what mysterious powers the Elyri might have, they were not going to destroy the entire Teren race with four or five daggers. Others claimed that the blades had arrived by way of the hordes that frequently troubled Hatu's southern borders. No end of unusual and exotic wares entered the Five Sovereignties across the Hatu borders, as well as from the great desert, giving a high degree of credibility to the possibility of the daggers migrating from elsewhere.

There were stories that the blades were living entities in their own right, demons from darkness that could possess the wielder, causing a man to commit any number of unspeakable atrocities before they turned upon its user and killed them. Not normally a superstitious man, that notion made Caol chuckle. True, the stories of its use invariably involved someone of foul and twisted character, but he could not believe that a weapon could overpower a man's free will, at least not without the man's consent. No, anyone who resorted to child sacrifice and the torture of innocent people was warped to begin with.

The most popular story circulating, and the one Caol put the most stock in, was the semi-historic legend of Dawid Coryllien and the bloodthirsty marauders who traveled the Sovereignties, save for Elyriá, kidnapping adults and children alike and murdering them in bizarre rituals meant to call up forces that would destroy the Elyri completely. The only way to defeat a sorcerer or demon lord…as many had once believed Elyri to be…was to call up an entity more powerful. That is what some had intended to do, the only way they could think of to defeat the Elyri. Everyone, Teren and Elyri alike, lived in terror that they would become the next sacrificial victim.

Indeed, during those years at the onset of the Elyri persecution, there were numerous unexplained disappearances, mostly of Teren children, and a great number of individuals were captured and convicted of kidnapping and murder. All of these individuals spoke of a Dawid Coryllien, but there was never any proof of his existence. There were rumors of his whereabouts but never could anyone definitively say they had seen him. What had troubled the authorities the most was not this mysterious man or the origins of the daggers, but why, if this man and his accomplices were attempting to drive off the Elyri, were they taking the lives of Teren children to accomplish it?

The Teren victims soon dwindled as the Teren perpetrators were apprehended and executed, but the rise in Elyri deaths by blade, bow, and poison, escalated out of control. Indeed, the poison that was usually lethal to Teren, which Caol had cautiously disposed of, was twice as deadly to Elyri. Occasionally Teren survived it; Elyri never did. And what killed Teren in a matter of hours or days took a matter of minutes to kill Elyri. The dagger most often associated with the poison became a symbol of impending death; anyone who saw it died within days. It had been strangely inevitable. The Corylliens were things of nightmares, creating them, bringing them, destroying everything they touched.

Eventually, the Elyri had fled behind the Llaethlágárá, to the land they considered theirs, and legend maintained that one by one three of the daggers were discovered and placed in safe keeping in the royal castle of Cordash. The fourth dagger had never been found. Then abruptly, the three remaining daggers were said to have disappeared, something that the royal family of Cordash would neither confirm nor deny. Whatever the case, the daggers were never seen again.

Caol chuckled, this time darkly. That, of course, was not entirely true. In the seamy world he had been privy to as a boy, there were always rumors, and rumors of rumors, of this or that criminal or family seeing a Coryllien dagger and being dead within seventy-two hours. Very few who saw it lived to tell its tale, and of those who told the stories, few could claim to know the details as facts. Yet still the mythology grew. Many on the underbelly of life grew up believing the daggers to be not a myth but a deadly reality.

How Halstatt's clan had come into possession of one of the daggers, Caol did not know. For as many generations as the two families had been feuding, the dagger was there, used as a challenge between them. That was what it was now. Once Halstatt had what he had come for, he would take the dagger and disappear into obscurity.

Not this time, the inquisitor vowed, his jaw tightening as he gripped the window ledge and looked behind him. He had to find a better hiding place for the dagger, somewhere Halstatt would never think to look…or where he would be caught while searching for it.

Deidre entered as he looked frantically around the room, and he forced himself to seem calm to her smile. He accepted her kiss, vowing to keep her safe. This time, Halstatt would not get what he wanted and the dagger would stay out of Tarmajien hands. The cycle of terror would stop with Caol.

## ❧Chapter 3❧

Kavan was alone on a bench in the courtyard, watching the sun set behind the castle's outer walls. His index finger tingled where Prince Hagan had touched him; he absently rubbed his thumb against it as if to be rid of the sensation. It did not work. Sighing, he pulled his robe closer to his chest to shield himself against the wind and shook his head. He still did such simple acts of self-protection, though by now he was adept at altering his body's temperature and did not need to think about it to make it happen. If it was cold, he was warm; if it was hot, he was cool. He generally felt himself to be at an ideal temperature. Things like wind and rain and snow, however, still caused him to react as any Teren…and most Elyri…would, both out of habit and out of a need to conceal. There was no reason for anyone to know the extent of his abilities. It was enough for people to know he was Elyri.

His thoughts circled back to the infant prince. Little Hagan would rule one day, of that Kavan was certain. So would Princess Diona. But the impressions he received at her birth were different than those he had felt with Prince Hagan. The youngest Lachlan would rule, but not very long. It troubled the bard to not know what would happen to the princes that would allow their sister to reach the throne. As much as he loved the girl, and felt she had the potential to be a good ruler, it grieved him to think that something would happen to the boys. He prayed it would not happen during the King's lifetime, or even within his own. It was a matter of fate he did not believe he could change, but he could pray he was wrong.

⮞*⮜

Lord High Chamberlain Guthrie McHador reined in his mount, took one last look at the thirty horses that would become the first of Enesfel's new cavalry, and then started in the direction of Rhidam. He had been absent from the castle for twelve days, surveying plots of land that could be used for a new military training ground. The military had been virtually nonexistent since Arlan had come to power; most royal funds and efforts had been funneled into famine relief and the restoration of the kingdom's infrastructure that had fallen into ruin since the days of King Donal's reign. Those had been bleak years for Enesfel and the Lachlans, though few within the castle walls complained and even the kingdom seemed willing to be patient in the hopes of recovery.

Fortunately, other than minor skirmishes with raiding parties along the Neth border, there had been no need for a standing militia, and while there was still no immediate or pressing need, it was time to plan for the future. It was Guthrie's experience that peace did not last forever, and it had been quiet for too long; his instincts told him that something would happen soon. Better to be prepared, he had advised the King, then to be caught off guard. Now that famine was behind them, and the basic restoration of roads and public places was complete, it was time to think about defense.

And náós. The chamberlain smiled. He had known of King Innis' desire to restore the Faith to the kingdom, and why it had not been done. Enesfel had been too involved in the war with Hatu, and the plague, to spend its resources on anything else. The plague had passed and Donal Lachlan had broken the cycle of war. Thanks to a one-eyed k'gdhededhá named Jermyn Tythilius and a devout Elyri bard, Innis' youngest son had accepted his father's vision of bringing the Faith once more to Enesfel and made it his own.

Until this year, there had been no funds to restore the old places of worship, but the past thirteen years had not been wasted. k'gdhededhá Jermyn and two other Teren clergy, who had trained in Elyriá, started a seminary in Rhidam, a place of instruction for any who wished to enter the Faith and serve the community as leaders. The first class of candidates had been ordained and received full blessings from k'gdhededhá Dórímyr of Elyriá. Funds were set aside in the royal treasury for the restoration of existing Faith buildings, and within the next two years, work would begin on Rhidam's Hes á Redh Náós.

His two loves, Guthrie sighed. He had always been a military man, but it had not been until one night seven years ago that he had entered into the realm of the Faith. His niece, the queen, had been in labor for nearly two days, only to have the baby, the King's third child, arrive stillborn. The entire household had been devastated. There was nothing anyone could have done, though both court healers had tried. Even Kavan had come to lay his hands upon the child in the hopes that some miracle might occur, but none came.

Like many within the castle, Guthrie had been unable to sleep afterward and had intended to go to the kitchen in search of something other than wine to settle his nerves. As he passed the upper oratory on his way to the stairs, he heard the comforting sound of Kavan's harp. Normally, he would have continued past, but that night either something in the music or something within his soul compelled him to enter.

Nothing appeared out of the ordinary. The Elyri bard knelt before the altar with the kestrel harp on his knees, which Guthrie knew he did frequently. To the bard's left, Ártur sat with young Muir upon his lap, rocking to the rhythm of the music. After watching the peaceful tableau, absorbing the much-needed calm of the atmosphere, the chamberlain approached and settled on Kavan's other side. There seemed no point in standing to listen when he could sit and find his peace here instead of the kitchen. The only acknowledgment he received was a nod from the healer, which he preferred over words he might feel compelled to answer. He had not come in to interrupt or talk. He wanted peace. He closed his eyes, listened to the night sounds of the castle and the crystalline notes of the harp, and allowed himself to feel the grief that he had, until that moment, hidden from everyone. Grief over the lost child, over his late wife Jezeel, over King Innis and his queen, Cordelia, over Prince Muir, over Prince Owain. If his companions could see or hear his sorrow, they never spoke of it.

It had not been until he thought that grief was spent that he became aware of what he had believed to be another presence, the overwhelming certainty that someone else had entered the room. He opened his eyes to discover that Ártur and Prince Muir had gone, leaving only Kavan with the music pouring from his hands as though of its own accord. There was no one else. Unable to shake the sensation, Guthrie shifted positions; the movement caused Kavan to lift his head and the two men's eyes met. Never before had Guthrie noticed their color the way he did then, a green of such intensity and brilliance like the finest emeralds or the freshest spring grass. He would have stayed there, mesmerized by the power of a man he had never understood, but the Elyri glanced towards the pyre figure upon the wall, a gesture that seemed to be a command, and the chamberlain looked too.

The crushing agony in his heart at that moment was the greatest he had ever known, greater still than what he had felt at the death of his wife, King Innis, or Lady Cordelia. Burning a living person upon a pyre was, to him, a barbarous practice, one he had refused to allow in Enesfel from the moment he had first become able to influence King Innis' decisions. As far as he knew, only Neth still carried out such sadistic brutality, and he would have eliminated the practice there if he could have. The sight of Dhágdhuán burning on the pyre always made him shiver in distaste, even though it was an inanimate image. This figure, however, was not inanimate, but appeared to be alive and writhing with the pain of wounds seen and unseen. Guthrie was helpless to stop the anguish either of them felt, and it made the emotion that much worse.

He closed his eyes, hoping to make the torment cease, but the effort failed; the image was too vivid in his mind's eye to block out. Kavan stopped playing, pulled him to his feet, and dragged him behind the altar to the foot of the figure upon the wall.

"Touch him," the bard had said in a whisper that commanded action. Guthrie obeyed after much inner protestation. The feet of the figure felt like hot, blistered flesh; even the smell of the soot and blood that stained Guthrie's hands was too realistic to ignore or deny. He was unsure of what transpired next, except that he had begun to weep and Kavan had held him as one would a suffering child. When morning dawned, the chamberlain had gone directly to k'gdhededhá Jermyn, made what he was sure must have been one of the longest purification confessions on record, and asked to be initiated into the Faith. It was a night, an experience, he would never forget.

The thought of Kavan brought a warm flutter to his stomach, something he was certain happened to everyone who knew the man. It was akin to being in love, he mused, though he would never have called it that. Kavan knew more about him than even King Innis had known, and Guthrie suspected the bard knew more about everyone than they knew of themselves. When he had first met Kavan, he could never have guessed that the seven-year-old child would have such a profound effect upon him, upon Arlan, and upon Enesfel. Had that really been thirty years ago? He smiled again and pressed his heels into his horse's sides.

Elyri had never made the chancellor nervous, but this one…he could not define exactly what Kavan made him feel. He was grateful he had made the white harper's acquaintance and that the bard had been supportive of him and Enesfel's royal family. If not for Kavan, Guthrie was not certain Arlan would be on the throne, or that things would be as prosperous as they were.

He glanced to his right where Lord High General Ternce Wyndham rode quietly, his sharp, deep-sunk eyes riveted to the road ahead. It had been Guthrie's suggestion to leave the military in Ternce's hands, despite, or perhaps because of, the unswerving loyalty the man had shown King Owain to the end of his reign. Guthrie had not wanted the position, and despite Arlan's misgivings, he had pointed out that if Ternce took the oath, he would likely be as staunchly loyal to King Arlan as he had been to Owain. Ternce Wyndham was a man of honor, one who kept his word, even when his word placed him in a precarious position or out of favor. He had not betrayed Owain but had kept his oath to the man despite his misgivings and his disapproval of some of the ruler's actions and deeds.

To the King's surprise, Ternce enthusiastically embraced the new position and had thus far done everything asked of him and more. There was no indication of discontent and he had, over the past years, softened slightly. The chancellor trusted him, though he knew that trust was not mutual. It would be many years, if ever, before Ternce gave Guthrie his full trust.

Rhidam seemed abnormally quiet as they rode through the city center. The usual gathering of colorless rabble filled the streets, trudging home for the evening, but few spoke or even looked up, leaving the atmosphere eerily still. The general met the chamberlain's gaze with matching curiosity as they shifted their string of horses aside to allow a wagon to pass. Nothing else seemed unusual as they approached the gates of the keep, except for a cloaked shape lingering in the shadows near the Eagle's Nest Inn. Guthrie might have confronted the suspicious individual if the familiar white-robed figure in the courtyard had not caught his attention. He dismounted his horse before the animal stopped and allowed the general to take the reins from him as the bard approached. Guthrie did not offer his hand in greeting, as such contact made Kavan uncomfortable, but he smiled warmly in welcome.

"Kavan…are you here by coincidence or were you anticipating my return? What is the news? Has something happened in my absence I should know about?"

The smile was not returned. "The queen has given birth to a son."

The range of emotions that crossed the chamberlain's face varied from joy to despair. The manner and form of the greeting told the chamberlain more than he desired to know, but he could not help asking, "How are they?" He knew from Kavan's hesitation and expression that he would not like the reply.

"The child is healthy, for which we are thankful. He is to be christened Hagan Guthrie tomorrow eve."

That brought a brief, bright smile to the elder man's face. He had not known he was to be the child's namesake. "Brenna? How is she?"

Kavan turned towards the door and Guthrie fell into step beside him. "It was a difficult delivery, as expected," he said. "She lost much blood and continues to weaken. Ártur and Syl are doing everything that can be done, but the outlook is not optimistic. The children have been to see her already. I think it would be wise for you to see her too."

The chamberlain's knees buckled, but Kavan's hand upon his arm steadied him before he collapsed upon the stone steps. Perhaps it was the bard's physical strength that kept Guthrie standing, or perhaps it was the gentle touch the bard possessed. Either way, he appreciated the escort through the halls to the base of the stairwell that would lead up to his niece's chamber. The tone of Kavan's voice, or rather the lack of inflection, told Guthrie more about the queen's condition than the words did. Such support was welcome.

"I would accompany you to the Lady's chamber, but I must see that the children are prepared for dinner. Please deliver my prayers to her and tell her I will return to her later this evening.

Guthrie nodded, hating to part with Kavan, but he steeled his shoulders and resolutely made his way to Brenna's room. It was silent and dimly lit and she was currently alone, save for the child. Thinking her asleep, with her eyes closed and her damp hair tangled about her on the pillow, he intended to depart, but a whisper, his name loud in the quiet room, pulled him back. He hesitantly drew nearer, settled on the edge of the bed, and took her pale, clammy hand between his.

"Uncle…you came."

"If I had known the child was coming, I would have returned sooner; you know it. I just arrived."

Her head bobbed in agreement once. "How are the horses?"

"Excellent; fine animals…"

"And the land? You did secure the land?"

With his brow knit in puzzlement, he replied, "Of course; it is a few hours southwest of Rhidam. But we shouldn't be talking about such things…"

She cut him off by clutching his hand. "I want to know. I want to be certain that you, Arlan, and Enesfel's army will protect my children when I am gone."

The chamberlain cleared his throat and squeezed her hand in return. "You are not going anywhere…"

A resigned flicker flashed through her eyes. "No one has said I will, but I know my chances are not good. It is something I feel in my soul…something I've seen on Lord Cliáth's face. I accept it…but I regret that I cannot do more for Arlan."

"Nonsense," he scolded in a voice thick with emotion. "You have given him two sons and a daughter, heirs to the throne of Enesfel. You have given him yourself. There is nothing more he could ask. But I wish I…"

She shook her head. "I know you feel responsible for placing me in the palace…for what happened with Owain…but you could not know he would come back to Enesfel…that he would do what he did. It is not your fault. Besides, I have given the world a very noble son from that, one with more heart, wisdom, and sensitivity than Bertram will ever possess. I believe Lord Cliáth is correct in saying that Muir would be a better king than Bertram…if Bertram is not steered differently."

The corners of the chamberlain's mouth twitched. He had never told Brenna the truth about Muir's bloodline, or Owain's. Despite her condition, he did not intend to tell her now. It would be better that she never knew "Kavan said that?"

"He has said it, or alluded to it, many times, though Arlan ignores him when he does. Arlan so wants to see himself in Bertram…"

"…that he is blind to the boy's faults and spoils him. Yes, I know. Such lenient treatment does not help Bertram, and will not help Enesfel." He got up and went to the cradle to look at the sleeping infant. Hagan's hair was not as dark as the twins, but there was no mistaking him for anything other than a Lachlan. "I am honored you chose to give my name to the new prince."

"It was Arlan's idea. He believes Hagan resembles you. Besides," she smiled weakly, "you are the closest thing to a father Arlan has known. He feels he owes you."

And Arlan was the nearest thing Guthrie had to a son. Raising him had been time and effort well spent. "I will thank him when I see him." Noting the flutter of her weary eyes and the twitch of pain at the corners of her mouth, he asked, "Is there anything I can do for you? Do you wish to sleep?"

She nodded. "Please…and when you see Lord Cliáth, tell him I wish him to play for me."

"I will. He said he will come later and sends his prayers."

"I need them," she admitted beneath her uncle's kiss upon her forehead. If anyone's prayers would help her, they both believed those prayers would come from Kavan.

☙*❧

The morning room was dark as the sun set on the opposite side of the castle. The lone figure slouched in the plush high-backed chair did not notice, or perhaps did not care, that he was now in darkness, for he did not attempt to light the candles or lamps. He was slumped, almost sagging in the chair; if anyone opened the door and peeked in, they would not see him. In his hands, he held a crystal chalice of Káliel sherry that he had poured when he entered the room several hours ago and had not touched since. In his stupor, he was not even aware that he had missed dinner.

His universe was growing bleaker every moment he remained there, but he could not bring himself to move or do anything. Upstairs, his wife, his queen was dying. Dying, and there was nothing to be done about it. They had tried to avoid this pregnancy, but it had happened, as though this child had been preordained. And this infant, this unasked for baby and k'Ádhá, would cause him to lose his cherished love forever. Kavan would chastise him for the thoughts he was having, 'blasphemous' the Elyri would have said, but at this moment, Arlan Lachlan did not care. Not about k'Ádhá, not about Kavan, not about himself. If she died, he would never be the same.

The door creaked but he did not hear it. A tiny figure in a white nightgown peered into the darkness, and, seeing no one, slid inside and closed the door. She tiptoed across the stone floor to the desk with the hopes of finding a candle and flint to light it.

"Diona?"

The voice startled her and she jumped back, dropping the candle she found and the cloth doll she carried. After her eyes adjusted to the darkness, she saw the figure in the chair that had straightened and set the glass of sherry on the table beside him.

"Father?" she squeaked.

"What are you doing? It is late?"

She shuffled her feet. "I could not sleep. None of us could…except Bertie. Wilred was crying, and since we could not sleep with the noise, Muir and I talked until he got too sad and went to the oratory. He's going to…" She stopped as if changing her mind about what she was going to say. "I would have gone there too; he needs me…but…"

"But?"

She sighed. "I always come here to stare at the stars when I cannot sleep. I'm not like Muir; praying in the oratory does not help me feel better. I need to think, not pray. And I could not talk to Lord Cliáth…not this time."

Arlan had not known the Elyri was his daughter's confidante. "Why not?"

"He is angry with us for what happened today. I did not do anything…but I think he believes I was on Bertie's side. I did not take anyone's side. Muir shares our mother…he's our brother. What Bertie did was foolish and bad; Lord Cliáth told him not to and…"

"I know all about it, Diona," the King interrupted in a weary, clipped voice.

The girl stared at her father with large eyes. "If it had been me…if I had done what he did…I would have been punished. Bertie hasn't been…"

Arlan motioned for her to come closer and pulled her onto his lap. He did not know if she had felt singled out for punishment all along and was now voicing it, or if this was a recent realization, but hearing her point out the same fault Kavan normally chided him for, stung. Bertram was special because he was the heir to the throne, but Diona was truly his favorite child, despite that outward favoritism. A daughter was different from a son, and in many ways, she reminded him of his mother. And of Brenna.

"I have not had the opportunity to speak to Bertram," he explained. "I have had too many other things to think about."

"Mother?" He nodded as she burrowed her face into his chest. He was different from Kavan, broader, softer, hairier. She treasured being near her father like this; it was rare that she saw him outside of formal circumstances. His beard pressed against her forehead as he kissed her.

"Is mother going to die?"

The innocent question made him feel cold and choke on his words. "I…"

"She thinks so…and I think Lord Cliáth does too. He looked sad at dinner and would not talk about her. He did not say much. Do you think she will?"

"I do not know," he admitted. His voice was more ragged than he intended, though he had hoped to keep fear out of his voice. His daughter did not need his grief, but it was too late to hide it. That Kavan feared the worst did nothing to ease his mind. Diona did her best to wrap her short arms around his neck; he embraced her in return.

"I hope not."

Winding his fingers in her curls, Arlan murmured, "I hope not as well, my princess."

## ❧Chapter 4❧

The melancholy cooing of doves woke Kavan before the sun's rays had brightened the horizon with their warming touch. Not even the house servants, save for the cooks, would be rising yet, but that would happen soon enough. He often woke at this hour; he relished the serenity and freedom from the cares of the new day. At this hour, there was no one to disturb him, no one demanding his time or attention. He could be himself.

He gazed idly around the room from the comfort of his bed. Every inch of this room was intimately familiar, though he did not consider himself to be home. Sighing, he pulled into a sitting position, his lone sheet falling away from slim, muscular shoulders that gleamed moonlight white in the dim light of pre-dawn. No external scars marred their perfection, but the occasional dull stiffness had never completely left his muscles after the floggings he had received with Owain Lachlan's permission over thirteen years ago.

Thirteen years. He had not traveled outside Rhidam in all that time except for the brief visit to Bhryell when Ártur and Syl had married. The home of his childhood had seemed foreign, as if it belonged to someone else or to another place and time. He had stayed in his own house, the small brick structure near the town center, and had not visited his family. He did not feel he could face them.

Tám and Dhâná knew little about the public adoration that followed their nephew, and even less about the flogging he had received or the miracles attributed to him. What they did know they either did not understand or did not believe. Jermyn had been with him in Bhryell during that visit and had whispered something about a prophet not being welcome in his hometown, and though Kavan did not consider himself a prophet, he shut his thoughts and feelings on such things deep inside. He spent the remainder of his stay in Bhryell alone in his personal oratory, or in the naós, refusing to see almost everyone, and to this day he refused to speak of the sensation of despair that visit had brought him.

As much as he wanted to deny it, there was too much truth to the man's words and Kavan hated it. The distance between himself, his uncle, aunt, and cousin Sámel, extended to everyone in Bhryell he had known as a child, except for gdhededhá Bhílári, who had tried his best to treat Kavan as he would any other man, and Tíbhyan, the bhydáni who had instructed Kavan as a boy. The sage knew what his student was capable of and believed in him; he had never condemned or criticized Kavan but rather had encouraged him to explore his potential. He had certainly never second-guessed those events for which Kavan had no explanation but that caused Bhryell's citizens to hold him apart in awe and fear. Perhaps it was the bhydáni's age and wisdom, or perhaps merely an insight and tolerance that others did not possess. Either way, it had been soothing to have at least one person accept him fully. It had been Tíbhyan's suggestion that he turn away from Bhryell and never look back. Kavan tried to take the elder's words to heart, though the effort was more painful than expected. He took those possessions dearest to him, locked the door to his private sanctuary, and left Elyriá behind.

Thus, the Lachlan Castle in Rhidam had become his residence. Not his home; he did not believe he had a home. Though he knew he was welcome here, and he felt he had nowhere else to go, he could not regard it as home. It always seemed there was somewhere else he should be, something else he should be doing; he felt as if he was waiting but did not know what for. Wanderlust was how one traveling minstrel put it. Once a traveling bard, forever a traveling bard. But Kavan had consciously chosen to put that part of his life behind, choosing instead to serve as tutor to the royal children and advisor to the King. He found too much despair when he traveled, too many reminders of who and what he was, things within him that he found too painful and awkward to confront.

Elyri. That much he accepted and was proud of. That he was a musician of extraordinary merit he also knew and welcomed as a blessing. It was the other aspects of himself and his life that troubled him. As Elyri, he could manipulate the natural energies around him to his advantage and was far more gifted in that way than anyone he knew or had heard tell of. He was ágdháni. Overall, that normally did not trouble him, except when he overheard anyone proclaiming the Elyri as tools of evil, demons, or sorcerers. He tried once to explain to a visiting minstrel that Elyri did not require spells, incantations, fetishes, or any physical materials or spoken words to do the things they did. They merely reached within themselves, or into the world around them, gathered the necessary energy together, and shaped it to meet a particular end. If that was true, argued the minstrel, why were Teren unable to do likewise? It was a question no one had ever been able to answer, and Kavan was forced to drop the subject. The question had haunted him ever since.

There was his fine face, the whiteness of his skin, and the androgynous, almost feminine edge to his voice. Those things set him apart from everyone. He could disguise that he was Elyri, could refuse to discuss the matters of faith that set him apart, could refuse to practice his gifts and to acknowledge what he was capable of. But he could disguise his voice only through silence, and his appearance could never be hidden. They marked him as what he was, different, unique, the means by which everyone recognized him and knew who he was.

He had hoped that after thirteen years of remaining in Rhidam, the rumors and stories about him that circulated throughout Enesfel would fade into distant memory. Instead, they had become their own full-blown tradition, made up less of truth than of myths. Every bard passing through Rhidam relayed the latest story about the White Bard of Bhryell. To many, Kavan was a saint, a prophet, a miracle-worker, all of which he frantically strove to deny. The harder he tried, however, the more he failed, because even he could not deny the miracles. A miracle had saved King Owain's life, and it had been Kavan's hands that had performed it. Too many people had witnessed that for him to deny it. And while he could deny the miracles others attributed to him, how could he know whether those things had happened or not? Denying the possibility was as wrong as claiming the miracles as his own. There were songs, stories, poems, and paintings, all dedicated to his existence. Most recently, he had heard that there was a movement to have him elevated as a Saint within the Faith. The idea of it hurt, frustrated, and frightened him.

Thus, he had allowed himself to become what other minstrels referred to as a tamed bard. Though he traded songs with the passing musicians he eagerly welcomed at court, only those within the castle walls heard his voice, his music. He had become, for all purposes, a recluse within the royal house.

Saint. He shivered at the word. Standing, he stopped in front of the full-length mirror and gazed at his reflection. The nude image revealed to him reminded him of the marble statuary in the sovereign court in Clarys. There was a compact quality to his lithe, athletic frame, the tautness of youth that belied his age of thirty-seven years. Broad shoulders and chest, trim hips, all well-proportioned, smooth, white, and flawless. Perfection, Ártur would have said, as would countless men and women who sent him gushing love sonnets, people who had never seen or met him and knew little, if anything, about him. They only knew what they had heard, and what they had heard was mostly untrue. He wanted to mar that perfection, prove to everyone that he was neither perfect nor a saint. Prophet, miracle worker, perhaps, but not perfect and most definitely not a saint. By Ethenae, he thought, he needed to get out of this place, needed to be somewhere else, away from the madness that every day threatened to draw him in.

He spun suddenly and thrust his clenched fist into the mirror, destroying the projected image, shattering the glass into thousands of sharp points of blue-white light. Dropping to his knees, he knelt amidst the shards, allowing despair to wash over him. There were no tears, but his anguish flowed outward all the same. Kavan wanted to give Arlan the happiness he himself was unable to find, but as with ever before, he could not. He suspected that Queen Brenna would die and he could not prevent it. He was not a healer and could not control the miracles that sometimes occurred at his hands. All of the longing in the world would not make it happen. He had been unable to save either of the two previous children and could not save the queen. He wanted to curse his ability to know events before they occurred, but he did not even know the words to use.

Behind him, his door opened slowly. "Lord Cliáth?" called the quiet voice as the blonde prince peeked around the door. When he did not immediately see his tutor, he pushed the door open further and slid into the room. He froze when he saw the naked figure huddled before the broken mirror.

Prince Muir waited, dead still, heart thundering in his chest as though it would burst. The sight of his beloved mentor and friend in the midst of that broken glass was shocking, but the overpowering beauty of the man overrode everything else. He wondered what he should do as servants passed in the hall. When Kavan did not move, he forced himself to speak. "Lord Cliáth…are you well?"

❧ 57 ❧

The only response he received was the continued trembling of the broad white shoulders. The prince pulled the sheet from the canopy bed and gingerly wrapped it around Kavan, averting his eyes as best he could, careful not to step on the glass in his bare feet. He retrieved the hand broom kept on the wall near the water closet and set about sweeping away the glass. Once done, he sat cross-legged before his tutor, not speaking, watching the man's face and wondering if he should touch him or tend his bleeding hand.

Kavan became aware of the linen sheet around his shoulders at the same moment he became aware of Muir's presence in the room. He was no longer surrounded by glass, and the room was considerably brighter. He met the prince's gray-green eyes with a start.

"Muir..."

The prince shrugged, hoping to hide his embarrassment at being caught staring. "There is no cause for concern," he murmured. "No one else has seen you like this. I was coming to speak to you when I heard the crash, and no one else has been here. I cleaned up the glass; you can tell Father I broke it if you want." What his heart longed to say, he could not. He did not have the words to express how he felt.

"Blaming you for my foolishness would not be right..."

"He will never believe you did this."

Kavan glanced at his injured, still clenched fist as though finally becoming aware of the pain. "He will when he sees this."

Muir smiled. "Then he will not see it. Come...I will remove the glass and clean it for you, and then we will find Lord or Lady MacLyr. By the time Father sees you, he will never be able to tell."

"My prince..."

Protesting proved useless as the prince pulled him to his feet, keeping his gaze elsewhere as Kavan pulled the sheet around himself with his bloody hand. The Elyri waited at the table as the young man filled the washbasin, found a clean cloth, and then joined him. Muir was not surprised when Kavan did not flinch as sliver after sliver was removed, but he was still confused. His tutor rarely showed any sign of weakness; it caused Muir to worry about the cause of this incident, worry about Kavan's health and happiness. He did not ask, however; Kavan would not likely answer his questions.

The effort to remove the slivers grew more difficult as the trembling of his hands increased. He had touched Kavan's hands before, but this time he was aware of their heat, their strength, and their gentleness, of each tiny line and crease, as he studied them carefully in search of splinters. A small sound made him look up to meet Kavan's gaze.

"I am fine, Muir," the bard murmured as if he had been reading the younger man's thoughts and was embarrassed by them. Muir hoped fervently he had not. Thankfully, if Kavan had read them, he gave no other indication of having done so. "It is the price one must pay for being too restrained, perhaps. Tension must be released."

"But striking a mirror, Lord Cliáth?"

"Not a wise choice for relieving tension, I admit, but I am not as wise as everyone thinks me to be." It looked as though the prince was about to protest, and Kavan quickly added, "Why were you seeking me at such an hour?"

With the last of the glass removed, the prince emptied the washbowl of its red-stained water and returned it to its place, hanging the wet cloth upon the stool next to it. He had come to tell his mentor the decision he had made but now felt that choice might be the wrong one. How could he do such a thing and hurt the man he loved dearly when the bard was clearly in a difficult emotional place. No, Muir decided. Say it. It was the best choice, the only way he saw to be free of what he believed to be an intolerable situation.

Head bowed, he murmured, "I want you to know, in case someone asks, that I will be leaving Rhidam. You and Diona are the only ones who know."

There it was. Kavan closed his eyes and sighed, trying to hold back everything he felt. After many years of torment, neglect, and rejection, the prince was finally fulfilling the prophecy Kavan had seen on the day of the boy's birth. There was no use in fighting fate, but Kavan did not like it. "Where are you going to go?"

Taken aback by what seemed indifference to him, the prince spluttered, "You mean you are not going to stop me?" Perhaps, he realized then, he had wanted to tell the bard because he had hoped that Kavan, like Diona, would try.

"Answer the question."

Muir shrugged his shoulders stiffly but would not look at Kavan. "I do not know. I think I want to go to sea."

"As a sailor or a fisherman? Not exactly princely work..."

Eyes flashing defensively, the blonde's head jerked up and he snorted, "The stories Captain Delamo tells about the sea...about Káliel...they are exciting. The Lachlans were once seamen. I should like to experience that life for myself. I am a good swimmer, and I'm strong. Either a sailor or a fisherman is fine with me. Besides, I am not a prince..."

"Your mother is the queen, your father was a king," Kavan interrupted sternly. "That makes you a prince, despite what others say to the contrary. Though Owain was not Innis' son and may not have been of the Lachlan line, he was of the de Corrmick lineage. He is part of a royal bloodline, a prince in his own right. Therefore, regardless of what Arlan, Bertram, or anyone else says, you are a prince."

Muir was still, his face creased with confusion. "I never thought of it that way," he whispered.

"I did not think you had. They also seem to forget those facts. I have known this day would come, that you would seek to leave home one day, since before you could speak, since the first time I held you in my arms. But I admit..." he lowered his gaze, "I did not expect this day to come so soon. Or perhaps I was being selfish and hoping I could give you reason enough to stay despite your unhappiness."

Muir watched the bard's face as the man stared out the window. Kavan? Selfish? That could not be any further from the truth. A lump formed in Muir's throat but again he could find no words. Kavan rarely showed emotion; this tiny glimpse of it caught the prince off guard. Getting no verbal response, Kavan asked, "When do you plan to leave?"

"I…do not know…tonight, I think…"

"Could I perhaps persuade you to wait?" The prince prepared to retort, finally getting the resistance he had anticipated, but the bard stopped him. "I am not saying you should not and cannot go. You would be happier away from Bertram…and I want you to be happy."

Kavan got up, clutching the sheet around his waist, organizing his thoughts as he went to the window where he stopped with his back to the prince. When he spoke again, it seemed to Muir that it took great effort. "More than anything, happiness is what I want for you. If we find the proper place for you to go, Arlan may even approve your departure. He may not think of you as his son, but he does want you to be respectable. If you will agree to wait…"

"Why should I? Bertram does not want me here, nor does the…"

His words were bitter and he immediately regretted them as Kavan shrank into himself. Or wilted like a flower under too much heat. "Your mother needs you, Muir, for a while longer. She will die, and it will break her heart if you leave when she is gravely ill. Your sister loves you dearly and will need your comfort. Can you at least wait until your mother is gone, until after her final rite? I will do what I can to secure shelter and employment for you wherever you wish to go if you will do this for them."

The prince bit his lip as Kavan knelt beside him and adjusted the sheet at his waist. His mother and sister. But the one person who mattered most to him had not been included on that roster. Had not been mentioned, either because Kavan could not bring himself to ask Muir to remain for his sake or because the bard believed he did not matter to the prince. Both thoughts hurt, as did the bad news about his mother, and Muir tried to turn away. But Kavan grasped his hands and held them fast. He had not meant to be blunt about Brenna's condition, but it was done, and he believed that Muir would appreciate his honesty far more than he would false hope.

"There will be much pain in this house, Muir…you are needed here. Your mother needs you. Diona needs you." He paused, swallowed, and admitted quietly, "I need you."

Muir rushed into the Elyri's embrace and clung to him, weeping against his shoulder. Kavan needed him. He could not recall ever being told he was needed, and with that one statement, the bard persuaded him to remain in Rhidam for a little longer. The love he felt for his tutor at that moment was the strongest emotion he had ever felt. The Elyri sighed, holding the young man close, smoothing the unruly blonde waves with his good hand. He did not want to let him go.

## ❧Chapter 5❧

Rubbing the sleep from his eyes, Justice Cornell stretched again before sliding from his horse. Duty had kept him awake too late last night and summoned him too early this morning. He was not ready for this day to begin, but he resolutely rapped upon the door. The abruptness with which it was answered by the stoop-shouldered balding man who motioned him in was not surprising.

"Can't talk here. Too many might hear and I hate gossip. Come into the back."

The justice followed the old physician through one room that smelled heavily of alcohol and death, into the parlor beyond. "You have examined the Elyri woman?"

"That's why I asked you here. I already sent her off to be buried, but thought you'd want to hear about her soon as I was done."

"And?" Minos did not like dealing with physicians, particularly ones who drank too much and put off answering his questions as this man normally did.

As if reading those thoughts, the old man grinned widely, a number of his crooked yellow teeth missing, and asked, "Would you care for breakfast, Lord Justice? It's mighty early for you to be here, so if you want…"

"I would rather hear what you've learned so I might make my report to the King. I do not have time for a meal, Sorvis. Not today. Tell me what you found."

"She was stabbed to death, milord."

Minos scowled and resisted rolling his eyes. "Nothing else?"

"Nothing that I could find, but if you think there's something more, or you want to know something more specific, call in one of the King's Elyri. The wound was unusual, I will admit…she bled to death…drown in her own blood I'd say from what was in her lungs…but I've never seen another wound like that in all my years."

"Was it three punctures or one?"

"The three points were too clean, too evenly spaced, to have been multiple entries. It seems likely it was one clean stroke. I would stake my career on that."

Reassuring to know the doctor was willing to risk his already meager practice on what he had found. "Where is the body?"

"Taken to the náós for burial, like I told you, milord. Are you sure you will not have breakfast?"

Justice Cornell was already out the door, mounting his horse and heading towards the náós. The doctor muttered something demeaning under his breath and went back inside.

ॐ * ॐ

Caol stretched, half asleep, and then jumped wide-awake when he realized his wife was not in bed beside him. Instead, she was already awake, sitting at the bureau, brushing her mass of honey-gold hair. Seeing the movement in the mirror, she turned to smile at him, blew him a kiss, and then returned to styling her hair. He leaned into the mound of feather pillows, his hands behind his head, and smiled back.

He still considered it a miracle that the princess of Enesfel had wanted to marry such a simple man and even more of a miracle that her brother, the King, had consented to the request. He had not known the King thought that highly of him. He had joined Prince Arlan's fight for the throne to avenge his father's death and to escape the cycle of criminal activity into which his family had fallen generations ago. He had never expected to come this far, for his life to change as much as it had. Now Halstatt's arrival threatened to destroy the existing trust between Caol and his king.

He scowled and scratched absently at his shoulder. He supposed he had been startled upon waking not because of Deidre's absence but because he was surprised to have awakened at all, especially in his own bed. If Halstatt wanted his death, Caol suspected the man could have made it into the castle compound last night without being caught. So what did Halstatt want? Money? Not likely, that would be too simple. Halstatt would demand something that would be nearly impossible to give. Caol wondered what it would be.

⟿*⟾

Rhidam's Hes á Redh Náós stood at the northeastern edge of town, its single Elyri spire lost in the early morning fog. It had been built in the centuries before the first Teren had arrived, and its thick stone walls had outlived every war and conflict that had occurred since then. Where once had been brilliant stained glass mosaics, there was darkness; the glass had been broken or stolen long ago, used for other purposes or simply destroyed. The external overgrowth of clinging vines and untrimmed trees had been lovingly tended or cleared away in recent times by the man Kavan sought within, making the ancient building more hospitable than it had been the first time he had seen it, but it still required much work to be the sort of place people would happily flock to.

Inside of the structure, with little sunlight to warm it, it was cool, damp, and dark. There were no candles lit in the sanctuary at this early hour. The bard approached the altar, touched his knee to the steps, and then placed the heavy candle he carried at the center of it, bowing his head as he did and murmuring a short prayer. He carried no lighter, but certain he was alone, brought a small tongue of flame to life in his palm and smiled as he lit the candle. Such a simple use of the energy he harnessed, yet the release was immensely satisfying. It had been too long since he had used it to any great extent. Perhaps soon he would leave the cares of court life and go somewhere where he could use it without concern for his safety.

But not yet. He turned to the side door that would take him into the thóres and was not surprised to hear k'gdhededhá Jermyn's voice within. The k'gdhededhá had always had a habit of talking to himself when he worked alone. Today, however, the man was not actually alone. The woman on the cot did not stir, as he wrapped her in linen and sprinkled her body with blessed water. The k'gdhededhá turned with the creak of the floorboards and motioned for Kavan to enter. "Would you care to assist me, Lord Cliáth?"

Kavan started to nod as he approached, but he froze as soon as he saw the woman's face. She was Elyri. His hands began to shake; how much like Gabrielle she looked. He had not allowed himself to give Gabrielle Dilyn more than a passing thought in many years, needing to force all of the troubling imagery of her out of his head to keep his sanity. This woman could easily be her except for the reddish tint to her blonde hair. Gabrielle had been more auburn. They shared the same short nose, however, small full lips, and the same upward slant at the outer corners of their eyes. He wondered what color her eyes had been. "Natural causes?" Few Elyri died young unless they were gravely ill or were killed by some external force. From where he stood, Kavan could see no injuries.

"Murder," the one-eyed man sighed. "She was found yesterday in the back of a merchant's wagon. No one knows who she is or how she got there or why she was in Rhidam."

"May I?" Jermyn nodded to the bard's question, knowing what he wanted to do, and stepped aside for Kavan to settle on the edge of the cot. "How did she die?"

"She was stabbed…"

The woman's hands were already bound, but Kavan could learn what he wanted to know in other ways. He lay one hand across her forehead and let the images flow. Water. Gate. Love. Gabrielle. Dark cloak. Thief. Pain. Dagger. Poison. The image of the dagger solidified but it was the poison that had killed her. Gabrielle again. Shaken, Kavan pulled his hands away and clenched them in his lap. He had been correct about her identity.

"She seems young," Jermyn murmured to himself; he had been around Elyri enough to know her age and appearance would not necessarily match.

"Do not finish her burial preparations yet, k'gdhededhá."

"Milord?"

Kavan looked over his shoulder. "I think her family will want to have the final say in her burial."

The other man's eyes lit. "You know her? You can contact her family?"

"I know her family…and yes, I can contact them. I will send Ártur to preserve her remains until I…"

He was interrupted by footsteps behind them. "Good morning, Your Grace. Lord Cliáth."

"Good morning, Lord Cornell." The clergyman's bow was slight, even though it was Minos that should have bowed to him. Somehow, Kavan noted, that had never happened, and the k'gdhededhá went out of his way to bow to nearly everyone. He seemed to forget what his position entitled him to. Or maybe he was as uncomfortable with such formalities as Kavan was. "I presume you have come regarding the woman."

"I had hoped to examine the wound again before she is buried, but I see you have already wrapped most of the body."

Jermyn nodded. "You can examine her if you wish. Lord Cliáth has instructed me to postpone burial until he can contact her family."

Surprised, the justice stared at the bard, asking, "You know her, milord?"

"I met her daughter many years ago," Kavan admitted uncomfortably.

"Daughter? She looks too young…"

Kavan's brow twitched. He estimated her to be ninety-seven years old, based on what Gabrielle had once told him and what his own research had taught, but he saw no need to reveal that. "Yes, she has a daughter…and for the record, the puncture wound alone did not kill her. She was poisoned."

The justice began to retort but stopped. It was no use asking how Kavan knew such things; the bard often knew things others did not. He cleared his throat and rubbed the back of his neck. "I suspected as much. She got to that wagon on her own, climbed into it herself. I'd stake my position on that. Doctor Sorvis suggested I bring in a healer to confirm his report, but if you are certain it is poison…"

"I am," Kavan assured him.

"Then there is no need for me to examine her again." He stared at the woman for several moments, lost for words. "Was there anything of value on her person? Any clues that might suggest who might want to kill her?"

"Her money purse, as you know…and this." The heavy gold brooch he placed in the justice's hand was antique, and of a design the man recognized at once.

"The Serpent of Káliel," he choked, rubbing his thumb over the red coral dragon. "This is worth a small fortune to be sure. I did not see it on her before…"

The clergyman smiled and adjusted his eye patch. "I would be surprised if you had. It was pinned beneath her corset. Any thief would have had to undress her to discover it." He stifled his laughter at Kavan's uncomfortable expression. "Have to wash the dead for burial, milord. It comes with the job. She obviously knew its worth or was simply determined to keep it out of sight. Is she related to the ruling family of Káliel?" The bard did not reply other than to brush the thick hair away from the woman's face. "It will look very bad for an emissary to have been murdered…"

"She was no emissary." Whatever she might have been doing in Rhidam, Kavan knew she had not been there to act as ambassador. "His Majesty will need to know of this, but I think it can wait. Until the queen's condition is…resolved…he does not want to be disturbed by anything short of war. We should allow Lord McHador to deal with this, I believe, Lord Justice?" Minos nodded in full agreement. "dedhá, I am derelict in my duty. The queen requests that you come to her bedside and pray with her for a few hours. If you will send Ártur to me here, I will stay with the lady."

Jermyn's face darkened. "I heard it was a difficult labor again; Wortham told me this morning, but he did not say how bad it is. Will she live?"

The bard refused to look at him. He did not want to tell the truth, not this time, but he could not lie. It went against his nature. "The odds are against her," he finally said with a groan.

Knowing those words were an understatement, Jermyn took the brooch from the justice, muttering, "She is dying…yes…I will send Ártur to you…" The brooch was placed on the dresser and then he bustled around the room gathering incense, blessed water, his pearl prayer beads, and anything else he thought might comfort the queen. Then he hurried from the room, his robes swishing behind him, his pudgy, balding features conveying sorrow and apprehension.

The justice was not as quick to depart. He watched the bard study the woman and toy with the hair around her face. Elyri always made him uneasy; they were different, mysterious, and he did not understand them, but he felt no hatred. The idea that someone could know his thoughts before he did, or could take them from his head, intimidated him in a way little else did. This pale harper was even more daunting. Other than Lord Chamberlain McHador and the queen, Kavan was the person closest to Arlan Lachlan, and Minos could not help wondering how much influence this Elyri had upon the monarch. Not that he had yet to steer the King in a bad direction, but was it possible for Kavan to make King Arlan do something he did not desire to do?

Kavan met the man's gaze somberly and sighed. It was difficult to close out such negative thoughts, particularly today when he felt raw around the edges. "You give me too much credit, Lord Cornell, and the King too little. I am his friend, that is all, and he is too strong-willed to be swayed by my advice unless he desires to be."

Minos drew back his shoulders, made a guttural huffing sound in his throat, turned heel and left. Kavan did not watch him, though he puzzled over why the man's thoughts had been so clear to him today. It occurred to him that the man's thoughts were always clear, as if the justice was projecting them. The bard wondered why that was.

Absently, Kavan reached for the brooch. In his hand, it felt cold, akin to the feel of the dead woman's skin. He had seen the one worn by Gabrielle's father when he had been on the island thirteen years ago, but Gabrielle had not explained its significance. He had not asked. It had been his studying in the years since that told him that the brooches were handed down through the family to the ruling child. It was square, as wide as his palm, and finely wrought of gold. On its face was a red coral dragon, the Káliel Serpent, each brooch slightly different from the other. This bit of jewelry supported his discovery that this was, indeed, Gabrielle's mother.

He knew that, while valuable enough as an art object and for the materials it was fashioned from, the Serpents real value was their political, ceremonial, and sentimental importance to Káliel's ruling family. But it was not valuable enough to anyone else that it should have been necessary for the woman to hide it carefully…unless…

His thumb rubbed over the dragon. Each brooch contained a hidden compartment, big enough to house a small bead or lock of hair or small image or message. Perhaps it contained something the killer wanted, or at least it might contain a message for Gabrielle. With that in mind, he decided that she should be the one to open it. The woman's thoughts had last been of her daughter; perhaps she had been on her way to see her child again.

Hoping to glean further information, he clenched the brooch tightly in his palm. No images presented themselves except for those of the woman pinning it to the inner edge of her corset. Whatever it might contain, she wanted to protect it from someone. Or something.

Gabrielle. He shivered but allowed himself to smile wistfully as the feelings the thought of her inspired filled him again. It happened less frequently, and enough time had passed since her unexpected kiss that he no longer felt the burning shame and embarrassment that fiery longing had once created. No other woman had affected him the way she had, and yet he had shut himself off from her. Completely. He knew nothing of her life since they had last seen each other, except that she had succeeded her father as Prime Magistrate of the islands. That had pleased him; he knew how much she had desired that position. Her interest in affairs of state had been too obvious and she had been far too intelligent not to convince her father and the Council of her ability to effectively govern the islands. Thus far, she had been very successful, proving herself to be one of the best leaders the islands had known.

"Kavan?"

Shaken out of his daze, Kavan blinked and looked up. "Pardon me, Ártur. I was…"

"A thousand miles away from the looks of it. k'gdhededhá Jermyn told me to come, that you were waiting." He gestured to the woman on the cot, the reason, he presumed, that he was here. "Who is she?"

"Will you preserve her?"

"Pre…I have not done that in…why do you make such a request?"

Knowing that his cousin always wanted information, always sought to understand Kavan better, the bard resisted being put off by his probing questions and replied, "I need to inform her family of her demise, and I do not know how long that will take. She would have been buried today, but I think her resting place and rites should be decided upon by her daughter."

The healer cocked one eyebrow. "You know her then?"

"I have never seen this woman before, but I do know her daughter." He placed the brooch in Ártur's hand and met his questioning gaze squarely.

"The Káliel Serpent? This is not…"

"This is Gabrielle Dilyn's mother," the words were a whisper.

The healer sank down on the other side of the cot, staring at the woman in stunned silence. She was very beautiful, and if Gabrielle looked anything like her mother, the healer understood why Kavan had been smitten with her. It would have been hard not to be.

"Has word been sent?"

"Not yet. I just learned of her death myself."

"How did she…?"

"Stabbed, with a poison blade. The wound might not have killed her, but the poison certainly would have…and did. You may confirm it if you wish."

Ártur took her face in his hands and allowed his eyes to close. He traced the paths of her cells with his thoughts, touching her organs and the wound, examining them without the use of his eyes. After a cursory inspection, he delved deeper: lungs...death. Swallowing hard, he withdrew his hands; he had seen enough.

"The poison killed her, as you say...a poison I'm not familiar with. And the wound is most unusual, like no blade I have ever seen. But Kavan...she was already dying."

After a twitching around the corners of his eyes, the bard's expression went blank. Whatever he felt or thought, the healer could not tell. "Explain."

Wiping the back of his hand across his brow, Ártur replied, "There was an infection in her lungs, something curable if an Elyri healer had tended her, but she left it too long...it would have claimed her life whether she was murdered or not. The poison compounded and hastened that death." Glancing back at her, he continued, "I hope this was not political; relations with Káliel have always been tenuous, and if this was an attack directed at the ruling family..." His voice trailed off, not needing to complete that thought.

Lifting his hand, Kavan studied the brooch still clutched in his palm. "Perhaps she was traveling to see Gabrielle...to bid her farewell. This was hidden inside her corset...perhaps to travel unrecognized, although I doubt she would have been noticed for anything beyond being Elyri. She may have wanted to return this...and unless her killer was familiar with Gabrielle, or she had otherwise revealed her identity, I doubt anyone would have known..."

"It is still conceivable, Kavan, and you know it. Does Justice Cornell know who she is?"

"He saw the Serpent; he knows she has ties to the islands. He is intelligent enough to determine that she has some connection to the ruling House, but I did not tell him she was the Prime Magistrate's mother."

"You should. If this is more than a random killing or even a random anti-Elyri act, he, Guthrie, and the King should know. You will tell them?"

The healer was rarely one to tell Kavan what to do or to offer firm opinions on affairs of state. Kavan took that knowledge into account when he reluctantly nodded and murmured, "I will, of course."

"Will you give Gabrielle this news?"

The flicker that crossed Kavan's face was gone before Ártur could identify it, but he knew he had struck a nerve. It was an idea he expected Kavan to resist but his cousin surprised him with a sigh. "I should. All of Káliel believes this woman died over twenty years ago at sea; Gabrielle was the only one who believed anything to the contrary. She was also the only one who seems to have been aware that her mother was Elyri…not even her father knew of it. I know her…and I know the truth about her mother. No one else on Káliel would understand; I do not think it would be proper for anyone else to share this news with her."

"Do you think you can face her?"

Kavan ignored the amusement in his cousin's voice, the gentle, teasing reminder of Kavan's reaction to the kiss she had given many years ago. "There is no choice; I believe I must. It is time to lay the past to rest."

"Or to reopen it." Ártur did not attempt to hide his smile. He clung to the belief that Kavan would be happier if he had a companion, a wife, in his life, to love him and for him to love in return. The solitude with which Kavan surrounded himself could not be healthy.

The bard's eyes narrowed in a moment of annoyance but the look and the emotion behind it did not last long before he turned his thoughts to practicalities. "I should not go until the queen…Arlan needs me here."

"You could take the Gate and return before noon," the healer suggested.

Kavan visibly blanched. He had not considered the Gate because he was, despite his words, resisting the thought of seeing her again. But he knew his cousin was right; there was no point in delaying the inevitable indefinitely, and there was no logical argument he could make against the use of the Gates. "Yes…it would be the fastest way…save me a sea journey…" he admitted. And if Gabrielle endeavored to detain him, he could use the queen's condition as an excuse for an urgent, abrupt return. "If you have need of me…you' know how to find me. As for anyone else, tell them I will return as quickly as I can."

It was a positive, brave step Kavan was taking, and Ártur would never dare refuse those small requests. "I will preserve her, Kavan, but then I must return to the keep. I do not wish to be away from the queen any longer than necessary. I will ask gdhededhá Claide or Tusánt to keep an eye on her." He clasped Kavan's free hand. "Good luck."

Kavan nodded without meeting his cousin's eyes. He did not dare risk undermining his courage by catching even a small morsel of humor in the healer's face. With the brooch clutched tightly in his hand, he left the thóres, padded silently across the open expanse of the worship hall and entered the Purification Chamber where the nearest Gate was. It had been many years since he had operated the k'rylag, and despite his nervousness about what lay on the other side, he was looking forward to the expenditure of energy this use would allow.

With his head dropped back and eyes closed, he took several breaths and sent a tendril of energy into the air, seeking the path to his destination. The cluster of tiny points of energy, like stars against the blackest sky, shimmered there, each within his reach if he chose to use them, each minutely different in subtle, almost indistinguishable ways. For Kavan, however, familiar with the desired path, it was a simple matter to quickly find the point he desired. Once contact was established, he pulled the tiny point of power towards him. Or perhaps he pulled himself towards it; he was never certain how it worked. The anticipated disassociation of his mind and body was followed by the sensation of floating through a cool, mist, and then it was over.

Prime Magistrate of Káliel Gabrielle Dilyn pulled the stack of documents towards her, raising her quill pen to sign the latest onslaught of amendments and proposals approved by the Council. Her maidservant, Delia, came to announce yet another visitor, interrupting her for the fifth time this morning. She straightened her hair, smoothed the bodice of her green velvet gown and waited for her visitor to be escorted in. Delia often questioned why her employer had taken to wearing mostly green over the years, but Gabrielle had never explained. Not that she needed to. Delia had been there when the Elyri bard had visited the islands. She might be growing physically feeble, but her mind was still keen and she knew that color choice was connected to the bard with the emerald green eyes.

In the back garden behind her, Gabrielle could hear her daughter Clianthe shouting childish obscenities at some toy that refused to cooperate with her. Gabrielle smiled, knowing that she had been much the same as a child and understanding now what her parents, particularly her father, must have endured to raise her. The servant woman knocked on the doorframe and bowed as she brought a gentleman into the room.

"Thank you, Delia…welcome, Lord Mancs." She forced a smile and did her best to sound pleased to see him, though she was tired of visitors today.

"Greetings to you, milady. You are looking exceptionally beautiful today," said the simple, average looking man with the dimples in his cheeks, a smile, and an awkward bow. He hardly looked like a lord with his saltwater stained trousers and sun-browned skin, but as such a look was common for seamen on the island, it was a look hardly noticed. He had taken the time to clean his hands and face, at least, and his hair, normally beneath the hat he held in his hands, was as tidy and clean as could be expected.

"I am not in the mood for flattery today, Lord Mancs," she said cheerfully, though her words were crisp and businesslike. "What can I do for you?"

Unfazed by the brush off, something that seemed no harsher than one would expect from a busy leader, he smiled in return and replied, "I have come to speak regarding the restoration of the south docks…"

Gabrielle listened as he rambled about the docks, the logistics of ship traffic, and the need for increased trading routes, but she did not fully hear anything he was saying. She had come close to marrying Elus Mancs; now, however, as she looked at his wind-dried face and listened to his low nasal voice discussing such mundane matters, she wondered why she had ever considered him. He must have seemed interesting to her at the time, and he must have been handsome, although he had not weathered kindly and seemed dull to her now. Despite her rejection of a future with him, he took every opportunity to be a spokesman for whatever group was lobbying the Council, any excuse to see her, even though he had his own family. Today, Gabrielle had no interest in boats or docks and certainly none in Elus.

A sharp stab of static charged the air, something she had not experienced in years, a touch of power that certain people could manipulate. Her focus went to the nearby closet, though her gaze stayed on her guest, a knot of fear and anticipation coiling in her stomach. Someone had used the Gate. There was no other explanation for that feeling. Someone was here, waiting in that closet. For her, she wondered? She cut her visitor short, eager to find out.

"I am sorry, milord, but this discussion will have to wait for another time."

"Milady…?" His tone and crestfallen expression reminded her of when she had turned down his marriage proposal. But today was business. Such children men can be, she thought.

"I have an appointment to keep that cannot be delayed. If these issues must be dealt with immediately, please feel free to present them to Felix. I am sure he can tend to your needs, and if the matters need my approval, he can discuss it with me later." Smiling, her eyes upon him still, she reached behind and to the side of her for the thick, blue rope whose chime would bring Delia to her, and waited with growing anticipation. Whoever was in the closet knew she had company and was either waiting for her visitor to leave, or was waiting for the room to be empty. That, she decided as Delia arrived, was nonsense. If someone wanted to come through that Gate unnoticed, they would have done it at night, and if they were concerned about being caught, they would have left as soon as it was clear that Gabrielle was not alone. Thus far, the Gate had not been reactivated; her visitor was still there.

Keeping the cordial smile in place, she offered her hand to her visitor as the woman came in. "Delia, please see Lord Mancs to the door…or to Felix if he wishes. And please, see to it that I have no further callers today. I have too many documents to study and sign; I'll never finish them as it is. I want no more interruptions."

"Yes, milady." Delia led Lord Mancs out of the room, but not before he cast Gabrielle a beseeching look. Gabrielle pretended not to notice it. Once certain she was alone and would be uninterrupted, she closed the window shutters so no one would witness whatever would transpire. Then she sat down, hands clasped nervously, and waited.

Kavan inhaled sharply, aware that Gabrielle was alone in the room now and that all he needed to do was to open the door between them and step out of the closet. Face her again. Thirteen years ago, he had fled her, through this same Gate, because of a kiss, the first and only one he had ever known. He stared at his still clenched fist, realizing that the sharp metal edges of the brooch were pinching into his flesh, close to drawing blood. Though he willed his feet to move, he was failing to take that final step towards confronting his past.

"I know someone is there," Gabrielle called in a low voice, one he recognized despite the years apart. "If you wish to speak with me, I am waiting. Otherwise, be gone. I have no time for games."

With his shaky, empty hand, Kavan pushed the door open, took another deep breath, and forced himself into the room where she waited behind the desk.

"Lord Cliáth!" The Prime Magistrate rose in haste, knocking the documents from their piles, her mouth open in amazement, her heart racing. She had not expected it to be him; there had been no reason to believe she would ever see him again, in spite of her hopes. He was dressed in a long white robe of heavy fabric and pale gray suede boots that she could see peeping out beneath the folds of white that brushed the floor. He was as she had last seen him, and to her eyes and her heart, he was as breathtaking as he had been thirteen years ago. He appeared not to have aged a day.

Shifting awkwardly from one foot to the other, Kavan would have stared at the floor, should have looked anywhere else, because her beauty brought back the overwhelming rush of physical responses she had previously aroused in him. He stood mesmerized, his eyes noting that she had changed very little except for small lines at the corners of her mouth and eyes and the thick auburn curls that were pulled into a neat bun on the back of her head rather than hanging loose upon her shoulders. She wore green, a green he knew closely matched the color of his eyes, and he did not have to ask why. He knew. When he completed his appraisal, his gaze stopped as his eyes met hers.

"I…pardon the intrusion; I should not have come unannounced."

Gabrielle nervously cleared her throat. "Nonsense," she murmured as she struggled to overcome the shock of seeing him again. "You know that as long as I live, you are welcome here. No other foreigner to my lands is as welcome as you." The sincerity in her voice and in her hesitant smiled allowed him to relax a little. He had thought she might hate him for the way he had left. "Pray tell, what has brought you back after such a long absence? Your prince became king, and I received your message of gratitude."

He bowed again. "We were most grateful for your assistance…"

"You do not need such formality with me," she laughed lightly. "Please…how is Captain Delamo? Is he serving you well?"

The bard nodded, wondering momentarily if the captain was serving him because of some oath he had made to Gabrielle. The idea was promptly dismissed. No man served another with such loyalty and devotion merely because a third party requested it. "He is well. I am very fond of him." It was an understatement, but he could not find words to express how much Wortham meant to him. "He is a favorite among the soldiers but has been placed completely at my disposal when I have need of him. I believe he requested that." The corners of his mouth twitched in an effort to smile. "He has successfully trained others in the style of the Káliel guard; his presence in Rhidam has been a blessing."

The news made Gabrielle smile. "Then we have contributed more to the mainland than wine and linen and a little aide to the current Lachlan monarch. It warms me to hear it and to know that you and Captain Delamo have become friends. He seemed to be the sort of man you would approve of; I chose him specifically with that hope in mind. And your King? How is he?"

That reminder of current events was sobering and brought Kavan back into the moment with painful abruptness. "He is well, though the house is in turmoil. The queen bore him a son yesterday afternoon, but she is in critical condition." Now he did look away from her, down at the desk between them, before adding, "She will die."

Gabrielle wanted to touch him, to offer comfort, but she did not. She knew he wanted nothing she could give him. He was deeply hurt and the most she could do was murmur, "I am sorry, Kavan. Is there anything I can do? Is that why you came? Does King Arlan require port on my islands or goods for trade?"

In answer to her query, Kavan extended his clenched fist towards her and opened it, revealing the smudges of blood from where the metal had bitten into his skin. Gabrielle had to come around the desk to see what he offered. She noticed first the blood, and then the brooch, and when her fingers brushed his skin as she took the brooch, their gaze met again. "You are bleeding…" she whispered.

Fighting to keep his breathing steady and to refrain from fleeing, he managed to respond, "It is nothing," as he hastily withdrew his hand and took a half step away. His gestures forced her attention back to her hand, and it was then that she gasped as she realized she held her mother's Serpent.

"Where did you get this?"

"It is not easy to explain…and I fear you will not like what I tell you…"

His words were dismissed with a wave of her hand; her curiosity was too strong to be deterred by any simple warning. "I will be the judge of that. Sit…please. Tell me where you got this. I have mine, and Father's passed to Felix after his death; Felix never takes it off." She sat on the bench near the door and patted the empty area beside her. "That can only mean…"

"A woman was found yesterday in the bed of a merchant's wagon in Rhidam. She had been stabbed once by a dagger laced with poison and was dead when she was discovered. I saw her this morning and I thought she was…until I touched her and then I saw…you. I believe her to be your mother."

"My mother is presumed…" What he was saying made sense, and the brooch was proof enough, but she found it difficult to accept.

"You told me you believed she had staged that boating accident…that her body was never found and you believed she had returned to Elyriá. I can show you the images I gathered from her if you wish; I may be wrong. Only you can verify her identity." He extended his shaking hands, palms up, an offer of one of the most intimate forms of contact any Elyri could give. Coming from Kavan, the gesture suggested certainty in his beliefs.

Overwhelmed by the unexpected news, Gabrielle stared at the brooch for many moments, wiping his blood from it with her thumb. He waited, half-dreading the intimacy of psychic contact as he watched the play of emotions flash and fade across her face. Finally, she set the brooch upon her lap and placed her hands upon his, her eyes closed as if afraid she might see something in his eyes that she did not want to face. It was that taint of fear that caused him to hesitate, but she did not retreat, seemed determined to know the truth, and he opened his thoughts, giving her access to those memories and images he wanted her to see. The dagger, the wound it had made, the dark-cloaked figure wielding it, and at last, the woman's head upon a pillow as Kavan had seen her.

Her mother.

The image took on more definition, as clear as if the woman was lying before her, and tears pooled at the corners of Gabrielle's eyes and broke free to slide down her cheeks. Kavan's hands impulsively tightened around hers; he regretted the hurt he was causing. When he started to disconnect, to take the image away, she fought him, using what little Elyri power she could muster, to savor this vision of a woman she had not seen in many years. Kavan relented, leaving the visage of the dead as vivid in his mind as if he were gazing upon her too, and through him, Gabrielle was able to see and grieve.

Both were unaware of the passage of time until a small voice intruded upon their thoughts, murmuring, "Mother?" with a note of concern. Contact was broken between them, the image of the dead woman vanishing as they looked into a small round face that nearly duplicated Gabrielle's, save for the more golden red tint to her auburn hair. "Why are you crying? Are you alright?"

Gabrielle bent to kiss the girl's head with a melancholy smile as Kavan gratefully pulled his hands back. "It is nothing, darling," she said as brightly as she could.

The child, however, was not fooled by the forced cheeriness. She pouted and stared at the unusual looking man sitting beside her mother. "Did this man hurt you?" she asked protectively, causing Gabrielle to chuckle and Kavan to tilt his head in amused surprise.

"No, Lord Cliáth would never harm me. He brought me unhappy news. I thought I told you not to come into the office when the door was closed."

The admonition made the little girl's stern expression fall away. "Father said I could play with Nona as long as I told you first. May I?"

Such a pleading tone, as well as the need to complete her discussion with Kavan, caused Gabrielle to smile and reply, "Of course you may." She kissed the child's cheek. "Now go, before Nona thinks you have changed your mind."

"Yes, mother," the child said with a grin and skipped out of the room with a backward glance at her mother's guest. Gabrielle, noting Kavan's pained expression, waited until the door was closed and they were alone again before speaking.

"My daughter, Clianthe."

He nodded once, but his troubled expression did not change. "I did not know you had married."

As the turmoil behind his words hit her, she felt her first moment of anger towards him. "You did not expect me to be unmarried forever, did you? Father wanted me wed before he died…it was necessary to ensure the line of succession…and I did not expect to ever see you again. If I had thought you would come back, I would have…"

Kavan's surprise was genuine, even though she did not finish what she had begun to say. "You would have waited? Married me if I asked?" The thought had never crossed his mind, and hearing that it had crossed hers was as unexpected as her anger.

"In an instant." She sounded suddenly sad, tired, and defeated, as if those flashes of anger had drained all of her strength. "You are surprised? I wanted to wait...to hope...but I knew..."

"Milady..." He tried to touch her hands but she returned to the desk, making a show of tidying the objects upon it. The separation between them was for the best, as touching her would have further inflamed the fire ravaging his soul. "I am sorry. I have no right...we hardly knew each other. You were the first...the only...I have kissed no one before you, or since. But I could not...marriage was not for me. May never be for me. I knew I would not have the opportunity to know you as I should...and I could not even consider..."

"I know." Back to him, she sniffed and dabbed at the corners of her eyes. "I knew by the way you fled. I knew there was no future with you...but I continued to dream...to hope. Just as every woman...and probably a few men... you have ever met has hoped and dreamed of a future with you. Do not look at me like that, milord. You know it to be true, even if you choose to deny it. Besides, a kiss is nothing, an expression only and not necessarily one of undying love. I doubt you have never kissed another woman because of what you feel for me. You are saving yourself for something greater, though Ethenae knows what that is. But," she turned to face him, a smile in place on her face, "Clianthe is my piece of you, in a way. She has her father's green eyes, and she is learning to play that old harp and enjoys it. I hum the songs I heard you play, and she has learned some of them. I even named her for you. It is all I have, all I will ever have."

He dropped his gaze at the unhappy note at the end of her words. Such knowledge made him sad, but there was also a flicker of relief that perhaps she would not pursue him, that he could find freedom from the desire he had carried for all of these years now that she belonged to another. "I did not mean to cause you pain...either then or now. You have the right to live your life as pleases you; I am not your judge or a dictator. Can we forget what cannot be changed and address the matters at hand?"

"You mean my mother." She brushed away the feelings of finality. It was for the best, she knew. He was beyond her reach, but at least she knew that for certain now. When he nodded, relief in his eyes that the past was put in its place, she asked, "Has she been buried?"

"No. My cousin agreed to preserve her body until I could ask you what you wish to have done. I can bring her here for burial if you desire."

Leaning against the desk, she gave the idea no more than a moment's consideration. "No; I do not think that would be wise. To bring her here, when everyone believes she died long ago, would cause unnecessary confusion and difficulty. Besides, she looks like my older sister, not my mother. How could I explain that without revealing that I am half-Elyri?"

The squealing of children came from outside of the room and Kavan eyed the door, expecting the child to burst through it at a run. "Is Clianthe…?"

Gabrielle shook her head. "She carries the power, but I do not know how extensively yet. She is only five. No," she came away from the desk and began to pace, "she cannot be buried here, but I would like to see her, touch her for myself. Would you object to my returning to Rhidam with you briefly? Long enough to see her?"

The bard hesitated, catching his breath at the thought of having to touch her in order to take her through the Gate. He had not considered that she might make such a choice. "I…would not…and I suspect the King would be pleased to welcome you…should you wish to meet him." It was the sensible offer to make, even if the idea was unsettling.

"Perhaps this can be the dawn of a new understanding between Enesfel and Káliel, initiated by my mother. It would be a fitting legacy." She stopped before him, shoulders squared with determination. "I will tell Delia I will be away…"

Kavan interrupted her. "I must ask you something further…or rather tell you…" Those details had almost slipped his mind. "My cousin says she was dying of an illness in her lungs. There was desperation in her thoughts…as if she was eager to see you again, perhaps to return the brooch to you. It was found pinned to the inside of her corset as if to conceal it, and I suspect she may have hidden something within that could tell you why she was in Rhidam…and possibly tell us who might desire to kill her and why."

The brooch was retrieved from the desk where it had been placed, and though the thought that her mother might have had some secret worth dying for was troublesome, she fingered the edges, seeking the small metal knob that would open its secret compartment. Inside was indeed a small folded piece of parchment. Casting Kavan a curious glance, her trepidation drawing her mouth into a frown, she lay the brooch down and unfolded the parchment in order to read the message, set down in tiny handwriting, aloud.

'Gabrielle,

I am delivering this to you through Lord Cliáth because I know he knows you and I know that, even if I could reach you in time, my presence would cause you difficulty. He can be trusted with this. I cannot allow this Serpent to fall into the wrong hands; there is much at stake, and if he gets this, all of Káliel, perhaps all lands, will be in danger. Lock the Serpents away, or better still, destroy them. If you do not, he will find them. Forgive me. I never meant for things to end thus. I live to see you again, but I fear I shall not. Take care, live well, and be happy, my child.'

Lísbhet.

Gabrielle's confused gaze turned on Kavan. "She knew I knew you?"

Kavan shrugged. "Stories about me are everywhere. If someone saw me here or spoke to Wortham or one of the others, it would not be difficult to find out."

"But I don't understand…why is Káliel in danger? Who is she referring to? Certainly not you, or else she would not have been delivering it to you. There is nothing about the Serpents that should place anyone at risk; why would I wish to destroy them? What danger could they represent?"

"They have existed for centuries; there could be a secret surrounding them, or their creation, that is lost to us, that could prove dangerous…"

Gabrielle snorted, although she was trying to take the matter seriously. "They're harmless bits of jewelry, not even particularly valuable. If there was a story or myth about them, I would have heard it, wouldn't I?"

Standing, Kavan came to her side. "Some myths fall out of circulation eventually unless written down or are changed in the telling until they are unrecognizable from their original form. People have been known to destroy whole cities for less wealth than these represent, and while they may not be valuable in a monetary way, they are powerful symbols. You might want to consider doing as she suggests."

Distracted by his proximity but wanting to think clearly, to make a decision not based on the influence of his personal magnetism, Gabrielle took a step away and shook her head. "I will not. They are, as you say, a cultural symbol, part of our history and part of my office. They are the islands. I will never destroy them, but…" She thought better of what she had first intended to say when she saw the disappointment on his face. "I will put them somewhere they will never be found. First, however, I must go to my mother. Wait for me, please…I will return shortly."

## &Chapter 6&

The man called Halstatt who was currently using an assumed name as he skulked around Rhidam, sulked in a tub of lukewarm water, scrubbing his nails with a brush, watching the large spider that hung to his left on a thin thread of web. He had neatly trimmed his beard with a pair of rusty shears his host had provided and he was almost clean again. The rented room was lit by a single greasy lamp and smelled of perspiration and rot, but as he had been short on funds and without the Association's assistance, this was the best shelter he had been able to secure on short notice. His quarters might be filthy and shabby, but Halstatt was compulsive about his personal cleanliness and manner of dress. Thankfully, his landlord had been able to provide him this tub and warm water.

There had been no move made by Caol Dugan yet, though given some military inefficiency, the soldiers at the gate could have forgotten to deliver the dagger. Or, quite possibly, the man, or someone else, could have recognized the weapon and kept it for themselves. Hopefully, if that was the case, the man's knowledge of what he had was incomplete; one mistake with that particular dagger could prove fatal. Halstatt would have to keep his ears open for word of an unexplainable death among the soldiers, and then swoop in to retrieve the dagger. Either way, he could only wait. As long as no one could identify him except Dugan, he was in no hurry to go anywhere. What he wanted was in Rhidam, and he would stay until he got it.

❧*❧

"I have made arrangements so that I might remain in Rhidam as long as I am needed," Gabrielle said with a melancholy smile as she entered carrying a large brown satchel. Kavan had picked up the scatter of documents that had fallen upon his arrival and replaced them neatly on the desk. She made note of his ponderous glance at her bag and laughed. "If I stay more than a day, I will need clothing."

"More than a…do you plan to stay long?" he choked. He had done his best to brace himself for a short stay in her company; he had doubts about being able to endure an extended one.

"Do you wish me to?" Her playful smile embarrassed him., but her expression sobered quickly. The reality of the need for this visit was too fresh and painful. "It is nearly noon and I do not think there will be time to bury my mother today. Besides, as you suggested, I would like to meet King Arlan while I am in Rhidam. I went to great effort and risk to assist him; it is time for me to meet the man I helped. I should like to meet your cousin also."

"Who will manage things here?"

"The Council can function without me; they generally do, and Felix is authorized to handle things that need a signature during my absence. He is a good man, but like many, he does not enjoy being ruled by a woman. He is annoyed that I am leaving without confiding my business, or my destination, but he knew how things would be when we married. He has nothing to complain about that he did not bring upon himself. He will be grateful for the chance to exert influence while I am away. Come…shall we go?"

Kavan nodded, wondering what sort of marriage she had, and followed into the closet, leery of being near her and trying to hide it.

"You will have to take us through," she continued. "I can no longer do it. Well…I can…but it would take too long to be practical."

The thought of losing his powers, of no longer being able to use them, made him feel vulnerable and ill. "I'm sorry…"

She chuckled at his reaction. "Don't be. Responsibilities keep me here. I only regret I may not be able to teach Clianthe to do it. Perhaps you will have to teach her."

"It might be best if she does not know her heritage." He did not allow Gabrielle to question him as he took her hands, refusing to hesitate any longer. The sooner they left, the sooner he could stop dreading that contact. The connection between Káliel and Rhidam was found and he took them through the Gate, leaving her breathless at the speed and ease with which they traveled. She looked at him with a pang of regret, both for that lost ability and the lost chances to experience more, and then she emerged from the Purification Chamber behind him.

"Hes á Redh Náós," she murmured, gazing into the high pointed arches of the ceiling. "I have seen drawings and have seen it from the outside, but it is much larger than I imagined…more dilapidated. I thought it would be…"

"It is scheduled for renovation; the King is putting a great deal of Enesfel's resources into the work. It will be magnificent when it is complete." She nodded, trying to imagine what this place must have been like when filled with candles, colored glass, people in their finest clothing, and lofty music. There had to be music. "Follow me; your mother is in the thóres."

There were arguing voices from the room Kavan led her to, but it did not deter Kavan from entering. He seemed comfortable in this place, more at home than he had been on Káliel. "Pardon the interruption, k'gdhededhá…"

The portly, balding man turned, his eyes lighting up at the sight of the bard. "Lord Cliáth! Praise be. Do you know anything about the

Serpent? It was on the nightstand when I left to call upon the queen, but it is gone. gdhededhá Tusánt has not seen it, and I doubt Lord MacLyr would have taken it…and Lord Cornell is demanding I turn it over to him as evidence…"

Gaze lowered, Kavan bowed contritely to the two men. "My apologies, milords. I did not consider that it might be evidence, thus I returned it to the lady's daughter. k'gdhededhá, Lord Cornell, this is Prime Magistrate Gabrielle Dilyn of Káliel. She has come regarding her mother's body."

"Prime…your mother…?" the justice sputtered, worried that she was here to demand retribution for the murder of a member of Káliel's sovereign family on foreign soil.

Until that moment, Gabrielle had been staring at her mother's body on the nearby cot. Though difficult to take her eyes from the woman who seemed far too young to die, when she realized that the justice was growing anxious, she looked at him sympathetically. "Do not fear, Lord Cornell. Lord Cliáth has explained the circumstances surrounding my mother's death. I do not hold you or Enesfel at fault for what has happened. My concerns are her burial and the apprehension of the person who did this."

The justice bowed. "We are seeking him. Thus far, there are no witnesses, but we will find something. The brooch…"

"Is in safekeeping," she finished for him and glanced at Kavan. "I have it. There is nothing unusual about it that should concern you. It is state property and I prefer to keep it where it is. If you have need of inspecting it, I will, of course, cooperate."

"Uh…" The justice groaned, at a loss for words. "Very good, milady. Lord Cliáth, there will be an assembly later today regarding this incident. Since you are the one that claimed she was poisoned, and you know her identity, the King has required you to be in attendance."

"As will I be," Gabrielle said.

"I…" A woman in a position of power made the justice uncomfortable. Such a situation was rare in Enesfel. He did not want to slight her and knew the King would want to meet with her, but this was a delicate matter. Surely, she would not want to hear the morbid details of her mother's demise. Hoping to discourage her, he said, "It will bring out the unpleasant details surrounding your mother's…"

Gabrielle gave her most disarming smile, something she had long ago learned worked on many difficult men. "All the more reason I should attend. I wish to know what you know, no matter how horrific. I would like to be there if King Arlan will allow it of course."

Now that the King was brought into the matter, the justice knew he could neither deny her nor talk her out of it. "I will make your request to the King," he promised, bowing and backing out of the room hastily.

When he was gone, with politics out of the way, Gabrielle turned her attention to Jermyn. "You are the illustrious k'dedhá of Rhidam?"

The robust man flushed and bowed. "k'dedhá, yes; illustrious, I do not know. I think you have confused me with someone else."

"Nonsense." She offered her hand, beckoning him to rise. "I have heard much about you, all of it pleasant. Will you oversee my mother's burial?"

"You wish me to come to Káliel?" He had never been there and knew the islands rarely allowed visitors.

Her smile faltered. She seemed to be surprising these men a great deal and found it entertaining. "No, she will be buried here. It is a long story, one that I do not wish to discuss, but she would prefer to be buried here, I believe. It is too late today and I am not feeling up for a burial. If it could be done in the morning, I would appreciate it, your grace. If you both do not object, I should like to be alone with her now."

Understanding that request from a long career of helping families cope with the passing of their loved ones, the k'gdhededhá bowed and headed into the sanctuary. When Kavan, feeling like he should remain close by for her, did not follow, Jermyn took him by the arm and pulled him out of the room.

Once alone, Gabrielle knelt by the cot, touching the cold, waxy-feeling flesh of her mother's face, the only part of her that was not wrapped for burial. She looked as Gabrielle remembered her. It had been long ago, when Gabrielle was a small child, but time had not touched the woman and when Gabrielle had come to believe that her mother truly had died in the boating accident, as was claimed, the woman returned to her. Returned, but was dead.

She was crying again, as she had been with Kavan a few hours earlier, but she did not restrain herself. What had her mother been trying to tell her? What words were there that she could not put in writing lest someone learn of them? Why would anyone wish to kill her? Not for money, since her purse had been untouched. Something more then. For the Serpent?

Head filled with tumbling questions, her cheek resting against the cold bosom that had once rocked her to sleep, Gabrielle closed her eyes and continued to weep.

᪐*᪑

The queen turned over in her sleep, then suddenly snapped awake, startled by the demons in her slumber. "My baby! Where is my baby?"

At her bedside, Syl was reading on a cushioned stool, taking her turn at watch in order that her husband could get some much-needed rest. At the queen's stirring, the lady healer reached for her hand and held it lovingly. "All is well, my queen. Prince Hagan is asleep in his cradle."

"Hagan...I must see him...bring him to me."

"Milady," the healer murmured, trying every skill she had to soothe her. "Please…be at ease. This state is not good for you. Prince Hagan is asleep…"

Not for long, Syl feared. The queen squeezed her hand roughly. "You do not understand. I must see him. It could be the last time."

Syl stifled the panic that gripped at her throat and cut off the flow of air. She had heard that the dying knew when the end was near but she had never believed it. She had known few to die, save for through violence or illness, thus had never seen the theory tested. Unsure of how to proceed, she tried to sound reassuring, to ease the queen's panic. "No, my queen. You will be well. You are healing…"

"I must see Hagan!" the bed-ridden woman begged. "And the children…bring me the children…"

Deciding not to argue lest she upset the woman further, Syl brought the now crying infant, stirred from slumber by his mother's distress, from the cradle and kissed his pink forehead before placing him in the queen's arms.

"Bertram first…then Diona…then Muir. Bring them…"

The worried healer retreated from the room.

Brenna breathed a little easier once Hagan was resting in her arms. How could she explain the dream, the gathering of záryph around her, telling her to bid farewell to those she loved to be free to go to them? The children, Deidre, Guthrie, and Arlan. And Kavan. He must be there at the end, she knew, and she did not question why. Bertram's boyish frame appeared in the doorway and she held out one hand to him. He trudged into the room, crawled onto the edge of the bed, but refused to touch her or come any nearer, as if he knew some terrible truth and wanted to distance himself from it. The queen motioned for Syl to close the door to keep the other children from hearing what she had to say. Now was Bertram's time. The others would come.

❧*❧

The stateroom was silent and tense as the gathering of royal advisors waited for the last few to arrive. Ternce Wyndham spoke in hushed tones to Minos, careful not to raise his voice. Across the table, Bhríd sipped a glass of water and watched Caol from the corner of his eye, curious about the man's nervous state. They were all edgy today, but Caol's agitation seemed different. Guthrie McHador sat with his head in his hands, rubbing his eyes, trying not to think about his niece, trying to focus on the purpose of this meeting…the murder of a woman Justice Cornell suggested was related to the Prime Magistrate of Káliel. Beside him, Ártur ran his hand through his hair, wondering why he was here when he should be upstairs with the queen or asleep as he had promised his wife. Wanting to be there had nothing to do with distrusting his wife's healing skills; Ártur preferred to be there himself should an emergency arise.

At the head of the table, the King looked small and weak, having gotten no sleep. He had meant for this meeting to begin five minutes ago, but the news that the Prime Magistrate of Káliel was in Rhidam and requested to attend this meeting concerning her mother had prompted him to wait. He did not know how she had come to be in Rhidam this soon after the murder was discovered but suspected it was Kavan's doing. If the bard thought it wise for her to be here, she would be welcomed. Once she, k'gdhededhá Jermyn, and Kavan arrived, they could complete this meeting and he could return to his wife's bedside. Why did a murder of this importance have to occur now?

The door opened and the three latecomers entered. The men at the table stood in deference to the foreign dignitary in their midst. She approached Arlan without hesitation and extended her hand to him. "I apologize for my tardiness and for keeping you from your duties, Your Highness. I was involved in my grief and did not consider that this house has enough of its own. My prayers and thoughts are with your queen; I hope she has a quick and full recovery."

He took her offered hand and kissed it; she in return did likewise to his. "Your prayers are welcome, Prime Magistrate," Arlan managed to say without choking on the words or stammering. "May your prayers be heard and answered. I am, likewise, sorry for your loss, which is the reason we are gathered. Please sit, if you will, and we shall begin." He nodded at Kavan in acknowledgment, always feeling a little better when the bard was near, and took his seat, with the bard relinquishing his usual position at the King's side to Gabrielle. Once everyone was seated and the introductions were made, he turned to Minos. "Lord Cornell…please."

The justice straightened in his chair. "Yesterday the body of a woman was found in the bed of a merchant's wagon in the cloth district; she had been dead for several hours when she was discovered, her body cold, the blood in the wagon and on the ground around it nearly dry. There appeared to be no attempt at robbery, as she was still in possession of a purse of bhelts. The merchant, Simin Dralski from Levonne, was questioned, but he claims ignorance of the lady's presence there."

"That name is known to me," Gabrielle remarked. Heads around the table turned in surprise. "His family is a contact for much of the linen we export. I have never met him, however."

"Would your mother have known him?" asked Minos.

"Is this woman your mother?" was the counter-question from Ternce, who leaned his elbows on the table and glowered at the woman suspiciously.

His stare did not deter her. "She is indeed my mother, Lísbhet Dilyn. As for whether she knew him, I could not say. His family has been in the linen export for generations, but he only came to my attention after my father's death. My mother has not been on the islands in many years; if he did not recognize her then they may not have met…"

"Or he was lying to protect himself," Minos snorted.

"Perhaps…there are trade records on Káliel if you require them."

The King raised his hand to cut off whatever retort Ternce was about to make. "You will allow us to review your records if the need arises?" It was an unexpected offer from the leader of the isolationist islands.

"I will do everything I can to see that you get them," Gabrielle agreed readily, almost producing a smile on the King's weary face.

Instead of smiling, however, he waved for the justice to continue.

"The facts are inconclusive. She did not appear to have been robbed, still possessed a purse, and though her dress was torn and soiled there is no evidence that she had been abused in any other way. She had been stabbed once and made it into that wagon of her own accord. As it is unlikely she traveled more than a day with that wound, less now that we know she was poisoned, we are questioning everyone within a day's walking distance." That this meant potentially every man and woman in Rhidam was not mentioned.

"What if she did not walk but had come by horse?" Guthrie asked, recalling the shadowy figure he had seen in the alley the previous day.

Or come by Gate, Kavan thought, considering the images he had gained from Lísbhet. He half listened to Guthrie and Minos arguing over the logistics of a woman riding a horse with such a wound. No. The merchant had dealt in cloth; the cloth and garment district was near Hes á Redh Náós. That suggested much to Kavan, and so he said, "I would suggest questioning those between where she was found and the náós…or those who had been there that day. She was attacked after leaving there…she did not have to travel far to find shelter. If anyone saw her, or her attacker, I suspect they will have been in that vicinity."

Both the justice and general were prepared to retort, still finding it difficult to accept direction from the bard when it came to matters of security, but a stern glance from Guthrie silenced them both. "Do as Lord Cliáth suggests; I trust his instincts." He did not remember the náós Gate and had no reason to suspect the woman had come through it if he had. He had not seen the body and did not know she was Elyri, but after thirteen years, he would not begin doubting Kavan's instincts. The bard's insight into people, and his foresight, had saved too many lives too many times, Guthrie's included, for the chamberlain to distrust him. "Your Grace, if you do not object, it might be prudent to search the sanctuary and the grounds for evidence."

The balding man nodded. "By all means, do. If murder was conducted on our holy grounds, I want to be the first to know."

"Is there anything more, Lord Cornell?" asked the King, pleased that his advisors and staff were on top of this matter without him needing to give commands.

"Yes, examination of the wound by both Lord Cliáth and Lord MacLyr confirmed that the lady had been poisoned…"

The King's face lost color. He had lost his mother to poison. This case was beginning to strike too close to heart. "Poisoned? What type of poison, Lord Healer?"

Ártur shrugged. "I cannot say. It was powerful; I do not think I could have stopped it…it was something I have never encountered before. Without having seen its symptoms, I could not hazard a guess as to what it was. For the record, however, I must point out that she was dying already, of an illness in her lungs. That illness, compounded by the poison, resulted in respiratory failure."

Caol's head snapped up and he stared at the healer as if the man had grown two mouths. Respiratory failure. That was one of the primary effects of the Coryllien poison, particularly for Elyri. He thought about the vial he had discarded in the fire last night and his throat went dry. It was coincidence, surely, he decided, but though he tried to keep his expression nonchalant, he knew the chancellor was scrutinizing him closely.

"How did the poison enter? Something she ate or drank?" Guthrie asked.

"She had been stabbed in the abdomen, below her left lung," the healer replied. "Judging from the condition of the flesh around the wound, I would wager it entered on the blade itself."

The King looked at the k'gdhededhá, seeking his opinion. "Did you examine the wound? Do you concur with Healer MacLyr?"

"Indeed, Your Highness…the strangest puncture I've ever seen, its three edges a faint purplish-black…as if the skin was beginning to rot where the blade had touched…"

The justice scowled. He had not noticed that discoloration when he had found her, and Sorvis had not mentioned it to him. Perhaps it had only become visible as the body had begun the process of decay.

"Three edges?" asked Bhríd, leaning forward, aware that Caol grew more agitated though few in the room noticed.

"It was a tri-edged blade, like this," explained the justice, indicating with his fingers, as best he could, the pattern the blade had made.

At the far end of the table, Caol's blood ran cold and his hands began to shake beneath the table where he kept them hidden. He did not otherwise react outwardly, as he had before, but the prickle at the back of his neck caused him to look into the green eyes of the harper. Not for the first time, he was unable to hold the man's gaze and quickly looked away.

Ternce drummed his fingers on the table. Ever the skeptic, he asked, "Are you certain it was a triple blade and not three separate entry wounds?"

Minos shook his head. "Physician Sorvis examined her; he swore it was too clean to be more than a single puncture. The man drinks to excess, but he has never been wrong before. It looked like a single entry wound to me."

"To get a wound like that, the edges clean, with three blows, would have required the woman to be unconscious or dead already," k'gdhededhá Jermyn remarked. Smiling at the responses, he continued, "Just because I am a man of Faith does not mean I am ignorant of the world. I know a little about medicine, and I know what I saw when I washed the body. There were no jagged edges that would suggest three entry wounds. The injury was too precise in both detail and location."

The justice agreed. "Even if the killer was a professional assassin, his victim would have had to be stationary to get a wound like that with multiple blows. I have never in my life heard of anyone standing still while under attack if they can help it."

With his arms crossed over his chest, the King leaned back in his chair and glanced at each person seated around the table. "What type of weapon could make that sort of wound?"

After that moment of eye contact, Kavan had been unable to take his eyes from Caol, though until this moment he had been unable to ascertain what he detected in the other man's demeanor. But the words that flashed through Caol's mind in response to the King's question came through as if they had been a shout, and the bard's stomach twisted into a tight ball. Kavan's whisper, when it came, brought a deafening silence to the room.

"A Coryllien dagger."

He knew the legends. Anyone well versed in history, especially Elyri history, did, and the Coryllien stories were still often used as precautionary tales to encourage children to behave. Kavan did not know why, with everything he had heard and seen, especially the images in Lísbhet's mind, he had not thought of that possibility sooner. At his side, Gabrielle grew pale and clasped her hands tightly in an effort to stay their trembling. Yes, she realized, the dagger Kavan had shown her could have been a Coryllien.

General Wyndham laughed. "Those are myths..."

"I would not be cer..." Bhríd started, though he was cut short by both the harsh glare Caol gave him and by Kavan's next remark.

Though he felt sickeningly chilled, the bard said, "I can describe for you the exact detail of the dagger that confronted Lísbhet Dilyn at the moment of injury; I saw the image when I touched her, although I did not…" He shook his head. He, more than anyone else here, should have recognized it sooner. "You may draw your own conclusions."

Closing his eyes, he described the deadly instrument line by line. The gold gargoyle handle encrusted with polished black stones of unknown type or origin, the gleaming blue-silver triple-edged blade like a three-point star nearly a foot in length. Each detail he revealed caused Caol's apprehension to grow, crowding around the corners of the image in Kavan's head until he had to push it aside to focus on the image. He would confront Caol later. This was not the time.

Guthrie rubbed his eyes and looked at Bhríd. They had talked about the Coryllien daggers last evening. But he, like nearly everyone else in the Sovereignties outside of Elyriá, believed those daggers to be more myth than reality. This unexpected revelation surprised him, but the chancellor seemed to take it in stride, appearing troubled but not astounded. The chamberlain wondered what connection there might be between their discussion and today's events.

"That description perfectly describes the dagger…the drawings I've seen," Ternce said in disbelief. "You have either seen those same drawings or have seen one of the daggers with your own eyes."

The bard ignored the implications in the general's words and used a soothing mind touch to calm his cousin when Ártur's anger flared. "I have not, but Lady Dilyn did. It was what she saw before it pierced her body."

But the general would not be put off. The possibility that the Coryllien dagger was real, that it could have surfaced in Rhidam, that it had been used to kill a noblewoman, was too surreal to grasp. "Where would such a thing have come from? No one alive has ever seen one, as far as I know. To murder this woman this way…"

"…is what remains to be discovered," said the King at last, studying the bard's flushed face. The Elyri was fighting away something unpleasant; Arlan knew his friend well enough to interpret that disturbed expression, and he did not like it. Kavan was not easily unsettled, and seeing it spoke to the King of bad omens ahead. Between them both, Gabrielle looked perplexed, as if she wanted to speak but was not certain she should, but Arlan leaned a little closer to her, and asked, "Lady Dilyn? What is it?"

Unclasping her hands, she smoothed the dress across her lap before speaking, as though stalling for time as she sought the words to say. "It may be nothing…but my mother's final message to me contained a request that the Káliel Serpents be hidden or destroyed lest they fall into the wrong hands and all of our lands be in grave danger. She had hidden the Serpent inside of her corset, where k'gdhededhá Tythilius found it, and she had hidden her message within it." She looked from the King towards Kavan. "There is one version of the Coryllien myth that claims that Dawid Coryllien was born on Káliel and that he returned there to die. Nearly all the myths I have ever heard claim he died there. There are numerous stories around the islands claiming different locations to be his resting place, and many believe there may be treasure buried with him. Believing his gravesite to be both haunted and cursed, few have gone in search of it…and of those who have, most have never returned or returned empty-handed."

"Could there be a connection then," the King asked, "between your mother's death, the Serpents, the daggers, and these tales of Coryllien?"

Kavan nodded, his expression grim. "If her killer knows the myths, which he might if he has such a dagger, then he could believe the Serpents are the keys to what he seeks." It made it more imperative that Gabrielle be rid of those brooches, although his personal curiosity about the mystery binding these seemingly random things together was strong.

"I have them in safe keeping; no one will have access to them except me; there is no cause for concern…"

The door opened, interrupting whatever more she intended to say, and the lady healer entered the room. "Pardon my intrusion," she said contritely in a strained voice that brought her husband to his feet. "The lady is awake and asking for you, Lord Chamberlain. She is being unreasonable, demanding that you come to her at once."

"Not unreasonable," King Arlan said hastily. Whatever his ailing wife wished for, he was prepared to give. "Go to her, Guthrie. Lord Cornell, continue your investigation and alert the watch to the possible existence of this dagger. I want to know if anyone has seen anything suspicious. Prime Magistrate, you are welcome in Enesfel for as long as you wish to stay. Perhaps while you are here, we can discuss a new relationship between our realms."

"I would like that, milord," Gabrielle said with a curtsey before the King followed his chamberlain out of the room, with Ártur behind them. Most of the others waited until the King was gone before leaving the table.

"Lord Harper, might I have a word?" Bhríd asked, noting Caol loitering in the nearest doorway, eyeing him cautiously. Kavan motioned to his kinsman and the two stepped away for further privacy, leaving Gabrielle alone. "This will sound odd, but it concerns Caol…"

That same cold fear as before knotted in Kavan's stomach; when he glanced at the inquisitor, the man hastily left in response. "What of Lord Dugan? Is there trouble?"

"I wish I knew. Last evening, someone left a box for him at the front gate; General Zarkosta delivered it. Caol told me without opening it that he believed it contained a Coryllien dagger…or a replica of one. I did not see it, but I know no reason for him to claim it might be something so exotic if it was not. I do not believe Caol could be responsible for the woman's death, as it would have occurred before he received the box and I was with him for most of the last two days. But with few daggers claimed to exist, what is the likelihood that more than one has appeared in Rhidam at the same time?"

"Lord Cornell is the one who should…" Kavan started, not understanding why Bhríd was revealing this to him. It seemed likely, if Caol possessed what he claimed, that he had the murder weapon. What had Kavan to do with that, beyond the desire to see it himself?

"You know Minos does not particularly like Caol and would likely act first and ask questions later. You are less threatening, more likely to learn the facts first, and more likely to give Caol a fair hearing. I know you sensed that he is hiding something, that something is troubling him; I do not think he will talk to me, but he might talk to you."

Kavan nodded. What his kinsman said was true. For reasons he never understood, the bard had a gift of getting people to relax, to talk, to be open about things that they might not otherwise speak about to anyone. And as Caol was one of the King's best friends, getting to the truth without unnecessarily disturbing the King at this troublesome time was paramount.

"I will speak to him. Let us pray that he is not somehow involved; Arlan would be devastated."

"Aye, he would be," the dark-haired Elyri said with a sigh as he bowed and departed to do as the King had bid him.

Alone in the stateroom, save for Gabrielle, Kavan stared at the portrait on the wall before him, trapped within the walls of his own whirling thoughts. It was a landscape, a portrait of the southern fields beyond the walls of Rhidam, which Ártur had painted many years ago, a painting the King had insisted upon displaying. There was something in that simple meadow with its rim of distant hazy trees that Kavan found especially soothing today. Not as soothing as it would have felt to shed his troubles on falcon wings, but soothing enough that he thought he would be able to face the world again after losing himself in it. Gabrielle, however, was not going to allow him that; she came to stand beside him, slipping her arm around his as she also gazed at the painting. Despite the awkwardness of physical contact, it was a comforting gesture, one that he found he did not mind.

"This is beautiful. Who is the artist?"

"My cousin."

"The healer? Ártur MacLyr?" The bard nodded. "Artistic ability seems abundant in your family…"

A prickle of discomfort crawled up his spine, but Kavan could not explain it. Instead, without taking his eyes from the painting, he said, "Ártur's primary talent is healing; painting is a diversion he has spent nearly twenty-one years perfecting."

Gabrielle side-eyed him at hearing that strained note in his voice, but his tension did not keep her from asking, "And your talents, Lord Cliáth?"

The purr of her voice caused him to step abruptly away; the throbbing it awakened in his body was unwelcome. "I am a harper, you know that. Come, I will find a lady to serve you and show you to a room for your stay." After a quick, perfunctory tour of the library, dayroom, and the kitchen, and after placing a plump serving girl at her disposal, Kavan deposited Gabrielle in an empty bedchamber, leaving her without further word. She watched him go, regretting her propensity for pushing him away when all she wanted was for him to stay.

## ❧Chapter 7☙

Guthrie came out of his niece's room into the King's chamber and went directly to the nearest window, not speaking, not acknowledging the King or anyone else. Three children sat on the King's bed, Princess Diona stifling her sobs as she tried to comfort Prince Wilred who was crying uncontrollably. Dangling his feet over the edge of the bed, Prince Bertram huddled next to her, kicking the nearby chair, an act of frustration and angry fear that no one could adequately address. Princess Deidre was at the desk with Caol behind her, his broad hands upon her shoulders lovingly. Now and again, they would look into each other's eyes, communicating with expressions, touches, and gestures that had developed in the years of their marriage. Syl curled into a huddle before the fireplace and occasionally cast mournful glances at the doorway that led into the queen's chamber. k'gdhededhá Jermyn stood next to the hall door, not certain he belonged here but knowing he was wanted, that his faith and support would be needed as the night wore on. Prince Muir had been sitting on the bed when Guthrie went in to visit the queen, but now he was sitting alone by the armoire, wide-eyed and unsettled looking, keeping his distance from everyone. He looked as lost as Guthrie felt. The older man gestured to Muir to join him, and though the boy hesitated, he did as requested, accepting the comfort of the strong arms of the man he knew as uncle.

There were many long tense minutes before Ártur emerged from the nearly dark room. He ran one hand through his hair. "My Liege, she wishes to see you. Syl, she has asked for Kavan and his harp. Find him, please."

Death was something that had never truly touched Arlan. He had seen men die in battle, yet that was killing. Murder. He had sanctioned executions, but those deaths had been impersonal, meaningless to him as anything other than a peacekeeping necessity. His mother and father had died, but he had been a newborn infant when his father passed; he had never known the man. And he had not been in Rhidam when his mother died; it had seemed more like they had merely stopped seeing each other. Two of his children, infants, had been lost, stillborn, but they had been tiny and helpless, dead when he first saw them. Watching Brenna lie frail and weak was different. Her life was draining away little by little and he was unable to plug the leak. Before the pregnancy, she had been vital, fun loving, and alive. Now she was pale and fragile, a faded shadow, and it pained him to see it.

He settled on the bed, longing to lie with her, to hold her, to make everything better. But Ártur had warned against unnecessary movement on her part and Arlan did not intend to contradict that order.

"Brenna?" he said, taking her hand in his. Her skin was hot to the touch. "I am here."

Her eyes opened, a flicker of her old self igniting at the sight of her beloved husband. "You came."

"I would be nowhere else." He kissed her knuckles and continued to hold her hand. "The family is in the other room…Diona said you told her…"

"I am dying."

"No. Do not…you must not say such things. You have too much to live for. I love you; I need you."

"You have always been strong, Arlan. Be strong now. For the children, for the kingdom, you must be strong."

"I was strong because of you," he choked.

The woman shook her head. "Because of my uncle and Lord Cliáth you were strong. Are strong. They were with you before I was; they will remain when I am gone. Trust them…let them help you."

"You will not go anywhere," he repeated firmly.

Though she tried to smile at his stubbornness, the effort fell short. "You want it to be so…but this time I think your commands will go unheeded. But please…you must promise me something."

"Anything." He kissed her knuckles again with pleading urgency. "I will promise you anything if you will stay with me."

"Promise me that you will not blame Hagan for my death. He did not ask to be brought into this world; this is not his fault." The King's face hardened and he growled, causing Brenna to squeeze his hand and struggle to sit. "Arlan, please…promise me…"

The effort to wring acquiescence from her husband brought with it a spasm of pain that caused her to groan and double over. With it came the slow creeping stain of red across the bed sheets that caused the King to jump to his feet, crying "Ártur!" The word was barely past his lips when the healer burst into the room; Ártur pushed the King aside, made the woman lie down, and placed his hands upon her abdomen, sliding them slowly downward until his healing senses located the newest source of bleeding.

"Arlan! Please!" Brenna begged, her need to hear that promise from her husband overriding any concern for self-preservation.

"Keep still," Ártur scolded between clenched teeth.

Arlan squeezed closer, took her hand, and clung to it. "I promise, Brenna. Please…do not leave me…"

In the doorway, a crowd gathered as the family tried to see what was transpiring. Guthrie stood inside to the left, with one arm around Princess Diona and another around Prince Muir. k'gdhededhá Jermyn came into the room, stopped at the foot of the bed, prayer beads in hand, his thick lips moving silently in fervent prayer. Deidre held Wilred, trying to silence his crying as her husband stood with his arms around them both. Prince Bertram stood beside his sister, less cocky and demonstrative as he watched the stain on the sheets continue to expand.

"Some light please," Ártur muttered. The k'gdhededhá was the only one to respond. As he lit two more candles and held one high to aid the healer's work, Prince Bertram gasped to see more clearly the red of that stain. Princess Diona buried her face against Guthrie's side. Muir bit his lip but refused to move or look away. At the rear of the gathering, Gabrielle had come in; her hand flew to her mouth when she saw what was happening. Then Syl arrived and elbowed her way into the room and to the bedside with Kavan in tow.

The bard had been in the upper oratory when Syl found him; he knew the state of things, knew the queen's condition, before he was summoned. His prayers had not been enough to alter the course of events thus far, and so he had been praying instead for strength and peace for the family that might soon be left behind. Syl had not needed to speak when she found him; he rose from the place he had knelt upon the altar steps and followed her. He took a quick appraising glance at the bloodstained sheets, set the harp on the bed, and took one deep breath before laying his right hand upon Ártur's and taking Brenna's free hand in his left. Ártur felt the surge of energy from his cousin, boosting his healing gifts, enabling him to stop the flow of blood more easily. He met his cousin's gaze with a mixture of thanks and regret. There was so much more he wished he could do for her.

"Not yet, My Queen. I came as you asked."

"Kavan," she whispered weakly, "do not let him hate Hagan. He promised…"

The King and bard's eyes met, both of them knowing that it would take more than a mouthing of a promise to make that happen. "I will do my utmost, milady. You have my word. Do you wish something from me?"

"A song."

Nodding, he released her hand and readied the quarter-scale harp upon his lap. "Any particular one?"

"Any…an offering to záryph…to greet them…when they come…"

"Brenna…" Arlan began, only to be cut off by a stern glance from the healer. The woman did not need emotional agitation.

Kavan stared at his hands upon the silent strings. It felt like an empty eternity to the others in the room. Nothing he had composed thus far felt appropriate for what she asked. No, he needed something new, something beautiful with which to greet záryph. Eyes closing, he pictured the tapestry hanging in his room, the black-winged záryph upon it, and allowed the music to pour forth from his hands. He wanted to sing, to give voice to the words pushing into his head, but he did not. The focus here must be the music and the queen, not his peculiarly androgynous voice. The song was alternately joyous and triumphant, and then mournful and breathtakingly beautiful. He was unaware of the tears shed in that room, or that Prince Muir had come to kneel beside him with his hands clasped in prayer.

But he was aware of the energy gathering around them. The presences, the forces that frequently came to comfort him in his time of need, were here, and he knew from the touch of his cousin's hand upon his leg and the k'gdhededhá's hands upon his shoulders that they felt it too.

Gabrielle cried freely as she watched the unusual display unfolding within the queen's chamber, and she was grateful when the dark-haired chancellor entered behind her and put his steady hands upon her arms; it helped her remain on her feet beneath the onslaught of raw emotion. The white harper played as if the queen's soul depended on it. The healer had one hand on his patient and the other upon his cousin's exposed white knee, while the k'gdhededhá clutched his prayer beads in one fleshy fist. Prince Muir knelt in prayer close enough to Kavan that he might as well have been in the harper's lap. The woman called Syl joined them and placed her hands upon the queen, closing her eyes as she aided her husband in his healing efforts.

Stranger still was the energy Gabrielle felt building within the room, the sensation of being in a crowded place with a multitude of others she could not see. Kavan appeared to glow with a faint, silver-blue light, but if anyone else noticed either that glow or the presences, they did not visibly react.

Blessed k'Ádhá, she thought, what is he doing? How powerful is this man?

One by one, the other family members came to the bedside. Bertram, Deidre, Caol, and Wilred stood at the foot of the bed, hands intertwined. Guthrie stood behind the King and put his hands firmly on the monarch's shoulders. Arlan glanced at him but quickly turned his attention back to his wife, praying desperately for a miracle at Kavan's hands. Diona climbed onto the bed and pulled her mother's head onto her lap, stroking the dark hair with its first strands of silver. Every face in the room showed traces of tears except Kavan's. Whatever was happening, it was a sight Gabrielle had never witnessed before and knew she would never see again.

"Perfect," the queen's raspy whisper broke through the music. "They approve. They are here...can you tell...?"

"Yes...I can..." Kavan's voice trembled with emotion he did not show, deeply humbled by the visitation of záryph.

"Take my hand, Kavan...they want you to..."

She said no more. The music slowed and one white hand closed around hers. Kavan continued to pluck a simple tune with his other hand; the music never faltered. Instinctively, as he held her hand, he lowered his internal defenses further to fully see what she saw.

The room was filled with silver-robed figures, most of whom were featureless to him. The one feature he could distinguish, however, was their wings, wings the color of storm clouds, as the Heretic-Saint's accounts described. A tiny gasp of awe escaped his lips, but the auburn rimmed face of the man who stood closest to him was unmistakable and calmed the initial anxiety. "Milord Kóráhm," Kavan whispered aloud, loud enough that the hands upon him tightened when the others heard.

He had not seen the Heretic-Saint in thirteen years; the last time he had, the Saint had been quite real, flesh and bone. He was not that now, or the others in the room would have known he was there, seen him with their own eyes. How a man could appear in both forms, Kavan did not know. This was not, however, the time to ponder existential questions.

The one called Kóráhm stretched his hand forward, beckoning. Do you want her to come to you, the bard's thoughts went out, not daring to voice words that those in the room did not need, or want, to hear. Kóráhm could hear him without spoken words.

Kóráhm's reply was a single nod of his head. Kavan refocused his gaze from his mind's eye to his green ones and looked into the queen's fevered face. Seeing two realities simultaneously caused his temples to throb. "Are you ready, My Queen?"

Twisting her head to the other side, she stared at her husband and squeezed both men's hands. "I am ready, Kavan," she whispered, before pulling Arlan's hand to her lips and pressing it there. "I love you…"

The bard focused again upon the saint and his entourage of záryph as she spoke, and extended his hand towards them, with the woman's still clutched in his own. Kóráhm took her hand from Kavan as she spoke those final words to Arlan, and before the King could interfere, Kavan murmured, "Farewell, My Queen." Finding peace in her serene expression, he released her hand.

Those in the room saw Kavan raise her hand and release it as he bid her farewell. The music ceased and the room fell silent. The two healers, whose hands rested upon the ailing woman, would never be able to explain what they experienced at that precise moment, but as Brenna's eyes closed and Kavan released her hand, they felt a familiar tremor run through her body. The queen's hand lingered in the air as if held there by an invisible force, and then dropped limply to the bed. Syl and Ártur looked at each other in awe as Prince Hagan began to cry in his cradle.

The King was the first, other than the healers and Kavan, to realize what had happened. "Brenna…" he begged, a squeak of despair pulling at his voice.

"She is gone, My Liege," Syl said gently, reaching for his hand.

The King eluded her grasp. "Kavan! You…" He growled and tried to reach across the bed, across his wife's unmoving form, but Guthrie's hands upon his shoulders prevented him from reaching his target. Inundated by the growing despair in the room, his eyes filling with tears, Kavan tucked his harp beneath his arm and squeezed out of the room, not even aware that Gabrielle was there. The child-like wail of grief that followed him down the corridor was like icy daggers piercing his skin and he was grateful to make it to his room without being followed, to escape as soon as he was able.

After placing his harp upon his bed, he stood at the window, trying to calm his trembling body. Had it been only this morning that he had broken the mirror? It felt as if that had been centuries ago. The mirror and Muir. Gabrielle, Caol, the Coryllien dagger, and Brenna. Kóráhm. Too much had happened today, most of it unpleasant. He looked into the sky, longing to fly but knowing he was too exhausted and agitated to keep the change for any significant amount of time. He needed a more immediate form of release.

His heart, and the need for escape, drove him through the deserted hallways into the quiet courtyard where he could lie upon the chilly stones and stare into the sky. If the guards in the watchtowers saw him, they likely pondered his behavior, if they gave the eccentric bard any thought at all.

There were no stars in the sky to offer comfort tonight; it was overcast with the pregnant promise of rain in the air. Let it rain, he thought. He was not above lying where he was, in the rain, if the experience would wash away his grief. The náós bells tolled midnight and from the second floor of the castle he could hear Prince Hagan crying, the King bellowing, and other voices jumbled into an incoherent stream of sound. He did his best to shut it out of his head, not wanting to hear anymore, wanting only the cold discomfort of hard stone and the peace of earth and sky.

It was over. The end of an era, Tíbhyan called it. Wise Tíbhyan, where are you when I need you, the bard thought. Where was anyone he could lean on? Ártur, Syl, and k'gdhededhá Jermyn would tend the body, and the baby who had not been consecrated today as scheduled. Guthrie would tend the King, if Arlan allowed it; otherwise, he would turn his attention to the children, as Caol and Deidre would. And while Kavan felt that perhaps he should be there for Prince Muir, right now the need to be alone was overpowering. No one could see his grief. He would leave Prince Muir to Guthrie.

How would he ever be forgiven for this? How would the King ever look at him again without seeing the man who had killed his wife? Not killed, but Kavan had been the gate; he had delivered the suffering woman into the hands of death, had made her way safe, had let her go. He knew he could not have stopped her without divine intervention. Kóráhm's expression had been set and her body had been too weak to continue. She had wanted to go; it was her time. But how would the King ever accept that Kavan had been a conduit of her death?

"Kavan?" Gabrielle settled onto the stones beside him, crushing the green velvet of her gown beneath her. She brushed the silver-white strands of hair from his face but he did not react or respond to her.

Catatonic he lay, his chest barely rising beneath the thin veneer of his robe, his eyes open but unfocused, unaware of her being there. Heart full of what she had witnessed, she remained with him, tracing the fine line of his jaw, wiping away the occasional tear that moistened his temples. Felix would rant if he heard of it, as he was too possessive to think she could have a male friend. But Felix be damned; Kavan needed a friend. To hell with anyone who thought otherwise.

The náós bells chimed the first hour before Kavan finally blinked and looked at her, his hand gripping her wrist savagely, preventing her from touching him further. There was a flash of anger in his eyes that startled her, as she had never seen him angry before, but he had already released her to get up and brush the dirt from his robe.

"Kavan," she begged. "I want to help."

"There is nothing you can do," he replied in a clipped tone without looking at her.

"I can try…"

"You!"

The shout surprised them both as King Arlan appeared as if from nowhere and spun Kavan towards him. "Bastard! You killed my wife!" He swung, catching the bard off guard; his fist connected solidly with Kavan's jaw. Gabrielle heard the crack of bone and gasped in alarm. Though the harper stepped out of reach, he did not otherwise react to the blow.

"Didn't you hear me? Traitor! You and your damned Elyri sorcery! What spell did you use? What demons did you call to take her away?"

Kavan did not speak and the King leaped forward again, mercilessly swinging at the other man who did nothing to fight back or defend himself, hitting him in the stomach, the chest, and the face again. This time he drew blood from the bard's nose and lips and sent Kavan sprawling onto the ground. Gabrielle backed towards the castle, wondering if she should call for help or if the King would stop this outburst before he killed Kavan. Where were the guards? Why did no one come to break up the fight? Why was Kavan not defending himself? She stopped moving when she bumped into someone and turned, startled. It was Prince Muir. The young man caught sight of what was happening over her shoulder and started forward, perhaps to break up the fight, but she caught his arm. In the rage the King was in, there was nothing the young prince could do without risking his life.

"Fight me, coward! Stand up to me!" The King straddled Kavan where he had fallen and pulled him up by his robe, tearing it as he yanked. "You are pathetic," he cried, seeing tears in the man's eyes. When he shoved him against the paved stone, there was the harsh crack of bone. By then, two soldiers had arrived but stood gawking, uncertain what to do. Did they dare break up the altercation since it was the King involved, especially since the King appeared to be winning?

Nausea and blackness swam in Kavan's eyes, but the ball of energy gathering within his chest was enough to keep him from blacking out. Remembering what that ball of energy had done to young Prince Owain some thirty years ago gave Kavan the impetus to pull abruptly away. The King stumbled backward, far enough that Kavan was able to get to his feet, fighting the dizziness as he tried to steady himself.

"That's right, coward. Fight like a man for once..." He lunged at Kavan again, knocking him back to the ground with a snarl. "...if you can."

Clamping down on the growing ball of energy, the Elyri growled. If this did not end quickly, he feared he would be unable to restrain that force and it would burst forth, as it had done when he had been a child. This time, however, the greater magnitude of his power would likely do more than give the King a headache. It might kill him. He pulled away, willed himself to stagger to his feet and prepare himself for Arlan's charge. He caught the King and held him at arm's length. Arlan swung wildly but could not reach his target. Agitated, he tried to twist away; Kavan released him, and though Arlan stumbled, he did not lose his footing or fall.

Rethinking his strategy, the King darted in, knowing he had to catch the bard off guard if he was to succeed in hitting him again. Fearing what the Elyri could do, the soldiers took a few steps forward but the King angrily waved them off. This was his fight and he meant to take Kavan on his own. He danced back, out of the bard's reach, after one quick thrust into his ribcage. He was surprised when Kavan, in turn, charged at him, but he saw it coming in time to spin sideways and attempt a kick in the bard's direction. Kavan caught his leg and brought Arlan crashing to the ground.

Kavan's eyes narrowed as he released the King. Arlan crawled to his hands and knees, panting for breath, then began to stand, before recklessly rushing forward, head down like a charging bull, aiming for the man's abdomen. Kavan brought up one knee into the King's face, flinging the man vertical. He took one swing, connecting squarely with the side of the King's head and Arlan was thrown several yards to the left as though he were a toy. On the courtyard stones, he did not move for several minutes. The night was silent once more. Prince Muir and Gabrielle were gaping wide-eyed, but neither spoke as the guards flanked the bard, wondering if he had killed the King, wondering if they should take him into custody, cut him down where he stood, or leave him alone.

As if to answer their dilemma, the sound of sobbing, a sound Kavan easily identified, broke the silence. With a deep breath, he dispelled the last of that ball of death inside of him, stepped away from the soldiers, and knelt beside the King.

"My Liege…"

Arlan sat, threw his arms around the bard, and wept. Kavan gathered the man against him, and though he had shed all of the tears he felt capable of, he still grieved. Gabrielle felt she could breathe again, and relieved that it was over, escorted Muir back inside, though not without both of them pausing several times to look back. The guards too, realizing the spat was over and that there was no animosity between the combatants, stepped a respectable distance away but they continued to watch to be certain the King was well and that Kavan did not retaliate.

"She is gone, Kavan. I can never get her back. There is much I wanted to say to her…now she is…forever…"

"She is in your heart, Arlan. She will always hear your thoughts." An owl hooted in the distance, a mournful sound that made him pause before adding, "I am sorry, Arlan…"

The bearded man shook his head, wiping his wet cheeks in vain. "There is nothing for you to apologize for. She knew it was coming; she asked you to be there…to take her through. But I wish…it could have been me."

"She knew you would not have let her go. And what I did, what I saw, I doubt anyone else did…or could have."

Arlan drew back to look at him. "What did you see? At the end?"

Dabbing the blood from his lip, Kavan considered his words carefully. He would tell the truth, of course, but he wanted to do it in a way that caused the least amount of pain. "The room was full of záryph…all around us…and Kóráhm was there to take her."

"Why Saint Kóráhm?"

Kavan shook his head. "I do not know. Perhaps because k'Ádhá knew I would trust him with her. Perhaps because I thought about him before I started to play. Perhaps merely because he wished to be there…and could be."

"Then she is safe?

"Free from pain, My King. She will suffer no longer."

Arlan rubbed the side of his face; it was tender and starting to swell. "Pain and suffering…I think my eye will match Muir's come morning."

Embarrassed, Kavan's gaze fell. "I am sorry, My Liege. I was afraid I might have caused you serious harm."

"It's nothing time and rest won't heal, I'm sure." His heart, on the other hand, he believed would never heal.

"At least I did not fracture your jaw or skull," Kavan sighed, still dizzy despite not moving.

"I…we must have Ártur look at you. I could not bear to lose you too…not tonight. I didn't think you would fight back…that you are so strong."

"All Elyri are. Have you never wondered about Bhríd's prowess? He is significantly stronger than I am, but even my strength would be more than a match for most Teren. My people are feared enough for what we are suspected of; why compound that with unnecessary displays of strength. Be grateful a black eye is all you have. If I had not hit you, if I had continued to be passive, and you continued to attack me, you probably would be dead, your brain exploded inside your skull." He did not react to the shocked expression on Arlan's face as the King helped him to his feet, though he did feel a sinking sensation that his honesty may have driven another wedge between them. "Do not ever do that again."

"I shall not. I shall remember this warning. I would like to keep my brain intact." Supporting Kavan as they turned to go inside, he asked, "Kavan?"

The bard looked at him tenderly, although there was much pain in his eyes, both emotional and physical. "Yes?"

"I am sorry. About hitting you, about the things I said. You are not a coward, a traitor, or a sorcerer. You are the finest man I have ever known. You could not have killed Brenna. It is not in you to kill."

A dark shadow crossed over Kavan's face. "It is in every man to kill…with the right incentive. You were angry; you needed a release. You chose me instead of a mirror." He shrugged away the King's puzzled look. "I will explain later. Let us find Ártur to be certain we will both live, and then try to rest."

The King groaned. "I do not know that I will ever sleep again, Kavan…but I will try."

## ❧Chapter 8❧

Halstatt looked cautiously about before stepping through the doorway into the bustle of noon in Rhidam. He had exchanged his dark clothes and cloak for a foppish yellow jerkin and leggings, and had obtained a brown leather eye-patch and wide-brimmed, blue plumed felt hat. With the beard he had grown specifically for this mission, Caol would not immediately recognize him, and if the royal militia were looking for the man who had delivered the dagger to the castle, they would likely be using the inquisitor's description of a smooth-faced, blond haired, wiry thug. Halstatt was no longer wiry and his hair had been dyed a dark brown. He smiled at a passing maiden carrying a water jug on her shoulder and would have offered to carry it for her, for a price of course, if he had not been out on business. Halstatt had never been one to ignore an attractive woman.

He had heard that the Queen of Enesfel had died during the night. While not particularly affected by the news, he regretted never having had the opportunity to see a woman that by all reports had been exceptionally beautiful. Childbirth complications, he had heard. All the better. Best way for a woman to die, he felt, doing what women were meant to do. Of course, any one of the women in his circle of acquaintances would have slapped him for that and a few would have knocked him to the floor. But he liked those spats, as they reminded him where he stood in the world.

The other bit of news did concern him, however. The body of an Elyri woman had been discovered in the bed of a merchant wagon. She had been stabbed with a triple-pointed weapon, a Coryllien dagger it was rumored, and it was said she had been poisoned. Her burial had taken place that morning in the náós plot. The town guard was perplexed that she had retained her possessions and did not appear to have been robbed or raped, only murdered.

Well, she would have been, he thought bitterly, spitting on the ground. She had been poisoned and would have been stripped of possessions and honor if the wench had not pulled away from him to flee into the early morning streets. She had been amazingly strong for such a slight thing. He pursued but lost her trail. Her escape angered him; he would have disposed of her properly, to keep anyone from finding her, if he could have. Now he had the authorities on his tail.

But they were looking for a man with a dagger he no longer possessed, a dagger that was somewhere on the royal grounds. Someone would either be eager to be rid of it quickly, delivering it to Caol if they had not already or turning it into the authorities. And if it was Caol who had it, the man would be squirming. He would know there was no way to trace the dagger to Halstatt, and if he spoke, if he turned in the dagger, his possessing it would raise serious questions about Caol's history and loyalties. Halstatt felt confident that he had little to fear.

Rather than fear, however, he felt anger, anger that he had lost the Serpent. She had it; he knew she did, even though he had not seen it when he grabbed her. Halstatt hoped that the good gdhededhá had found it and removed it with the intention of either sending it to Káliel or adding it to the náós' treasure store.

There were too many people around the dilapidated place of worship today, too many mourning the death of their queen. Halstatt would have to wait for a better opportunity to get inside. Tonight, perhaps…or tomorrow. Yes, there was a carnival setting up at the fringes of town, a festival in the making. He would not likely be noticed then. Turning into an alley, he backtracked to his room. He would busy himself by creating some sort of plan to get the soldiers off the trail of the Coryllien…and to get to Caol Dugan.

৯►*৯

The castle grounds were tranquil aside from the distant tolling of náós bells that called the townsfolk to the memorial in honor of their queen. She had been interred earlier in the garden sepulcher where decades of other Lachlans had been buried. The bronze plaque with her name upon it gleamed brightly in comparison to the others surrounding it. All of those monuments to fallen royalty suffered from varying degrees of tarnish and weathering and many were difficult to read, but Kavan made a point of coming here to polish the metal markers whenever he could. For such a long-lived people, remembering the dead was a very important thing.

He rubbed his fingers across the plate bearing the queen's name and then sank to the ground with his back against the marble wall of the mausoleum. All that remained of the queen was stone, metal, and memories. He closed his eyes, refusing to compare his age, as Ártur frequently did, to that of the recently deceased. Kavan refused to give in to that form of despair. It was not age that had claimed Brenna Weylin Lachlan, but the complications of childbirth and k'Ádhá's will.

Lísbhet Dilyn had been buried at dawn in the Hes á Redh Náós cemetery. It had been cold and foggy, with a slight mist in the air, but thankfully there had been no rain. Kavan hated when it rained at a burial. k'gdhededhá Jermyn presided over the simple ceremony at Gabrielle's request. Few attended, only Gabrielle, Kavan, Ártur, Prince Muir…who believed that someone should stand in as a representative of the Lachlan family...and in the distant shadows, Caol Dugan. Kavan found the inquisitor's attendance puzzling, but he was unable to question him. The man faded from the scene before anyone could speak to him. Kavan doubted anyone knew he was there.

The small group returned to the castle where a brief ceremony was then conducted to christen the baby Hagan Guthrie Brennan Lachlan. Then, at noon, the royal household gathered here in the garden on the east side of the castle to pay their final respects to the late queen. Again the k'gdhededhá presided. The fog had lifted by then, but the air was still cool, as if her passing had taken away the world's warmth. There was weeping, from all except the King who had stared into space as if he was present in body but not in mind. Because the King had not wanted a large communal ceremony that might require him to make a public spectacle of his grief, the k'gdhededhá arranged a memorial service in front of the náós where the public could mourn the woman's loss. It was the second hour past noon. Three funeral services in one day. Kavan was grateful he was not in the k'gdhededhá's place.

At last, the bard was alone. He had not spoken to Gabrielle except at her mother's graveside, and now she was meeting with the King to discuss trade policies and other matters of politics. Arlan was eager to get about life as usual, to pretend that last night and today were a dream, that Brenna was merely away visiting family. He requested Kavan's attendance at the summit with the Prime Magistrate, but Kavan politely refused. Not today. Unlike the King, he could not will these events away, nor linger in Gabrielle's presence while he felt raw and vulnerable.

She was a friend; that much he knew and intellectually accepted. Her marriage denied them anything else, and he easily admitted that he wanted nothing more from her. But intellectual knowledge and acceptance of their positions did not keep him from wanting to touch her, and whereas he had cleared his conscious of that desire once, now that she was married he felt dishonorable and guilty about physical responses he could not quell. But he could ignore them, refuse to act upon them, if he tried hard enough, which was what he was striving to do by keeping his distance. Ignore them long enough and perhaps they would cease to be a distraction.

Two sets of footsteps approached through the growth of flowering bushes. Princess Diona and Prince Muir. The princess truly was Muir's constant companion. They were as close as any brother and sister could be. He did not speak as they paused to look at the plaque that marked their mother's resting place, and then they snuggled on either side of him as close as they could get.

"Avoiding your lessons?" he murmured.

The princess shrugged. "Lady Ilene has gone to the náós with Father's permission…"

"And Lord Cáner has canceled our swordsmanship for the day. We had hoped to find you in your room…"

"But when you were not there, or in the oratory," the girl continued, "we thought perhaps you had gone to the service as well. We came here…and here you are." She tried to smile as she wrapped her arms around his neck and kissed his cheek, but the smile did not reach her eyes.

"Yes. Here I am."

In the silence that followed, Kavan studied Muir out of the corner of his eye, realizing for the first time how tall the youth had become. And how much like Prince Owain he looked. Unlike the rest of his body, however, his hands were still small, much like Kavan's more delicate ones, he noted, as he turned his attention to his own white hand against the young man's shoulder.

The sight of his hand gave him an idea. Relinquishing his hold on both children, he put his hands in his lap. "Here, sit up. Both of you. Watch my hands." It might not cheer them, but it would, he hoped, distract them from their grief for a few minutes. With his hands cupped, he focused his energy, causing the instant glow of a small yellow globe to gather there, pulsing and shimmering as if it were the sun itself caught in his hands.

"What is it?" Prince Muir gasped, his voice hushed in awe.

"Sunlight."

The princess looked up as if to make certain the sun was still in the sky and that Kavan had not somehow captured it. Seeing it was still in place, she looked at the smaller globe again. "How do you do that?" she whispered with a perplexed scowl.

Kavan was pleased that his efforts to distract them was working. "I cannot explain it in a way you would understand. It is just something I can do."

"Is it real?" In response, Kavan placed it in the prince's hands before Princess Diona gathered enough courage to touch it. "It is! It's like a warm, prickly snowball."

Her brother holding it was all the encouragement Diona needed to try again. But the glow was already fading and the ball quickly dissipated into nothingness. Pouting she asked, "What happened to it?"

"It went back into the air," Kavan explained. "Out of my hands, they do not last very long."

"Then make another one." When the second ball materialized in Kavan's hands, she clapped with joy and took it from him tentatively. "You are right, Muir…it is like a snowball!" She tossed it at her brother and he caught it moments before it disappeared.

"Can you do it with moonlight?"

"Of course, my prince. Or torchlight, or firelight. Any sort of light. Moonlight is cooler to the touch…"

"And prettier I wager."

The bard nodded. "I think so."

Diona grunted. "Nothing could be prettier than sunlight, Lord Cliáth. It is what gives life after all."

"But night brings peace and stillness…" Muir countered.

The girl scrunched her face. "And monsters."

Kavan interrupted the budding argument with a third ball of light, which he this time molded with his hands into a square block. The children poked and prodded at the shape in his hands, molding it to their whims, into faces and animals and objects, their minds no longer occupied by the loss of their mother. For Kavan, the use of the energy, the power he released into this simple diversion, was an immense relief after having allowed it to lie mostly dormant for too long. The recent use of the Gates, his brief psychic contacts with Gabrielle, Lísbhet, and the queen, and this easy, amusing diversion, were the most he had used his gifts in years. While it was a much-needed relief, the doing also filled him with the overwhelming desire and need for more, to empty himself of energy to the point of exhaustion. Perhaps tonight, he mused as the naós bells tolled three in the afternoon, he would take the chance while the castle inhabitants slept.

The children stopped their play and looked at one another, the mournful tolling darkening their mood. Reluctantly, Kavan allowed the light in his palms to float back into the air.

"Lord Cliáth," asked the princess, "did k'Ádhá take mother?"

Despite the painfulness of the memory, the bard managed a sad smile. "I saw the záryph there to welcome her, Saint Kóráhm as well. I am confident she is with k'Ádhá."

Prince Muir plucked a dainty pink flower from the shrub nearest him. "If Saint Kóráhm was there, she is surely safe and happy. There is no cause for mourning." His words were more certain than were the emotions behind them, and his sister looked far from convinced.

"Mourning, no," Kavan said. "But you are still allowed to be sad that she is gone. It is permissible to miss her and grieve the loneliness."

Kicking at the dirt with the heel of her shoe, the princess asked, "The service is over?"

"It should be."

Carrying the weight of their words with her, she got to her feet and brushed the grass and dirt from her gown. "I should go. Lady Ilene will be back soon."

Kavan caught her hand and kissed the back of it affectionately. "I want to apologize for scolding you the other day," he began, regretting that he had not had the chance to say the words before.

"I know you didn't mean..."

"You were a brave girl, to stay with your mother the way you did. It made her happy to have you there. Remember that you are allowed to miss her and it is acceptable to cry."

The girl nodded her head, impulsively kissed her tutor's cheek, and then wove her way back through the garden until she was out of sight. Only then did Prince Muir slide away from the bard a little and lean back against the stone behind him. Each thinking their own thoughts, the two men remained silent until the prince's musings demanded voice.

"Lord Cliáth?"

Kavan did not turn his head. "Yes?"

"Last night...after Mother...why did Father hit you?"

The bard's expression of surprise faded quickly. He had been unaware that the prince had witnessed the episode, as the tone of his question suggested. Hoping that perhaps the young man was merely responding to the morning's gossip, he replied, "He was angry and hurt..."

"I was there...I saw everything. That was not...you did nothing to deserve being beaten like that," the prince snorted with a scowl.

"Blaming me for your mother's death was easier for him than blaming k'Ádhá or himself, although I suspect he will do both in his grieving. And it was certainly more acceptable than blaming Hagan." He suspected, however, that the King would always blame that child, regardless of the truth. "Besides...I was there in those last moments with her. I let her go. Rather than cry, he needed to be angry."

"He hurt you," Muir growled, "and I hate him for it."

Taken aback by that fierce animosity and hoping he could diffuse it, Kavan faced him. "Do not hate him, my prince. He did not hurt me out of hate, and I do not bear him ill. It was nothing Ártur could not undo, and I am well, as you can see. Bruised, but nothing more. Arlan and I have made peace; everything is forgiven, and I beseech you to do likewise."

Muir shrugged and grunted. "Perhaps...but he should not have done that to you for any reason. He could have killed you if you had not...you..." His eyes widened. "You hit him back!"

Those words made Kavan groan and rub his temples. "Believe me, Muir...I had no desire to fight...but it was the lesser of two evils. I did what I had to do to protect him. He understands that, and it will not happen again."

Although he had no idea what his tutor was talking about, the prince detected the gravity behind the words and his frown deepened. "Still...I did not think you would...after...well...after the things you have said about strength and violence. I did not even know you knew how to fight."

"There is no special knowledge to self-preservation. My actions were not born out of anger or the intent to hurt or kill. I merely acted to prevent something far more terrible. I am grateful I succeeded, but I regret the way it had to be done."

"I am grateful too. Next time Bertie wants to fight, I will remember what you did." The prince relaxed against the wall, his thoughts jumping randomly between that fight and his mother. Beside him, Kavan sighed and wondered if he would have done anything differently if he had known Prince Muir was there.

❧*❦

In the encroaching twilight, Caol skirted the passers-by and stuck to the shadows of the alleys as he wove his way through Rhidam's underbelly. He looked nothing like the prince he had become by marriage to the King's sister. The collar of his cloak was folded up and his telltale red hair was covered with a floppy gray scarf he had wrapped around his head. He kept his head down, though he remained aware of everything around him, every small noise or movement or smell. He had no intentions of being caught off guard tonight.

He had tried each of his contacts, all of those underground elements he had used once before to orchestrate the kidnapping of Princess Deidre as a diversion to keep then King Owain occupied while Arlan fought to secure Enesfel's throne. No one was eager to tell him anything that might provide clues about Halstatt's whereabouts, regardless of what he tried. He had done his best to assure them that talking to him was not snitching to authorities, that he and Halstatt had personal, familial connections that stretched back for generations, but even that tactic failed. No one was willing to trust him because of his connection to the Crown.

The only thing he succeeded in learning was that there had been a second murder, one the justice was unaware of, the death of an eight-year-old child of one of the Association's local leaders. The child had been killed near the náós with the same sort of triple-edged blade that had killed Lady Dilyn. A witness to the other crime, no doubt, though even in the Association it was seen as shameful and without honor to kill a child for any reason.

Caol knew those rules by heart, knew that the murder of children was deemed unthinkable, even if the child was a witness to your grandest scheme or was the offspring of your worst enemy. It was a way of perpetuating the Association. Halstatt would know those rules too. That he had ignored the unwritten law revealed one important kernel of truth. Halstatt was desperate for whatever that woman had owned, or had known, and for that, he had gotten careless. Careless enough to kill her before a witness, careless enough to kill again, a child, to cover his tracks. Careless in the Association was dangerous. Children were not pawns. One way or another, at Caol's hands or those of someone else, Halstatt would pay.

Caol prayed that those hands would be his.

❧*❦

Bhríd flipped rapidly through the pages of the manuscripts he had taken from the library's shelves. He was looking for references to either the Coryllien daggers or the Dugan family. Judging by Lord Cornell's lingering distrust, it appeared that he knew something unsavory about the Dugan family, but Bhríd would question him only as a last result. Approaching the Justice too early in his investigation could implicate Caol in a murder that the chancellor was sure Caol had no hand in. At the very least, it would raise suspicions. Perhaps, Bhríd decided, if he examined the census records first, he would learn something, find a place to start, though he was uneasy about looking there. Taxes and census taking were his duties to the Crown; he had ready access to the records and no one would question his right to examine them. But he did not wish for anyone to question what he was seeking. Right now, he did not know what he expected to find.

He inquired about the person who had delivered the box to Caol, but Yorick was only able to question one of the two guards who had received the delivery. That man could not describe the messenger with any accuracy, but he did indicate that his partner had opened the box to examine the contents, a dagger it was said. Unfortunately, the second sentry had been given leave to marry and could not be reached for questioning. General Yorick had badgered the chancellor about his interest in that delivery, but Bhríd refused to discuss it and made the man swear to keep the investigation silent until the second sentry could be questioned.

Bhríd knew that Kavan had not yet spoken with Caol. There had been no opportunity last night or today, and except for the queen's burial, no one in the keep had seen the inquisitor, not even his wife and son. Bhríd had not talked about his suspicions to anyone else, and a quick search of the man's room failed to uncover the mysterious wooden box.

Caol, he thought, replacing another armful of volumes upon the shelf. What are you hiding? What are you afraid of?"

⮞*⮜

"Gabrielle Dilyn is as beautiful as I imagined she would be," Ártur commented, alone in the dayroom with his cousin for the first time today. He had been shocked last night to learn what occurred between the King and Kavan, but not truly surprised. Arlan had been initially more angry than hurt at the loss of his beloved wife, and he had, for innumerable reasons, blamed the bard. The anger appeared to be gone, only the pain remained, though the King had buried it deep within. The healer was grateful that Kavan had been able to stop himself from killing the King while allowing Arlan the emotional release he needed, but he worried about his cousin's state of mind.

"Yes."

The healer looked up from the painting he was completing. "Is that all you can say?"

"What should I say?" the bard asked in a strained voice. "She is married; she has a daughter. The past is in the past."

"But your reaction to her has not changed. Do you love her?"

Kavan scowled. "I told you; I do not believe you can love someone you do not know…"

"But you know her…" He saw that scowl deepen and quickly said, "I am sorry. I will not discuss it further. Have you spoken to Arlan today?"

Looking up from his book, grateful for the change of subject though he would have preferred silence, Kavan replied, "Not since the service. He has been with Gabrielle all afternoon. He has not told Muir about the Queen's Final Statement; I think Arlan is expecting me to tell him. And he refuses to grieve."

"It will come, in time. For some people, it takes longer…"

"He will never get over her death. He will not let go of the pain because it is all he has left of her. This pain will be with him forever."

The healer sighed. "I hope you are wrong." But he knew the assessment was accurate. Kavan was nearly always right about such things.

Kavan set his book aside, closing it, the Volume of Saint Kóráhm he had received from Ártur when he had been six years old. He long ago lost count of how many times he had read it; he almost knew it by heart. He left his chair and stopped at the window where he stared into the darkening sky; his fists clenched at his sides as his thoughts waded into darker territory. There was a gathering of individuals in the courtyard; he knew none of them, recognized not one face, but he suddenly felt as if he was being crowded. Entirely too many people. "And I could kill them all in a second," he muttered to himself.

Catching those words, the healer stared, barely believing what he had heard. "You are troubled about last night?"

"Shouldn't I be? I am a killer," Kavan replied without turning.

"A potential killer, like everyone else…"

"Not like this. I could will a person dead and never bloody my hands. No one would know how it happened…except, perhaps, you. Eventually, it will happen, Ártur. I know it. There is no release for this." He thumped his chest. "I feel trapped…people watching me, judging, expecting me to be wise and above reproach. It was…a relief…in a way…for Arlan to blame me for her death, though I know there is no blame. I am not what people think I am."

"I know…"

"Do you?" Kavan's fists clenched and relaxed several times. "Do you understand what it is to have this tremendous capacity to do things…this abundance of power…and not be able to use it for fear of someone discovering it?"

"Everyone here, or nearly everyone, knows who and what you are and what you can do."

The bard shook his head stubbornly. "They know but a fraction of what I can do; you know only a fraction. I can never reveal to anyone the extent of what I am capable of; you are sínréc and I hesitate even to show you. I do not want to do things to impress people; I want to be free to do what I am able without fear of repercussions. Instead, I am expected to be the perfect courtesan and advisor, which I know I am not. k'Ádhá…I should never have stayed in Rhidam…"

By now, Ártur had stopped painting, placing the brush aside to stare at his cousin's back, watching the tension ripple through his body like shivering waves. He turned his thoughts to healing, diagnosing what was happening to Kavan and how best to address it. Confinement, yes. And loneliness. Those were things that he knew often plagued his cousin. But he had never known Kavan to be this full of anger and hostility. His green eyes, which Ártur could see reflected back to him in the window glass, were like those of a trapped beast, though the compulsions to pace, to escape or lash out, were kept under tight control. Whatever was going on in his cousin's head, thoughts Ártur could not see, Kavan was on the verge of breaking. "You could return to Elyriá any time you choose," he started.

But Kavan shook his head. "No. Arlan needs me here. I gave him his throne…or so he says; I owe it to him to stay…to help him. Besides, even in Elyriá I would be stifled…perhaps more than I am here. In Bhryell…they are more afraid of me for my differences than anyone here is. Here, I am only another Elyri."

"Well, then…where would you choose to go…if you could go anywhere?"

Kavan gave a wounded sigh of defeat. "There are not many places I could go."

Knowing that to be true, Ártur did not try to refute it. The only way Kavan would ever be free to wield the power without any sort of backlash would be to go somewhere without people, something that would make him even more alone than he already felt. How frustrating that must be. It was a familiar impasse between them, and it made Ártur's heart ache because there was nothing he could do to ease his cousin's burden. Instead, he asked, "You did not tell me what happened to your hand yesterday."

Kavan's jaw twitched. "I broke a mirror, as Prince Muir said."

"How?"

Though he felt his cousin's psychic probe, he did not, for once, try to shield his thoughts, but instead turned to look at the healer as if daring Ártur to think him a liar. "I punched it."

More taken aback by that challenging gaze than the response, Ártur asked, "Why?"

"Does it matter?"

"Perhaps."

Kavan shrugged and turned to the window. "I was angry. I was helpless, unable to aid the queen, unable to give Arlan the happiness I cannot find for myself. Because what I saw in that mirror sickened me." He shuddered at the memory of that moment. "I had to mar the perfection, destroy it before it destroyed me."

"Destroyed you? How?"

"I cannot tolerate any more pressure to be what others want me to be." It was not an answer to the question, but it was all he could say.

"I wasn't aware there was anyone pressuring you…"

The bard's short, bitter laugh was like a slap. "Weren't you? People assume that, because they see no glaring mistakes in my life I must be without fault. They expect me to continue to live that way. The expectations of others weigh upon my every action and decision.

If…or rather when…that mistake comes, I fear a great many people will be disappointed in me, rather than being supportive and understanding. I fear losing their approval, Ártur. It is all I have. Which is why I must be away; the longer this goes on, the more trapped I feel." His pleading gaze met his cousin's. "Sooner or later something unfortunate is going to happen if I stay."

Ártur ran one hand through his hair as he leaned back on his stool. "Have you considered that the only one expecting you to be perfect is you? You have always pushed yourself, Kavan…balancing on a razor path that only you can see. The pressure you put on yourself is tremendous, and I wager that is what is hurting you, not what anyone else thinks or does not think about you. Who cares what they think? The only ones you have to satisfy are yourself and k'Ádhá. You should learn to relax, to enjoy life, not to take everything as seriously as you do. Most people's goal is to better themselves, but you obsess over it to the point of fanaticism sometimes. It is devouring you."

The younger man wanted to make some retort, but he could think of nothing to say. He had no idea if Ártur's words were accurate, and at the moment he was too emotionally fractured and charged to think it through, or to care. He wanted peace.

"Kavan…fly." The bard looked at the healer quizzically. "No one else is in this room; you could fly out the window and no one would be the wiser. It is nearly time for the evening meal, but I can explain your absence. Stay away as long as you need, cleanse this anger from your soul before it poisons your beauty. As healer to patient, though I have never been a proponent of raigháthá, you need the energy release. As you said, it has been too long and there is too much power in you to leave it dormant. I know that being unable to use it makes you angry; if you do not release it, you will grow more bitter than you are…and I would not want to be around you when you reach that breaking point. Go. Fly. Quickly."

He almost thought he caught the beginnings of a smile cross Kavan's face, but the look was gone too quickly behind the bard's usually controlled expression to be sure. As a little boy, Kavan might have hugged his cousin out of gratitude. It was not that he actually needed permission, but emotionally, he did. Instead of hugging the healer, Kavan willed his shoulders to relax and closed his eyes. Ártur saw the shimmer in the surrounding air, as if the world around Kavan had shifted out of focus; he felt the tingle on his skin as energy was pulled from the air and was then the sole witness to the creamy white falcon that appeared in the room where Kavan had been standing. The bird hopped from the floor to the sill and waited for Ártur to open the window as it ruffled its feathers expectantly. As soon as the way was clear, the healer watched the bird disappear into the darkness, smiling to himself, again astonished at how quickly and easily Kavan could make such a change. That alone spoke to the depths of his strengths.

The falcon soared over the castle walls, over the towers, consumed by the joyous relief of being free from cares. In the sky, high above the men and women who always watched him, there was no castle, no Lachlans, no lords and ladies to entertain and please. No one to judge him. No one to fear him. There was the earth and the breathtakingly open firmament. He flew west, into the sinking sun, and then turned north, for no other reason than he could. Balmy wind caressed his feathers, swept past his face as he turned east again and flew for over an hour, relishing the expenditure of power and the physical activity. On impulse, he eventually folded his wings and rocketed towards the earth, pulling up moments before he hit the ground, and disappeared into a grove of trees.

What emerged from the grove moments later, however, was not a falcon, but rather the great white hart of legend, the beast that had not been seen since the night Owain Lachlan was dethroned. As tall as the tallest horse at the shoulder, its antlers gleamed silver, wider than a man's arm span. It strode confidently towards a group of women trudging home from the fields for the night. All four stopped to behold the creature, frozen as it approached. Few had ever seen it, and yet here it was, before them.

It lowered its head and rubbed its velvet nose against the closest woman's hand. She gasped but did not move away. Then the hart bounded back towards the trees. Doubtless, Kavan thought, that young woman would become the pride of her village when the story spread that she had touched the fabled white hart. Whereas she had been a humble girl no one had shown much interest in, soon he expected every eligible man in her community would be vying for the hand of the maiden thus blessed. Good. Someone with a chance at the happiness he was denied.

But as he reached the trees, he decided that this form did not feel right tonight. Flight was what he needed. The kestrel reappeared and took to the sky, determined to savor freedom for as long as it lasted.

❧*❧

Extending his hand, King Arlan bowed. "This meeting has been most productive, Lady Dilyn. Thank you."

Gabrielle chuckled and clasped the offered hand. "I thank you…but do not be too hopeful. Unlike you, I cannot normally make decisions for my people. Only the Council may do that, and after centuries of isolation, they will not jump eagerly at any proposed alliance, no matter how beneficial it could be to both of our kingdoms."

"Surely they will see the benefits…"

"Seeing, accepting, and doing are different things. Public opinion is beginning to change, with a little help," she grinned, "but it may be many more years before they agree to a treaty with anyone other than Elyriá."

"Then perhaps Enesfel's relationship with Elyriá should be made known to them. We have nothing but goodwill between us. We can at least, you and I, keep a dialogue open?" He was hopeful of the outcome of such a dialogue. It was all he felt hopeful about today.

"Of course. Now that we have met, I would think of doing nothing less than continuing our efforts to work together. I am sorry to have come here...to have this discussion at such a time...but I think we have made promising steps."

The shadow of grief lowered over the King's face. "It could not be otherwise...but I too am grateful for this opportunity to build something out of our mutual grief. If you will excuse me, milady, I have been negligent of other duties that I should see to before dinner."

She gave a curtsey of respect. "Certainly. I understand the responsibility of ruling; I do not mean to detain you."

Returning the bow, Arlan said, "It was worth being detained."

They entered the Grand Hall together and that was where the King left her. Knowing the meal would be served soon, and that others were already gathering in the adjoining dining hall, Gabrielle paced the room, musing over what it must be like to be the lone decision-maker for thousands of people. The idea made her uneasy; she trusted her judgment for her personal decisions and felt she had a good head on her shoulders to guide others, but she did not dare presume to know what was best for all of the people on her islands. She was curious how those like Arlan could do it.

The royal scepter lay across the throne where the King had placed it after the burial service earlier. No one had bothered to return it to its proper place; she thought it a miracle it had not been stolen. She picked it up, perched upon the throne, and fingered the large crimson stone that filled its gold casing. Was it a ruby, she wondered, having never seen that particular stone as far as she could remember. There was coral on Káliel, and pearls, and someone had discovered an abundance of faint, chalky blue stone dubbed sea stones. All other gems on the islands were imported from Elyriá, but their quantity was low. How she could increase the wealth of the sovereign family, indeed the whole nation, if she could gain access to gems such as this.

Above her, hanging on each of the four walls, were the royal standards, black Lachlan eagles nested in amber, trimmed in crimson. Much more regal, she felt, then the simple red Káliel Serpent on its blue background that hung in the Council House. The Serpent did not even represent her family as this did Arlan's. The Serpent was the islands; to destroy the Serpents was to destroy Káliel. Why, she wondered, did her mother beseech her to destroy those brooches? It made no sense.

"Good evening, Lady Dilyn." Startled, she dropped the scepter and a masculine pair of hands retrieved it. "No harm done," he said with amusement. "This thing is indestructible, I think. It has been used as a weapon at least once and survived numerous falls. You did not damage it, I'm sure."

Relieved that she had not committed some sort of political faux pas, she sighed, "Lord MacLyr…thank you…"

"My apologies for startling you. I am on my way to dinner…and to the kitchen to inform the cooks not to hold Kavan's plate. I did not mean to startle you."

"Is he well?" she asked, hoping to sound less distressed by the thought than she was. She had not seen him today, save for her mother's burial and the queen's service, and she had hoped for his company over dinner. After the fight with the King, Kavan had not looked well this morning, but he had insisted on going through with the formalities duty and friendship required. Hearing that he would not attend the meal both disappointed and worried her. Perhaps his injuries and exhaustion had overtaken him.

"He had personal business to attend; I do not know when he will return." Gabrielle kept her face turned away as she stood in an effort to hide her regret, but the healer sensed it. Wanting to distract her with light conversation, he asked, "How are you enjoying your visit to Rhidam?"

"Not as much as I would under better circumstances, but that cannot be helped I'm afraid."

"Indeed." Being here would be a reminder of her mother's passing, and there had been few positive moments in the castle these past few days. "How long will you stay? I assure you things here are not always like this."

"I'm sure of it. I have done what I have come for and am expected home. I should be returning soon, tomorrow perhaps if Lord Cliáth is available to…"

The healer tried to smile, the twinkle in his eye brightening his expression. "I cannot say what his plans are, as he is not one to shirk duty for long but…there is a carnival in Rhidam tomorrow, the Festival of Saint Mátán. You will attend, will you not? It would be a bright spot to your visit. We would hate for you to leave with such melancholy memories."

"I…"

He inched closer with a teasing grin and then reached past her to put the scepter on the throne. "My wife, Syl, does not enjoy carnivals and plans to stay with the infant prince and his nurse. I may have to tend the children, but even so, carnivals are not as much fun alone."

"I don't suppose Lord Cliáth enjoys such things…"

That made the healer chuckle. "Not particularly. He is not interested in jousting or sport, nor does he like the press of people."

"And yet he is a bard."

"Ironic, I know. I have never fully understood it either. He is a bard because he needs the music and it is what he excels at. Music is who he is. He dislikes the company of too many others while fearing to be alone. He is a conundrum. If there are actors, he will be there, and if there are other musicians, he will find them. He cannot resist the lure of other musicians, regardless of their quality. He is supposed to take the children to the carnival, but if he does not, I have agreed to do it in his stead."

Despite what he had already said, she found herself asking, "You expect him gone long then?" as if asking again would change the answer.

"He did not say. If he does return in time, then my services with the children will not be required and I will be doubly appreciative of your company. Will you join me?" If Gabrielle went with him, it would mean sparing Kavan spending an awkward day with her. A winning answer for each of them, he believed. His questioning smile was sincere and inviting.

She wondered if that was what Kavan's smile looked like, and discovered that the healer had nearly won her over for that reason alone. "I might. Speak with me before you set off."

"I shall. Oh…" He grinned wider, his gaze darting towards the throne and scepter. "The King does not look favorably on people sitting on the throne who should not…but your secret is safe with me."

She laughed at his teasing and curtseyed. She liked this man. "Thank you for the warning…and for keeping my secret." If only he could help her with Kavan.

"My pleasure, milady." Ártur MacLyr was thinking much the same thing. "Come…join me for dinner."

Cinda Maylor stopped rocking the newborn prince, handed him to Syl, and picked up her own child, clutching her protectively. She had not realized there were so many Elyri in the royal house when she was sent to apply for this position. She could not help, after years of familial indoctrination, feeling uncomfortable in their presence. Although they showed no hostility or threat, even seemed friendly towards her, she worried constantly that they might harm her daughter, and carried the girl whenever she had the chance. Right now, the lady healer was in the room, having come to examine the prince as she often did, but familiarity with the woman did not soothe Cinda's nerves. There was something terrifying about anyone who could take away pain and illness with a touch.

"Milady?" she started, still uncertain how to address the healer.

"Yes?" Syl laid Prince Hagan across her lap to unwrap and inspect him. His undergarments were stained and looked as if they had been for some time. With an unnoticed side-glance at Cinda, the healer cleaned the infant and continued her examination.

"Are you attending the carnival tomorrow?"

Without looking up, Syl replied, "No; I do not enjoy such things. Do you wish to attend?" The assumption made sense. Cinda was young and saddled with the care of two children. Seeking a bit of fun was natural.

Cinda, however, was startled to be easily found out. "I…" her voice faltered. "I would…but someone must care for the prince…and I do not want to shirk…"

"I can watch him for a few hours, as long as you feed him before you go out and return to do so periodically throughout the day. I can watch your daughter if you wish." She looked up to catch the fading look of horror on Cinda's face. "I will care for her as if she were my own child. No harm will come to her, I swear it."

Patting her daughter's back, the girl turned away as if pausing to consider the offer. Finally, she said, "May I let you know in the morning?"

Syl nodded, although the gesture was unseen. "Certainly. You deserve a little entertainment, caring for two children will be a handful and will give you little free time. Let me know what you decide."

ᐁChapter 9ᐃ

I t was cool and damp and not yet dawn when the cloaked figure heard the approach of unexpected hurried footsteps. He had waited in the shadows of the foliage surrounding Hes á Redh Náós for the last hour, waiting for the best opportunity to slip inside of the building unnoticed. But even in the pre-dawn hours, there were peasants and townsfolk wandering in and out of the great structure to offer prayers and leave offerings before the altar at the start of this holy day carnival.

His weather-beaten oiled leather cloak kept out the morning moisture, but not the cold, and his uncovered hands grew more numb as time passed. As the footsteps drew nearer, he would have reached for the stiletto hidden in his boot if he had thought there was time to draw it without being noticed. As long as he was not spotted, he would have no need to defend himself, and a fighter by nature, he expected to get the better of anyone.

But the owner of the footsteps did notice him as she rounded the corner, stopping at the sight of the brown cloaked figure amongst the early spring shrubs. She took one hasty step back as a gloved fist crashed down on her. There was a muffled cry of pain and he caught her as she fell. The man looked around hastily; not seeing anyone, he took the sleeping child the woman held, placed it several feet away upon the ground, and then hoisted the woman's body over his shoulder, glad there was no blood to leave a trail. With one foot, he rubbed out the footprints in the damp earth and hurried away. Damn it, he grumbled. What was she doing here? This was going to complicate everything.

His other mission was going to have to wait.

❧*❧

Ártur shifted beneath the blanket, his knees brushing against his wife's thigh, but he resisted the urge to touch her. She had been up late last night as Prince Hagan cried for hours and Cinda had been at the end of her wits. While it was not Syl's position to be the prince's nursemaid and caretaker, Ártur knew Syl loved it. She wanted a child of her own, as did Ártur, but thus far, she had yet to conceive. Twelve years of marriage and no children. That was not unusual for Elyri, Ártur knew, especially at her young age. Conception was naturally difficult for their people, and the majority of Elyri pregnancies did not come to term. The belief was that it was nature's plan for them as a race; if they could conceive as rapidly and easily as Teren, the longer Elyri lifespan would mean overpopulation in a few short generations. A baby would come in its own time. In the meantime, caring for the children within the castle walls filled her longing for parenthood.

Syl expressed her concern last night that perhaps Cinda Maylor was not the right woman for the task of wet-nurse to Prince Hagan. The healer found the babe in its own waste more than once and he cried almost constantly despite being in perfect health. Not to mention, the young woman panicked every time Syl entered the room, making working side by side impossible. Though she sympathized with the girl's fears and the financial predicament of her family, Syl admitted that a new nurse must be found. She would talk to Cinda at the first opportunity regarding some other arrangement. There must be some other position in the castle she could fill that would keep her out of close proximity with the Elyri and not leave her penniless in the street.

Knowing sleep would not return for him, he sat, ran his hand through his hair, and willed himself to get out of bed and don his pale yellow wool robe to keep out the early morning chill. There was a faint glow in the sky, heralding the day's arrival. He rarely woke before dawn but today he was wide-awake; anticipating the day ahead must have made his mind and body equally restless for it to begin. Kissing his wife on the cheek, he left the room and stole down the hall to Kavan's chambers.

His cousin had demanded rooms separate from those of the rest of the household and had gotten them despite the King's initial annoyance. Kavan needed the perceived isolation, perhaps because he felt less alone when he was alone than when he was in the company of other people. Such great loneliness was something Ártur had yet to comprehend. Even in the midst of people who loved him dearly, the bard felt isolated. The healer thought briefly of Gabrielle, wondering if she could have eased that burden if Kavan had been willing to give her the chance. But it was not to be, and knowing that, Ártur dismissed all further thoughts on the matter.

Kavan's room was empty, his bed untouched. He had not returned to the castle last night. All the better. If a night of freedom restored his cousin's peace of mind, it was worth the lost sleep and worth Ártur taking responsibility for the children for a day. As excited as the children were last night, he presumed they were already awake. The carnival had come at a fortuitous time. It would ease the children's suffering for a day, and perhaps the rest of the family's too.

ॐ*ॐ

Captain Wortham Delamo, once a member of the elite Káliel guard, stumbled blindly in the direction of the royal castle, moving more on instinct than actual awareness of where he was going. Though he did not drink to excess often, he knew he had last night. It was rarer still that he ended up in an inebriated state. His bulky frame held its liquor well; getting drunk was too much of a chore for Wortham. But last night, after the death of the Queen and a brief conversation with his former employer, he had been more depressed than he had ever been and drinking had seemed the only choice worth thinking about.

Lady Dilyn was happy, or at least content, with her life on Káliel, but Wortham had detected the underlying melancholy, something he knew she would not discuss with him. But she did not need to; he could guess the root of it. He had heard through the line of military gossip that her mother was murdered and that this was the reason for the Magistrate's presence in Rhidam. Wortham had believed, as had all of Káliel, that her mother had died many years ago, but such appeared not to be the case. Gabrielle Dilyn had always been a private person, and thirteen years of distance between them, as well as divergent responsibilities, made her seem even more insular. Seeing her had brought him a vague sense of regret for leaving the islands that had been his home from birth.

But he liked Enesfel, liked Rhidam. There was land, trees, no miles of ocean and no constant smell of fish unless he happened too close to the river. He held great respect and admiration for the royal family he had agreed to serve at Lady Dilyn's request. And he deeply loved the Elyri bard who was his closest friend, far closer, in fact, than the other four Káliel countrymen who had agreed to serve King Arlan with Wortham. He could tell Kavan anything and often wished that sharing could be mutual. The few times he had seen Kavan yesterday, the Elyri seemed more distant and withdrawn than usual, more haggard looking than Wortham could ever recall seeing him, except for that trip at sea and the march that brought Wortham from Káliel to Rhidam when he first arrived.

A splashing sound, a muffled gurgle of distress brought Wortham out of his reminiscing thoughts and sobered him enough to allow his feet to follow the noise. There was a fountain nearby and a dark cloaked figure was leaning over it with one arm thrust inside. The splashing and gurgling had ceased.

"Halt!"

The figure looked at him, startled, and sprinted into the shadows of the nearest alley after releasing whatever he had been holding. Wortham knew that in his state, he would never be able to catch the perpetrator; instead of pursuing, he turned his attention to the fountain and what he assumed would be some sort of animal.

What he found, however, was a woman.

He pulled her out and laid her on the ground, trying to recall the proper protocol for aiding a drowning victim. He pushed the water from her lungs, a skill nearly everyone on Káliel grew up knowing, and tried to force air back into them. Despite his efforts, however, she refused to breathe. There was no pulse and her cold body was limp. He was too late.

Though dizzy and beginning to feel the throbbing in his skull that followed a drinking binge, he lifted the woman and staggered towards the náos. He did not know where else to take her. Regardless, Lord Cornell must be told of this. Wortham kept his guard up all the way, in case the woman's assailant chose to follow him; he was actually hoping the fellow would try.

❧*❧

Brown satchel packed, Gabrielle sighed and turned towards the mirror. Her reflection disappointed her today. She was thirty-five and looked perhaps ten years younger, but she had hoped that the Elyri longevity of her mother's blood would treat her more generously. Her mother had been ninety-seven at the time of her death and looked to be no more than thirty. Gabrielle sighed again. As with the power, the Elyri traits had come halfway with her. Perhaps, if she was lucky, she would live to be one hundred.

How long will Kavan live, she wondered. What was the Elyri lifespan? Her mother had never told her. So much her mother had never said. In frustration, Gabrielle tried to bring a flame to life in her palm as she had seen her mother do to light candles. Nothing happened. After several minutes of concentration, she gave up. Feeling tears rise, she turned from the mirror and wiped angrily at her face.

She had not spoken with Kavan's since the night of the queen's death and there was much she needed to know, needed to say before she returned to Káliel, because she suspected that once she returned home, she would never see the bard again. Fate had brought them together twice, but she did not expect fate to intervene a third time. Yet Kavan had not come back last night as she had hoped. Gabrielle waited in his room until midnight and then returned two hours later. At the fifth hour of the morning, she had given up, and though she had checked again before packing her bag, he was still not there. He was avoiding her; she knew it. "Innocent dove," she murmured to the air as if he would hear her, wherever he was, "what have I done to you?"

The sound of a child crying distracted k'gdhededhá Tythilius from his morning prayers as he knelt before the yet unfinished altar. The candle Kavan placed there two days ago had burned down and sputtered out, leaving a pool of hardened wax in its plain brass bowl. The k'gdhededhá had not had the heart to blow it out while the queen lived and discovered that it had gone out when he returned to the náós the night she died. Though not superstitious, Jermyn wondered if Kavan had expected that she would live as long as that candle burned.

He pushed up from his kneeling position and went to the náós door. Kneeling was becoming harder on his joints, he admitted grimly. Nevertheless, he would do it until the day he died, or at least as long as he was capable of moving. Perhaps if he ate less he would find it easier. He was chuckling when he reached the door and looked in the direction of the crying. Near the steps, a child, perhaps two years old, fidgeted uncomfortably on the cold, damp earth, looking around with a wide-eyed, frightened, confused stare. No one was in sight, no one who could have left a child. Jermyn picked the baby up and wrapped it in the folds of his robe.

"Well, little foundling, how did you come to be here?"

The child whimpered in response, clutched at the warm fabric, and began to cry. Detesting orphanages, Jermyn was going to have to decide what to do with the little girl, but first, he had to pay a visit to the castle. Perhaps, if he took the babe with him, Lady MacLyr would have a suggestion.

⮡*⮠

"You wished to see me, sir?" Prince Muir spoke the last word tentatively, as if afraid the King would punish him for saying it. Though he had lived his whole life with the King as his father, there had never been any level of comfort between them and he never quite knew what he should call the man. The solar was warm and bright this morning, though the gloom of the previous days still hugged the walls like moss. The prince stood in the doorway, waiting for permission to enter, noting the glass of untouched wine on the desk despite the early hour.

The King looked up from the scatter of scrolls and parchments before him. He had gotten little sleep over the past several nights and it was beginning to show. Dark circles rimmed his sunken, glassy eyes and his shoulders were stooped, sagging under the weight of fresh grief. Still, he conducted himself with the business-like air he always had on formal occasions and motioned Muir into the room with a wave of his hand. "It is regarding your mother's Final Testament." The prince did not speak as he entered and stopped out of the man's reach, carefully keeping his expression neutral. "As you know, she had one sibling, and because Lord Weylin had no heir, he left the Weylin estate in Alberni to his sister. It has been carefully maintained these past four years and is in excellent condition. It produces significant income, which should suffice for you…"

"Suffice…?"

The King quirked his brow as if he thought the prince should understand what that meant. "It was her wish that the estate be left to you."

"Me?" Muir's mask of calm slipped as his clasped hands began to tremble.

Misinterpreting that nervousness for distaste, the King continued, "If you prefer not to accept it, it will remain part of the royal holdings. Otherwise, upon your fourteenth birthday, you may claim legal ownership and assume the title of Duke of Alberni. Your birthday is still several months away, and I intended to tell you of this at that time, but Lord Cliáth felt it important that I inform you now."

The prince lowered his gaze, not sure what to make of Arlan's words. The King, his stepfather, had never lied to him, had always been brutally honest. He did not doubt his mother's wishes, but it surprised him that the King would willingly honor any wishes where Muir was concerned. If anything, he had expected the Alberni estate and titles to be given to either Bertram or Diona. Perhaps the King's decision had been influenced by the bard, who had undoubtedly insisted that Muir be told of this, giving him an option for his uncertain future. "I thank you…sir…" he stammered.

"There is no need to thank me; it was not my choice. Your mother was strong-willed and opinionated and I have chosen to honor her wishes."

Muir was grateful that the King did not continue. Arlan could have done nothing, leaving the estate to the Crown territory, to revert to Bertram when he became king. Or he could have bestowed it upon anyone he desired to make into an ally. Muir could later have contested that choice, fought for what was legally his due to his mother's testament, and so the King chose to circumvent later difficulties by being honest with his wife's wishes now. That his mother, at least, had desired to provide a future for him caused the prince to love her even more.

"May I be dismissed, sir?"

Absently, his attention having already returned to the papers on his desk, the King grunted, "Yes." He watched the young man leave without lifting his head. Muir was not a bad person. He was handsome, kind, generous, thoughtful, pious, and would likely make a good king. But he had one flaw that Arlan could not see past regardless of how hard he tried. Muir Lachlan was not his son.

❧*❦

"Are you certain it does not trouble you that Lady Dilyn is accompanying me to the carnival?"

Syl tilted her head and looked at her husband, an amused sparkle in her eyes. "Should it? You must go…Kavan is not here and you are required to attend the children in his stead…and it is best that Lady Dilyn not go about Rhidam alone after the attack upon her mother. It would not be safe for her." She laid the silver comb upon the dressing table, got to her feet, and slid her arms around his neck. "I have nothing to be jealous of, but I am flattered you think I might be. I abhor carnivals and festivals. You do not. This is the best alternative for everyone; go and enjoy your day. I will tend Prince Hagan and look forward to your return this evening."

There was a knock upon the door at the mention of the infant prince, and Ártur opened it as his wife continued to speak. Princess Diona entered, carrying her infant brother over her shoulder as she had often seen the older women do with babies. She wore simple brown hose and a green tunic, and her black curls were tucked beneath a green cap. She could easily pass for a commoner or a page and not a princess, which was the mode of dress the children had decided upon for the day. They rarely had the privilege of attending events outside of the castle and today, without their parents to watch over them, they were determined to mingle with the common folk as much as they could. Only the necessity of attendants and guards would give their station away.

"He was crying," she said. "I thought he needed something, but he stopped when I picked him up. I think he was lonely."

Casting her husband a sideways glance, Syl asked, "Where is Miss Maylor?"

The princess shrugged. "I do not know; she was not in the room, but there was this." Shifting her brother carefully to be sure not to drop him, she produced a folded bit of parchment and handed it to Syl. Hagan began to fuss again as she added, "I have not read it."

"Let me take him." Ártur took the child, rested him against his shoulder, and patted his back, rocking slowly as his wife's expression changed from worry to annoyance, both colored with relief.

"She is gone. It saves me the need of speaking with her, but Prince Hagan is going to need feeding…and I am not equipped to do that. She could have waited…"

"Do you want me to…?" Princess Diona's frown cut Ártur short.

"You promised to take us to the carnival since Lord Cliáth cannot," she began with a pout.

Syl took the prince from her husband and shooed him, and the princess, out the door. "I will manage. Go. Lady Dilyn will be waiting for you, as are the princes."

"Are you certain?"

"I am." Ártur kissed her once and did as she asked, confident that his wife could handle the situation duty had forced upon her. Once they were out of the room, she placed the fussy prince in the center of her bed, where he could not fall, and finished dressing. She was mentally reviewing the list of women she had interviewed before the queen's death when there came another knock upon the door. Expecting it to be one of the boys searching for Ártur, she called, "Come."

"Pardon the intrusion, Lady MacLyr…"

"You're not intruding, k'dedhá," she said with a smile, not looking at her guest as she checked Prince Hagan for soiled clothing. The clergyman was one of the few people in Rhidam with free run of the castle; like Kavan, he came and went as he pleased. His appearance at her chamber door was not that unusual.

He chuckled warmly. "I was wondering if you could aid me with this child, but I see that you already have…"

She looked at him, and the child he carried, with surprise. "Bianca? Where did…how did she come to be in your care, k'dedhá?"

"I found her upon the náós steps; you know her then?"

"She is the daughter of the woman retained to care for Prince Hagan…" She reached for the little girl; Bianca reached back and clung to the lady healer when the k'gdhededhá released her.

"Then her mother is here."

Shaking her head, Syl sat on the edge of the bed, trying to console two fussing children. "I wish she were, but she is not. She left a message saying she was leaving the Lachlan's employment. She must have departed during the night, or near dawn this morning."

"Does she have family nearby? Somewhere she would have gone?"

"I do not know. Her family name is Maylor; she was the oldest of seven children at sixteen years. I know little else about her."

"I suppose the queen did…which is of no use to us," the man grunted, twisting his sleeve as he often did when anxious. Whatever grievances the girl could have had with the Lachlan house that precipitated quitting her position, did not explain leaving the little girl at the náós steps. "I will look through our records and see if there is any family information, and I will enlist your brother to do likewise. I brought her to you because I cannot bear to put children in the orphanage if there is some other option. I was hoping that perhaps you could care for her temporarily."

Syl kissed the top of the girl's head at the thought of it. Two children would keep her very busy, but she missed the days of caring for small children and relished the notion the clergyman put forth. "I will be happy to, k'dedhá, if you could do me one favor in return?"

"That would be?"

After disentangling herself from the children, Syl took a sheet of parchment from the desk and wrote a list of the names that came immediately to mind. "Contact these women, and see if any are still willing to be Prince Hagan's nurse. Ask them to come to me immediately if they are interested, as he needs to be fed. Please, k'dedhá?"

Jermyn bowed with a smile. "Your wish is as good as granted, milady. I will hurry…and thank you."

❧*❧

The scuffs in the moist earth on the north side of the náós were too recent to have been made at the time of Lísbhet Dilyn's death, but the efforts to cover them were a little too tidy and hasty in General

Wyndham's opinion. Almost as if someone had not had the time to do it properly or was an amateur in such things. He pushed the soil around with the toe of his boot but found nothing there or in the bushes. There were broken branches, also too recent to have occurred at the desired time, judging by the still fresh sap that oozed at the points of breakage. The grass was moist and showed signs of having been trampled; much was flattened as if it had been stood upon for an extended period of time. With the foliage here, he mused, looking around him at what could be seen from this spot, people could have passed and not necessarily have noticed anyone hiding there.

Well, he thought, someone has been here recently. He wondered why. He could ask the k'gdhededhá if he had noticed anything unusual that morning, but the k'gdhededhá was not in the náós. No one else he had spoken to had seen or heard anything. For the moment, the general would continue his investigation alone, determined to find a killer and get to the bottom of this mystery.

☙*☙

Guthrie looked at the dead woman once more with a sigh, shaking his head before sending a page to inform Lady MacLyr that Prince Hagan's nurse had drowned. Or rather, had been drowned. He had listened to Wortham's tale twice before sending the soldier to sober up. They would both be part of the party accompanying the children to the carnival, and Wortham should not be seen on duty in his current condition.

It honored him to be able to carry out such a duty at his age. Most people were surprised at how fit and strong the sixty-three-year-old chamberlain was. He looked to be twenty years younger, though the ache in his joints kept him from any foolish notions of youthfulness. He remembered King Innis at sixty-four, frail, thin, barely able to move about of his own accord. Guthrie gave prayers of thanks every day that he was blessed with the fortune of good health, and he hoped that when the end of his days arrived, he would still be in good health, not weak and dependent on others.

Sounds outside the room brought his thoughts back to the drowned girl and he tried to fathom who would do such a thing. He huffed and covered her face with a cloth. Some people did not need a good motive. The slightest offense was sometimes cause enough.

"Lord McHador?" said Justice Cornell as he stepped into the guardhouse. "Lord MacLyr, Lady Dilyn, and the children are waiting in the outer courtyard. I will attend to this matter, if I may. Captain Delamo told me what has happened; he is waiting with the others. I have taken the liberty of sending Logros, Denyan, Avner, and Waljan with you." Noting the man's effort to protest, the Justice shook his head. "Not that I doubt your, or the captain's prowess. I do not think, however, that two of you will be enough to protect four children, the healer, and the Prime Magistrate of Káliel, particularly with the state the captain is in, should there be trouble. There's been too much of this," he indicated the dead woman, "recently...I don't want to take any risks."

"Of course." Though he had felt momentarily slighted, Guthrie knew the justice was correct in his assessment of the situation. It surprised him, however, to feel anything at all. Since his niece's death, he had felt very little. He strode out of the room, in the direction of the outer courtyard, leaving the justice to contend with the mystery of yet another dead woman.

## ❧Chapter 10❧

Morning sunlight wove through the boughs of the trees, caressing the man that slept in the midst of the thicket. His pale skin and hair were damp with kisses of dew, but he was unaware of it. The sounds of the birds in the branches above and the gradually increasing warmth upon his face eventually caused him to stir, stretch, and open his eyes. A new day. And he was far from home. He might have chastised himself for falling asleep in the forest, unprotected from the elements of nature, for not returning to Rhidam last night as intended, but he could not. The calm and peace within were too deep at that moment for him to feel anything other than contentment. He sat, gazing with wonder upon the spring growth, and began removing the twigs that had tangled in his hair during sleep.

Through the branches he could make out the lake; his lake, he had always felt, even though he did not own it. He had come here often as a boy but had not been here in nearly fourteen years. Though he had not intended to come, he was not surprised to end up in this place. It was the one spot in the world where he felt safe, secure, and at peace. He crawled from the thicket and went to the water's edge; without thinking he did what he had always done, shedding his white robe to stand white and gleaming in the morning light. Though he had no mirror, he recalled his reflection. Today, however, there was no horror at the image. Today there was only Kavan and a sense of pride and rightness in who and what he was.

With one graceful action, he dove into the brisk water and exhaled sharply at the icy shock of it when he surfaced. The cold was invigorating, not inconvenient, and he did not try to warm himself. Even the fact that the sun's position indicated he had slept until nearly noon did not trouble him today. He had taken what his soul needed and now felt right with the world.

After several minutes of swimming, he left the water and again stood upon the bank. There was no cloth with which to dry himself, but that was of no consequence. Head thrown back, he pulled upon the energy within and that, combined with the warmth of the sun, soon left his body dry and refreshed. He listened to the wind, felt the prickle of sunlight across his skin, and wondered if he could burn. He had never been in the sun long enough to find out, except in the guise of some other creature, when fur or feathers protected him. But this was not the day to learn the answer to that question. There was a carnival in Rhidam, and unless Ártur had escorted the children, they would be impatiently awaiting Kavan's return. After retrieving his robe, he pictured the soaring falcon in his mind as he drew it over his head. The form easily claimed him and he flew with leisurely purpose in the direction of Rhidam.

"I'm telling you, General, I did not see anything unusual this morning, or hear anything either, until I heard the child crying." Jermyn adjusted his eye patch and shifted in his chair. The King sat across from him, with the justice and general standing to the monarch's right. If the k'gdhededhá did not know the King as well as he did, he would have considered this an inquisition.

The King tilted his head, lost in thought for many minutes as the men looked at one another and waited. "All we know for certain is that Miss Maylor left the keep sometime after the second hour, likely taking her child with her, and then this same child was found upon the náós steps at approximately the same time Captain Delamo discovered someone drowning her mother."

"Apparently drowning," the justice tentatively corrected. "Captain Delamo believes he heard struggling but admits he was not sober and might have been mistaken about what he heard. She might have been dead already and the person seen was trying to dispose of her body. The examination by the physician will tell us if she drowned or not."

For once, the general found himself agreeing with the justice, but he did not admit to that directly. "It matters less how she died then the fact that she did, but it would seem likely that the person seen with her was also her killer. It is unfortunate that Captain Delamo did not get a look at the fellow's face. There was evidence near the náós that someone had been there, loitering, and it could indicate that either Miss Maylor was there and left the child herself, or that she crossed paths with someone hiding there, who dispatched her, left the child behind, and took her to the well."

"According to Syl, the nursemaid never went anywhere without her daughter; I doubt she abandoned the child herself. Do you think this is connected to Lady Dilyn's murder?" the King asked, rubbing his chin. "There was no other evidence there that might help?"

The justice shrugged. "There is no way of knowing if there is a connection, Sire, until we apprehend the guilty party. We are still questioning people, but we have learned nothing useful."

Though he knew he was taking a risk by speaking out of turn, the general cleared his throat and interrupted the justice. "Lord Cliáth's insistence that she was attacked near the náós may be in error. There is nothing there to indicate foul play, no blood or anything else. It is possible he may be trying to mislead…"

If the general saw the dark cloud descend over the King's face, he did not acknowledge it and the King did not directly voice his anger, though his abrupt turning to Jermyn, cutting the general off, was evidence enough. "Your Grace, question your parishioners. See if any were there the day of the murder and might have seen Lady Dilyn or anything that looked suspicious. Perhaps they will speak to you since they are not forthcoming to the justice. Lord Cornell, continue the investigation; make it your top priority. General Wyndham, I am taking you off of this matter."

The general was genuinely surprised, though the surprise was short-lived. "Milord…"

Again, the King cut him off. "Chamberlain McHador is eager to begin training our new military. Your job is, as it should be, training our troops and the new cavalry. Upholding law and order is Lord Cornell's jurisdiction. I do not think I need to remind you of that. You do your duties and allow Justice Cornell to do his. If he requires your assistance, he will request it."

The general bowed his head, mentally chastising himself for his error, though it was one he had made in full knowledge of the King's position. In the King's eyes, the white harper could do no wrong and was always correct. Though it was true that the military was his duty, and not the investigation, it was speaking ill of a man whom the King kept on a pedestal, which had worked against him. "I apologize, My Liege…of course, you are correct. I will see to the troops." It did not mean, however, that he intended to give up trying to solve these murders.

⮞*⮜

The crush of unfamiliar bodies around them made Muir nervous. He seldom had the opportunity to mingle with anyone outside of the palace staff and his family, and even within the castle, his socializing was generally limited to his tutors and the other royal children. Because of this relative isolation, he felt a degree of mistrust of the people whom his father, King Owain, had once ruled. Diona did not appear to share her brother's wariness, however, and the prince knew that Ártur felt as comfortable amongst common men as he was amongst royalty, perhaps even more so. Those facts, and the presence of the attending guards, were enough to ease the young man's fears; the longer they were out of the castle, the more relaxed he became.

Most in the crowd were peasants and townsfolk dressed in their finest attire, some in linen, others in muslin, leather, or wool. Silks and velvets were worn almost exclusively by the upper classes and the nobility, of which there were plenty on hand. They were fewer than the commoners, but traveled through the crowded avenues with considerably more pomp and grandeur, seeking the attention they believed their station afforded them. A woman borne on a litter stopped frequently to allow passersby to kiss her jeweled hand and then would shoo them away to allow her entourage to seek the next attraction. A mounted gentleman bearing the crest of the Duke of Erleta rode slowly, seeming ignorant of everyone and everything around him while managing to make certain that everyone who passed acknowledged who he was.

Vanity, the prince snorted in disgust as a breeze brought the pungent scents of spice and incense to him. If his companions noticed, they did not show it, although Muir suspected his love of incense would cause him to pick out that fragrance above those of baking bread, roasting meats, flowers, perfumes, and the smell of the unwashed rabble. He was grateful Bertram and Wilred had gone with Chamberlain McHador, otherwise, they would stop at every food vendor they passed until they were too sick to walk.

Ahead on the street corner was a motley collection of jugglers and tumblers. Temporarily forgetting the press of people, Prince Muir wove to the front of the crowd, aware that Ártur broke away from their escort and the women to accompany him. When one of the jugglers dropped a blue wooden ball, it rolled to the prince's feet. Muir picked it up and tossed it back, delighted that the man caught it and continued with his exhibition with barely a falter. Having seen enough, the prince allowed the healer to lead him back to where the rest of their party waited.

Further on, near a fruit vendor's stall, a balding gdhededhá in the habit of Saint Bhenádíctus swung a censer and cried for the repentance of mankind from the ways of wickedness. Muir smiled. The source of the incense. While his sister and Magistrate Dilyn selected fruit from the vendor, the prince pulled three silver coins from his purse and placed them in the iron pot at the gdhededhá's feet.

"Bless you, my son," the man said, tracing the Sign of Devotion upon Muir's forehead. He did not recognize Muir, either as a prince or as his father's son, which dispelled the last of his uneasiness. Diona made a face at her brother but said nothing about his donation.

They stopped under the shade of a vintner's awning and ate a delectable midday meal of sweetbreads, fruit, roast pork, and wine. From their places, they watched a troupe of mummers who, from all appearances, were acting out the ascension of King Arlan to the throne of Enesfel, a popular tale amongst the people as much for its inclusion of the White Hart as for the overthrow of an unpopular monarch. Their performance was mediocre at best and their blatant ridicule of King Owain made the prince uncomfortable. The healer, sensing this, reached for the prince's hand but Muir drew away. He was an adult, or nearly so; he could withstand the ridicule of the man who had fathered him. For all he knew, the stories could be true.

The sky was clear today, the spring air warm enough that there was no need for cloaks or gloves. Even Ártur had forgone his customary outer robe of pale yellow for a simple yellow tunic and brown breeches. Always yellow, Muir mused. Yellow was the color for healers in Elyriá, a way for the average person to know whom to seek out for help. There was no required emblem or designated color to tell the people of Enesfel one was a physician, but most had adopted the yellow robes and tunics of the Elyri healers or affixed a braided yellow ribbon to their day to day attire to signify their calling.

The Teren had adopted many Elyri things. Architecture, art, music, and a variety of day-to-day customs such as the use of yellow clothing for physicians. Now they were claiming the religion too. When Muir considered how much his people took from the Elyri and how little they gave in return, he felt guilty. Yet there was little Teren had to offer that the Elyri needed or wanted; all they really desired was amity and acceptance, and the prince could not understand why that should be difficult to give. Just because the Elyri were different. Perhaps, at least in his eyes, because they were in some ways superior.

He turned his thoughts outward, wondering how the jousting match was progressing, or if it had begun. He had not heard the usual chaos that generally preceded a tournament. The other carnival Muir had attended had been years ago when Diona and Bertram were too young to go. The prince had gone with Kavan, taking Captain Delamo as an escort. It was the first jousting match the prince had seen, and his last. He enjoyed the excitement of riders dismounting riders until one knight accidentally killed another's horse. For weeks afterward, Prince Muir awakened nearly every night in fright, hearing the agonizing scream the horse had made as the lance drove deep into its chest. Kavan had tried to reassure him that the death of a horse in a tournament was a rare thing, but the prince had never been able to gather the courage to attend again.

After their meal was complete and the mummers had moved further down the street, there were purchases to make. Ártur had not allowed the children to spend any of their coins until they had seen everything the vendors had to offer. The princess decided upon a gold braided chain very early in the day; it was the only thing she desired. It hung midway down her small torso when she slipped it over her head, but she wore it proudly. Her remaining coins were pooled with her brother's and together they purchased a peppered marble záryph to place before their mother's final resting place.

For himself, the prince selected a stoppered stone bowl of incense and a black-handled dagger. Ártur had objected, at first, to the purchase; however, as the prince pointed out, he was nearly a man and had every right to carry and own it. What he had not said, however, was that he would need it when the day finally came to leave Rhidam.

His other purchase, a very expensive one, was a large, leather-bound volume he would not allow the others to see. He wrapped it within waxed canvas and a leather satchel and clutched it tightly for the remainder of the day. It was a treasure worth guarding with his life.

ঌ * ๙

The light of a single candle drifted slowly through the rubble beneath Hes á Redh Náós, its bearer careful with his footing as he poked and prodded, hoping to find something of value. One wrong step and it could mean his death…and no treasure found here could be worth that. There was too much clutter and too many rats, and if he were injured, he would be unable to receive help. No one would rescue him because no one knew he was here, and he had no desire to be trapped in a burning building.

The three chambers below the náós were all in a state of ruin and disrepair, though he had only searched two of them thus far. The third was strong with the stale stench of death and decay and the two skulls that tumbled out at his feet when he pried the door open deterred him from entering. He had never heard there was a crypt beneath this particular náós, but then again he had never been much interested in religious history…unless there were treasures to be had in it.

If either of the two rooms he searched had ever been the náós' treasury, they were no longer used as such. Indeed, they had not been used for many centuries from the looks of it. What he sought was not here, he decided; it was time to leave. He could not risk overstaying his welcome. He made his way back to the crumbling stone stairway, blew out the candle he carried, and climbed. There was no sign of anyone in the room above; he pushed the trap door open slowly, slid out, and closed it behind him.

He searched the main thóres when he arrived and found nothing. Room after room, but none more sparsely adorned than this room. There was a bed against the far wall with a simple oak and iron chest beside it. There was a round wooden table, two chairs, and a cabinet with a washbasin and built-in armoire. This was the last place in the náós he could think to look since he knew the secondary buildings were still unused, and everywhere else he could think of that would make an obvious, or not so obvious hiding place for wealth, he had already searched. Perhaps what he sought was within this trunk. It seemed unlikely, but it was his last hope.

There was an old lock on it, a simple one that he had no difficulty picking. But the trunk merely contained a few articles of clothing, a large manuscript written in Elyri, a string of gleaming blue prayer beads, and a small silver knife with religious iconography engraved on both blade and handle. There was no trace of the brooch. Suddenly angry about the wasted time with no results made, he allowed the lid to bang shut before locking it again and starting back to the thol.

He lingered on the other side of the thol door until an elderly woman kneeling in prayer at the altar rose and left. Certain he was alone, he came into the room but paused at the altar when another woman entered the building also to pray.

Damn, he thought. Where was that brooch? Surely, he was not the only person to recognize the Káliel Serpent. They would not have buried her with it, would they? He detested grave robbing, but if it came down to that, he would do it, or hire someone else to do it. Alternatively, perhaps the brooch had been recognized and sent to the palace or was on its way to Káliel. He could not afford to go to the islands yet, not until he finished his business in Rhidam. Nor could he afford to charge after a courier that may or may not be on his way out of Rhidam. It seemed, therefore, his best chance was to funnel his concentration and effort on Caol Dugan, seek out the woman's grave, and try to learn if the brooch had been added to the Lachlan's treasure store or not. The reward awaiting him for the Serpents would have to wait a little longer.

He stood to leave, turned, and almost ran into a one-eyed man in k'gdhededhá' robes. He had not heard the man approach and cursed himself for not paying more attention. "P...pardon me, dedhá...I did not hear you."

Jermyn's expression was distracted as he waved a hand at the man as if he did not realize what had almost happened. "No pardon necessary, sir. Good day to you." He continued towards the thóres with hardly a break in his steps.

"dedhá?"

"Yes?" When he turned back to the man whose dark brown hair hung long and straight around his cracked and weathered face, it was with a touch of annoyance. The stranger appeared uncomfortable under his gaze but did not retreat, and Jermyn forced himself to put on a friendlier demeanor.

"I am newly arrived from Cordash...for the festival...and have heard the most disturbing rumors. Is it true the queen has died?"

"Aye," the k'gdhededhá sighed, "Disturbing indeed. It is a great loss."

"It is. Was she the one murdered with a Coryllien dagger?"

Jermyn blinked, wondering how and when that rumor had started, and how anyone outside of the King's council had heard about the Coryllien dagger. Perhaps a servant had overheard them. It was the only way that knowledge could have gotten out. Many people had already come to him, fearful of a tale of a mysterious murder, that he was getting weary of addressing. If the rumor of a Coryllien in Rhidam surfaced, his efforts to assuage the public was going to be more fervent. "The queen was not murdered."

"Someone else then?" the stranger prodded anxiously.

"There is nothing to fear, I assure you. You are safe in Rhidam, sir."

The corner of the man's mouth twisted as he tried not to smirk. He could hear the words the k'gdhededhá was not saying, and they pleased him. "That is good. I would hate to cut my business short because of an outbreak of violence...particularly if the Coryllien is involved."

"There is no need for that. Go about your business in peace. Now, if you will excuse me...and please, enjoy your stay."

"I shall," the man said, perhaps a little too enthusiastically. The k'gdhededhá did not appear to notice.

☙*❧

Caol swung his feet as he perched upon the hastily erected fence, watching the archers prepare for the upcoming contest. This was his sport, though he had never gotten up the nerve to compete despite the King's insistence that Caol was the best archer in Enesfel. Perhaps he was, but he had no desire for his name to spread through the Five Sovereignties when there were men like Halstatt who were eager to hunt him down for the sins of his father and family. Nor did he desire to embarrass every archer in the kingdom by defeating them the way Bhríd defeated other jousters and swordsmen. Caol was content with the private knowledge of his skill.

He had been unable to find any clue as to Halstatt's whereabouts and the man had not attempted to contact Caol again. Though he had removed the dagger from his room, hidden it somewhere Halstatt was unlikely to look, Caol was certain Halstatt would not leave Rhidam without attempting to retrieve it. Some other matter had distracted the man for the moment, or perhaps he was merely playing for time, waiting for Caol to let his guard down before striking.

The inquisitor's palms grew damp as he thought back to the meeting of the King's advisors. Bhríd was suspicious, Kavan knew something was amiss, and Caol wondered why neither had shared their suspicions with the justice or the King. Bhríd could corroborate his whereabouts for the time of the woman's death, but possessing the dagger, especially as day after day passed with it in his possession, was enough to incriminate Caol as an accomplice. He avoided being alone with either of the two Elyri and avoided the justice as best he could, to remain safe. He knew he was not guilty, but he could not risk any knowledge of the dagger getting out. At least if Bhríd chose to talk and Caol's rooms were searched, nothing would be found. He smiled. Perhaps the Elyri chancellor suspected he would not hide the dagger in his own room and thus had not yet spoken to avoid looking foolish. And because Kavan would never speak of suspicions without proof to support them, for the moment at least, Caol felt he was safe.

"Lord Dugan."

The voice was close, too close, and Caol spun. He would have knocked the speaker to the ground if the mountain of a man was not prepared for the swing and stepped back out of his reach. The stranger was tall and dark-skinned, with features that spoke of too much time in the desert sun. A black sash around his waist secured his simple gray trousers, his feet were bare and calloused, and his tunic was fashioned of a thin, white, gauzy material. The standard fashion of dress for most Cíbhóló tribesmen. But the heavy, ornate, foot-long dagger at his side was not the weapon of a commoner. As a resident of Durham, having met and seen nomads before, Caol recognized what it meant at once.

"Who wants to know?"

The man smiled, his teeth brilliant against the darkness of his skin. "I do. Wace Elotti."

Heart stopping in his chest, Caol struggled to breathe normally without revealing his anxiety. That was a name he had never hoped to hear at such close proximity. He had never crossed paths with a venador, although any member of the Association was well aware of the hunter-caste's existence. His hand inched unconsciously towards the dagger on his hip.

"No need for that, Lord Dugan." The man smiled again and stretched his large, rough hands forward to show the inquisitor they were empty.

Caol snorted, trying to cover his unease with bravado. "Your gesture of goodwill is admirable, but your reputation precedes you. If what I have heard is true, though your hands are here, you could easily slit my throat before I could draw my weapon to defend myself."

"You flatter me." The large man chuckled. "If it eases your mind, I am not seeking you…though I am familiar with your family's history. You, however, appear to have made a name and life for yourself outside of the Dugan business. Inquisitor…how fitting."

Hearing that he was not the target in the man's sights allowed Caol to relax. "That's been my intention. I have no desire for an early death to a hangman's noose or headman's ax. So…" he paused to watch the archers take position, "what does the distinguished Wace Elotti want with me if there is no price on my head?"

"No price I'm aware of," the man chuckled again. "If there was, if I wanted you, we would not be having a civil conversation, would we? I am looking for information I believe you have. I am looking for Halstatt Tarmajien."

Caol's face remained impassive, except for the slight tick at the corner of his eye. Fortunately, as he was looking at the archers and that tick was on the side of his face Elotti could not see, he was safe from discovery. "Why would I know anything about Halstatt?"

Wace leaned against the fence, the muscles in his bare upper arms bulging. If the gesture of contained strength was meant to impress or frighten Caol, there was no visible sign it did. "In my line of business, the feud between the Tarmajiens and the Dugans is well known."

That was certainly true. Almost everyone who had more than casual dealings with the Association had heard about the four-hundred-year-old feud. Caol allowed his legs to swing casually but it was many minutes before he replied. "Last I heard, he was in a prison in Neth. Something about slave running, I believe, though I didn't think Neth was too particular about that sort of thing.

"They aren't…unless it involves a member of the nobility. He kidnapped the youngest Cordashian princess and sold her as a slave to Prince Loris. It created a political incident when a Cordashian envoy learned what had happened and Neth had to make recompense that nearly broke them as a kingdom. Halstatt made the mistake of staying in Neth too long and Loris' men found him. I don't know why they didn't execute him. He escaped over a year ago; I have been on his trail ever since."

"Over a year?" Caol snorted. "I didn't think him capable of outsmarting you for that long."

Shrugging, Wace grunted. "He's kept his nose clean, for the most part…and I have had other more pressing business to tend to. I knew he would turn up in Rhidam eventually, looking for you. Your marriage to the King's sister makes you easy to locate. I merely had to bide my time and wait for him to come to you."

"Wanting me to do your work for you? You've gotten soft."

Elotti refused to be goaded. "Taking advantage of the feud, and your location…simplest way. Not soft, efficient."

Caol could not argue with that. Why expend unnecessary resources to find someone when you knew where they would turn up? It was why Halstatt had yet to come for the dagger, and Caol had not pushed his search. Eventually, they would cross paths. It was destiny.

"He is here in Rhidam?" he eventually asked.

A young blonde archer, perhaps twelve years old, was preparing to shoot. He would be the first contestant in the competition. Elotti watched him, his keen eye studying the youth's movements approvingly. "You know he is. You also know he was behind the murder of that Elyri woman in the garment district. No one else would dare use the Coryllien like that."

Caol had not expected the venador to believe the Coryllien daggers were a myth, and the matter-of-fact reference to them did not surprise him. "We have no evidence it was him, or that it was a Coryllien…"

"Come now, Lord Dugan," the large man snorted. "Do not insult me. We are far too knowledgeable about such things. You know the mark of the Coryllien when you see it."

"I didn't see it. I only know what I've been told."

"But you know the truth."

"Perhaps." Caol did not like the way the venador was visually devouring the young archer. He liked this conversation even less.

"He hasn't contacted you?"

"I do not know where he is, if that is what you are asking."

"Has he contacted you?"

Caol shrugged and jumped down from the fence; enough was enough. "If he had, why would I tell you? I have nothing to gain by it. That part of my life is over and I want nothing to do with you, Halstatt, or the Association."

It would never be that easy, and Elotti's smirk told Caol he knew it as well as the inquisitor did. "You will let me know if he contacts…"

"It won't matter. If he does, he would not tell me where he is staying. If he were foolish enough to mention it, he would relocate as soon as he realized his error. And if he asked to meet with me…that is between him and me, not you. If you want him, find him yourself. Get rid of him and do us all a favor."

He left then, interest in the match lost. The realization that Halstatt could be here, and could find him, especially at this event, was sobering. His curiosity about what his enemy had done to earn Wace Elotti as his hunter would remain unsatisfied; Elotti's services did not come cheap. It seemed likely there was more to the kidnapping story, or some other offense, in order to set the land's most notorious killer on his trail. Caol had no desire to get involved in the underground and the Association again, and no plans to cooperate with the infamous venador. He wanted to stay out of it…for as long as he could.

⮞ * ⮜

Most of the wooden bleachers were filled when Guthrie, Princes Bertram and Wilred, and the Káliel guardsman named Avner, arrived to watch the day's jousting match. Guthrie directed the boys into the king's box, though Arlan would not be in attendance today. Several armored horsemen waited to the left and right for their turns to compete; among them, it was not difficult to locate the crimson-plumed knight that was Bhríd Cáner. Tournaments were one of the few places that particular Elyri never looked out of place.

But Guthrie's attention was soon drawn from the tournament preparations to two disruptive men who pushed through the crowd and elbowed several people aside to obtain seating below the king's box and slightly to Guthrie's right. Sensing potential trouble, the chamberlain felt them worth keeping an eye on. No one went through all of that effort to get close to the royal box without a purpose, and Guthrie wanted to know their intentions.

One of the men was from the southern fringes of Neth; the cut of his clothing indicated that much, making him already suspect. He was tall, pale, and wore a single gold hoop in his right ear, a fashion men of wealth in Neth usually followed. They appeared to be kin, both bearing similar hawkish noses and narrow blue eyes, although his companion's appearance suggested less wealth and more hard labor. He wore no gold hoop, as his ear was torn at the lower edge, but the chamberlain wagered that he too was from Neth. They were loudly debating the political state of affairs in their homeland, a subject t not spoken of much outside that country for the last four years and which drew stares from those seated around the pair. Occasional reports of internal strife filtered into Rhidam, but those were often impossible to confirm. All Enesfel's spies knew for certain was that the roads between Enesfel and Neth were heavily guarded and what little trade had once been conducted between the kingdoms had trickled to an almost halt. The rumors that did reach Rhidam were of increasing disorder and mass slaughter. That these men were discussing it openly, within his range of hearing, excited the chamberlain.

"Loris should never have made it to the throne. For what he did, he should have been executed for treason, not crowned king," the taller, better-dressed man was saying. "At least Ander had a little sympathy for the people." He spoke of neither de Corrmick with a title or any measure of warmth.

"You would prefer the foreign prince over Loris?" his companion chuckled. From his expression and the tone of his voice, Guthrie wagered he agreed with his own sentiment.

The first uttered a string of unintelligible syllables below his breath. "Being born on foreign soil is not enough to make him a foreigner. He is of royal lineage after all…"

"So is Loris," the shorter man shrugged, reciting words that sounded like a memorized speech. "He is Ander's son, like it or not. The other…"

"Has pride, conviction, a heart, and courage, things Loris wouldn't recognize if they spat in his face."

That brought a laugh from them both but neither spoke again as the first jousters prepared for their initial pass. Lances poised, the knights spurred their horses into action. The rider in orange easily unseated the one in lavender on the first pass, much to the onlookers' delight. "What are you planning to do?" the shorter fellow eventually asked.

The other rubbed his right ear, toying with the gold hoop. He glanced in Guthrie's direction as if to be sure he was there and listening, before replying, "What can we do? The councils of Fiara and Ruidoso have convened together, but I do not know what they wish to accomplish...or can accomplish. If the king learns of this meeting, there will not be much left of either city to return to. They could never hold off royal troops. With few of us allowed to bear arms, an uprising is out of the question. We could never defend ourselves with farming and logging tools and hope to win."

He looked towards the chamberlain again, who made every effort to appear as if he was not listening. The speaker scowled. "And the prince certainly won't live long enough to have a chance of gaining the throne if that happens, blood or no. Loris has already slaughtered anyone he suspects of treason and made it clear he will not hesitate to continue the butchery. He won't hesitate to kill his own kin. It's probably a matter of time before it's over; with the borders closed to travelers, there's no escape and no trade. I was lucky enough to make it through with an arrow in my backside and a cart of grain. You were lucky to get out when you did. For now, we wait to see what the council and prince decide to do."

"I hope we do not drag everyone into a war. We don't need a situation that would leave the Five Sovereignties vulnerable to Elyriá."

Twisting his earring once before putting his hands on his lap, he snorted. "Curious thing is, Elyriá's the only country aiding us. They send food and supplies to the places hardest hit by Loris' troops..."

"But they do not send weapons or soldiers?"

Grinning, the taller man shook his head. "I do not believe Elyriá has soldiers. As for weapons, I don't know. Look...there's our man."

Their attention returned to the joust and they said no more. The chamberlain watched the match but did not see much of it as his mind feverishly dug through the implications of the conversation he was, it seemed, meant to hear.

An uprising to overthrow a king. That is what had placed Arlan on the throne of Enesfel. It sounded as if the same was about to happen in Neth. He had not known that King Ander had died and that Prince Loris had come to power. Who was the foreign prince of whom they spoke? Had Ander fathered a bastard child who was interested in making a bid for the throne? It would not be the first time in Neth's history, nor would it be the last. Nearly every King in Neth's history had been an unscrupulous, degenerate tyrant; was this prince any better than Loris, who was seemingly surpassing his predecessors' viciousness?

That these men wanted him to overhear their conversation intrigued him. Did they hope to prompt Enesfel into action, to come to their aid, or were they wishing to prepare the other kingdoms for the near-inevitable outcome of Neth's aggression? Or were they a ruse, something meant to cover for some greater, more deadly scheme in the offing? Guthrie leaned back, arms folded across his chest, and remained lost in thought for the remainder of the tournament.

❧*❧

Leaning on the sill, Enesfel's King stared across the bustle of the festival below. He had not attended the carnival last year or the year before; there had been too many distractions pulling at his attention, too many excuses not to go. His queen had attended without him. Thinking back, Arlan hated himself for that. He had promised her he would attend with her this year, but for Brenna, there had not been a carnival this year, and Arlan felt that he could not, in good conscience, go when he had promised to accompany her.

Next year, if all went as planned, the carnival and the Feast of St. Mátán would include the first official service in Hes á Redh Náós in over five hundred years. The reparations might not be complete by then, but Arlan hoped it would have progressed enough to allow worshippers to attend normal observances. The náós could manage small services now, but until he was confident there was no threat of collapse, until the reconstruction was complete, he did not want to open it for general use.

A group of children ran through his field of vision, laughing and screaming as they pursued a small brown dog. How were his own children enjoying the festival, he wondered? If he knew anything about them, he suspected Bertram would have insisted upon attending the joust and Diona would be scouring every merchant's cart for special treasures. Prince Wilred would be following wherever Bertram went. And Muir? What were his interests? The King had to admit he did not know. Actors and musicians, perhaps, since he loved to listen to the minstrels who came to court and tended to take after Kavan in his tastes and habits.

Where was Kavan? Arlan knew his friend had not come back to the castle last night, but he did not know where the Elyri had gone and Ártur refused to tell him. The healer had said that Kavan needed time to himself. The King had nearly given some bitter retort about Kavan's duty to be there for him when he required it, but said nothing. Kavan had been there for him, and everyone else, unfailingly for the past thirteen years without asking for anything in return. Yes, the King realized, he had taken the bard's presence for granted. They all had. He would have to make it up to Kavan somehow.

Right now, however, he could not concentrate on the needs of his friend or anyone else. Arlan felt empty and tired. What he needed was something to occupy his thoughts, some project that would take his mind off his recent loss. Brenna would have told him to go on with his life. Perhaps if he took a personal role in the training of his troops it would help. He had maintained his two-hundred-man castle unit and the one hundred and fifty man elite guard, but Guthrie had recommended increasing the troops to at least two thousand and suggested rebuilding the cavalry and perhaps preparing a navy. The cavalry was in the works, left completely to General Wyndham's capable instruction, but a navy would have to wait until the kingdom had the resources for ships.

A cheer arose from the jousting arena. The King sighed. He should be there; it was the King's place to open the tournament. But not today. Guthrie had gone in his place, though he would have been there regardless. Arlan had no interest in jousting; the festival would go on without him.

❧*❧

Horse snorting impatiently, Bhríd lowered the visor over his face and adjusted his position in the saddle. His mount was ready to charge but he held him back, knowing the animal would explode forward when he gave it rein. He disliked this heavy armor. It was hot, dark, and made movement difficult. Smiling within his helmet as the tournament master motioned the riders into position, he braced the lance against himself. If the armor felt heavy to him, he suspected it felt twice as heavy to his opponents. Bhríd did not feel guilty about his strength or that it gave him an advantage. He liked to compete, to test himself, to improve his technique. And he liked to win.

His other advantage, one he guarded more closely than his strength, was that he perceived a starter's signal to begin before any Teren opponent ever could. That, coupled with his almost empathic link with his fiery mount, inevitably enabled him to lurch into motion before anyone else. This was his last pass today; to win would bring him first place. Again. He tried once to refuse such prizes as a matter of conscience, but the second place knight had felt humiliated by such a gesture and Bhríd never tried to reject a win again. Instead, he had gained the title of King's Knight, the best jouster and swordsman in Enesfel and, in the opinion of many, the best in the Five Sovereignties.

From the corner of his eye, he saw the beginning of the starter's signal and allowed his horse to charge. He kept his concentration focused on the other rider, judging his weaknesses, looking for the optimum time and location to hit him. Lance poised, Bhríd clenched his jaw, readied himself, and felt the bone-jarring impact of his lance striking the stone gray armor of his opponent. The man lurched backward, tumbled from his horse into the well-trampled dust, his lance catching Bhríd's arm as he went down. Bhríd saw the impact before it came, tightened his leg grip around his horse's sides, and successfully remained seated when such a blow might have dismounted anyone else.

The gathering was on their feet, cheering and whistling as he reined in his horse and his squire Flannery caught the animal's harness. He pulled the helmet from his head, shaking out his damp black hair, glad to be able to see and breathe normally again. Prince Bertram and Prince Wilred were screaming in delight with the chamberlain beside them, smiling in satisfaction. Bhríd inclined his head in their direction and waved.

In response to the applause, Bhríd paraded his proud bay mount back and forth before the crowd. At the far end, he caught sight of a tall, red-haired woman joyously waving a bit of cloth. She wore a deep blue gown cinched loosely about her waist, the cut of which led him to believe she was a noblewoman though he had never seen her before. There was something about her that drew him. Coyly, she dropped her gaze when he stopped before her, and curtseyed, making him smile. In the hand she lifted towards him was a kerchief, a winning gift he realized; Flannery assisted him in removing his metal glove to accept her offering. In response, the chancellor removed the scarlet plume from his helmet, held it to his lips, and offered it to her. Again, her gaze fell, but she took what he gave with a smile and watched him ride back to the center of the arena where the tournament master was waiting to award him the prize. In his heart, he felt he had already received it; he looked back at the woman, relishing the warm sensation in his stomach at the sight of her. She smiled and waved.

❧*❧

Dressed as he was in beggar's rags, Halstatt knew he would not be recognized by anyone who might be looking for him. He had enough experience that hiding in the carnival crowd would be quite simple. He slid between them easily, stopping occasionally to slit some hapless fellow's moneybag or to empty someone's pockets of whatever money they carried. He had not played the pickpocket in many years, but today it was necessary if he wanted to continue to eat and sleep in a decent bed. However, picking pockets no longer held the allure it once had; it had become too easy. There was no sport in it any longer. For a few more days, it would give him coin to survive while he completed his business. The brooch was gone; it was time to concentrate on Caol.

He hoped to find the man amongst the festival crowd, but he saw no one who looked as he remembered young Dugan. Of course, that had been fifteen years ago; Caol had been a boy then and Halstatt had been little older. He had no way of knowing how much Caol might have changed during those years. Was he slim or heavy, short or tall, bearded or clean-shaven? The only things Halstatt knew he would recognize would be the hereditary Dugan red hair and those eyes. Thus far today, he had seen no one that even vaguely reminded him of a Dugan.

Moving casually, slowly around a corner, Halstatt recognized the two women who leaned seductively against a tanner's cart trying to persuade the man to come into the inn behind them. Their cohort, a young boy of perhaps ten, waited in the shadows to raid the man's goods should he succumb to the women's temptations. What delicious whores, Halstatt thought, licking his lips. As he sauntered past, he pinched the more buxom of the two, who wore a linen gown of gold and looked more like a lady of wealth than some ladies did today. She looked at him, smiled in recognition, and planted a kiss directly on his mouth, not noticing his beggar status. Feeling the heat rise within, he briefly contemplated spending his stolen coins on this lusty wench.

But movement caught his attention and he glanced further down the row of merchant carts. There at the end of the row, a dark-skinned man stood against a lamppost, arms folded across his chest. He was staring directly at Halstatt, it seemed, although his expression was not one of recognition. Halstatt recognized the blade hanging at the man's side and knew that if the man did not immediately identify him, he would before long. Halstatt knew there was a price on his head, thus it did not surprise him to be the target of any venador...nor this particular one. Forcing himself to remain calm, he gave his female friend a crushing hug, placed a gold crown in her plump palm, and slid into the crowd back in the direction he had come from.

He did not want to look back to give the man any indication he was nervous, but Halstatt did not want to be followed. Twice he ducked into alleys and once he allowed himself to be pulled into a swirling street dance, which allowed him to quickly scan around for the dark man's presence. Though he could not see him, Halstatt knew that Wace Elotti was there and looking for him. Elotti's reputation for success and accuracy was well-known; getting away from him would not be a simple task. Halstatt had to lose himself in the crowd for a few hours and lie low for a couple of days. He had come too far in his quest to be any hunter's prize.

But it seemed Elotti was not currently following him. No, Halstatt decided, he had been meant to see the man, to know he was being hunted, to see that the shark was waiting for him to make an error, to spill blood in the waters of Rhidam. Not on your life, Halstatt sneered, though the pang inside told him that he was not as confident of his future as he would like to be.

## ❧Chapter 11❧

Kavan lingered in the late afternoon shadows of the doorway watching the gathering of minstrels bantering jovially as they carried on what appeared to be a friendly competition amongst them. They had set up a platform near the palace gatehouse, as usually happened during every festival event, and attracted a sizable audience over the course of the day. He had seen them when he arrived at the keep, long after Ártur had taken the children to enjoy the day's festivities. It was just as well. As much as he loved the children, he had needed this day away from his duties. One day was not too much to ask for the sake of his sanity.

For many long minutes, he listened to the music as he donned a clean robe and combed out his dry hair. Then, as he stared out the window, enjoying the tunes though he could not see the performers from his window, he felt an irrepressible urge to do what he had not done in over thirteen years. Play before an audience that was not the royal household and its guests.

He stood apart from the main throng, face and hands covered to avoid recognition, although his white robe should have been enough to give him away. No one seemed to notice him, however, even with the black kestrel-shaped harp in his hands, as he waited with an uncharacteristic nervous flutter in his stomach. Even his hands trembled. Should he approach, he wondered, or bide his time? He had not felt this uneasy since his first public performance at the Festival of Candles in Clarys when he was sixteen years old. It had been far too long.

One of the musicians on the stage, a fresh-faced girl with a lute, waved in his direction. He did not move, not certain she was waving at him or at someone in the crowd near him. She leaned over and spoke to the elderly bearded man playing a set of reed pipes; the man nodded. She set her instrument down and slid off the stage to push through the gathering towards Kavan.

"Well, milord," she smiled, attempting to see the man inside the hood. She smelled of fresh straw and fruit, innocent smells. Her brown hair fell loosely about her face; her dress and stance were that of a woman but her features and figure and the smell of her suggested she was little more than a girl. "I saw your harp. Are you interested in joining us?"

"I do not wish to intrude," Kavan stammered, almost regretting that he had come this far.

"Nonsense. Others are encouraged to join in. As you can see, there is no harper amongst us; if you can play that thing, you're welcome to."

"I can play, but your welcome may be premature. You do not know who I…"

"I know enough." She looked too young to have heard him play thirteen years ago, or to remember him if she had. Rumor and myth persisted, but as he had not played publically during those years, it explained, perhaps, why none in the crowd around him were reacting to him. Whatever imagery of the White Bard they carried in their heads, he apparently did not match it.

The girl took his arm and led him towards the platform, her fingers digging gently into him. "You are a musician like us. That is all we need to know." She was hoping for more than his musical ability, he deduced. Awkwardly, he freed his arm, but by then he was already at the stage and could not easily flee without appearing rude or cowardly. The musicians greeted him enthusiastically, offered him a stool, and after a brief discussion about what songs he knew, began playing again. The ensemble consisted of the piper, twin boys…one with a drum and castanets, the other with a tin flute…a blonde woman with a mandolin, a man with a coiled metal horn, the lute player, and Kavan.

They played several pieces in unison, Kavan blending in as if he had always been there, the numbers sounding planned and rehearsed. His companions did not verbally question how he could play with gloves, but they did look at him curiously, as did the audience. The lute player politely encouraged him to remove his hood and gloves but Kavan refused. He could not, at least not yet. He enjoyed the chance to perform as part of an ensemble, something he had never done, and he did not wish to detract from that. Anonymity was something he was not used to. He knew what would happen when the audience discovered his identity and he was not ready for that.

The group took a break, during which the twins performed a series of jigs and dances, singing gaily with their bright youthful voices. The horn player gave a rousing march and then the two women, mother and daughter it appeared, performed a string ballad together. Beside Kavan, the piper guzzled several mugs of ale during that break and belched loudly as he gazed at the women with admiration.

"Your turn," he said as he wiped his mouth on his sleeve. The women completed their set and were retreating to the side of the stage.

"I…"

"We've been playing since early morning. We could use the rest. From the way you play…gloves and all…I suspect you are more talented than we've seen. Go on. Take those silly things off and let them see you, for pity's sake. You will never make a name for yourself hiding that way."

"I have no need to make a name for myself."

The stage was empty, the audience waiting with noisy expectation for what might come next. Kavan was stationary, looking from the stage to the audience, struggling with the urge to play as he had not done in years. The urge gradually won, and despite the anxious gnawing in his stomach, he went to center stage and with his back to the audience, removed his gloves at last.

There were gasps and murmurs from those closest to the stage, but the reaction was small compared to the response given when he sat upon the stool, his harp resting on his knees, and with one hand lowered the hood of his robe.

"The White Bard of Bhryell!" he heard someone exclaim, as the minstrels he had been playing with stared with awe and reverence. He was the idol of many; he had not been seen in performance outside of the castle walls since King Arlan's ascension and he had graced these lowly musicians with his presence. He had performed with them when everyone knew the White Bard played alone. There were whistles, murmurs, screams and other sounds of delight and admiration as the audience threatened to crush in around the stage. The great push stopped, however, when the first notes soared over their heads and brought immediate silence. Whether it was fear of rejection, or fear that he would be unable to give the audience what they expected, that had caused his nervousness, it vanished with the first chiming notes of brass strings. Eyes closed, mind centered on the music, he allowed the harp to speak, to reveal his soul to those who had ears to hear.

"What is that commotion?" Gabrielle asked, straining her head in the direction of the hoots, whistles, and applause.

The princess pulled at Ártur's sleeve and begged, "Let us find out, Lord Healer. Please."

Reluctantly turning away from a troupe of acrobats, the healer consented, following the sound of applause as long as it lasted, straining to see through the crowd. He stopped abruptly as his eyes and ears simultaneously identified the reason for this attentive gathering.

"The White Bard…" He could not hide the smile, his face alive with genuine relief. If Kavan was performing publically, then his time away from the castle had done him good. He pointed and Gabrielle followed the line of his gesture.

"Lord Cliáth?"

Lifting the princess onto his shoulders, Ártur nodded. Muir was tall enough to see through the crowd, though not very well. Ártur did not need to watch his cousin play; he had seen it many times before. Hearing it was enough. This time, however, it was different. Kavan was playing before a much larger audience then he played for within the castle. He was not performing because the King commanded it but because he desired to play. More importantly to the healer, his cousin's countenance was filled with peace and something akin to joy, not the anger, pain, and frustration he had been filled with a day ago. For however long it lasted, Ártur was happy to know that his advice to Kavan had proven correct.

Gabrielle pressed through the crowd, not caring that she was leaving her companions and escort behind. Her single desire was to be close to the stage, as close to Kavan as possible. She stopped when she reached the platform and placed her hands upon the coarse wood planks to steady herself as she stared at his serene face. She recalled the other time she had seen him perform; it had been at the Festival of Candles in Clarys, his first public performance outside of a náós when she had been thirteen years old. She had gone there alone using the Gates, unbeknownst to her father, and had been awestruck by the white harper who at the time had been sixteen years' old himself. He looked little older now. His music, his features, everything about him had awed and inspired her in a way nothing else ever had. She had not spoken to him then; despite her often-impetuous nature, she had not had the courage to approach him. He had filled her dreams ever since.

He was even more beautiful now than she remembered, his music more passionate and stirring as the years had replaced his naiveté and innocence with experience, wisdom, and knowledge. Physically he had changed little, though she knew that one look into his translucent green eyes would shatter the vision of eternal youth he portrayed. His eyes could speak volumes and revealed an understanding of the world that could never be possessed by the post-adolescent boy he appeared to be. Touched by the music and her memories, tears sprung into Gabrielle's eyes but she brushed them away, refusing to cry.

Feeling the wave of melancholy wash over him, Kavan opened his eyes, his hands not faltering upon the strings as he met Gabrielle's gaze. He had not known she was there. There was a tightening in his chest at the sight of her but that was all. No more pain, he decided, and closed his eyes again. He refocused his attention upon the music that continued pouring from his hands in an endless stream of sound. When he peered from beneath his lashes again, she was gone.

There was nothing promising in Kavan's gaze when he looked at her, nothing that told her what she wanted to hear or answered any of her questions. Gabrielle stifled the whimper in her throat and wove back through the crowd towards Ártur and the children. The healer did not appear to notice she had been gone, and the children paid her no heed; all of their attention was upon Kavan. Frustrated, she tugged upon Captain Delamo's arm.

"I wish to return to the keep," she demanded, not quite covering the distress in her voice.

The captain frowned as he tore his attention away from Kavan, an expression that gave his broad, bearded face an ominous air. "Milady? Lord Cliáth's performances are so…" He was prepared to stay and listen for as long as Kavan played. He did not want to leave.

"I must return home. Now. Káliel has been without me long enough...and I do not desire to remain here any longer."

Something had upset her, but Wortham knew she would not tell him what it was. His station was to obey, though it broke his heart to leave Kavan's music. "Very well, milady," he said with a low groan before leaning over to whisper in the healer's ear. Ártur nodded, an absent gesture that indicated he might not have actually heard what was said. As Wortham escorted Gabrielle away from the group, through the crowd, one of the other guards stepped in to fill the void at Ártur's side. As they were already before the gatehouse, it would not take long to escort the Prime Magistrate indoors, and if he was lucky, Wortham might be back before Kavan finished playing.

"Has something upset you, milady?" he asked as he pushed through the crowd, offering to hear her if she wished to unburden her heart.

"What makes you think I am...?"

"You're dead!"

Gabrielle gave a startled yelp as the dirty beggar with whom she had unexpectedly come face to face, drew a knife, equally startled, it seemed, to see her. He swung reflexively, intending to strike the woman, but as Wortham thrust her aside, the blade slashed across his face instead. Around them, people screamed, but the beggar disappeared into the crowd before he could be apprehended. Wortham covered his face with his hands. Blood seeped between his fingers.

"Ártur!" Gabrielle cried as she maneuvered Wortham out of the throng. "Someone find a healer!" The man was groaning as he stumbled, muttering something about his eyes as he allowed himself to be led. Behind her, she could hear the healer's voice above the commotion, but she did not pause to wait for him until they were out of the thickest part of the crowd.

"Logros," the healer was saying to one of the guards with him, "take Lady Dilyn and the children inside." He gathered Wortham into his arms and lowered the man to the ground. Gabrielle refused to withdraw, even with the soldier Logros pulling at her arm, and the man was reluctant to harm the woman who had once employed him. Nor did the children seem eager to leave, though the princess looked as if she would faint at the sight of blood and leaned against her brother for support. Then, without warning, Kavan was there, handing his harp to Prince Muir and kneeling beside his cousin, but the healer did not look at him.

It took much of Ártur's strength to pull Wortham's hand from his face. He heard several people gasp at the sight. The princess buried her face against Muir's shoulder. The gash ran from above Wortham's left eye to his mouth and was deep and bloody, and the moment Ártur released the man's hands to begin the task of healing, Wortham brought them back to his face. It was Kavan who pulled them away a second time, and though Wortham struggled, he could not break free.

"My eye," he moaned.

The bard lowered his head until it was near Wortham's. "Allow Ártur to tend it," he murmured. "I am here. All will be well." At the sound of that familiar, much loved and trusted voice, the soldier relaxed although he continued to grimace, groan and tremble in pain.

"I can stop the bleeding," the healer grunted as he strived to heal the man beneath his hands, "but I need a better place to work if I am to heal him properly. Take him inside."

Logros and Denyan lifted their injured compatriot between them and followed the healer, as Gabrielle put her arms around the children and steered them inside, the prince still entrusted with Kavan's harp. She made note of Kavan's tortured expression as the bard got to his feet, scanning the crowd for the attacker before he too followed. It was not the way he had wanted his performance to end.

Prince Muir's face was a mask and he said nothing, but the princess was trembling and beginning to cry. Other than her mother's blood, she had never seen anything like this, and she was fond of the soldier who most often accompanied them on outings. As soon as they were across the drawbridge, she released Gabrielle's hand and ran, sobbing, in the direction of the stables. The prince hesitated and looked at Kavan instead of following his sister.

"Will he be well?"

The blankness inside of Kavan, a void he could not read as he contemplated Wortham's condition, gave him no answers. He could not manipulate the Sight, no matter how much he wished to. "I do not know, my prince. He will live, of course, but…"

The boy nodded, understanding what his tutor could not say. He gave the harp to Gabrielle, rather than put it in Kavan's bloody hands, and said, "I will go to Diona. Will you be in the oratory?" The Elyri's blank expression did not change but he nodded.

Kavan neither rejected nor acknowledged Gabrielle's presence as he watched Ártur disappear inside the castle with Wortham. The man was silent, unconscious from pain and shock, which would allow the healer to tend him without the need of Kavan's soothing assistance. Yes, he decided, the oratory was the place to go. He might not be able to help his cousin, but he could pray, and prayer was something he felt deeply in need of. Gabrielle followed but stopped in the doorway of the oratory, watching him approach the altar, genuflect, and then kneel without ever taking his eyes from the pyre-bound figure that towered above him on the front wall of the room.

This was a part of Kavan that she had always been aware of but had never witnessed before. Never had she come across such rapt devotion, not even in those petty missionaries who somehow found their way past her patrols and onto her islands. Vows he may not have taken, but in his soul, Kavan was more gdhededhá than many of those men. Here, at last, she could see the truth about why he had turned from her, why he continued to push her away. These were his loves, k'Ádhá and music, and though he might feel something for her, it was not strong enough to gain equal footing in his heart beside those two passions. Physical passion he could, perhaps, live without, but he could not live and be happy without his faith and his music.

Harp left upon the first pew, she sat on the step beside him, gazing at his face in the glow of the lamplight. His eyes were closed, his thick, silver-white lashes barely visible against his fair skin. He did not seem to notice she was there, but eventually he softly asked, "You wish to speak?"

"I…" His voice in the silence surprised her. There were many things she wanted, needed, to say, but the first words to come out were barely a squeak. "Captain Delamo?" She felt responsible for what had happened. If she had not insisted on coming back to the castle, they would not have run into their attacker. Wortham would not have endeavored to protect her and would not have been injured. She wanted to know he would be well.

"I know no more than you. The wound was not life-threatening and Ártur is the best healer I know. But I do not know the final outcome."

"You knew the queen would…"

Kavan sighed. "I knew she would die because that was the course left for her. She did not have the strength to fight, and it was her time."

"How did you know it was her time?" The bard did not reply. "What happened? When she died? It felt like there were many more in the room than I could see…but that should not be possible." His eyes sparkled but still he did not speak. "I know you felt it too. I saw it in your face. What did you see?"

"záryph," he whispered, looking back at the figure of Dhágdhuán in anticipation of her reaction. "záryph and Kóráhm."

"Saint Kóráhm?"

He ignored the disbelief in her voice. "I have seen him before, many times. He came for the queen. He took her hand from me and I let her go. She…told me that I needed to be with her at the end. I suppose because Kóráhm wanted it."

"Why would Saint Kóráhm manifest himself to you?"

Her words should not have hurt him, but they did. It was foolish, he supposed, to expect anything different. "You do not believe me. No matter. Very few do, unless they see for themselves. I was born on the eve of the feast of his martyrdom. He, or a follower of his, came to my mother that same night…made predictions. I bear his name; he is my patron. If it is something more than that, I do not know. It is not my place to question why he comes, only to accept that he does." He met her gaze again, though this time she was the one to turn away from his scrutiny. She was afraid of what he was saying and afraid of what he might find in her eyes. "There is something more?"

Unable to voice the real question in her heart, she turned to the other topic that had been eating at her for days. "Why do you think it best Clianthe not know her heritage?" The question seemed to surprise him. "You did say that," she reminded him. "I want to know why."

"I did…I…" He looked at his clasped hands, noting that the blood upon them had dried. "Times are growing bleak for Elyri, Gabrielle. It has not manifested itself, but I feel the hatred growing. Not in everyone, of course, but it is becoming more pervasive than before. Perhaps because there are many of us in positions of influence to the King…I do not know. If Clianthe does not know what she is, and the knowledge of your mother remains hidden, perhaps she will have nothing to hide when the persecution begins. She will have no reason to be afraid."

"Don't you mean if the persecution begins?"

"No. When. It will come. Do not doubt that. Perhaps not as violent or prevalent or as long as it was in centuries past, and perhaps it will not come in my lifetime, but it will come."

His sincerity made her shiver and she gave an uneasy laugh to alleviate her anxiety. "If it does not come in your lifetime, I doubt Clianthe has anything to worry about. You shall outlive us both."

Kavan's expression darkened more. This was not a topic he liked to discuss. "Do not think I welcome the lifespan I've been given. It is not something I asked for. Besides, it is very likely that I will die before either of you, because of what I am."

Gabrielle's voice grew small and she shivered as she asked, "Because of...I have heard that you have the Sight. Is this true?"

"Yes."

"Have you seen your death? Is that why you say this? Is this what troubles you?"

"No, it is merely a feeling I have." Kavan shifted off his knees to face her. "Everyone knows me, by either name or reputation. It is well known that I am Elyri. My position and influence on the Crown of Enesfel does not endear me to many across the Sovereignties. That will make me an easy, and perhaps worthy, target in the eyes of many. I do not grieve my lot; k'Ádhá has given me this..." he looked at his bloodstained hands, "for a reason. Who am I to argue with the will of k'Ádhá?"

"So you give up? You will allow yourself to be killed?" Gabrielle asked with anger in her voice. She had never thought of him as weak, and his seeming so now troubled her.

Kavan cocked his head, perplexed by her reaction. "Giving up? There is no fight. I will do what I can to live, as I have no desire to die, but death will find me in k'Ádhá's time...if I can die at all."

"All living creatures can die, Kavan..."

Clenching his fists in his lap, he waited for her to continue, and when she did not, he spoke again. "Elyri can be killed, yes. I have seen Elyri killed by accident and disease and know we can die. But I have never known any of my kind to die of old age. There are few graveyards in Elyriá, and those who are buried in them have died of illness, fire, childbirth, or something similarly external. I remember the bhydáni, three of them...disappearing when I was a child. They went into the forest, not together but one at a time...different years…and they never returned. I considered it a coincidence, thought each could have encountered some wild animal, or that they had moved away from Bhryell. Now, however, I am less certain that was the case."

"No one is immortal…"

"We cannot know that. Maybe the same source of our gifts keeps us from dying. Perhaps our connection with the energies of nature allows us to bypass that end and go on to some sort of existence other than death. Teren have accused us of immortality…perhaps they are correct."

Gabrielle squirmed, toying with her dress as she realized the implications of his words. "But if that is true…then what of your…our souls? Can we…?"

She could not say it, and Kavan was glad. He did not like the idea any more than she did. "I do not know. Your Teren blood will save you. I will only know that answer if I die."

He and Gabrielle were spared the need to say more when the oratory door opened and Ártur entered, scrubbing his hand through his hair wearily. "I thought I would find you here."

Noting the exchange of eye contact that passed between the cousins, and the way Kavan bowed his head, Gabrielle realized she was going to have to ask questions if she wanted answers. "How is he?"

There was a long pause as the healer absorbed the melancholy in the room and wondered what they had been discussing. When he finally replied, his expression was sad. "I told him to sleep. His eye is healed, as is his face, but his vision…"

Kavan's head twisted to the side, and he stared at the pyre figure intently. Ártur followed his cousin's gaze towards the front of the room, feeling a faint tickle of energy run down his spine, a sensation that caused him to shiver uneasily. "sínréc?"

There was no spoken response. Kavan climbed to his feet and rounded the altar, moving as though in a dream. Once there, he wrapped his hands around the carved feet of Dhágdhuán. His body convulsed once and he groaned aloud. A static surge from somewhere above trickled through the carved figure and began to pool in his hands. It was happening again, Kavan realized. Nothing he could do would stop it. He could refuse to act, but he knew he did not have the will to refuse. Particularly on Wortham's behalf. Trembling, he managed to whisper, "Bring him to me…please."

Ártur was already on his way from the room. Though he had never experienced that building of energy before the miracles he had witnessed in the past, Kavan's distress was evident and the healer had known what to do before Kavan spoke. If there was even the smallest chance or hope for Wortham, this could be it. Gabrielle, too, felt the energy shift, and that, combined with Kavan's agitated voice and shaking body, distressed her.

"Kavan?"

He did not respond. He had not removed his hands from Dhágdhuán's feet though the static sensation beneath them was growing unbearable and pushing him to tears. There had been no miracles for thirteen years; he had believed that part of his life to be behind him. No, he thought. Not me. Not this again. I am not worthy of this. Then his cousin was there and Kavan lifted his head to look first into Ártur's eyes and then into Wortham's empty expression as the healer inhaled sharply. Tears. There were rarely tears.

The bard dropped his head between his outstretched arms, no longer looking at anyone. "Wortham," Kavan croaked, his quiet tone rough and strained, "do you believe in k'Ádhá's power?"

"Yes." The reply was certain, though confused.

"Do you believe in Dhágdhuán?"

"Yes."

"Do you believe in me?"

"Yes."

There was a long pause as Kavan shifted his weight from one foot to the other. "Do you trust me?"

"Of course." These seemed odd questions to the soldier, but easy ones to answer.

Odd questions, perhaps, but ones Kavan felt in need of asking. His second pause was longer; he had never asked this question of anyone in his life and he dreaded asking it, half fearing any answer the man could give him. "Do you...love me?"

Wortham groaned, partially out of frustration and confusion, partially out of surprise to hear such a question, and partially out of fear and relief to finally be able to speak his heart. "You know I do, milord...more than anything..."

Kavan too uttered a sound of relief as his heart swelled. "Wortham...would you do anything I asked, no matter how difficult?"

The soldier was anxious. These questions, the sight of the bard quaking with his hands upon the carved wooden figure, Ártur's proximity behind him as if to keep him from running, all were taking their toll. He did not know what was transpiring, only that he had lost sight in his left eye and that his dearest friend was clearly distraught. He could bear being questioned no longer. "Milord, you know me better than anyone ever has. You know my faith is strong. And you know I trust and love you more than my own life. I would do anything you bid of me. You know that is true."

Those words made Kavan warm inside and forced the brimming tears to break free. Rarely did anyone profess that sort of emotion to him with the honesty Kavan felt in Wortham's voice. "Then listen to me. When I give you the word, you must place your hands here...where mine are...and do not let go until I tell you to, regardless of what you experience. Can you do that?"

Not expecting anything unusual, and not doubting Kavan's instructions, Wortham nodded. "Yes, milord. I will."

Kavan stepped away from the figure and positioned himself behind Wortham, near enough that their bodies pressed together. Wortham tensed at the unexpected intimacy, but as Kavan slid his right arm around the man's broader torso, his hand pressed flat against Wortham's stomach, the man quickly relaxed. The bard's left hand covered Wortham's sightless eye, his palm pushing down gently as he pulled Wortham closer and began to pray, speaking in High Elyri, words that only Ártur understood.

"Touch His feet." The command was gentle but firm.

The captain did as instructed, but jerked his hands back with a squawk. "They are…"

"Do it!" This time, Kavan's command was a hiss and Wortham obeyed, refraining from pulling away again from the sharp, painful burning that enveloped his hands. Touching those feet that felt like flesh was like holding a hot coal.

"Milord…the pain!" But he could not withdraw his hands now. Something held him in place, something both internal and external. His whole being felt engulfed in flame, and both his hands and the places where Kavan's hands touched him burned hotter. Agonized tears came quickly.

Ártur watched in breathless anticipation. Beside him, Gabrielle was trembling; she had no idea what was happening. When the blood began to flow from the pierced feet of Dhágdhuán's image, trickling onto Wortham's hands, she gasped and nearly fainted. The healer steadied her, aware that Prince Muir had entered the oratory and knelt at the back of the room, afraid to come nearer to the source of incredible power.

"Lord Cliáth," Wortham cried, clinging to the title of respect even in his distress, "There is blood!" As it quickly covered his hands, however, he found that its touch soothed the pain of his burning flesh and leeched away some of his anxiety and fear.

When it was time, when Wortham's hands were bathed in red, Kavan dropped his hand from the man's face. The abrupt exposure of the area to the evening air was chilling. The Elyri released his hold and stepped around him; he touched his fingertips to the blood on the figure's feet and used it to trace a red X upon Wortham's sightless left eye. The captain screeched in excruciating pain, but the sound ended abruptly as Kavan moved.

"Come." Kavan pulled Wortham's hands from the figure's bloody feet; as soon as no one was touching the figure, the flow ceased. Gently Kavan guided the man to the consecration fount, lifted the heavy silver lid, and said, "Wash your hands."

Still trembling, Wortham stuttered, "In the fount, milord?"

"Yes, Wortham."

The man's hesitation was brief. It was not that he doubted Kavan's instruction, but the thought of immersing his red-stained hands into the chalice of holy water filled him with trepidation. Before Kavan could command him again, however, Wortham chose to act on faith and plunged his hands into the icy water. As the red swirled away from his skin and disappeared into the clear water, the burning sensation left and was replaced with an uncomfortable tingle, as if his hands had fallen asleep and were now waking. Amazed that the water did not turn crimson as expected, he fought to ignore his discomfort as he looked expectantly into Kavan's eyes.

"Wash your face."

Again, Wortham did as he was instructed, not sure why he was doing this but showing no hesitation this time. The moment the water, doubly consecrated by holy prayer and the blood of the Intercessor, touched his face, there was a flash of brilliant warmth and light and he stumbled backward into Kavan's waiting arms. There were several seconds of stunned silence. "Milord..." he stammered as Kavan steadied him. "My eye...I can see!"

With Wortham now standing steady, Kavan gulped and turned away from everyone, wanting to hide his tortured expression. "Yes, Wortham," he whispered. "Go and sleep…be at peace, my friend." He dropped to his knees before the altar and did not acknowledge the healer's comforting hand brushing his shoulder. Ártur, also shaken by the awe he felt, led the stumbling, babbling Wortham out of the oratory, passing Prince Muir on the way and giving him a small smile. The prince watched them leave, and when they were gone he approached Kavan. Almost afraid to touch him, yet feeling the strong compulsion to do it, he took the bard's hands in his, kissed first the man's hot forehead then the bloodstained hands, and then set about the task of cleaning the blood from the places on the floor where it had dripped with his tunic. To the side of the platform, Gabrielle had not moved other than to put one shaky hand to her mouth as if to silence herself. She watched the prince, then Kavan, and then the prince again, but Muir continued as if she was not there and Kavan seemed present only in body. Once the blood was cleaned away to his satisfaction, the prince kissed Kavan's hands again and then quietly left the oratory as silently as he had arrived.

When they were alone in the dimness of the quiet room lit only by three candles upon the altar, Kavan looked at her, his eyes burning feverishly, tears still present on his cheeks and lashes. He did not attempt to read her thoughts, but the expression on her face told him everything he needed to know.

"Say it, milady."

The words were hard to find, hard to formulate, but she finally managed to croak, "You…the stories…they are true. You are the most powerful Elyri that has ever lived…and you can perform miracles…"

He did not flinch before those words, but there was a miserable flicker in his eyes. "k'Ádhá performs the miracles. He uses my hands, but the power is His. As for being the most powerful…I do not know about that…"

"You are. I have never…I did not…believe…"

In miracles. He heard the words though she did not say them. "Do you now?"

Awkwardly, she looked away, unable to bear his gaze as she struggled to find an answer. "I cannot deny what I have witnessed these past few days. These events are forever seared into my memory…but why…why have I been allowed to witness such wonders?"

"I cannot answer that. Perhaps so that you would believe." He sighed. "I do not ask for these things to happen; they come of their own accord. If I could control it, I would have saved the queen."

She nodded, understanding what he meant. How horrible it must be to be at the whim of some other power, unable to control the outcome and help those he loved the most. "There is great love between you and Captain Delamo," she said wistfully, a touch of jealousy in her voice. "I sent him to you, hoping you would become friends…but there is much more…"

Kavan was about to retort, to address her words, but something else, a shadow across her face, her thoughts, flashed across his awareness, causing him to shiver. "You are leaving tonight."

It was not a question, but Gabrielle looked at her feet, suddenly embarrassed and uncomfortable. "I…yes. That is why I wanted to speak with you. I do not want us to part on unpleasant terms again."

Remembering their previous parting, Kavan admitted, "Nor do I."

"My things are in the purification chamber," she glanced to the tiny alcove. "But before I go…" Her voice caught in her throat.

"Yes?" He rose to his feet, feeling a sudden stab of fear at what she might do and finding his body prepared for flight should she try.

Thinking he had risen to face her fully, Gabrielle took a step closer. "I have to ask you…I must know…do you…love me?"

That stab of fear grew into a fire that fixed him in place. "I…cannot answer that…"

"Why not? It is a simple thing. There are only a few possible…"

"It would not be…it is not that I do not have an answer. I do not want to answer your question."

Again, she stepped closer until they were near enough to touch. She could feel the heat of his body and his discomfort at her proximity, but he did not retreat. "Is that because I am married?"

To his surprise as well as hers, Kavan took her face in his hands. She touched his in return; his were warm and trembling, hers were cool and steady. Gently he touched his lips to her forehead, ignoring the urge to kiss her mouth. He could not do that. He would regret it forever if he did. Because of that inner struggle, it took him many moments to speak. "It is because I do not wish to hurt you. I do not feel for you as you do for me, Gabrielle. You know that to be true. I do not know if I am capable of that sort of emotional attachment." She tried to pull away but he held her fast. He did not want to part on bad terms, but how could he change it? "But if I could…"

She freed herself, took a step back, and then hurried to the purification chamber, needing to escape before she said or did something she would hate herself for later. "Gabrielle." His voice halted her steps. "Do you wish me to take you through?"

"I do not think that would be advisable, milord."

Her tone stung but he could not fault her for it. He knew she was as angry at herself as she was at him. "I do not mean to hurt you. You do know that?"

Rather than answer, she murmured, "I desire two things from you, Kavan." She did not look at him but she did touch the bloody smudge on her cheek where he had touched her.

He was afraid of what she would ask, but said, "If I can give it, I shall."

"Tell me when my mother's murderer has been apprehended and punished."

"Of course."

"And when I am dead, do not forget me. For however long you live."

There was an uncomfortable pause as he weighed her request against what he had said earlier. "I have no choice in that, Gabrielle. I shall remember you always."

Her head bobbed, a nod of agreement, and she whispered, "And I you," before disappearing into the purification chamber.

He longed to follow, to stop her, but he did not. For both of their sakes, it was best he did not go after her. He felt the slow gathering of energy within the chamber; fifteen minutes later, she was gone. What Kavan had not said before, he whispered into the stillness. "If I could ever love anyone, Gabrielle…I think it would be you."

## ᚨChapter 12ᚦ

K'gdhededhá Jermyn adjusted his robe one final time and ran his stiff bristled brush through his sparse blonde hair. His first duty today had been a brief service for the ill-fated Cinda Maylor, and though disappointed, he was not surprised that only the court healers, Kavan, and Prince Muir attended. He was unable, thus far, to locate any members of the girl's family or anyone who knew of them, and it would have been disheartening to bury her alone. Kavan's presence, as always, had been more than adequate to bolster his mood.

Now he was off to the castle for the hopefully more pleasant task of a cordial appointment with the King. They were to discuss restoration of the náós, and with any luck, work would begin soon now that winter was past. The k'gdhededhá hoped Kavan would attend the discussion, as his eye for religious beauty surpassed anyone else's as far as Jermyn was concerned. Also, he admitted with a touch of guilt, he was eager to be within the bard's presence again. Like many others, he seemed unable to get enough of the Elyri's company.

He opened his trunk of personal belongings and rummaged through its contents. Finding what he sought, he turned the small velvet pouch upside down but it was empty. He frowned and began a slower, more thorough search, finally locating the blue prayer beads in the midst of his undergarments, though he did not understand why it had not been within its pouch where he kept it. He had never failed to return it there before. With a shake of his head, he chastised himself for growing old and forgetful. "Madness," he muttered, as he hung the beads about his neck, closed the trunk, and headed to the castle.

⮷ * ⮶

It was pleasing to wake in her own bed, Gabrielle decided as she stretched and looked at her husband beside her, the back of his head tousled from a restless night's sleep, even if home was not where her heart longed to be. She shivered. She had not been away from home for many years; those few days in Rhidam had felt like an eternity. Despite how much she appreciated being home, however, there was a hidden part of her heart that wished she had never had to come back.

Felix had been happy to see her, but try as she did, she was unable to return his affections with any enthusiasm. Kavan's face was all she saw in her mind's eye, and all she felt was the sensation of his hands upon her face and the great raw void that had filled her when she had entered the purification chamber to return home. It would be with her for a long time, she knew, like the last time, and while it healed, she could not endure the touch of her husband's hands. They were not the graceful, gentle white ones she longed for. But she would will this pain to pass as she had done long ago. Felix did not deserve this. If she threw herself into her work, offering King Arlan's proposal to the Council, Felix would think little of her turning him away. She had never been free with her affections. He likely, she hoped, would not suspect a thing.

Silently she crept down the marble staircase and went to her office, dressed in her nightclothes and dressing robe. She could hear Delia already moving about the villa. On the oak desk was a stack of documents waiting to be revised or signed; Felix enjoyed the power but hated the paperwork. Ah well, she sighed wistfully. It was a perfect excuse for keeping distance between them.

A rock crashed through the tall glass window behind her, hitting her in the shoulder, showering her unexpectedly with shards of glass. She cried out, more in surprise than fear or pain, and picked up the fist-sized rock. As quickly as the silence was broken, the world was silent again. She could see no one through the unobstructed window, just the waving of branches from the foliage planted behind the villa. There were enough shrubs that anyone might have been hiding there, and in the early light of day, it was difficult to tell if any of the movement she saw was anything other than limbs swaying in the breeze. Bouncing the rock in her hand, contemplating this unusual event, she could not recall the likes of it happening within her lifetime.

"Milady!" Delia burst into the room, panting with the exertion. "I heard…oh my! Are you injured?"

"Bruised, nothing more. Probably children playing…" That made little sense since the sun had barely risen, but it was a better explanation than the alternatives. "Set the guard to search the grounds for intruders, have this glass cleaned up, and see to it that the window is replaced. I will take these to the study. I will work there today; please see to it that no one disturbs me. Except Felix…when he comes down tell him I must speak with him. Such acts against this house cannot be tolerated."

"Lord Harper?"

Kavan did not look up from his kneeling position on the altar steps. He had been there the entire night; after what transpired the evening before he had been unable to calm his restless mind, unable to sleep, and he had feared whatever dreams he might have had after Gabrielle's departure. He left this position long enough to attend the burial of Prince Hagan's nurse. He was not surprised that Wortham sought him out, but Kavan wished he had not. He wanted to be alone. But, as he was unable to deny the man anything, he bid his guest sit with a tilt of his head. The soldier obeyed.

"I do not mean to interrupt, milord, but I need to speak with you before I return to duty. I must thank you…"

"There is nothing to thank me for, Wortham; you know it. I am only a man and could not have healed you."

Wortham smiled. "I know your humility is great, milord, and it is true that the miracle and thanks belong to k'Ádhá, but it was your hands…"

"I did not ask…"

"You never do…or more precisely it is often the miracles not asked for that are the ones allowed to occur." His smile widened at the bard's expression as it dawned on Kavan that this could be true. It seemed that the harder he prayed for a miracle, the less likely it was that one would happen. "There is no one else in the Five Sovereignties who is reputed to perform miracles," Wortham continued. "If you had not been here, the eye and sight would have been lost. I thank you for being here. You could have refused to help me, teach me a little humility."

"Humility you do not lack. And you know I could never deny you what I have the power to give. You are my friend."

Looking away in embarrassment at the deep emotion in the bard's voice, a tone that spoke of a love deeper than friendship, Wortham went on. "I owe you eternal thanks for that if nothing else. Please accept my gratitude, milord. I hope that someday I will be able to repay you. There is one other thing though…the incident…something I remembered on waking this morn that I find troublesome. I was hoping you could help me untangle my thoughts."

When Kavan did not speak, only bobbed his head, Wortham continued. "The attacker was a beggar or looked to be one. I was escorting Lady Dilyn to the castle when we came face to face with this man. He looked more startled than we, and said something puzzling before attacking. He looked at her and said, 'you're dead' as if he thought she was someone else."

Kavan leaned forward with interest. "Someone like Lísbhet Dilyn."

"I never had the honor of meeting the lady, but I have seen her portrait and I did see her from afar a few times as a boy. There is a strong resemblance between the two, I admit. He could be someone who had heard of the lady's death, knew of her, and thus recognized her daughter, but even so, lashing out seems a highly irrational act, even if he was surprised. I can think of no other reason, however, for him to wish to harm the Prime Magistrate."

Nor could Kavan. If this man had some part in the death of Gabrielle's mother, the attack on Gabrielle and Wortham made sense. Otherwise, it seemed random and defied explanation. "Did you see the attacker's face?"

"Briefly, as he fled as soon as he cut me. I could try to describe him, but given the circumstances, it would be clearer, easier, if you saw for yourself."

The soldier held forth his hands, eagerly awaiting the intimacy of Kavan's touch and the psychic probe it would bring. It had happened before between them, more times than Wortham could recall, because it was much simpler to let the bard describe what he saw than to have Wortham attempt to describe what he could barely remember. Memories seemed faulty at best, until Kavan touched them, read them, brought them to life and made them complete.

With a small smile, Kavan took Wortham's hands. Few Teren trusted the intimacy of two minds joined that way and even fewer welcomed it. Like Ártur, Kavan could barely bring himself to examine the thoughts of a resisting or unsuspecting individual. He hesitated to do it even with those who would welcome the rapport. When Captain

Delamo was wrongly accused of theft many years ago, instead of allowing Ártur to test his honesty, as the King usually asked for, the Captain had requested that Kavan do it. To the bard's surprise, Wortham's mind had been completely open and embracing, and since then, Kavan relished each opportunity to touch it, though he could never be as open as Wortham was with him. No other Teren, not even King Arlan, had shared this experience with Kavan, and the only other Kavan currently desired such contact with was Prince Muir.

The startled face of Wortham's attacker was clear to see, anchored as it was in the trauma of the nearly lost sight and the miracle that had given it back. Brown beard, brown clean hair…too clean to belong to any beggar, in spite of the man's tattered attire. He was of medium height, wiry build, and looked to be from thirty to forty years old. Details Wortham might never have recalled were also clear, such as the heavy bulge within the man's shirt that indicated a money pouch and the high quality of the wood handled knife used in the attack. But the man was no one Kavan recognized.

Pulling away, he did not speak until Wortham regained his composure. Despite welcoming the intimacy, Wortham, like any Teren, required time to pull out of that fugue state, to readjust to the loss of another mind merged with his. When the captain's dazed expression had eased back to his normal relaxed one, the bard said, "I will go to Ártur; he can create a drawing of this individual. It may be useful in apprehending him, and if he is connected to Lísbhet Dilyn's death, that is imperative. I suggest you tell Lord Cornell what you have told me, and tell him I will get the sketch to him as soon as possible."

❧*❦

"Are you certain you wish to do this, milady?" The stout woman who hustled around the room fretted as she hastened to do her lady's bidding. She returned with the silver and ruby comb the woman requested and assisted in nestling the adornment within her mountain of red curls.

"Of course, Elyn. Why should I not? He is a capable warrior and a wealthy, and handsome, man."

The servant continued to frown. "He is also Elyri."

"Yes, so I have heard. What of it? They do not frighten me, nor do I think they are the spawn of evil. This man is just that…a man like any other. He is nothing I need to fear, particularly if he is as much a gentleman as is rumored. You may accompany me or not, but I am going to meet him."

Finished with her lady's hair, Elyn curtseyed. "Of course, milady. I will accompany you." There was no way she would allow her mistress to do this alone. There might be no physical danger, but the scandal of meeting alone could be dangerous enough.

❧*❧

Lifting the moldering velvet drape to see into the street below, Halstatt was able to determine it was mid-morning and that the city streets were filled with the usually drab daily rabble. But as with every time he peeked outside last night, there was no indication he had been followed, no sign of Wace Elotti. He found it difficult not to believe that he had given the hunter the slip, as it was more logical than believing the hunter had given up. Elotti was not the type of man to give up. Time and again, however, Halstatt reminded himself that such foolishness was what Elotti was hoping for. If Halstatt grew overconfident, he would make a mistake. Halstatt did not intend to let that happen.

He let the drape fall and turned, waiting until his eyes readjusted to the darkness of the room. He had been here too long. It was time to find a new hideout. And it was time to plan his next step. Caol had nothing Halstatt truly wanted; he wanted the dagger, and the man's death, of course, and he knew Caol was aware of that, but beyond that, there was nothing. And the only thing Caol might want of him was his death. Thus, Caol was unlikely to agree to meet him, unless his sense of honor drove him to it. If Caol would not come to him, Halstatt would have to go to Caol. But how?

≈*≈

Kavan was kneeling in the upper oratory when the King entered, as Ártur had said he would be. The room was charged with static power, and though the sensation seemed weaker than it had years ago, the King could still feel the presences, the distant sensation of others he could not see watching him. He did not like it any more now than when he had first felt it. He crept forward, knowing Kavan could hear and recognize his naturally heavy footfalls. He settled on the front bench, the harp still there where Gabrielle had put it, and was absorbed in his own thoughts, willing to wait for Kavan to acknowledge him. In this setting, Arlan rarely demanded the bard's immediate attention. Today, as usual, he could wait.

"Is it time for your meeting with k'gdhededhá Jermyn?" Kavan finally asked, shifting sideways off his knees to face the King in one fluid movement. Arlan still marveled at his friend's grace.

"Soon…as soon as he arrives." Arlan did not speak right away as he concentrated on the diminishing sensations around him. "Kavan?"

"Yes, My Liege?"

"None of that today. This is friend to friend, not king to bard."

The flicker in Kavan's eyes acknowledged the request. "What did you wish to ask?"

"Those…presences. I still feel them, but they still do not approve of me. Why? I am restoring náósthé around the kingdom, educating gdhededhá, spreading the Faith. All of my children have been christened and taught the ways of Faith…even Brenna embraced it…"

His voice faltered and failed him for several moments. "Yet they do not seem satisfied…as if they want something more…and they seem to be fading."

"Fading?" There was a note of alarm in Kavan's voice.

The King held up his hand and shook his head, hastening to reassure Kavan. "Nothing to do with you, I am sure. But it is getting harder for me to feel them. It still makes me uneasy when I do, but I have gotten used to them over the years, and find it disturbing that they might soon be gone. What more can I do?"

Kavan bowed his head and gave the question thought. "Your works have been outstanding, it is true…and your heart is good. But pardon me for saying this…you have little belief in the ideals you are working for, in the tenants of the Faith…"

"Faith? I believe the tenants are right and good…that the Faith is a good thing…that the people need this…"

"What about you? Do you need it? Do you believe in the words, in the teachings? Do you believe in Holy Grace and Dhágdhuán's Intercession? I suspect that once you make your final choice about such things, what you feel will return to you, or it will leave you all together."

"Still seeking that conversion, aren't you?" The King's tone was gentle and warm, far from accusatory. He knew Kavan would not answer that question. "I believe in k'Ádhá. I believe we are meant to live peacefully, in harmony with others, helping those who need it. Beyond that, I am not sure. How can I believe in a man who would willingly accept a death like that," he motioned to the carved pyre figure, "for the sake of a world of others he would never know, who are largely unworthy of such a sacrifice?"

"All are worthy." Hands clasped in his lap, Kavan continued. "He knows the hearts of all men…and loves us despite our faults. That is enough. As for…do you believe in me?"

Arlan prepared to retort but then stopped and stared at his friend. "Yes…you would. I know no other man who might lay down his life for a stranger if you thought the cause was just."

"Then if you can believe in me, in my fleshly, impotent state, why can you not believe in one who was mortal but is now something more, a man who lived a life beyond reproach. I am not as close to k'Ádhá as Dhágdhuán was, but if I thought by sacrificing myself for someone else I could somehow atone for my own wrongs and redeem even one man, I would do it in an instant. Can you understand this?"

The King did not reply. Instead, he leaned back in the pew and clasped his hands behind his head, staring at the pyre upon the wall. There was blood on it still from the previous night, when Wortham's sight was restored. Once the King noticed that, recognized what it was, he quickly looked away. Sometimes he wondered if his hesitation to believe had more to do with his own stubbornness than with any lack of faith. Perhaps, he thought, I can believe in Kavan because I can see him with my own eyes.

The stillness within the oratory intensified in such moments since the sounds of the other rooms and outside world failed to penetrate here. He fingered the heavy silver medallion hanging around his neck, the matching half of the one Kavan also wore. It had been a gift from his father and he knew it somehow bound the House of Lachlan with Kavan for however long the bard lived and perhaps beyond.

"Whatever happened to us, Kavan?"

"My Liege?"

"Things between us seem…different…now. I use to feel connected, as if you and I could do anything together. Now…it seems that has changed. I guess I am missing my youth."

"Thirty years is hardly old, Arlan."

"Perhaps not for you, but I am almost half as old as my father was when he…and you look no older than you did when we met. You will not look much different in thirty years. I could be…I…oh, never mind." He cleared his throat and changed the subject to something less grim. "Lady Dilyn has returned to Káliel?"

Countenance darkening, Kavan replied, "Yes." The change of topics was welcome, but the new topic did not make him feel at ease.

The King did not fail to notice that change, though he did not understand what it meant. "I was hoping she could stay longer. I think we made great strides in defining a new relationship between Enesfel and the islands. With more time, we might even become allies." The bard did not react beyond a slight nod of his head, so again Arlan changed the subject. "I also heard about your performance outside…and Wortham's eye…"

Kavan squirmed. "I wanted to play; it had been too long…and I would prefer not to discuss the other."

Nodding, understanding that desire, Arlan sighed. "I am sorry I missed the performance. I think it would have done me much good to see it…and it would have done me even more good to have witnessed the other." He pushed reluctantly to his feet, watching Kavan's still bowed head. "There was a time when we could talk freely. But I have sensed a change of late. What has changed, Kavan? Are our paths really much different?"

Kavan lifted his chin and met the other man's gaze. "Maturity, Arlan. That is what has changed us. The years and events we have lived through have shaped who we are. And you know I have never shared freely with anyone. As for paths…you are a king. I am a harper. You do not have the luxury of being truly able to confide in anyone. You command; I obey…when I can." There was a touch of amusement in the Elyri's otherwise somber voice and expression. "You have responsibilities I do not, and I have freedoms you do not. And you will agree that, despite my tutelage, there are many areas in which the two of us do not share the opinions and outlooks."

"Muir."

"Not only him, but he is a good example."

"You relate to him better than you do to me, do you not?"

Kavan wondered for the first time if Arlan was jealous of his relationship with the boy. "Because I have been the one to raise and school him."

"You have schooled me, Bertram, Diona, Wilred…"

"You were taught by your mother, Lady Johanna, King Donal, and Lord McHador. I merely added to the foundation already there. Bertram has your influence to steer him and that of the soldiers he pesters. Diona had Brenna's, Deidre's and Syl's, and yours. Wilred has his parents guiding him. In those ways, Muir is alone…although Lord McHador does what he can, as did Brenna."

The King frowned. "Will you hold that against me forever?"

"I do not hold it against you, Arlan. I understand your reasons…but I cannot approve of them. However, my love for you is not hampered by my love for Muir, nor do my loyalties to you affect my loyalties to him. I try to keep you separate as best I can."

"Then you are a better, wiser, man than I shall ever be, Lord Harper. And more honorable I believe. I pray k'Ádhá grants me more of your compassion and wisdom. Are you coming to meet with k'gdhededhá Jermyn?"

"I may arrive later. I must speak with Ártur regarding Wortham's attacker."

That news hooked the King's interest. "You learned something?"

"I was able to draw imagery of his assailant from Wortham; if Ártur will sketch the individual, we could display it throughout Rhidam and perhaps someone will come forth with information. It seems likely, from what I was told, that this may be the same individual who killed Lady Dilyn; I would like to see that he is arrested before anyone else is harmed."

The King smiled; it was the first good news he had heard in days. "Excellent. I want that as well. Sketches would be useful. I hope you will arrive at the meeting on time too…as I'm sure the k'dedhá does."

❧*❦

"Good morning, Lord Chancellor."

Bhríd looked up from his manuscript at the young man who had come into the room. He, too, tried to show the eldest prince extra attention to make up for the lack he received from his surrogate father. It was easy to do, as Prince Muir was bright and eager to learn and very rarely cross, irritable, or difficult. "Good morning, Prince Muir. Is there something I can do for you?"

The prince settled in a chair across from the chancellor, scanning the cluster of books and documents piled upon the desk. They were not from the library shelves; they appeared to be ledgers and legal manuscripts, in which the prince had no interest today.

"It is nearly time for my lessons, but I wished to speak with you beforehand."

Marking his page with a length of ribbon, Bhríd closed the book. "This sounds serious."

The young man nodded. "You are aware that my mother left the Weylin estate in Alberni to me?"

"Of course. I drew up her Final Testament and had the opportunity to see the estate and assess its value. You have questions regarding the estate?"

"Fath…Arlan says it will become mine upon my fourteenth birthday. Whose is it now?"

"Legally, it is yours. It belonged to the Crown while she lived, but now it is held in trust for you until you sign the documents and take full possession. If you were to die before then, it would revert to the Crown's ownership, and while in trust the Crown gains the benefits of its income, but by right and law it is yours. Upon your birthday, you will gain the formal title of Duke of Alberni, the use of its income and lands, and become responsible for its upkeep. Now, the Crown is currently responsible for those things and no one holds that title."

"Am I free to do what I wish with it, or must I wait until I am Duke?"

Curious, Bhríd steepled his hands, his elbows on the desk, and leaned forward. "That depends upon what you wish to do. If you wish to create knights or commission buildings, you will have to wait; your signature as owner will not become valid until your birthday. You could freely change the personnel in the house and ground staff, since you are part of the Lachlan family, though I would recommend learning about those who are there before you do. If you wish to appoint public officials or change them or to sell the estate or bequeath it to someone else, you would need to wait until your legal signature becomes valid."

"But if I made a decision now," Muir leaned back in the chair, "one that would not go into effect until later, when I am old enough, would that be acceptable?"

"I would think so. Once you are of age, the land and title are yours. Your decision might still need to pass the King's approval, depending on what you intend, but I cannot imagine him denying a reasonable request. Why? What is it you wish to do? I am at your disposal should you wish to draw up any contracts."

"Thank you. I may need your assistance…I do not know if what I wish to do is possible. If you have time later in the day to discuss it further, I should like to do that."

Bhríd stood and offered his hand. "I shall make time, my prince. Come. It is time for your lesson."

## ❧Chapter 13❦

Making a tidy bundle of his purchases, Chamberlain McHador handed the merchant a handful of coins, slung the bundle over his shoulder, and left the shop. This was his favorite place to make purchases. His late wife, Jezeel, had always bought her household supplies here when she lived, and though she had been gone from his life for nearly forty years, he continued that trend, though now it was a habit and had little to do with her. In fact, he realized as he closed the door behind him, today was the first time he had thought about her in quite a long time. There was no pain in those memories any longer, no loneliness, just the fond memories of a love that had been. There had been too much to do since her death, many other losses and much history, to afford her constant thought.

He trudged towards the keep, feeling bored and restless. General Wyndham had not needed him today, and while Guthrie could have insisted upon tending the new cavalry with the general, he knew that Ternce disliked close supervision, particularly by the chamberlain. Guthrie agreed to remain in Rhidam, if for no other reason than he had arranged to meet with the King to discuss the latest rumors out of Neth.

He had learned nothing more since the carnival and was unable to locate the two men overheard at the tournament. But he had sent Hewett Colson north to gather any information that could be found. If war was in the offing, Guthrie refused to be the last to know. It looked as if his premonition of needing a military might be accurate and timely after all.

Impassioned swearing rose within the Eagle's Nest Inn as he approached, followed by the sound of smashing furniture, glass, and pottery. It was not his place to break up a brawl; the innkeeper would have his own men to do that and royal interference would be unwelcome. When four individuals crashed through the front window within ten feet of him, he decided it was his problem to take care of, particularly since it was three men against one. Four others from within the inn rushed through the door and tried to wrestle the antagonists off their prey.

The chamberlain pulled the victim from their midst and the broken man sagged into his arms. One burly assailant surged forward but stopped short of the tip of Guthrie's sword. The other two were apprehended; one of the innkeeper's men caught the third man's arms, allowing Guthrie to sheath his sword and kneel beside the fallen man. There was no pulse, no breath, and no sign of life. And, the chamberlain noted, he was Elyri.

Standing, he wiped his hands on his leather pants. The innkeeper emerged from the inn and stopped in the doorway, looking pallid and distressed upon seeing the chamberlain's familiar face in the midst of this matter. "What is going on here?" Guthrie demanded.

"No Elyri swine should be allowed in a reputable…" started one man who bore an ugly black eye. The man who held him squeezed his arm around the man's neck and the fellow grew silent. The innkeeper crept closer.

"You…" Guthrie motioned to him. "What happened?"

Expression apprehensive, the stooped man cleared his throat. "These…" he indicated the three attackers. "They were at the bar when that one came downstairs." He glanced at the man at the chamberlain's feet, not knowing if he was alive or dead. "He has been here for two days, renting a room. He came to the bar for a meal…he's paid all his bills and caused no trouble. When they could not bully him into leaving, they…" His mouth snapped shut as the second assailant snarled and tried to break free of the man who held him.

"He doesn't belong here! He's not one of us! I will not associate with filth!"

Guthrie exhaled slowly, barely believing he was hearing this. "You could have left if you did not like the company. He has as much legal right to be here as you. But you need not worry about him any longer; he is dead." He watched their expressions to gauge their reaction. "Now you have me, Justice Cornell, and His Majesty the King to be concerned with instead. Bring them to the castle. And you, sir, will be required to testify regarding this matter."

Face ashen, sick and disgusted by the death that had taken place within his establishment, the innkeeper nodded hastily.

The second man cried, "He started it! He would not leave as he was told…"

"If he had a room here and has paid his debts," the chamberlain growled, "there was no one to tell him to leave save the innkeeper. There are no laws restricting the travels of…"

"There should be!"

"Enough!" Guthrie had become annoyed with this business and was finding it difficult to refrain from punching the next man to open his mouth. "His Majesty will decide your fate after hearing all arguments. But I will spare you some worry and tell you that your fate will not be good. Come."

❧*❧

Sitting beneath the shade of a small tree in the northern courtyard, Kavan watched Prince Muir practice his swordsmanship with the chancellor. Though not as strong or as experienced as his Elyri instructor, the prince was doing a remarkable job of holding his own. With experience, the prince could be a great swordsman; Kavan felt certain. Having the best swordsman in the Five Sovereignties as a tutor was an advantage, but neither Prince Bertram nor Wilred showed such promise. Wilred's passion was the bow, like his father, and Bertram's interest was in jousting. Memory drifting back to his childhood sword practice, wondering if he should try to train Prince Muir, Kavan leaned against the tree with a wistful sigh.

He could not remember falling asleep, but suddenly he sat upright, trembling, his blood pounding in his ears. He had been dreaming, something he rarely did. In his dream, there had been a child crying, a child that had sounded like Prince Wilred. A group of seven horsemen, some of whom he recognized…Caol, Wortham, Prince Muir and himself…were stopped in a field. He was not sure who the others might be, though one wore clothing suggestive of a Nethite. An odd assortment of companions. There was a feeling of dread and apprehension in the dream, a sense that this was somehow more real than a dream should be. Now that he was fully awake, the images did not fade as those from a dream normally did. Not a dream then, but a vision. Of what? Muir leaving Rhidam under armed accompaniment? What did Neth have to do with that and what interest did Caol have in the prince's departure? Why was Prince Wilred crying?

On the practice field, Bhríd was trying to teach Muir to feel an opponent's advance when he could not see it. A difficult feat for someone who was not Elyri, but the prince was, as usual, proving to be more proficient than his Elyri teacher expected. Perhaps his constant exposure to Elyri had sharpened the boy's natural intuition. A small flame of pride flickered within Kavan but he extinguished it quickly. Muir could have been his son for all of the pride he took in the prince's accomplishments.

Vision blurring, the bard lost sight of the men on the field and the castle walls beyond. Instead of struggling against the vision he knew was coming, he relaxed into it, hoping to avoid the worst of the usual nausea and dizziness that came with them. Two in such rapid succession was rare and thus important. This time he Saw Muir standing at the foot of a cliff, in a musty cavern, a sword raised above his head as though he was preparing to drive it into an unmoving opponent at his feet. Kavan could hear Prince Wilred crying again, and somewhere far off he could hear Caol arguing with someone. Several paces to Prince Muir's left, a body lay face down amidst a scatter of jagged boulders and stones. The form was regally dressed, though dirty, but from this distance, it was unrecognizable. Though Kavan strained to push the Sight towards the figure, the vision would not allow itself to be molded. He could see only what it allowed. Within the vision, there came a loud crashing of falling rocks and Kavan's view went dark.

Groaning, he pushed himself off the ground, knowing better than to ask how he had come to be face down in the grass. The Sight did strange things to him sometimes, and he long ago stopped trying to understand it. Prince Muir and Bhríd ceased their practice and rushed to him; the prince was already there helping him up with concern on his young face.

"What is it, Lord Cliáth?" the prince asked. "Are you well?" He worried more for his tutor since his mother's death. He could not bear to lose Kavan as he had lost her.

"I am. It is nothing that should concern you, my prince…"

Bhríd squatted beside him and placed a hand upon his kinsman's shoulder. "llánec?"

The bard nodded. Bhríd understood. Only an Elyri could understand what the Sight could do to a person. And in many ways, Kavan believed that only an Elyri could respect the ramifications of the Sight.

It was a term the prince had heard before, and he knew what it meant. Brow knit in worry, he knelt and asked, "What did you see? What has happened?"

"I…" Kavan shook his head. "It is something that will happen…or could happen, but it was not clear enough to say any more about what it means." He raised a hand to stop the boy's questions. "The Sight is not always obvious, my prince. Often its images are cryptic. I can know what it wants me to see and no more, and right now, what I have Seen makes very little sense."

Thankfully, the sound of horses entering the courtyard drew their attention away from the conversation, deterring Prince Muir from asking further questions. Three riders, two women and one young man, approached, and though Kavan and the prince did not recognize them, the red-haired woman who dismounted with the help of her squat male escort was known to the chancellor. He went forward with a smile and bowed when he reached her. It was too much to ask for that she had come to see him, but he was hopeful that was the case.

She studied him as he approached and smiled before speaking. Without his heavy armor and the horse, he was not as intimidating as he had been yesterday, but he was still taller than she was and heavier built than any other Elyri she had seen. His ebony hair was also unusual for an Elyri, but his eyes were a pale green, the color of the froth at the ocean's edge, a color not unseen amongst his people. Her smile widened and she held forth her hand. "You are Chancellor Bhríd Cáner." It was a statement, not a question.

He took her hand and raised it to his lips. "I am."

"Madalyn Dubuais, Duchess of Levonne."

His bow was deeper than it had been yesterday. She far outranked him. "Milady, it is an honor to have you in Rhidam. Are you here to seek an audience with the King?"

"Later, yes. For now…" Movement behind him drew her attention as Kavan and Prince Muir got to their feet. Her eyes widened. "The White Bard of Bhryell?"

As illogical as it seemed, Bhríd felt a stab of annoyance, but thankfully, it passed quickly. Kavan was not one to seek attention, save through music; it was not his fault that people recognized him whenever they saw him, and thus knew who he was. "Lady Dubuais, this is Prince Muir Lachlan, and this is Lord Kavan Cliáth."

Her gesture of supplication to the prince was genuine and sincere. If she knew his history, it appeared not to trouble her. "At your service, my liege," she murmured before offering a hand to Kavan with another curtsey. "I believed you to be a myth, milord. I am pleased to learn you are not."

Kavan kissed her hand because it was expected, and bowed in response. Technically, he had no title, but because the King insisted upon calling him Lord Harper, everyone over the years had grown to assume he was a lord by birthright. "Much about the White Bard is a myth, milady. I am not what the stories claim me to be."

She chuckled. "You are modest, milord. There is surely some truth to the tales, although very few are ever precisely what stories make them out to be. I shall be happy to avoid comparing you to the myths if you wish."

"I do…it is appreciated." Many people had difficulty separating myth from reality where Kavan was concerned; if she could do it, he would find her company more tolerable. "Come, my prince. Let us leave the duchess to her business." Both bowed again and left Bhríd to attend to the visiting dignitary.

"As I was about to say," she continued, picking up where she had left off as though they had never been interrupted. "I do have matters to discuss with the King, but they are inconsequential compared to recent events in Rhidam. I can speak to him at his convenience and offer my sympathies. I came here today, however, to speak with you."

Bhríd blinked and struggled to keep the impending silly grin from his face as he asked, "Me?"

"Your meekness becomes you. May we talk somewhere out of the sun?"

"Of course." He motioned and a scatter of servants came running from all directions, some taking the three horses to the stables while others escorted the group into the castle. Bhríd led them to the library, which was usually unused at this hour of the day; there the pages left them alone and the duchess' servants remained outside of the door. It was her right to have them in the room with her, but she was the one to bid them stay with a hand gesture. With a quick visual perusal of the room as the door closed, she settled into a cushioned chair and waited for her host to make himself comfortable.

"Would you care for a drink?"

"No, thank you."

Bhríd poured himself a glass of water before sitting, an attempt to hide his apprehension. This was not like him; he was not a man prone to nervousness, even around kings, but something about this woman made his hands tremble and dulled the edges of his usual calm. He sat across from her, cupping the metal mug between his hands, and cleared his throat before beginning, "What may I do for you, milady? Are you in need of my services in a professional capacity, be it a matter of taxes and census or a matter for the sword?"

She shook her head, and for a moment, Bhríd was mesmerized by the red curls that slid across the slope of her shoulders. "Nothing so mundane or drastic, Lord Cáner. I have seen you compete many times and have heard a great deal about you. After I saw you yesterday, I decided it was time to make your acquaintance while I was in Rhidam."

"For what purpose?" Her straightforward manner added to his uneasiness, but it was an unusually pleasant sensation. He judged that she knew what she wanted and allowed nothing to prevent her from reaching her goals. It was an admirable quality for the only woman in Enesfel to have strict control over her lands. Her father had died, leaving no other living relatives, thus ensuring her right to his lands and title. Bhríd was aware of how prosperous she had been for the last nine years, though he had expected her to be older and not nearly as beautiful.

"It is a delicate issue that I am not certain you will agree with, particularly since I have heard such things are handled differently in Elyriá. However, I am willing to compromise on this matter, as much as I am able, if you will but give ear to my petition."

"What petition is that, milady? Of what do you speak?"

"Why, marriage, of course." She laughed at his expression as words failed him and he struggled for something to say.

"Marr...you do not mean..." Deciding that he must have misinterpreted her intentions, he gathered his wits and coughed. "If you are asking for recommendations of a suitable partner, I do not think I am qualified to make that choice. I do not know you."

"I have already decided upon a suitable partner, and for that, you do qualify. I know marriages are not arranged in Elyriá, nor is it customary anywhere for a woman to approach a man with such a proposal. But I have no father or brothers or cousins to arrange such a thing, and there are few available men worthy of my station. The men I know wish to marry me to control my lands and wealth, and that is something I will not accept. I know we do not know one another..."

"You are proposing I marry you?" For all of the attraction he felt towards her, he could not believe he was hearing her correctly.

"Yes."

Bhríd stared, dumbfounded and silent for many minutes. "Why...do you desire this marriage, duchess, when you could have anyone you choose?"

She leaned forward, elbows resting on the table between them. "I am under pressure from my people to marry and produce an heir to my lands. I have told them I have little interest in marrying, but they continue to implore me. It is their sole complaint against me, and I do understand their viewpoint. I have no living relatives I am aware of. My subjects fear civil unrest upon my death or the returning of the lands to royal holdings. I think that troubles them the most, the thought of what autonomy they might sacrifice if that were to happen. I have agreed that if they will allow me to marry the man of my choice, regardless of who that may be, regardless of his rank or station, I will do as they request as soon as I am able. If I do not…cannot find a man I am willing to marry, I will relinquish my estate."

"Rel…is that necessary?" He could not believe she could do such a thing.

"It is the best agreement we could reach," she said with a sigh. "They want a secure future. They want a man to lead them, though they will not say that. I offer them prosperity but they feel security is more desirable. I thought it fair to agree to their conditions."

"Surely there are eligible men of your station who are better qualified than I am…"

"Social standing is not important. There are no qualifications except that I like him, that he is willing to allow me to maintain my position and control of my lands, and that I am willing to spend the remainder of my life with him. Of all the men in Enesfel, you have impressed me the most. Your accomplishments are many, your reputation unblemished, your loyalty to our King noteworthy and commendable. And you are a handsome sight to behold." She smiled as his cheeks flushed crimson. "I think you may be precisely the man I seek; I would be willing to marry you, as long as we can come to agreement about the lands and title…"

"I am Elyri," he stammered.

"That makes no difference; I bear no prejudice or fear of your people, milord…"

"Perhaps not…but I could easily outlive you by several centuries."

Taken aback by the admission, she stared at him as he stared at her until eventually, her shoulders shrugged once. "And you could die tomorrow. If you do outlive me…by a day, by an hour, by a lifetime, the estates will be in excellent hands, won't they?" What she did not admit to was her other reason for choosing him, a reason that hinged upon his answer and would only be revealed should he decline her proposal.

He had to admit that she had a point. "I have duties to attend in Rhidam…and you in Levonne…"

"I am not asking you to relocate to Levonne. Since you would not be taking full responsibility for the estate, it would be a simple enough thing for you to reside here…"

"A marriage in name, then?" He felt more confused and flustered as he tried to follow her logic; the words made sense, but his emotional state was twisting them into things he could almost not comprehend.

Again, she smiled. "Not at all. I am attracted to you…and you to me…or am I wrong?"

After the dream he had of her last night, and the way she made him feel by riding into the courtyard, he murmured, "You are not wrong."

The duchess reached across the table and covered his hands with hers. "I am a flexible woman. I doubt there are any habits you have which I would find too distasteful that I could not bear to live with you…unless you enjoy senseless torture, mindless violence, and unnecessary cruelty. I doubt too that I have unbearable habits …we would have as much, or as little, contact between us as we wish. It is not such a distance between Levonne and Rhidam. Once there is an heir to the estate, my subjects will be satisfied…"

Withdrawing his hands from hers, Bhríd stood and went to the window where he watched a pair of birds perched upon a nearby shrub. No Elyri man could imagine himself in a situation like this, he mused; he had certainly never expected such a thing. "Milady, I do not know if I can do as you…"

"I am not pleasing to you?" She sounded sad as she came to his side. "Or is there someone else…?" That he might already be betrothed or married had never crossed her mind. He had never been seen in the company of a woman, but perhaps she resided in Elyriá, away from possible Teren threats.

"No…there is no one…you are exquisite…an intelligent woman if the success of your estates is any indicator…but I do not know you…

There was a sigh of relief upon hearing that he was not already promised. Gently, she took his arm and turned him to face her. "I can wait a while longer. I can set my affairs in order at home and place the upkeep of the lands in competent hands for a time. Then I will be free to remain in Rhidam for however long it takes to gain your affection and trust…or at least your admiration and respect. Everything about you is pleasing and satisfying to me; I could easily accept you into my life, milord. Could you not do the same for me?"

There were tears in her eyes that refused to fall and he hated seeing them, but his voice refused to cooperate, keeping him from answering her question. When he did not respond immediately, she pulled away, swallowed and regained her composure. "I do not mean to plead; begging is beneath me and I refuse to do it anymore. I detest the haste with which my people want me wed; it leaves little time for things like a proper courtship. I thought this worth a try, but if I was mistaken, I will return home and trouble you no further…"

Feeling that he was being unfair, Bhríd clasped her hands. He could understand her predicament and could not fault her for making some effort to salvage her situation. "Lady Dubuais…I am afraid I have been inhospitable and there is no excuse for it. I…perhaps I could learn to accept you…love you…but I have always believed that love came before marriage, not the other way around. It is the way Elyri are raised. I cannot fault you for a difference in customs. I can secure a room for you; you are welcome to stay in Rhidam for as long as you wish. Give me time to consider your proposal, for us to discuss the details. But consider this; I am Elyri. My lifespan is longer than you can imagine. I do not know the odds of a Teren-Elyri union producing children…it may be possible, but likely difficult. And if recent events are any indicator…if what my kinsman says is true, then Elyri hatred is rising. You could be placing yourself, and any children, in grave danger by associating with me."

After staring at their joined hands, she looked into his face. "I do not believe that to be the case. I am guarded and can defend myself, and my estates. My father saw to that. I also have no doubts about your ability to protect me. As for children…conceiving is not determined by race. It is possible that I cannot bear children at all, as many women in my father's family have been unable to bear children. Your longer life would secure the safety of the lands until you found someone else to care for them if that should be the case. But…" she smiled again in an effort to remain positive, "I will give you time to consider this if that is what you need. That is a reasonable request. I am sorry if I was presumptuous in coming here. I would never force anyone, let alone you, into a marriage they did not desire."

Her apology, while unnecessary, helped him relax enough to smile and offer his arm. "Let us see what happens. Would you care for a tour? Perhaps I can assist you with the matters you came to discuss with the King." It was a good way to get to know her better, and any time with her would be time well spent. He might not be prepared to consider marriage, but he did not want her out of his company yet.

The change of tone and his offer made her smile. "That would please me, Lord Cáner." She took his arm. "Very much."

❧*❧

The King leaned back in his throne, the communication passing between him and Guthrie entirely nonverbal, born of years of familiarity with the other to understand what they both were thinking. Nearby, the three men apprehended for the beating and killing of the Elyri traveler were fidgeting, fuming, and fretting about their circumstances. Arlan could see in their faces that they had not expected to kill the man, even though their rage demanded nothing less. They were genuinely concerned about their fate. But he could also see there was little remorse for what they had done, and he guessed that if they were released without punishment, they would perpetrate such a crime again to any unfortunate Elyri who happened to cross their paths.

Across the room, Ártur sat with his hands folded in his lap, eyes downcast. He had examined the deceased and gathered what little information there was about him. The man had been a painter and had come to Rhidam to offer his talents to the royal house. He took a room in the inn while he waited for an audience; from it, the healer collected three complete portraits and one incomplete sketch, the quality of which was enough to make Ártur feel his efforts paled in comparison. The man had died of multiple fractures and heavy internal bleeding. The corpse was bruised from head to foot. It was the healer's opinion that they might not have intended to kill the painter, but the amount of damage they inflicted could have done nothing else. The three men were guilty of his death and showed no remorse, thus deserved to be punished. However, Ártur knew his place and would not voice his opinion unless it was asked for. His thoughts were not the ones that counted here.

The King stared at the healer for many minutes, knowing much of what the man was thinking without asking. Reading his mind was not necessary. The last malicious anti-Elyri crime on record, other than the terror King Bowen had inflicted upon Enesfel, had occurred early during the reign of King Innis. Ártur remembered that time, as he had first come to Enesfel to serve the Lachlan's under that King. Arlan was determined this should stop here, the violence contained to a single incident, but he was not prepared to condemn these three to death. There had been few royally ordered execution in Rhidam during his years as king, and only Ula de Corrmick, a killer, a conspirator against the crown of Enesfel, and Owain Lachlan's mother, stood out in his mind. Her execution had been a necessary, if unpleasant, task. He was not certain execution was necessary now.

Justice Cornell, on the other hand, thought it was necessary, vital and appropriate and ground his teeth, glaring harshly at his prisoners. He took the recent outbreak of crime as a personal affront and was quite prepared to execute these men as an example to anyone else in Rhidam who was contemplating murder. Three deaths in four days was more of an epidemic than he desired to have upon his record as Justice. But he refrained from tapping his foot impatiently or otherwise expressing his annoyance, particularly after Guthrie, who stood beside him, nudged him as a reminder.

Finally, the King stood and laid his scepter upon the throne. He paced before the prisoners, stopping before each one to stare into their faces. It reminded him of the first time he had interrogated prisoners, three soldiers from Neth. The memory made him smile wickedly before stepping out of earshot of the three and motioning the healer to his side.

"Ártur, this painter…could he have defended himself against these men?"

"My Liege, I…"

"Kavan fought bravely, expertly against me…but I know he held back. He could have killed me, couldn't he, without this other extraordinary ability of his?"

Ártur nodded, his expression grim. "It is possible. I have no idea how strong he is, or how well trained."

Knowing Kavan, if he had trained to fight, he was as skilled in that as he was in everything else. Kavan did nothing part way. The realization was sobering. "He says all Elyri are strong. Could he have fought off three men such as these?"

"Not easily, perhaps, but it might be possible…"

"Then this painter could have defended himself? Why did he not fight back?"

The healer shook his head. "Elyri as a whole are nonviolent, My Liege. And comparing Kavan to anyone is unfair…his skills are unique to him alone. Even if this painter had the knowledge to defend himself, he likely sought every peaceful way out of a fight, even to the point of submitting in the hopes they would relent."

"In other words, these three refused to listen to rational reason, or to mercy, and killed a man who would not fight back."

"They are tradesmen, laborers by nature, strong men who work with their arms. He was an artist. The injuries he received show knowledge of where to hit a man to cause the greatest damage. A painter would never have known such things."

The King glanced over his shoulder and stared at the three prisoners. "Would you," he asked absently, "agree to show these fellows a taste of Elyri strength?"

Ártur's pale face went ashen. "I do not think it would be of any use; it would likely fuel their fear and hatred."

"And make you uncomfortable. Hmmm…" The King returned to stand in front of the captives, his face blank although the healer felt sure Arlan had made up his mind. "I should have the three of you executed for killing a defenseless, innocent man."

"He was Elyri! He was neither defenseless nor innocent," one spat before being hit roughly in the back by the justice's big fist.

"He was guilty of no crime; being Elyri is not a crime. As for defenseless, why did he not fight back if he was capable…"

"He was a coward," hissed the man with the black eye, interrupting the King mid-sentence. His interruption gained him a blow from the justice as well.

"You are in the habit of brutally beating cowards to death? Interesting."

Though one of the men clearly saw the trap they had fallen into, the one with the black eye snarled, "He was not defenseless. Elyri can do things…"

"Then why didn't he?"

The King received no response until finally, the man replied, "He gave me a black eye."

"One you deserved, an act of self-defense. You beat him severely enough that even if he walked away from the fight, he might have died before he found a healer. If he could have defended himself and stopped you, I think he would have done it before he died, don't you?" Again, there was no response. "Captain Cornell." The High Justice stepped forward with a sharp click of his heels. "I want these men imprisoned…"

"My Liege!" Minos began to protest, not caring that he was interrupting.

But the King's mind was set. "They will be held until they each pay a fine of one hundred crowns. And on your way to the dungeon, please do them the courtesy of sharing their victim's pain. Do not kill or maim them, is that understood? I want them to live with pain, to understand what it is to be beaten when helpless." He turned his back, signifying the end of the sentence, and the attending guards and justice led the prisoners away, their expressions mirroring their shock or dismay. The King met Ártur's gaze.

Once the doors closed and the King settled upon his throne, the healer knelt before him. "Is such brutality necessary, My Liege?"

"They need to learn that I will not tolerate such nonsense. Elyri are not inherently evil; I do not want you, Syl, Bhríd or Kavan to be the next victim. A prison sentence would teach them little, execution even less, and a lesser fine would be too easy to pay."

Guthrie, who had also remained behind, snorted. "One hundred crowns is a little excessive."

"I am in no hurry to collect it. There will be no pressure put on their families, if they have any, to pay. The longer it takes, the longer they have to consider what they have done and why. If they appear to have learned their lessons once they are released, then I may return a portion of the fine to them. As for the beating…" He smirked as he met the healer's troubled gaze. "I am willing to allow you to tend their injuries. They will have the choice of either excepting help from someone whose race they despise or they can live with the pain. That choice will be theirs to make."

"As you wish." Ártur bowed before retreating, leaving Guthrie alone with the King. He could see the logic of the King's choice, perhaps even the wisdom of it, but he was not comfortable with his part. There were some aspects of politics he would never be comfortable with, no matter how many decades he lived in Rhidam.

Aware of his chamberlain's stare, the King growled without looking at him. "Yes?"

Guthrie raised his hand in a submissive gesture of supplication with a smile on his lips. "I was merely thinking, Arlan, that your father would be pleased with the king you have become. As am I."

He left the room when dismissed and Arlan watched him, feeling a rush of relief. He wondered often what the father he had never known would think of him and his choices. To hear such praise from Guthrie, a man who had intimately known them both, was precious indeed.

# ❧Chapter 14ᴥ

S quatting in a darkened alley where he had hidden for the better part of the past two days, Halstatt peered from beneath the piles of dirty rags, rotting food, broken crates, and other discarded rubbish. It was not a comfortable or pleasant smelling hiding place, but it sheltered him enough from passers-by that he was unnoticed and it gave him the best vantage point he could find from which to watch the castle's main gate. There was one window in particular on the third floor, barely visible over the outer wall, in which he often saw his quarry standing, watching the city with what Halstatt hoped was apprehension. Was Caol wondering what had become of him, wondering why there had been no further contact? There would be, Halstatt thought with a smirk. Very soon.

He had no more sightings of the venador, Wace Elotti, nor had there been any made by those underground elements he had employed since his arrival in Rhidam. Halstatt was almost convinced that the man had never been there, or if he had been, that Elotti had not been in Rhidam looking for him. He breathed a little easier, but he never let his guard down. If Elotti was not looking for him, Caol would be. He could not afford to be careless. Soon, he would make his move, get what he had come for, and be gone from Rhidam before any hunter caught him. He had things to do and could not linger in Enesfel on this side mission much longer.

❧*❧

The morning room was empty when Kavan arrived, which was how he had hoped it would be. It was too early for the children to be awake and he wanted to be alone. For the past two days he had been having continual visions and dreams, the same snatches he had seen of Muir with a sword, Prince Wilred crying, Caol arguing, a body amidst rubble. Each time it came, the sounds, the sights, and the smells became more vivid, as if whatever event he was foreseeing was rapidly bearing down upon him. But still, he had no idea what it meant, or what he should do.

The dream that had forced him awake this morning had been the most realistic and intense of all, and the most disturbing. He had to talk to someone about what he was seeing before the dreams ceased, before the events came to pass, but he continued to hope that if he waited he would know exactly what was to transpire. That was too much to ask of the Sight, however; it had never offered him a complete picture of events before and he knew, despite his hopes, that it was not about to give him what he wanted now.

"Oh…pardon me. I did not know you were here, Kavan."

The bard did not turn from the window. "No need to apologize, My Liege."

The fact that Kavan did not look at him when he spoke, remained distant and formal with an uncharacteristic tension in his shoulders, made the King frown. "Is something wrong? Shall I leave you alone?" He would rather know what was troubling his friend, but he doubted Kavan would tell him.

"Your company does not disturb me."

"Good." Arlan came further into the room and settled into a chair. "I need to talk to you, and since we have some time to ourselves, this may be the best chance. Please. Sit." Though he hesitated, Kavan did as the King asked and then waited in silence. Why that stillness unsettled the King, he could not say. "I must ask a favor of you."

As soon as he said the words, Arlan realized he did that far too often, asked favors of his best friend, but often the things he asked were those that no one else could do. He wondered what would happen the day Kavan refused, but today would not be the day to find out.

"Anything."

The King sighed, glanced away as he structured his thoughts into words, and then spoke again. "Ever since the events with Captain Delamo's eye, Muir has done nothing but talk about it, and you, and your sanctity…"

Kavan scowled. "A great many people are doing that; far too much attention is being paid to the worker instead of to the miracle itself and to the power behind it. I was aware that it had touched the prince…that he was there…but I was not aware that…"

"I have heard mention of it from a few sources, Guthrie and Ártur to be exact. I thought little of it until he came to me last night and told me he wishes to enter the prelacy." He watched the bard's scowl deepen. "You did not know of this?"

"No," Kavan replied. "He has not spoken of it with me. What do you want me to do?"

"Talk him out of it."

The bard's gaze fell and his scowl froze into place. "Why?"

"He's a prince. Royalty," Arlan huffed. "The prelacy is no place for a prince."

"Would you prefer him to become a fisherman or a sailor?" The King started to reply, but Kavan continued. "Deny him this and that may be the path he chooses. What other options does he have, milord? He is the eldest, but he will never see the throne. Even Wilred could become king before him. He feels he has little of value to look forward to in life."

"He has the Alberni estate. That is a proper place, a proper life, for a prince."

"Not the proper place for the eldest. The world knows nothing of his bloodline; they see him as your son...and yet you deny him any rights that position should afford him. Sending him to Alberni, as good of a life as that may provide, is your way of avoiding potential embarrassment and he knows it. He cannot help the circumstances of his birth, but he can live in a way that gives him self-worth. Would it not be better for him to do something that makes him happy? There is nothing shameful about entering the prelacy, and I suspect if you deny him this, you will do more damage than good."

Somewhere in the midst of Kavan's speech, the King went to the cabinet to pour himself a tall glass of wine, despite the early hour. "I should have known better than to ask this of you," he muttered. "You always take his side and are more inclined to follow faith than duty."

"My faith is my duty," Kavan frowned. "I have always done my duty to you, milord; there is little conflict in that. However, if I do not take Muir's side, no one will. I agree that he is young, though not too young to make such a decision about his future. I suspect this whim may be entirely based upon the overwhelming nature of what he witnessed instead of honest dedication to Faith. He likely has not mentioned his plans to me because he knows I will point that out. I will speak to him, test his conviction. If he is not completely certain, I will dissuade him from making a hasty choice. But if his conviction is firm, I will not talk him out of it. Such a decision is between him and k'Ádhá and no one should interfere with that. I will, however, explain to him the ramifications of such a life, if he has not already considered them."

"At least you will talk to him; you are the only one he will listen to." It was a compromise the King was reluctant to make, but he knew that Kavan would not be bullied. After swirling the wine in his glass, watching the red liquid slosh to and fro, he looked back at Kavan. "Something is troubling you. I knew it when I came in. What is it? Talk to me, Kavan." The bard's worries were rarely petty. The more troubled he was by something, the more important it probably was.

"I…yes…you should know. I will try to explain what the Sight has shown me…" Perhaps the King would know what to do.

"The Sight?" The King inhaled sharply and sat back down, perching on the edge of his seat and giving Kavan his full attention. "What have you Seen?"

"The visions started two and a half days ago…and vary a little each time they come, but they are basically the same. I have seen a raging battle, similar to one I saw on the day of Muir's birth…this time I know that the green and black flags are of the de Corrmick family. I hear Caol arguing with someone…though I do not recognize the voice or hear the words…and I can hear Wilred crying. Muir, Lord Dugan, Captain Delamo and I are traveling with three others…one of whom I believe is from Neth…and then I see Muir with a sword raised in readiness to kill someone at his feet. I do not know what it means, but I do believe all of the events are connected."

The King set his glass down and slid back in his chair. "From what Guthrie has been telling me, war with Neth might not be out of the question. He overheard talk during the festival that gives us cause to prepare for such a possibility. But what has this to do with the children? They are too young to go into battle."

"Muir is nearly old enough, but I am not certain the children are involved in the battle I witness. What I do know is that Prince Bertram is in grave danger." He took a quick breath and pushed on, not giving Arlan a chance to speak. "I have seen his body…broken upon the rocks at the foot of a cliff, with a dagger protruding from his back. I fear I have seen his death."

The King blinked and straightened. "That cannot be…are you sure it was Bertram? Are you certain he's dead? Perhaps this is a dream connected with…"

"Dreams do not occur when one is awake," Kavan murmured reluctantly. "And even my dreams I have learned to take seriously. It is Prince Bertram I have seen. I cannot know his fate for certain, but from the location of the dagger…"

Interrupting because he did not want to hear the words spoken, Arlan barked, "He cannot die. He is my heir. Are you certain?"

Kavan was still, recalling his premonitions from the days the children were born, that Hagan and Diona would rule but that Bertram would not. He wondered sometimes if he should have told Arlan that truth earlier, but he had always prayed that he would be wrong. Such premonitions were not always infallible, were they? He bowed his head, unable to voice those thoughts and fears. His duty was to assure his friend, despite his own misgivings. "Events can be altered. Perhaps if he is kept within the castle, if his personal attendants are increased and closer watch put over him, this can be avoided. It may be a warning of what could happen if great care is not taken; I cannot say with any certainty. I can tell you no more than what I have Seen. Do what you can to protect him, Arlan. That is the best advice I can give."

"You…Captain Delamo…Caol…the boys…Neth…" The King wearily rubbed his face, sounding older with every word. "What is this, Kavan?"

"I do not know. I wish I did. I will let you know if I learn anything more, but I advise you to act swiftly. Every time I See this, it becomes clearer, more real; to wait could mean disaster. The longer we dally, the more danger there may be. I may have waited too long to speak as it is, but I wanted to be sure."

The King understood that. Kavan was rarely a man to leap to conclusions. "Bertram will have every protection that can be arranged. Captain Colson has already been sent north to learn more about the situation with Neth, and General Wyndham will be instructed to hasten military preparation. If you say there will be war, there likely will be; we will not be caught unaware." Arlan escaped quickly, ignoring the fact that he could easily put faith in half of Kavan's prediction but ignore the other half as a warning rather than a certainty.

Kavan watched him go, feeling the knot in his stomach slowly tighten again. Arlan's glass of wine sat untouched upon the table. Picking it up, Kavan held the glass to the light, fingering the etchings, studying the shimmers in the deep red liquid. It was likely more than his Elyri metabolism could efficiently tolerate, but some unspeakable compulsion urged him to drink. Without hesitation, for reasons he did not understand beyond a desire to forget the burden he faced, he raised it to his lips and drained the glass in a single breath. It burned on the way down, cinching the knot in his stomach, blurring his vision as it coursed through his blood. Not a wise choice, he decided. He staggered up the stairs, feeling the alcohol's numbing effects spread quickly before he was halfway there. By the time he reached his door, his head was pounding, the walls and floor were swimming and rocking around him, and his stomach ached with dull fire. He barely reached his bed before losing himself into a blackness that erased all thoughts of Prince Bertram's fate from his mind.

❧*❧

In the warmth of the noonday sun, the courtyard was empty except for two servants chatting in hushed tones upon one of the many stone benches. They paid little attention to the inquisitor who sat on a different bench several yards away, although both kept an eye on him should he make sudden demands of their services. He appreciated their inattention more than they could know, and they knew he was unlikely to call upon them. The things Caol disliked most about his current social status were the constant attention and presence of both guards and servants. He had not grown up with these things and they made him feel awkward and uneasy. Privacy was a rare thing within the castle walls unless one demanded it, and Caol was not very good at demanding anything from those he still viewed as his superiors.

Since the carnival, he had seen no sign of Wace Elotti. He hoped the hunter had caught up with Halstatt, captured him, and taken him away. That would explain why there had been no further contact from either of them. No messages, no threats, no sightings. Nothing. Caol had hidden the Coryllien where no one, especially Halstatt, was likely to find it. No one would ever see it again; he felt confident of that. Hopefully, because of it, the feud that had plagued the Dugan clan for decades was finally behind them.

Right now, he was berating himself, feeling that he should apologize to his wife but not knowing how. Since the carnival, with his concerns about his past dogging him, he had been unnecessarily harsh and abrupt and he knew he had hurt her by not confiding in her. But the issue of Halstatt and his family history was not something he could discuss. He could not risk the condemnation, or worse, he might receive when she and her brother the King learned what he really was. Or rather, what he had been. He wanted to forget the past and concentrate on the present. Deidre wanted a second child. Perhaps, with Halstatt out of his life, that could be arranged; perhaps it would make up for whatever failures and shortcomings she saw in him.

Across the courtyard, Justice Cornell appeared with a parchment roll under his arm, leading his horse towards the main gate. Always curious about the justice's business, as the duties of justice and inquisitor often overlapped and intersected, Caol sauntered towards him, keeping one eye open for signs of trouble as he had been doing diligently since Halstatt's return into his life.

"Good day, Lord Cornell. What have we here?"

Minos grunted, still annoyed that the King had not executed the three men who had killed the Elyri painter. He shrugged without looking at Caol. "Sketches of the man who attacked Prime Magistrate Dilyn and Captain Delamo. They will be posted and used to question people."

"May I see them?"

By now, the justice had mounted his horse. He had no reason not to show the inquisitor; in fact, it was the right and logical thing to do. But the delay annoyed him further, and he grunted as he reluctantly unrolled the sketches and held them out for Caol to see. One quick glance was nearly enough to make Caol turn away, but he forced himself to smother his initial response and hold his ground. Though he had not seen Halstatt in over a decade, he recognized the man's features. He had no doubts about the man's identity and coughed to cover his nervousness. "Ugly fellow, isn't he?" Minos grumbled in irritation and rolled the sketches. "How do you know this is the fellow? Who gave you the description?"

"Captain Delamo. Lord Cliáth pulled it straight from his head and Lord MacLyr sketched it. If Lord Cliáth says this is the man, you can believe it is. Now, if you will excuse me…"

After stepping back to let the horse and rider depart, Caol did not move for many minutes as he tried to still his pounding heart. The Elyri knew. Kavan knew. But what exactly did they know and how much had been shared with the King?

At least he knew that Halstatt had been in Rhidam during the carnival, and had again made the mistakes of allowing himself to be surprised and attacking someone in a crowd of people. How unlike a Tarmajien. The reassuring thing about those sketches was that if Halstatt was still in Rhidam, he would see them. That would either force him to flee or force him to act. Caol knew from experience that a Tarmajien would likely act before admitting a mistake and leaving. Deidre and a second child would have to wait a little longer. Caol would not put another Dugan child at risk. He had to prepare himself for whatever action his rival would make next.

Syl rocked Prince Hagan, watching Bianca play with the gaily dressed doll the k'gdhededhá had brought for her. Lady Faylyn, Hagan's new nurse, was purchasing supplies for the nursery today, and Syl had enthusiastically agreed to watch the prince. She treasured her moments with the children and was as much a nurse to them as Lady Faylyn. If she had been able to feed the prince, Syl would have cared for him by herself. At the moment, though, it was Bianca who concerned her. The girl looked lost, her liquid gray eyes staring about her as though dazed, occasionally murmuring, "Momma?" as though she expected the woman to appear at any time. Syl motioned the girl onto her lap and rocked them both.

There were no Maylors in Rhidam, and according to Bhríd, none in Enesfel. Jermyn had sent letters to his contacts in Hatu and Cordash in the hopes that Bianca's true family could be located. After many days of caring for the girl, however, Syl had to admit that she was beginning to hope no family would come forward. She had tentatively brought up the subject of adopting Bianca with Ártur, but he gently reminded her that it would be best to refrain from such hopeful thinking until it was clear that the girl had no kin to claim her. She had seen in his eyes that he was not opposed to the idea, however, and as each day brought her closer to her desires, she prayed he would not change his mind.

❧*❧

The dark-skinned man looked around him with what appeared to be no more than a casual perusal of his surroundings. In truth, his dark eyes missed no detail, no matter how small, that might be somehow important, and many that were not. He held a tightly wound roll of parchment in his left hand while his right hand rested on his hip inches above the ornate dagger he always carried there. There were many people about, peasants and merchants and travelers, but they were of no interest to him. He took one lingering glance at the nearby castle walls and then into the alley behind him. With a satisfied smirk, he unrolled the parchment and proceeded to nail it to the lamppost.

Halstatt watched from beneath his pile of rubbish, scolding himself for believing that Wace Elotti had given up. The hunter had been standing near that lamppost much longer than Halstatt liked. Now he was posting something upon it. He was curious as to what it was, but not curious enough to give away his location.

Task completed, Elotti pocketed the small mallet he had used, smoothed the parchment on the post to prevent it from curling, and wiped his hands on his trousers. He stared at his handiwork with satisfaction and then unhooked a ceramic jug from the strap on his belt. After uncorking it, he took a long drink and then tossed it in the direction of the rubbish heap. It landed three feet from Halstatt's location, shattered upon impact, and showered the pungent red liquid it contained across the ground. Halstatt flinched and held his breath but did not try to wipe the wine from his face or take his stinging eyes off the venador.

Elotti laughed as the jug exploded, and then turned and disappeared to the left. When Halstatt found he could breathe again, his breath came out in one terrified gush. He pushed the panic into his knotted stomach and out of his head. If Elotti knew he was there, why did he not come for him? Why taunt him? Was the hunter trying to scare him into making a mistake, or was he letting Halstatt know he was still there…waiting?

It was nearly an hour later before Halstatt emerged from his cover. He waited, he watched, he listened, and eventually concluded that Elotti was gone, making it useless to hide any longer. He did not want to stay here long enough for the hunter to return. Besides, he had things to do before tonight.

Making certain that he appeared casual and innocent to any who saw him, Halstatt approached the lamppost to see what Elotti had posted. The sketch on the paper caused him to swear, rather more loudly than he intended. How had anyone gotten his description? Had Caol talked at last? No, he decided. The Halstatt in the sketch had a beard, and Caol could not have known he had one. Elotti, then…or someone had seen him at the carnival. Infuriated, he ripped the image from the post and shoved it inside of his shirt. A man's deep-throated laugh reached his ears but he saw no one laughing nearby. Perhaps he had imagined the sound. But it was enough to cause the panic to rear, making him swallow hard and bolt for shelter. If he was careful, he could make it back to his lair without being tailed, and after tonight he would be gone.

҈*҈

When the children had come to him earlier that morning claiming that Kavan would not wake up, Ártur had been deeply apprehensive and dropped his paintbrush to follow the princess to Kavan's room. Princes Wilred and Bertram stood in the doorway, as if on guard, while Prince Muir sat cross-legged on the bed beside the bard, holding one white hand in his, the look on his face that of a man about to lose his best friend. Not wanting to worry the children any more than they already were, Ártur insisted they leave the room to allow him to examine his cousin and try his best to help him.

Kavan's skin was flushed, cool and moist, his breathing was shallow, and his pulse slow and faint, though steady. There were no injuries the healer could see. Laying his hand on Kavan's forehead, Ártur pulled the healing forces from within and sought the source of his cousin's condition, fearing poison. What he discovered caused him two simultaneous reactions, for Kavan was intoxicated. Part of Ártur found it mildly amusing that his normally wise cousin could allow this.

At the same time, however, he was concerned about what could have led Kavan to such uncharacteristic behavior. He was in no danger of dying, thankfully, but alcohol was one of the few substances that were detrimental to Elyri. One glass of anything stronger than wine could be toxic and fatal. Kavan, like all Elyri, had been taught this from a very young age, and though he had sampled wine before, it had never been in sufficient quantity to put his life at risk.

There was little the healer could do except allow his cousin to sleep off the effects. It might not take much alcohol to get an Elyri intoxicated, but often it took them twice as long to recover from the effects. Ártur assumed Kavan's tutoring duties for the morning and reassured the children that their tutor would be well. It was nearly noon before he returned to his cousin's side. The bard was not yet awake, though he had shifted into a more comfortable position and was no longer as wan and weak looking as he had been.

When his green eyes fluttered open, it was to mid-afternoon light through the open window that made him groan. There was a throbbing ache in his head, his eyes hurt, and his mouth felt dry and pasty, but he felt otherwise well. It took several moments to realize he was in his own bed, though he could not recall how he had come to be there. He sensed his cousin nearby at the same moment the healer heard his groan and realized he was awake. Ártur loomed into view, expecting Kavan to be either embarrassed or mortified at his condition, but if he was, it did not show. His face was a blank mask, save for the occasional grimace of discomfort.

"Have you been here long?" Kavan croaked, his voice rough and scratchy. The healer gave him a glass of water, which he drank slowly as Ártur held his head.

"Since the children came to me earlier saying that you were late for their lessons and they could not wake you…though I did leave to tutor them for you. I feared there might have been something seriously wrong…" Kavan did not look away but did not speak either. He saw no need. "There could have been, you know. You were lucky. What did you drink?"

Kavan closed his eyes and thought back to the last thing he could remember. "A rather large glass of wine…red… I do not know what kind. Arlan poured it for himself but did not drink it. I saw no point in wasting it."

Ártur snorted. "Making yourself ill, risking your life, was certainly putting it to good use. Any particular reason you felt compelled to drink yourself into a stupor? Or was this an experiment?"

Kavan pushed himself into a sitting position, expecting the room to spin around him. He was pleased that it did not. "I do not know," he admitted. "The glass was there. I drank it. Thank you for assuming my duties…"

"There is no need to thank me." The healer put the empty water glass on the nearby table. "Are you sure there is nothing troubling you? Gabrielle Dilyn, perhaps?"

Realizing that Ártur was not going to stop his interrogation until Kavan told him something, and not having the energy to evade the questions today, the bard sighed, "You know me too well."

"I am your cousin and might as well be your brother; we are sínréc. What I do not know about you by now I likely never will. What is troubling you?"

Reluctantly, Kavan explained his visions and watched his cousin's face darken with each new revelation. Finally, in a shaky, small voice, he concluded, "I know Prince Bertram will die, Ártur. I cannot say when, and I cannot be certain how, but it will happen. If not in the way I have been Seeing, then it will be some other way. If my premonitions are right, he will not live to become king. How can I face him every day knowing what I know?"

Ártur took Kavan's hands in his, an affectionate gesture he had not made in many years. "You know Arlan will die, right? You do not know when it will be, or how it will happen, but it will happen, most likely within your lifetime. Yet you face him every day and you treasure the time you spend with him. You know I will die, but not when or how…" If the healer saw the pain that crossed Kavan's face, he neither acknowledged nor questioned it. "Bertram may be killed in battle, die of a fever, or die in an accident. These things could happen whether you knew about them in advance or not. Since you say you have known he will never rule, this particular revelation should not be shocking…although I can understand why it is upsetting. There is little use in worrying about something you cannot change…you can only pray that you are wrong."

Kavan's head bobbed grimly. "I will try. I think, however, for the children's sake, it might be wisest if we find them a new tutor…at least a temporary one until I can face them again."

Squeezing Kavan's hands, Ártur replied, "I will see to it. I may not be the philosopher and historian you are, but I think I can do an adequate job of it. But you will need to offer a plausible excuse for your absence."

"I…"

"Do not worry about it today. I want you to sleep until the last of this is out of your body, which should be by morning. I will have something sent up for you to eat, and it might help you feel better to bathe; I will have water heated for you. Will you do as I say, or must I stay and supervise?"

"That will not be necessary…I will do as you ask. Go. Believe me, I have no intentions of doing this again."

Ártur was much relieved to hear it. "Good. I would hate to see this become a habit…or see you kill yourself."

## ᢒ•Chapter 15᠊ᡧ

U nfortunately for Halstatt, or perhaps fortunately, he found it entirely too simple to get past the guards at the gatehouse and across the bridge into the inner keep. It had not been difficult to grasp hold of a passing wagon and cling to its underside until the wagon stopped in front of the palace stables. There had been no challenge in it and he wanted a challenge. There was little glory in reaching his prey too easily. When he was sure no one would see him, he dropped from the wagon and rolled into a nearby mound of hay where he remained hidden until dark. No one noticed him there, no one disturbed the haystack, and when the náós bell chimed midnight, he emerged to go to work.

Carefully he removed all traces of hay from his hair and clothing before pulling a clay pot from the dark sack he carried. Within was a thick black paste that he smeared over his face to mask it. After wiping his hands clean with several handfuls of straw, he made sure his dagger was secure inside his boot and pulled on his gloves. He was clean-shaven and his hair was considerably shorter than it had been that morning and was hidden beneath a tight-fitting cap he had secured for the night's adventure. Dressed in black, with his face blackened, it would be harder to spot him as he slunk through the night. Everyone was looking for a bearded beggar. He was no longer that.

He knew that to go around the south side of the castle would be the most direct route to his destination, but he would need to pass the guards' barracks if he did, and Halstatt had no desire to take that risk. The north side of the building housed servants and livestock, who should all be asleep, making it the safer route to take. It was pure luck that the wagon he had used for cover had gone there to begin with and he intended to take advantage of that good fortune. If he entered from the north, he believed he could easily make his way through the castle halls, assuming there were few guards about, and reach his destination without difficulty. Clinging to the shadows, he crept out of the stables without the horses paying him heed. As anticipated, there were no visible guards here, and he assumed there would be few along the western wall. If he was careful, the soldiers in the outer towers should fail to see him.

With a shiver and a start, Kavan sat up in his bed, sleep leaving him abruptly as he felt the surge of nervous energy gather. Across the room, his harp sat upon the dresser, its black kestrel form glistening in the pale starlight that filtered through the open window. Thinking that perhaps another dream had brought him awake, he tried to recall it but could not. If not a dream, something else. He slid from beneath the sheet, pulled on his white robe from where it hung on a hook beside the bed, and went to the window. No moon tonight, he realized, and there were signs of gathering storm clouds to the east. He closed his eyes, focused on the sensation that had awakened him, and leaned upon the sill, grateful for the cool night air.

From this close, the third-floor windows were higher than Halstatt had calculated, but that would not deter him. Walls were a simple enough obstacle to get around, or over. Halstatt did not require ropes, at least not with walls of this type of stone construction. He removed his gloves, held his dagger in his teeth, and found the first hold on the large stones. Before he could hoist himself up and begin his climb, however, the sound of approaching footsteps caused him to drop back to the ground and flatten himself into the shadows.

It was a soldier and a young woman, either a servant or a whore. They were walking arm in arm, whispering and giggling. Halstatt remained still and silent until they passed his location without noticing him and entered one of the servant houses. Servant then. Sooner or later that guard would come back. Halstatt knew he had to hurry. The night was silent again and he looked towards the towers. There was no moon, and the approaching clouds would block out any starlight. It might make the climb more hazardous, but it meant he was less likely to be seen, and he hastened to begin his climb again.

The energy Kavan felt solidify behind him, near his harp, caused him to turn to face it. He recognized the shimmering figure that stood there and he dropped to his knees before it. The familiar scarred hands bid him rise and pointed towards the chest of drawers. Extending his senses outward, seeking whatever the figure bid him find, he allowed the power to direct his feet to where the Saint stood, and guide his hands. The chest was heavy, but he managed to push it aside, moving his harp first to avoid damaging it. But he saw nothing behind the chest except the wall. He glanced at Kóráhm, who still pointed to the space in front of Kavan with an urgency that made the bard uneasy. What was the Saint trying to tell him? Why did he not speak?

Foot slipping from its purchase, Halstatt clung to the sill as a shower of stone particles scattered upon the ground below. He remained still and steeled his body for the necessity of a very long drop to the ground should someone in the room have heard the sound at their window. He hung there until his hands began to ache, but no one came, and after finding a better foothold, he worked into a position that would allow him to open the window. When prying with his raw fingers did not open it, he slid the dagger's blade between the two panels to nudge the latch out of its clasp. The left panel swung inward on loose hinges, while the other stuck but gave way with a slight push.

There was no one in this room and it seemed to have been unused for some time. Halstatt smiled as he hoisted himself through the opening. He made little sound as he hit the floor, but the clink of a passing soldier's armor stopped in the corridor outside the door. There was no time to find an appropriate hiding place, thus Halstatt did the first thing he could think of. He climbed beneath the blankets of the four-post bed and pulled them over his head.

The door opened and the soldier peered inside. He was young, barely an adult, and thus had drawn the less desirable duty of night watch. Seeing the window open, he entered the room, intending to close it, and then noticed someone in the bed. He could not recall being advised of guests in this room, which showed little other evidence of being in use. He stared at the figure for several moments, saw that it did not stir, and then left the room, closing the door behind him. Rather than disturb a possible guest, he would discuss it with the duty officer. Perhaps it was a household member who merely wished to sleep alone.

Halstatt waited as the footsteps hurried down the hall. That was the worst part of these things, he thought, as he got out of the bed, noticing the black smear across the linen pillow sham, but not having time to do anything about it. He hated the waiting involved in being cautious. It slowed things down. Still, it would be worth the price to do what he had come to do without being caught, and by the time anyone discovered the soiled pillow, he intended to be gone.

The footsteps of a soldier passed the room, but Kavan did not pay it heed. He found the protruding sharp edge of a stone block slightly out of place as he explored the wall behind the dresser. A quick glance at Kóráhm as the apparition lowered its arm told Kavan that this was what he was meant to find. It took some effort to slide the stone out of its tight-fitting slot, the grating of stone against stone sounding harsh to his ears in the nighttime stillness. Removing the block revealed the empty chamber behind it, something Kavan had never known was there. No…not empty. There was a wooden box within the chamber. Kavan removed the box, disliking the violent jolting sensation he received from touching it, and when he turned towards Kóráhm, the Saint was gone. This was what he had been searching for.

Rising from his crouched position, Kavan stretched, the ache in his back prevalent tonight. Effect of the alcohol, he assumed, or else a product of the effort to move the dresser and remove the cover stone. He sat on the stool before the chest, hesitated with a shaky breath, and opened the engraved wooden box. What he saw within made his vision blur, his breath catch painfully in his chest, and his heart stop beating.

The Coryllien Dagger.

Without considering what he was about to do, he reached for the dagger. Not the blade, came the warning within his head. Do not touch the blade. The designs upon the gold hilt, the twisted, demonic form of it, repulsed him, but he closed his fingers around it, bracing himself at the shock of contact, closing his eyes at the visions that came unbidden through the touch. Faces flashed before him, victims and killers, generations of faces he had never known. Some were Teren, some were Elyri, many were women and children. But three faces struck him like a blow between the eyes. Lísbhet Dilyn, the man who had attacked Wortham, and Caol Dugan.

The dagger clattered to the dresser and rolled to the floor. As Wortham had surmised, his attacker had been responsible for Lísbhet Dilyn's death. But what did Caol have to do with that? That the inquisitor had been the one to hide the dagger here, Kavan knew, but how had Caol come into possession of this particular dagger…and why? Why had he not spoken to someone of this? Why hide it in Kavan's room?

He recalled what Bhríd had said about Caol receiving a box the day Lady Dilyn's body was discovered, a box claimed to hold a Coryllien, or a replica of such. This was no replica. This was an artifact, a true weapon, and it made the inquisitor's claim true. In all likelihood, Caol knew the dagger was the murder weapon, or suspected it, and that was the reason for hiding it. Did he know the murderer? The more worrisome question, however, was Caol Dugan involved?

Kavan retrieved the dagger from the floor, studying the detail more closely before replacing it in its box and returning it to its hiding place. Better for it to stay out of sight until he determined what was going on. He wanted no innocent man, particularly a friend of the king's, to come under suspicion prematurely. Once the chest of drawers was in place, Kavan sank down upon the stool, lost in thought.

Though Halstatt had never been in Rhidam's castle, indeed no castle beyond a Nethite dungeon, he had judged from the number of windows approximately how many rooms were along the west wall on the third floor. He was pleased to see that he had been off by a single room, but one less door meant room for error. And the sound of footsteps approaching meant that he had little time to make his choice. Correction, he realized as the steps drew closer. Two sets of footsteps. He chose a door, opened it, and slid into the room, closing it behind him before anyone could see that it had been open.

Trying to calm his rapid breathing and pounding heart, he allowed his eyes to adjust to the darkness of the room. It was too small, he knew immediately, to belong to the princess of Enesfel, and the pale reddish hair of one of the figures in the bed was too light to be Dugan's. Ah, he realized, but this was the Elyri healer he had heard about. It would be satisfying to be rid of one more of that cursed race. This was not the time, however. He had to find Dugan. The hall was quiet, the footsteps past, and he slid back into it and to the next door down, confident of what he would find there.

This time he entered a small sitting chamber furnished with a table, two plush high-backed chairs, and a short divan. At one end of the room were a locked cabinet and a low chest of drawers. Over the back of one chair hung a dark amber cloak. He touched the velvet, crushing it between his fingers, and then pushed deeper inside, easing open the door that led into the second chamber. Beyond it, in the light of a single, nearly extinct candle upon the nightstand, he recognized the flaming red hair of one of the sleeping occupants and smiled wickedly. He should kill the man, but first, he wanted his dagger back; he withdrew to the outer chamber to begin his search.

Kavan pushed Caol's door open, sending out a tendril of energy that he hoped would wake the inquisitor and bring him into the outer chamber to speak with him without disturbing the princess. He had noticed the two guards coming from the room next to his, but they stopped to confer together and did not speak to Kavan or even look at him. He was known to have odd hours, to spend many late nights in the oratory; his being in the corridor meant nothing em. Now, however, he stopped short, aware that someone else was in that chamber, a darkly attired figure attempting to pick the lock of Caol's wine cabinet. Kavan allowed the door to close behind him loudly enough that the intruder could hear it.

The thud and click pulled Halstatt around in surprise. The figure behind him, in the doorway, might have been a phantom with his white garments, skin, and hair. But the fiery intensity of his eyes, noticeable even in the near darkness, told Halstatt this was no ghost. Both men stared at each other expectantly.

It was too dark, the stranger's face too expertly blacked out, for Kavan to distinguish any clear features, but when the man hissed, "Elyri," Kavan knew who he was. He intensified his silent summons to wake Caol for assistance, wondering if the guards in the corridor would hear him if he called out.

Halstatt knew he was trapped. To attack this man would cause a ruckus, create too much noise, and alert others to his presence. He began backing towards the inner door, hoping to rush into the bedchamber, kill Dugan, and make it to the window before he was apprehended. Forget the dagger. In the grand scheme of things, it was less important than his life. But the Elyri was following him like a relentless dog, with no overt threat in his actions, but he clearly had no intention of allowing Halstatt an easy escape. When the door unexpectedly opened behind him, Halstatt jumped and spun.

"Hal…" Caol started, his voice a squeak of surprise that was cut short as Kavan rushed forward and forced Halstatt to the ground, knocking the blade he carried from his hand. The man struggled to be free, rolling easily with Kavan because the bard had no practical knowledge of wrestling, and managed to regain the dagger. A quick study, Kavan used the same maneuver, but the intruder was able to maneuver the dagger between their bodies and thrust it into the Elyri's abdomen. The bard fell away, eyes wide in shock and pain. That unexpected tussle was long enough to leave Halstatt vulnerable to Caol, who jerked him to his feet by one arm and drove a knee into his groin. With a howl, Halstatt freed himself but staggered unsteadily. The hallway door opened again; the Elyri healer gave a quick glance at the fighting men, called out for help, and then turned his attention to where his cousin slumped on the floor, the red stain on his robe spreading rapidly.

The princess, awakened as Halstatt shoved Caol against the bed, might have cowered in fright if not for realizing immediately that her husband needed help. She reached for the decanter of water on the bedside table, intending to use it as a weapon as soon as the intruder was in the open again.

By now, Halstatt knew he was outnumbered in a fight he could not win. There was one recourse. He shoved Caol backward, this time into his wife, and charged for the window. With a crash of glass, he was gone as a trio of soldiers burst into the room.

"Out the window!" Caol cried, rolling from the bed to pick up Halstatt's fallen dagger and race out of the room after the guards. The princess regained her balance and saw the healer kneeling over his cousin's bloody body, ripping Kavan's robe away. She retrieved the washbasin, emptied into it what little water the decanter held, and hurried to fetch more.

The healer nodded in appreciation but he barely noticed her. His focus was on his cousin's wound and the ragged breathing it had created. The blade had punctured his lung, and Ártur knew that if he did not heal him quickly, Kavan was going to drown in his own blood. Unable to bear the thought of living without his cousin, he willed the healing energy to surge through his hands. With Syl's hands suddenly upon his shoulders, the energy he used was not entirely his own. The assistance was appreciated. Fingers in the wound, seeking the damage done, he worked feverishly to set it right.

Below Caol's window, the scatter of palace sentries studied the point of impact in the decorative bushes where Halstatt had landed, but there was no other trace of the man there. Caol glanced towards the outer wall in the most direct path and thought he saw a length of rope slither over the walls and thought he heard the sounds of something large hitting the water of the moat. "Outside," he cried, the guards already hearing it too and breaking into a run. "He's over the wall." Caol did not bother to follow them this time as they rushed to lower the bridge. By the time they made it to the other side, Caol knew that Halstatt would be gone.

Gone. Caol trembled and began to collapse beneath the realization of what had happened. In spite of the odds of such a thing being successful, Halstatt had penetrated the castle fortifications and would have killed him if Kavan had not been there. Caol would have to thank the bard for that, ask him how he had come to be in the inquisitor's room at that precise moment...if the man lived. A groan escaped as he doubled over, feeling suddenly weak and ill.

"Easy, Caol." The chamberlain's strong hands were there, steadying him. "Are you well?" Caol nodded, not willing to trust his voice. He was physically well, but he would never admit to anything else. "What happened?"

He took the time to catch his breath and be steady on his feet before finding his voice. "I don't exactly know...I woke to find Lord Cliáth and this...man...in my room. We tried to apprehend him, but he stabbed Kavan and jumped out the window before we could. I think he made it over the outer wall..."

Guthrie grunted, staring at the commotion near the wall. "Minos will find him. Did you get a look at him? Anyone you may have seen before?"

Caol swallowed the bile in his throat, knowing he could not tell the truth, no matter how badly he wanted to. He did not want to lie, but the truth was more than he could admit. "His features were blackened; it was difficult to see him, but he vaguely resembled the drawings Ártur made...the ones Minos was posting earlier...except this fellow had no beard..." At least he spoke that much of the truth.

"Hmmph...same fellow perhaps. Must be a professional..." How else would he have made it into the castle, and over the exterior wall, without being noticed or caught? "Wonder what he wants. Let's check on Kavan, talk to him if he's well enough, and see what he knows." He had no idea how serious the bard's injuries were; he needed to see them for himself and get some answers.

"I..." Caol choked on his words. "He's likely to be indisposed for some time...if he lives..."

The chamberlain's face paled. "That bad?"

Caol nodded. "If it's the same to you, I would like to help with the search. I saw him…this man invaded my rooms…endangered my wife. I want restitution…" And he did not want to be there if Kavan had anything to say…or if the bard should die.

"Yes…very well…" Distracted, the chamberlain looked towards the castle door. "But be careful. If this man is after you, that dagger in your hand will not offer much protection."

Looking at the dagger he had forgotten he held, Caol offered it to Guthrie. "This is evidence…he dropped it…"

"Good." The word was grunted as he snatched it away. "I'll give it to Minos. Here…take this…" With his spare hand, he drew the sword from his side and handed it to the inquisitor. "Find him, Caol."

The weapon was accepted into shaky hands. "Yes sir…" he murmured. That was exactly what Caol intended to do. Find him. And kill him.

Ártur rocked back on his heels and allowed his wife, who knelt beside him, to close the wound. He was empty, drained; the intensity of his effort had exhausted him in less than fifteen minutes. The last time he had needed to heal anyone so quickly had been upon a battlefield in the aftermath of war, and then, as now, it had been Kavan dying through his connection with Arlan as the prince had fought for his life. Never before had it been Kavan's life directly beneath Ártur's hands. He felt he should have done better. He should have healed every trace of damage. Yet with his energy reserves depleted, that was left for Syl to do. Sensing the King in the nearby doorway, he lifted his head; their eyes met.

"He will live," the healer said, "but he should have at least two days of complete bed rest. I will make certain he gets it."

"Yes, you will," the King grunted with a nod, his expression no less grim upon the news that the bard would live, though his eyes shown with tears of relief. "Deidre woke me. What happened?"

"I want to know the same thing." Guthrie's voice came from behind Arlan and the King sidestepped to allow him to enter the room.

"I don't know," the healer replied earnestly. "I heard noises and when I came in, Caol was wrestling with an intruder…and Kavan…" His glance down at the man's bloody chest said enough. "Maybe my arrival spooked him…or calling the guards…because he jumped out the window as soon as I came in and called for help."

"Did they catch him?"

The chamberlain shook his head. "Not yet…I wish they had. They're still looking, but it seems he made it over the outer wall…though how he survived the fall from this window, I couldn't say. Justice Cornell has every available man looking for him. Caol did get the man's dagger, however, which could be read, and he believes this man may be the same one that attacked Captain Delamo and Prime Magistrate Dilyn. He saw the sketches and said the two bear a strong resemblance."

"Indeed," the healer agreed. "I did not get more than a glimpse of him, but there did seem to be some similarity between them."

Staring at Kavan's still form, hands clenched at his sides, the King growled, "Guthrie, I want this madman caught. He is terrorizing my household and I will not have it. I do not care what needs to be done to find him. Ártur, see to Kavan's health, but I want to know the moment he is well enough to answer questions. He might have the answers we're looking for."

## ❧Chapter 16❦

"Emissary from Cordash to see you, My Liege."

The King looked up from his chair in the stateroom, where he had been waiting all morning for any sort of good news regarding the hunt for the palace intruder. The realization that someone had breached the castle defenses meant that Kavan's warnings about Prince Bertram's safety had to be taken more seriously. There was no way of knowing if Caol had been the intruder's target, or if that had been the intruder's first stop of the night, but Arlan would take no chances. Guards and attendants were ordered to be with the heir at all times, and if the King had thought he could keep the boy with him, he would have. But Bertram could be unruly when bored, and Arlan could not afford that sort of distraction while trying to conduct the business of running a kingdom.

"Did they state their business?" he asked wearily. He did not think he would ever sleep normally again.

"No sir, only that they carry an urgent message from Prince Renfrid Valdis."

A message from the Cordashian prince warranted attention, but Arlan hoped it truly was urgent and not something frivolous. He had never known the Cordashians to be frivolous, and he had never had contact with Prince Valdis before, thus such a thought was unwarranted and unfair, but he was not in the mood to be trifled with.

"Very well, Yorick, bring them to me, please." He stood to straighten his hair and his garments, hoping to appear more confident and alert than he felt. Soon, two men, both tall and fair, were escorted into the room and the King inclined his head in greeting.

"Welcome to Enesfel and to Rhidam, gentlemen. On whose behalf do you come?" He knew what Yorick had told him, but he wanted to hear their words for himself. He chose to speak in their Cordashian tongue for their sake, believing it more diplomatic than speaking in Trade and less presumptuous than expecting them to speak Enesi.

Their reply, however, came in Enesi, showing their willingness to address the monarch they were visiting in his native tongue. They were well-trained diplomats indeed. "On behalf of Prince Valdis, heir to the throne of Cordash, and on behalf of the holy k'gdhededhá Tymothy Borlad. We carry messages from both."

The King sat, smiling at their formality and their respectfulness. "General Zarkosta, thank you. Please let me know immediately if Lord Cornell has anything to report. Come, sirs. I shall hear your message. Please speak freely."

The other staff in the room, servants, guards, and pages were not dismissed. After what had happened during the night, the King was not going to risk being alone in a room with strangers, emissaries or not. The pair did not sit, as it was not their place, but instead, they bowed and the younger of the two spoke first.

"King Ahern and his family send their regrets for the death of your queen and wish you peace in this troubled time…"

Arlan frowned, disliking the reminder but accepting that such diplomatic well wishes were to be expected. He inclined his head and the young man continued. "k'gdhededhá Borlad sends word regarding the infant in your house's care, a Bianca Maylor, of whom k'gdhededhá Tythilius inquired. Records are being searched but thus far, there is no family by the name of Maylor found within our kingdom. The search will continue, but it is the k'gdhededhá's stance that no Maylors will likely be located in Cordash."

Steepling his fingers, the King imagined that news had been given to him to relay it to Lady MacLyr, although it had also likely been given to Jermyn who would do the same. Giving it to the King seemed redundant, but Arlan chose not to point that out. "I shall be sure to make it known to all interested parties. Is there something more?" He presumed there must be, as their expressions were too grave to have merely wanted to relay such formalities.

A look passed between the two before the eldest squared his shoulders and spoke. "Our Glorious Lordship, King Ahern, has not long to live. The prince is of age to assume the throne, and there is no doubt about his ability to rule. However, Neth has been a great thorn to us of late and the prince does not feel experienced enough to effectively deal with war."

"War?" The King leaned forward with interest. After what his chamberlain had told him, and Kavan's warning, hearing this sort of confirmation was intriguing. "Are you at war with Neth?"

"Not at this time, but both King Ahern and Prince Renfrid feel it is inevitable. There was trouble with Neth prior to your ascension, as you may recall, and though there was a respite at the onset of their internal difficulties, they have again begun to raid our borders. Raids we can manage, but war at such a tenuous time would be a different matter, and that appears to be the direction Neth is pushing. Prince Renfrid wishes an audience with you to determine a mutually beneficial course of action, should such an event be brought to pass."

The King rubbed his bearded chin. "If the Prince wishes an immediate audience, I shall have to send an envoy in my stead. Matters in Rhidam require my full attention at this time, and if we wait until I am able to be there, Neth could overrun us all."

"An immediate audience is not required, but as you say, action must be swift if the Nethite threat is to be circumvented efficiently. The Prince is willing to travel to Rhidam if you will have him."

While he could not tell the envoy the entire truth, Arlan felt compelled to be honest with them for the sake of the Cordashian throne. "In all fairness, I should warn him that his safety may be a concern if he comes here now. We have had an outbreak of anti-Elyri violence recently," it seemed the best way to phrase the issue, and was, at least, true, "and until I am certain it is contained, I would hesitate to say that Rhidam is a safe place for visiting dignitaries and royalty. He will, of course, be afforded every possible protection, if he chooses to come. It is not that I do not desire a meeting with him, but I think he would agree that his safety is paramount, particularly since his father is ailing."

Again the pair looked at each other, speaking words in that glance that Arlan could but guess at. "Agreed, sir. Circumstances do not always permit us to act when we should like. Your honesty is appreciated. In anticipation of such a response, the Prince has sent this." The older man produced a scroll sealed with the Cordashian King's personal, unbroken seal. "This document puts forth the suggestions he and our King have considered; they are expecting a response in kind, if not with us then via your own courier when you have had time to study this. If it pleases you, we can either wait in Rhidam or depart and inform His Majesty that your response is forthcoming."

The King nodded at the smugness and efficiency with which these two carried out their diplomatic function. It pleased him that this Valdis prince had the foresight to anticipate all possible responses from Enesfel's king. "I will tend to this at once and send a reply to Prince Valdis and your king as quickly as I am able. I dismiss you to return home; give them both my regards and best wishes." The two bowed stiffly and were escorted from the room by one of the attending guards, leaving Arlan to peruse the document in relative solitude. At least studying it would keep his mind off of Kavan and last night's intruder.

The second search party had set out of the palace at dawn, shortly after Caol and the original search team returned. Nothing had been found yet, no sign of the intruder outside of the castle walls and very little of it within, save for the dagger and black-stained straw and bed sheets. With Captain Cornell leading the second team, confidence was still high that if the man remained in Rhidam, he would be located and apprehended. Though on the verge of exhaustion, running on nervous energy and adrenaline, Caol rapidly consumed a large breakfast and set out again under his wife's pleading gaze. The man had almost killed him, might have killed her, Caol explained, and had certainly wounded Kavan gravely. He knew that Deidre read more into the incident than anyone else, perhaps because she knew him best, and he could not risk remaining here, waiting for her to discover his secret, waiting for Halstatt to be found. Until Kavan was capable of speaking, there was nothing in the palace for Caol to do that would help.

It was approaching noon and as the search teams began to regroup in the courtyard again to report to Captain Cornell, there was still nothing to tell. No one had learned anything useful and no sign of the man they sought had been found. Or almost no sign. Caol's face was grim as he listened, fingering the slip of parchment in his trouser pocket. He had read it twice, each time feeling a raw core of ice expanding within him. Halstatt wanted to meet with him in a small grove east of Rhidam, the place known to many as Hangman's Grove. Halstatt had certainly chosen a fitting place. He had made no demand for money or property, not even the Coryllien dagger. No questions were asked. There was nothing more than the request to meet.

Caol knew the place Halstatt referred to. And Halstatt knew that Caol would come. The inquisitor wondered whether he should speak of this to Captain Cornell, but he could think of no way to explain why this man wanted to meet with him, of all people, or even knew his name. Supplying any information to the justice that indicated he knew who Halstatt was, was akin to signing his own death confession.

The third search party set out; Caol following wearily several paces behind everyone else. If he could go underground, contact a member of the Association, he might locate his quarry that way. But there were too many royal soldiers combing Rhidam, meaning that he could not easily slip them, and after his last failed attempt to work with the Association, he was not sure they would help. Now he was running on very little sleep and too much nervousness, both of which made him ineffective in searching for details.

"Are you still going to deny that Tarmajien is here?"

Caol jumped, not having noticed the large man who had fallen into step beside him. He stopped, Guthrie's sword drawn and poised for attack. "I never denied he was here," he growled with narrowed eyes, "I said I did not know where he was. If I had known, I would have dealt with him myself and would not have spent the last ten hours scouring Rhidam. If I knew where he was, he would be dead."

Elotti snorted. "Dead…that would be unfortunate."

"Unfortunate for you maybe. He thought to kill me last night and critically wounded the king's bard. He nearly blinded a fine soldier and has killed at least one defenseless woman and a child. This in eight days. I would hardly call his death unfortunate, nor would anyone else. It would be a blessing to all mankind, and I intend to see that he dies."

"I could assist you if you wish…"

"I do not want, or need, your help, hunter," the inquisitor growled. Seeing a slow grin begin to creep across the dark man's face, he snapped, "Unless you know where he is…"

"You said you do not want my assistance…"

Caol's fist balled at his side and he waved the sword beneath the man's chin. He barely refrained from striking him. "Damn it, Elotti! If you know where he is, tell me. Or at least have the decency to get him yourself and stop playing games…or are you too much a coward for the job?"

The insult melted the grin from the hunter's face and left him wearing a hard expression. "Coward?" Both men stood their ground, the hunter leering, Caol refusing to be intimidated, until eventually, the bigger man's smile crept back into place. "In all fairness, I do not know where he is. He has moved around quite a bit while he has been in Rhidam. But I would be willing to assist you in his capture if you agree not to kill him."

So that was why he waited, the inquisitor thought bitterly. By waiting for his prey to strike at the royal family, he hoped to increase the potential payout once he caught Halstatt. Caol shoved the sword into its scabbard with a grunt. "If you want your reward, find him yourself. I cannot risk him escaping punishment. If I find him first, he will die."

Bhríd folded the letter neatly, enjoying the warm flush that came as he held it to his lips. He had not expected to be this happy to receive word of the Duchess' safe return to Levonne. But it was not only her safe journey that pleased him. She missed him. He had never been told that by anyone except his family, and this felt considerably different. Besides, he knew she meant it. The psychic impressions he allowed himself to read from the folded parchment and from her hand when she had bid him farewell told him of her sincerity. That he had dreamed of her every night since their first meeting also confirmed that he had become attached to her though he barely knew her.

There was a strange sort of rationale to her request, something reinforced by Bhríd's own logic, thoughts that had been coming unbidden to him since her departure. There were few Elyri in Enesfel, and none of them were available women. Bhríd had no intention of returning to Elyriá anytime soon; the chances of meeting a compatible Elyri woman were slim. Even if he should return home, he was not likely to find one willing to relocate to Rhidam. If he were to marry a Teren, whom he would likely outlive by many decades, why not Madalyn Dubuais? If the match proved unbearable, she was willing to live apart, and instead of a divorce he could not give her, he could wait until her death to remarry. While he was in no hurry to start a family or take a wife, he could think of no logical reasons to wait. He could think of no reason for a marriage to the Duchess to be unbearable; it would benefit her, and to be honest, the more he considered it, the more appealing the idea became.

On impulse, he withdrew a quill and ink from the drawer and retrieved a sheet of blank parchment to send her a letter in reply. But he would not give her an answer. Not yet. Not like this.

No word had come from Caol, but Halstatt had not expected any. Caol had no way of finding him. But Halstatt was certain they would meet tomorrow and he would make certain the inquisitor paid for the minor injuries he received in his leap from that window. He examined the new sword one last time in the dimming candlelight and then laid it beside his new knife. Both were purchased for tomorrow's encounter and both would be disposed of afterward where no Elyri was likely to find and read them. While the Coryllien would be lost to the Tarmajiens, a single branch of the Dugan family would be all that remained. They could be easily dispatched without the Coryllien. The feud would be over.

❧*❧

There were rocks sprinkled on the ground and scuff marks on the outer wall of the castle a distance away from Caol and Deidre's window, and the bushes beneath that window were crushed and misshapen from the intruder's fall. Captain Cornell studied it carefully though the evidence told him little they did not already know. That the intruder had entered through one third floor window there was no doubt, and the justice had the black smeared pillow sham, the handful of dirty straw, and the discarded dagger as evidence. A stable boy had also discovered one black glove in the courtyard as he was preparing the chamberlain's horse that morning. A sack containing tar makeup and a second pair of gloves were found on the banks of the river beside a muddy rope that could have been used to scale the outer walls. The items confirmed that there had been an intruder and that the man was a professional. Careless, perhaps, but a professional.

It was the unanswered questions that were the most troublesome. Why had the intruder chosen the princess' room when there were others between the point of entry and that one? Had it been an accident, intentional, or merely his first stop of the night? What, or who, had he been looking for? And why had Kavan been the one to find him?

Minos glanced at the towers. No, in the darkness, anyone there would have been unable to see a black-clad figure scaling the dark gray castle wall. The justice's best recourse was to intensify security, both of the castle and of Prince Bertram as the King demanded. It was not the justice's place to question his orders, but he wondered what had prompted the King to make such a demand. Did he have reason to believe the heir was in danger, or was he, perhaps, remembering his own childhood, the efforts made to take his life when he was slightly younger than Prince Bertram was now? Or did the King know something the justice did not?

He growled. How could he do his job if details were continually kept from him?

"Yes," Caol wrote, "I know this is not a good time. But I have discussed it with the justice. This friend is in Rhidam tomorrow and would very much like me to hunt with him. I will be gone for the morning. I should return by noon, or evening at the latest if the hunting is particularly good."

His wife looked squarely into his eyes until he broke her stare by gesturing for a response. She took the stylus with a huff. "There is more to this than you are sharing. You do not lie well, at least not to me. You never have. I cannot hear, but I know. Remember there is a man out there who may want to kill you. Go…and be careful."

In response, he embraced her tightly, pulling her towards the bed. Yes, there was a man out there trying to kill him. One way or the other, this would be over tomorrow. He had a duty to his family and the Crown to end it, and the gravity of what lay ahead made this moment with her even more precious. Tonight might be their last together; he did not want to waste it.

The creak of the bedroom door caused Ártur to look up from his book. Prince Muir made no attempt to enter. His blue eyes were rimmed with dark circles, his face was pale, and he could not bring himself to look away from the unmoving form on the bed. Only when the healer motioned to him did the prince blink and close the door behind him.

"He will be well. The damage has been healed; now he needs to rest."

The reassurance did little to change the prince's expression as he drew a chair nearer to the bed and sat beside Ártur. "What happened?"

Surprised that no one had told him, Ártur shifted in his seat. Like the King, Muir's curiosity demanded immediate satisfaction. The prince would not be put off by evasive answers, particularly where Kavan and his welfare were concerned. In that regard, the King and the outsider prince were much alike. "Kavan found an intruder in Caol and Deidre's rooms. He tried to apprehend the man but was stabbed in the tussle. Fortunately, I was nearby and arrived in time to save him."

The prince nodded but continued to frown. "Is it my imagination, or has he changed?"

That was not the sort of question Ártur expected. "Changed? How do you mean?"

The prince smoothed the sheet over Kavan's leg absently. "The fight with the King...now this. And he broke the mirror in his room...by punching it. He has never been thus before, violent...angry. Is it me? Something I have done?"

Ártur ran his hand through his hair, a familiar gesture he often did when he collecting his thoughts. He shook his head no, but it was many moments before he tried to explain. "Not you, my prince. It is...for much of his life, Kavan was a solitary person, more out of necessity than choice. He grew accustomed to doing as he pleased, when he pleased, not being surrounded by others whom he has to consider first. Arlan changed all of that. Kavan has been cooped up too long; he needs space, freedom, lack of responsibility..."

"Then it is because of me. He agreed to stay in Rhidam as my tutor..."

"He would have found something else to do, another reason to stay. He loves Arlan too much to leave him, and he believes Arlan needs him here...which is probably true to some degree. And he believes he has nowhere to go. He does not think he would be welcome anywhere else. Besides, Kavan would never abandon you. You are important to him too. He loves you as he does the King. Believe me, though he cares for many people, his love is a rare and precious gift that he does not easily give. There are few people in this world who can claim to be loved by the White Bard. You are one of them."

The young man leaned his elbows on the bed before brushing Kavan's hair from his forehead, his fingers unconsciously tangling in the thick silver locks. Ártur noticed but said nothing. The sun had set many hours ago. The candles at Kavan's bedside cast twisting shadows upon the tapestry of Kóráhm upon the wall. The prince looked away from the bard's face long enough to study the wall-hanging. "I had a dream about Saint Kóráhm last night."

"Really?" asked Ártur, as he too glanced at the woven image.

"I do not recall it clearly. He stood at the foot of my bed and spoke to me, but I could not hear him…and then I woke up to the commotion outside."

"Perhaps Kavan can help you with its meaning when he awakens. I am sure it means something. For now…would you stay with Kavan while I check on my wife and the children?"

"May I?" It was the first ray of light the healer had seen on the prince's face, and he was pleased with his instincts.

"If you promise to stay until I return, to not leave him alone. If you need me…I will know if Kavan needs anything. Stay with him."

Muir's head bobbed emphatically. "Yes, Lord Healer. Gladly."

☙ * ❧

Unable to sleep, Caol wandered the corridors until he ended up in the Great Hall perched casually upon the throne. Being a prince had its advantages, but he had no desire to be king. That much responsibility for the welfare of others was intimidating. He preferred the benefits of the royal life without that much work. His wife was asleep in their room; he had not wanted to leave her but he had been too restless and did not want her to wake. Besides, if he slept at all, it would be best to do it away from her so that she could not try again to talk him out of going in the morning, and would not know precisely when he left. He did not want to say goodbye.

There was a cold gnawing in his stomach and he wondered if it was the same feeling a condemned man experienced the night before his execution. Not that he was condemned; he had every intention of coming away from Halstatt as the victor. But he was realistic. There was always a chance, no matter how remote, that Halstatt would win this fight. Deidre would be alone, and Wilred would be without a…

"Father!" Wilred squeaked, as he and Prince Bertram bounded into the Hall and came to an abrupt halt.

Caol narrowed his eyes. "What are you two doing awake at this hour?"

"We were on our way to…" started Wilred.

Prince Bertram, however, silenced him with a jab of his elbow into the smaller boy's ribs. "We could not sleep; we are going to the kitchen."

One eyebrow twitched and Caol frowned. "Are you so hungry that you could not wait until morning?"

"I'm not hun…" Again, Wilred was silenced by his cousin's elbow.

"Starving," said the heir.

Rolling his eyes, Caol got to his feet. This was no new behavior between the pair; he was not the first to catch the boys up to mischief. He scolded or punished Wilred each time, but the elder prince continued to bully him into situations that were not of his making. "Then come to the kitchen. I'm a little hungry myself; I shall join you." He pretended not to see Bertram's exasperated expression and ushered the boys into the kitchen where he located a pitcher of milk, some bread, and a round of cheese. He served it and sat with them as they ate. Neither consumed much, however, confirming his suspicions that the kitchen was not the destination they had intended.

The older boy sighed sullenly, hating to be caught in such a position. "I guess I am not as hungry as I thought."

"Where were you really going? I want the truth."

After a brief exchange of glances with his cousin, Wilred mumbled, "To the stables."

Considering what had happened the night before, the stables were no place for the boys to be alone at this hour of the night. "Why on earth would you go to the stables tonight?"

"There are kittens! Six of them. Diona said so. Bertie wants to see them…"

Caol's frown deepened. "Kittens can wait until morning. You know it is not safe for either of you to go out alone…in the dark. How did you get past your attendants, Bertram?"

The boy shrugged, as though he did not care, although his quavering voice suggested otherwise. "They thought I was asleep…they went to sleep."

That was not good and Caol intended to do something about it. "I shall see to it they carry out their duties more efficiently in the future. Do not do this again. Off to bed, both of you…now…or must I accompany you…?"

"No," Prince Bertram said abruptly. "We will go now." If Caol went with them, he would undoubtedly wake the sleeping guards, and possibly his father, and the prince would rather not face possible punishment tonight. Caol seemed distracted, so it might enable him and Wilred to get out to the stables after all if he appeared cooperative.

Both children sighed and got up from the table. They made it as far as the door before the inquisitor spoke again. "Wilred?"

"Sir?" He glanced back, afraid he was about to be punished rather than simply sent to bed.

But tonight there would be no punishment. "I want you to know I am going hunting with a friend in the morning. I should be back by noon, or by evening at least. I want you to do as you are told and stay out of trouble."

The boy's eyes lit. "Hunting? May I go with you? Please?"

His father shook his head. "No, not this time. You are not yet old enough. Next summer, perhaps, if you continue with your bow…"

"Next summer is too far away! I want to go hunting now! What are you hunting for? Bears? Rabbits? Harts?"

"Whatever we can find." He was not going to allow the boy's pleading to get to him. He might have, if this had been an honest hunting trip. "You are not coming with me this time…and I want you to obey your mother. Do you understand?"

The child pouted but lowered his head and murmured, "Yes, sir." He rejoined his cousin in the doorway and said over his shoulder, "Good luck."

"Thank you." What Caol did not express was that he would need that luck. He returned the milk to the ice house and nibbled at the cheese the boys had not eaten.

In the Grand Hall, out of earshot of the inquisitor, Prince Bertram took Wilred's hand. "Do not worry," he said. "I will take care of everything…just do what I say."

## ❧Chapter 17❧

I t was not yet light outside when Caol fastened his sword about his waist and wedged his dagger securely in his wrist sheath. He was no prince today, at least not a prince of the royal persuasion. Today he was what he had been born to be, the prince of the Dugan clan. There was one goal, profit, and today's sought-after profit was the death of Halstatt Tarmajien, the last of his family's most hated rivals. The simple brown leather breeches, boots, and jerkin were barely sufficient to keep out the early morning chill, but the day would grow warmer and the inquisitor did not want a bulky cloak or coat to hamper his movement. Speed, dexterity, cunning, and strength were what would matter today. They alone, coupled with luck, would determine which man walked away from this day alive.

The castle gate was already open as the servants and palace staff hurried about their early morning routine; Caol slipped through unnoticed and unhindered. He looked for any trace of Wace Elotti, and when he thankfully saw no sign of the venador, he started east. He failed, however, to notice the pair of figures following several yards behind him.

❧*❧

There was a stab of pain as Kavan rolled over; it brought him abruptly awake with a gasp as his body tried to recoil away from the sensation. The room was dark but he could see the beginnings of dawn through the window to his left. He was alone. Initially, he did not understand the reason for that pain in his breast until he recalled the intruder in Caol's room. Several things flashed through his mind, demanding attention, fighting for prominence. A dagger in his ribs. Caol. The intruder. Kóráhm. The Coryllien. The fight. He groaned and eased back into his pillows. So much to know, but he did not have the willpower to rise. His bed felt unusually comfortable this morning and he was unready to leave it. Besides, everyone was still asleep. Ártur would come soon enough, and then Kavan would get his answers.

Hesitantly he fingered the area where the dagger had penetrated his skin. No scar. He groaned. A scar would have marred his flawless physique, set him apart, but he was not surprised Ártur had seen to it that no blemish remained. Kavan remembered the shock as the blade had bit into his flesh; it was a feeling he had never known, had never expected to know. If he tried, he could evoke the exact physical sensation, causing the bruised flesh to throb in recollection. No, that was nothing he wanted to remember. With a sigh, he closed his eyes to sleep again, banishing the residual pain from his memory.

⪼ * ⪻

After his second inspection of the morning, General Wyndham retreated to allow his five subordinates to begin the daily drills and exercises. Guthrie had briefed him on the situation with Neth and stressed the need for Enesfel's troops to prepare immediately, in case they were needed. The five-thousand-man infantry and two-thousand-man cavalry he currently commanded would be a far cry from Neth's last known military strength, but if fortune favored them, and Cordash fought with them, it might be enough.

It would have to be. After the King's meeting with the emissaries from Cordash, the call to arms had been made and the troops were already converging upon Rhidam. By the time they were needed, if they were needed, the number would swell to twenty thousand, the cavalry to five thousand. It was nothing compared to the military strength Ternce recalled existing under King Donal, but too many had died in the years since. Though the population was beginning to recover, it would be at least another twenty years before there were enough men in Enesfel to create such an army. Unless war reached Enesfel first and devastated the kingdom again.

The general rubbed the back of his neck and stared towards the rising sun. He had not been in Rhidam at the time of the break-in, but he had heard about it from Guthrie and several of his men. His first reactions had been shock and relief that the intruder had done no harm to the royal family. Then, after thinking about it for several hours, his relief turned to suspicion. How had Kavan known this intruder was there? Luck, perhaps, or his unique brand of Elyri intuition, but maybe the bard had been involved. Ternce could think of no way to test that theory, nor could he explain why the intruder had brutally attacked the bard if Kavan were involved in some plot. Nor was there any reason to suspect the bard of treachery. If Kavan had wished harm to any of the Lachlans, he had almost fourteen years to have done something. Ternce knew better than to express doubts about the Elyri bard's loyalties. He had already experienced the King's displeasure for voicing such an opinion. The general did not want to experience that again. But his doubt was there, despite the illogical nature of it.

⮞*⮜

The early spring grass and freshly budding trees had never looked so green to Caol. The condemned man syndrome again, he smiled grimly, pushing a silent path through the foliage. He circled the clearing twice to be certain there were no ambushes, traps, or hidden surprises, and a glimpse into the grove had revealed that Halstatt was not there yet. That was a relief. It allowed Caol to take his time selecting a vantage point from where he could await the other man's arrival. He decided upon a low hanging tree branch thick with leaves. Climbing trees had been one of his favorite pastimes as a boy, and something he still did whenever he was away from the prying eyes of the royal household. It was useful as he perched in the dense vegetation, waiting patiently with his dagger in hand. He could wait there for hours if necessary.

ༀ*༁

"Bertram!"

The force of the panic that seized Kavan was great enough that he barely felt the stab of pain as he sat straight up in bed. Ártur's hands grasped his shoulders and tried to ease him back down into the pillows. "Easy, Kavan. Everything is fine."

"nai." The bard took hold of the healer's wrists, his eyes wide in distress. "ghytim kedhá Bertram. naethád gaeth dhi osté. uhwlth."

Ártur had no illusions about Kavan's sanity or sincerity. Kavan rarely spoke in his native language since coming to Enesfel. His eyes were wide, pupils dilated and his hands, his whole body, shook. Whatever his cousin had Seen, Ártur would not remain idle and question it. He squeezed Kavan's shoulders to reassure him and hastened to the children's' room. The prince was not there. His sister was asleep but both Wilred and Muir were also gone, although the eldest prince was found in the oratory. Apprehensive, the healer closed the door to the holy room without distracting the prince from his meditations, and pondered what to do next. He knocked on the chamberlain's door, and then knocked again more insistently when there was no immediate response.

"Hold on," came Guthrie's sleepy, irritated reply. He opened the door as he attempted to pull on his trousers the rest of the way. "Goodness, Ártur...what is it?"

"I would not have...but Kavan..."

Guthrie's throat constricted in response to the panic in the healer's voice. "What has happened to Kavan?"

"He says Prince Bertram is in danger, but neither Bertram nor Wilred are in their room. I would look for them myself, but I do not want to leave Kavan...in case he sees something more...says something..." Or does something foolish in his current state of fragile health, Ártur thought grimly. "Please...you must find the boys before it is too late..."

After the King's admonition about increasing security around Prince Bertram, the chamberlain grabbed a tunic and hastily threw it over his head, not heeding its unwashed, disheveled appearance. He had no doubt that if Kavan believed Prince Bertram was in trouble, he likely was.

"I'll get a party and find them. You tend to Kavan." He was running down the hall towards the stairs before Ártur could say anything more.

❧*❧

There was no sign of his prey when Halstatt entered the clearing, which both surprised and pleased him. It pleased him to have arrived ahead of Caol, but it surprised him because it was past sun-up. Halstatt had been detained trying to lose a trio of royal soldiers who had seemed to be tailing him, and he had expected Caol to have already reached the meeting place. Perhaps the inquisitor too had been detained. Or perhaps he had decided not to come. Either way, Halstatt could but wait and watch for a potential ambush.

He strolled around the grove, senses attuned to anyone's approach, appearing to admire the flora. He stopped beneath a tall tree as the crack of twigs from the east made him turn. Anticipating that Caol would emerge from the bushes across the clearing, he rested his hand upon his sword hilt and waited. Something dropped from the tree behind him and he found himself in a headlock with a dagger at his throat.

"Expecting someone, Halstatt?" Caol hissed. The man struggled to free himself. "Getting careless in your old age…but I suppose you realize that."

Though he was surprised that Caol had not already slit his throat, Halstatt realized he could not break that grip in any conventional way. With a quick snap, however, he was able to throw the man over his back. Free of that grasp at last, Halstatt had time to draw his own knife, and once Caol was on his feet, the two began to circle each other. Caol regretted not killing him quickly when he had the chance, but there were answers he needed first.

"What do you want, Halstatt? You could have killed me before Lord Cliáth found you, but you didn't. What were you looking for?"

Halstatt lunged but Caol leaped back, avoiding the blade he suspected was poisoned. "Looking for my dagger, of course. You did get that message?"

"I do not have it." Seeing Halstatt's doubtful expression, he smirked and continued, "You could have searched my entire room and you would not have found it. You are not skilled enough to search the entire grounds without being caught. You couldn't even kill me without…"

"If it had not been for that cursed Elyri…" He again slashed forward, making Caol laugh when he missed. It was like a dance, the inquisitor thought; the more Halstatt swung and missed, the angrier and more reckless he would become.

"On the contrary," Caol sneered. "That Elyri is more blessed than any man you or I shall ever know…and not just because he saved my life. What is it you really want?"

"Your death."

The dagger cut across Caol's arm, ripping fabric but not drawing blood. There was no burn to suggest poison, but he knew he could not count on being safe. The fun was quickly seeping out of this charade, he mused, as he tripped his opponent and danced back. Halstatt sprawled into the dewy grass and mud but recovered quickly enough to avoid the stab of Caol's dagger. "And? Surely you did not track me all the way to Rhidam for something as simple as that. No money? No treasure?"

On his feet again, Halstatt growled, "The Káliel Serpents." There was no harm in admitting it when he was confident Caol was going to die.

The inquisitor feigned left as another jab thrust past him. "So, it was you who murdered the lady. King Arlan will be pleased to hear it."

"You have known all along it was me. You have not exposed me yet. You will not have the chance now and the matter will go unsolved."

Caol sneered again. "On the contrary. There is at least one person who knows you are responsible." Caol did not know this to be true, though he suspected it, but his words were enough to concern Halstatt. The brief hesitation his words brought allowed Caol to cut across the man's chest, drawing blood. Halstatt snarled and rushed forward, knocking Caol to the ground. They wrestled, both men trying to stay out of the reach of the other's blade while simultaneously trying to injure their opponent.

A sharp slam into Halstatt's wrist sent his blade flying across the grove. The man reached for his sword but could not draw it without disengaging himself from Caol's hold. When he did manage to free himself, he belted the inquisitor across the face and knocked him to the ground. Caol's vision blurred as he fell, and for a few seconds, he did not move. Seeing his opportunity, Halstatt pulled his sword and readied to drive it through Caol's heart.

"Father!"

Wilred broke free of his cousin's restraining grasp and dashed forward. Prince Bertram stood in surprised response. The brambles they had been hiding behind no longer provided cover.

Astonished, Halstatt hesitated long enough for Caol to roll away from the sword and cry, "Wilred! Run!" Sensing that movement, Halstatt brought the blade down into Caol's thigh, driving it through into the earth before retreating. Caol bellowed, motioning for the boys to run. But as he pulled the sword free, Halstatt seized both boys with an arm caught beneath their arms, around their small torsos, and disappeared into the forest. Caol pushed painfully to his feet and tried in vain to follow the terrified, angry shouts of the boys, but once he heard the thundering of hooves and caught a glimpse of Halstatt on a departing horse, he collapsed, weak from blood loss and pain. There was no way he could hope to catch them on foot, especially when injured.

❧*❧

"It's too late," Kavan murmured when Ártur returned to the room. He was sitting, slumped forward, the sheet fallen away from his shoulders. It was difficult to call his white skin pallid, but he did look gaunt and frail.

"What do you mean?"

Kavan rubbed his temples, trying to will away the ache. He was not certain what he meant, only that he knew it was too late. "Prince Bertram... it is too late. There is nothing more to do."

The healer's face lost color. "Is he dead? Have you Seen his death?"

"No…" the bard shook his head. "But I know it is too late."

Sitting on the bedside, reaching for his cousin's hand, the healer said, "Guthrie is looking for them. He will find them."

"Them?"

"Prince Bertram and Prince Wilred…"

The bard appeared to shrink deeper into himself. A ball of realization was forming within him and he did not like it. "Wilred…then it is so. It is too late. I told you what I have Seen. Wilred crying…Bertram's body…"

"No…if Bertram is not yet dead, then it is not too late. They might merely be out playing. You do not know that this event is connected to what you Saw…"

"And you do not know it is not," Kavan countered.

"Do you think…?"

Kavan sighed. "I know what I feel…and it is not good."

If Ártur was going to protest further, he refrained. The sinking sensation within him was too real to ignore. "You have never been one to give up; do not now. We will need your strength, sínréc…" He stopped and looked away, realizing how selfish those words must sound, though Kavan would never call him selfish.

Changing the subject, Kavan lifted his head and asked, "Will I live?"

Ártur nodded. "For centuries. Lucky for you, I was next door. I managed to keep you from drowning in your own blood. You slept all day yesterday. How do you feel?"

"There is some pain here," he indicated the area where the intruder's dagger had pierced him, "otherwise, I feel well. You left no scar…" His cousin shifted uncomfortably before placing one hand upon the point of injury, closing his eyes, and seeking out the source of Kavan's pain. When he heard Kavan's sigh of relaxation, the pain now eased and erased from his body, Ártur took his hand away. "Thank you. Has the intruder been caught?"

"He jumped from the window…survived the drop. Apparently, he is a professional; he climbed in through the room next to yours and made it over the outer wall into the moat before anyone could catch him. No one knows what he was after, but everyone wants to question you. They seem to believe you hold the key to this mystery."

"I do not want to talk to anyone." There was little he could say, and much of what he did know he did not feel ready to reveal.

"Would you tell me what happened? What you know? My curiosity will be satisfied and I can answer everyone's questions and keep them away from you. What were you doing in Caol's room?"

"I…" The memory of the Coryllien came to him and he resisted looking towards the wall where it was hidden. "Something woke me. When I could not sleep, I decided I needed to ask Caol some questions."

"What kind of questions?" Kavan looked away. "You are not going to answer that, are you?"

"No. Not until…and do not try to probe my thoughts, Ártur. I will slam my defenses down hard enough that you will have a headache for days, one you will be unable to sooth or remove." The healer looked down at his hands, withdrawing his probe; he had no doubts that Kavan could do what he threatened. The bard continued in a gentler tone. "I do not know what woke me, but when I got to Caol's room, the intruder was attempting to gain access to the liquor cabinet. I backed him against the middle door, and Caol opened it. I attempted to knock the intruder down while he was distracted, and though I was successful, you know what I got for my efforts."

"Did you see him? Can you describe him?"

"He is the same man who attacked Wortham and Gabrielle. The face is the same…the voice too."

"That's what both Caol and I thought; it is what everyone wants to know. Will you be well if I leave you alone? I will send up food, and then I want you to rest."

Though he did not feel the need to rest any longer, Kavan replied, "Yes, sínréc." At least resting in his room meant he might be able to avoid the host of people who wanted to interrogate him.

Relieved not to have to fight Kavan on the issue, Ártur embraced him. "I will tell them what you have told me. That ought to keep them from bothering you today." As would the search for the boys, he thought grimly.

Though still uncomfortable with the physical intimacy of embraces, Kavan was better at enduring it, and Ártur usually knew when to release him before that comfort threshold was crossed. "Before you go…"

"Yes?"

"May I have my harp?" The request made Ártur smile and he gladly retrieved the instrument for his cousin. "Thank you. Please…if there is any news about the boys…"

"You will be the first I tell."

❧*❦

Caol had no idea how long he had lain in the mud in that clearing, or whether he had blacked out, but the searing pain in his leg brought him to full awareness. A young man, handsome and delicate, knelt beside him; he had already cut away the bloody leg of Caol's trousers and was dressing the freshly cleaned wound. The bag at the man's side and the yellow braid upon his lapel indicated he was a healer. Caol tried to clear his vision to focus on the stranger. That he could not remember this man with the ash brown hair arriving confirmed that he must have passed out, but how long had he been here?

"Easy, milord," the young man said, his voice as light as his features. "I have taken every precaution and step to ensure that your leg will heal, but you must not strain it."

"Who are you and where did you...?" Approaching steps through the brush stopped him mid-sentence; he expected it to be Halstatt, but instead, Wace Elotti emerged into the clearing. "You!"

"It looks like I arrived in time, but it puzzles me why Tarmajien did not finish the job of killing you when he had the chance."

The reminder jolted Caol to sit, but the physician pushed him back down. "The boys!"

"Not yet..."

"Now! Did you see him? Any sign of him? He has taken Prince Bertram and my son!"

The hunter's face hardened. "Why did you...?"

"I didn't bring them! I didn't do anything! They followed me; I did not know they were here! When it looked like Halstatt would...my son ran out...there..." he pointed to the spot where he had last seen Wilred. "He did this! He took them! There was a horse...I tried to follow..."

"Valiant," muttered the venador, squatting at the place Caol had pointed to study the ground. "Children are not pawns. I suspected Tarmajien was a fool, but not this much of one. I found evidence of a horse, but we encountered no one."

"We must find them."

Elotti got to his feet. "You are in no shape to do anything until your Elyri healer tends you. Rouvyn is a good doctor but no substitute for an Elyri." He tousled the young man's ash-colored hair at his crestfallen expression. "Still, he has other uses. He will take you to Rhidam; I will find Halstatt."

"You should have already found him! Then none of this would be happening!"

The dark-skinned man glowered at him and Caol glared back. Normally, Elotti would have been offended to be insulted in such a way, but in this situation, his child in danger, it was understandable and Elotti chose to overlook it.

When he did not rise to the challenge, Caol too backed down from his anger. "Find them and I will pay you double the reward. Triple if Halstatt is alive for me to rip out his still-beating heart. But you cannot tell anyone of my family connections with the Tarmajiens. I'm hiring you to find a band of thieves who attacked me and took my son...a band led by the man who broke into the castle the other night."

It was Elotti's professionalism and his respect for the life of children that kept him from finding amusement in Caol's desperation. He shook his head. "We want the same things. If I return Halstatt to my benefactor, that shall be reward enough. I will help you find him because it is my duty, and because of the children. Once the Association learns of this..." He smirked, thinking of the repercussions Halstatt was likely to suffer because of his ill-advised actions. "Rouvyn, take Lord Dugan back to Rhidam, to the palace. Do not answer any questions; allow Lord Dugan to do the talking. I will come for you later..."

Caol grabbed Elotti's arm and held it tightly, fingers biting into his flesh. "Let me join you. At least for a time. I cannot return...without my son...not until I know something...not until he is safe."

A tense pause followed, the two men again staring at each other, one with desperation, the other with annoyance. Dugan was trying his patience, but again, he decided the man's actions were justifiable. "Very well...but only for a while." That the boys might not ever be safe went without saying.

๏*๏

The mournful, plaintive resonance of brass harp strings drifted into the corridor; Prince Muir heard the sound as he reached the top of the stairs. A silly, joyous grin sprung onto his face as he ran to Kavan's door, but he stopped short of opening it. The healer had given strict orders to allow Kavan to rest, that he was not to be disturbed. But he was not resting, and the prince needed to see him, talk to him, be certain he was well. That need won out and he rapped on the door and waited.

"Come."

Pushing the door open slowly, the prince peered inside, his grin both excited and concerned. "I apologize for disturbing you, Lord Cliáth. Healer MacLyr said you should rest but…"

He doubted Kavan's expression could have been more sincere; though the bard did not smile, it was clear he was happy to see the prince. "I have been resting all morning, and all day yesterday. It is past noon and I have had more rest than I desire. Your company is welcome. It has been lonely."

"I thought you preferred to be alone," Muir murmured as he approached the bed. He could not interpret the emotions that crossed Kavan's face, but they made him uncomfortable to see.

"I prefer being alone to the company of those who are not dear to me." He changed the subject, not wanting to talk about himself. Brushing his fingers beneath the boy's eye, he said, "The bruising is nearly gone."

"Almost, yes. Though I had gotten used to it." He wanted to touch Kavan in return, to assure himself further of the bard's reality, but he could not bring himself to try.

As if reading his wishes, Kavan took the prince's hands in his. The boy looked away to conceal his embarrassment and joy. Assuming that Muir already knew the news of the day, he asked, "Has there been any news about Bertram?"

"Not yet, at least I have not heard anything. I would be the last person to be told." He looked at Kavan meaningfully. "It does not surprise me though. I told Wilred he would end up in trouble if he did everything Bertie asked."

"Trouble may be an understatement this time."

The prince nodded his head, though he had no inkling of the seriousness of Kavan's reference. "How are you feeling?"

"I am well, my prince. Do not concern yourself with me. How is Ártur as tutor? Are your studies progressing?"

The boy smiled, though his concern for the bard's well-being had not dissipated. "You know they are. I do not shirk my studies, regardless of who is teaching me. But Diona has made his task nearly impossible with her usual questions. Lord MacLyr does an admirable job, but he is not accustomed to the way she thinks. And unlike you, he frequently does not have answers for her, which of course means he gets no peace and we get little accomplished. We miss you. It will be better when you come back."

"I will not be your tutor any longer, my prince." It had been a difficult decision to make, but in his hours spent alone, Kavan had concluded it was for the best.

"Wha...why not?"

While prepared for the questions, Kavan realized he was not adequately prepared for the force of emotion behind them. "Diona is old enough to require a woman tutor, and you, my prince, are nearly old enough not to require a tutor at all...though there is more you can learn from me if you are willing. Besides, I thought you were leaving Rhidam. I cannot be your tutor if you are not here."

Prince Muir shrugged his shoulders but his expression did not change. "That is true. But while I am here...will you...it is the things you have taught me outside of formal studies that have proven most beneficial. Will we still be friends?"

The bard's mouth turned up in a rare hint of an embarrassed smile. "We will always be friends. You do not need to ask me that."

It was a relief to hear it, even if the previous words sounded like excuses. He would not pressure Kavan for his reasons, however. If they had something to do with Kavan's need for freedom, as Ártur had mentioned previously, the prince did not want to know. He did not want to be responsible for trapping Kavan in any way. Instead of speaking, he pulled free of Kavan's hands and stood before the tapestry. He ran his fingers over the gold threads in Dhágdhuán's robe reverently; it had taken him many years to gather the courage to touch it as if it were some ancient holy relic, and when he did, it was with the greatest respect. "Lord Cliáth…is it wrong of me to want to be gdhededhá?"

Inhaling slowly, Kavan placed the harp on the bed beside him and rested back into the feather pillows piled high against the headboard. It eased the stiffness in his back and the slight ache in his ribs. He had not had the chance to bring up this topic with the prince before and was pleased Muir was bringing it up on his own. "It depends on your reasons for the choice. If you are merely doing it to escape an unpleasant life here, or because I have somehow influenced you, that is not reason enough. You do not need to be gdhededhá to do k'Ádhá's work. I am not gdhededhá, nor is Ártur. Each person serves in their own way, religious vows are not required. Why have you decided upon this path?"

For many minutes, the prince was silent. Others had asked him the same question, and he had always answered defensively as if knowing they were trying to talk him out of his decision. He did not think Kavan was trying to do likewise, however, thus he had to give his answer careful consideration.

"I want to serve k'Ádhá. It is not a disgraceful occupation for a prince. There is much I could learn and…" He paused to look at the tapestry but did not complete his sentence. "I dreamed about Saint

Kóráhm the other night. He was at the foot of my bed, trying to tell me something, but I could not hear his words."

"When was this?" To his knowledge, the prince had never dreamed of the Heretic-Saint before.

"The night of the break-in…the night you were injured. It was the first time I…and he seemed real. Then last night I saw him again; this time, though I still could not hear him, I know he uttered the word father…"

"Father? What has…?"

The healer came into the room, smiling as he entered to see his cousin awake and looking better. "I did hear voices. I thought I said…"

Though he was teasing, Muir looked chastised and crestfallen, and Kavan said, "I invited him in, cousin. I have had enough bed rest. The pain is nearly gone. I feel well enough to fly." He stopped abruptly as though he had forgotten Muir was in the room before speaking. The healer was about to say something, but the prince, who was staring at Kavan with incredulous confusion, interrupted.

"Fly? Men cannot fly…"

After a quick visual exchange with Ártur, Kavan sighed and said, "Go and let Ártur do whatever he has come to do. Perhaps tomorrow, if Ártur will let me out of bed, we will discuss it further."

The prince did not complain about being expelled from the room; he was too intrigued and puzzled by Kavan's mention of flying, and too concerned about the bard's welfare to keep the healer from his work. Ártur looked exasperated but did not chastise his cousin as he placed both hands on Kavan's chest and closed his eyes. Kavan did not speak until the examination was complete and Ártur drew back. "I did not mean…"

"Such an indiscretion is not like you, Kavan. You are the one most apprehensive of what people will think of what you can do. Very few Teren know that is possible, and even fewer believe it…"

"sínréc." The healer stopped and they stared at each other. "I have been hoping to show him. He is going to leave Rhidam soon; if he does not enter the prelacy, he may simply run away. I want to share what I am in the time I have left with him. He would never betray me. You know what he means to me. Can you blame me for wanting that bond with him?"

Ártur stomach knotted with a twinge of jealous apprehension as if the prince could somehow come between them. He bit his lip, took a breath, and released it slowly. "I suppose not. But I hope you are careful if you go out tomorrow. Arlan is not likely to allow either of you out of the grounds without guards, not after recent events."

Those words told Kavan what he had been hoping not to hear and his gaze fell. "The boys have not been found?"

"No. The grounds have been searched but there is still no trace of them. We hope that they may have gone hunting with Caol, but we will not know until he returns. In the meantime…"

"Hunting? Caol has gone hunting?"

His vision blurred and before his eyes a wooded grove formed, still and empty except for the stain of blood upon the spring grass. Shaking his head to clear it, he met Ártur's gaze, the healer knowing from the momentary distance in his cousin's eyes that the bard had Seen something. He also knew, from the distress on Kavan's face, that it was not good. "What? What is it?"

"Hangman's Grove…blood on the ground…but no one was there…I could not hear anything…"

Exasperated, Ártur squawked, "That could mean anything Kavan!"

"I see what I am meant to see…you know that. I believe it is connected to this hunting trip…but whether it is connected to the boys…what it might mean…I can only speculate."

"I will tell Guthrie to have someone search the grove. If there is anything there, I pray they find it. And you…" He looked his cousin over affectionately, "If you will stay in this room and rest for the remainder of the day, I will allow you to return to your activities tomorrow. Is that satisfactory?"

"It will have to be, won't it?" His faint smile undermined the sarcasm in his words. As much as he disliked being confined in his room, being under his cousin's care meant he did not have to face a castle full of concerned and curious faces and questions. It was a tradeoff Kavan was willing to make in such instances.

"Good. I will have dinner sent up to you soon."

❧*❧

Caol was not prepared for the chaos he encountered when he returned to the castle, nor was he prepared for the flurry of people who surrounded him with questions and concerns. He, Elotti, and the physician Rouvyn had ridden in broadening circles from the point where the children had disappeared, but there was no indication outside of Hangman's Grove that Halstatt had passed. Elotti had stopped twice in Rhidam to send word to his various contacts in the hopes of tracking Halstatt that way. But such contacts and leads could take days to produce results; as the sun began to edge lower in the west, Caol's only recourse was to return home to face his wife and his best friend.

Fortunately, Elotti's menacing presence deterred most of those who would have hounded Caol for answers, but it could not stop Guthrie who was in the courtyard as the trio rode across the bridge.

"Caol, have you seen Wilred and Bertram?" Caol looked sick and faint as he slid from the horse and collapsed when his injured leg refused to hold him. "Good word, man! What happened to you? Who are these men?"

"I was hunting…" he started.

"I know that…"

Elotti growled. "Will you let him finish?" The venador and chamberlain glared at each other, but Caol spoke quickly before the tension could explode into a fight.

"Before I could meet with my…I was attacked…bandits…led by the same fellow who broke into the castle, I believe. He had the same voice. I did not know the boys were following me until Wilred came out of the brush…trying to warn me…they…I could not stop them." He sagged in Rouvyn's arms as the physician tried to help him stand.

Elotti added, "What he is trying to say is the bandits have taken the children."

Turning sharply to glare at the larger man, Guthrie barked, "Who is this man, Lord Dugan?" He was tired of a stranger interrupting their conversation.

"Wace Elotti." Caol's voice was small and weak.

Guthrie inhaled sharply, started to speak, and then snapped his mouth shut. Though he had never met nor seen the man, he knew the name, the venador's reputation, and knew that like many in his caste who made their living off of hunting other men, Wace was a man who always accomplished what he set out to do. The chamberlain was impressed by that, as well as by the man's stature, apparent even while astride a horse. But he was not intimidated.

"He and his…friend…found me…I knew who he was…I hired him to find…"

"The King did not agree to…"

"No matter," Elotti interrupted again with a stiff, cold air. "From the description Lord Dugan supplied, one of the individuals who assaulted him is likely someone I have been tracking. He is wanted for crimes in Neth and Cordash. I am being paid handsomely for his capture; if I require more funds, Lord Dugan has agreed to pay me from his own purse. Your king does not need to hire me; I will stop this man regardless and find the boys. I brought Lord Dugan back to

Rhidam because he was in no condition to walk far on his own. Come, Rouvyn. Lord Dugan, I will be in touch."

Caol did not respond to the almost smirk on Elotti's face. If Guthrie had not offered to support him as Rouvyn mounted his horse, Caol would have fallen to the ground. The chamberlain helped him to the door, past others who wanted to question him, as the venador and physician rode out through the gate.

"Arlan is not going to like this one damned bit," the chamberlain muttered bitterly to himself.

"If I had known they were following me, I would have sent them home…or at least protected them…" He should have taken them to their room during the night, roused Bertram's guards, made sure they were attended the way the King had commanded…but he had not. His failure had enabled the boys to sneak out after him, and his failure to realize they were there had allowed Halstatt to take them. Caol blamed no one but himself.

"No one is blaming you, Caol." At least, Guthrie was not. Like many in the castle, he knew how headstrong Prince Bertram could be and knew from experience that the younger boy would follow him anywhere.

You would if you knew the truth, Caol thought, his jaw thankfully tight and unmoving. He did not have the courage to be truthful.

The chamberlain called to two idle soldiers. "Dervis, take Lord Dugan to his room. Tedor, please see that one of the healers attends him immediately."

Dreading what came next, Caol asked, "What are you going to do?"

Guthrie waved his hand dismissively. "I must report to the King; we have to decide what to do next."

Caol wisely did not attempt, or consider, arguing, even though telling Arlan that his son had been kidnapped was the last thing he wanted to do.

The chamberlain found the King in the stateroom, nursing a glistening silver goblet of something, studying a map of the Neth-Enesfel border. It was an effort to distract himself from problems he could do nothing about. He looked up from the map as Guthrie entered, long enough to see who it was.

"Oh, good, Guthrie. Perhaps you can give me some suggestions."

"I do not think this is a good time, My Liege…I have come with news regarding Prince Bertram and Prince Wilred…"

Attention diverted, the King looked up, eyes eager for good news. "Ber…out with it. Where are they? Are they here? Safe?"

The chamberlain did his best to stay steady, despite being the bearer of bad news. "Unfortunately, no…he and Wilred took it upon themselves to follow Caol on his hunting expedition…unbeknownst to Caol. He was ambushed by a band of ruffians, led by the same man who entered the palace the other night. During the scuffle, the bandits discovered the children at the same time Caol learned they were there…they have taken the boys. Caol was injured during the confrontation and was unable to mount pursuit…"

The King's face went from white to vivid red and then back again in the span of a few seconds; it took him great effort to find his voice. "Send out a search party, comb the city…the country…post a reward…"

"Milord…" The King stopped. "A search party would be unproductive, I fear; Caol has people looking but we have no idea where the boys have been taken…"

"They could be dead!"

The chamberlain sighed. "Unlikely. The kidnappers must know who they have, and thus will likely seek a ransom; to injure their captives would not be to their benefit. Besides," he coughed nervously, something he did not normally do, "thanks to Caol, we have the best venador in the Five Sovereignties working on this." The King's eyes narrowed. "You have heard of Wace Elotti?"

"The Cíbhóló venador? Who has not heard of him? Justice Cornell mentions him every time someone goes missing or a criminal escapes. How did Caol ever meet up with him?" The man was known to have traveled most of the Sovereignties; it seemed a peculiar twist of fate that the infamous hunter happened to be in Rhidam just when the Crown could use his services. It was no wonder some authorities accused Elotti, and other men like him, of perpetrating the crimes they solved to extort money from the wealthy.

"Elotti found him injured and brought him back to Rhidam. Seems our burglar, or one of his cohorts, is wanted in Neth and Cordash, and Elotti tailed him to Rhidam. If anyone can find the boys, he can."

The King sank into his chair, stroking his beard, tracing the smooth scar that marred his face with his fingertips. Following a criminal from elsewhere into Rhidam might have been legitimate; Elotti had a reputation after all, but Arlan was not willing to give anyone the benefit of the doubt when it came to the safety of his son. "I would feel much better if we had some of our own men on this. But I do not know whom I can spare. Neth and Cordash appear to be on the brink of war and our help has been requested if it comes. Our troops are green. If we go to war, I am going to need our best minds to keep us ahead of Neth. I have sent word to King Geir, but he is likely as short of troops as always. I do not expect much help from him. What do you think, Guthrie? Can we trust this hunter? Is this a fight we can win? You were my father's general…and Donal's…"

"I do not wish to go into battle again," the chamberlain said evasively.

Arlan shook his head. "I am not asking that of you unless the situation turns desperately grave. But will you at least command the armies from here? Will you put your knowledge of tactics and warfare into service for me one last time? Will you help me arrange a division of labor that will enable me to find my son?"

Sighing, Guthrie gave in. He loved Arlan as he would have a son, and he had loved Arlan's father equally. He could not deny the King's request. "First thing…all we can do for the children tonight is continue looking, wait for a ransom request, hope that Wace Elotti lives up to his reputation, and pray. I am following a lead that Ártur gave me, something he learned from Kavan, and I will tell Justice Cornell what we know. He will direct his men accordingly. I will dwell on the situation with Neth overnight and present solutions in the morning." He placed his hand on the other man's shoulder, one of the few close enough to the King to be allowed that sort of intimate gesture. "I cannot tell you not to worry, Arlan, but I can offer you one piece of advice."

"What is that?" The King's voice teetered on the edge of exhaustion and despair.

"Tell Kavan what is happening and place the matter in his hands. If k'Ádhá will listen to anyone's prayers, it will be Kavan."

## ❧Chapter 18❦

The thick haze of cold fog wove between the trees that formed the walls of Hangman's Grove. It was not yet dawn and there were no birds or animals nearby that he could hear. He had been in this place more times than he could recall throughout his life and found it much less menacing now than it was when filled with people here to witness an execution. He could identify the exact trees where men had gasped their last breaths, and if he tried, he could recall many of those swinging faces. Those memories had not faded over the years as others had, even though this place had not been used for executions in years. He regretted having walked to the clearing instead of riding; he had not considered how long the trek would be on this cold morning. Breaking into the clearing, he paused to catch his breath.

It was not difficult to locate the site of the scuffle. There were loosed clods of earth and grass, the long skid marks of dug in heels, and the dark stain of Caol's blood marring the ground where he had been told it would be. Caol had conceded, when pressed, that the attack had occurred in Hangman's Grove, although Guthrie found his tale of meeting a friend here to be suspect. He supposed it was a landmark that those unfamiliar with Rhidam and its surroundings would be able to find, and the forests around it teemed with prey that only those with a dispensation from the King were allowed to hunt, but it seemed to be an odd place for a meeting between friends. Squatting, Guthrie held his lantern nearer to inspect the scene more closely, but it told him nothing of consequence. He stood, rolled his head from side to side to relieve the stiffness in his neck, and wiped a gloved hand across his face.

A glint of light reflecting in the grass pulled him several feet away from the scuffle sight. A knife, one of high-quality workmanship with a finely carved oak hilt, lay discarded in the mud. Unusual for a fighting knife to have a wooden hilt; surely it would make it simpler to trace the owner. As he recalled, Captain Delamo's attacker had wielded a wood handled knife. And, he noted, the design of it matched the short sword Caol had given him yesterday, the weapon that had been driven into his leg. All the better, Guthrie thought. It meant that Caol was likely right; this must be the same man who had broken into the castle. Guthrie shoved the knife through his belt and continued his investigation.

By the time the sun had risen enough that the lantern was no longer necessary, Guthrie had learned little more of importance. He found scuff marks on a tree, broken branches on some bramble bushes, horse tracks, and the path of a large animal moving through the foliage. That someone had ambushed someone from that tree he had no doubt. But if, as Kavan had Seen and Caol had indicated, this was the sight of the abduction of the princes, there were too many things that did not quite add up in the chamberlain's mind. He was not sure, however, what they meant.

ও*৻

There had been a time fifteen years ago when Arlan would never have imagined himself involved in such intrigue. Of course, fifteen years ago, he had little idea or hope that he would ever return to

Rhidam, no belief that he would ever become king of Enesfel. All of that had changed thanks to the Elyri bard whom he considered his truest friend. But under such trying circumstances, he felt alone with his fears and doubts because, as Kavan rightly pointed out, Arlan was the king. It was his decisions that determined the fate of men and no amount of counseling from anyone, including Kavan, could be blamed for the choices the king made. Success was shared amongst those who advised and assisted him. Blame was entirely his own.

He rarely regretted his decision to take the throne. The people loved him and he enjoyed the rank, privileges and the responsibilities. If he had not claimed his rightful heritage, Owain Lachlan might still be king. Perhaps, with time, Owain would have adjusted to his role and become the sort of King Enesfel needed, but time was one thing the land had not had, and the people had not been willing to give. It still troubled Arlan that Owain had surrendered so easily that night, and he often wondered what had caused Owain to renounce legal claims to the Enesfel throne with so little final effort. It had not been cowardice. This had been something more. Kavan knew the reasons, as did Guthrie it seemed, but neither had ever shared that secret with their King. He did not even know what had become of Owain in the years since. But Arlan did not particularly care, either. As long as he did not have to see that man ever again, he would be content.

Today, however, as he tried to relax in the morning room sipping a glass of honeyed nectar, watching the sunrise, he did regret his decision to take the throne. He could have remained within Elyriá's safe borders and lived a full, happy life with Brenna and their children. Brenna, perhaps, might still have died too soon, but if Arlan had not become king, Bertram would certainly be safe and Arlan would not be concerned with the complexities of another war.

The war that had brought him to this day, the war that had given him the crown, had seemed like a game, albeit a serious one, a crusade against injustice, a noble cause. A war with Neth, a kingdom historically violent and scheming, was different. Neth had thus far done nothing to directly gain Enesfel's wrath, but Arlan could not remain idle while Cordash faced this threat, even if Cordash did currently have the strongest military in the Sovereignties. A Neth victory would end the stability and peace of the entire region. Even King Geir of Hatu would offer whatever resources he could spare, and Hatu was the least threatened by Neth's activities. Arlan had already made the request for troops the day after the carnival when Guthrie had smelled war in the offing. King Arlan had seen no alternative but action.

A small knock sounded on the door behind him. Princess Diona's expression was sullen and fearful as she asked, "Am I disturbing you, Father?"

"Certainly not. Come here." She climbed into his lap without speaking. She did not need to; her father knew precisely what was troubling her. "Bertram and Wilred will be fine, Diona. They will be home soon."

"When?"

He brushed her hair from her eyes. "As soon as we find where they have gone."

"Don't you mean as soon as you find where they have been taken?" When he did not reply to her blunt question, she looked into his face apologetically. "Muir and I kept telling Wilred not to do everything Bertram tells him…"

Arlan's sharp expression silenced her. He was used to her directness, but today it stung. "Did you know they were going to do this? That they were going to follow Caol hunting?"

"No, sir…but Wilred would not have done it on his own. He is not that…brave."

The King gently pushed his daughter from his lap and went to the window. He did not want to admit that she was right, but he knew she was. Wilred was bright and could be scheming, but not particularly daring. He might come up with ideas for mischief, but he lacked the initiative and courage to follow through on such plans. And he often gave in to Bertram's bullying and persuasion, whereas neither Muir nor Diona did. Wilred was a follower, not a leader, and Bertram was one to take advantage of that quality to the fullest.

"Father?"

Her tiny, forlorn voice made him look over his shoulder at her. None of this was his daughter's fault. There was no use in punishing her with his silence and distress. "Yes?"

"May I stay and watch court business today? Lady MacLyr is tending the babies, Lord MacLyr is caring for Uncle Caol, and Lord Cliáth is taking Muir out. Even Lady Ilene is away. There is no one to play with."

Arlan lifted her onto his hip, barely noticing her slight weight. Winding his hand in her dark hair he replied, "There will not be much court business today, but let me suggest this. I will read with you for a time, and then I shall have Lady Alba teach you to needlepoint."

The princess rolled her eyes. "Must I?" She might have looked dainty and feminine but she was not the most lady-like girl Arlan had ever known. Perhaps because she had grown up surrounded by boys, even though her mother had tried to steer her differently. Perhaps, he realized, he should find other girls for her to associate with the way Deidre had grown up with Brenna at her side.

"Your mother would want you to learn. Since she cannot teach you, I will have someone else teach you. Please do it for her, if not for me."

She sighed and said, "Very well. I will learn it for her. Now, what shall we read?"

Her father managed a weak smile and walked hand in hand with her to the library, grateful for the distraction from the day's worries.

❧ * ❦

Bitterly, Princess Deidre wiped away her tears and stalked from the room, leaving Caol lying in bed, facing away from her. He had refused to speak to her or acknowledge her presence since he had returned yesterday, even when she asked about Wilred. His response was a sick expression given before he turned away. Syl tried to assure the princess that his injury and the guilt he felt over what had happened were causing him to withdraw, that he was not trying to be insensitive to his wife's feelings. Perhaps, Deidre thought, but she was not convinced. She was Wilred's mother; she had the right to know what had happened to him. She had heard the story from Ártur, who had heard it from Guthrie, but she wanted to hear it from her husband. Whatever his tale, she would see things in his face that they, most likely, would not.

In the back garden, she sank down upon a stone bench, sobbing, and casting longing glances at Brenna Lachlan's final resting place. She had envied her friend's ability to hear her children cry; now all she wanted was to see her child again. Caol had not wanted children, though she had never understood why. He had finally relented to her persuasions and the result had been Wilred. If she lost this child and he refused her another, she did not think she would ever forgive him.

But she loved him. That, she had never doubted. Even when she had been betrothed to Owain, when Caol had come to Rhidam as a man of little importance and kidnapped her for the sake of her brother and his followers, she had loved him. It had not given her the courage to break her engagement when she had been uncertain of her brother's success, but his daring roguish character had played a major part in her decision to support her brother's bid for the throne.

She wondered what had become of Owain after that night. It had been painful to watch him be pushed off the throne and she had been terrified that her brother would execute him. But something had passed between Guthrie McHador and Kavan that had kept that from happening and she still felt grateful to them for it. Because despite everything, she had loved Owain too. Not as deeply as she had come to love Caol, but she had loved him nonetheless, a secret she kept locked deep inside since the night her twin had become king of Enesfel.

❧*❧

Kavan's slender white mare and Muir's sturdy bay gelding trotted ahead of their three attendants. Conveniently, Wortham was among them, partially at Kavan's insistence he knew. Gabrielle Dilyn had originally sent him and his compatriots in Kavan's employment until they could be placed directly under King Arlan's command, but Wortham had continued to consider himself Kavan's man, despite the bard's periodic attempts to convince him otherwise. And because Kavan requested Wortham's services whenever he had need of an attending guard, it was clear that the bard favored him too. The captain was intuitive enough to know that a private excursion shared by Kavan and Prince Muir might not be a typical jaunt in the countryside; though he rode behind his two charges, he was more alert than usual, wanting nothing to happen that should not. Nor did he want to miss any detail that might make this day a memorable one.

They traveled at a leisurely pace a couple hours north of Rhidam, past the peasants and farmers who toiled in the fertile black fields. When they passed all signs of inhabitation, Kavan slowed the pace further, watching around them as if seeking something specific. Finally, he reined in his horse and slid from her back beneath the shade of a cluster of ancient trees. The landscape here was open, with no significant obstacles to hide enemies. The area appeared safe enough, though Wortham still commanded his fellow soldiers to search the nearby vicinity thoroughly to give him peace of mind.

Harp in hand, Kavan sat with his back against the oak's trunk and strummed soft melodies as the guards searched, satisfied themselves with their security, and then returned to share the noon meal, which Muir had quickly, silently, readied for them. The prince felt no need for them to serve him. He was satisfied to treat them as equals and friends. Despite their duty to guard, the three men accepted what was offered and took a position a respectable distance away, allowing the prince and his tutor as much privacy as could be afforded.

"Are you certain you do not want any?" the prince asked as he uncorked the wine bottle. "Káliel's finest burgundy."

"Does Arlan know you have that?" Kavan countered.

Muir shrugged. "I got it from Captain Delamo, not...do you want any or not?" He was already filling his own tin cup.

"No, thank you."

"Why not?" He secured the cup on the ground to keep it from tipping and corked the bottle. "I have never seen you drink wine. You do not know what you are missing."

"Yes," the bard sighed, "I do. Do you remember the day when you could not wake me?"

"Mmmhmm," came the reply, mumbled over the edge of the cup.

Kavan watched him tip it back and drink. "I drank one glass of wine...a rather large glass, I might add."

The prince choked on his drink and stared as if he could not believe what he heard. He knew that some people could drink more than others, but he could not imagine anyone passing out after a single glass of wine. It took every effort not to laugh, but seeing that Kavan was quite serious, he swallowed his amusement along with a mouthful of wine.

Kavan continued. "Elyri cannot tolerate much alcohol. One glass of anything stronger than wine can kill us. I have heard of it happening, though I have never seen it. Thus we do not drink..." He took the wine bottle from the prince, passed it under his nose to smell it, and added, "Usually, that is."

Instead of saying something inappropriate, Muir took another long swallow and looked away. Kavan saw no indication that the prince understood the depth of trust it took to reveal that bit of information. Instead, the young man got to his feet and returned with something from his horse's pack. He held the large object forth to Kavan, but the bard did not take it.

"There is no occasion…"

He had intended to give his gift to Kavan today anyhow, but after the bard's words, the prince felt like he should give something in return. He had no deep, hidden secrets to reveal, but he could give this. "Do I need an occasion, Lord Harper? I found this at the festival and thought you should have it. You were not there to purchase it for yourself; I did it for you. Will you take it, or must I throw it at you?" He laughed at Kavan's perplexed expression but the bard took it at last, though he did nothing more as Muir sat. "Open it."

The stiff waxed canvas felt smooth beneath his fingers as he took the contents from its leather pouch. As he pulled back the folds to reveal the treasure inside, Kavan realized his hands were shaking. His breath caught and he cast an incredulous glance at the prince before studying the book closer. "My prince…"

"Do you like it?"

The works of St. Kóráhm, written in High Elyri, leather-bound, embossed and illustrated, a work that was surely several centuries old. It was not the Heretic-Saint's own writings, but it was still a magnificent treasure, something that had somehow escaped the destructive fires of the prelacy, and Kavan could not have dreamed of such a work if he had tried. Tracing the gold lettering on its cover, he managed to whisper. "How could I not?"

"I thought you would," the prince said with a smile. He continued watching Kavan study the book. "I doubt the seller knew what he had…except that it was old and expensively made. I do not know what it is exactly, but I recognized his name, and from the illustrations, I assumed it must be some sort of biography, is that correct?"

The bard nodded, taking a bite of the cold roast beef they had brought and then wiping his fingers clean before gently turning the delicate pages. Muir watched his jaw move, marveling that even that simple action filled him with warmth, awe, and joy. If such scrutiny disturbed the bard, he did not show it. He did not even seem to notice.

Many quiet mouthfuls later, the prince asked, "Do you think my dreams about Saint Kóráhm mean something?"

Looking up from the books, Kavan replied, "They might not have been dreams, my prince. Not the way you describe them. He might actually have been there with you. He came to me the night of the break-in too."

"But how do I know?" Muir scowled. "How could you be sure it was Saint Kóráhm? How do I know what it means? I could not hear what he was saying, but I swear he was speaking to me…"

"The first time I saw him, I did not know who he was. Now, when he comes, in whatever guise he chooses, I know it is him. Perhaps it is a matter of faith, or of recognition, or some connection to him that I do not understand. Do not concern yourself with whether it was a dream. Dreams can be as important as a visitation. That is not the main issue. As for the meaning, since you could not hear his words, I cannot offer much assistance, but I suspect when it is important for you to know, you will know."

"You are a lot of help." The bard noted the teasing tone with a raised eyebrow. The meal lapsed into silence again, Kavan's attention back on the book while the prince watched Captain Delamo stare absently at the horizon. "The King allowed us out today because he wants you to talk me out of becoming gdhededhá, didn't he?"

Meeting the young man's gaze, Kavan closed the book and pushed the hair from his eyes. "Do you expect me to try?"

"If he asked you to, as I am certain he must have, then you would because he asked it. He is your friend, and he is the king."

A faint flicker of amusement crossed Kavan's face. "You do not know me as well as you think you do, my prince."

"You mean you are not going to try?"

Kavan shrugged. "I agreed to test your conviction. It is not my place to decide what course your life should take. It is your life, your choices to make, your mistakes to make, to learn from, and live with."

"Then you do think I am making a mistake," snorted the prince.

The bard would not be put off by either annoyance or attitude. "Am I correct that this idea of entering the prelacy came to mind after you witnessed the healing of Wortham's sight?" The prince nodded. "How many days ago was that?"

"Six."

"Six days to consider the implications of your choice. Perhaps the prelacy is your destiny, but such a brash, abrupt decision could also be a mistake. You are...you have recently lost your mother. You are unhappy and wish to leave the painful life you have known behind. And you have witnessed an event of profound spiritual significance."

"A miracle."

Kavan reluctantly agreed. "A miracle. Thus, you have decided that this resurgence of faith must be acted upon, that the prelacy is the tonic that will remove the ills from your life, erase your trials, tribulations, and sorrow. Being gdhededhá is not an escape from life, Muir; it is a commitment of faith. Are you certain this is what k'Ádhá wants?"

A long, awkward silence was the only response he received but it was enough to tell Kavan the truth. "I once contemplated entering the prelacy, and though the idea reoccurred sporadically for a few years, I was never convinced it was the right path for me. Now I know it was not. The prelacy in Elyriá is a tricky thing. The gdhededhá are respected and revered for what they are called to do, but there is often an undercurrent of disdain. If, as many Teren believe, we are inherently evil for the things we can do, then any of us serving as gdhededhá is a hypocrite of the worst kind. In Elyriá, it takes great conviction to enter the prelacy. I did not have it. I ask too many questions…carry too many doubts. If I had entered the Faith that way…Arlan might not be king and I would certainly not be sitting here with you." The affection in his eyes was genuine. "It may or may not be the same for you. If it is the path you are meant to pursue, you will know. I am asking that you give yourself that time to think the choice through completely, that is all."

"How long?" the prince murmured, feeling deflated of purpose beneath those words.

"Until you are either certain that it is what you want or you know it is not. It might be to your benefit to speak to the k'ghededhá or one of the others about this. They can answer your questions and may allow you to assist as an altar attendant to give you a taste of what the prelacy entails. Will you do that?"

Grinning despite his disappointment, the prince stretched back upon the ground and asked, "Lord Cliáth, has anyone ever told you that you are very persuasive?"

"Ártur tells me that often…and the King frequently agrees."

The prince laughed. "That does not surprise me. I promise to think about the matter further…until I am certain, as you say, and I will talk to k'dedhá Jermyn as soon as he is available. There is one condition, however."

Knowing that the prince was teasing, though still nervous about what the young man would request of him, he asked, "That is?"

"I wish to nap. If you will play for me, I will do as you ask."

Kavan sighed in relief. "A simple and pleasurable request, my prince."

The quarter-scale black harp lay at Kavan's side, waiting for the white hands of its lover to stroke it to life. As the brass strings brought forth an impromptu medley of several of Kavan's compositions,

Wortham turned his attention more towards Kavan than it had been. Within minutes, the prince was lulled to sleep, but rather than allow the strings to fall silent, the bard continued to pluck and strum absently. By evening he knew he would have at least one new work to add to his vast repertoire. Tonight, he would read.

ᚼ*ᚼ

Not for the first time, k'gdhededhá Jermyn wished for the lost luxury of passing through the streets without the company of either of his fellow clergy or his personal guards. Once, years ago, Jermyn had been anonymous enough that few remembered his name, and few were affected by his words it had seemed. It was his association with the White Bard and the act of becoming k'gdhededhá of Enesfel that caused people to take him seriously at last. People constantly showered him with attention, or at the very least demanded attention from him, and privacy was a luxury he rarely experienced.

Beside him, gdhededhá Claide, the other Teren clergyman in Rhidam, was chirping with excitement about something he had recently read as they returned to Hes á Redh Náós from a morning of administering to Rhidam's sick and infirm. It was his way, Jermyn knew, of erasing the depression of a morning of facing the ill and dying. Claide's nasal, reedy voice irritated Jermyn, today more than usual. Of course, neither Claide nor the Elyri gdhededhá Tusánt had been told about the missing boys yet, and therefore Claide had no reason, beyond the morning's duties, to be glum. Still, it took a great force of willpower to keep Jermyn from quieting the other man.

There was the matter of the picture he had seen, the drawing of a man said to be Captain Delamo's attacker and Lísbhet Dilyn's killer. The k'gdhededhá had seen that face before, but he could not recall where or when. He was searching his memories for that detail, hoping that if he remembered it might somehow aid in the search for the missing boys.

Something Tusánt had confessed to him that morning had strengthened the need to remember. Someone had come to Tusánt in confession, claiming to have witnessed an attack on a beautiful woman on the náós grounds. Further questioning had led Tusánt to conclude that the woman had been Lady Dilyn and the attacker had been the man on the flyer. The parishioner had not told the authorities what he had seen for fear of retaliation and Tusánt had wanted Jermyn's reassurance that urging the person to go to the justice had been the right thing to do. He had absolved Tusánt for breaking the oath of confession, perhaps because Jermyn had been excited to learn something helpful. Now, however, the k'gdhededhá was saddled with the burden of either keeping silent or speaking out. If he spoke to the King, who would absolve him?

He abruptly stopped, listening to the sounds around him, his face skewed in concentration. It took Claide several steps to realize he was walking alone; he turned back and asked, "What is it, Your Grace?"

"Do you hear that?"

The man cocked his head. "Hear what?"

"That sound…like a child crying. It sounds like…" He looked up at the curtained second-floor window of this particularly dilapidated building, trying to pinpoint what he was hearing. "It couldn't be…"

Still, Jermyn had spent enough years in Elyriá to know better than to ignore his intuition. Something about that sound, which had stopped now, had touched a nerve. Sending Claide back to the náós alone, Jermyn headed for the castle instead, his two attendants immediately behind him.

❧*❦

If Caol was aware of the comings and goings in his room, he gave no indication; he responded to nothing. He refused to acknowledge his wife when she sat by his side, holding his hand. The healers were forced to lift his head to feed him, and when the King came into the room all he got from his friend was a blank stare at the distant wall on the other side of the room. It was the Elyri's healing sense that told Ártur that Caol was aware, not in some sort of catatonic state. If he had thought it would be useful, Ártur would have attempted to probe the man's thoughts, but he saw no reason to doubt Caol's story, except that Kavan insisted upon being the first to speak to the inquisitor when the man decided to talk. If Kavan wanted to speak to Caol, then there was something everyone else was missing. The bard was not going to reveal his reasoning, however; the healer could only relent and maintain his vigil.

And Caol knew it. He had heard the healer and bard discussing it before Kavan left with Prince Muir that morning. If his leg did not continue to ache, if he had not been under constant surveillance since his return to the castle, he would have bolted from the keep and stayed away until he had the boys safely in his care. He had to escape the questions and Deidre's accusing eyes. The children were gone and it was his fault…even if no one else believed it.

❧*❧

In the coolness of the third-floor day room, with the windows open and the day's breeze filling the space with the fragrances of the world outside, Princess Deidre paced. Other than the library, this was her favorite room in the castle. It was brightly lit, posh, and generally empty except for when the children were playing. But today there were no children here. Of the four, only Princess Diona was home, and Deidre had not seen the girl all day.

She had been surprised when Guthrie requested an audience with her rather than with her brother or her husband. Despite the years they had lived beneath this roof, and the fond memories she had of her childhood, his presence continued to strike a note of fear in her. He was a legend, a relic from the world of her mother and father, from a time so long ago it seemed to have been another lifetime. He never did anything to frighten her, but she was rarely comfortable with him nonetheless.

His expression, when they met, had been contemplative, though otherwise blank, but he had brought no news of the boys. Unlike other times, however, it had been his questions, not merely his presence, which had given birth to her fears.

While the chamberlain had not voiced opinions, his questions had revealed doubts that mirrored her own. Who had Caol been going to meet that day and why? Had this friend come to the castle to see him when they failed to meet for their hunt? Had Caol ever mentioned the name Wace Elotti before? Most of the questions she had been unable to answer to the chamberlain's satisfaction, but by the end of their discourse, the princess was more certain that her husband was not telling the truth. And she believed, from things Guthrie did not say, that whoever had her son's life in their hands was far more dangerous than any pack of common bandits could be.

☙*❧

The dingy upstairs apartment was vacant when the justice arrived and secured permission from the owner to search it. Though it was dusty and untidy, the scuff marks in the grime and the smell of cooked meat lingered in the room, all too fresh to have been there long. A half-eaten wheel of moldy white cheese was haphazardly wrapped and set on the wobbly bedside stand. Red wine stained the table, still damp in places, and the bedclothes were rumpled as if recently slept in. The rusty washbasin bore a small pool of water from recent use. There was no evidence of a rush to vacate, which led the justice to conclude that either the occupant had left some time ago or there had been very few belongings to take. Either would make a search of the room a relatively short and simple task.

He was grateful that the k'gdhededhá remained in the doorway talking soothingly to the agitated owner, keeping the man from interfering. Minos wanted no clumsy, inexperienced helpers to mar whatever evidence remained. He was able to conduct his investigation without interruption.

But there was little to find. The occupant had been a man named Malizar Caliph, of Cordash, a private, quiet man the owner rarely saw. He had seen no children with Caliph, nor could he recall having heard any. The justice found two gold malcs in the folds of the bedclothes, but while it supported Elotti's claims that the man they were seeking had spent time in Neth, there was no way to tell how long the coins had been in this room or who had lost them.

Correction, he thought with a grunt, pocketing the coins. Perhaps the Elyri could learn something useful from them. It was worth a try.

There were smudges in the dust on the windowsill and a clay jar of a black greasy substance he guessed to be make-up, a substance and jar similar to what was found near the castle the night the intruder had broken in. Wanting to compare the two jars, he took that too. His other discovery, however, seemed to support the k'gdhededhá's claim and gave the justice the first small ray of hope. It was a boy's cap. There had been a child here at some point. He met the k'gdhededhá's gaze and nodded. After ordering that the room remain vacant until further notice, and paying the owner handsomely to ensure cooperation, Justice Cornell stalked from the building. Jermyn did not question him and had the good sense to return to the náós rather than follow the soldier to the keep, though he was dying to know what the justice had determined. From the look they shared, the k'gdhededhá believed they had concluded, and were hoping for, the same thing.

## ❧Chapter 19❧

Wortham felt sleepy beneath the warmth of the mid-afternoon sun as he listened to the song Kavan was perfecting. To his left, the other two guards dozed, and Prince Muir had fallen asleep over an hour ago. It was inappropriate for soldiers to sleep while on duty, but try as he did, Wortham was unable to wake them. Sensing his bewilderment and frustration, Kavan caught his attention with an almost impish twinkle in his eyes. Ah, the captain realized, relaxing but refusing to sleep. This slumber was somehow the Elyri's doing. He got up, dusted off his trousers, and came to squat at Kavan's side.

"There is a reason you want us to sleep, milord?"

Kavan set the harp in its case. "Not everyone...just them." He indicated the two sentries with a tilt of his head. "I promised Muir...well, you shall see soon enough. I thought it best they not witness what transpires."

"You do not care that I do?"

"Wortham," he sighed affectionately as the prince, no longer lulled by music, began to stir, "You know I trust you with my life. If I thought you would betray me...besides, this will not be entirely new to you."

Prince Muir yawned, stretched and rolled onto his side to face the two men. "What will not be entirely new to him, Lord Cliáth?" he asked, unconcerned that he might be interrupting a private conversation.

The question was sidestepped with ones of his own. "Did you rest well, my prince? Do you require refreshment?"

"No, Lord Harper…I am fine and you are avoiding my question."

"Did you consider the conversation might not concern you?" Kavan chided. The prince frowned and looked away, chastised and embarrassed. Instead of saying more, Kavan stood, went to his horse's pack and brought out three small, leather, sawdust filled balls, the sort sometimes used to train falcons and hunting dogs, from his bag. "I made you a promise for today, did I not?"

Relieved that his mistake did not have lasting repercussions, the young man scrambled to his feet. "You said something about flying," he began as the balls were placed into his hands. "What did you mean? Did you mean flight as in leaving Rhidam?" He prayed that was not the case, that Kavan had not brought him here to say goodbye.

"If I show you, you must swear to me that you will never speak of it to anyone, not even your sister."

It was the sort of serious request Kavan rarely asked of people, and it made the prince aware of the gravity of whatever Kavan was about to share with him. Nodding his head, he replied somberly, "I swear, Lord Cliáth, I will never speak of our time together this day to anyone if that is your wish."

Believing the prince took much of the weight off the bard's shoulders. He was still wary of the young man's reaction, but it was a risk he was willing to take. "Wortham, if you will slowly count to three. On three, I want you to throw one of these as high into the air as you can, Muir. Watch what happens. After that, I will leave it to you to decide what to do with the other two." His eyes closed; he drove all thought from his mind and willed his body to relax, and murmured, "Wortham…when you are ready."

The captain began his count, paying more attention to the balls than to Kavan. On three, he and Muir watched the largest ball fly high into the air, expecting it to transform into something else. Both were equally startled to see a snowy white kestrel dart after the ball, catch it deftly in its talons, and drop it to the ground at the prince's feet. The bird circled above them until Wortham, more intuitive than anyone when it came to the bard, and more familiar with his abilities, held out his arm. The kestrel landed easily and gripped into the man's leather gauntlet to remain steady.

"Kavan, where did…" But when he turned, the prince saw that the Elyri bard no longer stood beside him.

The kestrel screeched and Wortham grinned. He had forgotten about this particular ability of Kavan's but one look into the bird's green eyes was all it took to know the truth. "He is here, Prince Muir."

The prince drew closer and the bird screeched again. "That cannot be…" he started. The kestrel hopped to the ground, and with a shimmer in the air around them, Kavan reappeared, sitting on the ground as comfortably as if he had been there all along.

Muir could not recall ever seeing Kavan look so amused, likely at the shock on the young man's face. "You look skeptical, my prince. It is called raigháthá…the taking of another life shape. About a third of all Elyri can do it, though most refuse even if they know how. It is one of my few vices." Not a vice, perhaps, but it was the one gift he treasured above all others, the one he practiced at every available opportunity, especially if it meant flying.

Still wide-eyed, Muir stared at him as he struggled to grasp the ramifications of such an ability. "You can do that whenever you want? Be anything you want?"

"As far as any living creature…I believe so, though I have never tried to be a water creature or another person. It is limited to creatures with which I am familiar. Wolves, ravens, cats, rats…" He chose not to mention the White Hart. That was a legend he preferred to leave alone. The Hart had disappeared the night Arlan reclaimed the throne. It had been seen only once since. "Kestrels are my favorite, however, as there is nothing else like flying."

"Would you do it again…please?" The prince wanted to see it this time, wanted to see how such a change could happen.

Kavan smiled.

This time the prince watched the bard, though he could not determine how Kavan accomplished such an extraordinary change. One moment he was there, standing beside Muir as usual, and the next moment he was gone, the white kestrel now in his place. Realizing he would never understand how the change was made, that he was not meant to, the prince threw two of the balls into the air and grinned as the kestrel shot into the sky and caught one ball in each claw. The third ball was thrown behind the bird, higher than the first; the kestrel had to spin backward to catch it in his beak. Muir laughed in delight. Spiraling to earth, the three balls were deposited into the prince's open hands before the kestrel pulled sharply skywards as if saying 'again'.

Games of catch had often been played with Wilred, Diona, Caol, and even Bhríd, but those games were nothing like this. To realize that Kavan was playing when he was customarily restrained made Muir feel warm and happy. It was the most delightful, deeply special experience he could imagine sharing with the bard. For Wortham, who knew how closely Elyri, especially this one, guarded their abilities, this was the consummate gesture of trust. He hoped the prince would come to realize that, once the joy of this outing had faded to memory.

Neither could truly appreciate nor comprehend, however, what this experience meant to Kavan. When he had shared this skill with Arlan and Guthrie, it had been a matter of necessity and survival. The King was his friend, deeply loved, but Kavan had never felt comfortable sharing such things with him, perhaps because on some level, Arlan was never comfortable with them. There had never been a reason to share with anyone else. To be able to trust a Teren in such a way, without fear of recrimination or rejection, was an act of ultimate freedom.

Kavan would gladly have continued for hours until exhaustion forced him to stop, but after nearly thirty minutes of their game, his superior kestrel eyesight caught a glimpse of a group of horsemen traveling towards them from the north. Even at this distance, there was something familiar about the lead rider, though the manner of dress the four men wore made Kavan uneasy. He let the uncaught balls fall to earth and flew towards the riders, wanting a closer look before he came to any conclusions about the prince's safety. If he had been capable of stopping mid-air, once he reached them, he would have done it. As it was, he slowed, circled the riders twice to be sure this was no manifestation or illusion, flying lower each time before returning swiftly to the prince's side, his heart thundering nervously.

Both Muir and Wortham started to follow the departing falcon, thinking this a new twist to the game. But the urgency of the bird's flight caused the captain to stop, huff with narrowed eyes, and then hasten to rouse the other soldiers. By the time the kestrel returned, the prince too had stopped following. The captain had obviously seen something with his experienced military eyes that warranted waking the others which meant it was wiser for the prince to stay where he was. Unlike his half-brother, Muir was not impertinent enough to look for trouble when there was no need for it. The kestrel descended behind the tree, out of sight of the waking attendants, and Kavan stepped around it, face flushed and perplexed.

"Captain Delamo," he ordered, automatically speaking more formally in the presence of the other soldiers. "Guard the prince." He grabbed his horse's reins and mounted.

"Milord…?"

"There are riders approaching…and I think it best I face them before they reach you here." There was a tight, nervous feeling in his belly and a certainty that it was imperative to the future of Enesfel, although he could not explain why he believed this. He dug his heels into the mare's flanks and galloped north, ignoring Muir's protests.

Once within sight of the riders, Kavan stopped his horse and forced himself to be calm. Blessed k'Ádhá, he thought, am I doing the right thing? These four were clearly from Neth, and Neth's hatred for Elyri was notorious. If his intuition proved faulty, he could easily be facing death. But the riders came with purpose, foreigners likely to obey the laws of the land they were in, and the fourth rider, the leader, a man with an unadorned black helmet which hid his face and black gloves which hid his hands, had a different aura than the others. That aura reassured Kavan he and Prince Muir would be safe. It was that belief in safety that Kavan was counting on.

The Nethites slowed when they saw the lone rider facing them with unexpected confidence and without hostility. Nearly everyone they had encountered on their journey through Enesfel had either fled at the sight of them or else had charged with threats and bravado that had caused more than one near fight. This individual, however, showed no trace of fear or enmity, leaving them perplexed as to how to proceed. They looked to their leader for instruction, and when he raised his hand, they stopped.

At this distance, any facial features of the lone opposing rider were indistinguishable, but the leader did not feel threatened. Rather, the white-robed figure gave him an unexpected tingle of anticipation. Another hand signal bid his companions to stay where they were and he rode forward alone. The closer he drew to the rider in white, the stronger his anticipation and excitement grew until he stopped, barely able to contain himself.

Kavan felt no threat in that approach, though he could sense anticipation and uncertainty. There was an almost tangible tension in the silence between them until the rider in black removed his helmet.

"Lord Cliáth...I did not believe I would see you again." The man spoke in Enesi, as he did not speak Elyri and had no knowledge of what other languages, beyond Trade, Kavan might speak. It afforded them a degree of privacy, as he knew his traveling companions did not speak the native tongue of Enesfel.

Though Kavan tried to contain his smile, he could not; a wash of joy flooded through him and sparked on his face, causing the other man to fully relax. "Milord. I knew this day would come...though I was not expecting you today. Are you disappointed to see me?" They had an unpleasant history between them, after all.

Shaking out his damp, thick waves of blond hair, the other man replied, "Surprisingly, no. I have wondered often what would pass between us if we met again...after the things I had done. I am pleased to find myself happy to see you. Can you honestly say the same after what I...?"

"I harbor no resentment, milord. You had my forgiveness when you departed Rhidam, and I have had thirteen years to reach an understanding of those troubled days."

"Lord Cliáth, I believe you understood everything from the beginning, more than the rest of us...long before we did. If we had gone to you for wisdom and heeded your words, I suspect history would have progressed much differently." He looked over his shoulder and motioned his comrades forward. "What fate causes you to greet me here?"

"There are far too many forces guiding my actions for me to guess what led me to be here. I am entertaining one of the princes today..." An unanticipated shiver passed as he realized what was about to transpire. It would be the first awkward situation of many. "What has brought you into Enesfel?" It had to be important if the man was willing to break the conditions of his exile and risk his life, and that of Guthrie McHador.

The man's voice dropped and he continued in Enesi, grateful he would not be understood by his own party. "I do not expect the King to be pleased to see me, but this is a matter of great diplomatic and political import, one that may have a profound effect upon the future of the Five Sovereignties. It was not my choice to come, knowing what sort of reception I will receive, but it was because I know Enesfel and the customs here that I was chosen to be the voice and mediator in these matters. It is a mission of peace between Enesfel and myself, I assure you."

"Come then. I will be your escort. No one will harm you if you are in my company, and if you speak to me of your business, I may be able to intercede with the King on your behalf."

"I wager your influence tempers his behavior a great deal," the man said in a low voice heavy with regret. "At least...it should."

Kavan shrugged. Some believed he had too much influence on the king, when the truth was that Arlan Lachlan was too strong-willed to do anything he did not want to do. More often than not, he chose a path that ran contrary to Kavan's thoughts, the way it should be for a strong ruler.

The riders reached the place where Prince Muir and the others waited, none of them speaking as they rode. The knot in the bard's stomach grew ever tighter until they stopped and he watched both Wortham and the prince closely for their reactions. There was no sign of recognition in the young man's face; Muir had never seen the painting Arlan refused to hang in the library with the other portraits of Lachlan kings, even though Bowen's hung there...by far, the worst king Enesfel had endured for centuries. The prince did not recognize the similarities he shared in features with this man. But Wortham remembered; it was evident in the way his hand rested on his sword hilt and the nervous way his gaze flickered uneasily between Kavan and the newcomers, waiting for whatever command the Elyri gave.

"Do not be alarmed, Captain Delamo," the bard said calmly. "They come on a mission of peace; they have matters to discuss with the King."

Emissaries then. Prince Muir straightened in his saddle, cleared his throat, and asked, "You are from Neth?" in as diplomatically neutral a tone as he could manage. He had never met anyone from that land, but he had seen envoys at court and recognized their manner of dress and the language.

The prince might not recognize similarities between them, but Kavan knew the other man did; the mounting tension in the air around them confirmed it. If he spoke, the truth would be out, but it could not be avoided. And after all of these years, it was time for such secrets to be laid to rest. "Prince Muir, this is Prince Owain Lachlan."

Muir pulled his horse back several steps, shocked more than afraid, as he stared at the stranger in disbelief. There was a flicker of confusion and dismay that crossed Owain's face, but years of experience allowed him to regain his composure quickly. Prince Muir looked at Kavan, wanting to ask if Owain knew who he was, and though he did not speak the question, Kavan saw it in his eyes and shook his head. There was no way for Owain to know, although he could, perhaps, guess. Reluctantly, knowing he needed to be diplomatic, regardless of his conflicting feelings, the prince inched forward and offered his hand. "Welcome to Enesfel, Prince Owain."

A curious glance was cast at Kavan, but Owain could not read anything on the Elyri's face. He grasped the prince's hand, pleased with the strength of the boy's grip and his willingness to deal with him in a diplomatically respectful fashion. He could imagine what sort of tales the King had instilled in his children and his subjects of the sort of man his predecessor had been. "It is an honor to make your acquaintance, Prince Muir."

"The honor and pleasure are mine." Now that the initial shock had passed, the prince seemed to have recovered and relaxed. "It is growing late, Lord Cliáth; it will be nearly dark when we reach home, and I am hungry. No doubt, Prince Owain and his men are hungry too. If he has business in Rhidam, we should escort him there at once."

Relieved that thus far the encounter had gone more smoothly than anticipated, Kavan agreed. The odd assortment of companions started for Rhidam, with Kavan and Owain in the lead, Owain's soldiers behind them, followed by Wortham, Muir, and the remaining Enesfel guards. As they rode, Owain explained his mission, all the while casting curious glances over his shoulder and then meeting Kavan's gaze again with growing torment.

The bard's sincere belief that Owain would not be harmed while in his company was tested as they reached the city's edge at sundown. Owain had replaced his helmet to avoid being recognized by the people he had once ruled; he did not share Kavan's belief that he would be safe without it. Even hidden, or perhaps because he was disguised, they were still met with inquisitive, fearful expressions on the faces they passed. Kavan could not blame them; it was not often an envoy from Neth came to Rhidam. Owain confessed to Kavan, as they neared the castle, that he felt more secure with his unexpected escort than he would have riding into Rhidam with his small unit of men. At the castle gate, it was Wortham's reassurance to the palace guard that allowed them to enter the courtyard and guaranteed that the foreigners and their horses were tended. Wortham took Owain's three men to quarters they would use during their stay, leaving Kavan with Muir and Owain.

"Lord Cliáth, I should like to speak with you later," the young prince said, a little less authority in his voice now that they were home where the King's word would rule over his. "And I should like to speak with you, Prince Owain, if you can spare the time while you are here."

Wondering what the young man could have to say to him, Owain bowed and said, "I will endeavor to do so." He watched the boy depart and followed Kavan into the castle. He could have found his way to any room Kavan directed him to, but he was a guest, not a resident, and was willing to obey any restrictions placed upon him. The bard did not speak but kept his senses attuned to the approach of anyone he did not wish to encounter yet. The news of Owain's arrival was best not made public until the King knew it too. They made it to the largest billeting room without incident, and then he breathed a sigh of relief.

"I think," the bard said as he closed the door, "it is best for you to remain here until I speak to the King. Since I brought you, I believe he should hear the news from me. As you say, it may temper his reaction. I can have your basin filled if you wish to bathe, and food sent."

"I will be well enough." He removed his helmet and gloves and looked around him. Though he had never spent time in this room, it felt familiar. It was a welcome feeling. "There is water in the washbowl with which to refresh, and I swear to you I shall not leave this room until you summon me. As for food…speak to the King. If he wishes to speak immediately, a meal can wait. Otherwise, I would be honored if you would join me."

Kavan bowed his head to hide his smile. "I shall strive to, milord."

The bard backed out of the room, closed the door, and leaned against the opposite wall to steady the tremors that erupted throughout his body. He had known when Owain was forced out of Rhidam and Enesfel thirteen years ago, that they would see each other again. And he admitted that he had looked forward to this meeting, despite the beatings he had once received under the man's command and despite some of the things Owain had done as Enesfel's king. Kavan was, perhaps, the only person in Enesfel who had forgiven Owain for the history they shared. He was, therefore, possibly the only ally the man had, and he would fulfill that duty to the best of his ability.

When he entered the Great Hall, he nearly collided with his cousin, the healer charging through the door with a determined intent to find someone. To find him, Kavan guessed, from the way the healer caught his arm, stopped mid-stride, and demanded, "Is it true? Are there Nethites here? You escorted them to Rhidam?"

"Yes," Kavan replied, not asking how the healer had heard the news so soon, or why the healer was troubled by it. Emissaries were common. Emissaries from Neth, while less so, were nothing to find shocking.

"What do they want? Why are they here?"

Kavan looked at him, perplexed by his cousin's unusual curiosity. Or perhaps it was not unusual given the relationship of distrust between Nethites and Elyri. "I am on my way to discuss it with the King. Do you know where he is?"

"In the stateroom with Guthrie the last I saw him…but I do believe he will want to be disturbed with this…whatever it is."

Knowing the healer would follow whether Kavan asked him to do otherwise, the bard nodded and suggested, "I know why they have come and I am not certain Arlan will agree to listen…your presence may be helpful."

"If you brought them, then listening will be worth it," Ártur said earnestly. Kavan rarely did anything without good reason. Curiosity, and belief in his cousin, made the healer follow him across the Hall, resisting asking questions that he knew Kavan would not yet answer. He would know the truth soon enough. Kavan rapped on the stateroom door and waited. When they finally heard the King's muffled command to enter, the bard pushed the door open and went in with Ártur on his heels.

"Well, Kavan…I assume you have come for something important." The King looked up from the maps he was studying, pushing them to the corner of the table with an expectant expression that suggested he was hoping for good news about his son.

"I have."

The King gestured to a chair; when Kavan refused to take it, the healer did so. "Am I going to have to drag it out of you? Is it about the boys?"

"No…though I wish it was, My Liege."

"What then?" the King snorted with disappointment. "Do not play games with me, Kavan. Guthrie and I are busy."

"Planning strategies against Neth."

The King's eyes narrowed a little. The maps were self-explanatory, and Kavan was adept at linking seemingly unconnected bits of information to make an accurate assessment of any situation. Sometimes it annoyed Arlan that the bard knew far more than he was told, but today his annoyance had less to do with Kavan and more to do with the danger his son was in, danger he was trying not to fret over even as he had men scouring Rhidam and the surrounding lands. "Yes, and I do not have time to…"

The bard cut him off. "I have information that may have bearing on your plans."

That made Guthrie turn from the window. "What sort of information?" he asked, while the King continued to stare.

"While out with Prince Muir, we encountered a four-man emissary from southern Neth, on their way to speak with you, My King. They do not come on behalf of King Loris, but on behalf of the joint councils of Fiara and Ruidoso. They have revealed enough to me that I feel their offer will have great benefit for the future if you will hear them. I escorted them to Rhidam and they have been given quarters for the night."

Looks of excitement and interest passed between the King and his chamberlain. "Did they tell you what they want?"

Kavan nodded. "Their message was explained, yes, but I think it best if they present it to you themselves. Their spokesman was chosen by their councils to come before you; he has asked for an audience at your convenience."

"What are you waiting for then?" the King snapped. "Bring him to me at once..." He stopped, dark brows knitting in confusion, as the bard hung his head. "You can bring him to me, can't you?"

"I can, but it would be wise for you to know something before you meet."

The bard's evasiveness was grating on the King's nerves. "What? What aren't you telling me? Is he a criminal? Malformed? A de Corrmick?"

"The last...indirectly. He is none of those other things, though it would be easier for you if he were." Knowing what the monarch's reaction would be, he instead met the chamberlain's gaze. "The man chosen to speak on behalf of the people of southern Neth is Prince Owain."

Guthrie remained standing by the sheer power of Kavan's gaze. He heard the healer choke as the King pushed to his feet, eyes flashing as his heavy chair skittered backward. "You brought Owain here?" the King hissed. "You of all people should know..."

"...that despite what was done in the past, he is here on a diplomatic mission..."

"He killed my wife!"

Undaunted by the King's anger, Kavan stood his ground. "The complications of childbirth caused Brenna's death, milord. Owain had nothing to do with that. He did not..."

"I do not want him here!"

The chamberlain finally found his voice, compelled to speak on the previous king's behalf. "As king, you owe him diplomatic courtesy. He did abdicate the throne to you with less resistance than we expected, and whatever else he might have been, he is not foolish enough to come here to reclaim something he should never have claimed to begin with. I told you the councils were planning something. If he has come on their behalf to make an offer, or present a plan, we should hear it."

"I want nothing but his head!"

"Arlan." The King glared at Kavan, holding the bard's sad gaze for many moments. Yes, the bard seemed to be saying in that silence. You had cause for bitterness, but thirteen years was far too long to hold a grudge, and Owain was not responsible for every problem in Arlan's life. Despite his desire to remain angry, the King knew his friend was correct and he could feel his anger melting with each passing moment, taking with it some of the sadness from Kavan's face.

He snorted. "I do wish I understood you, Lord Harper. You forgive a man's injustice towards you for no other reason than he is a man." If anything, Kavan had more personal cause to hate Owain than Arlan had, and yet, there was no hate in him. The King went to the liquor cabinet to have time to arrange his thoughts. "I will speak with him in the morning. I want you, Ártur, Guthrie, Bhríd, and General Wyndham there. The hospitality of the House of Lachlan is his…and I expect him not to disappoint me."

The bard bowed. "I shall inform him. Your welcome is more than he expects."

As he retreated from the room, Kavan was again followed by his stunned cousin. "Owain is here?" Ártur gasped. "You…I thought after what he did…"

"That I would hate him? Do you think I am capable of that, sínréc?"

Ártur chewed his lip. "No…I suppose not. Still, you seem pleased he is here."

"I am." Kavan kept walking. "The moment I knew who he…why he gave up the throne, I forgave his transgressions. I understand his actions. I knew when he left that I would see him again, and he has brought such hopeful news for Enesfel. He deserves to be heard on that count alone."

Taking Kavan's arm, Ártur asked, "Why did he give in the way he…?"

"That," Kavan sighed, pulling his arm free of the restrictive hold, "is not for me to reveal. I must see that our guests are supplied with their meals."

Free of his cousin, though he knew Ártur wanted to press for answers, Kavan retreated to the kitchen. It was bustling with activity, as there was always cooking and cleaning to do to keep up with the demands of the royal family and palace staff. He waited patiently out of the way for a tray to be readied, noting as always that the staff shied away from him as best they could while still being polite and respectful. When it was prepared, he took the tray to Owain's room, relieved to escape that uncomfortable atmosphere.

A reply did not immediately come to his knock and he momentarily feared the worst. But the door finally opened; Owain, his face and hair damp from washing, was dressed in black silk that contrasted strikingly with his pale skin and blonde hair. He took the tray and set it on the cedar table, waiting for Kavan to enter and close the door. Seating himself, he motioned for the bard to sit across from him, but Kavan did not move.

"What is it, Lord Cliáth?" There was plenty of food for two on the tray, and plates and utensils enough, causing Owain to assume they would be dining together. Perhaps he was mistaken. Or maybe it was something else. "Do you not trust me?"

In response to the hurt in the blonde's voice, Kavan murmured, "I trust you. You are not armed and pose no physical threat to me. But you…how can you be certain that I am no threat to you?"

"You are too honorable to do something like poison my food; if anyone was to do that, it would be someone else. Nor do you seem capable of violence…" He stopped at Kavan's crestfallen expression, finding it both odd and heartbreaking that the bard should react that way. "Even if you are," he continued, "one of us must take the first step in trusting the other. You have never meant me harm, though you have had many reasons to. If you can trust me after the things I have done, then I can trust you. Please…sit and eat."

Kavan accepted the seat, though he picked at his food, eating because he felt it polite though he was not hungry and his nervous stomach was too clenched in knots to easily take food. He did not interrupt as Owain talked of the last thirteen years, except to ask an occasional question or answer one. He absorbed everything he heard for further analysis, happy to hear the man was doing well. Despite his pleasure at being in the prince's company, and his gratefulness that Owain had not suffered during those years, Kavan was still uneasy, feeling that he was on the verge of some great turn of events he could not foresee. Perhaps it was because of the news Owain had for the King. That could be cause enough. Any entanglement with Neth could bring great changes throughout the Sovereignties.

Owain cleared his throat and it startled Kavan to see how much the movement reminded him of Muir. Perhaps, he realized as he watched the man drain the last of his wine and wipe his mouth, holding knowledge that Owain might not like also added to his discomfort.

"The King has agreed to meet with you and several of his advisors in the morning," the bard said after many moments of awkward silence. The meal was complete, or as complete as it would be, and he could avoid the inevitable no longer. "He will not be without hostility when he meets, but he will at least hear what you have to say. With myself and Chamberlain McHador…"

"Guthrie?" The man's face turned gray. "He will be there?"

Understanding Owain's discomfort, Kavan nodded. "The King has asked it. His position at court requires it. There was no tactful way to argue against his attendance without revealing the truth…and I am sure he wants to see you."

"No one knows?" Owain was surprised that the truth was not public knowledge.

"Only I and Lord McHador knows. He asked me not to speak of it, and I have not. As you are…age and a beard would have made you…"

Owain gave him a half-hearted smile. "That is why I shaved it shortly after leaving Enesfel. I know how much a beard makes me look like the man I am. I decided to spare him and myself the indignity of unwanted questions. Too much history was manipulated by my mother's lies; I felt it best not to compound the issue further. Thank you for keeping that secret."

"There is no need. There was no reason for anyone to know, and I saw no need to speak of it to appease curiosity. A man's past, or his present, should not be open to speculation, ridicule, or gossip. I would never betray you."

The prince's cheeks flushed. "I believe you. I wish I had believed you when we were both much younger." He noted for the first time that Kavan appeared no older than he had the last time Owain had seen him. "Your friendship might have spared me much grief."

"Perhaps," was all Kavan chose to say.

Owain folded his napkin and placed it on the table before sliding backward with his chair. "At least he will meet with me. The rest will take care of itself, I hope."

"There are some things you should know…" Kavan rubbed his eyes. It would be difficult to broach this subject and he saw no way of doing it gracefully. "The queen, Brenna Weylin Lachlan, died ten days ago." Owain's expression spoke for itself, dark, grieved, and burdened with past regrets. "Complications of childbirth. Nothing could be done to save her, but Arlan feels you are somehow responsible."

The silence was uncomfortable as Owain tried to determine what Kavan knew of those events of many years past. The depth of understanding in the Elyri's green eyes suggested that Kavan knew more than Owain cared to remember and he looked away, shaken and embarrassed. That he saw no reproach in those eyes made him feel more ill at ease. "I never meant to do what I did, you understand. I was young and angry at everything and had an ill grip on the concepts of right, wrong, and personal responsibility. Those are things my mother never taught me, and the de Corrmick court is not a good place to learn such values as compassion, generosity, and kindness. I know that does not excuse my actions, and I can never make amends…"

"Not with her, and Arlan will never accept anything as payment enough, but there is someone else." He watched Owain's face as he continued, "It is best you know this, as Arlan may confront you with it and we should avoid an unwanted incident. Prince Muir is your son, milord."

Their gazes held until Owain slid back further, got up, and retreated to the window. There was more Kavan wanted to say, thought he should say, but he stared at the array of plates before him instead. When Owain did not speak for many minutes, the bard continued, "He was born in Bhryell, Elyriá, before Arlan moved to claim the throne. He will be fourteen in three months' time."

"Does he know who I am…about his heritage?" He turned at last to face Kavan, his expression tortured as it had been earlier that day.

"He does. Arlan has never been able to accept him, especially once his own children were born. Muir has always been the outsider. Once Prince Bertram, Arlan's eldest son, discovered the secret, Muir has been spared no amount of ridicule and torment. He is aware of his status, his place in the family, and that you are his father, although until today he had never seen you. He knew you by name alone. He knows little about you other than the method of his conception and what little I have been capable of telling him in your favor. But I have never told him why you relinquished the throne to Arlan. I did not think it would be wise. That is for you or Lord McHador to do."

Owain looked away again. He should have known. Muir looked his age, which would have put his birth very close to the ascension of Arlan to Enesfel's throne, too close to have been conceived after

Brenna's flight from Rhidam. His face was wide, like his father's, his eyes the same gray-green. There was very little of Brenna in Muir, and definitely none of Arlan. And the blond hair was another marker, neither Brenna nor Arlan were blond. Owain had feared she would conceive a child, though at the time it had been fear for himself and his throne. Now that the years had changed him, he was saddened to have missed his son's youth, saddened that an innocent child had suffered because of his anger and stupidity. Owain had left Enesfel without knowing he had fathered a child, and he had never guessed that what little news he heard about Prince Muir over the years might have been about his own son.

He was unaware of the tears on his cheeks until he felt the Elyri's hand upon his shoulder. The strength and support he felt in that touch were too much to tolerate, something he had never known, and he had to retreat before he broke down and wept against Kavan's shoulder. Kavan let him go.

"I think it is why he wishes to speak with you," Kavan murmured. "To learn more about you, to learn the truth for himself…to connect with someone to whom he might matter. It might be his best chance to belong somewhere…" Somewhere other than with Kavan, who, while beloved, was no substitute for the family Muir had been denied.

Owain nodded. "Will you send him to me? I shall wait up for him…if he wishes to come."

"I am certain he does."

T he atmosphere in the stateroom was strained, but no more than Kavan expected. Bhríd seemed not to care that Owain was there, that there was a history with him, and merely listened to the arguments, speaking only when some mention of money came into the discussion. His thoughts were preoccupied with some other matter. The King was snappish but tried to keep his temper, and his tongue, controlled, and when he could not, a sharp, forlorn look from Kavan turned him back to civility. Guthrie was subdued; after the initial welcoming handshake, he had not brought himself to look Owain in the eyes. Ártur studied the pair, and Kavan suspected that by the time this meeting was over, the healer would have deduced the truth.

It was Ternce Wyndham who was most uptight and who spoke not at all unless directly questioned. He had served as this man's general, had believed him to be the rightful king of Enesfel, had also been the man's best friend, and had been stunned when Owain abdicated the throne. Once Owain was gone, he quickly entered King Arlan's employment, and he fretted over what Owain must think of him now. He would have avoided this meeting if he could have, but the King would not hear of it, and now that he had learned the nature of this gathering, he was glad to be included.

Having heard the details before, Kavan did not actively listen to the discussion but rather kept attuned to the emotions of all involved in the hopes of keeping talks going smoothly. He was also thinking about his brief talk with Muir that morning over breakfast. While the prince had been quieter than usual, he was also, it seemed, more self-content than before. He was up most of the night talking to the man who had fathered him, which accounted for the dark circles beneath Owain's eyes. Some measure of peace had been made with the past, and Muir felt able to move forward in life. Kavan had yet to determine if Owain felt the same way.

"Let me make sure I understand, milords," Bhríd finally interjected. It was nearing noon, he was hungry, and wanted this to be over. "In sum, the entire region south of Lake Curo, between the Dagar and Kelari Rivers, has decided to throw in their lots together, with you…and desire Enesfel's assistance to overthrow King Loris?"

"Overthrowing Loris is not practical," Owain clarified. "They would make me king if they thought they could, but I do not believe I have enough supporters to put me there…or rather keep me there once I was on the throne…they know it. Treachery is such a part of the de Corrmick family, I would probably not live a week as king without the military backing me. And gaining military support is nearly impossible without the right connections…and the whole of the de Corrmick purse behind you. I do not want to live my life…or end it…like that. It leaves the southern regions with two options…"

"Succession from Neth to become your own kingdom, or becoming part of someone else's." Guthrie met Owain's gaze at last as he finished speaking.

Owain did not shrink from that scrutiny. He, at least, was comfortable with the relationship that bound him to the chamberlain. "Exactly. Yes. Becoming our own kingdom is not realistic. We do not lack resources, but most of the region is forest; we could not supply enough food to adequately feed ourselves without clearing it. A kingdom that cannot provide its own needs is destined for quick ruin. Nor do we have sufficient force to protect ourselves, should Loris rise up to fight. It has always been illegal for the common man to bear arms in Neth, save for bows and knives for hunting, and King Ander enforced that law more strictly than most. Loris inherited a kingdom almost devoid of military capability. Only nobility and those in the armed forces can be trained…legally. I have trained a number of men during my years there; a prince needs armed attendants after all. Ander and Loris neither had the desire to supply me or the will to stop me and there are always ways to discreetly gather arms and train more men than I require, and then work an amicable dismissal with some in order to train more. Other nobles have done similarly…although far more discreetly than I have. Still, it would never be enough men to face Loris and Neth's militia. Any attempt to break free of him without foreign assistance would be suicide."

"Why Enesfel?" asked Ártur. "Why not Cordash?"

"Cordash is the stronger kingdom, it is true. But our region borders mainly on Enesfel and Elyriá…and Elyriá is out of the question for obvious reasons," Owain explained. Most of those gathered at the table understood the logistics of such a choice, but Ártur was not a military strategist. "They have no reason to want our little piece of land, particularly when defending it would leave them exposed and open to war. If we offered it to them, chances are high they would decline on principle. They have given us more assistance than we ever dreamed…food, clothing, materials…but they have no desire to involve themselves in a war. Cordash is fending off raids from Loris; no one on the council believes that King Ahern or Prince Renfrid would believe our bid for peace. To merge with Cordash would awkwardly divide their territory and would be difficult for them to defend. It is not practical for them, or for us. Because I have prior dealings with Enesfel," Owain's face flushed as he said it, "the council believes Enesfel is our best hope. Our sole hope, in all truthfulness.

We are prepared to submit to Enesfel laws." He paused to look at Ártur and Kavan. "Including those pertaining to Elyri. Everything we have would be subject to your rule."

The King leaned forward, elbows on the table, his eyes narrowed. "Would you be willing and able to submit to me...Owain?"

Owain started to say something, to rise to the challenge in Arlan's voice, but he stopped. He also suppressed the impulse to turn to Kavan. He had never been one to lean on anyone else and it troubled him to feel this way. Arlan was not an obstacle that Owain could not handle. Instead, he took a single breath and squared his shoulders. "I should never have been king of Enesfel, Your Lordship, but I am a prince. As a subject of Enesfel, I would submit to your rule, but, as a subject of Enesfel, one with a substantial amount of wealth and land within this new addition, as well as a member of the nobility, I would expect to be treated with the same fairness and equanimity you bestow upon other subjects of similar status."

It was a counter challenge and Arlan knew it. He stood, wandered to the liquor cabinet to pour himself a drink, though he could have ordered any number of servants around them to do it. It was his usual means of stepping away from an issue long enough to think. Grudgingly, he had to admit that Owain was nothing like he had anticipated, not the self-centered, cruel, and vicious man Arlan's dreams painted him to be. He also had to admit that the offer put forth by the joint councils of Fiara and Ruidoso was tempting and logical. Such a maneuver would strip Neth of a third of her territory and further cripple her military. If they could successfully oust King Loris in the process, it would be an added bonus. Maybe Owain would take the Neth throne then and Arlan would not have to worry about ruling over him. If Owain was the sort of man he appeared to be, it might improve the overall relationships between all Five Sovereignties and lead to a lasting peace.

"Allow me to think about this…" he began as the door burst open. Heads turned when Justice Cornell stumbled into the room, disheveled and breathless.

He did not close the door but paused long enough to straighten his posture. "I apologize for the interruption, Your Majesty, but this was left with the sentries at the gate towers. Tedor thought the messenger looked suspicious; I took the liberty of reading it. It is about the princes…"

He did not finish before the King snatched the parchment from his hand. Sensing Arlan's anger, the healer came to his side under the guise of emotional support. But he did not anticipate the King turning on Owain instead, crumpling the parchment in his hand before pulling the prince up by his shirt.

"You come expecting peace and kidnap my son to extort money?" he howled.

"Milord!" the chancellor cried, the only one not too stunned to speak. Bhríd leaped to his feet as Guthrie tried to separate the two men. In the end, it was Kavan who forced them apart roughly and abruptly enough that Owain stumbled to the floor before anyone could catch him. Both King and prince were surprised, but it was Arlan who received the brunt of Kavan's anger.

"Fool," he hissed, a word that caused both Ártur and Guthrie alarm as the chancellor held the King back. "He has nothing to do with the children…"

"He arrives after they are taken and this arrives while he is here! It is a plot…"

"A coincidence, nothing more. Any fool would know that. But you would sooner jeopardize your son's life and the future of the Five Sovereignties for the sake of old grudges than discover the truth."

The men around the table knew Kavan was right but none would dream of speaking to the King that way. Kavan never had before either, which made the moment more tense. Snapping around to Ártur, breaking away from Kavan's heated gaze, the King snarled, "Lord Healer, I want the truth."

"I can do it," the bard started.

"No. You are his ally, his friend. You think I would believe a word you say where he is concerned? You defend him as you do Muir!" The King's voice was high and laced with uncharacteristic venom. "Lord Healer, do it."

In the agitated silence that followed, as Kavan and Arlan glared at each other, the healer stood still, more from shock than a desire to put off the inevitable. Owain looked around the room at the shocked faces, not knowing what Arlan had ordered the healer to do but knowing that this was an unusual standoff between King and bard. Kavan was the first to look away, realizing Arlan was not going to back down. He held a hand to Owain to help him to his feet. In a voice colored with contained rage, a rage Owain had never imagined possible from the bard, Kavan said, "Present your hands to Ártur, my prince, and remain calm. He will touch you, probe your thoughts, and that is all. He will not harm you. You will feel no pain, likely feel nothing at all. Trust him as you would trust me."

Apprehensive, understanding that there was to be an invasion of his thoughts, Owain shakily did as instructed because Kavan guaranteed his safety. What if the healer learned something he did not like, something unrelated to this moment? Would it be used against him? But Kavan's promise proved true. Owain felt nothing except the healer's hands and a tickle between his eyes that made him feel like sneezing. It lasted no more than ten seconds and then the healer backed away and spoke to the King.

"He has no idea what he is being accused of, Milord. He knows nothing about the boys, did not even know they are missing. He is guilty of nothing."

The King snorted and crossed his arms. Owain might know nothing about the missing boys, but Arlan would not believe he was guiltless. "Lord Chancellor, Lord Chamberlain, stay. We will discuss this demand. The rest of you, out. Now. Including you, Lord Harper."

Kavan was the first to leave the room and did not look back. He was as horrified at his own behavior, at the anger behind it, as he was at the King's. Arlan had an excuse for his touchy temper. Kavan, as far as he knew, did not. The healer stopped pursuing him when he realized his cousin was seeking solitude. Owain stood in one of the tall archways to the Great Hall. Ártur beckoned him to follow and the two stepped into the courtyard, away from anyone likely to overhear them.

"You should feel honored."

"Why?" Owain asked with a sigh, shuffling his feet, looking more like a lonesome, sullen child than a man of thirty-eight. It was a posture, an action, an expression Ártur recalled from Owain's childhood and he regretted that he had been unable to do anything to ease it then. He could try now, however. "I fear your cousin has risked recrimination, his status in court, on my behalf, and I have done nothing to deserve such compassion or loyalty."

"Precisely," the healer said. "That is one thing Arlan fails to understand. My cousin's compassion is great, yes, but he only gives such loyalty to those he deems of worthy character. That he gives it freely to you proves you are more than any of us sees. And that he offered to be the one to read you, when he rarely makes that offer for anyone, also speaks highly of your worth. He loves you, my prince. Please remember that."

The last might have been an admonition or a warning, but the healer was already leaving the prince alone in the courtyard, giving him no chance to ask more. Owain was alone in seeing the white kestrel as its shadow crossed the mid-day sun."

❧*❧

The second-floor balcony was well shaded at this hour of the day Madalyn noted again as she gazed across the vineyards towards the ocean in the distance. The vines glistened with blossoms and soon the grapes would come. She liked this view of verdant foliage meeting the azure sea, a vista that gave way to the brilliance of the powder blue sky. This was her favorite place to take her meals, though today she did not feel like eating. The bedroom behind her had been empty and unused since her father's death. It was too large for one person, she had rationalized, and thus allowed it to become dusty and cold. Of late, however, she was beginning to consider refurbishing it in case it should become necessary to use it again.

A small tapping came on the wood of the doorframe behind her. "Yes?" she asked absently without turning.

"Pardon, milady, this arrived for you. I thought you would wish to see it at once."

Madalyn held out her hand for the rolled parchment the servant put in her palm. It was the seal that told her why her handmaiden would think she would want this immediately rather than when she came down after her midday meal. Madalyn smiled, murmured her thanks, and began unrolling and reading the scroll before Elyn was out of the room.

Commotion in the field below distracted her several minutes later. Two workers arguing over their duties, she deciphered, rolling the letter and sliding it inside of her chemise near her heart. Let the two men come to her for help; she was going to see about cleaning this room. Her mood was greatly improved and she did not want petty squabbles to break it. After all, Bhríd Cáner had invited her back to Rhidam.

❧*❧

Princess Deidre was alone in the library, reading a collection of sonnets written by a poet she had never heard of. The words bored her today, failing to stir the strings of her heart as love poems generally did. Her heart was too full of other things to respond to tender words, she decided, and closed the pages. Caol was not bed-ridden today, yet he did nothing but stare out the window with Syl or Ártur ever present in the room. The princess did not understand why they were there, although Syl mentioned a fear that he would do something irrational and unwise. What that something could be, Deidre could but guess, for she did not think him foolish enough to take his life. For him to do anything at all would be preferable to his doing nothing.

She gazed out the window towards the soldiers' barracks, watching men coming and going with little interest in their actions. Not long ago she had seen a white kestrel, unusual she knew, and assumed it was an omen of some kind. A good omen, she hoped. Right now, Rhidam needed a good omen and some good fortune.

Picking up the book from her lap, she rose to replace it upon the shelf, but stopped in near panic as she saw the tall, smooth-faced blonde man in the doorway. She remembered Guthrie telling her last night that Owain was in Rhidam, but she had not expected to see him. They stared at each other until he gestured towards the table and sat. At first, she could not move, stunned by memories and the sight of a man who was still handsome, a man she had never thought to see again. When he began writing with her ever-present quill and paper, she sat across from him to see what he wished to say.

"I mean you no harm. I never have."

There was no malice in his face, rather there was melancholy and loneliness. She felt pity for him and wondered what his life had been like since being banished from Enesfel. "I once had doubts, but I know that now."

He nodded, his gaze straying to take in the line of eight portraits upon the wall. Those doubts had been justified; he had not been the most likable man in the days they had known one another. "I am not surprised your brother did not hang my portrait. It would be inappropriate for it to hang with the others. Do you know what has been done with it?"

"It is in the storage rooms, beneath the Great Hall. I would not allow him to destroy it." Of course, Arlan might have done so when she had not known it, but to her knowledge, that was where the painting resided.

The thought of her fighting for his portrait's survival made him smile. "I should like to have it, if you think that would be allowed. It will keep it out of the wrong hands."

That seemed reasonable to her. "Very well. I will arrange it."

Again he smiled. "Thank you. I have heard you are married. Does he treat you well?"

"Yes." But a change in her expression belied her words.

"And your son?"

There was no hesitation in her response. "Is missing."

Ah, it was not just Arlan's son, but Deidre's too. The pain of that she could not hide and Owain felt angry on her behalf. "Is there anything I can do? I will find him, if I can, or offer what resources I have to pay for his ransom, if that will help. It is the least I can do."

She sniffed as she shook her head. "You owe me nothing. What about you? Have you married? Do you have children?"

He could not hide the tremor in his hand as he took the stylus from her. "No, I have never married." He had told her he would never love another as long as she lived, and thus far those words had proven true. "As for children…there is the one you know. I mourn the method of his conception and the lost opportunity to watch him grow, but he is a fine young man, a credit to Lord Cliáth I am told. But yes, I do owe you. My unchecked anger drove Lady Weylin from you and kept you in fear for too long. I should never have subjected you to the dungeon.

If finding your son will make up for even a small part of the misery I caused, I gladly offer my services."

His written words, and those he did not write but she knew were there, brought tears to her eyes and she traced the words with her fingers, smudging the ink on the page. "You do love me."

"Some might call it obsession, but yes."

"I loved you once…"

He closed his eyes and calmed his ragged breathing before writing again. She had never said those words before. "But not enough to marry me. I understand, though it saddens me to accept it. Please…allow me to help find your son."

"Any assistance is welcome. Thank you." She stood and drew close to him, touching first his face, then his hair, watching tenderly as he closed his eyes and touched her hand with his fingertips. Kissing his cheek, she took the paper and left the room. Owain did not open his eyes. He could not watch her leave again.

ᵒ⨾*⨞ᵒ

Caol did not turn from the window as the door opened behind him. He heard Yorick speaking in a low voice to Syl, though he could not hear what was being said. Then the man went out, leaving Caol alone with the lady healer. He could overpower her, force his way out of the room, but what was the point? It would turn more people against him, and he did not have the heart to hurt her.

"Lord Dugan? General Zarkosta brought this for you. He said it was left at the gatehouse. Do you want to read it or shall I read it for you?"

For the first time in days, Caol reacted, grabbing the scroll from her hand before she could open it. Her bemused smirk was covered as she went back to the garment she was sewing for Bianca. There was no need to read it out loud, he reasoned, not wanting to alert her to the possibility of anything unusual. There was no seal, no identifying marks, but he knew it had to be from Halstatt. A ransom, perhaps, or further instructions for what he wanted Caol to do to get the children back. He hoped to read it later when she was paying less attention, but his curiosity, his need to know, demanded appeasement. He retreated to the water closet and read it by the dim light of the single candle burning there. The children were well, it claimed, as Caol had anticipated they would be. He did not believe Halstatt would be stupid enough to risk harming them yet. He demanded that Caol come to him, with or without the price that had already been asked of Enesfel's king. Then the children would be released…as long as the Coryllien was on his person when they met.

But how could he get away to meet Halstatt, he wondered, rolling the scroll. The single clue to Halstatt's whereabouts was the request to meet in the place they both knew. Durham. Caol believed he knew where, even though Halstatt had not been specific. It would be the place where their fathers had fought, and their grandfather's before them. Syl could be heard in the main room talking to someone who had entered, though he could not hear their words. Damn, he swore, holding the scroll to the flame and watching it burn. He had to destroy this before anyone saw it. And he had to figure out how to get out of the castle unnoticed. That was going to be a much harder task then ridding himself of the letter.

He froze when he came into the main room, finding that Syl was no longer there, but that Kavan was in her place, his back to Caol, looking out the window where the inquisitor had been minutes ago. Caol judged the distance, calculated his odds, and let the closet door close before trying to slide cautiously towards the main door.

Without turning, Kavan asked, "Why must you sneak away, Caol?" The voice was quiet and gentle yet the words stopped the redhead in his tracks as if he had been caught in the midst of a crime. Sweat broke out along his upper lip and the back of his neck. It had been a long time since he had felt this trapped, and being trapped by words was the worst possible feeling. He had not felt this way since his father had last caught him in some random act of childish disobedience. "I will allow you to go; I know what you intend. I do wish, however, that you speak with me before you act."

"And if I don't? Will you report what you know, or think you know, to the King?" It was his greatest fear, but he was unsure if Kavan would betray him.

The bard turned around. The intensity of Kavan's gaze felt like it was burning him until the inquisitor felt forced to look away. The bard muttered an inaudible sigh. "What is there for me to tell that will be of use? I know a Coryllien dagger was delivered to you the day Lady Dilyn's body was found, and I know you hid that dagger behind my dressing table. I have seen it, Caol, held it in my hands."

Caol's knees grew weak. He could not imagine how the bard could have known it was there, but Kavan tended to know a lot of things he should not. Caol realized he should have known better than to hide such a powerful object in the room of the kingdom's most powerful man. The bard looked at him as he grew pale, Kavan's face an unreadable mask, but Caol could feel his intensity as if it were a blade holding him at bay. Kavan did not need words or facial expressions to convey anything.

Kavan continued when Caol did not speak. "I know that this man, the one who killed Lady Dilyn, attacked Captain Delamo, broke into the castle, wounded me...kidnapped the boys...you know him. Chamberlain McHador has surmised that there was no band of thieves but one or two individuals involved with you in the skirmish in Hangman's Grove. He questions why the friend you were to meet never found you and has not come to the keep to learn what became of you. It will not be long before he pieces together more."

"You...have not told anyone..."

"No one except you and I know where the dagger is. To tell anyone would lead to your premature imprisonment…and I would prefer the dagger remain where it is. It is safer there."

Hearing that allowed Caol to breathe easier though he wanted to know what Kavan had to gain by keeping this knowledge to himself. He did not believe the bard was keeping quiet merely to protect him. "You think me a fool for not speaking of this to the King the moment it began…"

Kavan shook his head. "I would be the fool to make such a judgment without knowing the facts…which is why I come to you. If there is anything I can do, I must know what is going on."

"I don't believe there is anything you can do…that anyone can do." Caol collapsed onto the edge of the bed, shaking, eyes closed as he envisioned the end he was likely to meet when the truth came out. Still, he wanted to confide in someone, and felt that Kavan was the best person to fill that need. "His name is Halstatt Tarmajien; our families are part of the Association." He was surprised to see that the bard knew what he was referring to and seemed neither unsettled nor surprised. "We have been feuding for the last four or five hundred years at least. No one knows any longer how it started, or why it continues. My father killed his, his grandfather killed mine, his great-grandfather killed mine…for generations it has been this way. Now the tale has turned, unfortunately, to Halstatt and me."

He stood and began to pace. Frankly, it was a relief to be talking. "I wanted out. I never really wanted in, but when you are a boy born into the Association, into the Dugan clan, you do not have many options, particularly if you show any degree of talent. I was pretty good at stealth, at breaking and entering, and I can shoot any bow you give me with near flawless accuracy. There was some hope that I might have made a good assassin. Then I saw my grandfather die…and when my father was caught smuggling…I don't know what…King Owain's soldiers beheaded him. I did not want that fate, and I did not want to be an assassin; I resisted training, tried to prove myself less useful then my family wanted, until I was able to join Arlan's troops. I was caught up in the adventure of rebellion, and then Deidre expressed a desire to marry…by then I had heard that Halstatt was in a prison in Neth. I wanted to believe that my past was buried with him…behind me."

He shook his head. "I should have known Halstatt could not be held by any prison not designed to detain him. The Tarmajiens have always had a talent for getting out of traps, getting away unscathed…though I've never known anyone else to escape from a Nethite prison. But somehow he did…it took him over a year I've learned, but he finally caught up with me here. I think it may have been coincidence more than anything. He could not have gotten much news in prison. He was in Rhidam looking for a Káliel Serpent and learned that I was here is all."

"Why a Serpent…and how does that tie in with the Coryllien."

"I don't think they do. I don't know why he wants the Serpents…he did not tell me. The Coryllien…it's a challenge between our families. His family has had that one dagger…forever as far as I know. When a Tarmajien wants to challenge a Dugan, he delivers the dagger. Usually, there is a confrontation a day or two later and one of them dies…and somehow the dagger always finds its way back into Tarmajien hands. I do not think he intended to challenge me, but sending it to me meant that the murder weapon was no longer in his possession, meant he could not be implicated in Lady Dilyn's death. Maybe he was hoping I would be. When I did not look for him, he came to me."

"By breaking into the keep. He must be very…talented."

"Lucky," Caol snorted. "I could have done the same thing if I set my mind to it, but I would have been more careful. Every apprentice in the Association learns things like that, though not all of us have the skill to succeed. When he failed to find the dagger and kill me, he wanted to meet in Hangman's Grove. Perhaps I should have told someone, brought someone with me, but it was a family matter…and I believed I could handle it, settle the score."

"But it would not have ended there, would it? If he has a son, the feud would pass to Wilred, and the royal house would have inherited the Tarmajien-Dugan feud. That is why you resisted having children."

Caol nodded, surprised that Kavan had realized there was a reason behind his delay in having a family. "The Dugan clan would die out, except for my sister's family, but at least the feud could end. Without access to the Associations information, I do not know if Halstatt has children…I pray he does not. That day…one of us should have died and it should have ended there. I could have brought my bow, killed him from the trees with a single shot…but that would have been a dishonorable way out; at the time it did not cross my mind."

"A little dishonor might have spared everyone much torment."

"I know," Caol groaned as he rubbed his eyes. "I regret not doing it…but I had no way of knowing what lay ahead. The whole Association honor code is so ingrained in me; I do not know if I could have done anything differently…except made sure that Wilred and Bertram stayed home. If I had known they were there, I would have protected them, I swear it. When Halstatt had the advantage, Wilred ran out of the bushes to protect me; he might have saved my life, but Halstatt put his sword through my leg…took the boys. I could not follow a man on horseback when I could barely stand, and by the time Elotti showed up, we had no hopes of finding them."

"I would like to meet Wace Elotti." Kavan smirked at Caol's near horrified expression. "You are surprised? I have heard much about him, most of which I do not understand. Meeting him might answer my questions."

"You do not want to meet him. He is a twisted, perverse man. Good at what he does, it is true, but twisted nonetheless. Do not taint yourself with the likes of him." Kavan's perplexed scowl made him stop and shrug. "He brought me back to Rhidam; he has been hunting

Halstatt since his escape from Neth. I do not know why he delays in catching him, but if anyone can find him, he will…eventually. My concern is how much havoc Halstatt will create in the interim. I should have told someone…"

Kavan nodded. "Yes, you should have. I understand why you did not. You wished to hide your past from others; I understand that. But I do not think most would judge you as harshly as you believe. A father's transgressions should not be placed upon the shoulders of his son, and you cannot be blamed for the things you were taught as a child. When you were mature enough to choose a path, you chose Arlan's cause. You have lived your life for that cause ever since. I think Arlan would be flattered to know what you have given up for him."

"Flattered that I gave up the Association?"

"Being Association had its advantages and rewards, did it not?" Caol did not reply. "It surely offers more freedom in some ways than you have here, even if it is more dangerous. There are pros and cons to every life choice, Caol, and when something is such a part of a family's history, it is difficult to break from tradition."

"Do you think I should tell him?"

"No. Not now. He will likely blame you for the children's disappearance."

"Rightly so."

"Rightly so," Kavan conceded. "You know that the King received a ransom demand?"

Caol shrugged. "Yes, but it does not matter if he pays it. Halstatt wants me, the Coryllien, and the Serpents."

"Does he think the King has them?"

"I don't know. He thought Lady Dilyn had one and might believe it is in our treasury. As I understand it, they are not particularly valuable, but I have never understood what he wants anyhow…"

"But he saw Gabrielle…"

"And thought she was her mother. It probably has not occurred to him that, whoever she was, she might have taken the Serpent to Káliel…or maybe he doesn't care. I doubt he expects to get them from the King, but it cannot hurt to throw them into the ransom. He will try to get them some other way if they are so important. Same with the Coryllien; he will hunt for it forever if I don't give it to him, but in the end, neither the dagger nor the Serpent are really important. If he gets me, I believe he will release the children…but it may only be Bertram who comes home alive."

Kavan shivered, refusing, this time, to give in to the images of death crowding into his head. "Halstatt wants you. Where would he be? How can we find him?"

"He…" He realized as he paused that Kavan might be his way out of the castle, out of Rhidam. The corners of his mouth twisted into the shadow of a grin. "Durham, where we grew up. I was planning to…"

Nausea swept over Kavan, causing him to double over and reach out with one hand to steady himself. Caol caught him. The image of riders flashed through his mind's eye. Muir, Caol, Wortham. Owain? Yes, that was one of the other riders he had been unable to identify before. The feeling of foreboding returned. Eyes focusing, he looked beseechingly at Caol. "You will not succeed alone, my friend…there is to be a search party…"

"Arlan cannot send a search party when he does not know who he is looking for…or where to look…and if he sends too many…Halstatt will never allow himself to be caught…may never return the children…"

"He does not know where…but we do. Or at least, we have a place to begin. Leave the logistics to me. There will be a search party and we will leave at dawn."

"You? Why?" It seemed a peculiar idea to him, and Caol did not like peculiar.

"I…" Only because he knew that the inquisitor was more open-minded than most men, and had faith in Elyri abilities, did he continue, "I have Seen it."

The inquisitor cocked his head, his eyes wide. The Sight. "Then who am I to argue with providence," he said with conviction. If it meant getting out of the castle, if it meant a chance of finding his son and the royal heir, then Caol was eager to try anything.

"There is something you should know. Prince Owain will be with us."

The redhead's expression hardened but he grunted and said, "Deidre mentioned that he is willing to search for our son. I can work with him if I have to, Lord Cliáth. I am bitter about what he ordered done to my father, but he was not without justification. My father was the one breaking the law, after all, knew the risks of it. I think my nearly killing him made up for that debt. If he is willing to help, if you deem his company necessary, then so be it."

❧*❧

With darkness fast approaching, the King knew he should retire to a better-lit room, but he did not have the will to rise. He and Guthrie had spent most of the day discussing first the ransom demand, then the situation with Neth, and then the ransom again. He would have spared no amount of wealth or lives to retrieve his son, particularly after recalling Kavan's prediction that Bertram was to die. But the demands had been for a greater amount than Enesfel's coffers could afford and Arlan had no way to get the Káliel Serpents in time, even if he thought Prime Magistrate Dilyn might be willing to give them up. Bhríd promised to go over the kingdom's finances and see what he could arrange, but the King knew in his soul that there would not be enough.

Guthrie had devised a rough plan that might resolve the situation in Neth more quickly than Arlan thought possible, provided Cordash was willing to work with them. The chamberlain felt it was feasible with a little more adjustment, and believed that the Valdis' would be agreeable to the undertaking. It would need to be discussed with Owain before anyone set foot in Neth, but the King had no desire to speak to the man. Kavan had been right, Arlan reluctantly admitted. He had behaved like a fool."

"Milord?"

"Kavan." Arlan sat up and placed his empty wine glass on the nearby table. "I was just thinking about you. My apologies for the darkness…"

"No need." A tongue of flame sprang to life in Kavan's outstretched palm, with which he lit the three fat tallow candles in the brass candelabra. The King smiled in spite of himself; it had been a long time since he had seen the slightest display of Elyri power from his friend.

"Showing off?"

There was a brief appalled expression on the bard's face until Kavan realized the King was teasing. "Taking advantage of an opportunity."

"You do not have much chance to do that, do you?" The lowering of the bard's gaze was the answer the King received. "I owe you an apology, Kavan. No…do not stop me. I behaved like a fool for exactly the reasons you said…assuming Owain was responsible for things he could have known nothing about. I should have believed that if you said he was innocent of such crimes, it was so. Your integrity is untouchable. It was surprising to hear you get that angry with me…"

The bard did not lift his head. Embarrassed, he murmured, "I apologize for that…"

"Apologize?" Arlan snorted. "I think your anger was what I needed. I take advantage of you too often and do not heed your advice when I should. Having you angry with me for once helped put our relationship into proper perspective. I do not know what has brought out these changes in you…"

Not wanting to discuss his recent volatile state, Kavan cut him off. "I have not been myself of late…and I apologize. I should not have called you a fool in front of the others…"

"I am a fool. I did not take your advice seriously enough and Bertram got out of the keep…"

Kneeling before him, Kavan hung his head. "I would try to assure you all will be well, but I do not know that to be the case. I know things will be the way they are preordained to be…"

"And Bertram is preordained to die." The King got up and passed Kavan to stare out the window. "These things you say, the things you See…they have always come about in one way or another. I have seen it numerous times. Regardless of what you consider yourself to be, you are a prophet of sorts. You saw a battle with Neth the day Muir was born; you told me that. Now that he is old enough to…that prediction looks to be coming to pass. I doubt this instance will be any different."

The bard chose not to voice his thoughts. He knew Arlan was right and that his silence would confirm the King's doubts. Fingering the Kílyn Cross he wore, he sighed. "I do not mean to change the subject, but I have come to ask what has been decided about the Council's proposal."

"It has the potential to benefit Enesfel greatly, and benefit the oppressed people in that region even more, if we are successful. Guthrie and I have a few ideas; if Owain and the Valdis' agree, it should result in crippling Neth enough that they will be less a threat to anyone. I will discuss it with Owain in the morning, if he is speaking to me…"

"If you wish to talk to him, you will need to do it tonight."

The King scowled. "Why? Is he leaving already?"

"That is what I came to discuss. I want permission to look for the boys."

They stared at each other. "You want to lead the search?" Kavan nodded and the King continued, "How do you propose to find them? What has this to do with Owain?"

Kavan leaned back on his heels. "I have a premonition about where they have been taken. Prince Owain promised your sister to help find Wilred. I have spoken to Lord Dugan, who also wishes to journey with me because he feels responsible…and because he has seen the man we seek. With Captain Delamo's help, I believe we can find them."

"Alive? Where do you think they are?"

Evasively, Kavan looked away. "It is a feeling…I am going to follow my instincts wherever they lead until we find the children. From your mood, I doubt the ransom demand can be met, and if our forces are occupied with Neth, there is nothing else to do. You will need every man; who else can you send? Allow me to do this, Arlan."

The King considered the request. Kavan would be no good to him in battle and sparing Captain Delamo and Caol Dugan would not affect the outcome of the war. It made sense to him; if anyone could find the boys alive, it would be Kavan.

"Your instincts are the best. If they can be found, you will find them, more quickly, I believe, than that venador can. When will you leave?"

"Dawn." He was relieved he did not have to argue with Arlan. "There is no time to waste. Lord Owain is prepared to leave his men at your disposal, either to take messages to the Council or to escort you if you decide to travel into Neth."

"That will be useful. We will need them. Tell them your party leaves at dawn, and tell Captain Delamo to choose a partner. I want at least one other soldier with you, Kavan. Do not refuse me. As for Owain, send him to me."

"You wish to speak with him alone? Now?"

The King straightened, understanding the bard's concern. Alone would be difficult, but at this hour, it was the way it had to be. "I will need to see him before he leaves…this is as good a time as any…and it will be easier to apologize if no one else is present."

## ❧Chapter 21❦

**K**avan had stood in the outer courtyard staring into the overcast sky long before the first hint of dawn, long before any of the palace staff began their day's work. He hoped this search party was the right thing to do, hoped his absence would not be detrimental to the King and his plans for war. Durham was many days ride from Rhidam; if Arlan needed him, Kavan might not be able to return in time to be of use.

The few belongings he would take were at his feet, a satchel with extra clothing, the Coryllien dagger, sketches Ártur had drawn of both the princes and of Halstatt, and his harp. He packed those things last night before trying to sleep, but his rest had been troubled with dreams he could not recall upon waking; he eventually gave up on sleep, picked up his pack, and came here to think and be alone beneath the sky. He heard the crunch of boots on stone behind him but did not turn; he knew the sound of those steps. Wortham stopped beside him, his breath misting in the cold air as the moisture condensed on the fringes of his beard.

"I'm bringing Darius Corbin. He has little field experience but he's strong, quick, and trustworthy. That's probably the most important thing. He has sworn to do whatever you ask of him." Kavan nodded in response, appreciating Wortham's insightfulness. "Shall I get the horses?" Again, the bard nodded and Wortham left him alone.

But he was not alone for long. Caol was next to join him, and then Owain. No one spoke until the King came to bid them farewell, his amber cloak wrapped around his shoulders to block out the cold. The chamberlain was with him, watching Owain without giving the King cause to notice it or question it if he did. From the expression on Owain's face, Kavan assumed he and the chamberlain must have had some sort of conversation; he had never seen either the chamberlain or the prince at peace. Wortham and the horses were not long in joining them.

"Do you need anything?" the King asked, nervous and concerned with their well-being since he would not be with them. "Food? Money?"

"Captain Delamo has seen to those details. Besides," the bard glanced at his harp, "I do not think members of the royal family, two royal soldiers, and the White Bard will have difficulty finding lodging and food if we need it."

The King reluctantly agreed. He recalled the hospitality and generosity received thirteen years ago while in Kavan's company. Things were different now, Arlan was king instead of a prince, but Kavan had not changed and he had been away from the public for so long that many would be eager to accommodate him. Caol, Owain, and the young soldier Darius were already mounted and eager to be away. Wortham secured Kavan's belongings on his horse and held the animal's head, waiting for Kavan to mount. But the Elyri hesitated. The party was not yet complete and there was something he needed to say to Arlan before he left. He saw Ártur in a second story window and waved; the healer nodded and disappeared from view.

"You will have gone to war before we return," he said quietly. "I suspect it may be over before we make it home as well."

The King's expression fell. "You expect to be gone that long?" What did that suggest about his son's chances of survival?

"It will not take Enesfel long to do what must be done." Kavan did not know why he felt his own journey would take longer than expected, but he believed it. "Are you going into battle with the troops?"

"I do not know. I must think of the future…and until Bertram returns I do not know who would rule in my place should something happen to me."

That the man did not consider his daughter was telling, but Kavan said nothing. The girl would rule one day, he knew, whether her father appointed her his heir or not. "Nothing detrimental will happen to you, My King…at least you will not die in battle. Of that, I am certain. It will do much for the morale of our forces if you lead them, and will do much more for the citizens of Fiara, Ruidoso, and southern Neth. Think on it, but please be cautious."

"Aren't I always?" The King touched the scar on his cheek, his constant reminder of his impetuousness. Another horse joined them; Guthrie glanced at the new arrival, then at Owain without speaking or changing expressions. The King, on the other hand, scowled. "Muir, what are you doing?"

There was the slightest awkward pause from the prince before he cleared his throat and replied, "I am joining the search for Bertram and Wilred."

"Why on earth…?"

"Despite what anyone says, Bertram is my brother…and Wilred is my cousin and friend." Not an actual cousin by blood, but cousin by upbringing. "I want to find them and bring them home."

"It might be dangerous, Muir. You cannot…"

Responding to the imagined condescension in the King's voice, Muir drew his sword from the side of the horse Arlan could not see. The chamberlain inhaled sharply but no one interceded. No one, not even the King, thought Muir would actually use it. Arlan held his ground. "Lord Cáner has trained me to the best of his ability; I have more to learn but I am not weak and not a coward. You have never bothered to see how my swordsmanship, or anything else I do, is progressing; do not tell me I cannot defend myself."

The King's cool expression sapped the bravado from the prince's tirade. He felt Kavan's gaze and sheathed his sword, wondering if the bard disapproved of his outburst. "Besides, I am not wanted or needed here. Without Lord Cliáth, I will be left to my own devices. If I join them, I will be out of your way, I may be able to make a difference, and," he looked at Owain, "I can know my father better. He, at least, desires my company."

There was nothing the King could say to that. Nothing he would have trusted himself to say if he could find his voice, and the Elyri's hand upon his arm kept him from trying. Muir's defensiveness was surprising, as had been the sword at his throat. It was awkward to realize how quickly Muir had accepted Owain as his father, and to know that the prince had easily turned away from the man who had raised him. Not raised…clothed, fed, and sheltered, but not raised. Arlan coughed. The chamberlain's expression was a mixture of astonishment, amusement, apprehension and something more the King could not define. Rather than say something inappropriate, Arlan looked at Kavan and changed the subject. "You do not have a healer with you. What will happen if someone is injured?" It was as much permission as he could verbally give Muir to do what the young man would do regardless.

"Captain Delamo knows basic medical techniques. If we need something more, we will locate a physician or pray k'Ádhá sees fit to tend the problem directly. You will need Ártur on the battlefield, and Syl must remain here to care for Prince Hagan and the household. Do not be concerned about us."

The King snorted. "Not concerned? My best friends are…and my children…" He stopped, realizing what he had said, realizing that for the first time in memory he was concerned about Muir's welfare and had referred to him as son. Kavan heard it too. Hoping to cover the slip, the King waved his hand. "Go, Kavan. Find the boys. Blessings and fortune go with you, my friend."

"k'Ádhá watch over you, Arlan. If you have need of me, believe me, I will know." He mounted his mare, nudged her flanks gently, and led the five riders and their lone packhorse out of the keep. It was going to be a long day.

ॐ*ॐ

There was a cold rain falling when Gabrielle Dilyn awoke to find her husband not in the bed beside her. Dawn was breaking, and in the gray stone fireplace the fire had gone out some time ago, making the room miserably chilled. How unlike Felix to awaken and not tend the fire, she mused. There was no need to summon Delia or one of the boys, however. The serving woman was fast approaching the age where it would be necessary to hire additional help, but Gabrielle was loath to do it. Delia had been with her as far back as Gabrielle could remember. For something as simple as starting a fire, there was no need to burden the woman when Gabrielle could do it herself.

The heavy red robe that hung on the bedpost was also cold but warmed quickly once wrapped around her body. Grateful for the Hatu woolen rug with its blue and black concentric patterns, she padded barefoot to the hearth and got the fire going to her satisfaction. She gave the blue cord hanging in the corner of the room a single tug and heard the chimes of it echo throughout the house as she settled upon the hearth.

Life had nearly returned to normal; her time in Rhidam felt like a distant dream. She had been busy with first Council business, and then the illness that had kept Clianthe in bed for days; there had been little time to dwell upon Kavan. It made getting over him again much easier. But when she heard her daughter plucking at the strings of the old family harp, as she had last night, the familiar pain returned. It was truly over, over before it could begin, she knew, and that hurt. Even if she had not been married, things between her and Kavan could never be different. He did not want what she wanted. Though her mind knew it, her heart struggled to let him go.

A knock came upon her door and the servant' woman's head poked in. "You are awake, milady. Shall I bring breakfast?"

"Yes…I think so, thank you, Delia. Have you seen Felix?"

The white-haired woman nodded. "A message came early, calling him to the docks; he felt it best to take care of the matter before the storm worsens, but he did ask me to tell you he did not know how long he would be out."

"Oh." It made sense. With the docks being the livelihood of the islands, business there was always important and often lengthy. "As long as it is raining like this, I do not wish to be disturbed by anyone other than family. I will be right here by the fire." Delia curtseyed and retreated. Pulling her bare feet beneath her, Gabrielle sighed and stared into the flames. There was nothing as cozy as a cold day of rain and warm fire to rest by. It looked to be a good day ahead.

❧*❧

"You are certain these coins and dagger belong to the man who broke into the castle, that the kidnapper is the same man?" Justice Cornell did not know why he bothered to ask. Ártur MacLyr was one of the most honest men the justice knew. The healer nodded, his attention focused on the King's glassy-eyed stare rather than the justice's questions.

"If you do not believe me, ask Lord Cáner or Syl. Or wait until Kavan returns if you feel it necessary…"

The justice looked insulted. "Milord. To do that would be a waste of valuable time, and the princes may not have much of it. This Malizar Caliph has already vacated one hiding place. If what Lord Cliáth suggests is true, he may no longer be in Rhidam." When he saw the King's eyes close wearily, he hastily added, "But wherever he is, I will find him. We will search all of Enesfel and the Five Sovereignties if we need to. There is nothing…"

"Do it, Lord Justice," the King interrupted weakly. "Enough talk."

"Yes, milord, at once."

The King went to the liquor cabinet for a drink but stopped with his hand on the cabinet door. He realized he was doing that more frequently since Brenna's death, as Guthrie had pointed out to him yesterday. His chamberlain urged him not to turn to drink to ease his pain, claiming to know from experience what it could cost. Sighing, he dropped his hand.

"That was Prince Wilred's cap," the healer said.

The King nodded. "I know."

"Are you going to tell your sister?"

"I do not know. There is not much to tell, is there?"

"But to withhold what you do know? It would be useless to tell you not to worry, but I am confident the boys will be found. Lord Cornell is hard at work, and Wace Elotti is on the fellow's trail. And if they fail, there is Kavan. There is nowhere in the Sovereignties, or indeed the world, where kidnappers can hide from him."

"But will Kavan be able to get them back if he does locate them?"

The healer put his hand on the King's shoulder. "Kavan can do anything he sets his mind to."

❧*❧

The search party had not traveled much beyond the city's outer limits when they heard a shout behind them, pleading for them to wait. A figure in healer yellow hurried after them, puffing breathlessly in his haste to catch them. When he was close enough to be identifiable, Caol felt his stomach lurch as if he would be sick. Muttering a string of obscenities, feeling this was the last thing they needed, he stopped his horse and waited. The others in the party did likewise.

"Lord Dugan! Lord Dugan! Please! Wait!"

"What do you want?" the inquisitor yelled back, his voice sharp with annoyance. "Don't tell me Elotti sent you to stop us."

Hazel eyes red and puffy, cheeks stained with wetness that might have been tears or a matter of exertion, the ashen-haired doctor shook his head fiercely as he reached the riders. "I do not know where he is," he choked as he gasped for air. "I have not seen him since the day we brought you back to Rhidam. He told me to wait for him but I cannot…" He paused as if embarrassed. "I know he must be looking for the man who attacked you…that is what you are doing, isn't it? Searching for him too?"

Caol glanced sideways at Kavan before replying, "Yes…that is what we are doing." Knowing what was coming, he hoped Kavan would exclude the physician.

Scanning the riders, Rouvyn asked, "May I accompany you until we find Wace? There is no physician among you; if someone is injured you will be at the mercy of strangers…"

"I don't think…"

But Kavan, recalling that the search party he had Seen had consisted of seven riders, interrupted. "No, Lord Dugan, he is welcome to join us. His company will not hinder us and might be of use. What is your name?"

"Rouvyn Talis, milord." Whether he knew the tales of the White Bard or not, he stared at Kavan with fascination, already under the Elyri's spell as so many were.

Paying no attention to that stare, or perhaps not noticing it, Kavan said, "Very well, Rouvyn. We do not have a horse for you; you will have to ride with one of us." He cast a quick glance at each member of the party. He did not want to encumber the fighters in the group, should they enter a skirmish and he could not expect Prince Muir to share his horse. Caol's expression suggested that if this doctor was placed with him, he might resort to irritated violence. There was no other choice. "Come up with me."

Rouvyn climbed onto the horse awkwardly, wrapping his arms around the Elyri's waist in a way that made Caol shudder and caused Muir to look away from the bard self-consciously as if the physician was doing something he longed to do but had never had the courage for. Owain side-eyed the doctor but his face showed little reaction, though Wortham's expression was the only one truly neutral, the one who kept his eyes on their path and his attention on the surrounding countryside. If Kavan noticed any of it, he did not mention it. He started his horse forward as soon as Rouvyn was settled and the others fell into formation behind him.

Standing on the main dock, Gabrielle tried to pull her cloak closer as protection from the driving wind and rain, but it was a fruitless effort. The water had soaked through to her skin over an hour ago, leaving her cold and shivering, and her hair had become impervious to the persistent tugging of the wind, clinging fiercely to her skull instead. To anyone who saw her as she struggled alongside her people, she was likely a pathetic sight. But those scurrying around her, pulling boats to moor or holding lanterns as close to the water surface as the waves would permit, paid her little heed. Their job was not to appraise her appearance but to find the man the suddenly worsening storm had pulled into the turbulent sea.

A particularly large wave crashed over the wooden dock, drenching those there, pulling another hapless man into the water. Fortunately for him, his nearby mates were able to throw a line in and pull him to safety before the sea claimed him. Gabrielle coughed and spluttered, wiping a strand of seagrass from her face and blinking salt water from her eyes. She strained to see into the darkness, but without a lantern of her own, she was restricted to the moving glow of search lamps and the occasional flash of lightning. This morning she had welcomed this storm and the forlorn feeling it brought. Now she wanted it to be over.

Normally, of course, she would not be out in a storm of this magnitude. She was not a seaman, and the islands could not risk their leader to the deep water. But she had an especially strong interest in the proceedings today, even if there was little she could do to help. A hand on her arm caused her to jump.

"There is nothing more to be done, milady." The gray face was unrecognizable in the rain, the voice indistinguishable as its owner struggled to make himself heard over the wind and surf.

"You cannot give up…"

"The storm is too strong! We will have to continue once it subsides. He will be…"

Gabrielle did not hear the remainder of his words. Her next coherent memory was of waking before the fire in her own room, though there were vague recollections of Delia peeling off wet clothing, wrapping her robe around her, and depositing her on the bed. Beyond the windows and walls, it was still raining, though the storm appeared to be slowing. She wanted to ask what had happened, how long she had been unconscious, what time it was, if the search continued, if there was any news. But she was alone with the fire. Head throbbing in a way that suggested she had hit it upon the dock, she forced herself to sit and wrapped her arms around herself as she stared into the hot gold of the flames.

Without anyone's words to say it, she knew that the sea had won this round. It was the primary danger of the islands. The sea had claimed thousands of victims over the centuries and this one would not be its last. Delia would tell her not to give up hope, that all would be well, but Gabrielle knew that was not true. She might never know what business had called Felix to the docks, and though she did not know the entire story, she did know he had slipped upon the rain-slicked dock and fallen into the water. The undercurrents around the islands were strong, even stronger during a storm, and Felix was one of the few on the islands who had never learned to swim. Even a strong swimmer like Gabrielle would have found survival difficult under those circumstances. For Felix, it would have been impossible.

She knew that too much time had passed with no sign of his body. Perhaps he had been swept out to sea, perhaps he lay at the bottom, wedged between rocks below the docks, or perhaps he would wash up on the shoreline somewhere else. The man on the docks, whoever he had been, had been right. There was nothing more to be done until the storm passed. When the waters calmed, a thorough search would be made of the coastline of all five islands. Until then, she could but pray. And though her thoughts filled with guilt that she had been too distant from Felix lately, she was too numb to mourn him. Oddly enough, she did not think about Kavan.

## ৯৽Chapter 22৾ঌ

R ouvyn tended the roasting rabbits, struggling to pay no attention to the others as they prepared the camp for the night. He was not untouched by the way most avoided or stared at him, but he knew there was little he could do to change their opinions. Since the start of the expedition, he had felt compelled to behave more independently than he was accustomed to, but Caol's knowledge of the man's relationship with Elotti had seemingly spread throughout the party, or at least the inquisitor's distaste had done so, and Rouvyn's initial clingy response to Kavan's welcome had intensified the belief in his inability to be a strong man. Try as he might, he knew if he did not find a way to prove himself, this would be a very tedious journey.

Prince Muir set the bedrolls while Darius and Wortham gathered wood to last through the night's watches. Caol had built the fire and now tended the horses. It was Owain's hunting prowess throughout the day that gained them the rabbits; he skinned and cleaned them as they rode and now settled near the fire to watch them cook after seeing that every water skin was filled from a nearby creek. The elder prince's attention turned occasionally to Kavan while the rabbits sizzled, as he found it inevitably did when he had nothing else to occupy his thoughts since coming to Rhidam and seeing the bard again.

Owain had known very few Elyri, only the healer Ártur when both lived in Rhidam during Owain's first eight years of life. He had very little firsthand experience with their abilities. After that frightening encounter with Kavan when they had been children, Owain's years in Neth had filled the knowledge void with rumors and wild tales of the atrocities Elyri could wreak with their demon-spawned magic upon unsuspecting Teren. He did not believe the stories any longer, due mostly to his adult encounters with Kavan. Kavan might be different, might possess abilities unknown to Teren, but he was certainly not a spawn of evil. No servant of a demon would have saved Owain's life the night Arlan claimed Enesfel's throne.

Still, he harbored an innate discomfort with the unknown. He wanted a comprehensible explanation for everything he saw because for many years he was denied explanations for anything. How could the Elyri do what they were rumored to do? Were any of the rumors true? Everyone knew about healers, and he had seen Kavan transform into the White Hart and back, but what else was there?

He did not believe Kavan, or any other Elyri, would volunteer such information, thus he refrained from asking. If he were Elyri, he knew he would not trust people who hated and feared him with that sort of knowledge. But sometimes, as with now, when Kavan met his gaze with those translucent, wisdom-filled eyes, Owain believed Kavan sensed his thoughts and the flicker of torment and loneliness in those same eyes made Owain sure that the bard wanted to confide in someone, answer those questions, if he could. Knowing that longing was there somehow made Owain's ignorance bearable.

Rabbits cooked, the party ate in silence. It had been the same since the start of their journey. Caol gave everyone a wide berth, particularly Owain and Rouvyn. That Muir and Kavan were comfortable in Owain's company eased Wortham's mind, but he was confused about the part the late King of Enesfel played in this and why he was on such intimate terms with Kavan when he had once been the enemy. Rouvyn, the outcast with the gentle demeanor and features, seemed to cast an uneasy pall over everyone except the bard, especially because he stuck as close to the bard as he could. If Kavan noticed this attachment, he did not seem uncomfortable, but being the physician's sole social outlet created strain as the others vied for the Elyri's attention only to then draw back with hesitation.

Kavan sighed as he finished his meal, wiped his hands, and reached for his harp. But as with the last seven nights, the music refused to come. The surrounding tension pushed its way into his core and allowed him no peace. Until there was harmony among them, or at least more harmony than existed currently, he could do little more than pluck at the brass strings with distraction.

"Lord Dugan," he finally said across the fire, determined tonight that the silence would not prevail. "We will reach Erleta by noon tomorrow. We are far from Durham, but is there anything we should look for? Anyone to contact? Anything you would recommend us doing?"

The inquisitor cast uncomfortable glances around him but no one seemed suspicious of the bard's questions. No one knew why they were headed for Durham except that Kavan had chosen to start the search there. Most in the group knew that Caol had grown up in this corner of Enesfel, unlike Darius who hailed from the port of Kilmacud to the south and Rouvyn who had spent his entire life in Rhidam. The kidnapper had gone after Caol twice, either intentionally or accidentally; beginning in a region Caol knew made sense. Asking him about region-specific details was logical.

He took a long drink of lukewarm ale to cover his hesitation. "I don't know. I know people of course and will contact them when we arrive. But they might not want to talk to me…might not recognize me after all this time…might even be dead by now…and there's no guarantee they will know anything." He did not need to see the bard's expression to know Kavan understood what he did not say.

"We have no indication the bandits came in this direction with the children," said Darius, wiping his hands upon his trousers. "I'd think they would be in Rhidam still, waiting for the ransom. Durham's quite a distance…this could be a waste of effort."

"On the contrary," Kavan replied, appreciating the challenge. "Lord Dugan also received a ransom demand." He did not acknowledge Caol's surprised spluttering. "It has led me to suspect that the responsible party has taken the boys to Durham."

Wortham leaned forward, hoping for a better view of Kavan's face in the firelight. The bard met his gaze and whatever the captain saw there was enough to satisfy him.

"Does the King know about this second ransom demand?" asked Darius.

"I informed him that I had reason to believe the children had been taken to Durham. As for the rest, there was nothing significantly different from the one the King received. As burdened as he is, there was no reason to add to his concerns."

"The King trusts him," Wortham grunted. Kavan hoped he would continue to be worthy of that trust.

"And I'm sure he knows Caol would receive one too," offered Owain. "One of the boys is his son; the kidnappers would cover every angle, hoping to get what they could out of Caol that they might not get from the King."

The inquisitor nodded, surprised with the supportive words from the previous king. Feeling more at ease, he began to lie back, intending to sleep.

"One more thing," the bard said, interrupting him. "If we are to be successful in this undertaking, it will require cooperation. This means communication, trust, and an end to whatever is happening amongst us. Caol, you do not trust Lord Lachlan because of past events between your father and Enesfel's troops." Curious glances passed amongst the men but Kavan did not explain. "However, as you said, he was involved in dealings which contributed to his fate. Lord Lachlan pledged support to your wife and the king, promised to find your son. He is willing to do this despite the fact you nearly killed him. Accept his offer as sincere and let us work together."

He then looked at Owain. "Milord, I know you have every reason to mistrust all of us. You have not been treated with compassion in the past, with or without cause. Mutual trust is as difficult for some of us as it is for you, but we must strive to that end. Physician Talis deserves our trust too. As a physician, he did not join us to cause discord and has caused no offense. It may not be easy to trust a stranger, but it is necessary. If we are to make the most of our time in Erleta, and elsewhere, we should divide into smaller units, pairs when we can. The doctor has no weapons and it would be foolish to allow Prince Muir to be alone…"

"I can protect myself, Lord Cliáth," the prince said indignantly.

The corners of Kavan's mouth twitched. "I have no doubt of that, my prince, but if the kidnappers are near, they do not need another Lachlan to add to their collection. You are royalty and must not forget that. We should protect you accordingly, as much as we are able."

Wortham nodded. "I think the best plan, for now, would be for Darius and me to stick with the prince and pose questions as official representatives of the Crown."

The prince reluctantly agreed, despite his annoyance.

Grateful for Kavan's tact thus far, knowing that any doubts about their mission, and Caol's involvement in it, could be detrimental to their success, the inquisitor said, "Let us wait until we get there. We will secure rooms and I will reach out to a few friends, learn what I can. Like I said, we might find nothing in Erleta and it is best not to arouse suspicion…in case we are being followed and watched."

"Very well." Kavan felt he would know if he was being watched or followed, but taking precautions was wise. He wrapped one arm around his harp, no longer feeling like making music, and prepared for the first watch with Rouvyn. He felt significantly better for having spoken.

"Milord?" asked Wortham. He glanced at the physician, took a deep breath, and continued, "If it is the same to you, I would like to take this first watch with Rouvyn." No one would ever accuse Captain Delamo of cowardice, and he did not want to disappoint the bard. Besides, he knew Kavan was right. His jealousies might be eased if he got to know the physician better. At the very least, befriending the man would mean Kavan was not saddled with the task of being the only person Rouvyn had to talk to. That, in turn, would mean the physician spent less time with Kavan and leave less for Wortham to be jealous about.

The smile the bard gave him was praise enough.

&#x2619;*&#x264b;

"Welcome to Rhidam, Lady Dubuais." The King took Madalyn's outstretched hand and pressed it to his lips before allowing her, in turn, to kiss his ring. "I regret I did not see you when you were last here, but other matters demanded my attention."

She smiled and curtseyed. "I know. My problems, such as they were, were trivial compared to yours, and your chancellor dealt with them in a most expedient and masterful fashion." The smile she cast on Bhríd was warm and all-encompassing though he could not see it without turning his head. "I am honored you agreed to see me. My father spoke highly of your father and brother Donal, and I am pleased to see you uphold traditions of fairness."

"Fairness is the most effective way to rule. As some in my family failed to learn, you do not succeed without it. You and your family have been a great asset to Enesfel; I hope we can count on you in the days ahead."

"The rumors are true then? There is to be war?" The King neither confirmed nor denied it. "I have alerted my household, my advisors, and my people, to be prepared as soon as I heard the rumors. They can be summoned immediately should you request it."

"I shall, very soon, I assure you. Lord Cáner?" Now that he was included in the conversation, the chancellor lifted his head. "See to the Lady's comforts. I am due in conference with General Wyndham and Chamberlain McHador. I shall endeavor to see you later this evening, or in the morning, Duchess, and you can tell me to what we owe the pleasure of your delightful company."

"I would be honored, Your Majesty." She and Bhríd bowed and waited until they were alone in the library before she spoke again. "I will not be able to tell him, however, until I know what brought me here."

"Your horse?" Bhríd said with a teasing chuckle. He could scarcely believe how excited he had been at the thought of seeing her again, and since she arrived, he had been unable to stop smiling. It strengthened his conviction about what he was doing, but it did not make it easier. Her laughter at his words made him smile. "Actually, you came because I asked it, though I did not expect your arrival to be prompt. Did you have a pleasant journey?"

"Yes," she replied. "I would have come the evening I received your letter, but other matters detained me. I came as quickly as could be arranged. It seemed the proper thing to do…and it pleases me to be here, to see you again."

"Likewise. Have you eaten?"

"I ate as we traveled. I knew it would be late when I arrived, and I have no desire to trouble your staff."

"It would be no trouble, believe me. Since the hour is late, shall I show you to a room and have a bath drawn for you? Then you can rest and we shall speak in the morning?" He extended his arm and she hooked hers through it.

Though she would rather spend more time in his company, tonight, as happy as she was to be here, propriety demanded something else, and she answered, "I would like that very much."

&#x221E;*&#x221E;

The study was dark; Gabrielle had put out the lamp long ago and stared into the starless sky through the piazza window. The household staff was asleep, Clianthe put to bed much earlier, and there was no one to disturb her. She smoothed the black velvet of her gown beneath her palms and sighed. She looked stunning in black, everyone told her that, even her father, but today she did not feel stunning. She felt old and tired. Wiping her cheeks with her kerchief, she pushed down the sob that tried to escape.

After seven days of intense searching, no trace of Felix was found and Gabrielle reluctantly allowed herself to be persuaded to call off the search. Today there had been a short service held in his honor. The people of Káliel were not known for lengthy rituals, at least not where death was concerned. Beyond the occasional stifled sob, Gabrielle felt too stunned, too dead inside, to weep. That he was gone hurt, although she had never loved him in the way he had seemed to love her. Nor did it surprise her that Clianthe was as restrained with her tears. Felix had not been good with children and no bond had ever developed between him and his daughter.

Now it is just Clianthe and me, Gabrielle thought, rising, at last, to attempt to sleep. In truth, much of her life would be little different, but the loss was still painful. k'Ádhá rest your soul, Felix. Wherever you are.

&#x221E;*&#x221E;

"No news yet, My Liege, on any front," Guthrie sighed as he placed himself in a chair across from the King. He was amazed at how empty the palace felt without the princes and several of the King's usual entourage. The chamberlain had been busy thinking and rethinking strategies for dealing with Neth, discussing them with both Ternce and the King, and had not noticed the emptiness before today. Nothing seemed the same. From the King's haunted expression, Guthrie knew that Arlan felt it too.

"What is the status of our troops?" The general was unable to attend the agreed meeting, but as Guthrie had already talked with him, neither King nor chamberlain felt they were being detained by the man's absence.

"Those men from the holdings nearest Rhidam are here and training vigorously. I suspect most of the others will arrive within the week. There is going to be little need for cavalry in the southern forests of Neth; General Wyndham is diverting those men into infantry. I think it would be prudent to discuss plans with Cordash before we proceed further."

The King shook his head. "I do not trust anyone else to explain this matter to Prince Valdis, and I cannot justify sending you or General Wyndham when we are this close to war. Without Kavan…" He rubbed his eyes. "Who else do you recommend? Any suggestions?"

Guthrie pondered the question before replying. "There must be Gates in Cordash. If so, Ártur may be willing to take me to the Valdis court." He knew that the King had made it a personal policy to avoid relying on Elyri abilities, at least those abilities other than healing, and that Arlan would not want to start now. "They have placed their talents and skills at your service; why not make use of them when the need arises. This is as near to an emergency as we shall ever have; it cannot hurt to ask him. If he is unwilling, he will say so. It is the fastest way to get there and back, and the surest way of giving Prince Valdis the complete, accurate details of the plan we wish to execute."

Though he did not like it, the King knew it would be wise to agree this time. Time was pressing upon them; the need to act swiftly was undeniable. "Ask him. But I will not send you to Cordash and commit ourselves to action until Ternce believes the troops are ready."

Guthrie sighed. "I will ask his opinion, but I believe we should commit. We are as ready as we are going to be without a full year's training...and a year is a luxury we cannot afford."

❧*☙

The lush velvet of her gown flowed around her feet like water passing in a stream as Madalyn came to the library, expecting to meet the chancellor there as he had requested the night before. The gown was chosen because its hue matched the red of her hair and was cut to accentuate all of her best features, the swell of her hips, the curve of her breasts. Although it appeared Bhríd was leaning in favor of a union between them, she was determined to positively sway him in any way she could. From the doorway, she saw him lounging in a low cushioned chair, a book across his lap, his eyes staring across the room as if he was lost in a dream or deep thought. When he did not react to her presence, she smiled and said, "Good morning, Lord Chancellor."

Bhríd blushed as he faced her, wondering how long she had been watching him. He stood to welcome her, smiling at her beauty and the way she brought radiance to the room. "Actually, it is nearly noon," he teased. "Did you rest well?"

"Yes." It was her turn to blush. "I suppose the hasty journey took more out of me than I thought. What have you been reading?"

Looking at the book in his hand, he closed it and placed it on the nearest table. "Various accounts of Enesfel's battles with Neth. I am studying the layout of their countryside, what sort of terrain we will encounter, and what tactics they are likely to use, to be properly prepared."

"Know thy enemy?"

"Exactly."

She tried not to frown. "Do you anticipate going into battle then?" She did not savor that thought.

Realizing this, he took a step closer and murmured, "I am the King's champion, and as I am often told, perhaps the best swordsman in Enesfel." Whether or not it was true, he was at least acknowledging what others thought without trying to boast about it. "Do not be afraid. The King has not said I will go…but I think I must, and I have every intention of returning. I can fend for myself. Besides, from what I have heard of Chamberlain McHador's plan, I do not expect Enesfel's forces to do much fighting. That duty will likely fall to Cordash."

"It should," she huffed. "This is their problem; they ask for our aid though they know we are not prepared or manned for that." Something in his expression, in his eyes, gave her pause. "Is there more to it? What is it?"

Bhríd shook his head. "I cannot say. I can tell you that there is more at stake than Cordash' current squabbles with Neth." He smiled again, hoping to change the subject. "You missed the morning meal. Would you like to take something to the garden? We can dine there if you wish."

As much as she wanted an answer to her queries, she had not expected details of what lay ahead. A wise ruler never tipped his hand. Accepting the redirection, especially at the mention of dining with him in a garden, she smiled. "That would be lovely. Would you answer one question for me?"

"If I can." He offered his arm.

"Why did you invite me back to Rhidam?"

He grinned. "To learn more about you, of course."

She could see in his eyes that there was more to his invitation than that, but his answer still made her heart soar. Taking his arm, she grinned and walked with him out of the room.

❧*❧

Ártur stared across the courtyard in the direction of Durham, feeling the familiar tingle at the back of his neck that indicated Kavan was reaching for him. He wanted to open to that contact, but he did not. Not tonight. The events of the day had left him drained and he did not want his cousin to fret. Finding the missing princes was more important than any emotional stress the healer was contending with, and he knew he had been through worse.

He would go into battle with Enesfel's troops. He had not been asked, but he had known he would go since the first whispered rumors of war. Syl was not trained in that capacity, and though she served Prince Arlan during his push for the throne, her temperament was better suited for caring for the royal family and household in Rhidam. Ártur, on the other hand, had come to Rhidam originally to serve King Innis on the battlefield. It had not been pleasant work, seeing so many dead, so many dying, so many mutilated beyond healing. Though he had found the work rewarding and satisfying, he had been grateful when the King elevated him to head physician of the Lachlan House. Donal kept him on in that capacity and Ártur remained far away from war until he too gave aid to Prince Arlan. It did not surprise him that the King might desire his military experience, but he did not like it.

The chamberlain asked Ártur to take him through the Gates to Cordash, to King Ahern and Prince Renfrid. The healer understood the reasoning and could not offer a good reason for refusing. He could claim he did not know the locations of any Cordashian Gates, but as Kavan had spent many hours during the past years teaching him how to identify other Gates, the healer no longer had that excuse. Since he could not adequately voice the cause of his discomfort, he said nothing and allowed himself to be swayed, agreeing to take Guthrie as soon as the King permitted. It was his duty and he did not have to like it, but he felt ill-at-ease in such political situations and he would have preferred not to go.

Yet neither of those matters affected him as much as discovering that one of the three men incarcerated for the killing of the Elyri painter had died during the night. Normally the fate of prisoners did not trouble him, but the circumstances surrounding this death were disturbing and suspicious and Ártur worried about what it meant.

It had been the youngest of the three, and the single one to allow Ártur to tend to the wounds of torture. He had several talks with the healer while ignoring the derision of his accomplices. He managed to pay the entire fine the King had imposed and Ártur convinced the King that the man was no longer a threat. He had been scheduled to be released the following day. But come morning, he was found dead and Ártur's examination indicated the cause of death was poison.

The ensuing investigation had included everyone with access to the prisoners or who had contact with them, from Guthrie and Minos to the guards. When that proved futile, attention was turned to the kitchen staff who provided the meals. If the King had not insisted that the healer probe the thoughts of each suspect, they might never have discovered the intense hatred one of the serving staff harbored towards Elyri, or that she was distantly related to one of the three prisoners. Fortunately, the woman had not been on the palace staff long enough to do the damage she intended. Elyri hatred was not unusual, but his cousin had been the intended first target. Only Kavan's absence from Rhidam on the mission of finding the princes had spared his life. That unsettled the healer more than he cared to admit. He had not revealed that news to the King, however. The King had enough to worry about.

Kavan did not need to know such things either, and Ártur would not be able to hide it if he allowed contact. The healer turned from the window, forcing himself to ignore the tickle at the nape of his neck until it became fainter and finally stopped. But he knew Kavan would try again. Ártur could not avoid him forever.

&#x2767;*&#x2768;

It took Kavan several hours and much playing before he was able to break away from the tavern gathering and go up to the room he had secured for the night. He had not expected to be anonymous; he knew how far the stories and legends of the White Bard had spread, and he had been in this town and tavern before. That was many years ago, however, and he had thought perhaps after so long away he might have been forgotten. He had not anticipated the enthusiastic welcome he received. He chose to enter the town alone; the crowd gathered around him as soon as he was spotted, followed him to the inn Caol recommended, and stayed in the tavern with him until after midnight, which allowed his companions to come into town without harassment and conduct their business unnoticed.

And though Kavan disliked the press of a crowd and could feel the occasional flash of anti-Elyri hostility, it felt good to be playing for the people again. It had been fourteen years since he had played in a tavern and entertained the common folk. He had forgotten how much these people seemed to need him. To be needed was something Kavan desperately wanted.

Wortham, Darius, and Muir rode into town under an official banner, representing the Crown in their search of kidnappers. The prince wore Caol's gauntlets and mail shirt, which were slightly large for him but allowed him to blend in as a squire. They purchased supplies for the next leg of their journey and took rooms in the same tavern as Kavan, though they did not interact with him. Since their noon arrival, they had questioned people in and around the tavern and retired to their room long before Kavan could do likewise.

A short time after their arrival, Rouvyn and Owain followed, Owain disguised beneath the folds of his cloak. It would be unethical for Rouvyn to disguise his physician's calling, thus he posed as

Owain's doctor, secured a room in the town's other inn, and while Owain found refuge in a corner of the bar, Rouvyn attempted to engage the patrons in gossip. The news of the kidnapping had not spread this far north, and he learned nothing; in fact, Rouvyn's mention of it was the first anyone in the region had heard of the matter.

Kavan lay upon his bed, the dull, well-worn bedsheet wrapped around his waist, hands behind his head, staring at the ceiling. Except for the gnawing concern about why Ártur had shut out his contact, Kavan was content. He was emotionally drained and raw, but it was a satisfying feeling, a relief to be empty of everything, particularly the anger that had plagued him for the past several weeks. He knew from a veiled exchange with Wortham in the corridor that no one had learned anything of use, nor heard from Caol, who entered town alone and not been seen since they separated at dawn. What if the inquisitor decided to make the rest of this journey alone, Kavan mused, as a knock came upon the door.

As if reading his thoughts, when Kavan called, "Enter," Caol nudged the door open and slid inside, pushing the cloak from his face after the door was closed behind him. He turned to face Kavan, froze, and stared at the bard as if he had never seen him before.

When Kavan sat to look at him, he stammered, "I…I'm sorry, milord…I…I know your hands and…I never realized the rest of you was…white…" He felt stupid after saying it, but it was the truth. The thought of what might be beneath Kavan's white robes had never crossed his mind.

"What else would I be?" He did not sound slighted, but the inquisitor suddenly felt as if he had said something inappropriate. "Do not be embarrassed," Kavan admonished as he pulled his robe over his head. "I am sometimes as shocked at my appearance as you are."

"I am not shocked, milord, just…" Awed was the first word that came to mind but it stuck in his throat and refused to come out.

To relieve the awkwardness in the room, Kavan got up and turned his back to Caol long enough to adjust his robe. It gave Caol time to regain his composure. "I hope you have learned something; no one else has."

Caol shifted his weight and eyed the edge of the bed, though he decided against sitting. "They were here...or at least Halstatt traveled through Erleta. The Association...he was seen. It was days ago though, and he appeared to be alone. He did not stay long; news of what he had done reached the local members before he arrived and they refused to offer aid or sanctuary."

"Why would they do that?" Not knowing the rules of the Association, Kavan presumed the man would have a nearly unlimited supply of resources from an organization that spread throughout Enesfel, Cordash, Hatu, and Neth.

"Part of the code. Children are never pawns. They are not to be killed, kidnapped, or harmed. They can be threatened, they can be punished within the rules of the Association, but the children of other Association members and nobility are off limits. It is a built-in means of perpetuating both the Association and the monarchy. The last things the Association wants to do is kill off its own preparatory members or get involved in royal intrigue that would cause the nobility to take notice of them. Kidnapping the boys has cost him their respect and his place among them. The Association has no jurisdiction in the Dugan-Tarmajien feud; they cannot interfere directly, but he has taken the feud outside of personal jurisdiction and broken the rules he agreed to live by. His access to supplies and assistance is cut off and any member who finds him is permitted to kill him without question."

"Does this mean the Association is willing to help us?" That could be a helpful thing, a stroke of fortune for their efforts, as long as the boys were not harmed in the process.

"As far as they are concerned, I am a security threat because of my proximity to the King, so no. They acknowledge that thus far I have not been a liability; instead of killing me, as they usually would with someone like me, they will spare my life for my continued silence. They have released me from the bonds of the Association, which unfortunately means my access to their information may be restricted. Out of respect for my family, however, and because of the boys, the Association has agreed that if there is anything they think I should know, I will be contacted."

Kavan frowned. "Which may or may not provide us with anything. It is better than nothing, I suppose. Do we start for Durham tomorrow?" He saw no reason to stay where they were if there was nothing further to be gained.

"Might as well. The most we can do here is waste time…"

"Agreed. Tell the others we will rendezvous outside the city as near to dawn as we can manage." Caol nodded, pulled the hood of his cloak up and started out the door, both men hoping, as he left as silently as he had come, that they would have better success in Durham.

## ❧Chapter 23☙

gdhededhá Tusánt left the Purification Chamber and crossed the sanctuary, passing gdhededhá Claide who knelt before the altar conducting his evening devotional. Tusánt considered himself pious, devout, and sincere, but Claide's behavior often bordered on fanatical, which disturbed the Elyri gdhededhá on nights like tonight. Like most of the Teren gdhededhá serving now, Claide had trained in Elyriá, yet Tusánt knew the man felt superior to those who had trained him, felt purer in the eyes of the Faith. He might never say it, certainly not to Tusánt, but it was obvious even to k'gdhededhá Jermyn.

Tusánt had been tempted during the last confession to lift the veil and see whom he was speaking with, despite Claide being nearby. It had started much like any other concession, something about lying to his wife to spend a few hours drinking with friends…and then claiming to have been robbed to explain the missing money spent on drinks and whores. It was the man's tone of voice and Elyri intuition that tempted Tusánt to lift the veil, as the man felt much more sinister than his words suggested. The temptation to look, however, knotted into fear when the speaker's voice dropped low and he made an abrupt change in subject.

"If I were you, gdhededhá, I would leave Enesfel before someone slits your throat. Your kind are not welcome here. If you remain, I will not be responsible for what happens to you."

After the fellow left, Tusánt remained rooted to his wooden stool until Claide's voice punctured the silence. The man's devotionals were usually or supplication silent, but he often punctuated them with verbal words of praise. Tusánt had not been in Enesfel long enough to learn how deep the prejudice had once been, and as Enesfel had been peaceful for many years, he had never been threatened before. He felt no panic, no cause to rush out and seek safety, but he would now admit, if asked, that only duty and faith would keep him in Rhidam.

"Is something wrong, Tusánt?"

"I…" He turned as he reached the side door to the thóres and met Claide's gaze. "No. Why do you ask?"

The kneeling man shrugged, his expression bland and bored, and replied, "You seem agitated." He returned to his devotions and Tusánt hurried out.

How could he have known Tusánt was troubled when the man had been deep in prayer? The thought unsettled the Elyri. Perhaps he was being paranoid, but Tusánt had the distinct impression that the look on Claide's face before he bowed his head in prayer was anything but concerned.

"Something's not right."

Kavan looked to his left at Caol, wondering what the man sensed. He detected nothing, but the inquisitor's expression mirrored his words of concern, and because Caol was from this region, knew it better than Kavan, the bard was inclined to heed him. A portion of the main road had been washed out by the spring rains, causing the search party to take an alternate route to Durham. It was a path Caol agreed was feasible, but would delay their arrival at their destination by several hours. The sky was almost dark and they were still too far from Durham. None of the others shared Caol's anxiety; even Rouvyn seemed unusually relaxed. With a tilt of his head, the bard beckoned Caol closer.

"Explain," he said softly so the others would not overhear when the inquisitor's horse pulled alongside his.

Caol shrugged. "I can't pinpoint it…something about this detour troubles me. The sign looked official, and what damage we saw looked natural…but it's not right somehow."

"How much further to Durham?"

"Two hours, more or less…although in the dark we will need to travel more cautiously…maybe three hours."

Glancing at the fading red in the sky, Kavan frowned and absentmindedly toyed with the slack reins as he pondered the situation. His horse shook its head in agreement to his unspoken thoughts and then tugged at the lead. "Do you suggest continuing or is it wiser to set camp and continue in the morning?"

"By the time we reached Durham tonight," he scoffed, "we would be lucky to find rooms…not to mention it does not give us time to look around before getting settled. I would prefer to meet Halstatt in the daylight if possible. There is a stretch of dense forest ahead; if anyone wanted to set an ambush, the darkness and trees will provide effective cover, if not for Halstatt, then for anyone else hoping to rob passing merchants. It's happened before."

The bard remembered passing through that stretch of forest, with Prince Arlan and his forces many years ago. It was not the sort of place to be caught unaware. "You believe Halstatt arranged this detour."

It was not a question. Caol shrugged again. "I don't know…but I would not be surprised."

"Then perhaps we should stop."

"I doubt that would make a difference." His lips twisted into a wry smirk at the bard's perplexed expression. "He knows how long it should take to travel between Durham and Erleta…and how long it should take from the detour to reach the outskirts of Durham. If he has an ambush planned and we do not pass tonight, he will either wait until morning or have the ambush come to us. I doubt we'll be able to avoid it, if it is indeed what he has planned. But we might have one advantage." He nodded at the bard's curious expression. "He has been traveling ahead of us; without the Association, he probably has no way of knowing I am not alone. I've taken precautions to not be recognized, and I was alone in Erleta. If there's an ambush waiting, it can't be much of one."

Kavan kept the party moving forward, thoughtful as he considered their best choice, until he saw the rim of trees far ahead, silhouetted against the darkening sky. A glance at Caol made the inquisitor nod. Decision made, Kavan stopped his horse, turned, and waited for the others to catch up.

"Why are we stopping?" the young prince asked sullenly. He was an able rider but he had never spent so much time astride a horse, or out in the open. While he did not regret his decision to come, he missed the comforts of home. After the past several days, he was rethinking his dreams of going to sea.

"Lord Dugan suspects an ambush ahead. The woods are a common place for bandits. It would be prudent to camp and travel the final distance in the morning when we will have light to our advantage."

"And be extra vigilant on our watches," Wortham added, sliding from his horse. "Anyone would be able to come for us in the night, but with the distance, we should have fair warning."

Muir groaned, dismounted, and took out his bedroll. "Fine. I guess that means no fire. I am going to sleep. Wake me when it's my watch."

One by one, the party prepared for the night, but other than Prince Muir and Rouvyn, no one was particularly interested in sleep. There was too much military training, Kavan thought, wondering how he could do what he wanted with everyone awake and watchful. Correction, he thought. Wortham would not be a problem, and both Owain and Caol had witnessed a shape-change before, though he suspected Caol had forgotten about that incident. Owain would never forget those events, and Darius had not been part of that day.

"I don't think scouting would be a good idea," Wortham commented, hand briefly clasping Kavan's shoulder with an expression that suggested he knew what the bard was thinking. "We could all use the rest. No sense in looking for trouble; if it wants us, it'll come looking." He rolled his cloak into a lumpy mass and laid his head upon it, facing Kavan as he readied for sleep. Reluctantly, Kavan acknowledged that the captain was probably correct.

"Same plan for tomorrow, as in Erleta?" Darius asked, scratching at his knee and peering through the darkness in Kavan's direction.

Caol answered first. "It would be best. We cover more ground when we split. We can hit the market, the inns, the tavern, and the náós. That is where the most people will be gathered. If anyone has seen anything…"

"Riding in separately is asking for scoundrels to ambush us."

Caol ignored the young soldier. "We don't have any other options. I think we can get through unscathed if we are careful. I doubt Lord Cliáth will be in danger from common thieves…" He cast a sideways glance at the bard; he did not know the Elyri's abilities, but instinct told him that Kavan could defend himself. "Physician Talis and Lord Lachlan can attach themselves to the royal unit without looking suspicious, and all of you combined have the ability to protect yourselves."

Owain leaned forward. "What about you? You are the one these fellows want, right? They could be the ones waiting in ambush. They could be in contact with every rogue in Enesfel, all waiting to get their hands on you." No one had told him such details, but Owain was a smart man, and both he and the captain had reached similar conclusions. "If they are here…as Lord Cliáth insinuates…what are you going to do?"

"If I ride fast enough, they will not have the chance; then I make it known I am in town and wait for further contact." It was growing increasingly more uncomfortable as it seemed others knew more details of his business, but he trusted the captain, at least, to keep quiet.

"Someone should go with you," Wortham murmured sleepily.

"They are expecting me to be alone…"

"Lord Cliáth can do it without anyone knowing he is there."

Feeling Wortham's eyes upon him, Kavan nodded imperceptibly. He had considered doing precisely such a thing, without Caol's knowledge, but having his approval and acceptance would be better. The inquisitor started to protest, stopped, and then lay down. It was several minutes before he spoke.

"That might be a good idea," he muttered sleepily. "You certainly cannot gather much information with the crowds clinging and following you around town. You may not be of much use with a sword, but you may pick up something I would miss…"

"I am better with a sword than you think." The bard's tone was a little cooler than intended; he regretted it at once, particularly since his reaction prompted Wortham to prop himself on one elbow to look back and forth between bard and inquisitor. "But yes, I will be of more use to you in a capacity other than as a swordsman." Even Owain was glaring at Caol with annoyance, although, as far as Owain could recall, the inquisitor's assessment of Kavan's abilities was accurate.

"I did not mean…"

Kavan sighed. Caol's unintended affront, and Kavan's overreaction to it, had brought tension back into the group and Kavan knew he had to dispel it. "I know, Caol…no offense taken. There is merely much you do not know about me…and that is not your fault. Those of us not on watch should rest. We may be in for an eventful night and should sleep as we can." He lay down, though he did not doze until both Caol and Wortham slept. Caol's embarrassed discomfort and Owain and Wortham's protective hostility accompanied his dreams.

ঙ্গে*৵

Except for those men coming from the southernmost reaches of the kingdom, Enesfel's entire military force was assembled. General Wyndham's second in command, the swarthy, bulky, young Cíbhóló known as Agis had already taken those men most prepared and begun the long march north. They would wait for the General and the remainder of the troops on the south side of Lake Tarsee, far enough from Neth that detection was unlikely, but close enough that an invasion would not take long to accomplish. Because that region had served as a military encampment for training in the past, having troops there should not cause any Neth spies much concern. It would certainly not be an unusual thing for Enesfel to do.

Rhidam's resulting chaos caused by the increased number of men in the vicinity was not as bad as Justice Cornell feared, and it did not detract from his search for the missing children and their kidnapper. But aside from the anonymous merchant who came saying he had seen Lísbhet Dilyn coming out of the náós the day it was believed she had been murdered, Minos unearthed nothing of value. At least he knew that Lord Cliáth had been correct to say she had been in the náós. If only his other visions proved accurate…save one.

Guthrie paced the library, alone again, pondering the justice's latest report. The chamberlain empathized with the justice's frustration as he had very little constructive work to do in the face of war. He carried out his everyday duties and conducted a daily inspection of the troops; otherwise, he was left to brood about the safety of the three princes and the overall state of Rhidam. It was nearly the same before every military undertaking, the delicate balance between uneasy pall and partisan excitement and the flurry of activity that came from preparations. To busy himself, Guthrie most often reviewed strategies, both with the King and on his own, hoping to work out all discrepancies and problems before it became necessary to implement the plans on the battlefield.

"Lord Chamberlain?"

"Yes?" He turned from the row of portraits on the wall, recognizing the voice of Bhríd's squire, Flannery. Guthrie liked him, and because he knew the squire would never replace his master as King's Champion, he was grooming the youth for the office of chamberlain. He also knew that Bhríd was preparing Flannery for the chancellor's office. With any luck, Flannery would have a broad range of choices when he graduated from squire to knight, although Guthrie suspected that what the young man truly wanted was to be a knight in the service of the King.

"There is a messenger from Hatu for the King. I could not find him and presume it rude to keep an envoy waiting. Will you see him?"

A messenger? The possibility for news both intrigued and excited the chamberlain. They were not expecting anyone from Hatu, as far as Guthrie knew. "Of course; bring him to me. I believe you might find His Majesty in the back garden, though it would be best if he is not disturbed." It was the first time, to the chamberlain's knowledge, that the King had gone to his wife's burial site. Disturbing him there did not seem appropriate.

The squire bowed, retreated, and returned quickly with the messenger. The ebony haired man looked little older than Prince Muir, and from his deep blue silk tunic and turban, Guthrie knew this was no simple messenger. Flannery was right not to keep this man waiting.

"Welcome to Rhidam." He offered his hand. "I am Chamberlain McHador. May I assist you while the King is indisposed?"

The man seemed nervous but determined. He swallowed, accepted the offered hand with the awkwardness of facing unfamiliar custom, and bowed. "Prince Espen Harcourt, milord. I come on behalf of my father, King Geir, to offer what support we can spare in your efforts to subdue Neth. I have spoken to one of your officers, Sir Gabersdon of Nelori, and he and the southern forces are escorting the two hundred soldiers my father was able to muster to send to King Arlan."

Guthrie bowed, mirroring the other man's posture, using the action to cover his surprise at having the youngest Harcourt prince in Rhidam. "We are honored to have you here, Your Majesty. King Arlan was not expecting such a response from your father, for him to have any forces to spare, circumstances being what they are in Hatu."

"The circumstances in Hatu never change," the prince snorted with a touch of humor in the otherwise resigned statement. "If Hatu waits for her own stability, she will be as isolated as Káliel. We have maintained a strong relationship with Enesfel since King Arlan's ascension, and wish to continue doing so. We might require a similar favor someday. We do not have many men to spare, but my father has sent what he can. He and I were with this unit in Kílyn when your messenger rode through. I came as swiftly as I could to tell you. The men should be in Rhidam within five days."

"Well…" The chamberlain curbed his natural inclination to pace. He liked this prince, he could tell that already. He could not recall meeting Prince Espen while in Hatu thirteen years ago, but he had been preoccupied with other matters, and the prince would have been quite young at that time, little more than a toddler. "This is very good news. You are welcome to wait and tell King Arlan yourself, of course, or I can relay it if you are in a hurry to return to Natrona."

"I am in no hurry." His gaze wavered but his stance did not. "I am waiting for the troops and will ride into battle with them."

The chamberlain scowled. "I...does your father know your intentions?" He did not want to be responsible for the death of a prince if King Geir did not know Espen's plans.

"Of course," the prince smirked and produced a gold-encrusted scroll case. "I am older than I look, Lord Chamberlain. According to my father, it is past time for his youngest son to prove himself in battle. This is a more honorable cause than our border skirmishes. I will obey his wishes."

"His..." He began to open the tube. "Would you consider it rude of me to ask...?"

Anticipating the question, Prince Espen said, "I will consider it so if you tell me that seventeen is too young to ride into battle."

The chamberlain's brow crept up but his expression stayed neutral. He was more surprised by the prince guessing his question than he was the young man's age. The prince did not look seventeen, it was true. Enesfel often took in soldiers of that age. The two lands had different customs, but it was common knowledge that Hatu drafted much younger soldiers out of necessity. If this prince had avoided going into battle until now, he was a lucky man indeed. He would have been trained by the best warriors in Hatu in the use of the slim, slightly curved sword he carried on the white sash at his hip, but that did not necessarily make him an adequate soldier.

"I apologize for any impropriety," Guthrie said, rerolling the scroll he had hastily read. "I worry about men in battle...well-trained or not. I will send word to General Wyndham regarding you and your forces and see a room is prepared for you. Then I shall let King Arlan know you are here." He gave the scroll back to the prince. "I am sure he will wish to speak with you."

"The hour is late; if he would prefer to meet tomorrow, that is adequate. I should rest and bathe. And, milord...as my father says, for the time being, I am your soldier to command. Please do not hesitate to ask anything you need to know…or to demand a demonstration. I want you to be as confident in my skill as I am in yours."

Guthrie smiled. "Tomorrow you will be a soldier. Tonight you are a prince who deserves his rest. Welcome again, Prince Harcourt. Thank you for coming."

Smiling back, it was the prince's turn to offer his hand, wanting to prove his willingness to learn new customs and fight for the cause he was sent to support. "I thank you for welcoming me."

❧*❦

The etchings on the cold bronze could not be seen in the starless darkness, and the King had not brought a lamp with him, but without touching it, he knew exactly what it said. The name and the memories that accompanied it were fixed in his heart. He wondered which would last longer, those he carried in his soul or those on the bronze placard he had finally gotten the courage to face, that occupied a slot next to other family members…most of whom he did not recall. He remembered his mother and his brother Donal, but his other brothers were shadows and rumors. His father was a legend that parents would tell their children for generations to come; Arlan had never known the man who died the night of his birth. Brenna did not belong amongst people who had lived long, full lives, or who were cut down in their prime because of their mistakes, apathy, or cruelty. Brenna had been none of those things; there was no logical reason for her to be dead.

At least she was spared the torture of worrying about their son, of knowing that Bertram was destined to die too soon. There was a vulnerable deadness in Arlan's stomach when he recalled the bard's warning, and he prayed constantly that this one time the bard would be wrong. k'Ádhá help you, Kavan, he begged. Find my son, bring him home alive, and I will never take you for granted again.

A stifled cough roused him from his thoughts. Guthrie stood beside him, staring at the plaque, giving no indication how long he had been there. "It is good to remember, Milord, but it does no good to brood over what cannot be changed." He knew that lesson too well.

"Does it get better?" The chamberlain had been close to Arlan's father, had chastely loved his mother, and had lost his own wife and a beloved friend in King Donal. If anyone could answer that question, it had to be Guthrie.

"Memories fade, pain subsides. You miss what you no longer have, but it does get better. In time."

"Time." The King snorted and got to his feet. "I hope you are right. Did you want something?"

"Prince Espen Harcourt is here. He and two hundred of Geir's men have been sent to assist us. The troops will arrive with Sir Gabersdon within the next five days but the prince took the liberty of coming ahead. I gave him a room and saw to his needs. He wishes to meet with you tomorrow if you are agreeable."

That was good news and a welcome distraction. "Of course I am. I look forward to meeting him. See to it that an appropriate dinner is prepared for tomorrow, something from his homeland. There has never been a Harcourt in Rhidam. I want him to be welcomed with all possible courtesies."

The night had been uneventful and Prince Muir was allowed to sleep, but his mood was no better than it had been the evening before. Only twice during the journey had anyone roused him for a watch, and he suspected that was because Owain wished for his company. Though Wortham swore they allowed him to sleep because he was royalty, and a prince should be catered to as much as possible, Muir stubbornly held to the notion that he was being treated like a child. When camp broke that morning, he was sullen and silent. He did not look at Kavan, the perceived leader of this expedition, nor speak to him. If Kavan ordered the others to include him, they would, therefore being excluded and treated like a child was Kavan's fault. They parted company not knowing when, or if, they would see each other again, but the prince would not budge from his position.

Caol rubbed his hands together to warm them and watched his breath swirl in misty plumes. He did not move or speak until the others were out of sight, although he was aware of Kavan sitting quietly on the ground behind him. When Wortham mentioned Kavan joining him in disguise, the inquisitor wondered what sort of disguise the captain was referring to. Much later during the night, the white hart in the castle's Great Hall the night Owain had been deposed flitted through his memory as he pondered the possibilities. He knew that had been Kavan, although he had never given it any consideration before. He wondered what the bard intended to do.

"Would Halstatt be uncomfortable with a hound in your presence?"

"I...I don't think so. It would depend on how threatening the animal looked and whether he felt it would go after him if he attacked."

Kavan almost laughed to think of it. "I can guarantee he would not feel threatened, but I cannot guarantee I would not try to protect you should it seem necessary."

"I do not need protecting," Caol grumbled, sounding like Prince Muir as he gathered his belongings.

"I have no doubt of your ability to protect yourself, but there are times in everyone's lives when they require assistance. I am willing to allow you to conduct your day as you see fit and will only intervene should the need seem dire. Fair enough?"

Rather than answer that question, because he did not want anyone fighting his battles for him, he asked, "You would be the hound?"

Kavan's response was to close his eyes, form the image he desired behind his lids, pull the energy together, and in the time it took to draw a deep breath the change was complete. Caol watched the air shimmer, and then the bard was no longer there. In his place was a tall white hunting hound, thinly muscled, sleek and elegant, built for speed not strength, with the greenest eyes he had ever seen on a dog. When the animal pressed its wet nose against his hand, Caol laughed with amazement.

"Lord Cliáth, if I...that is one ability any member of the Association would kill to have...if it were possible. Too bad the Association has never been able to recruit Elyri. Would you like a job?"

The dog woofed and loped in the direction of Durham. "Hey! Wait!" Caol jumped onto his horse and followed at a gallop.

༄*❧

Alone for the first time since her return to Rhidam, Madalyn Dubuais strolled through the back gardens, appreciating the lilacs, roses, honeysuckle and other flowers the royal gardeners cultivated. Bhríd had shown himself knowledgeable about flora and the proper means of tending harvest plants; that it was also one of his passions pleased her. He had offered a few suggestions he claimed could result in a greater yield from her vineyards, and Madalyn was eager to return home to try them.

Their lengthy conversation of the previous day had been precisely what Bhríd had claimed it would be, their opportunity to get to know one another better. Though their choices of pastimes were largely different, they at least shared the same fundamental outlooks on life, politics, religion and morality, and culture. She saw no reason they should find a life together as husband and wife to be intolerable.

Except that he was Elyri and she was not. He asked her bluntly how she would feel in thirty years when she looked every bit her age and he looked no older than he did now. She laughed at the question, not able to take the notion seriously, until he pointed out that this Ártur MacLyr that served King Arlan was the same man who had served kings Innis and Donal and was, in fact, sixty-five years old. When Madalyn commented that he looked no older than twenty-five, she realized the point Bhríd was trying to make. She might be able to live with potential ridicule, scorn, or threats their union created, but could she live with a man who would one day come to look more like a son or grandson than a husband?

That had been their parting words last evening, words that kept her awake much of the night, occupying her thoughts. She had heard that Elyri had longer lifespans, but she had never imagined how long that might be. Could she live with it? She did not know.

Her mother had died while Madalyn was quite young. She remembered her mother looking thin, frail and gray, not at all the picture of a woman her age. When Madalyn's father had died, he had been nearly seventy though his unwrinkled features and copper colored hair had made him look nearly half his age. Perhaps age had less to do with one's countenance after all.

A pair of swallows caught her attention as they swooped down above her and disappeared into the stable rafters. The sight made her smile. No, this mortality thing did not matter, she decided. Life was too short and precious and she knew she would rather risk the discomfort of watching herself age next to Bhríd's unchanging, handsome features than risk losing her lands and spending the rest of her life alone. Mind made up, she found her way back inside, hoping to find Flannery. She had a message for Lord Cáner.

❧*❦

The hound followed close upon its 'master's' heels, eyes drinking in the various faces and locations they encountered as Caol made the rounds of his family's haunts. This was a side of life that Kavan was aware of but had never taken the opportunity to study. The men and women Caol spoke with, even the children, all likely attached to the vast organization called the Association, exhibited tension, wariness, and pain. But there was another common bond among them, a passion for living, for the excitement that this life provided them. Whether a part of the Association by choice or chance or birth, the people in it were all very much the same.

At some time during the day, Caol ceased to think of the dog as Kavan and became freer with both his language and his actions as he reverted easily into the old habits that had once kept him alive. Seeing it broadened Kavan's understanding of the inquisitor; it made it much easier to not harshly judge the choices the man had made in his handling of Halstatt's arrival in Rhidam.

The building that Caol once called home was now a cobbler's shop. His sole living direct relative, an older sister, had escaped the Association by marrying into the wealthy family of the town's sheriff. She refused to divulge information to her father-in-law and her husband never asked for any. The Association cut her off and left her family alone, although Caol suspected, upon meeting them, that her second oldest son had taken up the calling, either via recruitment or simply on his own. She welcomed her brother with open arms, however, as he too had escaped their past. She mourned his predicament, but other than enlisting her husband and father-in-law to aid in watching for any Tarmajiens, she could do little to actually help him. She had not seen Halstatt since childhood and she had every desire to keep it that way.

Thanking her, Caol and his hound went again into Durham's streets. It was nearing evening as they returned to the room they rented early in the morning. There were no instructions left for them and no sign of Halstatt. There were also no messages from their party members. Instead of lingering in the tavern to drink, Caol chose to retire to their room to clean up.

Once there, Kavan gratefully resumed his own shape and sat trembling upon the floor. Surprised by the sudden appearance of the bard in the room, Caol jumped with a yelp, tripped, and fell upon the bed with a laugh. "My apologies, Lord Cliáth…I forgot…"

"That your hound was not a dog?" The bard smiled weakly, his body radiating exhaustion as he stretched. "All the better. It kept others from being suspicious."

"Indeed. Isn't that hard? To stay that way for so long? The bard's white skin was flushed and he breathed harder than normal as he crawled across the floor to rest before the open window.

"Yes…and no. It should not have been as difficult as it was, but I have not done anything like that in a long time. Twelve hours is about my limit."

Worried, Caol frowned. "Would you rather not join me tomorrow when I go to the meeting place?"

It was not the man's worry speaking and Kavan knew it. Caol hoped to meet Halstatt alone, but Kavan was not going to let that happen. "You will not be rid of me easily. On Arlan's behalf, I must be there…and you might need me. I will sleep, and by morning I will be rested and ready." Caol nodded, got up from the bed, washed his hands and face in the water basin, and then started for the door. He was hungry and food was downstairs, and he had things to think about, possibly people to meet.

"And if you believe you can slip away, Caol," Kavan murmured, "you will find yourself mistaken."

The inquisitor rolled his eyes. He went out to allow Kavan to rest; the bard was asleep at once, curled up on the floor in front of the window.

❧*❧

The náós was vacant tonight except for gdhededhá Tusánt who sat at the table beside his bed, reading by the light of twin candles. The k'gdhededhá had gone to the castle to participate in the dinner given in Prince Espen Harcourt's honor. Tusánt had no idea, as usual, where Claide was, nor did he care.

He wished someone was with him tonight, however, even if that someone was Claide. He had hoped the uneasy feeling would pass after that unsettling concession, but instead, it grew worse every time he became aware of a parishioner's discomfort with, or dislike of, Elyri. Is this the one, he would wonder. Is this the person who has come to take my life? He did not know, could not tell without invading their thoughts, and he hated the constant suspense and suspicion. If there had ever been any illusions about whether his own mortality mattered, they were gone. He wanted to live.

A noise in the nave startled him, a creak, and the sound of something falling. He jumped and then froze, listening intently, but there was silence. Throat tight with fear, he fought for air and pushed his blonde hair from his face. They were here, he thought. It was over. He was going to die. Certain of that, he managed to find his voice and croaked, "Is anyone there?"

No reply. No sounds. Nothing. Perhaps they could not hear him. Or perhaps an old piece of plaster had fallen; it would not be the first time. In spite of his fear, he knew he should investigate. Someone might be there in need of his help. He could not turn his back on the possibility of a parishioner in need, no matter how terrified he was. He got up, focusing all of the energy he could gather into his senses. One dragging footstep at a time got him to the thóres door, where he called out again, but there was no reply and his senses told him there was no one present. In the darkness, he could not tell what, if anything, had fallen. Relieved that he was alone, believing he was safe, he turned to retreat with a deep breath of relief.

There was a sudden presence behind him, in the main doorway of the náós, someone from outside stepping in. He heard the click and twang of a bowstring and then a crack as the deadly bolt embedded itself in the door frame near his head. Spinning, Tusánt instinctively lashed out with everything he had, the power of it knocking the dark figure in the doorway to the ground outside. But his assailant was not injured; he scrambled to his feet and disappeared into the night. Shakily, the gdhededhá pulled the small bolt from the frame, returned to the thóres, and locked the door behind him.

There would be no sleep for him that night. He had no doubt of it.

Prince Espen tried to appear more at ease than he felt as he glanced at the others seated around the two long tables in the dining hall. The honey-glazed lamb and roasted potatoes smelled delightful, not quite what he was used to but similar enough to wet his appetite. But if this was home, he would feel relaxed; this would be another of his father's unnecessarily lavish dinners with advisors and friends. There would be no women present and no one would be watching him for indications of incompetence or treachery.

This, however, was dinner at a foreign table, a first for Prince Espen. He had never traveled outside of Hatu, never served as the sole ambassador for his father, and he feared doing or saying something that would jeopardize the relationship King Geir and King Arlan had worked diligently to cultivate. If only his brother, Noreis, was here. Noreis Harcourt was the diplomat. Prince Espen did not appreciate being the one in the position of outsider.

Watching the girl who entered the room, he realized he was not the only outsider tonight. She was tall, still a child he guessed, though

Espen could see she would be a beautiful woman one day. She was the youngest guest present, and from her expression, he decided she felt as out of place at this function as he did. Her attendant escorted her to the empty seat opposite him; King Arlan sat at the head of the table between them.

"Prince Harcourt…my daughter Diona. Diona, Prince Espen Harcourt of Hatu," the King said, confirming what Prince Espen had already deduced.

"A pleasure, milord." The girl curtsied before sitting, her bowed head barely hiding a coy smile and the blush on her cheeks. Taking the King's puzzled look as disapproval, the prince pushed the awkward feeling in his stomach aside and bowed his head. "Likewise, milady."

The princess's smile widened.

There was little chance for serious talk after that, as course upon course of Hatu delicacies were produced from the kitchen and presented for Prince Espen's approval. He had spent the day discussing the situation with Neth and strategy with the King, his advisors, and the two councilmen from southern Neth who had come to Rhidam with Owain. Their presence unsettled and mystified the prince at first until the plan was outlined, and then he marveled at the brilliance of it. Why, he wondered, were Hatu's military experts incapable of devising similarly brilliant strategies?

Once the meal was complete, the King led the gathering into the secondary hall where a trio of minstrels awaited. The King spoke with them, took his seat upon the throne, and bid them play.

Leaning closer to the King, Prince Espen asked, "If I may, Your Majesty…where is the White Bard this evening?" Anyone who came to the Rhidam palace hoped to hear the White Bard play. For many years, that had been the only way to hear his music.

A shadow fell across the King's face, but his voice showed no emotion. "He is on an errand. I doubt he will return before we travel north."

The prince decided not to probe further. "That is unfortunate. I was hoping to hear him …it would be my first time."

Sighing, his eyes scanning the dancers as if looking for something specific, the King said, "I would prefer to hear him too." It had not been many days since Kavan left Rhidam, but the King continued to hope for his speedy return. Every day the bard was away was one more day the boys were at risk.

And truth was, he missed having Kavan there.

Soon there were few who were not dancing, as people knew this might be one of the last evenings they could enjoy before war was upon them. The prince stared awkwardly at the dancers, wondering if he could excuse himself. The King was involved in a quiet conversation with the k'gdhededhá of Rhidam, whom Prince Espen met earlier in the evening. On the other side of the k'gdhededhá, Princess Diona swung her feet, gazing longingly at the dancers. The prince followed that gaze and then looked back at her. She turned her head to catch his eyes, smiled, and blushed. He could see that she wanted to dance, most women did he had been told, but he was considerably older than her. Such an issue would never come up in Hatu, as men and women did not mingle for most public events. He did not know how such things were done in Enesfel. Did he dare approach her?

She spared him the indignity of asking someone about the appropriateness of the action. With the grace and assurance of a much older woman, she came to him, curtsied, and said, "Dance with me, Prince Harcourt."

It was not a question, but rather a command. Men in Hatu would never take a command from a woman and he could feel the King's eyes upon him, judging him, wondering what he would do with his daughter's uninformed request.

"Are you…would it be appropriate?" he inquired, asking as much for the information as to show that he did not know the customs of Enesfel.

The princess, however, was not old enough to grasp that subtlety, or else chose to ignore it as she countered, "Why would it be inappropriate?" with a defiant smile.

That boldness on her face and in her words struck him with amusement, hinting at a fiery intelligence and stubbornness to rival most men. Prince Espen could not help but smile. "I do not know. I am unfamiliar with your ways and would not want to offend…"

"No one will care." She cast a look at her father, challenging him as she grabbed Prince Espen's hand and pulled him onto the floor as a new melody began. Feeling that he could not refuse without appearing rude, Espen decided to treat this as a test and follow her lead. Her father would either disapprove and stop it, or he would allow the dance as the harmless diversion it was.

Prince Espen did not know these dances and felt clumsy; dancing was a rare custom in his homeland, reserved for the few occasions when men and women were allowed to intermingle in a formal setting. The princess had to lead, which suited her. She danced well for her age, he decided, although as the evening progressed through several more dances, he began to view her less as a child and more as a peer in a way he had never considered a woman before. She was more intelligent and more outspoken than any woman he had met at home.

The k'gdhededhá smiled at the King's expression as the monarch watched his daughter dance. "Is something wrong, milord?"

"No, I…" He frowned, skewed his face, and continued. "Until now, I had not realized how lady-like my daughter is. Where did she learn this…coquettishness? When did it happen?"

"I suppose it is a gradual process," Jermyn replied with a chuckle. "There are a number of ladies for her to observe, and she has had ample opportunities and subjects upon which to practice…you included. Besides, it has been my observation that it may be an inborn female skill…an instinct even. Some women are naturally better at it than others."

"And my daughter appears to be one of those."

"Yes…she does."

The King watched silently for a while longer, seeing Brenna in his daughter's behavior, and remembering wistfully everything he had lost. "At least," he muttered absently, "she has chosen a respectable target for her attention." Prince Harcourt was not contemptuous, brusque, arrogant, or disrespectful. Coming to command Hatu's unit at the tender age of seventeen could not be an easy task; it showed courage, fortitude, and skill if his father thought him capable. There was no appearance of Espen being the sort of royal embarrassment that a king might be prompted to be rid of by sending him to his death in a war far away. Arlan had yet to see the young prince in action, but he suspected he was an adequate leader. Such a man might be a good match for his daughter…if the cultural differences could be overcome. Diona would never settle for being hidden away like a precious prize. His daughter was too gregarious for that.

"Indeed," agreed Jermyn. "I believe she has."

## ❧Chapter 24❧

P rince Muir kicked about him in annoyance, hitting his foot against anything that looked solid enough to offer resistance. While the captain could not keep the prince from accompanying him and Darius, he could, and did, prevent Muir from questioning anyone, citing experience as his reason. Wortham continued to insist he was protecting an important member of the royal family, doing his duty, and that, rightly or wrongly, people took older men more seriously. The prince, meanwhile, continued to assert he was being treated like a boy rather than a man, and today, instead of participating, he refused to cooperate and instead stayed alone in their rented room.

It was nearing noon, he was hungry, and was feeling more embarrassed than annoyed. The captain was right to do his duty, to protect Muir, and considering the responses they had been getting to their questions, the prince suspected it would not have mattered who was asking. For some reason, the people in Durham seemed to be rude to Wortham and his company. The prince would have demanded better treatment, and realized he might have ruined the investigation with his lack of tact and experience.

What he wanted more than anything was to talk to Kavan, to hear reassurance that he was a necessary part of this undertaking and not a burden, to know that Kavan was not annoyed or hurt by the way they had parted. But there had been no contact with the bard and inquisitor since last evening, even Rouvyn and Owain had not heard from them. Worried about the Elyri's safety on top of feeling embarrassed, Muir settled at the window to wait for the captain's return, formulating a much-owed apology.

ᐓ*ᐗ

"I am sorry, sir," Rouvyn stuttered, glancing around the tavern for anyone who might assist him. There was no one. Owain had gone to the náós in the guise of a pilgrim, hoping to find information there, and the doctor insisted he would be able to survive on his own until the man's return. It was the noon hour, but thankfully the tavern was quiet and unpopulated except for two promiscuously dressed women at a corner table and the hulking man with the washed out features who had thrown his bulk onto the bench across the table where the doctor was seated.

"I cannot come with you," he continued. "I am awaiting a gentleman who is in need of my skills and requested I meet him here. Since you have told me your demands are not of a medical nature, I am obliged to wait."

The fellow's pasty face leered nearer and he grabbed the front of Rouvyn's tunic with one beefy hand to pull him forward. He started to speak, his breath reeking heavily of ale, but the barkeeper whistled. The doctor knew his eyes betrayed his fear.

"None of that unless you plan to pay for the damages, Forst."

The fat man released Rouvyn with an annoyed and reluctant shove and crunched back onto the creaking bench. "I know who you are, pretty one. I've seen you with the hunter." At the mention of Wace Elotti, Rouvyn looked away. "I know he's looking for the youngest son of Belas the Blade since the scoundrel escaped prison in Neth. I've got word from some of his friends that he was here but has left, having business in Fiara. See that the hunter gets that news and tell him that Forst McLenum wants his share of the reward for helping catch him."

Rouvyn swallowed his nervousness and revulsion long enough to find his voice. "Who is the son of Belas? Why do you think Wace will know you or know who you are talking about?"

Grinning, the heavy man called Forst wiggled his way off the bench and stood. "Oh, he knows me alright. I've done him some favors…as you have." The physician found that the way Forst spoke of favors made him feel uneasy. "Give him the message. He'll know."

After the man waddled through the tavern door and was no longer in sight, Rouvyn's shoulders slumped. It would not hurt to give Elotti the message if he ever found the man again. It might get the doctor back into the hunter's good graces…if that was indeed why he was left behind. He resumed watching the door, waiting for Owain's return, praying it would be soon. He did not want to run into the likes of Forst McLenum again.

❧*❧

Prince Espen paced the morning room, studying the artwork and sculptures, longing for the company of friends and peers, longing for home. He had never been away from home for more than a few weeks, but there had always been other countrymen to keep him company and he had always been within Hatu's borders. This trip to Rhidam had taken nearly two weeks and he had been in Kílyn with his father for five days before that. It would be a long time before he returned home, and while Rhidam was pleasant and the Lachlan castle lusher than his own, he found the weather too cold and he missed what he was accustomed to.

"Oh…excuse me, Prince Harcourt. I did not think anyone was here."

Recognizing the voice, he turned to find Princess Diona in the doorway. She looked little different than she had the night before, except that her gown was less formal and her ebony hair was loose about her face and shoulders. And, he realized, she was without an escort. The noble women of his homeland were rarely seen, staying separate from the men for most of their lives, and were always in the company of other women and their male attendants, frequently eunuchs, when they were seen. That this fiery sprite was forward with him was both unnerving and intriguing. She clearly did not know the customs of his land, or else did not care to follow them, a fact that he found more pleasing than the attempts by most to impress him with their knowledge of his customs. He much preferred to see others as they lived, not as they thought he expected to see them. Her behavior caused him to wonder if all women outside of Hatu were like her.

"There is no disturbance, milady," he said with a bow. "I was pondering what to do with myself until my troops arrive or someone requires my presence. I know very little about Rhidam, I'm afraid. What would you suggest I do while I am here?"

She stared at him from a chair near the window, surprised that a grownup would ask her such a question. "I suppose that depends on what you like to do," she replied.

"Like to do?" It seemed an odd question.

The princess giggled. "Interests. Diversions. Healer MacLyr paints. Lady MacLyr enjoys reading. Lady Deidre enjoys needlework and poetry. Do you hunt? Fish? Joust or make contest with swords or bows? Play any instruments? Pray in the náós?"

"Oh." The prince furrowed his brow as he considered her question. "I do not know. I have never thought about such things. I have not had much free time to consider what I enjoy, I suppose."

Her young mouth pursed in annoyance. "I know boys spend a great deal of time learning things girls do not...combat and hunting…but there must be hours of the day not occupied by education and duty. What do you do then?"

"I ride…mostly. I am not much of a hunter, but I do like to ride."

That made her smile and she leaned forward with interest. "Do you have your own horse? Did you ride him to Rhidam?"

"Yes…and yes I rode her here. She probably did not appreciate the long journey, as she is not used to such continuous riding."

Her smile melted into a small pout as the princess crossed her arms over her chest. "Then I suppose riding would not be a good suggestion. I can show you around the castle, show you where everything is, if you wish. I do not suppose anyone has done that, have they?"

Prince Espen shook his head. "To be honest, no." Their time was filled with preparations for war, with little thought being given to much else.

"It has been very busy here with soldiers coming and going all the time," she said as she stood, almost as if she had read his thoughts. "No one has time for me either. I shall be your…"

"Escort?" he asked with a note of wonder. He was less surprised by her offer than by his own interest in it.

"Why not?" Her pout morphed into an expression of defiance. "Or would you prefer to have one of the men do it? Squire Flannery perhaps?"

He shook his head, trying not to chuckle at the petulant display. "I do not know who Squire Flannery is, but I would be honored to have you show me your home, that is if it would not be improper…"

Rolling her eyes, she grabbed his sleeve and pulled him into the corridor. "You and your concern for propriety. What is proper?"

Prince Espen was beginning to ask himself the same question.

❧*❦

The clearing in the ancient pine forest was empty of most forms of life, with no indications that anyone else was there or had been there recently. Caol made his circle of the area twice, more cautious than Halstatt had been in Hangman's Grove. If the man had been here, he was not here now. The inquisitor kept one eye on the white hound that padded around the perimeter, sniffing bushes, trees, and the ground. When it stopped beside him, it sniffed the air and then shook its head in a very person-like fashion before lying down at his feet, its dainty narrow head upon its paws.

Halstatt had not come and it was past the designated meeting time. Rather than sitting, Caol paced, knowing that though he was listening closely for the signs of anyone approaching, his canine companion would probably know it before he did. Still, knowing that did little to ease his tension. He had hoped this would be the final confrontation between the Tarmajiens and the Dugans. The man had no children, at least none in Durham, and no other kin here save for two elderly aunts, and it seemed safe to assume that Halstatt's death would mean the end of the feud. If Caol was lucky, Halstatt would have the boys with him when he arrived, they could fight, and the matter would be settled. If he did not survive the conflict, he at least felt confident that Halstatt would not survive either. Kavan reassured him that he would do everything in his power, whatever was necessary, to secure the boys' freedom and safety, including killing Halstatt if it came to that.

But as morning gave way to mid-day, and then mid-day to evening, as the shadows cast by the sun setting behind the pines stretched their fingers across the clearing, both the inquisitor and the bard knew Halstatt was not coming. They had been duped. Either Halstatt knew Caol was not traveling alone, something had happened to the man, or else he had not planned to meet Caol there at all.

Tired, annoyed, and defeated, Caol returned to the town, cursing himself without knowing what had gone wrong, the white hound trotting beside him. For the sake of their cover, he took the dog back to their shared room and prepared to leave, feeling in need of a drink, but the dog took its true form before Caol could close the door.

"Do you think he knows you are not alone?"

Caol ground his teeth and shrugged. "I don't know. We have taken every precaution we could, and I do not believe the Association would give him any information. That is not to say, however, that he does not have his own friends and spies."

Rubbing his eyes, Kavan sat on the corner of the bed. "Shall we wait a few more days or depart?"

"And go where?" The bard's eyes widened in response to the vehemence in Caol's question. "We have no leads, no idea where he may be, where he could have taken the children…"

"Then we shall wait." It seemed the best thing to do. Perhaps Halstatt had been detained, kept from meeting with Caol through no fault of his own. Waiting another day would give them a chance to try again. Kavan was interrupted by a knock on the door and braced himself for the necessity of an abrupt shapechange as Caol put one hand on his dagger and the other on the door handle.

"Who is it?" Caol growled.

"Physician Talis, milord. May I speak with you?"

A look was exchanged between inquisitor and bard; Kavan relaxed and Caol opened the door to yank Rouvyn into the room, making sure that no one in the hall had seen him.

"What do you want? You're not supposed to come here…"

"I am sorry," Rouvyn said nervously, head bowed, "but something happened today I thought you should know about."

"We don't have time for gossip…" Caol took a few stormy steps towards the window, wanting to put distance between himself and the physician, but Kavan caught his arm.

"Hear him, Caol; I am sure he would not endanger our cover on a whim. After our lack of success, the least we can do is hear him."

Rouvyn bowed and leaned against the nearest wall, his arms folded across his chest, a sour expression on his face. "Thank you...Lord Dugan...you hail from this city? Are you familiar with a man named Forst McLenum?"

There was a long pause, as Caol scratched his chin and thought about the question. "Forst? I know some McLenums...or I did...but not..." He cast a sidelong glance at Kavan. "Association." The bard nodded.

If the physician knew what that meant, he did not show it. "He approached me in the tavern and asked me to take a message to Wace..."

"I am not Wace. What has this to do with...?"

"He said that he knew Wace was looking for someone, the son of someone called Belas the Blade..."

Caol choked and stared at him until Kavan's movement broke his daze. "Belas the Blade...assassin of the highest order," Caol muttered. "Halstatt's father..." It was because of Belas that Caol's family had wanted Caol to be an assassin. They had seen it as their best chance of winning the feud with the Tarmajiens. To Rouvyn he asked, "Did he say anything else?"

"He was blustery and rude and I thought little of most of what he said at first...thought he was trying to intimidate me. He said this son had been in Durham but had recently continued towards Neth, to conduct business in Fiara. But when he mentioned that this person had escaped from a prison in Neth...knowing that the man Wace is tracking had likewise...I thought it might be the same man we are seeking."

"Fiara?" Tapping his foot against the wall, Caol wondered what sort of business could possibly have taken Halstatt to Fiara. "That's miles..." His face lit up. "Forst...of course..." No one interrupted his train of thought. "There are a lot of McLenums...I think I met Forst when I was a child…that family's always been impartial mediators in our feud…chosen to keep the Association out of it…"

"This could be a message from the Association?" Kavan began.

"Or from Halstatt…it's difficult to tell."

Pulling off his boots, the bard said, "It appears we are bound for Fiara. Rouvyn, please inform the others we shall depart as early as we can tomorrow, regrouping at our previous campsite, but do not give them any details of what we have discussed and do not reveal our destination. I will do that when the time comes."

Caol frowned. "Can we do that, Lord Cliáth? Get into Neth, I mean? There shall be war soon, and you are…"

"Elyri." Kavan took a breath and exhaled slowly. "I know the risks, Caol, but I do not think we have a choice. You are not carrying on this quest alone. Owain resides in Fiara; he may provide the leverage we need to travel unhindered over the border."

"I hope so," the inquisitor muttered, knowing Kavan was right, that there was no choice but to take the risk. "While Rouvyn talks to the others, I'm going to my sister. She'll provide provisions…and tomorrow we start again."

"Our daughter?"

Syl was unable to hide her smile as she embraced her husband. Ártur chuckled and returned the embrace, but said, "Unless Miss Maylor was from Neth or Káliel, she seems to have lied about her background, or her name. There appear to be no Maylors in Enesfel, Cordash, or Hatu, and her background is certainly not Cíbhóló or Elyri. There is little hope of finding family in Neth; unless Prime Magistrate Dilyn is able to identify the family, or some other relatives come forth to identify her, Bianca is to remain with us. Your brother has already drawn up the necessary documents to allow us to raise her…that is if you still wish to."

"Ártur!" she squealed, tightening her embrace. "You know I do!"

Smiling into her hair as he kissed the side of her head, satisfied to have made his wife happy, Ártur murmured, "That is what I thought."

ↀ*ↄ

Gazing longingly through the open doorway of his barrack room, Bhríd wondered what Madalyn had been doing since he was called away from the keep that morning. There was no time to speak with her; he barely had time to write a message and give it to Flannery to pass on. He wondered if she would be hurt or offended by his abrupt departure without a farewell. Perhaps she had already left Rhidam to return to Levonne.

No, he decided; Madalyn was too levelheaded and not one to be ruled by wild passions. Flannery would explain to her that General Wyndham had demanded his immediate presence, some business about the troops and preparations for the upcoming campaign. She would understand that duty called him away, not some whim, and that he was obligated to obey.

But neither knew when they would see one another again and the future of her lands still hung in the balance. He drafted a letter after Flannery's departure, but he did not want to send it. He hoped to be able to get away in the morning, leave long enough to return to Rhidam and speak to her properly. With the troops' departure imminent, it might be his last chance. Otherwise, the letter would have to suffice.

ↀ*ↄ

It was late evening before gdhededhá Tusánt convinced himself that he needed to inform someone of the previous night's incident, even if that someone was his superior. He did not want to talk about it for fear he would be sent away or worse, not be believed, but the inborn need for self-preservation told him he must. He had hidden the bolt where he expected no one to find it, but even a single crossbow bolt might not be proof enough that someone had intended to kill him.

"You wanted to speak with me, Tusánt?" Jermyn looked up from his devotions, his nose and eyes red as if he had been weeping. Having learned about the kidnapped princes, Tusánt assumed it was for them, or the late queen, that the k'gdhededhá had been grieving.

"If you would rather I come some other time…" Jermyn had set the appointment time, but Tusánt almost hoped that he would be dismissed to avoid discussing his troubles.

Jermyn shook his head and dabbed his nose. "You are here, as I asked. Please. What is troubling you?"

There was a long uncomfortable pause, filled by murmured voices outside, dogs barking in the streets, and the occasional sniff of the k'gdhededhá's nose. Finally, Tusánt murmured, "I cannot be certain, your grace…but I believe someone tried to kill me last night."

The k'gdhededhá's round face grew red with alarm. "Kill you? When? How? Where was this?"

"Last night, while you and Claide were out. I was, in the thóres…in my room…when I thought I heard something fall in the Gathering Hall. I went to investigate, but it was too dark to see anything. When I turned to come back, there was this…sound, and a bolt…from a crossbow…flew past my ear and embedded in the doorpost inches from my head. I did not want to speak of it…"

"Show me where you were." The command was absolute; Jermyn followed Tusánt to the doorway where he had been standing, muttering under his breath all the way. Tusánt pointed out the place, the gouge in the centuries-old wood. There was no way to prove that an arrow had made that mark since the bolt was no longer there; the only proof was that the size of it and the fresh splintering of wood meant it was a new mark of the right size and depth for an arrow tip.

From the angle of penetration, Jermyn could believe that the shaft had been fired from somewhere near the main náós door, as Tusánt claimed.

"Where is this arrow?"

"I removed it. I did not think it prudent to allow our parishioners to see an arrow embedded in the wall of the náós. I did not want whoever fired it to be able to come and reclaim it either."

Jermyn's head bobbed up and down. "Wise reasons, of course, but it would have been useful for Justice Cornell to see it himself. It would lend credence to your tale."

Tusánt took a startled, disbelieving step backward. "You do believe me, your grace…don't you?"

The k'gdhededhá clasped the Elyri's hand. "Of course I do. You are the finest gdhededhá I know, and an honest man. There is no reason to fabricate such a tale. Do you have any idea who might wish you harm?"

"No." Tusánt shook his head, thinking about the threat he received during the Purification. While he had been warned, he had no idea who the individual had been, or whether the man himself had intended harm, had been his attacker, or had merely been warning him that someone else would do so. "But I am Elyri, your grace…that would be reason enough for some."

"Hmmph," Jermyn snorted. "It would be…but I find it hard to believe…" He shook his head. "It does little to narrow down a field of suspects. I suggest we discuss this with the justice first thing in the morning."

Shuffling his feet, Tusánt asked, "Must we?"

Jermyn put an arm around his friend's shoulders, intending to escort him to the man's room. "We may never learn who did this, but the justice must know…so he can be on the lookout. I don't want this to happen again."

Neither do I, thought Tusánt. Once was more than enough.

⤙*⤚

Caol's sister supplied him with everything the search party would need to get them to Fiara, including two mules to carry the extra rations. Having her backing made him feel better as he and Kavan returned to the spot where they had previously camped outside of the forest, but it did little to ease the heaviness of worry inside for his son and Arlan's. He watched the road, looking for the others as light kissed the morning sky with pink and gold. He was the first to arrive, the first awake because he had slept badly, his night filled with nightmares that centered around a single man. Unable to sleep, he spent his time polishing his sword, his dagger, his boots…doing anything that kept his hands busy and his mind off Wilred.

He did not believe Halstatt would kill the boys, at least not yet. But if Prince Bertram got some idea of escaping into his head, Wilred would go along with it, and Halstatt would likely not tolerate that. If Halstatt had the Tarmajiens' fabled temper, Caol could imagine what punishment might follow. He prayed that for once Prince Bertram thought better of doing anything impetuous.

A low woof came from the dog at his feet. The inquisitor had forgotten it was there. After the last few days, he quickly forgot the animal was Kavan within minutes of the bard assuming the form. He even found himself scratching the animal's ears and patting its head and later wondered what Kavan thought of such actions.

Following the dog's gaze, he saw the five horses approaching and knew from the size and ebony coloring of the lead mount that it was the rest of their party, with Owain in the lead. The riders slowed as they approached, but once they were close enough to recognize Caol, they did not hesitate further.

"Where did you get such a fine hound?" Darius was the first to speak.

Caol shrugged, seeing in Wortham's amused expression that the man already knew the truth. "He's been following me since we arrived." Unsure whether the others knew about Kavan's abilities, he thought better of saying anything more. "I think he likes me."

Rouvyn reached down from the horse he rode and touched the dog's nose when the animal stood and stretched towards him. "He is a beautiful specimen. Perhaps he will fetch us dinner."

"He might," Wortham said with a laugh, "But I would not count on it." The dog barked in response.

Prince Muir, meanwhile, was looking around them, hoping to see Kavan, still feeling he owed the bard an apology. Kavan's horse was there, with the harp strapped securely to its side, but there was no sign of the Elyri. "Where is Lord Cliáth?"

"I…he is scouting áhead; he was eager to be gone and did not want to wait for the rest of you," Caol replied quickly, the answer ready as he had anticipated such a question.

Wortham gave Owain a teasing grin but the elder prince shrugged away any embarrassment. "Can I help it if the stirrup broke? I can ride as easily with one, but you, Captain, insisted we fix it before departing."

The broken stirrup itself was not funny, had actually seemed suspicious to the captain, but Owain's surprised squawk as he tumbled into the straw had seemed amusing at the time. "Better to fix it now then to find ourselves in a skirmish later and have you thrown from your horse because you didn't have the proper equipment, Lord Lachlan," the captain laughed easily.

"True enough," Owain agreed.

The friendly shift in the relationship between the Káliel captain and Enesfel's former king surprised Caol, but the dog barking again distracted him from it. Kavan had said they needed to trust each other if they were to succeed; it appeared their relationships were indeed moving in that direction. "We should go. We do not want to keep Lord Cliáth waiting."

When they started traveling again, Caol drew his hood over his head to hide his face. If Halstatt was watching, he did not want to be recognized. The order of the riders shifted to allow him to lead, with Owain behind him and Darius and Rouvyn in the back. No one spoke for many minutes until the dog, which had been loping beside Caol's horse, broke from the group and disappeared into the trees.

"There goes our dinner provider," Darius commented with a pout. Prince Muir was already frowning, worrying that they were either leaving Kavan behind, that something had happened to the bard...or maybe that Kavan was avoiding him. The others watched the dog until it could not be seen and then Wortham nudged his horse closer to Caol's.

"Are we following a new lead or returning to Rhidam, milord?" he asked, willing to voice the question the others would not.

The inquisitor shook his head. "Lord Cliáth will discuss our plans when we join him. He has asked me not to speak of it until then."

"So we have learned something," the captain said with a nod and fell back into his place in the line. Sometimes, the inquisitor thought with a grunt, the captain was too perceptive, but it was precisely why Kavan trusted Wortham Delamo.

They passed through open country and forest, the warmth of late spring making their travel tolerable, the days of rest making continued riding bearable. Instead of taking the fork that would take them south towards Rhidam again, they continued east. It was mid-day, good progress made, when they found Kavan in a roadside meadow roasting five large birds over a crackling fire. From the smell of it, the meat was nearly ready, and when he looked up as they approached, he nodded at Wortham's happy smile. Overjoyed to see the bard safe, Muir quickly slid from his horse, but he refrained from throwing himself at Kavan. He would never gain the respect of the adults if he acted like a boy. Owain, however, did not share that hesitation, and rushed towards Kavan to clasp his hand in welcome before taking care of his horse.

"Think you scouted far enough ahead, Lord Cliáth?" Caol asked, partially teasing, partially seeking information about what the bard may have seen without actually asking.

Kavan shrugged. "We cannot be too careful. Our directions could have been another ruse…with a trap laid for us on the way. But I've seen nothing suspicious; I think we are safe."

"A trap would still be the best explanation for all of this, even if we haven't found it yet," the inquisitor muttered as he settled on the ground near the fire with a wine flask and a water flask that he handed to Kavan. "Still, that we have not encountered anything yet may be a good sign."

Rouvyn passed around a loaf of bread as Darius cut chunks from a block of cheese, all provided by Caol's sister. The food and wine were of the best quality, for which they were grateful. Much of the best would be eaten within a few days while still fresh. The lesser rations would come later, but as long as they could hunt, they would not be hungry.

Kavan knew the others were waiting for him to tell them what their plan was, but he was reluctant to broach the subject. Entering Neth as the White Hart, something he had done years ago, had been one thing. To enter in his true form, even with the assurances of Owain's words to King Arlan, was courting danger. He was willing to take that risk, but he was less willing to place the others in harm's way.

But each man, even Prince Muir, had come knowing they might face dangers on this quest. Few, if any, would turn away from the risk, even if Kavan urged them too. Having eaten all he could stomach, Kavan wiped his hands and asked at last, "Owain, can you gain us safe passage into Fiara?"

The expressions of astonishment, interest, and concern, were expected. If anyone wanted to make a negative retort, however, they must have thought better of it, because none did. Owain leaned against the tree behind him. "Fiara itself will be no problem. It is my city; they will do as I instruct or ask. As for the surrounding territory…it may depend on how quickly Arlan has moved. If Enesfel's troops are in place, no one will think twice about a few more men in Enesfel's armor…especially if I am with you. If we arrive ahead of them, we will likely encounter difficulty crossing the borders if Loris still has troops there. There are places to breach the line, where his soldiers aren't stationed…"

"Which you used to cross into Enesfel?"

Owain nodded. "Crossing the border is not as difficult as Loris would like it to be…but it is not easy either. It might help if we can procure nondescript armor or strip what you have of the Lachlan colors…"

"But what about you, Lord Cliáth?" asked Muir with obvious concern. "You will not wear armor…"

"And an Elyri in Neth is risking his life," Kavan completed his sentence. "I know. But it is a risk I must take. We have word that the man we seek has gone to Fiara, quite possibly with the boys, and I mean to pursue him."

"He could be leading us on a wild chase. We could be going away from where we need to be…"

Caol growled. "Yes, Darius, we could be…but we found nothing in Durham that led us to believe the boys or the kidnapper are there. Our other choices are to wait in Durham, wander Enesfel without any leads, or return to Rhidam empty-handed…and I won't do that…"

"We follow this lead to Fiara," Wortham finished, looking at Kavan. "Very well. If you are willing to take this risk, milord, then you know I am with you."

"As am I." Owain first met Kavan's gaze and then Wortham's, an exchange that warmed the bard's heart. That the two men had become friends pleased him. "I will do everything in my power to protect you."

"As will I." Caol closed his flask. "I don't have a choice. Wilred is my son, Bertram my nephew, and I mean to get them back whatever the price."

The remaining three men looked at each other. Rouvyn had nothing to lose, and had the hope of finding Elotti in Fiara, if he too were on Halstatt's trail. Darius was duty bound to go wherever Lord Cliáth and Captain Delamo bade him. Prince Muir, on the other hand, had no such obligations and was unsure he wished to travel into Neth, even with his father beside him.

Kavan reached for the young man's hand. "No one will fault you if you choose not to travel into Neth, my prince. Such a choice carries risk, as you say, I have no desire to place you in danger. We can arrange housing in Tarsee and rejoin you after…"

"And the King will think me a coward," the prince protested bitterly, knowing what he had to do. "I do not want it to be said that I am a coward. I am coming with you." He had chosen this expedition and he would not back out. He would find his brother and prove to the man who raised him that he was as worthy of respect as Prince Bertram was.

## ❧Chapter 25❧

The Valdis court in Cordash's capital city of Aralt was as opulent as Hatu's court was sparse. Guthrie had been in both castles more than once, in the service of Kings Innis, Donal, and Arlan. As he and Ártur waited in the mahogany, marble, and velvet stateroom with its long carved table and cabinets with stained glass doors, he concluded he much preferred Rhidam's balance to either. Here he was afraid to touch anything, afraid to sit or cough lest something be broken or soiled. The healer appeared equally uncomfortable as the two remained standing, waiting to be seen by the King. The chamberlain had not brought written details of his plans, just maps of the regions he wanted to discuss. It would be easier to keep information out of the wrong hands, a necessity if they wanted to guarantee success against Neth.

Not that the Elyri beside him was a threat. There was no need to keep anything from Ártur. Guthrie had known the healer for so many years that Ártur was the closest family the chamberlain had. While the healer was not the most politically savvy person, Guthrie trusted him with his life, and with the King's. Both had placed their lives in the healer's hands more than once, and Ártur had never failed them. Anything Guthrie revealed to the healer would be safe.

He knew that Ártur felt differently, however. The healer had been reluctant to make this journey through the Gate to Aralt; though he gave no reason, Guthrie thought perhaps the healer felt he was being used. He had argued that providing the healer with details about the upcoming campaign might ease Ártur's fears, but the King refused to allow it. In the King's eyes, there was no strategic reason for the healer to know anything and ignorance, he hoped, would keep the Elyri safe. Watching the healer, however, as they stood in front of the blue velvet divan, his hands clasped before him and eyes downcast, Guthrie decided he was willing to take the risk. The healer would soon jeopardize his life on the battlefields in Neth just as the soldiers would. He deserved to know what to expect.

The wooden double doors behind them opened at last. The man who entered was of medium height and build, his long blonde hair tied back from his mustached face. His jaw was round, his features soft, the similarities he shared with his father were undeniable. The chamberlain bowed from the waist, his hands at his side; Ártur did likewise. Their host returned the gesture.

"Welcome back to Aralt, Chamberlain McHador," the prince said, sweeping past his attendants and taking a seat at the head of the table. "I apologize my father is unable to attend; he was looking forward to seeing you again. Perhaps later this evening he will feel strong enough for a visit."

"I would be honored, Prince Renfrid. I hope you will convey Enesfel's best wishes to him."

"I will, of course. I must say, I am surprised at your hasty arrival. We were not anticipating a rapid response. Nor were we anticipating King Arlan would send you, of all people, to speak about this situation. Daneel informed me that you brought a plan to put down this foolishness. General Marym is in my writing room and is quite eager to hear what you have to say, as am I. As for…" He looked past Guthrie to the healer standing behind him.

"Forgive me, My Liege. Allow me to introduce our court healer, Ártur MacLyr…"

The prince's face looked stricken. "My word; you are well, are you not?"

Guthrie smiled. "I assure you I am." He could think of but one way to guarantee that Ártur remained with him. "I have been suffering a stomach disorder, however, and the King has demanded he stay with me…in case I have need of his services…and if you wish to have him attend your father, that can be arranged as well." Not knowing the king's condition, or whether the Valdis' had access to an Elyri healer, such an offer might make the difference between the monarch's life and death. He could feel Ártur's surprise over the fabricated story, but fortunately, the Elyri did not comment. "I swear to you, he will speak of nothing he overhears while we are here."

The prince appeared thoughtful as he stood, as if trying to decide whether to risk the chamberlain's health by demanding the healer leave them alone. Knowing that healer's had to take oaths of privacy, however, and assuming that such an oath would apply to this situation, he said, "Yes…when my father awakens…we would appreciate such attention," he agreed. "As for…you are welcome to join us, Healer. Shall we join General Marym then, gentlemen? I am eager to hear what you have to share, and breakfast is waiting."

❧*❧

The large dun wheezed heavily, glad to have come to rest and be free of its rider. The man gave the reins to a stable hand and hurried to his room. It was nearing noon and from the state he was in it would be at least an hour before he was presentable enough to attempt his mission. He had ridden hard all morning; General Wyndham had given him two days, understanding that when a man's mind was where his heart was, it was difficult for that man to concentrate on the job at hand. Go home, he had said, and do what must be done. Two days, and then he must return and prepare for combat.

Two days would be enough, though a day and a half was all that remained. Each minute that passed was one less available. Once in his room, he pulled off his boots and was about to remove his sweaty clothing when a knock came upon his door. He bid his guest to enter, praying that it was not someone come to summon him back to the general already.

"Ah, milord, Tedor informed me you were here. I did not expect you until the campaign was complete. Is something wrong? Is there some matter with which you require assistance?"

"It is good to see you too, Flannery," Bhríd said with a smile. Sometimes, in his efficiency, the young squire did not always remember the rules of courtesy. "At the moment, all I need is water for a bath and clean clothes."

"I will see to it," Flannery said with an earnest bow.

Before the squire made it out of the door, however, Bhríd called him back. "Oh, Flannery…is Lady Dubuais still in Rhidam?"

"She is," the young man nodded. He had wondered why, when it seemed she had come to see the chancellor and Bhríd had left, but it was not his place to questions such things.

Relieved to hear it, Bhríd said, "Please inform her I must see her at once."

"The lady is out, milord; she, Princess Deidre, and Princess Diona have gone to the cloth district. They are not due until evening…"

The chancellor sighed, some of the urgency now sapped from his quest. He did not understand Princess Deidre's need to go to the cloth district herself when the merchants were eager to come to her, to indulge her passion for sewing new garments. "I shall wait to speak with her then. I will have dinner in my room this evening, if she will join me…"

"Of course, milord," the squire bowed again. "I shall send her to you as soon as she returns and see that dinner is brought up. Is there anything more? Other than bath water, I mean?"

"A favor?"

Surprised, Flannery cocked his head and asked, "A favor, milord?"

"I know you have hopes of riding into battle with me, but after speaking with General Wyndham, I am sorry to report there will not be much riding. But if what I need to speak with Lady Dubuais about comes to pass, she may have need of a strong arm to protect her while I am away."

The squire straightened. "You wish me to be the Lady's protector? I am not yet a knight, milord."

"But your arm is good and I trust you. It will be good experience." If anyone did wish the Duchess harm, they might not expect the squire to pose a significant threat. Bhríd knew, however, that Flannery would be more than a match for most men. "This is not an order, Flannery, but I would appreciate if you would do this for me."

Flannery squared his shoulders and tried to hide his smile. "Oh no, Lord Cáner. If the lady requires a protector, I shall see to it that she is protected. And I will see to your bath water at once."

❧*❧

Pacing his small barrack room furiously, Justice Cornell cursed under his breath using every word he could think of. For reasons he never understood, anti-Elyri violence always galled him more than anything else did. Though he had never known Elyri before coming into the Lachlan's employ, tales of such violence had always unsettled him. Before King Arlan appointed him High Justice, before he entered the military as a young man, violence against Elyri had angered him in a way little else could. Now that he was Lord High Justice, he viewed such incidents as attacks upon himself. That someone had tried to kill another Elyri was bad enough; that the intended victim had been a gdhededhá was infuriating.

Though gdhededhá Tusánt had feared the justice would not believe him, Minos accepted the story without the slightest trace of doubt. The bolt the gdhededhá gave him had a hollow metal shaft and metal head, not the standard arrow of a hunter but one of a marksman or assassin. Someone who aimed to hit their target from a further distance than a hunter might. No hunter would use a crossbow of the small sort this one must have been. The justice assumed he had a professional assassin at hand, or someone who fancied themselves as such. Of course, if this was a professional job, why had the bowman missed his mark? Had the shot been meant as a warning?

With little else to go on, the justice bade the clergymen to be watchful and to report to him anything suspicious or unusual they might see or hear. This might be a random incident, but after the attack on Lady Dilyn, the Elyri painter, and the arrest of the anti-Elyri sympathizer in the King's kitchen staff, Minos did not intend to let this matter pass. Nor was he going to take any chances. It was time to post a reward for any information that led to the arrest and conviction of any anti-Elyri sympathizers in Rhidam.

"Those are all your men?"

From the window of the dayroom, Princess Diona and Prince Espen had seen Hatu's troops arrive. They had passed time over the last few days engaged in a variety of games that proved to the prince that this young lady had a brilliant head on her shoulders and an untiring desire to know more. No one looked twice at the time they spent together; in the pre-war chaos, Prince Espen was not sure anyone, even the King, had noticed.

"Not all of them," he replied. "Two hundred of them are with me. The others must be troops from southern Enesfel."

"Who is that?"

The prince followed her pointed finger and awed voice to find the tall, well-muscled, brown-haired young figure she indicated. Not that locating him was difficult. The individual she spoke of, in gleaming well-kept armor would have stood out among any crowd. The prince's stomach knotted in what might have been jealousy if she had been an older woman. "Sir Balint Gabersdon of Nelori," he ground out through clenched jaws.

"Sir Gabersdon! Of course! I should have recognized him; I remember when he was knighted, but that was a long time ago. He looks different…" She stuck her head through the open window to see better.

"Older," was all Prince Espen chose to say.

Though she did not understand his tone, she looked over her shoulder at the prince trying to guess what he was thinking. "Should we greet them?"

Bristling, the prince stepped away from the window. "I should, but you cannot."

"Why? Because I am a child…or a girl?" Her features were set with a mixture of disappointment and defiance. His first reaction to her question faded when he realized she wanted nothing more than to be involved in the world of her elders. As the only child around, she undoubtedly felt left out too often. It was a feeling he, as the youngest in his family, had often felt.

"Partially, my princess. In Hatu, a woman's place is not the same as here. Women do not mingle with men; at least respectable noblewomen do not. My troops would respond badly and would not take me, or you, seriously, even if you are royalty. I must see to them, but I will return this evening to complete this game, if you wish it?"

Her eyes lit up, whether because he took the time to explain his reasons to her or at the prospect of an evening with him he did not know. He hoped for the latter. "Oh yes! I would like that very much…if you are able to get away."

Wondering how anyone could ever dare to disappoint her, he smiled and said, "I will do my best to see that I do."

❧*❧

Ártur was not surprised at the simple intricacies of Guthrie McHador's battle strategy. Despite his years of inactive military service, the chamberlain was still the best military strategist in Enesfel, likely the best in the Five Sovereignties. Though the man was still in excellent health, perhaps, thought the healer, it was time for him to school an apprentice. Not that Ternce Wyndham was inept; King Arlan's current general did not have the special insight that had made Guthrie's military career remarkable. To lose that knowledge would be a shame.

Nor was the healer surprised that Prince Renfrid whole-heartedly embraced the plan and sent his general to begin the necessary preparations. Cordash' troops were already mobilized since they had been dealing with Neth for many months, and the ships the Valdis court sometimes used as a navy already rested at their moorings awaiting instructions.

There was an Elyri woman present during the discussion, though with her short hair and slender figure she looked at first more like a boy than a young woman. Ártur had been surprised to find an Elyri woman as the Valdis court herald. He suspected she had taken the necessary orders to the coastal cities of Wynett and Lindumn to prepare the ships for departure and then had likely taken General Marym to Matina and Edug to give orders to the troops stationed there.

This whole campaign could be underway within a matter of days. It was amazing to the healer how quickly the plan was taking shape.

What surprised him the most, however, was that Guthrie had included him in the discussion. He had no doubt that if Kavan had been here the bard would have been included. But Ártur had neither the political astuteness nor the insight his cousin possessed and though he did not resent that his cousin was often included when he was not, Ártur did often wish his allegiances were taken more seriously. He was a healer, however, and as the King had said to Guthrie, there was no reason for Ártur to know the details of a military campaign.

He had been an integral part of Arlan's push for Enesfel's throne, and after thirteen years of peace, he could admit that there was excitement he had not experienced since that campaign, an excitement he found exhilarating. He hoped to be included in this undertaking as he had been in the last. But Arlan had been a boy then, in need of advice and ideas from his elders for an undertaking with which he had no experience. Now he was a man, the King of Enesfel, with years of leadership experience behind him. Ártur's place, as it had been with Kings Innis and Donal, was as Lachlan healer. That was all.

For the first time since King Donal's death, Ártur missed him. Their friendship had been cherished and something he had not found since. He and Guthrie were brothers in a sense, and Kavan was sínréc. But neither relationship was the same as what he had shared with Donal Lachlan.

A tickle crept up his spine and up his neck, the telltale sign that his cousin desired contact. Until that familiar sensation began, Ártur had not considered how much he missed his cousin and how much of his depression might hinge upon the bard's absence. He allowed the contact, overjoyed that Kavan and the others were well, dismayed that they had not yet found the missing princes. There was no despair in Kavan, no loss of hope, though the healer knew Kavan did not expect to find Prince Bertram alive. Kavan was anxious but would not disclose the cause. Ártur tried to reassure him that success was in the hands of k'Ádhá. The bard acknowledged the sentiment and broke contact, distracted by whatever was happening around him. Disappointed to lose the link, to be alone with his dark thoughts, Ártur turned to the late afternoon sun and let loneliness overtake him.

❧*❧

"You wished to…oh!"

Madalyn had changed her gown as soon as she returned to find Flannery waiting for her with the news that Bhríd was back and wanted her to join him in his sitting room. It was not necessarily the proper setting for a gentleman to meet with a lady, perhaps, but certainly the best place to ensure a private conversation in the bustle of pre-war Rhidam. She had not expected to see him until after the campaign and still hoped he would not be going into battle with the troops. While she anticipated a conversation, she had not expected a meal. His nervousness made her guard go up and she wondered why she felt apprehensive about sitting.

"Please, Lady Dubuais. Will you join me for dinner?"

His formality was not unusual, but his edginess was contagious and she hesitated, saying, "It appears as if I am not being given a choice, Lord Cáner."

His gaze wavered and the hand held to her, an offering to join him, dropped to his side. Perhaps there was some better way to do this, but after their previous time spent together, he believed she would appreciate such a gesture. Perhaps he had been wrong.

"Milady always has a choice," he said, trying not to sound as disappointed as he felt. "If you would prefer to dine with the King, or have made other arrangements, I will not feel slighted."

Not slighted, Madalyn decided, looking from his face to the table and back again, but definitely hurt. She had not intended to hurt his feelings and felt guilty because of it. "My company might be missed…but dinner with you would be preferable." She managed a sincere, if nervous, apologetic smile, one that brightened when, like a child, he grinned and hurried to pull her chair out. She waited as he filled their glasses with burgundy and sat across from her.

"Káliel?"

"Aye," he replied.

"You spared no expense, I see…"

Maybe she thought he was trying to buy her somehow, but he could not imagine giving her anything less than the best. "I rarely do," he admitted sheepishly.

Once more, she realized she had hurt him, or at least embarrassed him, and Madalyn turned her attention to eating. Neither spoke for many minutes but rather watched each other across the table in an attempt to determine what the other was thinking. It was Madalyn who eventually broke the silence in an effort to make him comfortable. "Have you returned to Rhidam then?"

"Briefly." Discussing the upcoming war seemed safe enough, even though he knew she would not like his reply. "Once Chamberlain McHador returns from Cordash, we will know more. Knowing him as I do, I would not be surprised if we set north the day he returns. It will likely be within the week. I returned to Rhidam because I have matters to attend to beforehand, that could not wait."

She nodded, wondering what those things might be, but Bhríd seemed disinclined to reveal them. With one matter hanging heavy in the air between them, the one matter she wanted to take care of before war pulled them apart, she lay her napkin upon the table and said, "I have considered what you said the last time we spoke, milord…about your age…and mine."

"Yes?" It was difficult to say more, knowing that she might have decided against their union before he could agree to it.

The nervous squeak in his voice told her that this was a topic on his mind also, that she was likely one of the matters he wanted to see to before going into battle. That made continuing easier. "In the end, age does not really matter. When my mother died, though she was quite young, she appeared ancient, tired, and worn. My father...you met him once...you know how young he looked despite his advanced age. Age is but a small factor affecting appearance, and not necessarily the worst. Appearance is irrelevant, and nothing is certain. As I said, we could each live to be ancient, or we could die tomorrow. With war at our heels..."

"I have no intentions of dying in battle," was his response. Dinner conversation drifted onto lighter topics as he pondered her words. They discussed the cloth she purchased that day, the agricultural information she had gleaned from the Lachlan library and gardening staff, her developing friendship with Princess Deidre. With no news about the missing boys, each passing day brought a darker cloud over the King and his twin sister; a new friendship helped to dull that pain a little for the princess.

Meal complete, Bhríd pushed back from the table after stacking the dishes to make it easier for the servants to clear them away while Madalyn sipped her wine. In the candlelight, her red hair glowed as if it was the flame itself and the pale blue of her gown faded to nearly white. He caught himself staring at the gentle rise and fall of her bosom before she noticed. He stood hastily to retreat to the window, finding it safer to look elsewhere instead of at her. Madalyn watched him, confused by his actions and the emptiness in her stomach that grew despite the meal. Rising, she stood with him at the window.

"Is there some reason you wished my company tonight, milord. A final meal with a lady before battle?" She did not believe that was the reason he had invited her here, but she wanted to hear him say it.

He shook his head without looking at her. "I would never treat a lady's honor in such a fashion. I...want you to know...I am leaving my squire as your protector in my place. Make use of him as your needs dictate…"

"My prot…I do not need a protector, Lord Cáner."

When he turned to face her, his expression was grimly serious. "Perhaps not. But since I will not be here to defend you, or your honor, or deflect any insults, I want someone with you I trust. Who knows what manner of indignities you shall have to endure if you agree to marry me."

"Manner of indignities…?" She stopped, eyes growing wide as her face tilted towards his. Had she heard correctly?

Surrendering to the impulse he had controlled since he had first seen her, to the temptation she represented, Bhríd cupped her face in his hands and crushed her lips to his. He had kissed women before but always chastely, properly. It was nothing like the passion that ignited between them, and the way her body yielded against his increased his certainty of choice. Afraid that if he did not stop, however, he would do something improper and besmirch her name, he broke the kiss and nestled his face in her hair to catch his breath.

"I will marry you, Madalyn, if you will have me."

She giggled in a child-like fashion and embraced him, her face pressed against his chest. "After a kiss like that, Lord Cáner, I do not think you have a choice."

☙*❧

When Kavan abruptly awoke, it was still dark, though a faint hint of yellow was creeping over the horizon in the east. Something had roused him, but what? Not a dream. Not the Sight either; since his quest for the princes had begun there had been no further flashes from the Sight, no further details that might help him find the boys.

He looked to where Rouvyn and Darius were keeping watch and frowned. The physician fingered the bow Caol provided for him when they stopped earlier yesterday to supplement the armor of the fighting men in their midst with items more nondescript. Rouvyn was no warrior, but he had learned the bow in order to hunt, and it was a pursuit Elotti had encouraged. Whether or not the doctor would use it, he should at least look like he would.

Beside him, however, Darius slept. The day had not been particularly grueling and the young soldier was not one to disobey orders by falling asleep on duty. Seeing him slumbering was troublesome, but before Kavan could consider it further or try to rouse him, he heard it again, that same faint, almost inaudible sound of breaking twigs and crushing leaves that had jarred him awake. Not the sound of an animal passing, and Kavan sensed no predators around them. He had not wanted to stop in this densely wooded glen, but the others, except for Wortham, had voted in favor of setting camp. If the bard had been able to offer a valid argument against stopping, even if he had been able to foresee danger or trouble, they might have been persuaded to continue on. Instead, they chose this spot to build their fire and rest for the night.

The sound came again from a different direction. There were several aggressors, whoever they were. Refusing to show alarm or panic, Kavan reached his thoughts to those sleeping minds, hoping to wake them. With a sinking in his gut, the bard realized Rouvyn had taken the second watch with Prince Muir and that this watch should have been Darius' and Owain's. Rouvyn had been awake all night.

Kavan moved cautiously, but casually to sit beside the physician and whispered, "You have not slept."

"The others…no one would wake up. I did not mind keeping watch alone," Rouvyn said with an embarrassed shrug.

"It is almost dawn."

Rouvyn glanced at the sky with surprise. He had not realized how long he had been awake. "I am not a very good judge of time passage, I fear. Shall I try again to wake the others?"

The bard shook his head. "You cannot. They are…" His head snapped to the north where the sound was more audible that time. Rouvyn heard it too. "Can you shoot in the dark?"

Knocking an arrow with trembling hands in response to the bard's question, Rouvyn whispered, "I can try, milord."

"Be prepared for anything."

The fire sputtered and died abruptly, its flames going out as if doused by an unseen hand as Kavan endeavored to even the field between hunters and hunted. Rouvyn jumped to his feet in surprise and then shrank back as an arrow whirred past his left ear. What followed was the sound of bodies crashing through the underbrush. Catching sight of one vague outline, his heart pounding in his throat, Rouvyn let his arrow fly. Someone cried out. Someone else grabbed at his arm as something sharp and jagged caught him in his calf. Rouvyn twisted free of the hands as he fell, closing his eyes, expecting the attackers to fall upon him.

But there was silence. Movement and sound, abrupt and unexpected as it had been, had ceased. In the increasing light of dawn, Rouvyn cracked his eyes open to see the man who had grabbed him frozen in place, contorted in his efforts to reach his escaped prey, the faint flicker of panic in his gray eyes indicating that the man was aware of his predicament. Around the clearing, another six men were similarly held as motionless as statues while the seventh lay where he had fallen, an arrow protruding from his neck. Rouvyn's arrow. The physician felt faint and sick and knew he would have collapsed if he were not already lying on the ground almost in the still warm ashes of their fire.

Not far away, Kavan stood, his eyes closed, breathing deeply and steadily in concentration with his hands outstretched as if reaching for something or trying to stop someone from reaching him. Though Rouvyn had little experience with Elyri, it was not difficult to guess that the bard was responsible for the condition these men were in. Pushing off the ground, he croaked, "What now, Lord Cliáth?"

Kavan did not open his eyes. "I can hold them this way long enough for you to tend your leg…then you will need to find every available rope, strap, or string to bind them before I release them." Rouvyn did not budge. "Please hurry, Rouvyn. I can maintain this for a while longer, but the longer you dally, the harder it will become."

"Yes…right…" The physician tended his leg, the wound not as bad as it felt since the arrow had snagged the top of his boot, keeping it from embedding too deeply. He found enough rope to bind five of the seven, tore the hem from his tunic to bind the sixth, and used the reins of Kavan's horse, at the bard's insistence, to bind the last. Once they were no longer a threat, Kavan released his psychic hold upon them and nearly collapsed from the welcome exertion. The sun had cleared the horizon as Rouvyn rounded up their prisoners into a small group but the others in their party still did not awaken. The seven men glared and struggled against their bonds, their cries of outrage muffled behind gags that Rouvyn was able to create, but they were not a threat.

Only when he stopped to study the clutter of weapons at his feet, did Rouvyn give in to the trembling of adrenaline. He had killed a man. He had never killed before, and though he had not taken the same oath that Elyri healers took, he never anticipated taking a life. While the act had given him none of the pleasure he knew it gave Elotti, it had not been nearly as difficult as expected either. He had just done it, instinctively.

"Self-preservation," the bard murmured. "The others will look at you differently now."

"If we can wake them," the physician grunted. To cover his embarrassment, he examined their companions. Their condition perplexed him for he could find no reason why they would not wake. To his eyes, they appeared to be sleeping normally, nothing more.

"A sleeping agent?"

Rouvyn grimaced. "I…yes…it could be…perhaps the wine…" He met the bard's gaze as both men made the same realization. Darius received a flask of wine from a well-wishing merchant in the village and Kavan and Rouvyn had been the ones not to partake. "A trap?"

"Perhaps." It seemed unlikely this was connected to the princes; to Kavan, the men they had captured seemed to be nothing more than common rogues. Still, it was possible, which meant they would have to be more careful in the future any time they bought supplies.

"I could give them a purgative to rouse them…though after so long asleep, the only sleeping agents I am aware of should be out of their systems. They should be waking on their own soon enough."

"Then we wait. Sleep, Rouvyn." The physician deserved his rest and Kavan was comfortable watching over their prisoners alone.

❧*❧

"It is good to have you back in Rhidam, Guthrie." It was the first time since the queen's death that the chamberlain had seen the King look excited about anything. Perhaps, in some fashion, this conflict with Neth was what the King needed to go on with his life. "Sit, please. How did you fair with King Valdis? You returned very quickly…did you gain an audience?"

The King sounded worried. "Do not fear. The Valdis' and their general agreed wholeheartedly with our strategy."

Arlan relaxed. "Wonderful. When do they want to get underway? We can be ready within the week…"

Knowing what was coming, Guthrie cleared his throat. "Prince Valdis has already given mobilization orders to his troops."

"We are not ready!" The King had expected swift action, but nothing so immediate.

"We are as ready as we can be. You said as much when you sent me to Cordash…and we both knew the Valdis' would want to act swiftly. Cordash has taken the brunt of Neth's aggression for too long; the raids are taking their toll on morale and resources. The four of us agreed that quick action was necessary. If we wait much longer, it may be too late. If our troops leave Rhidam in two days, all should go as scheduled. I know it seems abrupt, but I am confident it will work."

The King perched on the edge of the table, arms crossed over his chest, his expression somber. "If you think it sound strategy, Guthrie, you know I support you…but I wish we had more time."

Guthrie nodded. "So do I." A rushed war was a lost war, but the chamberlain was confident in this plan. Whether Enesfel's forces were strong enough to carry it out remained to be seen.

## ❧Chapter 26❧

Stretched out on his cot with two royal guards posted outside of his door, gdhededhá Tusánt's life seemed to be going from frightening to deadly with each hour that crept past. First, there had been the threat, and then the shot fired at him within náós walls. Yesterday, someone had rained a pail of rocks upon him as he walked in the market. Today he had been accidentally, or so it had seemed at the time, drawn into the midst of a brawl. If Justice Cornell and k'gdhededhá Tythilius had not passed and broken up the fight, Tusánt had no doubt he would have been killed or at least badly beaten. He was bruised and sore but nothing was broken or missing, and what bleeding there had been had been tended to by the healer.

When the k'gdhededhá went to the keep for Healer MacLyr, he had immediately gone into conference with the King and Chamberlain McHador. He had been there all afternoon, seeking a way to keep the Elyri cleric safe. What the King could do to help Tusánt, the gdhededhá did not know. Anything they could do, anything at all short of sending him to Elyriá, would be a blessing he would welcome.

❧*❧

It was nearly noon, the day warm and fine without a trace of cloud or trouble, when Owain rolled onto his back and opened his eyes. He was the last to awaken and scowled when he realized it was much later in the day than the party normally began to travel. Feeling sheepish, he looked around at the others, each man already awake, and tried to judge their moods. He expected them to be angry for sleeping, but most of his campmates' faces were blank and evasive. It was not until he noticed the seven bound figures and the single dead man, that he scrambled up, clutching his pounding head with a groan.

"Ah, you are awake." The physician knelt beside him, felt for his pulse then felt his forehead, and added. "Strong and normal. How do you feel?"

"Like my head was kicked by a horse," he muttered.

"That is normal and will pass. You have suffered no other ill effects…"

"Wine was drugged," Darius muttered bitterly, feeling responsible for this situation although he could not have foreseen it.

"And them?" Owain asked, indicating the bound men to one side of their camp. There was no sign of Kavan, but Owain trusted the bard to fend for himself.

"There was a little action during our wine-induced stupor," Wortham replied with a grin as he brushed crumbs from his mustache and beard. "Lucky for us, Elyri do not drink alcohol and Rouvyn chose not to. Kavan's looking for more troublemakers."

Rouvyn squirmed, embarrassed with everyone looking at him. "I did nothing," he protested weakly.

Determined that the others knew the truth, Wortham clapped the physician on the knee. "Nothing except kill a man and help Lord Cliáth capture our attackers. If not for the two of you, the lot of us would have been butchered in our sleep."

The grateful expressions of the others agreed with Wortham's assessment, although there appeared to be some reluctance from most to admit they might owe their lives to the man they originally shunned.

Owain, however, felt no such reluctance; his life had been saved once before by the most unlikely of sources, and he appreciated any man's kindness. "Allow me to extend my gratitude," he said, offering his hand to Rouvyn as Kavan emerged from the tree cover. Though no one spoke, there was the beginning of a tacit understanding amongst them; even Caol had begun to accept Rouvyn Talis instead of merely tolerating him.

They broke camp, put the dead man on the back of one of the pack mules, and herded the prisoners along in their midst in search of the nearest town or village. There was no time to waste, but no one wanted to leave these fellows here to possibly harm someone else.

❧*❧

After days of having someone interesting, foreign, and handsome pay attention to her, someone who treated her as an equal rather than as a child, Princess Diona was unhappy that her new friend had to go away to war, particularly when it seemed to her there was little age difference between them. In her eyes, Prince Espen, like her brother Muir, was too young to be riding into battle. But as he often pointed out to her over the last few days, Hatu's customs were different from hers and she had no right to ask anything else from him. He had a duty to perform and he intended to do that. Perhaps she had no right, but she was used to getting what she wanted from most people; foreigner or not, custom or not, and she was determined not to lose him. She was a Lachlan, after all. That had to count for something.

But he was going, regardless of her determination, and she realized she would miss him when he left. Having seen her mother die, she dreaded the notion that he might die young. A talk with her aunt eased her fears somewhat and told her what she needed to do. A coy smile on her lips, the youngest princess of Enesfel bounded down the stone stairs in search of Prince Espen.

ॐ * ॐ

Twisting the string of delicate white stone beads in his hands, Ártur watched as the last of the night's dinner guests gathered at the table and the King bid them sit. It was a relatively small number compared to the usual company found at Enesfel's table, and he knew that none of them had adjusted to the absence of many of their loved ones. Despite that melancholy, however, he noted that Princess Diona was grinning mischievously at Prince Espen, who seemed not to notice as he spoke in polite tones with the k'gdhededhá who was also in attendance tonight. The healer wondered what designs the princess had on the Hatu prince.

The empty chair across from him should have been his cousin's, and he knew that all of his present kin agreed Kavan should be there sharing this evening with them. They believed only an Elyri would understand the importance of this night, and while it should have been done in the midst of family in Elyriá, Ártur knew that was not possible for a variety of reasons. Instead, it was he and Syl who stood beside Bhríd tonight. His wife touched his knee with hers; she shared his sorrow over missing family but also his joy for what lay ahead.

Once everyone sat, Bhríd nodded and the healer got to his feet. "If I may, My Liege, there is an Elyri tradition I wish to uphold before we dine."

Heads turned, surprise and curiosity passing between them as they looked to their King. Whether the monarch was aware of what was happening, or even cared, was unclear as he waved his hand and said, "Please do." He respected the Elyri who served him, and as they rarely called any of their cultural practices into play in his court, in a way that might intrude or make others uncomfortable, it did not trouble him when they did ask.

The healer rounded the table and knelt between Bhríd and the Duchess of Levonne, facing her as she turned towards him. Behind him, Guthrie concealed a burst of laughter. The chamberlain remembered what this ritual meant, even if no one else did.

"Lady Madalyn Dubuais, it is the custom of my people for me to present this to you." He extended the white stone necklace towards her, holding it up for all to see. "In my hands, the Pheslátkag, that which binds. It is said that the very first of our kind gave a like emblem to his beloved when he asked her to come with him from that which was our home to that which became our home. Accepting it bound them forever, not as common bonds that bind men to women and women to men, but as a bond between souls. Where one goes, the other follows. It is made of earth, and the earth binds us all."

He stood, turned, and touched the string of stones to Bhríd's forehead. "nudhá sun nudhá, nune sun nune, yho lís kelémim kíteni." He touched it next to Bhríd's chest, repeated the words, and turned to Madalyn. "Tonight I come as a representative of all who came before, to present the Pheslátkag, honed from the heart of the earth, to bind your heart as it shall never be bound again. Will you accept this, on behalf of hwudhá ibh gaeth, he who is my kin, as a symbol of his honor and humility before you, his promise to keep you safe, to respect and cherish you as he does himself? That until you may be joined before k'Ádhá and the generations, you may wear this and remember he who is your other self?"

Madalyn rose, trembling, aware that the King's face, and others, bore decidedly confused expressions. She faced Bhríd, opened her mouth, but could not find her voice. She had been told he would pose the question formally in traditional Elyri fashion, but she had not expected this.

"Oh, get on with it, Lady Dubuais," the chamberlain chided gently. "Say you will marry the man and let us eat."

"Marry?" asked the King, whose face then turned crimson as he recalled his court had gone through this same elaborate display of words when Ártur had asked Syl to be his wife. That development he had anticipated. This time, there had been no indications that his chancellor had been courting the Duchess of Levonne. Or if there had been signs, he had missed them.

When Madalyn, flushed with embarrassment, still did not speak but rather stared at Bhríd with a smile on her face, he took her hands and said, "In the proper form of Enesfel tradition, since you have no male kin to ask, I beseech you directly to do me the honor of taking my name and joining your blood to mine. Will you be my wife?"

Her head bobbed yes several times before she managed to squeak, "Yes, Lord Cáner. I will." Ártur clasped the beaded choker about her neck and then pulled a small velvet pouch from his pocket.

Removing the simple stone band from within, he held it forth to his cousin. "To complete this union of spirits, hwudhá ibh dhi, do you accept the Pheski, taken from the same piece of earth, to bind you forever to she who wears your heart?"

"aelibh aiándás, thae dást mál aihwelys aelá át, thae mal aighlaiph átaelás síuínthé aelá it aikáchá át bhair," the chancellor replied. He watched Ártur slide the white band around the first finger of his left hand, believed to have the most direct line to his heart. The healer then took that hand and placed it at Madalyn's throat bringing the ring and necklace into contact. There was a static pop, audible to most in the room, and the wearers felt the stones tingle and grow warm against their skin. Madalyn gasped in surprise, her hand coming up to cover his, to hold it there as she searched his eyes for the meaning of what she felt. What sort of magic was this?

The chancellor and healer smiled as Bhríd took her hand, kissed the back of it, and helped her sit. Ártur returned to his chair, where his wife took his hand with a smile. Once seated, the healer spoke again. "Normally, if this was Elyriá, the marriage would occur seven days from now as did my own. However, given the state of affairs in the land, that does not appear likely. Instead, the duchess and chancellor agree that the ceremony will take place within a month of Bhríd's return from Neth. In the interim, with the blessings of the Faith and k'gdhededhá Jermyn, all necessary legal documents regarding property and union are to be drawn up and signed by mutual consent and will be deemed in effect as if this marriage has already been entered into."

There were bound to be questions about such an unorthodox agreement, although most would assume the choice was made in case Bhríd were to die in battle. Rather than wait for those questions to begin, or for the barrage of congratulations to join it, Bhríd smiled and said, "May we eat? I'm famished." Madalyn squeezed his hand, her laughter joining that of the others around the table.

❧*❧

"Why the smile, Lord Cliáth?" Prince Muir asked as he and the bard took first watch that night. There had been little to smile about on this journey thus far, not a hint of good news, thus the prince thought that smile to be suspicious. It had taken the use of royal prerogative to oust Captain Delamo from the duty of first watch; the Káliel captain smiled when he relented to the prince's wishes but he had taken up his usual sleeping position where Kavan was within sight and reach. He was not asleep yet, however. He rarely slept while Kavan was awake.

Looking up from the silent harp strings, Kavan murmured, "There is good news…"

"About Bertie and Wilred?" the prince asked hopefully. If Kavan had seen something about his brother and cousin, Muir wanted to know.

"No, this is…Bhríd is going to wed."

Wortham scratched at his beard and yawned. "I was not aware he was courting anyone."

"Very few knew," Kavan agreed.

"Who is she?" asked the prince.

"Lady Dubuais…"

"The Duchess of Levonne?" The prince was there the day she had come to the castle, but he had not thought anything of her visit. "Will he be a Duke then?"

"If things follow their normal legal course, then yes, I suspect so."

The prince leaned his back against a log and looked at the sky. "I wish we could be there when the announcement is made," he murmured. "I wager there will be a celebration."

"It is too late for that; the announcement has already been made." Kavan too wished he could have been there for it; with few Elyri traditions to uphold in Enesfel, he would have cherished the chance for this one.

"Then I hope we make it back with Bertie and Wilred before the wedding," the prince said with a pout. "I've never been to a wedding."

"I hope we will too, my prince…" It would be a day to be cherished if Kavan could bring good news as his wedding gift.

❧*☙

After a late night of signing documents and making the necessary preparations for his time away, Bhríd set out at dawn the following day, along with Guthrie McHador and Ártur MacLyr, to rejoin General Wyndham and the troops. With them, Sir Balint Gabersdon, the southern forces, and Prince Espen Harcourt and the two hundred soldiers from Hatu. Somewhere in the midst of the ranks, gdhededhá Tusánt joined them as the spiritual cornerstone and a confessor for the troops, a measure designed as much for their benefit as it was to get him out of Rhidam until whoever was threatening him could be found.

The chancellor bid his sister farewell, gave Flannery his final instructions, and kissed Madalyn goodbye. Ártur restricted his farewells to his wife and the child Bianca, while a newly reinstated General McHador straddled his mount, expression stony, not speaking to anyone. There was no family, save the King and healer, for him to bid farewell and the chancellor pitied the man for that. But it was Guthrie's choice to ride with the troops, Guthrie's choice to carry out this service for his King and country while he was able. He was not planning on going into battle, but he wanted to be at the front in support of the men he had fought beside and led for so long.

As they marched through the castle gates and across the drawbridge, picking up men and women as they went, faces peered out of many of the castle's windows. Word had reached everyone in the keep and they had all come to see the men off. Come tomorrow at dawn, the reunited troops would begin the long march towards Neth.

Enesfel was at war.

ಎ⊸Chapter 27⊸ᶭ

"We are too late."

The smoke wafting up around the young Elyri woman told her and her companions to expect a grim tale as they entered the village, but it did little to prepare them for the horror. Gingerly, she rolled over the first body she found, the first of what would become dozens more. An entire village slaughtered, many in their sleep or in the acts of fleeing or protecting others. Not even the smallest children had been spared. Identification of the dead would not be easy or pleasant, as most of those found who had not been burned beyond recognition had been beheaded, mutilated, or both. All fifty-eight of the tiny village's population. She had never seen or imagined this degree of brutality in her eighteen years of life. It sickened and revolted her, but she was not truly surprised.

She and the others, seven from the region where she lived, had come to this village for the last nine months bringing food, medical supplies, and clothing, goods that could then be distributed to other villages in Neth where they were most needed, the places hardest hit by King Loris' rampage. All of her companions, and the villagers, had known that once Neth's king discovered where those relief supplies were coming into his kingdom, he would retaliate. Now he had.

The rain was coming down hard, making the pathways slippery with mud. Blood and ash mixed with the water, rinsing the corpses clean before eventually collecting into ugly, viscous puddles. She heard the squish of boots behind her and looked up from the hole she had finished filling with her bare hands, the grave of an infant she could not leave to the elements.

"Mílne, we can stay no longer. There may be troops in the region still. There are no survivors; there is nothing we can do."

The woman named Mílne pushed wet strands of blonde from her forehead and stared at him. "We cannot leave them like this Dhórdh. It would be sacrilege."

"I think k'Ádhá will forgive us for not seeing to their burials. We need to get the supplies back home, find a new inlet. The longer we dally…"

Someone in the distance screamed. Dhórdh pulled her to her feet behind him, fingers gripping tightly into her arm as though to keep from losing her. There was more screaming and both realized in the same instant that the sounds were coming from the abandoned náós that had been their point of arrival, the náós that housed the Gate. The rest of their group was waiting there while Dhórdh went back for Mílne. The others should not have waited, should have gone home without them, but they had stubbornly chosen to wait for the last of their number to rejoin them. To linger had proven to be the worst possible thing they could do.

Dhórdh was dazed, struck dumb by the rising panic in his chest. They could not get home through the Gate. King Loris' soldiers were here, it seemed, and there was nowhere safe to flee. His usually quick mind was blank and numb and all he could do was run without knowing where he was going.

But Mílne's mind was not thus affected. Running, his hand still on her arm, she turned him towards the village edge and the direction of the forest. Dhórdh thought they would disappear amongst the trees, but instead, Mílne pulled him into the charred and crumbling remains of a hovel, still hearing the cries of their comrades as they were slaughtered one by one.

"Make the change, Dhórdh."

"Change…?"

"We have to leave undetected…in some other form. They will assume that if the others were waiting, they were waiting for someone…and they will come looking. We have to go…"

Dhórdh nodded. It was not something he was accustomed to doing, not many Elyri practiced the art of shapechanging, even if they had learned how to do it. But at this moment, there was no other option. He hesitated but the shouts of soldiers, the clanging of armored bodies roaming nearby streets, gave him the impetus to act. A small yellow cat took Mílne's place and darted into the forest. Dhórdh followed her example and the two cats disappeared into the brush as several Nethite soldiers came into view. Neither waited nor looked back to see if the soldiers had seen them or given chase.

❧*❧

The opulent halls of the Valdis castle in Aralt were silent, empty, devoid of the merriment and bustle that usually filled them. This was in part due to the lack of soldiers and guards within her walls. The castle was a fortress, built to be exceedingly difficult to breach. It was nestled between the Nekan and Vela rivers, in the heart of Cordash; should any army wish to approach and besiege her, the occupants would know of those intentions long before the attackers arrived. Hence, Prince Renfrid and General Marym felt secure in leaving a minimal number of troops to defend her. Every other available fighting man was off to the Cordash-Neth border. The time for petty raids and skirmishes was past. It was time for war.

But today it was not just the absence of soldiers that created the bone-deep silence in Aralt. It was the silence of death. Their king, Ahern the First, had succumbed to the ravages of illness and age. Prince Renfrid Valdis had been elevated to king and was about to start his reign with the first war in over two hundred years of Cordashian history. If the chroniclers were to remember him positively, he needed success. He hoped General McHador's plan would bring him that.

๛*๛

After two hours of riding under ever darkening skies, the search party was forced to stop as the clouds opened and rain fell in torrents. They had tried to continue, not wanting to lose more time, but it had not taken long to determine that the rain was falling too hard, reducing visibility, making the path treacherous, and the thunder and lightning made the horses too skittish to control. Wanting to be dry and sheltered themselves, they located a dense patch of foliage with room enough for all of them, tethered the horses securely, and spread the large waxed canvas they had purchased to serve as a covering in the case of just such an event. The ground beneath was wet, as were their clothes, but the covering kept them from getting wetter. Despite finding nothing but rain-soaked kindling, Kavan managed to start a fire large enough for the men to gather around to warm and dry themselves.

"It is fortunate you thought to bring this covering, Lord Cliáth," Muir remarked through chattering teeth. "I would never have thought of such a thing or imagined we would need it."

The bard did not speak. His gaze was fixed upon the fire, every thought and ounce of energy focused on maintaining their source of warmth. He wanted his harp; there was a deep agitation in his soul today that he could not identify and had yet been unable to purge through prayer and meditation. Music might soothe him, but he dared not risk exposing the instrument to the weather. At least this outpouring of power kept his mind occupied and away from that roiling internal discomfort.

As Kavan did not appear to desire talk, and since Prince Muir seemed hopeful for conversation to distract himself from the cold, Wortham said, "He has had more experience with such travel than you have. I should have thought about it…it is spring and that frequently brings rain…but having grown up on Káliel, the thought of rain rarely troubles me."

Shifting closer to the fire, Owain muttered, "Likewise…I should have anticipated this."

"At least we know that Halstatt didn't set this delay upon us," the inquisitor grunted.

Owain nodded. "Not unless he has figured out how to produce rain at will or control the weather." If anyone noticed that Caol had verbalized the name of the man they were seeking, the man who had kidnapped the princes, they made no mention of it.

There was silence again, punctuated by the splatter of raindrops on the canvas above their heads angled to allow the water to run off the edges rather than pool in the center. Rouvyn produced a set of dice from his pouch and a flask of spirits from his horse and quickly had Darius, Muir, and Caol engaged in a game. Owain spread his bedroll and lay upon it. Over the course of the day, he had developed a cough, but when the doctor offered him an elixir, he refused. He was trying to sleep under Kavan's concerned eye. If the man's health did not improve by morning, the bard would force him to take that elixir. They could not afford for Owain to be ill. Wortham watched the elder prince as well, but once the man was asleep, the captain got up, circled three times around the perimeter of their shelter, watching through the trees for any sign of danger before he came back to Kavan's side.

"You are creating the fire, aren't you," the captain asked, keeping his voice low to avoid being heard.

Surprised, Kavan looked at him. Without his full concentration, the fire diminished but no one appeared to notice. "How did you…?"

"Wet wood does not burn, milord, particularly wood as wet and green as what we found." He gave a crooked smile.

"No one else…"

"If they chose to dwell on it, they would realize it too. The wood is barely charred after two hours. You add more wood to the pile periodically, but it makes the fire taller…it does not add fuel to the flames."

Kavan chuckled. "You are observant and perceptive, my friend." That he did not need to hide what he was doing from at least one man in the party was a relief. Wortham's smile brightened as Kavan turned his focus back to the fire and neither spoke for a long time, even when Wortham reached across to put more wood onto the pile. The captain enjoyed this sort of stillness, this closeness with the Elyri that did not require words or action. He watched the dice game, deducing that Muir was winning. It would likely do much for the prince's mood. The captain had not been comfortable bringing the prince on this journey, despite how much he liked the boy, but he was pleased that it was doing the prince good to be away from Rhidam and amongst the company of men who did not treat him as a castoff.

Eventually, he was distracted by a sound from the man seated beside him. He looked into green eyes filled with unexpected anguish and the bard asked, "How do you think I do it, Wortham?"

Kavan had called him by name, which brought the question, the discussion, down to a personal level that was not there minutes before. Unsure how to answer, the captain asked, "The fire?" The bard nodded. Wortham thought about his reply for several minutes before he gave it. "The same way you fly. The same way you travel from one place to another quickly. The same way Lord MacLyr heals. Not a miracle…but something else."

"How can you be certain it is no miracle?"

"I just am." He rubbed his bearded face. "When there have been miracles, there is an energy…an external force at work. I have felt it each time. Now, with the fire…I do not feel anything; it must be something internal to you that allows it to be done."

"If you cannot feel anything, how can you…?"

Wortham pressed his hand on Kavan's knee. "Deduction and faith. I have no trouble believing anything of you; I cannot explain why, but thus far, nothing you have done has shocked me."

"It does not trouble you that I can do these things? That miracles pass through my hands?"

There was a heavy note of sadness in Kavan's voice, a sense of loneliness that Wortham had not noticed earlier. He could feel it for the first time, although he realized it had always been there, always part of who Kavan was. He clasped the bard's hand tightly, hoping Kavan could read his thoughts through the contact. "Why should it trouble me, Kavan? You are a man. Elyri. Different, yet the same. You are my dearest friend. I love you with everything I am. Whatever may be to come, whatever you may do, nothing can change that. There are no words to explain it any better."

Kavan's eyes closed as his face turned towards the fire. In the light of the flames that sputtered and nearly died, Wortham saw the wetness glistening on the bard's cheeks and the tips of his pale lashes. The other men glanced at the fire; Wortham hastily added more kindling and watched the blaze flare again. No one else noticed those tears or suspected anything. Once the gaming was resumed, the captain discretely handed Kavan a kerchief to dry his face. The Elyri took it and wiped his eyes. When he met the captain's gaze, there was relief that Wortham was pleased to see. He smiled and stared into the fire.

⤜*⤛

As dawn arrived, Mílne and Dhórdh were miles away from the remains of their companions and the supplies they had left behind. They stopped out of utter exhaustion, unsure of their location, unsure of their safety. Yet they could not continue. They had tapped into all the energy adrenaline and fear had provided and were weary to the core. They had to sleep if they were to continue. They prayed they were far enough from the reach of Nethite soldiers to do so. Arms around one another for comfort and warmth, they curled against the back wall of the empty cave they had found and slept.

❧*❧

Captain Cornell glanced at the soldier who entered his quarters before returning his attention to sharpening his sword. With General Wyndham, Chamberlain McHador, and General Zarkosta gone north with the army, the scope of the justice's responsibilities expanded drastically. Not that he would complain. He rather enjoyed the fact that this was the first time in all of his years of service to King Arlan that he would be able to show how much he was capable of, without others there to overshadow him or steal attention.

He waited for the man to speak, and when he did not, the justice looked up again. "Well, soldier? What is it? Are you going to stand there or do you have something to say?"

The young soldier shuffled awkwardly and stammered, "I did not want to speak until you bid it, milord…"

"Then I suppose if I said nothing, you would remain there in silence all day?"

Blushing, the soldier shook his head. "N…no sir. I…Edgar Fielding, reporting for duty, sir."

The justice's demeanor perked up to hear that name. "Fielding. Right. You have returned from personal leave? A marriage, correct?"

It took great effort for the young man not to shuffle his feet again. "Yes sir, I am newly married, sir."

"Congratulations on that."

Flustered to receive those words from the justice, Fielding beamed. "Thank you, sir. I was told you wanted to see me…about my last day of duty?"

From his tone, the justice assumed the young man believed he was about to lose his position. That would be bad news for a recently married man; the justice could understand his nervousness. "Yes, the eve before you took leave. A parcel arrived for Lord Dugan, yes? I was told you received it?"

It took Fielding mere moments to reply, "Yes, sir. I did, sir."

"Do you recall anything about the delivery? What it was? Who delivered it?" After this much time, the justice had little hope of the man remembering anything, but it was worth asking.

To his surprise, Fielding nodded. "He rode a yellow gelding and wore a dark cloak that hid his face…and he wore no gloves. He delivered a box…"

"Any idea where he might have been from?"

"I could not say, sir. I detected no accent; I presumed he was from Enesfel. There were no marks on him or his horse for us to guess."

"The delivery? Mr. Baine said you opened the box? What did it contain?"

Again, Fielding struggled not to shift his weight. Fearing he was being accused of theft, he mumbled, "A dagger… like the man said it was…but it was the strangest dagger I'd ever seen in my life."

Minos leaned across his desk, awaiting more. "Strange how?"

Fielding had not been back in Rhidam long enough to know of the events of the past weeks, and the justice's interest worried him. "I did not take anything, milord, I swear it. I opened the box, but I did not touch anything. I took it directly to General Zarkosta and told him it was for Lord Dugan. I know nothing more about it."

"I am sure you carried out your duty properly, Mr. Fielding. I want to know what was in the box. What the dagger looked like."

The words were meant to relieve him, but still Fielding stuttered, "It had a gold handle with monster faces…and a black stone in the pommel. But the strangest part was the blade…like a three edged star that ended in a point…"

Minos straightened and barely kept the look of accomplishment off his face. "Are you certain of this, Mr. Fielding?"

"On my honor, sir. I couldn't make something like that up…and I'll never be able to get that thing out of my head as long as I live."

The justice sighed and leaned back in his chair. No doubt, he agreed silently. Such an item would defy imagination, and if one had never heard of the Coryllien, they would have no idea what they had seen. But he had no doubt that a Coryllien dagger had been, at least for a short time, on royal ground. "Thank you, Mr. Fielding. That will be all. You may return to your duties first thing in the morning. Oh…and welcome back to Rhidam."

Only then did Fielding believe his job was secure. He saluted and began whistling merrily as soon as he got outside the door. Propping his feet on the desk, the justice took the pieces of the puzzle surrounding Lady Dilyn's death and began to put them together again, hoping that when he was done, he would be closer to solving that murder…even if that meant implicating Inquisitor Dugan.

☙*❧

Having made little progress the previous day, Kavan roused the party before dawn, once he believed the storm had passed, and pushed northward again at the quickest pace the horses could manage on the slippery, muddy road. He had tended the fire all night, making certain the men were warm and safe. Keeping the fire burning, however, left him weak, disoriented, and exhausted. When they stopped to water the horses in a large puddle, not long after beginning their day's travel, he dismounted, spoke quietly to Wortham, and then climbed up behind the Káliel captain. The rest of the party watched with curiosity, concern, and envy, as he clung to Wortham, his head resting between the captain's shoulders. Very soon, however, he was unaware of their stares or anything else as the motion of the horse and the captain's steady breathing and heartbeat lulled him into much-needed sleep. Wortham kept his eyes upon the road, heart swelled with love; he failed to notice anything except where he was going and the man on the horse behind him.

≈*≈

The mid-day meal was his least favorite. Everyone in the de Corrmick palace knew that and the royal chefs had an increasingly difficult duty to make each day's meal more pleasant than the last for their demanding, unforgiving king. To fail, to be perceived as having made little or no effort to please King Loris, meant dismissal at best, death at the worst. The pudgy, whimsical looking chef with the square face and stringy, beaded mustache, peered from behind the heavy wool curtains, watching the king's portly frame devour the offering of berry-glazed pheasant, rice bread, Káliel sherry, and roasted apples. From the gusto with which the monarch ate, the chef felt he had surely passed the test again today. That the king was laughing with his once lovely mouse of a wife and his daughter meant that his mind was not on the food and thus not on the fate of his kitchen staff.

A courier came through the main dining room doorway and bowed with a flourish, a habit learned early by those in the de Corrmick court. The more flourish one used, the sooner you would get the attention of the king. Though his expression suggested he was in a hurry to deliver whatever message had brought him here, he maintained his bow until the king acknowledged him. Sometimes messengers and visitors were forced to stay in such positions for nearly an hour as the king otherwise amused himself. Today, perhaps because of his apparent jovial mood or out of boredom and a wish for something out of the mundane, the king spared the courier minutes of needless torture.

"What do you want?" he burped, wagging his thick finger, beckoning the messenger closer.

"Your Majesty...I come from Lord Demris; he says that Cordash...that the Valdis' have declared war and are amassing their troops in Edug and Matina. The details are here." He held forth the tattered scroll he carried and drew his hand back quickly as the king snatched it from him.

Everyone in the room fell quiet. The possibility of war was not to be taken lightly, though it was a normal enough state in Neth. In the kitchen doorway, behind the curtains, the chef began to tremble as the king's face grew redder by the moment.

"How dare they declare war on me!" he bellowed, causing those around him to shrink back in fear. The messenger did not flinch, though his expression showed he had withdrawn far within himself to endure whatever unpleasant punishment the king might inflict. "You!" The king grabbed the front of the courier's tunic, bringing him back to attention. "Fetch General Glucke at once; send him to the rear chamber. We will show that coward Valdis what it means to declare war on Loris de Corrmick."

The King started from the room, stopped, and then looked back. "And see that someone clears away this filth," he barked, indicating the uneaten portion of the meal.

The chef behind the curtain wilted visibly and scurried away.

∂◦*◦∂

Mílne faintly heard the sound of footsteps upon gravel that entered the cave and she opened her eyes, expecting to find that Dhórdh had risen first and provided them a meal. But the figure in fur-lined boots was unfamiliar and instantly terrifying. Her mind screamed formless words as she registered first the blood dripping from his blade and then Dhórdh's eyes, wide with surprise in a head that was no longer attached to his body. With all the energy she could gather, she threw the Nethite sideways against the cave wall at the same moment his blade drove through her chest. The satisfaction of knowing she had killed their murderer was the last thing Mílne ever knew.

ঌ৯*ঌৰ

The riders had not stopped for their noon meal, as they hoped to make up some of the distance lost due to the rain and mud. The setting of the sun, however finally forced them to stop. Kavan was still asleep upon Wortham's horse, clinging to the captain, somehow not falling as they traveled. Owain helped him down, allowing Wortham to dismount while Muir prepared the bard's bedroll. Kavan was placed upon it, each man in the party protective of the bard who was keeping this expedition going when there was nothing but hope to guide them. No one had the heart to wake him for the meal, but Rouvyn did examine him to be certain Kavan was sleeping and not suffering some worse condition. Owain accepted the physician's recommendations for his cough in order to be fit enough to take care of Kavan like everyone else. The thought of disappointing the bard again was more than he cared for.

With each doing his utmost to stay quiet to allow the bard to sleep, and the land around them being peaceful and still, the evening passed uneventfully until they prepared for sleep. Suddenly, Kavan bolted upright with a strangled, fearful cry that jolted all of them and brought each to his side.

"Easy, milord," soothed Rouvyn, laying his hand upon the bard's forehead to check for signs of fever while his eyes looked elsewhere to see if the man had been bitten or stung.

The terror in Kavan's eyes spoke not of illness or injury, but of something more powerful, and Muir, fearing he had seen something about Prince Bertram and Wilred, clutched one of his hands and squeaked, "Lord Cliáth?"

With his free, trembling hand, Kavan motioned for the water skin that lay beside Darius; the soldier gave it to him and everyone watched anxiously as he drank, each one thinking the same as the prince, that the worst had happened and their pursuit of the kidnappers had come to an abrupt and dismal end. Knowing he had to dispel those fears, regardless of his inner turmoil, Kavan whispered, "It is not the boys; it is…I have witnessed…felt…"

Wortham's large hand rested on the bard's shoulder, hoping to calm him. If Kavan said this was not about the missing boys, the captain believed him. "Do you want to tell us, milord?" If not, he would not force the issue, though others in their party might wish it.

Kavan gave the water skin back to Darius as he buried his face in the captain's neck and clutched his arm. The Sight had shown him many things over the years, from births to deaths, but few visions had been as real, as immediate, or as disturbing, as this had been. Like his very first vision, this was not an event that would happen, but rather one that had happened, happened at the moment Kavan experienced it, making the incident all the more terrifying. He welcomed Wortham's strength and support. Though there was no reason for any man here to know what had happened, he answered the captain's question, not caring if the others heard him or not.

"Mílne…Ártur's…my…tyne…murdered by…in Neth…"

In the heavy silence that followed, the men looked at one another as Wortham rubbed Kavan's back tenderly. One of Kavan's kin had been killed in Neth. A woman. Even Owain, for what little he knew of

Elyri, was aware that women in Elyriá were honored in a way they were not anywhere else in the Five Sovereignties. In a household, men and women were equal, but if a dispute arose, most often it was the woman's wishes that were considered. Men headed the religious establishment, but most bhydáni were women, and all matters of politics fell into female hands, from each village council all the way up to the High Mother herself. This murder, however it had occurred, was no small thing.

Eventually, Kavan struggled to his feet, leaning upon Wortham until he could steady himself. He pressed his damp face against the bearded one in what looked to the others to be a kiss, something none of them had ever seen from Kavan before, before he broke away and staggered into the forest. Knowing Kavan's penchant for private prayer, no one stopped him, in spite of their fears for his state of mind.

Kavan knew he had to tell Ártur and Syl. Tám and Dháná. Most importantly, he should inform his cousin Sámel that his eldest daughter had been slaughtered for no reason other than she was Elyri. He had been the sole witness to the crime, and no one would ever think to look for her in a cave in the mountains of Neth. While his bond with most of his family was not strong enough to allow contact for the sort of communication necessary to convey this message, he could reach Ártur, though the healer would likely be on his way to Neth with Enesfel's troops. The others should be told face to face…but how? Did he dare go home with such news?

Shaken, Kavan fell to his knees, face into the damp leaves and spring soil, and screamed a silent scream.

❧*☙

Struck into a panic by the urgency of the mind touch, Ártur opened himself to the contact his cousin insistently demanded. The healer had been too agitated to rest, but he would have felt that call even if he was asleep. When the contact was made and his cousin's story spilled through, it was all Ártur could do to maintain the link between them. Every fiber of his being wanted to deny what Kavan had revealed, but it was certain that Kavan spoke the truth. Kavan would never have told him something like this otherwise. Why Mílne had been in Neth, Ártur did not know, but he knew what he had to do.

Feet heavy with the weight of this burden, he trudged to where Guthrie and Bhríd slept. He roused his kinsman and, rather than relay such shattering information with insufficient words, he let the thoughts pass through his touch. Bhríd too was stunned, and the two stayed that way for many minutes, mental contact maintained, feeling each other's sorrow and comfort. Though they did not touch or try to wake him, the chamberlain stirred, yawned, and opened his eyes, awakened by the healer's proximity and sounds of grief the Elyri made.

"Ártur? What is it?" he asked with a sleepy groan.

Apologetically, the healer bowed his head. "I must send an urgent message to Syl. I would take it myself...but there is no Gate and I know I am needed here. Please, I must request someone take my message to her in my stead."

Before Guthrie could ask what sort of message warranted such immediate action when their march north had been uneventful thus far, Bhríd murmured, "It is from Kavan...regarding one of our kin...a death in the family. Syl must take the news to our kin at once. Please, milord...send someone to her."

A death in the family, especially when the news had come from Kavan, was important enough to Guthrie to warrant action. "Send that young soldier Curran. He has one of the fastest horses. Tell him to be swift about it. I want no delays in his return."

"Thank you, Guthrie," Ártur said gratefully, wiping his face on his sleeve before going with Bhríd to draft letters and find the messenger.

⊱Chapter 28⊰

For the first time since she was a small child, Syl found herself gnawing on the knuckle of her thumb. It was something she had done then as a relief for stress and frustration. At the moment, watching Princess Diona dress Bianca with all of the jewelry she could find, Syl could think of nothing further from stress. And other than missing Ártur, she did not feel frustrated. It was their first extended separation, the first time they had been apart by more than a few rooms or at most the size of Rhidam since their marriage. That Ártur had gone as a witness to war did not sit well with her. He would not be in danger from the actual fighting; if he suffered an injury it would be at the hands of some Elyri-hating Nethite. Guthrie had sworn to make certain Ártur was protected and guarded at all times. Somehow, that did not give her the peace she had hoped for.

More than likely this habit had resurfaced as a result of last night's restless sleep. She felt sad, vulnerable, and afraid for no discernible reason. There was also a sick feeling in her stomach, and an image of a sword red with blood in her head that would not leave. Syl did not have the Sight, nor was she particularly gifted beyond her ability to heal. She could only attribute such imagery to the nearness of war.

Hurry home, Ártur, she prayed as Bianca scurried back to her and climbed onto her lap to show off her treasures. Bianca needs a father. And as much as I love this child, I want one of my own. One of yours.

❧*❧

After the night's emotional ordeal, Kavan was quieter than usual when they broke camp the following morning. Normally one to pack his own belongings and do his share of any work to be done, he could not bring himself to act, and no one was inclined to complain that he did little more than stumble about in a daze. It was the first time someone close to him, a member of his own family, had died. Phyóná Térari had died but Kavan had not known her as anything other than a name mentioned by family members. Phaedr Cáner had died, but for whatever reason, Kavan had not felt that death and had not known about it until long after the fact. That Phaedr met a hero's death in battle, despite his blindness, had somehow softened the pain of that loss. Mílne was born while Kavan still lived in Bhryell, and the day of her birth had been the single time, after being expelled from his uncle's home, that he was allowed back. He had held the little girl when she was a few hours old, watched over her when there was no other family member available, and saw her often during Gatherings. He watched her grow from an infant into a small girl and had seen her again when Ártur and Syl married. Now with the thrust of a sword, she was gone.

He knew he could find her body if given the chance. Ahead, a day and a half ride from where they were, he knew they would reach a small village. There was a náós in the village, a náós with a Gate. But without knowing where she was in Neth, he did not know how he could hope to Gate close enough to her location to find her.

He was still pondering her death, the method of it, and her reasons for being in Neth, as his party started up the slope of the mountain ravine. The path was wide enough for a wagon, but rather than riding two by two, they elected to travel single file away from the ledge. With Kavan struggling to come back to himself, Caol insisted on being the one to lead and no one chose to argue. Below, the mountain river made by the melting of winter snow tossed and swirled, churning over the boulders that had tumbled down the mountainside in times past. The path grew gradually steeper, slowing their progress as they evaded rocks and holes in the road and worked to coax the animals along.

The inquisitor unexpectedly shouted, "Hold!" a word and tone that snapped Kavan out of the daze he had been in all morning. As the others reined in their horses and pack mules, Kavan dismounted and came to Caol's side. The redhead had already gotten off his horse and was examining one of the animal's hooves. "I think we should walk them," he murmured, not seeing anything that might make the animal skittish. "It's getting too rough and steep, and I would rather avoid tumbling into the ravine if my horse loses his footing. Besides, the grade will be easier on them if they don't have to carry us too."

Agreeing to Caol's suggestion, they continued up the trail on foot, the prince and physician grumbling about the difficulty of the climb all the while. They were caught in the heat of the morning sun where it broke through the trees on the far side of the ravine and reflected off the red stone wall beside them. They traveled for a little over an hour before they were forced to stop, the cause of yet another delay clearly visible before them. A scatter of rocks and debris littered the road, the largest being too big to get around with the horses. In the azure sky, the sun had almost reached its zenith.

"Just as well we stopped," Wortham grinned, unconcerned about an obstacle he believed they could surmount. "I'm hungry."

Prince Muir, weary and footsore, muscles aching in ways he was not used to, leaned against his horse and looked around with dismay. With the rocks ahead of them, the mountainside to their left, and the river to their right far below, he saw no way to continue, and though he hated the delay, he was grateful to have stopped. "What do we do, Lord Cliáth?" he groaned.

"The only thing we can," Kavan replied. "We eat, rest, and clear the path."

"Move those rocks? Some of them are as big as the horses."

Kavan arched one eyebrow. "Do you doubt me, my prince?" he asked, crediting Muir's irritability for his lack of faith.

The prince did not reply, not having an answer that he could put into words, and instead helped Rouvyn ready a meal as Darius examined each horse's condition. The Elyri, meanwhile, studied the rockslide that had cut them off. Some of the boulders were very large, but it was nothing he could not tend to. Part of him protested an open display of power this close to Neth, but it was either that or spend unnecessary hours and energy toiling to remove the blockage, or else turning around. The last two options were not worth considering.

Sudden prickles of ice raced up the back of his neck seconds before he heard the rumble of rocks. Too late, he cried out and spun, throwing out a wave of energy that he hoped would shield his companions from the second landslide. He could hear the cries of fear and astonishment from the others, but he could see nothing through the dust and rock until the shower ceased and the noise of falling stone ended in a series of splashes in the river below.

When the dusty yellow-grey haze cleared, he tried to determine the success of his efforts. Three horses were visible, those three closest to him. A large boulder pinned Wortham against the wall of the mountain, but from Kavan's viewpoint, he could see no one else. The Káliel captain looked at him with a stunned expression but was, at least, alive.

"Wortham?"

"Aye. I don't believe I am hurt...though I seem to be trapped."

"What about the others? The horses?"

The captain craned his neck. "I saw two horses go over the edge...I don't know about the rest."

A groan echoed, interrupting him, then came Prince Muir's faint call for help. Without a thought as to difficulty or danger, Kavan began moving rocks from his path, a task that to Wortham looked easier than it should have been. Within a few minutes, the bard uncovered Owain lying face down atop Muir, both still covered with small rocks, dirt, and dust, but at least accessible and in good health.

"Lord Cliáth?" the prince mumbled, his head turned away from the bard and unable to turn back because of Owain's position.

"Be still," the bard murmured. "I am here." He brushed the debris from Owain and lifted the man easily once he was sure there were no injuries other than bruises and a bump on the back of the man's head. Owain, propped against the mountain wall, began to stir as Kavan assisted the younger prince to roll over and sit up. "How do you feel, my prince?"

"Sore...but okay..." began Muir.

"Like death," said Owain simultaneously, thinking the bard was talking to him since he had not yet opened his eyes. He met his son's gaze with relief and added, "I have the worst headache and I feel like I was trampled under a stampede of horses...but it seems I am in one piece." Kavan assisted Muir to sit next to Owain where they would be out of the pathway.

"Nothing as bad as that, though it could have been worse," Kavan said. "Both of you rest but stay awake." If either had suffered a significant head injury, they could not fall asleep and succumb to it. As he stepped back, more small rocks rained down from above them, but not enough to cause harm. At the same time, behind him, he heard a skittering of gravel from the ledge. On his hands and knees, Kavan crept to the edge to find Caol grasping onto an outcropping of rock, trying to hoist himself onto the pathway.

"Good to see you…" The words were strained as if it took all of the man's concentration to retain his grip.

"Do not move, Caol…" Glancing over his shoulder, he asked, "Owain…can you hold my ankles?" He had the strength to pull the inquisitor up, but wanted the assurance of someone to steady him. Ignoring the pain in his head, Owain did as Kavan asked.

Lying upon the ground with Owain bracing him, Kavan inched closer to the edge and reached over. He was about to instruct Caol to take his hands, but the inquisitor's grip began to slip on the rock edges he clung to. Kavan shot forward, feeling Muir's added weight behind him, praying they would not all career over the edge as he wrapped his hands around Caol's wrists and held tightly. Caol's eyes were bright with the adrenaline of fear and surprise but he said nothing as inch-by-inch, Muir and Owain pulled, adjusting their weight and position as necessary. With the added aid of Caol's limber legs and feet to push himself up, he and Kavan were eventually secure upon the ledge.

When he felt the firm earth beneath him as he stared at the sky, panting with exertion and relief, Caol muttered, "You've got the surest grip of any man I've ever met, Lord Harper. I did not know playing the harp could strengthen a man's grasp; perhaps I should take it up." Joking was easier than a solemn thank you, but that would come, in time.

"I don't believe that would help you, Lord Dugan," Captain Delamo chuckled with relief from his place behind the boulder.

At the rear of the slide, Owain and Kavan found Darius and Rouvyn; the soldier had both legs pinned beneath a large slab of sheared off rock, while the doctor was caught beneath one of the horses. Both men were alive, though unconscious, but the horse was not. It took Muir's help to lift the awkwardly shaped slab off Darius and to unpack the horse and move it off of Rouvyn. Though the physician stirred as the weight was removed, he did not immediately wake, even when the dead animal was pushed over the precipice. Caol and Owain stood at the edge of the road, watching as the horse hit the water. Kavan, meanwhile, wrapped a blanket around Darius and began cleaning the blood off his face.

Upon waking, the first thing Rouvyn did was conduct a quick self-examination that told him nothing was broken. Though bruised and disoriented, he pushed to his feet and went to Kavan's side. Thus far, he had survived a bandit attack, a thunderstorm, weeks of relying on himself, and a rockslide. If he could survive all of that, then he saw it as his duty, even his honor, to heal those who had given him this new sense of confidence.

"Milord, allow me." Kavan moved to allow the physician to work. "How is everyone?"

"Bruises and cuts mostly; Owain has a bump on his head, but it appears that Darius has the worst of it."

"It could have been worse," snorted Caol, kicking at something amid the debris that he picked up to show the others. It was a plank of wood, splintered and cracked at one end as if it had broken off a much longer plank. "I don't think either avalanche was a natural occurrence.

Kavan remembered the cold prickle felt before the disaster struck; he nodded at Caol, agreeing with the inquisitor's suspicions.

"Someone did this on purpose?" Muir stammered, realizing for the first time how much danger both they and the other boys must be in. "Someone tried to kill us?"

"It's entirely likely," the inquisitor grunted.

Filled with fear, Muir glared at Kavan, the safest person he felt he could lash out at, and snapped, "Why didn't you warn us? You know things before they happen! You should have warned us. We lost horses…supplies…"

"Enough," barked Owain. Not expecting to be scolded, Muir bit his lip but continued to glare. "I do not know much about Elyri, but no man is all seeing or knowing. Claiming he knew about this and did not warn us is no different than accusing him of being in league with the kidnappers. I, for one, am not prepared to accuse him thus. Are you?"

Those words made the younger prince hang his head with a sense of shame he never experienced when Arlan chastised him. "I am sorry, Lord Cliáth," he whispered.

Rather than trust his voice, the exchange having struck a raw chord, Kavan started clearing away more of the rocks, pushing them over the ledge to tumble into the river. Owain and Caol joined him, and once Wortham was free of his confinement, he did likewise. It was a long process, and by the time the sun disappeared below the rim of the mountain wall, the road was cleared of all except the two largest boulders, one that had been part of Wortham's prison and the largest that lay in the direction they were traveling. Rouvyn had revived Darius, but the man had suffered from multiple fractures where the slab had crushed his legs; he would not be able to continue the journey.

Without enough wood to make a decent fire, they consumed a meal of bread and dried cheese. It would take another few hours to reach the other side of the canyon and the crossroads that would take them either east to the city of Bryn, north to Neth or south towards Rhidam. They discussed their options: to camp where they were and risk their attackers burying them in another landslide in the dark, or to continue forward and risk the ledge. Neither was a good option, but in the end, it was decided that if Kavan could remove the obstacle and provide light to travel by, they would take their chances with the chasm and continue.

Sparse meal finished, Kavan shooed the others back from the boulders. It was the twilight hour, but the shadows of the mountainside cut much of the light they would normally have. With the rising full moon, however, there was enough illumination for the men to see Kavan place his hands upon the first boulder, his back to them. It looked as if he might push it, a feat none of them could imagine any man doing alone.

Anxious that they might judge him for what he was about to do, Kavan took a breath and focused his concentration on harnessing as much energy as he could into himself, shaping it, sharpening it, holding it at bay. When he had enough, his focus shifted outwards, seeking the heart of the obstacle beneath his hand, its weakest point. There was an uncharacteristic tremor in his body; this was an ability he had not used since bhydáni Tíbhyan taught it to him, other than to practice it on his own in the desire to perfect it. He had never imagined he would need such a skill, and never thought to display it in the company of Teren. He trusted Wortham and desired to share that same trust with Prince Muir, even though the prince seemed uncomfortable at times with some of Kavan's abilities during this trip. In the last few weeks, Owain had also begun to garnish a deep level of trust, but that still left Caol, Darius, and Rouvyn. He could not prepare them for what he was to do or make them accept it. The boulders had to be moved and there was no easier way to do it.

When its most fragile point was located, Kavan shaped the energy he had gathered and directed it towards that point. It flowed from his hands, pushed into the core of the rock, and was held there until he was ready to release it. When it discharged, the boulder exploded, its shards and dust propelled away from him and the men behind him with a loud pop and bang that echoed through the canyon around them. Kavan jumped back, startled at the violence of the explosion, and the remaining animals whinnied and snorted in fear. Destruction of the obstacle was one thing, but he had not anticipated such an explosion.

Wortham whistled in awe, a sound much preferred over the gasps from the others. "I am grateful we were not on the other side of that."

"It was...I apologize. I have not done that in many years. It appears I am out of practice."

Owain cleared his throat and found his voice. "If that is what happens as a result of lack of practice, I do not wish to see the results of practice."

Approaching the second boulder, the bard replied, "The result would have been much more controlled." With his hands upon the second stone surface, he repeated the process, though this time he encircled the rock with energy; when the explosion came, the blast was contained. To those watching, it appeared that the stone merely cracked and crumbled to dust in relative silence.

"Controlled?" chortled the inquisitor, moving forward to get a better view. "It didn't look nearly as impressive as the first one."

"But just as effective. Actions do not always need to be violent to be effective, Lord Dugan. Now if everyone is ready…"

"With all respect," Caol began.

Kavan shook his head. "It is dark. I can provide light."

"But milord, if you are in the front, those in the back will be less able to see. The moon will help, but not enough. If we secure the horses to the rear, with Darius mounted, of course, Captain Delamo and I can lead. If you take a middle position, I think it would provide light for all of us."

It was logical, but the bard did not want to be surrounded by the wash of emotions he knew would continue to grow stronger when the light came. Already there was apprehension and shock over what they had witnessed. The safety of the group, however, was more important than his personal comfort, and he sighed and gave in. "Very well."

Their travel order was assumed, and once the others were ready, Kavan held out his hand. A large tongue of fire, equal in intensity and brightness to the light of several torches, sprung to life in his palm. Behind him, he could feel Muir's agitation as the prince moved subtly away from his teacher. Kavan's chest tightened and he blinked away the pain. Arlan's reaction had been the same when he had learned about the power Kavan wielded. It was too much to expect of any Teren, he supposed. He looked up as Wortham touched his fingertips, the captain's hands inches away from the strange fire that did not burn.

Their eyes met. It was too much to ask, perhaps, of anyone other than Wortham Delamo.

"Shall we be off?" the captain murmured. Kavan nodded, thankful to have such a friend.

✤*✦

Madalyn spent her day scouring the garment district, this time alone except for Squire Flannery. The other difference, this time, was that she was looking for something specific, both cloth and tailor suitable for her wedding trousseau. King Arlan did his best to assure her the campaign would be short and that Bhríd would return home safely and soon, and though she was not convinced, she was going ahead with planning in the hopes that he was right. Military engagements tended to take longer, and use more resources, than anticipated. There was no telling what might happen to a man in battle. It was hope that let her try to believe her king.

She finally located two bolts of the finest Elyri lace to be had in Enesfel and placed an order for the purest Káliel silk money could buy. There were few tailors in Rhidam that met her expectations, and the one man she approved of rejected the job when he discovered she was to marry the Elyri chancellor. Gladly washing her hands of him, she promised to put him out of business before storming out of his shop. She decided it did not matter if she found a tailor here; she had her own brilliant seamstress in Levonne who would be perfect for the job, and as it turned out, she was Elyri.

The day waned and as she and Flannery started back to the castle under the light of the too rare street lamps, she pondered the look of dismay on the squire's face during that exchange of words. She knew he had no prejudices against the man he served, but he obviously was too schooled in the arts of courtesy and diplomacy to speak as she had to the tailor and had probably been surprised that a woman of her station could have spoken thus. He was also unsettled by the tailor's prejudices. Well, she mused, he had much to learn, but at least he was good company.

Approaching a street corner not far from the castle gates, Flannery stopped, one hand out to stay her and the other upon his sword hilt. Madalyn started to protest but a wave of his hand silenced her before he pulled her behind him. Four men, unrecognizable to either, stepped around the corner as though they had been waiting, their unwashed faces contorted and cruel.

"It's the Elyri's whore," one of them chuckled darkly, taking a step closer. He, at least, smelled strongly of too much alcohol.

"Be gone," Flannery said tersely. If he was afraid of these four larger men, he gave no hint of it. It seemed likely that the tailor had sent them, or that he had spoken of the lady's threats to his questionable friends and left it in their hands to solve the matter. "The lady is in my protection and I will have no mercy for any who intend her harm."

"A lady? A wench who shares a bed with evil's spawn is what she is. Under the protection of a boy. What do you take us for?" Not recognizing the squire, or not caring who he was, the second man guffawed and stepped forward, to find the tip of Flannery's blade pressed between his eyes.

"One more step and I shall be forced to take your lives."

His stance and words were valiant, but outnumbered by larger opponents, Madalyn feared he stood no chance of success. The first of the four dodged left and grabbed her arm despite her efforts to elude him, as another dodged right, and came up behind Flannery. A flick of the squire's agile wrist sent one of the four to his death as he plunged his sword into the man's chest. When the last of the four tackled him, Madalyn screamed, but the man who held her clamped his hand over her mouth, cutting short her cry.

Kicking and flailing, Madalyn tried everything she could to be free of her captor, but he was too powerful. His grip bruised her flesh; she twisted to escape and felt the crack of bone and a stab of pain in her chest when his arm squeezed more tightly. Someone pulled her hair, struck her face, and from the corner of her eye, she could see Flannery wrestling with an opponent who wielded a large knife.

Biting the hand that gagged her won her enough time to cry, "Flannery!"

Too late, the blade slashed into the squire's left arm as Madalyn's captor threw her to the ground. "I'll show you the fate of anyone selling out to Elyri," he hissed, "and I'll teach you how a real man treats a woman."

His cohort placed a foot upon each of her wrists, immobilizing her under their weight. The first fumbled with her skirts and irrationally, she thought for the first time, she was glad women wore many layers beneath their outer skirts. It made this man's efforts much more difficult and might give her enough time for someone to come along the conspicuously empty street to help.

Frustrated, the attacker finally resorted to tearing the expensive fabric. A sound like a war cry erupted behind him as Flannery unexpectedly leaped upon his back, driving the knife he had wrested from his second conquest into this third opponent's neck. The man fell sideways, his eyes glazing over as blood trickled from his lips. The squire pushed him away, freeing the blade as the last of the four yanked Madalyn to her feet and pressed his own knife to her throat. The force of pulling her from between his feet caused Flannery to stumble backward but he quickly regained his footing.

"Be gone, boy. Leave this wench to me or I shall have her life."

Flannery shook his head. "You will take her life regardless…and on my honor to the houses of Lachlan and Cáner I serve, I would sooner die than allow harm to come to her. If you have any honor, if you are half the man you claim, you will release her and accept my challenge." He smirked and brandished the knife he held. "Or are you afraid of a 'boy'?"

He doubted the fellow would release the duchess but gambled that a charge of cowardice would be enough to sway him. It was. Madalyn was shoved into the wall, where she crumbled to the ground with a cry and lay still.

The squire's hesitation at the sight of his unmoving charge was enough to give his opponent an opening. He lunged, his short sword drawn, and caught Flannery's sword arm above the elbow. Flannery was fast enough to yank away before his arm was severed however, though he was forced to drop the knife as his body recoiled in pain. With his other hand, he drew his sword and the two began to circle one another like angry dogs.

"Surrender, boy. She's dead, nothing to protect, and you cannot hope to win with that disadvantage." He indicated the two deep gashes the squire had suffered. "Surrender while you still have your arm."

"Never!" he cried, leaping with what he expected would be his final blow. One miscalculation and he would be dead. But despite using his off hand, despite the growing weakness from blood loss, his blade found its mark. The man collapsed with an astonished look on his face and the squire's sword embedded between his ribs.

Flannery let the sword drop as the man fell and turned his attention to helping the woman he had been fighting to protect. "Lady Dubuais? Please…wake up, milady." She did not, though she was breathing, and thus he did the first thing he could think of. In the absence of anyone to help them, he ignored the agony in his injured arm, lifted her body, and staggered in the direction of the castle.

⮞*⬳

Camp was finally set near the crossroads, complete with a fire and a full meal that they had not had in many hours. It was a true fire tonight, Wortham knew, because the expression on Kavan's face read pure exhaustion. He wanted to speak to his friend, ease the anguish he sensed rippling beneath the blank façade, but the attention of the others in their party was too tightly focused upon the bard to allow the man even the smallest bit of privacy. The captain wanted to protect him from the questions, the curious stares, from the thoughts he knew Kavan could hear and sense, but since he could not, he simply set up his bedding in between Kavan and the others and gestured for the Elyri to sleep. Kavan closed his eyes, arms wrapped around himself, curled into a ball as though he were a small child in need of comfort.

They had decided that tomorrow at dawn, Rouvyn would take one of the remaining five horses and continue with the injured Darius to the town of Bryn, where the soldier could receive better medical care than could be had on the road. To Caol's surprise, the doctor had not mentioned Wace Elotti since departing Durham and had shown little desire to locate him. Perhaps, the inquisitor thought, the trip had done the physician good.

The remaining five would take the other three horses and travel towards Neth, and with any luck, they would reach the small village on Enesfel's side of the border by nightfall. They could restock supplies and obtain more horses. Once there, there was something Kavan felt he had to do, something regarding the murdered kinswoman he had spoken of, something he claimed might take days. The inquisitor fumed about the time they would lose, about how they might never find the missing boys, but Kavan's icy gaze silenced his tirade. It was only the second time Caol had ever seen the bard look angry, and this time he found himself wondering where Kavan's loyalties lay. But he knew he would have done the same thing for family, and as Owain pointed out, if their quarry was in Fiara, he would likely wait for them there. They had not been given a deadline, after all, and were likely assumed killed or at least delayed in the avalanche. If the kidnappers were not in Fiara, they had probably never intended to meet there. Caol had the sinking sick feeling that Owain was right.

∽*∽

"Are you saying those ruffians attacked you because Lady Dubuais intends to wed Lord Cáner?"

Flannery shifted his weight in his chair anxiously, feeling responsible for the injuries the duchess received despite everything he had done to protect her. "That is what I said, Lord Cornell," he replied, though he was side-eyeing the King with barely concealed concern. "It would be impolite to repeat the words they used to describe her perceived affront…but it was uncalled for and inaccurate in my opinion." He adjusted the cloth upon his arm, trying to hinder the flow of blood as he waited for Lady MacLyr to return. He had insisted she tend to the duchess first, even if it meant losing the use of his arm.

The King stood near the window, wondering at the cause of this sudden upsurge in violence and how he could stop it. When he met the justice's gaze, the man said, "I will make certain all four are apprehended, Your Majesty."

"I am afraid," murmured the squire self-consciously, "that will not be possible. I had to dispose of them to protect the lady…someone has already been sent for the bodies…" Flannery could not recall whom he had spoken to at the castle gate, but he knew the soldier there had done as he asked.

"You killed all four of them?" squawked the justice. "Alone?" From the tale the squire had told, he could not imagine it.

Syl entered the room before Flannery could reply, her face flushed, her expression strained. "Pardon, Your Majesty, but I wished to inform you that Lady Dubuais will live." There was a collective sigh of relief from the men in the room. "She suffered fractures to her wrists and ribs, and there was some internal bleeding and bruising, but no injuries which would prove fatal. She will sleep tonight; you may question her tomorrow if you wish."

The King took the woman's hands and kissed both palms. "Thank you, Syl. Will you stay with her after you tend to Squire McGranis' injuries?"

She curtsied without pulling her hands from his. "Of course, Your Majesty."

"Good." The King offered his hand to the squire. "Mr. McGranis, see to it that I mention this to Lord Cáner when he returns. I think he will be pleased with your actions and success…and impressed. I know I am. Well done."

Accepting the handshake, a rare gesture to be shared between a squire and a king, Flannery bowed his head. "Thank you, My Liege." It had been his duty, but he was pleased with the recognition and clearly flattered.

## ☙Chapter 29☙

The west wind whipped his sparse, tied back hair as the lead ship of the Cordashian navy cut swiftly through the waves of the northern sea. In the east, the sun had cleared the horizon and to the south, the port city of Wynett disappeared behind the fleet as the wind propelled them on their way. Captain Leocroft stood on the bow of his vessel, excitement pounding in his veins. It had been centuries since the navy had been needed for anything other than routine patrols and the occasional repelling of pirates. Not that he expected to encounter combat. His orders were specific; he would keep his fleet of twenty-nine cutters and cargo ships offshore, close enough for Neth to know their intentions but not close enough to engage the land troops. That gave the captain considerable leeway, however, and he intended to push the limits as far as he could. This might be the best opportunity for glory in his lifetime, the only time his fleet might pursue something more than pirates, and Captain Leocroft would be certain to make the most of whatever came his way.

☙*☙

It was midday before the search party, minus Rouvyn and Darius, reached the sparse village of Dun's Hollow. Twelve miles to the northeast, through the dense forest that served as the barrier between nations, lay the southern border of Neth. The proximity to that perceived enemy made most of the party wary and anxious, particularly Prince Muir, who glowered, frowned, and fidgeted more with every passing mile and hour. Owain tried to reassure his son that crossing the border under his standard would keep them safe. People they met would either treat them decently out of respect for Owain or out of fear that King Loris might retaliate if they mistreated his cousin. As long as the group stayed together, Owain anticipated no problems.

But when Kavan left them, entering the tiny, disused local náós alone, Owain's efforts to assure Muir proved fruitless. They discussed the importance of staying together and the first thing Kavan did was leave them to pray. At least, Muir assumed that was his purpose for entering that place. It was the only reason that made sense. Three hours passed and when the bard did not return, the prince stole away from the company of his elders at the leaky-roofed guest house where they had found lodging and returned to the náós to discover his teacher was not there. There was no indication the bard had ever entered.

To his consternation, when he raced back to the guest house, he discovered that Caol was missing too and that neither Wortham nor Owain seemed particularly concerned about either of them. The pair were attending the new horses they had purchased from a young man more keen on coin then animals he could barely afford to feed, preparing the extra supplies bought to replace what was lost in the rockslide, and saying very little. Wortham sought to remind the prince that Kavan had spoken of a duty to tend to, that he planned to return to them by nightfall, and that he was in no danger. While Muir reluctantly admitted he had forgotten Kavan's words about duty, he remained skeptical of the Elyri's safety as the older men tried, unsuccessfully, to engage him in a game of dice.

If anything, Wortham was more concerned about Caol's absence than Kavan's, but he did not intend to chase around the village in search of the inquisitor. Caol could take care of himself, seemed a resourceful and bright enough fellow and would, Wortham trusted, rejoin them before Kavan was ready to travel again.

Kavan, meanwhile, emerged from the charred remains of a Purification Chamber into the smoldering remnants of what had been a Nethite náós, ancient and long unused as anything more than a public meeting house. Here, in this place, stepping over collapsed timbers in the wake of whatever devastation had befallen these people, he was as uncertain of his own safety as Prince Muir was. Limbs, heads, and torsos were strewn across the altar steps, a slaughter of the most heinous kind in a holy place; he counted six individuals, all Elyri and all quite young. His stomach lurched, tightening with sickness and remorse at such senseless butchery. Senses tuned to detect the approach of anyone who might remain in the area, Kavan knelt to each severed head and touched each face to glean what information he could, a repellently unpleasant task but one he deemed necessary if their families were to have closure. From each, he took personal objects, a ring, a necklace, a dagger…anything he could use to identify each of them to the loved ones left behind.

They were all from Bhryell. He had known some of them as children, contemporaries of Mílne's. They had come to this place on a mission of mercy, delivering supplies to a poverty-stricken people suffering at the hands of a sadistic, apathetic king. Owain had indicated that Elyri were providing aid, but Kavan had never imagined it would be Bhryell's young ones doing the giving. They had been butchered because of their mercy…and because they were Elyri. Only one of these six had carried a weapon, the dagger more ornamental than practical. None of them had been wary enough to detect the danger until it was upon them, and none of them had possessed the opportunity, the will, or the knowledge to fight back when the threat burst upon them.

Mílne had been here, Kavan knew, but she had not met her fate in this place. She was not in the village at the time of her death. Still, believing her body would keep a little longer, he wanted to see this village for himself, learn why she had risked being here, what she had hoped to accomplish. Before leaving the meager shelter the náós provided, however, he felt around him for the presence of anyone else in the village, determined not to make the same mistake these unfortunate souls had. There was no one he could sense. As long as that did not change, he would be safe.

His excursion through the settlement, however, did little to reveal her fate, where she had gone, how she had died. Very few buildings, made as they had been of wood and thatch, escaped the fire's rage, and none of the inhabitants appeared to have survived the fall of the sword. Everywhere he looked was carnage and death, two small graves being the single bright spot in the village, and the most tangible indication he found that Mílne had been here.

By the time his search ended, the sun was setting low in the west, heralding the arrival of evening. He should return to Dun's Hollow, as he had told the others he would return to them tonight, but it had taken longer than expected, when bombarded with such grisly visages and his own grief, to search the village. Despite what he had told Wortham and the others, he could not leave Mílne's body to the elements any longer. She had to be taken home, to Sámel, to her family.

Thus, he chose his path. Pulling the energies together, he claimed the familiar kestrel form and focused on the images of Mílne he had last seen, the flashes of her murder that came to him at the moment of her death. A tiny spark pulsed within his mind, creating a thread of power that drew him into the peaks southeast of the village. Not in the direction of home exactly, but if she fled in panic, perhaps she had lost her way. Puzzled, and dreading actually finding her, he followed that thread through the clouds of dusk in search of she who was his kin.

❧*❧

She was lucky to be alive and in relatively good health; she knew that. She also knew that Bhríd had been wise to warn her of the dangers she might face if they agreed to marry, dangers she herself had believed would not touch her. That illusion was shattered now. Anyone who worked with, employed, or associated with Elyri, knew the prejudices, as she had known them, but she had never imagined that she, the Duchess of Levonne, would be subjected to them. Now that she had experienced such things first hand, she felt anger. Not fear, which she could have felt at the realization of how close she had come to death, but anger that anyone would dare assault her over her choice of a husband. Though she had not yet decided what the focus of her anger was, or if it had a specific focus…her attackers or a much broader spectrum of individuals, her anger fueled her desire to go through with her wedding plans rather than be deterred from them. She would show every bigot in Enesfel and beyond that Elyri were no worse than Teren, were in many ways better, and that she was neither a pawn nor a patsy.

A knock on the door of her room drew her attention from the sunset she was watching without actually seeing it. "Please, come in," she called, grateful for any company that might distract her from her darker thoughts.

Squire Flannery entered, regal-looking in his dark blue hose and tunic, his arm bandaged securely since he had insisted that Syl only needed to tend to the worst of the damage so that he could use his arm again and allow the remainder to heal naturally. He wanted those scars as badges of honor, a reminder of his first combat. His feathered blue cap was held between his trembling hands and after initially meeting her gaze, he looked at the floor.

"Please, won't you sit, Flannery?" she asked, indicating the empty window seat across from her in an effort to ease his discomfort.

The squire shook his head. "I have not come to sit, milady…I have come to offer my apology…"

"Whatever for?" she asked.

The hat changed hands a few times before he replied. He had rehearsed what he wanted to say, but those well-practiced words left him as he faced her. He felt humiliated to have to name his shortcomings and hung his head as he replied, "For allowing you to receive injury while under my protection. If I had done my duty, you would not be suffering pain."

"It hurts where that thug pulled out my hair, nowhere else," she assured him. "You could not have done your duty any better if you had been Lord Cáner himself."

"Milady…"

Madalyn stood and offered her hand. "Come now, Flannery. King Arlan told me how you single-handedly killed all four of our assailants. That is as good as any man could do alone. You saved my life. That is the best I could ask for, and I am grateful for it. A little pain is good for us now and then; it reminds us we are alive." She smiled, but the smile faded when she saw that the squire was not prepared to let himself off the hook. "Besides, I have learned some valuable lessons from this."

"You have?" He sounded frankly curious as his head lifted to look at her.

"First, and foremost, I have learned that Lord Cáner is more of a gentleman than many Teren I know. No matter what others might say, I will marry him and we will be an example of how Teren and Elyri can coexist peacefully. Plus, I have learned that he is a wise man…because he chose you as squire and left me in your care. If I ever need a champion and he is unavailable, you can be assured I will come to you."

Flushed, Flannery made a deep bow. He did not feel he deserved her praise and trust, but he did believe she meant what she said.

"Thank you, milady, for your confidence. I shall make every effort to prove worthy of your faith."

"Good." She smiled and patted his arm. "I am happy to hear it. You can be assured I do not hold you responsible for anything that transpired…except for saving my life…and that is a responsibility I am grateful you accepted."

Flannery smiled with relief, kissed her hand, and retreated backward from her room. Watching him go, Madalyn could not wait to tell Bhríd that he had the finest young squire in all of Enesfel.

❧*❧

The sky had grown black, the night cold, long before Kavan reached his destination. Ahead, in the cave some twenty feet above his current position on the mountainside, three bodies lay where they had drawn their last breath. He had not yet seen them, but he knew they were there as he climbed the craggy slope. One of the three was Mílne, but he had no idea who the others were. Scrambling over the final precipice, he braced himself to confront whatever he would find.

With his handlight illuminating his way, Kavan slid through the narrow opening, feeling his robe snag on the uneven stone and pausing to free himself before making the final drop to the cave floor. It was damp here, the runoff from the spring rain had trickled into murky pools inside the mouth of the cave, but further back the floor and walls were dry. The Nethite, despite the sword he had used, appeared to be a hunter rather than a soldier; he lay crumpled and broken against the cave wall to Kavan's right, his head misshapen from the impact with the stone and his neck twisted awkwardly to the side. Several feet away, a young man, an Elyri, his head severed from his body, lay beside the woman he had tried to protect.

Mílne. Kavan had not seen her since Ártur and Syl's wedding; she had been six years old then, a sprite of a girl prone to laughter and flower chains and a melodic, birdlike voice. Now she was a beautiful woman; she looked much like Dhángá except for her golden hair that shone like sunlight in the dim light of the flame in Kavan's hand. From the position of the short, battered sword, Kavan knew she had died quickly, if not instantly, having been spared the agony of drowning in her own blood. He took her wan face between his trembling hands, closing her eyes with his thumbs as he absorbed her death images into his memory. From the self-satisfied expression she wore in death, and those remembrances she gave up to him, he discovered she had killed the man who had murdered her. Though the sentiment was uncharitable, Kavan was satisfied with her final act of vengeance.

Except for the bloody gaping gash where the sword was still nestled between her ribs, she had not been otherwise marred by death; no animal had yet to discover the deceased. He removed the stone ring from the first finger of the man's left hand and looked back at Mílne in astonishment. Yes, she wore the Pheslátkag; she was to have married this young man. She had chosen the old customs, which meant that she had been planning to wed soon and Ártur had not known.

A cold twisting knot formed in his stomach. It seemed he was not the only one to be cut off; the family had apparently done the same to Ártur. Tám's doing, no doubt. Now Kavan had to return to them for the first time in years, carrying the girl's lifeless body. Face his uncle. He had disavowed his nephew when Kavan had been not yet an adult, a painful experience but one Kavan had known was coming, and something he long ago accepted. For Tám to turn against his own son was something else entirely. Hoping he was wrong, that Ártur had been informed of the intended marriage while Kavan was away, or that Mílne had intended to inform her uncle herself, Kavan pocketed the ring the man had worn, took the sword as evidence, and then lifted the woman's slight body with ease. There was another village no more than a mile to the south. He had seen it as he approached. If Kavan were lucky, there would be a Gate there. Otherwise, it would be a very long trek to Bhryell.

∾*∾

The cracked náós bell, the only thing in that abandoned building still in use, clanged midnight and in the crowded room behind Muir, his father, Wortham, and Caol already slept. The inquisitor had not spoken of whatever he had done during his hours away from the party, and no one had asked questions. Each assumed that, if there had been news…good or bad…Caol would have told them. They had shared the substantial meal provided by their host, paid a handsome sum for it, and then after too much drink and hours spent listening to the other guests gossip about local events, they had retired to take advantage of a roof over their head and the absence of cold wind and the potential attacks of man or beasts. The prince, however, was too restless for sleep, and stood at the window, watching in the direction of the bell, hoping for some sign of Kavan's return.

His father. He glanced behind him in the dimness to stare at the back of the man's blonde head. The three slept upon the floor, leaving the bed for the younger man, out of deference to his social status. From the stories Muir had heard growing up, from the hatred the King displayed whenever mention of Owain was made, the prince had expected his father to be a bitter, brutal, sadistic man with no redeeming qualities. He had no doubt that the man had made grave mistakes in the past, but rather than hide them or deny them, Owain confessed to them, including the method of Muir's conception. But those things had happened long ago, and the man Muir had come to know was no crueler than King Arlan. That Kavan had forgiven the outcast Lachlan and taken him as one of his closest friends spoke highly of the former king, no matter what anyone else said. Unlike

King Arlan, Prince Muir easily accepted that if Kavan approved of someone, there was something in that person worth approval.

With his thoughts turning back to the bard, the prince began to fret again. Though Kavan had not said Neth was his destination, he had said the woman he was hoping to find had been killed in Neth, and Muir fretted about him facing potential dangers alone. Why the woman had been in hostile territory, the prince could not guess, but he worried that without someone to fight for him, Kavan might not survive if he encountered King Loris' troops.

Floorboards creaked behind him, alerting him that someone else was awake, but the prince did not turn. "He will not come to harm."

The young man closed his eyes both relieved and disappointed it was not his father joining him. "How can you be certain, Captain? I know he can fight…" he had seen that firsthand, "but would he?"

"He does not need to. If he can perform miracles, if he can remove boulders from our path…I believe he can outwit anyone he chooses."

"But a whole army?"

Wortham chuckled, the sound less amused in tone then he hoped. "If he meets the whole army in southern Neth, then Cordash is not doing their job and Enesfel is going to be in great danger." It was no humorous matter, but because he did not believe that would happen, he meant to use the notion to calm the prince's fears. "Knowing him as I do, I do not believe an army could stop him…and we have our orders. If he has not returned to us by tomorrow night, we leave the next morning and continue the search under Lord Dugan's leadership."

"Can we do that? Abandon him, I mean?" The prince looked back in time to catch the shadow that washed over Wortham's face.

"I would rather not. But in this instance, Prince Bertram and Prince Wilred are my priority. Lord Clíath can fend for himself; they cannot. I swore to my duty. Regardless of what I want, I would never break a promise to him."

Scowling, the prince grunted. "I am not bound by such a promise."

"How would you locate him? We have no knowledge of where he has gone. Neth is a large kingdom, a perilous one. For a prince of Enesfel, traveling alone, it would be doubly so. He has given us little choice." Wortham shrugged and lay down. "We do as he wishes…or wait…or go home. I do not believe either of the last two are options."

❧Chapter 30❧

hydáni Tíbhyan hunched at the desk, an ancient sturdy piece bequeathed to him by his grandfather and older still than that he believed, still reading beneath the light of his dented brass candelabra though it was long past the midnight hour. He found he rarely slept any longer, and when he did it was most often during the brightest, warmest part of each day, when the glare of sunlight made his eyes squint and burn. His sparse white hair fluttered upon his head, ruffled by the breeze wafting through the open window beside him as his head bobbed up and down in cadence to the words upon the page. Knobby joints aching more than usual tonight, he leaned back in his chair, closed the manuscript, and stared into the flames of the dwindling fire across the room. He could choose to sleep, could have been in bed beneath comforting blankets already like most of those in Bhryell, but he did not feel tired. He felt old. Nor did he feel like reading any longer. He was bored and restless but there was nothing for it at this late hour.

What he needed, he realized not for the first time over the past several months, was another pupil. But he had not taught a private student since young Cliáth had left his tutelage many years ago. That remarkable young man had taken everything the bhydáni had offered, had given much in return, and now was gone the way of any grown man, into the world to forge a path of his own. The bhydáni was not sure he had the interest, will, or desire to give another person that much of himself. It had been too long since he had seen or heard from Kavan, and he wondered again what had become of his beloved student.

A small tapping sound came at his door, intruding upon his thoughts. It might have been a knock, but it was too soft to be sure it was anything more than the wind. Wizened instinct, however, drew the man to his feet and pulled him hobbling to the door as quickly as his crippled legs would take him. The nearer he drew to the door, the more certain he was of the source of that sound, an answer to an old man's unspoken prayers, a sign from k'Ádhá surely.

"Kavan…it is you…" The words came out as the door opened, but his voice faltered as he beheld the woman in his protégé's arms. "Please, come in; put Mílne down and tell me what has happened." The blood spread over her torso left no doubt that she was dead.

"You knew her, bhydáni?" Kavan asked as he laid her on the empty table his mentor indicated. He did not have to look around to know that nothing in the sage's home had changed. This familiar, heartening place was as much a home to Kavan as anywhere had ever been. Enough of his childhood had been spent within these walls, that he knew every inch of it intimately.

"Indeed." Tíbhyan brushed the girl's hair from her face. He did not mingle freely any longer, but he knew every face, every name, of Bhryell's residents now just as he had when Kavan had grown up here.

"She was in Neth…with others…when they were discovered by King Loris' soldiers." The old man's expression suggested he knew what they had been doing in Neth. "The others were slaughtered; she and her young man escaped, but were found later as they slept, by a hunter…who carried this…" The sword he had brought with him was removed from the tie at his waist and placed upon the table beside the body. "I Saw her death, bhydáni…I felt it…" He gripped the edge of the table with trembling hands as his voice broke beneath the weight of that unpleasant recollection.

"thenárá phyl haeles. Sit. There is no need to tell me more. I will learn what I need to know…please." With a hand on Kavan's elbow, he guided him to the nearest chair, stroked the younger man's hair with gnarled fingers, and then touched Mílne's face as Kavan had done. Though she was dead, though Kavan had taken her death memories, some of the images were ingrained in her still. Likewise, he read the sword, the item further supporting the dead woman's tale.

"You might want these, bhydáni." From his coin pouch, Kavan produced the objects he had taken from each of the deceased. "I could not bring them back with me…not in the condition they were in…but I did want to bring something…for the families."

After what the sage had learned, he nodded and took the items, reading each one before laying them beside the sword and reaching for the next. By the end, he closed his eyes, leaned against the table weakly, trying to dispel the grief clawing through him.

"Have you informed your family?" he finally asked, despite already knowing the answer.

"I…" Kavan almost squirmed in his seat, something that no one except those who had known him long and well would have detected. "No…not those here. I did not think it wise to see them at this hour. Besides, if they could not inform Ártur of her betrothal…"

"átaelás mai," the old man said as he patted Mílne's clasped hands, "There was no time. Their announcement was made the day they took that delivery…" He pulled over a nearby stool and lowered himself upon it to speak face to face with Kavan. "Yes, many knew what the young ones were doing. Several did not approve, as you can imagine…your uncle included…but others believed in their cause. Your influence…and that of your cousin…is more powerful than you know, opening our village to the world beyond our borders. Mílne was going to tell Healer MacLyr upon her return…was going to go to

Rhidam and seek him out…which now…" he sighed sadly as he looked at the girl, "she cannot do. This is one wrong you cannot place at your uncle's feet…but coming here first was a wise choice."

"Or cowardly," the bard murmured.

Tíbhyan smiled affectionately. "A coward you are not. As you say, it is too late to have taken her anywhere else. By bringing her here, I can support your claims; no one, not even Tám, will be able to discount you. I am always your ally, Kavan, you know this. Stay, rest…regain your strength and your heart. You will need it. I will see that gdhededhá Bhílári retrieves her body; he will be one more voice to support you. No one will doubt your integrity with us behind you."

"I would rather succeed or fail on my own merit, bhydáni."

The old man patted his arm again. "I know. But you also know how difficult that shall be."

To that, Kavan had nothing to say.

❧*❧

"What are you studying, Prince Harcourt?"

The Hatu prince tried to shove the slip of cloth he had been caressing into his bedroll before the Elyri healer could get a better glimpse of it. His efforts were unsuccessful, however, and the healer pointed to the visible corner of white lace. The prince remained silent, self-conscious and unsure of what he should say.

That embarrassment made the healer grin. "You have a lady at home?" Despite his years of service on the battlefield in the war between Enesfel and Hatu, Ártur knew little of Hatu's customs. Those customs had never been important enough for him to learn. His questions were based on the assumption that courtship rituals in Hatu were much the same as anywhere else.

The prince shook his head. "Not at home…and not a lady exactly." When the healer did not continue but appeared to be waiting for him,

Espen reluctantly sighed, drew the kerchief from beneath his bedroll and added, "Princess Diona asked me to take this while I am at war."

"If you had refused her, you might have had a royal tantrum on your hands," the healer acknowledged sympathetically, recognizing the familiar lace pattern as belonging to one of the kerchiefs the late Queen had given her daughter.

"No...it is not that...I was honored to accept her token since it seemed important to her. I do not understand the significance of the gesture, however. Such things are not shared between men and women at home. I do not know what it means." His fingers traced absently over the lace as if memorizing the pattern.

Noting the action, Ártur nodded with a teasing smile. "I believe you understand it better than you think, milord...but if I may. In Enesfel, a lady often gives a token of affection to the man she fancies before he goes into battle...whether it be real or a tournament contest. I would say Princess Diona has set her sights on you."

"She is a child, healer..." Not, he knew, that such things mattered. Girls her age throughout most of the Five Sovereignties were often betrothed and sometimes wed within a year or two of that if the marriage was deemed politically essential. As far as he knew, the princess was not spoken for, but he had not dared ask anyone, lest someone mistake his question for a suggestion. With their differences in culture, the royal houses of Enesfel and Hatu had never intermarried; Prince Espen did not see either family approving of such an arrangement now.

Ártur laughed. "Everyone knows that except the princess, as you may have noticed. For one so young, she knows her mind quite well." The healer continued to smile as he stood. "I will give you one word of advice. The princess often gets what she wants, one way or another." Chuckling at the prince's expression, one of a man not interested in being a 'trophy' but also intrigued that someone should have interest in him, the healer left him to contemplate those words and decide what, if anything, he wanted to do about it.

ॐ * ॐ

Syl stared at the parchment in her hand, then at the one that had already fallen to the floor. She recognized both her brother's, and her husband's handwriting, and knew from their words and the emotions that bled from the paper through to her fingertips that the words were true. Little Mílne. Dead at the hands of a Nethite. If not for Kavan's extraordinary gifts, no one would know what had become of the girl, only that she had disappeared, never to be seen again. She would lie wherever she had fallen, far from home, where none would think to look for her. Syl knew it was her charge to return to Bhryell, to tell Sámel that his daughter was dead, but it was not a task she wanted.

As the second page slid from her fingers and floated to land upon the first, she lifted her head from the emotional fog that surrounded her and sighed. Retrieving the letters, leaving the children in the hands of the wet-nurse, she moved resolutely into the corridor. She spoke to no one until she reached the stateroom, where she could hear the rise and fall of the King's voice behind the closed door. Unsure of whom he was speaking to and whether she should interrupt, she decided there was no harm in trying, and reluctantly knocked on the door.

When summoned, she was relieved to find that the King was reading to his daughter. The girl needed her father, with the danger surrounding her brothers and the death of her mother, and Syl believed the King needed his daughter for much the same reasons. He looked up, noted the healer's grim air, and gently nudged Diona from his lap.

"There is no need to send her away, My Liege. I do not mean to intrude. I have come to ask for a few days leave to return to Bhryell."

"Leave?" The King's brow knit in concern. The only time she or Ártur had left Rhidam was when they had gone to Bhryell to marry.

Perhaps her request had something to do with her brother's upcoming marriage, but the woman's expression spoke of something weightier. "Is there something I should know, Lady MacLyr?"

Though she had hoped he would grant her request without asking why, she had not expected that to be the case. "This," she murmured as she handed the brief letters to the King. He read them hastily. "I must return home to tell Ártur's brother of this; I do not expect it should take more than a day, two at most. Everyone here is in good health; Lady Dubuais is out of danger and Squire McGranis is healing as expected. I shall take Bianca with me; Lady Faylyn will need only care for Prince Hagan. I will return as quickly as I am able, My Liege, if you will allow me to see to this matter."

The King nodded. Knowing how it felt to have a child missing, to think to never see him again, to not know if that child was alive or dead, he could sympathize with how Ártur's brother must feel. Arlan waited every day for someone to bring him word; it was fair to allow this man the courtesy the King wished for himself. "Of course, Syl. Please relay my sympathies to her family…and tell them that if there is anything I can do, they are to ask it. I will do whatever I can." He could not give the man his child back, but if he could, he would have.

⁊*⁊

The House of de Corrmick, as unstable and chaotic as it was by nature, was in more of an uproar than usual. For the first time in two centuries, Neth was at war. Not against its own people, as King Loris' and those monarchs who had come before him often seemed to be, but against Cordash, their traditional nemesis. Cordash was less tainted by the love for things Elyri then Enesfel, and beyond the border forest had so much flat, agriculturally viable land that the Nethite kings had long sought to claim that land for their own. Neth was largely a land of forest; farmland was a boon they desperately needed.

And somewhere in their early history, a feud between brothers had resulted in the division of a people, the splitting in two of familial territory that resulted in the creation of the kingdom known as Neth. While the feud was lost to the void of time, those in modern times having forgotten the cause of that ancient feud, the hope of the de Corrmick's to reunite the whole of the lands north of Enesfel had never faded. It meant raids, it meant kidnapping of heirs and assassination attempts, and it meant the occasional threat of war.

This time, it was war.

Or at least, they would be at war very soon, the raids his forces conducted along the Cordashian border finally having pushed the Valdis' to action. In truth, Loris, as any other de Corrmick king before him, would have admitted that it was about time Cordash rose up and took up arms against them. As a rule, the de Corrmick's respected those with the courage to fight back…even if fighting got those opponents slaughtered. There was even a grudging respect for those of his own people who pushed back against their cruel king; even though those ill-fated people were most often executed for their folly.

Eager for a real war, for the chance to bathe swords in the blood of those weaker than themselves, all of the troops not already spread along the Cordashian forest line were pulled from the base of the Llaethágárá and all but skeleton units were withdrawn from the edges of Enesfel. Elyriá was not inclined to fight; the de Corrmicks knew this from experience regardless of what myths claimed to the contrary. And Enesfel was weak, her strength depleted by years of internal unrest and famine. Neither would pose a threat to King Loris.

What troubled and infuriated him, however, as he drew together his plans, was that none of his messengers were able to find the handsome Prince Owain, anywhere within the castle or the sovereign city of Glevum. Not that Loris had seen his cousin for several weeks; the King seldom spoke to Owain when the man was around, and Owain had a habit of rarely announcing his comings or goings to his king-cousin. This necessitated sending a messenger to Owain's Fiara estate in the hopes of gaining his campaign aid. Owain had many faults, being the bastard child of a Lachlan king was one of them, but as far as Loris knew, disloyalty and cowardice were not among them. His cousin would not dream of missing the glories of war. No true de Corrmick would.

ᐅ*ᐊ

Kavan waited on the opposite side of the thóres, silent and sullen, watching his family gather around Mílne's washed and wrapped body. He should stand with them; it was his right to demand inclusion because he had found her, brought her home, and he was her family too. But he had mourned her already, as he carried her body home, and none of these people had. He also had no desire for a confrontation with Tám over the girl's corpse; conflict would arise soon enough. This was not the time or place for it. Sámel was conversing in a low voice with gdhededhá Bhílári and bhydáni Tíbhyan, gaining the details of her death and making preparations for her burial. Dháná held the Pheslátkag and Pheski in one hand and stared at her granddaughter's face that still smiled with self-satisfaction. Kavan had noticed that none of them had touched their kinswoman, not even Sámel, possibly out of fear of the deceased or for fear of knowing what her last moments had been like.

Sámel's other two children, Aleski and Bhendhámyn stood with their grandfather; no one looked at Kavan but them. Aleski had been four years old the last time Kavan had been home, and Bhendhámyn had not yet been born. To them, Kavan was a legend, the White Bard of Bhryell, Bhryell Prophet, Bhryell Saint. He was a collection of stories, many embellished and perverted; he was not a person, not real, despite being directly related to them. Tám had done little to dispel those myths, if he allowed any talk of Kavan to surface in his home at all. With a sigh, Kavan watched them both turn away when Tám's labor-etched hands clasped their shoulders, but Bhendhámyn looked back one more time and smiled. He seemed neither afraid nor prone to obey his grandfather when it suited him to do otherwise.

Tám caught the turn of the boy's head and glowered; Kavan met that gaze evenly. He wanted to speak but could not find words that did not sound either like a verbal attack or a guilty apology. Sámel spared him the need for speaking, however, and kept Tám from doing so, by approaching and squatting down before the bard. He and Kavan had never been close, as there was too much age and too little commonality between them, but Sámel had never been afraid of Kavan and never condescending towards him.

"Thank you, tydhá," he said, clasping Kavan's hands. "You brought my daughter home when I had no hope of seeing her again.

"How could you possibly have known…?"

Tám's bitter, hate-filled question was cut short by the opening of the door and a voice familiar to all of them replying, "llánec."

"Lady MacLyr." It was the gdhededhá who spoke as the others in the room turned to greet her. "What an unexpected blessing."

Syl shifted Bianca on her hip to better greet the family she had gained by marriage. "I received word of this tragedy just today…from Bhríd and Ártur. I came to tell you as soon as I was able, but," she graced Kavan with an affectionate smile, "I had not anticipated Kavan would come, or that he would find Mílne and bring her home."

"llánec is a myth…"

"Tám," scolded Dháná uncomfortably, not wanting this fight.

Awkwardly, Syl produced the twin parchments from her cloak and gave them to Sámel. "You should have these," she said, hoping the comforting words of kin might help ease the man's sorrow.

Tám, however, was not finished, his grief seeking the outlet he felt he needed to address. "He had a hand in this," he muttered under his breath, though loudly enough that everyone in the room heard it.

Kavan clenched his hands on his lap, fighting to restrain his anger. Given his emotional state recently, perhaps facing his uncle was unwise, though it had needed to be done. He had to bring Mílne home.

The bhydáni poked his gnarled finger into the eldest MacLyr's chest and squawked, "I read him myself, read her, read every item he brought from the others. So did Bhílári. You have not touched any of them. He is no guiltier of this than I am. To accuse him is to dishonor your brother's name. To accuse me and Bhílári of lying is a grave charge. Do you wish to go that far, MacLyr?"

Kavan knew his uncle would never do that, regardless of how he might wish to. To accuse a bhydáni of lying was to challenge his or her right to retain their status, and to accuse the clergy was to risk censure by the Faith. Without evidence to support his claims, Tám would never oppose what the bhydáni, the gdhededhá, and his son's wife all held true, would never risk the family's repute and good name in such a way. There were too many items retrieved from the dead that supported the spoken facts, even without Kavan's confession. Tám did not have the fortitude to make such a risky accusation.

"I did not come to cause distress; I am aware my company is not desired." He could have said nothing, but for once, Kavan felt obliged to speak in his own defense. There was an angry edge to his voice; Tám heard it, and for the first time Kavan realized his uncle was afraid of him. It was not anger or loathing that drove them apart, or even the matters of Kavan abandoning his father's trade, failing to uphold the Cliáth name and tradition or even his occasional conflicts with the Faith. Watching his uncle back away, Kavan understood that the real reason for Tám's conduct and demeanor was fear.

Noting this did not cause Kavan to change his tone, however. "Since no one else knew of her death…I was the one who had to find her while there was still something left to find. I did what was necessary. I did not do it for you aendhá, but for her family, for her. And for myself."

With the peculiar gentle touch that strengthened many, he laid one hand on Aleski's head, the other on Bhendhámyn's and then took Sámel's hand. "I mourn your loss; it is my own, and I pray for her repose as I would any of yours. She will be missed."

Sámel nodded, unable to speak the words of grief that lodged in his throat. Deciding it was best that he left, Kavan gave a parting glance of acknowledgment to both the bhydáni and the gdhededhá. The clergyman bowed, accepting the silent farewell in the spirit it was given, while Tíbhyan touched the bard's mind long enough to reassure him that he had done the right thing…and that he, at least, appreciated seeing Kavan again. Syl, however, caught Kavan's arm as the bard passed and murmured, "A word please," before following him out.

As soon as they were in the nave of the náos, she continued, "I wish to thank you, since many of them cannot, for bringing her home. It was honorable and brave considering what awaited you here."

"I did what was necessary."

She smiled gently, knowing that was not true. No one else would have known if he could have found the girl's body or not, and as he was carrying out a duty for the King of Enesfel, he could have found a reason not to seek Mílne or bring her home. Kavan had done these things because he could, because he wanted to, and Syl was grateful.

"The princes?"

Kavan shook his head. "We have not given up…make sure Arlan and Deidre know that. There are leads to follow still and we will pursue them until there are no more paths to take. We have sent Darius Corbin back to Rhidam; he was injured in a rockslide. He is in the care of a physician in Bryn, and once transport is found, he will return home. He will need your care if he is to serve again."

"I will tell the King…and will await Mr. Corbin's arrival. You should know that Bhríd…"

"Is to wed Lady Dubuais." It did not surprise Syl that Kavan already knew, but she would prefer to tell him something he might already know than to withhold information that he might not. "Convey my best to her…and to your brother, if you get the opportunity. I look forward to attending their wedding."

"I will." When she hugged him, he did not pull away. His cousin's wife was the only woman he felt comfortable enough with to allow that distinction.

"Go back to them, Syl…they need you…and you must be there in Ártur's stead. I must return to my own duties."

"Good luck, Kavan. My prayers are with you."

Kavan drew back and let her return to the thóres. He was going to need those prayers if he was to succeed in finding the King's son alive.

❧*❧

The horses were saddled, the supplies packed, and Muir stared across the street at the náós, willing the bard to emerge from it as he waited for the others to be ready to leave Dun's Hollow. Kavan did not appear. The second night passed with no sign of the bard, and the older men had decided it was time to continue on towards Fiara. When all were mounted, they rode northeast without a word. Each felt as if they were leaving something important behind, and each worried that without that missing piece their chances of success were diminished. But three, at least, did not intend to give up, and because they would not, the prince would not either, no matter how miserable he felt about departing without Kavan.

Within three hours of leaving Dun's Hollow, the riders crossed into Neth without incident. Muir expected some sign, some indicator, some natural border like a river or a road, but there was none, only the unending forest and continuing incline of the land as if north meant up. They had chosen to travel off the road to avoid posted soldiers, and thus encountered no one as they pressed through the dense forest. There might be no visible border markers, but Owain knew, and his announcement of their crossing translated into further uneasiness amongst the party.

Their tension was relayed to their horses, making the animals skittish and edgy, but after an uneventful day, they made camp amongst a thicket of brambles and wildflowers near a slow running creek. Owain insisted the shrubs and water would help shelter them, and to help in masking their location, they made camp without a fire as the last of the day's light faded from the sky.

With dinner behind them and the need to sleep not yet taking hold, Owain took the opportunity to teach Muir the best way to use a dagger while Caol, taking the first watch of the night, paced up and down the creek bank, sat and fidgeted with his pack, and then paced some more, his thoughts kept private behind his nervous facade. Captain Delamo tried to sleep in preparation for his third watch. The sound of the inquisitor's pacing, however, made rest difficult, even when Wortham rolled to face away from him and covered his head with his cloak.

Feeling a soft tickle at the back of his neck, Wortham drew back the blanket and tried to brush whatever it was off with his fingers. An insect, perhaps, or errant blade of grass. The effort failed. Annoyed, he opened his eyes and, thinking he saw movement in the brush on the other side of their encampment, sat up to watch more intently. Caol, already ill at ease, followed the captain's line of sight, and soon Prince Muir and Owain were looking as well.

"Is there something…?" started the prince.

Wortham waved him silent. Something, or someone, was there. He knew it. He detected no threat; perhaps it was an animal watching them as they were watching it. Despite knowing they were not alone, however, none expected the figure that emerged out of the forest, white raiment and pallor appearing as a ghost. In their shock, it took each of them several moments to realize that the Elyri bard was there, standing amongst them again, not as a spirit but in the flesh.

"Lord Harper, you have frightened the breath out of us," Caol chuckled nervously when he could speak. He left the creek-side and returned to the fire where the others waited in greeting.

"Speak for yourself," Wortham said with pleased relief and a welcoming smile to Kavan that drew a weary look of affection from the bard.

Muir looked at the captain skeptically, his heart still thundering, his relief at Kavan's return drawing up an unmanly impulse to cry for joy. "You can honestly say he did not startle you?" It was easier to ask that than to bombard Kavan with the host of thoughts and feelings cascading through his head.

Settling into his bedding once again, propped up on one elbow, Wortham shrugged. "I knew something was there, but I admit I was not expecting it to be you, milord." He noticed that Kavan was avoiding looking most of them in the eye, and what eye contact he did make with Wortham was brief and insecure in nature. It did not surprise him when Kavan chose to sit beside him, using Wortham's prone body as a shield. The bard immediately opened his harp case and touched the instrument he had not played in days. Music, he hoped, would dissuade the others from asking too many questions.

"It was not my intention to startle you...I apologize if I did."

Also sensing Kavan's melancholy mood, Owain murmured, "There is no need to apologize. We're thankful to have you back."

Kavan's hair hid his face as he hung his head. Owain's words were sincere and mirrored in the expressions of everyone present. Though he had not thought he would be unwanted here, the intensity of their welcome was still unexpected. "I am sorry I did not return when intended. There were things I needed to do...if I am to focus on Prince Bertram and Prince Wilred." All he wanted was music and peace. "You found nothing in...?"

"Didn't expect to," Caol grunted.

Kavan nodded, his eyes closed.

The first chiming note from the brass harp strings caused Prince Muir to glance around with panic in his eyes. "Should you be…?"

"If he thought it would endanger us, he would not do it," Wortham grunted in the bard's defense. "If anyone approaches, he will know. Do you object to music?"

To keep his son from saying something inappropriate in his youthful inexperience, Owain put one steadying hand on Muir's shoulder and rumbled, "We would be fools to object to the honor. We are as safe here as we could be anywhere else."

Even Caol had to nod in agreement. He stopped pacing, and once the music began, found himself at ease for the first time that day. Muir eventually relaxed enough to sleep and Owain listened with his eyes closed determined to do likewise. Wortham, after watching barely perceptible emotions flitter across Kavan's face like wind-driven ripples on a smooth pond, drifted into blissful sleep certain he had never heard anything more beautifully mournful in all of his life.

❧*❧

The Cordashian navy was in place except for those ships that were sent further down Neth's eastern-most coast towards Glevum. Those would take a few days still to reach their destinations, but as far as Captain Leocroft was concerned, his men were in place. With ships strung out along the Nethite coast as far as the cliffs of Elyriá, he was curious to see the faces of the people upon the shore, to know what they were thinking. After all, how many of them knew their king had dragged them into war?

By land, King Renfrid's troops had converged in the city of Kor on the Dagar River and had, from there, begun to fan out along the border the kingdoms shared. Another group was equally split between the cities of Edug and Medina; after receiving their orders they too had spread along the kingdom's edge. Of Cordash's vast military machine, there was one small unit that remained un-deployed, awaiting a special mission from their king.

With the troops in position, Cordash braced for combat. Their goal was to push to Glevum and depose King Loris if they could, or at least strangle Neth's military until they thought twice about rising up against their neighbors again. On the twenty-sixth day of the sixth month of Kailar, in the first year of the reign of King Renfrid the Third, Cordash initiated the invasion of Neth.

## ❧Chapter 31❧

Guthrie knew, from the gently rising slope of the land and the gradual thickening of the forests they passed through, that the long string of Enesfel's troops marching behind him was nearing its first destination. He mentally reviewed every detail of the plans he, King Arlan, and the now King Renfrid had decided upon. If all progressed as scheduled, at dawn yesterday, Cordash would have initiated hostilities by now. With luck, King Loris was ill-prepared, a state of affairs that would mean fewer casualties for Cordash.

By mid-morning, the chamberlain and those with him reached the outskirts of Tarsee to find messages waiting for them. General Agis had proceeded towards Bryn as instructed, where he and his three thousand men would begin their push into Neth. General Zarkosta traveled east to the region where the borders of Neth, Enesfel, and Elyriá converged, where his two thousand men would do the same. As each general left Tarsee, they were to post four, five-hundred-man camps along the border, and the remaining one thousand men would continue towards Cordash along the Dagar River to assist Cordash's men in dividing the heart of Neth.

The last one thousand men, those following Guthrie, were officially under General Wyndham's command, although the planning and final strategic decisions were to be left to Guthrie McHador. They and the two hundred Hatu soldiers made camp on the north side of the Lake of Tarsee for the night; come morning Enesfel would begin their own invasion. If what Owain had told them was accurate, Enesfel would be able to strip Neth of a significant portion of their kingdom with little, if any, resistance.

Guthrie, however, knew there would be bloodshed. No king would give up a third of his country without a fight. The chamberlain prayed that Enesfel's green troops were prepared for what lay ahead.

𑰉*𑰉

"Will you take something to Prince Harcourt for me, father?"

The princess stood before her father, her hands behind her back, her face blank. A habit she had learned from the court bard, no doubt, although unlike Kavan, she could not keep the mischievous sparkle out of her eyes as she waited for her father's reply.

King Arlan was behind schedule as it was. He intended to start for Tarsee at dawn, but there had been one interruption after another that kept him from leaving. First, k'gdhededhá Tythilius had come with a two-page list of instructions and admonitions for gdhededhá Tusánt that he had, it seemed either forgotten to give the other clergyman before his departure or saw necessary to give again. Then his lady healer had come, returned from Bhryell, with messages for her brother and husband from herself and other family members. She also brought word from Kavan that, while he had yet to find the boys, he had not given up the search. That bit of news made Syl's interruption a worthwhile one, though Arlan did not like the news. Try as he did, he was unable to keep the bard and his son out of his thoughts for long; any morsel of news concerning them was welcome.

Then, as he gave his trunks to his staff to be secured for travel, his sister had come to him with a tearful farewell. She and Justice Cornell would manage matters in Rhidam in the King's stead for the weeks he would be away. Though the King had no doubt, despite his sister's handicap, that between the two of them, the kingdom would continue to run smoothly, he was still uncomfortable with releasing the reins of power. He trusted his sister and his justice but worried he was placing Deidre in danger with his choice.

There had been other servants and advisors interrupting him too, verifying what he wanted packed, what should be done about this matter or that during his absence, and now there was his daughter. His first impulse was to brush her aside, but her wide, dark eyes, much like Brenna's, demanded a response. As annoyed as the King was with another delay, he squatted before her and held out his hand. How could he be angry when it was his wife's face he saw every time he looked at her?

"What is it, Diona?"

"This." She held out one hand; in it, a black velvet and lace pouch that the King recognized at once.

"Your pearl prayer beads? The ones Lord MacLyr gave you?" Though she, like him, did not seem to harbor strong religious ideals, the King knew she carried those beads with her at all times. That she was willing to give them to anyone surprised him.

"I have told Lady MacLyr my intentions," she said, "I can get another. Prince Harcourt does not have one; I thought he might appreciate this."

Brow quirked, the King took the beads but said, "Their religious practices are different from ours; they do not use these…"

"Neither does Lord Cliáth," the princess replied with a shrug, "but he still admires the beauty of well-made things. I think Prince Harcourt will too. He might not use them, but it might help him feel closer to k'Ádhá…especially when he is fighting. I do not think killing people can make anyone feel closer to k'Ádhá…even if it is for a good cause."

The King shook his head with a bemused, small smile, and placed his empty hand on his daughter's head. "I think, little one, you are much smarter than you should be." Not because she was a girl, but because she was so young.

Smiling at his compliment, she curtsied and giggled, "Lord Cliáth says so too. Will you take it to Prince Harcourt? Please?"

Baffled by his daughter's interest in the older prince, an interest he did not think her old enough to have, Arlan kissed the top of her head and then her cheek. "I shall if you wish it. I do not know if I will see him, but I will see that he receives it. Now, I must be on my way or he shall never get it at all." He stood and offered his hand. "Will you see me off?"

"Yes, father."

❧*❦

The small, square, wooden structure, a house judging by the crooked stone chimney, askew wooden door, and two boarded-over windows they could see, looked as if it had been erected in the midst of a man-made clearing decades ago. The dark green ivy vines that snaked up the sides had long been undisturbed and appeared to have merged with the wood and plaster walls in most places. To the left was a stable and corral housing a single mule, goat, and cow. An abundance of chickens clawed the ground around the house without restraint and a yellow dog lounged on the mossy steps scratching his neck, watching them approach but showing no signs of concern or interest. From the stone chimney, a curl of white smoke perfumed the air but there were no sounds save for the animals and no other indications that this place was inhabited. Unsure of what they might find, not wanting to startle the owners with the arrival of an Elyri on their doorstep, Kavan held back, his face and hands covered as they had been since crossing into Neth, while Owain knocked upon the weathered wooden door.

Owain could hear the slow shuffling within before the door finally cracked open, revealing a grizzled face through the slight opening. At the sight of Owain, the woman's expression twisted with a combination of awe, annoyance, and fear. "Lord Lachlan!" Owain was surprised to be recognized. "What brings you to our home? This is far from Fiara. Or," the old woman croaked with sudden suspicion, "are you here to demand taxes?"

Owain cocked his head. He had never bullied his people into paying taxes, although knowing it was a common de Corrmick practice, it did not surprise him the woman might think him the same. "No, good woman," he said earnestly. "I am returning to Fiara from a mission of peace and seek shelter for myself and my companions for the night."

Whether out of defiance or a desire to test the lord at her door, the thin little woman puffed out her chest. "I've no room for freeloaders, even if you are royalty…or is this a demand?"

Swallowing back the moment of affront and insult, Owain opened his mouth to respond.

"We make no demands and ask no preferential treatment," Kavan murmured as he stepped forward, drawing the woman's attention away from Owain and cutting off any retort the man was about to make. "We offer labor if you have need of it, and I am a harper. I am willing to play for shelter. Or we can offer monetary reimbursement for lodging if that is more suited to your needs. We have spent many nights in the open and would appreciate a roof over our heads."

Eyes wide at the prospect of both payment and assistance, and swayed by Kavan's easy tone, the woman murmured contritely, "I have no room but you can use the stable; it needs mucking though."

"One minute," Caol snapped. "If you expect payment, you will need to do better than a dirty stable…"

She coughed and shifted uneasily. These must be important men if Prince Owain allowed them to speak in his place. The fact that none in the party demanded shelter, as many noblemen would, meant a great deal, even if the redhead sounded irritable about her offer. "Well…if you could clean it…gather the eggs in the morning before you go, feed the animals, you may sleep there without payment. Ral and I," she looked at the white-hooded figure, "would appreciate entertainment too…he has been sick so long…it would do him good to hear something beautiful."

The terms were accepted after glances exchanged between the men, despite Caol's initial annoyance. These people had little, likely had few visitors, and their age and diminishing health made upkeep more and more difficult for them. An afternoon's labor in exchange for a little hospitality seemed a fair enough trade.

By sunset, Caol and Wortham, the former with gradually diminishing complaints, had the stable and corral cleaner than either had been in many months. Owain, after helping Muir feed the animals, paid the old woman with a fistful of coins for two chickens which he killed, cleaned and roasted for dinner over a fire pit in the yard. The prince, meanwhile, used a curry brush and comb to groom the dog; the work revealed a beautiful animal little older than a puppy.

Kavan, meanwhile, took it upon himself to clean the interior of the house while the woman tended her stew pot. Her husband lay motionless upon filthy sheets, his body skeletal and gray though his bony chest rose and fell with his shallow, labored breathing. He watched Kavan's movement with bleary eyes as the bard worked, until Kavan felt compelled to kneel at the bedside. Other than the obvious refocusing of his eyes upon Kavan, he was unresponsive. The others came in as their host set their meal upon the table. It was not much, the roasted chickens, vegetable stew that had been simmering over the fire for days, and flat, unleavened bread, but Kavan suspected it was the best meal these people had eaten in a long time. He lifted the old man's head, trying to feed the fellow broth, as he listened to his companions dine.

He felt little desire to eat and settled for a morsel of bread and a few swallows of broth; his stomach still felt cold and knotted from the encounter with his uncle over Mílne's death. He was thus the first to finish and chose to play a few simple melodies to accompany them as they supped. Their host, surprisingly, showed no objection or fear because he was Elyri, and once the music began, she did not even notice he was different. Requests were made, the evening growing more boisterous as Owain, Caol, and the old woman Inga, jostled to see who could sing the loudest and who could come up with the wittiest lines and songs. It was good to see them relax, good to give the old woman a bit of merriment, and even the corners of Ral's mouth twitched as if he meant to smile. Wortham sat detached from the merriment, focused instead on Kavan, lost in thought. Prince Muir, unaccustomed to such an atmosphere, having been excluded from such lewd entertainment because of his youth, did not participate but listened and laughed when it seemed fitting. Kavan was not sure how much, or how little, the prince understood.

When Wortham suggested they turn in for the night if they wanted to get an early start in the morning, there were disappointed groans from Owain and Caol. Inga begged for one more song and Kavan relented, ending their night with an airy, hymn-like lullaby, and then as the others aided in clearing the table, he went out into the misty night air. Muir and Wortham followed soon after; both men were asleep before Owain and Caol emerged from the house. Kavan did not climb into the loft, did not rest, until both men had collapsed into exhausted, intoxicated sleep. It was good to see that they had gotten past their differences, and Kavan mused over why two men drinking together often either resulted in a closer friendship or a brawl. There was no need for watches tonight; they would each be able to enjoy a full night's rest, but Kavan wanted to be sure everyone was together and settled before allowing himself the luxury of sleep. The horses and dog would give warning enough of someone's approach.

Some time later, after his body had succumbed to exhaustion, the bard bolted awake, the scent of smoke strong in his nostrils. Outside, the dog was barking furiously. Wortham woke as he did, and both men hastened from the loft and out of the stable to find the house nearly engulfed in flames that were determined to leap to the thatched stable roof. A scream broke through the crackle but it was barely discernible over the roaring fire.

"Get the others...and the animals..." Wortham was already running to fetch those in the barn, grabbing first Kavan's harp and an armload of supplies as he shouted for the others to rise and join them.

Kavan faced the fire. He had two choices, contain the flames or go inside to help their hosts. The screaming had ceased, or at least he could no longer hear it as the blaze's voice grew louder in his ears. In all likelihood, both elderly people were dead, but without proof to the contrary, Kavan could not knowingly condemn them to such a death. Knowing he could protect himself, the thought of going inside was still a frightening one, but no one else stood a chance of surviving, of rescuing their hosts. As much energy as he could gather was thrust around him as a shield and he plunged through the cabin's door as the others burst out of the stable, carrying supplies and leading animals.

"Kavan! No!"

Owain dropped his armload of goods and restrained his son with one hand. "You cannot go after him; you will die."

"But he..."

There was nothing Owain could say. He had no idea why the bard would rush unprotected into a burning building or how any man could survive such an action. With the animals safe though terrified, Caol pumped water from the well into three nearby buckets. Rather than focus on the Elyri's fate, Owain grabbed the first bucket, bid Muir to take another, and began attempting to douse the flames.

Kavan heard the prince's cry but the sound was quickly swallowed by fire as he entered the building. The heat was stifling but the flames could not touch him, nor did he feel the intensity of the heat to the degree anyone else would have. Scanning the one-room hovel through the smoke he could see no sign of Inga. Ral lay upon his bed still, the bedclothes alight around him. Kavan had no idea if he could protect another with the power that shielded him, no idea if the flames and smoke would affect him then, but he could not leave the man there if there was the smallest chance he was alive.

He lifted Ral's slight frame with ease. The contact of Ral's dirty, smoldering nightshirt with the energy surrounding Kavan caused its protection to collapse unexpectedly. Running for the door, Kavan struggled to reestablish that shield but it was too late. His robe was burning and his lungs were filling with smoke by the time he and Ral were clear of the collapsing building.

Caol saw him come out, but rather than quit pumping water, he shouted to Owain, who was closest to the bard. Enesfel's former king took the old man from the bard's arms, instructing Kavan to drop and roll upon the ground to put out the flames. Rather than do as Owain instructed, however, Kavan stopped moving, closed his eyes, and caused the flames to choke and go out through the force of his will and control of power. Though he was quickly successful, little remained of his robe and his skin was blistered and bleeding in many places.

Ignoring his pain, seeing it as inconsequential, Kavan reached for a pail of water, but Wortham stopped him. "It is no use, milord. The stable has caught. We can never hope to contain it; it will need to burn itself out. The animals are safe; our supplies are rescued…"

That one of their hosts was missing was a grim reality that went without mentioning.

Kavan looked at the silhouette of the forest's outline through the orange, smoke-filled air. Enough of the trees had been cleared that, unless a strong wind developed, there was little chance of the flames igniting the forest, but the flames had already claimed too much and Kavan decided not to take any more chances. Voice ragged from smoke-inhalation, Kavan croaked, "Keep the water ready," as he staggered back towards the flames. Fearing that he intended to go back into the crumbling building, Wortham followed, but Kavan went no closer than the searing heat of the blaze allowed. Focusing energy was difficult; his body hurt and where some of the blisters had broken open the charred bits of his tattered robe clung to his flesh. It took longer than he wished, but eventually, he drew in a deep, abrupt breath, threw his arms open wide as if casting a net, and stopped.

As the fire began to pull in upon itself, the flames receding from the edges of the buildings, coming together to a point in front of the bard rather than continuing to climb and spread outward, Wortham's knees began to buckle. It took all of his strength to remain standing. He knew this was no miracle, but rather another aspect of that incredible power the Elyri bard harnessed, and though it was not frightening to behold, the magnitude of the act was still astonishing.

Little by little, the flames moved inward, and when it appeared that they could shrink no further, buckets of water were hastily brought to extinguish what remained. In the light of the breaking new day, Kavan stood alone, staring at the sooty sky, knowing that the others were either gawking at him or at the charred remains of their shelter.

"Ral…?"

"Was dead when you brought him out," Owain answered grimly. Kavan hung his head. "It was a noble effort but his lungs were not strong enough to survive the smoke. It's what killed him, not the flames. You did what you could."

Wortham put one hand gingerly under Kavan's elbow. "Allow me to tend your wounds…"

"No."

"We cannot travel with you in this," the captain began.

"Yes, we can…"

Stubbornly, Wortham forced Kavan towards the blanket Prince Muir was spreading upon the ground. "I am sure you can, or more precisely you would force yourself to endure whatever pain might come, but," he looked to where Caol and Owain, who had both begun circling the fire's perimeter, squatted to examine something upon the ground, "why put yourself through such torture? We should bury Ral at least, find Inga if we can. By allowing me to tend the worst of the damage, you should be capable of traveling by the time the others are ready. If you insist on enduring useless pain, that will be bad enough."

Kavan did not have the will to fight him, and surrendered, allowing Wortham to pull the remains of his robe over his head and remove his singed boots. With his dagger, the captain cut away most of Kavan's pant legs, revealing pale skin that appeared to glow in the early dawn light. His big, rough hands began to smooth salve, which Rouvyn had left with them in case of an emergency, over Kavan's hands, arms, legs, and chest, anywhere the flames had eaten through his clothing. He was in the middle of dressing those burns when Prince Muir presented them with what meager breakfast he could manage without a fire to cook on. The yellow dog was with him, its sad eyes watching the prince's every step. Muir sat on the blanket too, his eyes filled with a mixture of concern and envy and the dog sat with him.

When Caol and Owain rejoined them, the red-head was carrying a dagger that he wiped clean as soon as he was seated. "I found Inga…face down…an arrow in her back…" The disgust he felt at such a cowardly killing of an elderly woman colored his voice. "Couldn't have been much of a struggle."

"Then the fire was deliberate?" the prince asked.

"Seems so…though we can't be certain."

Weakly, Kavan asked, "Halstatt?"

Caol shrugged, aware that Wortham had picked up on the second use of that name. He handed the arrow to Kavan. "Could be. I can think of no other reason anyone would want to harm those old folks. They weren't troubling anyone and had nothing worth killing for. I might have ruled it an accident…a fallen candle or something…but that arrow…" He shook his head. "No, I think it was us they were after…whoever they were."

The image from the arrow was a face Kavan did not recognize. Not Halstatt, and not any of those men they had captured and turned in to the authorities in Dun's Hollow. A relative of one of them, perhaps, but without apprehending the killer, there was no way of knowing what the murderer's motives had been, or whether he had set the fire or it had been accidental.

"Since Captain Delamo has ordered me to stay rest, would it be an imposition to ask you to see that our hosts receive a decent burial? It is the least we can do for them."

"I will see to it," Wortham promised. If Kavan was willing to do as he asked, Wortham would do anything Kavan wished. "What of the animals?"

Owain looked at the dog at Muir's feet. "He seems to have taken a liking to Muir…we could keep him around. And we could use the mule, I think. The cow and goat however…there is a village two days east of here, before we reach Fiara. We could take the animals there…sell them or give them away. We could kill a few chickens…take the meat with us?"

Kavan's head bobbed in agreement. The animals would slow their travel, but leaving them to fend for themselves in the wild did not seem right. If he and his party had not been here, none of this would have happened; the old couple might still be alive to care for them. He knew the deaths were not their fault, but knowing did not ease his guilt.

Neth. Thus far, as Ártur rode within the cluster of soldiers directed to protect him, the countryside looked no different than the mountainous forests of northern Enesfel. There had been no border guards, no one to prevent them from crossing into the northernmost kingdom. The only people they met had been a collection of drab peasants in colorless clothing who at first ogled them fearfully and then, when they recognized that the standard did not belong to King Loris, began to either cheer in the hopes of salvation or flee in panic. Thankfully, they had yet to encounter trouble, which was what Guthrie had hoped for. They had come to fight, they all knew it was unavoidable, but each man hoped the day of battle was a long way away. Being in enemy territory when camp was made that first night, Ártur knew he was not the only man to sleep uneasily. Many, he suspected, did not sleep at all.

## ❧Chapter 32❧

Admiral Leocroft spent much of the night watching the small Neth town on the shore, an idea germinating in his head as the fires and street lanterns went out and left the shoreline in darkness. Capturing a Neth port was not part of his orders. If he attacked and failed, he would not likely live to return home. His orders had been not to engage land troops. But there were no troops here to engage and no one had told him he could not try to capture an unfortified port, that he could not raid and resupply his ships from their stores. This particular harbor was the closest to Cordash; it would provide a supply line for King Renfrid's troops if it was captured. At the very least, trying to take it would provide an interesting diversion for Leocroft and his men.

Taking thirty-six men from his ship and the sister crafts sitting off his prow, he rowed four dinghies to shore, using the cover of night to shield them. Shore patrol spotted the boats, as the captain knew they would; the klaxon sounded, but fortune was with Cordash since none of the arrows fired at the captain's men found their mark. The small boats ran ashore and were swarmed by villagers almost before the men could disembark. Killing innocent people was not high on his list of desires, but Leocroft was committed. He either fought or died.

His men were well-trained. Despite being outnumbered, after many minutes of combat with villagers who had little military training, the port was surrendered to Captain Leocroft's command. To his surprise and delight, he discovered King Loris' sister and her son in one of the wealthier houses. High profile captives were a bonus he would not ignore. Both were taken to the ship where he could watch them. He did not expect to hold the port for long; if the king learned of his sister's capture, he might send troops to rescue her. By keeping her on his ship, it would be easier to defend her, and harder for King Loris to win her back.

It would make for a more interesting game.

Twenty-four men were left to act as guards within the town and Leocroft took his wounded back to the ship as dawn broke. Whether or not King Loris sent reinforcements to reclaim his town, he might be willing to pay a ransom for his sister. If General Marym had done his job, however, Neth troops would not likely arrive for many days. Since King Renfrid would be unable to send support troops of his own, Leocroft would eventually have to relinquish control of both the port and the Nethite king's sister. In the meantime, however, he would take whatever supplies and valuable goods he could from the port and its surrounding area, capture any Neth vessels that tried to dock here, and amuse himself with his new toys.

And he congratulated himself with having taken very few lives.

Of all of the units of troops Enesfel sent into Neth, General Agis and his men were the first to meet resistance from Neth's militia. His drive north along the tumbling Poldris River was hampered by his scouts' reports that Neth had troops in the area. Pulling out, heading for the Cordash border where King Renfrid's troops had begun their invasion, but in the area nonetheless. Agis was a tactician, however, and had no interest in risking his meager forces if it was not necessary. If he could allow the enemy to pass, to meet their fate at the hands of Cordash's stronger forces, it was the more prudent course to take.

However, despite his efforts, it was impossible to hide three thousand men. Shouts of disorder from the back of his ranks told him that Neth's troops had found his. He was far from the fray and wished that this was a mounted fight. He was more proficient upon the back of a good sturdy horse. Nethites swarmed from the forest, falling upon the road behind Enesfel's men, leaving them no way to flee. Fighting was a necessity, one the men took to with relish. The general drew his double-headed ax as he reached the thick of the fighting and charged into combat swinging. He doubted the first few men he cut down knew what had hit them.

The largest man in the Nethite troops, a man with well-aged piecemeal armor and a long, braided grey mustache, picked Agis out of the crowd at the same moment Agis spotted him. Each knew at once that the other was the one to eliminate and began pushing towards one another, killing any foe in their path. The Cíbhóló stopped first, planting his feet, waiting, taking the opportunity to gauge the other man's strengths. He carried a shield, a luxury that Agis' two-handed ax did not allow, but to Agis, the shield hindered his opponent's range of motion, and Agis intended to use that against him. As the Nethite swung, the Cíbhóló danced back, killing two other soldiers with a swipe of his ax. The act created an opening that allowed his opponent another lunge, but Agis again dodged the attack and took his own shot. The blow was blocked by the man's shield, but the impact was enough to splinter the wood and render it useless.

Agis howled in satisfaction. Wooden shields did not offer much protection against a well-honed ax and a strong wielder. The Nethite dropped the useless shield and hopped sideways as another of Enesfel's men swung at him. I don't think so, the general thought with a second howl. No one was taking this prize from him. With his opponent distracted on two fronts, Agis swung again, this time separating the man's head from his shoulders with a single blow.

Not as much fun when a man was not paying attention, the general thought grimly. Ah well.

By the time Enesfel's army finished, by the time no more Nethites came from the forest and those who had lay dead along the well-traveled dirt road, Enesfel had lost fifty-three men, most in the initial moments of the unexpected assault. Regrettable losses, but Agis consoled himself with the knowledge that he was leaving behind a large number of Nethite soldiers who would not trouble King Renfrid's forces and who could no longer fight for King Loris de Corrmick. All in all, he praised himself and his unit, a job well done.

❧*❦

Despite the hardness of the timber bench, it was a welcome relief to rest there after being astride a horse for a day and a half. Riding had never been a discomfort for Kavan, but he had never ridden while covered with burns, blisters, salve, and wrappings. That the bench did not jostle him and rub his wounds the way a moving horse did was a relief to be savored.

The dog, which Prince Muir had named Coris, followed them to the village and trailed the prince everywhere as father and son sought the local sheriff to report the fire and the death of the couple. They intended to turn over the arrow that had killed one of their hosts as evidence, reveal their suspicions that the fire had been deliberate, but they knew they could offer no theory as to who had done such a thing to the aging couple. Only Owain's name and status would protect them from suspicion and possible arrest.

Wortham and Caol, meanwhile, sold the cow and goat, bought more supplies, and sought information about the missing princes and the man who had taken them. Because it was still mid-morning, they did not plan to stay in this village. Instead of paying for a room to rest in, Kavan opted to wait upon this well-weathered bench in front of the village tavern for the others to return. All he needed was the cessation of movement for as long as possible. Without considering the necessity of disguise, he leaned against the wall with his eyes closed and tried to will away the pain to be able to continue traveling when the others rejoined him.

The sun was warm on his face and shoulders, the spring breeze filled with the usual village aromas, and soon he was asleep despite his intentions to the contrary. With no idea how long he dozed, Kavan was jolted awake by someone yanking him to his feet. He blinked, dazed, expecting it to be Wortham or Caol to awaken him, but instead, his eyes fell upon a tall, pale, broad-shouldered fellow with a gold hoop in his ear and several missing teeth behind twisted, stained lips. Perhaps, Kavan thought too late, staying here alone without hiding himself had been a bad idea.

"You're not wanted here."

His assailant released the front of Kavan's robe. Dazed from sleep, lingering pain, and surprise, the bard stumbled, lost his footing, and fell backward to hit his head upon the bench's iron armrest.

"I said get up and move on!" The Nethite kicked him in the stomach and someone's derisive laughter told Kavan his attacker was not alone. He understood the Nethite tongue but there was no way these people could know that. He imagined they were giving him commands in their own language with the hopes that he would not understand or respond, thus giving them a reason, however flimsy, to attack. Another pair of hands, fleshier than the first, caught his arm to pull him to his feet, and dislocated his shoulder in the process. The pain of it shot down his back. He groaned but succeeded in yanking away from that grip, an act that resulted in a shower of rocks and vegetables and anything else the crowd had on hand as accusations of his attacking one of them took root and spread like a fire.

Unprepared, emotionally, mentally, or physically, for this assault, Kavan could not think clearly enough to defend himself. Fire raced through him each time something struck his blistered skin. Slumping to the ground, he tried to curl into a ball, hoping to limit the surface area his attackers could reach. The hard toe of a boot cracked into his hip. Something heavy struck his head and he prayed desperately for rescue or relief.

That relief came in the person of Owain Lachlan who, upon hearing the commotion in the street, grabbed the constable, pulled him out of his office, and raced to find the rabble gathered in front of the tavern…where they had left Kavan not long before. He could not see the bard, and it did not occur to him at first that the Elyri was involved. After all, with what Owain had witnessed during the past several weeks, he presumed Kavan would never allow himself to be at the center of such an attack. But as he pushed through the melee, leaving Muir at the rear out of harm's way, he realized the crowd was attacking someone upon the ground…someone, he saw at last, dressed in white.

The tavern wall and bench were all that kept Kavan from being surrounded.

Swinging in rage, Owain caught one man in the throat with his fist and another in the nose before anyone in the crowd recognized him. "The prince!" someone cried. Almost as one, those in the throng halted the attack or pulled back and fell silent. A few further back in the chaos broke free and ran.

Nose broken and bloody, while the other man lay at his feet gasping for air as he clutched his throat, the man who had started the bout began to babble excuses as Owain shoved him aside and bent over Kavan's unmoving body. The Káliel captain appeared at his side as if out of the air. Knowing the soldier had more medical expertise than he did, Owain grudgingly allowed Wortham to tend Kavan while he lurched to his feet and seized the bloody man by his lapels.

"I did not know this Elyri was in your employ…"

"He is not in my employ," Owain snarled, "He is my friend! Any man who assaults my friends…"

"I did not know…"

"You do now!"

"Is there a problem here?" Heads turned towards the speaker and Owain drew himself taller, recognizing the balding man immediately. He was neither scared nor intimidated like the villagers were.

"Nothing I cannot manage, Captain Venitt."

Not having expected the Lachlan prince, the Nethite captain stood at attention and offered a bow. "Milord…I did not recognize you." He looked at the two men on the ground, one Elyri, one not, and the burly man bending over the Elyri, and then at the crowd. "Is everything under control? Do you require assistance?"

"I am on my way home, stopping to conduct business with the constable; these men assaulted my friend." The Nethite captain looked between the two on the ground as if trying to decide which was the prince's friend. Owain continued, expecting to halt any questions before they were asked, "I have matters in hand."

"Very well." Venitt's short sword was nested back in its sheath. "Will you be joining us on the front, milord?"

It was a trap of a question, something he had to answer quickly and decisively, and with the expected answer, or risk exposure and an accusation of treason against his de Corrmick king cousin. Owain cleared his throat, knowing he could show neither weakness nor hesitation, and replied, "Once I deliver this man to my home…"

"I can have someone do that for you, milord," Venitt offered.

Owain shook his head with a growl, his expression still dark. "No, this is something I will do myself. He was beaten once…would have been killed. I will not entrust his welfare to anyone else."

If the other man thought his reasoning suspicious, he did not say so. "A sound choice," he said instead. "Very well." He turned to the constable and remained in the area long enough to assist in rounding up the agitators and clearing the street. Despite his lingering, Venitt did not appear distrustful, which made him comfortable enough to kneel beside Wortham and Kavan, now that Caol and Muir had pushed through the thinning crowd to join them.

"Is he…?"

Wortham did not look at him. "He's alive, but that beating did little good for his burns. He can't travel like this. His shoulder is dislocated and there's a chance his ribs are broken…maybe his hip." The bone beneath the captain's hand did not feel right to him. "There could be more damage…but I'm not a healer."

"And we do not have a decent one available," Owain muttered something under his breath. "The closest trustworthy doctor is in Fiara, and he's not Elyri…"

"Can we get him a room, Owain?" It was the first time Wortham had called the former king by name. His voice was strained, as though he were on the verge of cracking. "I will not leave him in the street."

"Of course. You will carry him?"

Wortham nodded grimly. "I hesitate to move him…but we must."

Once they secured a room in the inn next to the tavern and had Kavan resting upon a bed, peeled out of his bloody, dusty robe, the captain conducted a more thorough examination. Boarding an Elyri had not pleased the innkeeper, even though the man was injured and thus no threat, but Owain's status and purse gained them a single small room in which to care for the bard. Trying to give Wortham space to work, Owain insisted that Muir and Caol remain with him in the tavern, out of the Káliel captain's way.

"Thought you said your people were willing to abide by Enesfel's law protecting Elyri," Caol muttered.

Stung by the accusation, one Owain had been repeating to himself since he had first seen Kavan lying upon the ground under siege, the elder prince hissed, "Many are. Keep in mind, the majority of these people do not know about the Council's deal yet…we could not risk word of our plans getting back to Loris. Besides…get a man drunk…like that buffoon…and they say things they might not when sober, do things they would not normally do. And despite the laws, you know even Enesfel is not immune to this sort of thing." The blonde man rubbed his eyes. "We should not have left him alone. I am truly sorry…"

Muir stared into his tankard. Coris lay at his feet, his nose upon his paws, his brown eyes cutting back and forth between the young man and the door as if keeping watch. "He was so tired…in so much pain…and we…"

"Even more pain now," the inquisitor grumbled.

Without excusing himself, Owain pushed away from the table and stalked out the door. The truth was, he blamed himself for what had happened, and he could not bear to hear words that echoed like accusations in his ears. It had been his promise that the bard would be safe in Neth, his duty to protect Kavan while they traveled here, and he had failed. His negligence, his mistakes, had caused the bard untold suffering. Kavan might have forgiven Owain for that first time, but how could he ever forgive this?

Instead of going to the room to discuss Kavan's condition with Wortham, Owain made three circuits of the village's perimeter, partially to assure himself that Venitt's troops were no longer in the area and partially to allow sufficient time to berate himself.

When he did return to the tavern, as the sun sank over the treetops at the edge of the village, it was to discover Caol and Muir were no longer there. Not that he expected them to be. They would have gone to Kavan's side, which was where Owain, after quickly downing a pint of ale, went as well. Both Prince Muir and Wortham sat at Kavan's bedside in the lantern-lit room, but Caol was not with them.

After staring silently at Kavan's bruised, swollen face, willing the bard to open his eyes, to forgive him, Owain asked, "Lord Dugan?"

"Has gone to Fiara…to fetch the physician and check our lead."

"He should not have gone alone."

"Perhaps not," Wortham agreed, "but who else was there? Only you, and you were not here to stop him." Wortham felt reasonably certain that Owain would not have wanted to leave Kavan's side and Caol would have gone alone regardless. "I believe he wanted to undertake this search alone anyhow; the rest of us are here because Lord Cliáth insisted we be. Without his influence, I could not hinder Lord Dugan or affect his choice."

Knowing that was true, Owain grunted. Caol had wanted to be free of them from the start. "Have either of you eaten?"

"I am not hungry..."

Owain sighed and clasped the captain's shoulder. "Wortham, it will be a long night. You should eat. Muir and I can stay with him while you..."

"I do not want to eat alone...and I do not think any of us should go about on our own...even you, Owain."

"I..."

Prince Muir caught the shuffling of his father's feet and recognized it as a gesture he himself often made. There was something in the man's demeanor that Wortham either did not see or did not recognize, but Muir did. He wanted to stay with Kavan, to be there when his tutor awoke, but he suspected that would not be for some time, and Owain needed, more than anything, to have a few minutes alone with the bard.

Standing, the prince said, "I am a little hungry, Captain Delamo. I will join you...if you will accept my company."

The captain tore his gaze from Kavan after several moments of thought, gave a half-hearted smile, and said, "I would be honored, milord."

When he was alone in the room with Kavan at last, except for the dog that was curled up by the warming stove, Owain knelt beside the low framed bed and tentatively touched Kavan's bruised face. He wondered if Kavan had looked anything like this when he ordered the man to be beaten some fourteen years ago. Owain had not bothered to confront the Elyri then, after giving that order, and now he understood why. Despite the pervasive anger and self-loathing that had filled his life in those days, he had instinctively known that he could not endure the sight of such a beautiful man broken and suffering. If he had seen this man's face bruised, his body twisted and wracked with pain, Owain would have released him and Enesfel's history would likely have been very different.

Head upon the bed, one hand tangled in the silver-white hair that felt like spun silk against his fingers, Owain gave in to weeping as he never had before. Crying was something his mother had forbidden. At last, he felt free of her, but all he truly wanted at that moment was for Kavan's absolution, Kavan's forgiveness. He wanted to be forgiven for everything, and only this man could give him that.

☙*❧

Prince Espen had volunteered for scout duty tonight, as had Bhríd Cáner and the soldier called Tedor. Their orders were to make certain there were no Nethite troops close enough to detect the encampment of Enesfel soldiers. If there were, General Wyndham wanted to know about it in order to deal swiftly with the threat. Other scout units explored the rear, the west and east sides of the camp, while Prince Espen and his partners scouted north, the direction in which Enesfel's troops were traveling and one of two directions where they were most likely to run into trouble.

There had been a minor incident earlier in the day when four Nethite scouts stumbled into General Wyndham's path. Enesfel's forces had dispatched the four quickly enough that the majority of the men never knew what had happened. Prince Espen knew about it because he had been near the front of the column and witnessed their swift, bloody demise. Seeing it gave him a thrill unlike any he had ever known, but seeing it had also left him feeling sick, and then disappointed that he had been unable to participate in their capture or slaughter. His father had sent him here to gain his first taste of battle, to gain the experience expected of a Hatu prince; however, from what he knew of Lord McHador's plan and from today's events, he was beginning to believe he would return home with no kills to his name and no honor for his family.

He had volunteered for scout duty this night with the hopes that something exciting would happen.

Bhríd's greater experience and superior senses allowed him the point position. Prince Espen felt in no way envious of those things as he trailed to the right, and Tedor to the left, all three moving through the dense, rocky forest as silently as they could. There was little forest in Hatu and what there was, was not nearly as thick, which made the prince extra cautious. This sort of stealthy maneuvering, blending into the foliage and listening for the differences between animal noises and people, was new to him, exciting in its' own right but not the experience he was seeking.

It was not, that was, until he found himself yanked upwards off his feet, left suspended by one leg, upside down, several feet off the ground with his dagger and pack falling away. His squawk brought seven men crashing from the brush around him, all enemies save two.

The five Nethites turned their attention to Bhríd and Tedor, the more significant threats. What they failed to notice, however, was that although most of Prince Espen's belongings lay scattered on the ground, his sword remained in its sheath when he was yanked off his feet. Some dexterous flailing and maneuvering enabled the prince to draw his sword, but no one was close enough to strike.

True to his reputation, Bhríd had already dispatched two of the five and was involved in swordplay with a third. Tedor was faring less well, having the final two men concentrating on him. But when he saw the sword in Prince Espen's hand, he took a step sideways and began inching towards the swaying prince, whose head throbbed as the blood drained into his skull.

Hanging upside down affected Espen's vision. The two Nethites were fuzzy, the edges of his sight growing black, making it difficult to concentrate. When they were in striking range, however, he began swinging wildly, hoping he would hit at least one of the targets he could barely see. A scream as his sword met resistance told him he had succeeded; he could pray it was neither Tedor nor Bhríd. But that opening, the distraction of a scream, cost the final opponent his life as Tedor took the opportunity to run him through.

Prince Espen did not fully hear the praise and laughter from his companions through the blood pounding in his skull as he was lowered from the snare. He rested his head on his knees to recover his senses while the others clapped him on the back and searched their attackers. He knew and cared about only one thing. Regardless of whatever else occurred in this 'war', he had made his first kill. He could return to his father and brother with honor.

## ॐ•Chapter 33•॰ॐ

King Arlan stood on the unsteady wooden pier, the world seeming to sway around him, looking across the agitated lake, knowing from memory that he would not be able to see the far shore, but trying nonetheless. His arrival in Tarsee had been accompanied by all of the pomp and grandeur he had expected, far more than he had met the last time he was here thirteen years before, but the one thing he wanted most was not to be had. There was no news from the troops that had gone ahead, and none from Kavan regarding his son. His forces had been here; Guthrie had made sure that the King would know they had passed through Tarsee on schedule. By now, if everything had gone as arranged, the bulk of Enesfel's troops had reached Fiara. It was not far into enemy territory and was the largest city in southern Neth. It would be a good staging area, as long as Loris' forces had been drawn to the western border by King Renfrid's troops. Holding Fiara meant further assurance of success.

The King had not actually anticipated finding word from Kavan. The bard would not have known of Arlan's decision to travel to Tarsee unless the Sight had shown him, and Arlan doubted the Sight would show his best friend anything so mundane. As the weeks had crawled past, dragging despair behind each empty day, part of Arlan's soul grew more resigned to the inevitable. Kavan claimed Bertram would

die; his son was lost already, leaving Arlan with things left unsaid and undone…the way it had been with Brenna. Though he clung to hope, the more time that slipped away, the harder the effort to believe became. As he turned from the lake in response to a call behind him, Arlan wondered what he would do if he ever saw his son alive again.

❧*☙

His cousin Owain was nowhere to be found; at least, that was what his messengers reported back one after another. Such news did not please King Loris, but knowing his cousin was a hunting man, it was not inconceivable that he was somewhere in the mountains on an extended hunting trip…even if his servants did not know it. What kept the king from yet another murderous rampage, from demanding Owain's entire household be slaughtered, was that one of those servants had suggested to him that Owain might have gone on a reconnaissance mission into Enesfel when it was learned that Cordash was preparing for war. Such a notion made Loris happy. Enesfel was weak, yes, but they were capable of surprises, and King Loris did not want surprises. He was not concerned enough to spare men to perform an investigation; such initiative on his cousin's part was welcome. If Owain learned something useful, good. And because Owain would not be welcome in Enesfel, if the man was captured, Loris would not be terribly offended if the Lachlans executed his kinsman. It would mean one less person to watch.

He was more annoyed, however, by the news that the Cordashian navy had the audacity to capture a town, kidnap his sister and her child, and demand a ransom for their return. He believed his sister was strong, however, and could hold her own for the few weeks it would take to beat King Renfrid's troops into submission. At that time, Loris would demand her release and take the head of any man who dared lay a hand on her.

Early reports spoke of sporadic encounters with Cordash in the western forests, combat for which Neth's troops were well-trained, and Cordash's flat-landers were not. Nethite soldiers had to be trained for it since nearly two-thirds of the kingdom was blanketed with forest. For now, Neth had the advantage. If they could keep the Elyri-loving foreigners in the trees, Neth would remain safe and victorious. King Loris would teach them a lesson in warfare they would not soon forget.

❧*❦

Having ridden without stopping, as fast as his horse would take him, Caol reached Fiara before sundown, too late to do any serious investigative work since he did not know his way around the city. He had no desire to be broadsided in a dark alley when he would rather be making progress in his quest. It was not too late, however, to seek the local doctor and contact the Association's leading members in the area, names he knew but had never had reason to meet. Without Owain's support, he could not hope to gain access to whatever quarters the man's home might have offered, and he had no proof to present to show the two men knew each other. The Association, on the other hand, seemed a safe enough bet. He was banking that his name was not well-known in this place, and since he knew all of the proper codes, customs, and etiquettes, the people in this Association cell might be willing to assist him where members in Enesfel were not.

One name after another, one dirty, ill-kept back room after another dark, dead-end alley eventually gained him the access he sought. He was taken to a garish room above an inconspicuous tavern, a room whose contrast to the Association's underbelly spoke of expensive whores and prosperous thieves, and it was there he came face to face with Onea Pantel for the first time. The current head of the Pantel family, for all of the secrecy and anonymity, proved to be a woman. A very beautiful woman with the blackest eyes he had ever seen and a thick ebony braid that coiled around her head and over her shoulder like a serpent. She had looked him up and down silently for many minutes, her underlings turning Caol this way and that so that she could examine him as one might an animal or slave at auction, before eventually bidding him to speak.

By the time he opened his mouth, it was all Caol could do to maintain some degree of calm and decorum.

There were many women in the Association, but few cells in Enesfel were led by one. The Pantels were an old family, and if she was the last of the bloodline, or the oldest or most talented, she would naturally assume the leadership position, as long as she was capable of holding it. While she was able to direct him to secure shelter for the night, she claimed no information regarding those he sought. She promised to have word for him by noon the next day if there was any to be had. If the individual named Halstatt, or either of the two children had been in Fiara, she would know it soon enough, and if they were still in town, she would have their current location. She also promised to locate the physician for him, although the man was believed to be out of town, but he would be found. Caol had no doubt she would do as she promised. A woman in such a position of power, he thought with a smile, was normally prone to getting what she wanted…one way or another.

If Caol was not already happily married, Onea Pantel would have had him without a single word spoken between them.

☙*❧

Hours passed but there was no change in Kavan's stationary, unstirring condition. The bruises continued to darken, the open blisters crusted over, but he had not awakened and had not moved from the position Wortham first put him in. His companions' consolation was that the inquisitor should have reached Fiara. Each man carried concern that if Caol learned anything about the princes he might not return to them, or worse, he would forget to send the physician. After some discussion, it was decided that if the inquisitor did not return within two days, or if the physician had not arrived in that time, Owain would ride to Fiara to find the doctor himself. His dedication to the bard's welfare left Wortham no doubt about the type of man he was…regardless of what sort of king he had once been.

❧*❧

"I apologize, Lord Dugan," Onea said, her dark honey voice sincere with regret as he took a seat on the stool nearest her. At least, it sounded sincere to Caol. She was dressed in apple red today, as she had been during their previous meeting, draped languidly over a divan in the murky light of an oil lamp, the room, a different location than before that was absent of windows for security's sake. Her black hair hung straight and loose about her exposed shoulders and her feet were bare, though dusty as if she had recently been outdoors. "No one has seen anyone, man or child, that match your descriptions. If they were here, or are here, they have been well-disguised."

Caol shrugged, trying to keep his voice level and his emotion off his face. He had expected nothing less, despite the hope he clung to. Years of gut instinct told him she was being honest, although it was always possible, he mused, studying her impassive features, that she was a better liar then he was a judge of character. "More than likely they were never here…nor intended to be. He sent me here to throw me off, play games. It's his way…not your fault." He could not imagine what Halstatt hoped to gain, but he expected nothing less.

"I assume you have your own people working on this?"

"Not exactly. I have not been completely honest…" He rubbed the back of his neck as Onea's rouged lips pursed and her hand tightened on the arm of her chair. He was taking a risk in confiding in her, but he believed that the best way to gain her continued cooperation was to be honest. Besides, despite any possible foolishness, he liked her. "I grew up as part of the Association; my family has been with them as far back as our bloodline goes. But I have not been personally involved since I married the sister of King Arlan..."

"You are that man?" Her surprise displaced her annoyance as she grasped the seriousness of his situation and leaned forward to see him better in the lamplight. "There are always stories...but I did not believe...this man Tarmajien...he has kidnapped royal children?"

"My son and the heir-apparent." He was reluctant to admit that, but he was committed to finding the boys and he needed an Association ally he could trust. He believed this woman was his best bet. "Hence the urgency. The Association cells in Rhidam and Durham do not want to be involved, despite Halstatt's inappropriate actions and choices. Beyond my comrades and myself, and the Lord High Justice, there's Wace Elotti..."

That name made Onea smile, a look that reminded Caol of some sort of predatory creature on the hunt. "I know him well," she murmured, her tone suggesting how well she knew the venador, a tone that made Caol both shudder and fidget in his chair. "It is unusual that he has not yet produced results..."

The inquisitor snorted, trying to cover his discomfort. "I think he's up to something. He says he is working for someone, supposed to apprehend Halstatt himself, but it seems he's doing nothing more than following him. I don't like, or trust, him; I'll have better luck doing this myself. I'll find them...somehow...if it's the last thing I do." He stood with a stretch. "The physician?" If there was nothing further to be learned here, it was time he be on his way...before the temptation of Onea's seductively crossed legs proved to be more than he could fight against.

"Got home last night...three doors from the Sheep's Head Tavern. His name is Daens." She rose, and with her arm hooked around his, led him to the door. None of the others lingering in the shadows, young boys and girls who served her needs as servants, messengers, and apprentices, moved. "He is not a young man, but he is the best physician in the area. I know of one other, but I would not trust him with my cat." It did not concern her what business Caol had with the physician, but she wanted to be sure to recommend the best one. "I like you, Dugan…you seem to be an honorable man…one with integrity…and an edge." She grinned and traced her fingers along his cheek and jaw. "I will be your eyes and ears in Neth; if I learn anything, you will know. I hope to see you again."

She gave him no chance to reply as she opened the door, quickly scanned the narrow alley outside, and nudged him into it before closing the door behind him. There was no obvious trace of the door once it was closed; he had been brought here blindfolded to protect its location, but as Association, he could identify it if he tried. He knew the marks, the codes, the tells of any Association spot. It was a testament to the trust she was giving in exchange for his honesty.

Cautiously, he inched towards the main street, aware of every movement, every sound around him. Two women arguing in a room above. A baby's hungry cry. Children playing. The white and gray cat that stalked along a brick ledge and disappeared through an open window. The scratching of a dog that's foot thumped against a broken wooden crate. None of those things represented a threat. By the time he reached the street, he was able to merge into the daily bustle without raising eyebrows. Dressed in plain clothes, wearing nothing marking him as royalty, he asked a passing merchant with a cart of tanned leather hides for directions to the Sheep's Head, and then went in search of the physician, hoping he was not too late to help Kavan, barely consoling himself with the fact that the doctor had not been in town when he arrived and would not have traveled with Caol in the dark if he had been.

Tumult behind him, the sounds of horses and marching men, made Caol duck into the nearest open doorway, as many others on the street were doing. He had the sinking feeling it would be King Loris' troops passing through Fiara, perhaps seeking Owain, the one encounter Caol did not need. No one would recognize him as either a foreigner or as nobility, but he did not want to risk the possibility.

As the sound drew closer, however, and he saw the lead horses of the large group, he recognized by the armor and posture of the lead riders that these were no Nethites. With General Wyndham and Chamberlain McHador leading the way, it meant Enesfel was in Fiara.

Caol whistled, a shrill sound that drew eyes in his direction as he elbowed through the crowd towards the riders. The chamberlain was the first to spot and recognize him, while other soldiers around him prepared to put down an assassin if that was what Caol was.

"What are you doing here, man?" he asked, surprised to see a familiar face in this place and hoping that the coincidence meant good news. "Have you found the boys?"

With one hand on the horse's side to keep it calm, Caol shook his head. "We were led to believe they were here, but they are not. We're still looking. We're not giving up until we find them. Is the King...?" His eyes scanned the nearest riders. "Or Healer MacLyr...?" Why settle for a doctor when he could get the best Elyri healer there was?

"The King's coming behind...we're securing the way. Ártur's here, yes..."

"May I borrow his services for a few days? Lord Cliáth was attacked...not fatally but we have no physician and he needs treatment. Until he's..."

"Say no more." Turning in his saddle, Guthrie motioned the nearest soldier closer and grunted, "Bring Healer MacLyr at once."

Though he had been quiet, leaving the talking to Guthrie, General Wyndham moved closer, grabbed the chamberlain's arm and growled,

"We might have need of him…" He had nothing against the bard, did not wish him ill, but war changed priorities…at least it did for him.

"We have five other doctors with us, plus whatever local doctors there might be…" Guthrie started coolly, staring at the offensive restraining hand.

"Then send one of them," the general snapped. "Lord MacLyr is the best we have; it is his duty…"

"And Lord Cliáth is his family. Would you do your duty before assisting your kin?" Knowing he had hit a nerve by the flicker of emotion that shimmered across the other man's face, Guthrie grunted, "I thought not. You forget how well I know you. We should meet no resistance here; the city council has already secured Fiara for us. We can spare Ártur for…how long do you think, Lord Inquisitor?"

"If we leave promptly…three…maybe four days at most," Caol replied. He did not know if the healer was capable of endurance riding, but for the sake of Kavan's well-being, he suspected Ártur would endure anything. By the time he finished speaking, the healer's horse had drawn up behind Guthrie's; he saw Caol, prepared to speak, but Guthrie cut him off.

"Go with him, Ártur. He has need of your help."

"The princes?" the healer asked, his face paling. After what his cousin had predicted, the thought of one of the boys being injured made him feel sick.

"No…Kavan." The remaining color drained from Ártur's face. "Go, and come back as quickly as you can. I will leave men in Fiara to escort you to us if we are gone when your return. Caol, is there anything more?"

The redhead shook his head. "No…we have all of the supplies we need and can travel fastest with fewer men. Lord Healer, if we leave now and travel all night, we will reach him sooner. He needs you."

"Of course," Ártur said emphatically. "Whatever it takes."

Almost wishing he could go to Kavan's side, at least long enough to deal with whoever had attacked him, Guthrie waved the inquisitor and healer away, calling, "Blessings go with you." Unfortunately, duty kept him here. They could spare no delay in Fiara if they were to keep on schedule. He hoped there would be no need for combat or healing in store before the healer returned to them.

Ártur followed Caol to where the inquisitor had stabled his horse, wanting to ask questions but deciding there would be time enough for that as they traveled. The sooner they got Caol's horse saddled, the sooner they would reach Kavan. When they turned west onto the road that would leave Fiara behind them, the healer finally found his voice.

"Where are we going? Where is he?"

"A village not far from here. We should reach there early tomorrow. He was…" He swallowed, reluctant to recall the memories long enough to provide them. "He was attacked by a mob…beaten and stoned. Not fatally…at least Captain Delamo did not think his injuries were fatal…but I came for a physician because there were none there to be had. Fortunately, I have found the best healer anyone could want. He suffered burns before that…any help you can give him will be appreciated, I'm sure."

"By k'Ádhá…" Such an attack on an Elyri in Neth was not unheard of, and Kavan's unique appearance made who and what he was visible to all. But burned? How had that happened? What in k'Ádhá's name had Kavan been doing?

"We've not found the boys yet…" He knew the healer would ask; it seemed best to tell him up front. "A lead turned us to Fiara, but it was a ruse…nothing there I could find. I don't know what we shall do next except wait and see what Lord Cliáth says…provided he lives."

Expression grim, more worried than before, Ártur fixed his eyes on the road and mumbled, "He shall live. I will make certain of it."

❧*❧

The slow-moving depths of the Dagar River started high amongst the peaks of the mountain range that separated Cordash from both Enesfel and Neth and flowed northwards until it emptied into Lake Curo, in the heart of central Neth. It was a wide river for most of its flow, with enough breadth that the fleet of boats riding her current could travel three by three, occasionally four by four with a safe distance between them. Some of the troops that waited in the town of Kor now began sailing the river, others marched her southernmost shore. Every ten miles, without incident, an outpost was established. Five hundred men were left at each. Their objective, planned in detail by Guthrie McHador, was to cut the north of the country from the south, leaving any Nethite troops left in the south to the mercy of Enesfel and keeping any from the north from coming through and leaving them at the mercy of the Cordashian war machine. At the rate the flotilla was progressing, and the speed with which the soldiers erected their outposts, it would be a matter of days before the lake was reached, and then there would be no stopping the division of Neth.

⬥*⬥

The welcoming commotion that rose from the towers of the walled city of Ruidoso was unexpected. Agis looked at the men standing along the walls waving banners, blowing horns, Nethite men, cheering the arrival of Enesfel's troops. He had understood, from the stories passed through the ranks and from his briefings with Chamberlain McHador and General Wyndham before leaving Rhidam, that there was unrest throughout Neth, but unrest did not necessarily lend itself to an enthusiastic welcome from people with whom one shared a longstanding history of enmity.

Once Agis and his troops had left the forest, traveling became easier and they made good time, arriving in Ruidoso a day ahead of schedule thanks to Agis' determined command. It was exactly as the

Cíbhóló preferred it. Expecting little to no resistance, there was no reason to delay arrival merely to keep to a predetermined schedule. Besides, he had confidence in his men, and if doing his duty more efficiently made it easier for others to do theirs, he would be proud of his accomplishment.

His forces set camp outside of the east wall of the city where he had the most advantageous view and provided the largest area for his men to rest. He had been told to defend Ruidoso at all costs, and that was what his unit would do. Thus far, however, there had been few enemy encounters and he was not expecting more. As the sun set and he watched the horizon in every direction, he made a decision that he believed would be for the best. He would leave most of his men to carry out the mission they had been given. Agis, however, would take the remaining number, not quite one thousand strong, and continue north to the shores of Lake Curo. He would sweep the country of Nethite troops on the way, and wait on the shore to rendezvous with the Cordashian forces coming down the Dagar River. There would be time enough afterward to decide what to do next.

꼬*꼬

It took a half day longer than anticipated to reach the village because they crossed paths with a cluster of Nethite hunters on the road and Caol did not think the straight path worth a skirmish that he and Healer MacLyr were not equipped to win. The delay made the healer irritable, but he knew the precaution was wise. He would be unable to reach his cousin, to help him, if someone caught or killed him. By the time they reached the village, however, wisdom was the last concern on Ártur's mind.

His thought, his only care, was Kavan, and his first reaction to the sight of his badly battered cousin was the same as it had been fourteen years ago when Kavan had escaped the dungeons of Enesfel. He could not imagine what Kavan could do to deserve such brutality and he, despite his healer oaths, wanted to hurt whoever had dared do this. Captain Delamo briefed him on what had happened, how Kavan had been kicked, beaten, and stoned on top of having previously been burned in his efforts to rescue a bedridden man from a building fire. Kavan had not been conscious in the four days since the attack, had not moved other than to breathe. Some of the external wounds appeared to be healing and did not, themselves, seem to warrant a comatose state, and thus the captain was gravely worried for the bard's health. Having noted the knot upon Kavan's head from the impact with the iron arm of the bench, he feared that injury was the cause of Kavan's coma.

Banishing everyone from the room, the healer laid his hands upon his cousin's bare chest, feeling the extent of internal damage with the tendrils of healing power he controlled. Broken ribs were mending of their own accord; Kavan's inactivity made that process much easier for his body. And the captain had done an effective job of resetting the bard's shoulder. Ártur was left the task of completing nature's healing work; he saw to it that there were no internal injuries, mended the cracked ribs, hip, and skull, and then turned his attention to the bruises and burns. He could do little for bruising; those marks would need to heal and fade on their own. He could heal the burns, however. It took longer than it should have, his determination for perfection demanding slow and steady care, but by the time he was finished, no trace of the fire's damage remained on Kavan's flesh. It was as smooth and pale and perfect as it had ever been. His hands lingered longest over Kavan's face and hands, knowing the bard would prefer that he left the burn scars, but Ártur could not do it. He wanted his cousin to be whole again, to open his eyes, to smile, and make music.

When there was no further healing to be given, he settled back on the stool, gazing at his cousin's face as he tried to read him. Though the bard's mind was as tightly sealed as always, making intrusion from any outside source impossible, Ártur read a trace of something disturbing on the fringes. It was not the physical damage keeping Kavan from waking; so distressed had the bard been by the attack that he had withdrawn into himself, away from the terror into a place where he could feel no pain to keep from lashing out at his attackers with that touch of death he feared he could not control. It was a drastic, but effective, means of protecting others, perhaps the only sure measure against that ability Kavan worried about containing. But doing it had left Kavan defenseless, and his willingness to die concerned Ártur more than the possibility of Kavan killing someone else.

The lack of physical pain and the sensation of healing energy trickling through his body nudged Kavan's consciousness enough to draw him out of that dark, safe place. "Ártur?" The cracked, parched whisper was almost inaudible. He did not open his eyes, but he recognized that touch and the presence in the room without a doubt. "What are…where…?"

Ártur put his fingers to his cousin's lips, relishing the sensation, elated that his company had given Kavan reassurance enough to awaken. "In Neth…in the village where you…Caol brought me to you from Fiara." Rather than talk, or allow Kavan to strain his parched throat, Ártur answered his cousin's questions through the touch of his hand. He knew little of how the campaign as a whole was progressing, but General Wyndham had yet to meet resistance. He, Guthrie, and those they led had reached Fiara without significant incident.

The creak of the door behind the healer brought them out of their silent communication. Whether it was concern and curiosity that made them look, or some instinct that told them Kavan was awake, the four faces in the doorway showed relief at the sight of Kavan's open eyes.

"I'm glad bringing Ártur was the right thing to do," Caol remarked with a sigh. It had been worth the delay. "Unfortunately, that was all I could find in Fiara."

Kavan frowned. "No sign?" If there had been, Caol's demeanor would be different, but Kavan needed to hear the words.

"None…I don't think he was ever there. Whatever game he's at, it's tiresome…but if he thinks it'll make me sloppy, he's a fool."

The bard turned his head to look through the open window. He had no idea how much time had passed, how long he had been in this bed, but he could guess, from the position of the light, that it was after mid-day. As he recalled, they were not far from Fiara, and he knew without asking that Ártur would be needed there again. He flexed his arms, his legs, and feet, and finally nodded his head once.

"We still have daylight to travel by…"

"You are in no condition…" the captain immediately retorted.

Kavan held his hand to the man, and Wortham clasped it. "On the contrary, Wortham. I am stiff…sore in places…but Ártur has seen to the worst of it. I can manage a horse long enough to reach Fiara. Ártur must return quickly." And he felt, for reasons he could not name, that Fiara was where he needed to be. The clues to the boys' whereabouts had directed them to Fiara; though Caol had found nothing during his brief time there, Kavan clung to the hope that his certainty about being there meant the boys would soon be found. "If I feel the need for further recuperation, I can rest in Owain's estate while we plan our next course of action. His home will be safer and more comfortable, and I would rather not stay here any longer." The memories of this place filled him with uneasiness that was worse than any lingering physical pain. "Please…let us depart from here."

His companions fell over themselves in their haste to oblige him. No one wanted to be accused of being insensitive to his discomfort, the suffering they could hear in his voice without his needing to put it into words. The bard rarely expressed any sort of pain; his doing so now needed to be taken into account. Ártur remained with him, at Owain's insistence, as they packed belongings, settled their debts, and prepared the horses and mule for travel. The former king did not want harm to come to either Elyri; them remaining in the room while travel preparations were made, was for the best. Kavan had suffered enough. In less than two hours he was leading them on the road to Fiara, looking forward, at last, to being home.

❧*❧

The first day of Tord, in the seventh month of the year, was Prince Kjell de Corrmick's birthday. It should have been spent in merriment; a night of feasting and music following, he hoped, a day spent hunting with his cousin Owain. But war had changed everything and left no one in the mood for celebration. His father's doing, Kjell thought with annoyance. The same as always. Somehow, his birthday was always overlooked, or at best was celebrated by some brief mention of the occasion over dinner before his father became too drunk to remember anything. It was different for his brothers, particularly Earle, the eldest, who celebrated in any fashion he chose and got whatever he wanted…especially their father's attention and favor.

Being the youngest de Corrmick was his only fault, although he was aware of the persistent rumors that he might not be the king's son. King Loris, of course, denied these whispers, and Kjell could not imagine anyone else wanting his frumpy mother. Realistically, however, he knew that some men would do anything, including bed the king's wife, for a small morsel of power, and he admitted to himself that he looked nothing like his father or his brothers. Maybe, despite Loris' words to the contrary, the rumors were true; it would explain why the king most often ignored him. Or, at least on this occasion, perhaps his father was angry because Kjell was not old enough to go to war. Being so young, Kjell had little contact with the planning and knew that his father did not wish him to know about such things if he could not spill blood for the Crown. And Kjell had little interest in politics and war…or thus he led the king to believe.

❧572❧

For a boy of twelve, Kjell was more politically astute, he knew, than any of his siblings, and also more intelligent…or so General Glucke claimed during their occasional tutoring sessions. "You would be the greatest king in Neth's history," was one of Glucke's favorite sayings. Kjell, knowing the de Corrmick history by heart, had no doubt the general was correct. With the long bloodline of degenerates, miscreants, tyrants, and fools that had ruled Neth since the kingdom's formation, being the greatest would not be difficult.

Kjell was certainly wise enough to know that with Glucke's favor came the backing of the military. Military support and favor were necessary for any ruler in Neth. He was also smart enough to suspect that if he were to become king at this very moment, Glucke would be one of his regents. The general had his own designs on the throne; though no general or outsider had ever successfully overthrown a de Corrmick king, many had tried. Glucke would assume that his praise of the prince's intelligence would give him sway in the decision-making process. But Kjell believed he knew enough to make his own decisions. He would never allow any regents to make choices for him and believed he could manipulate the general, or anyone else, into thinking his ideas were theirs. He was well-practiced in that skill already; it kept him one step ahead of the throne seekers, his tutors, and his brothers.

But such thoughts were fantasies, amusements to entertain himself with in the hot summer afternoons while his brothers were off to battle and his father raged through the castle halls, swearing and fuming about injustice and paranoid perceptions in his usual drunken haze.

What a stupid man, Kjell thought, brushing his blonde hair out of his eyes. Neth had no business conducting raids on Cordash. Neth prided herself on being a self-sufficient kingdom, relying on little trade or outsiders to remain strong and independent. Raiding their most powerful neighbor to prove they could, had been a game for too long, and the king should not be surprised or affronted that Cordash finally chose to strike back. Loris should have backed down, or at least attempted to talk peace, while they could maintain dignity and manpower. Instead, precious resources were squandered in another fight. Short of a victory over Cordash, one that would guarantee access to Cordash's resources, Neth was going to face an ever struggling, uncertain future.

More foolish still, at least in the prince's eyes, was the abuse King Loris, like many other de Corrmick rulers, heaped upon his subjects. Kjell knew his father was delusional and paranoid; everyone within Glevum who had ever been in the king's company for an hour had experienced the mood swings and ramblings first hand. Knowing Glucke the way he did, the prince understood some of his father's fear that someone was after his throne, and the odds were, Glucke was not the only one seeking it. But the majority of the kingdom, the common people of the realm, had nothing to do with that. Glucke, whom Loris refused to see as a threat, and a handful of others in the royal employ or who shared de Corrmick blood…they were the threats. Any purge of traitors should have begun closer to home, not in the villages in the far-flung reaches of the kingdom. Kjell, however, by Loris' thinking, was not old enough to worry about such things, should not be aware of them. He was safe from such intrigue, at least for a few more years.

The king's voice could be heard from the main hall all the way to the back garden where Kjell planned his own battles as he traced patterns in the damp soil. A name came with the string of nonsense, Ibyll, the second de Corrmick heir. Kjell cocked his head to hear better. When that did nothing to improve his hearing, he got to his feet, brushed the dirt from his blue trousers, and went seeking information.

He found his father in the main hall as expected, wailing over Ibyll's bloody, headless body while Merkar, the prince closest to Kjell in age, stood to one side with a blank, emotionless expression. At least, from the man's clothing and the ring on his right hand, it appeared to be Ibyll. From where he stood, Kjell could not see the man's head.

Merkar was explaining how Ibyll's death had come at the hand of Cordashian scouts and how the entire unit Ibyll had commanded had been slaughtered, but the howling king did not hear any of it.

Kjell, however, heard it all. He was not close to Ibyll, had not liked him, but the elder prince's death, if this was not some sort of deception, left a cold knot in his young stomach. Prince Merkar looked at his little brother, a glint in his eye that was not lost on the youngest de Corrmick. In typical de Corrmick fashion, Kjell decided, backbiting had ostensibly taken its toll again. Ibyll's blood was, he guessed, on Merkar's hands, perhaps the blood of Ibyll's regiment as well. How could the de Corrmick's be expected to win a war against Cordash if they slaughtered their own soldiers in a quest for personal power?

Kjell wondered, for a moment before he crept out of the room, who was more stupid, his father, or Merkar.

Ȿ*Ȿ

The messages received were good ones. King Arlan's forces, as meager as they were, had reached Fiara. And the armies of Cordash had begun their trip along the Dagar River towards Lake Curo. There had been conflict, as expected, but nothing particularly devastating for either kingdom. Now that his way was clear, his safety secure, the King could continue north. He was ready. Come morning, the King of Enesfel would ride into southern Neth for the first time in decades to stake his kingdom's claim.

## ᐦChapter 34ᐦ

The three hundred Nethite soldiers were the last to retreat from the Elyri border, the last to begin the march towards Cordash where the fighting was claimed to be. Their commanding officer was quite inebriated when the orders arrived and the document had been lost in the scatter of debris in the man's quarters. To his credit, as soon as he discovered the misplaced page, he had his unit assembled and marching west within two days. It would not spare him a reprimand, possibly death, but at least his men would not be accused of treason. A charge of treason punished not only an individual but, if the king felt so inclined, their entire family as well.

Expecting eventual combat with Cordash, they were surprised to encounter a significant number of soldiers marching north under the Lachlan standard, far from where Neth's militia was instructed to be. At first, it was believed to be Owain Lachlan's standard, but they realized too late, as the force grew larger before their eyes, that it was not. It was King Arlan Lachlan's standard. Enesfel's army. Though vastly outnumbered, no soldier in Neth would allow the odds to hinder them in defense of their country; to flee such a confrontation meant death at King Loris' hand. Already facing punishment because of the delay in reaching the front, combat with these invaders was the best recourse. Rather than attempt to circumvent the intruders or talk their way past, the commander gave a battle cry that brought his men bearing down on the trespassers with all the fury they could muster.

Enesfel's generals saw the small force before they kicked into action, having enough warning to pull the noncombatants from the ranks and rally the soldiers into a defensive position. Without thinking, acting on decades of instinct, experience, and reflex, Guthrie did what he had always done. Though he had not intended to enter combat, he slammed the visor of his helmet closed, drew his sword, and thrust his heels into his horse's flanks, making the animal jump into action.

Bhríd, Prince Espen, and Sir Gabersdon saw him charge, leading the troops in the place where General Wyndham should have been. All three sped after the chamberlain, Prince Espen because he was worried for the old man in combat and Sir Gabersdon because he was itching for a good fight and would rather die at McHador's side than anywhere else. Bhríd followed for the fight, for duty and honor to Enesfel, and because he knew that, despite the chamberlain's excellent health, the man was no longer in top battle form. The King's champion was bound to the chamberlain's side.

With a violent clash of metal and horses' hooves, the two forces met. Enesfel quickly had the Nethites swallowed in their masses, surrounded with no hope of escape. A swift death with as many kills to their names as possible was the best the Nethites could expect. Guthrie grunted, swinging expertly, slashing through one man after another, tearing them from their horses or knocking them off their feet. He was aware of the Elyri knight behind him and was grateful that Bhríd tried neither to stop him nor slow him down. As far as Guthrie was concerned, this was his fight, one more accomplishment for the annals of his life story, one last bright star, he expected, for the legacy he would leave when he retired.

Thinking the same thing, Bhríd hung back, killing more than was his share, watching the chamberlain from the corner of one eye and Prince Espen from the other. He liked this prince and understood the strategic necessity of fostering a good relationship with him. He did not want the Hatu prince injured or killed on this day or any other. Fortunately, the young man proved to be a more proficient horseman than he was a foot scout.

Head turned as he gutted another opponent, the Elyri chancellor heard a scream. At least, he thought it was a scream, although it was something that reverberated more within his soul than in his ears. He yanked his horse around in time to see Guthrie tumble backward, knocked free of his rearing horse. The animal, with a bloody gash along its flank, kicked as the chamberlain fell, catching Guthrie in the ribs and causing him to fly into someone's shield. Bhríd leaped from his horse; the animal, well-trained to run for freedom when not mounted in a battle situation, charged through the fighting ranks. Cutting through the knees of two Nethites with his razor sharp, Elyri-hewn sword, Bhríd came to stand over the fallen man, where Prince Espen already stood. Back to back, they fought off attackers until bodies lay thick around them, while Sir Gabersdon, who had also witnessed the fall, rode around their position in a tight circle, killing those who tried to get past.

General Wyndham was at the rear of the field, having gotten separated from the chamberlain in Guthrie's initial charge. It was not until Neth's soldiers lay dead, wounded, or were captured, that he was able to weave his horse through the bodies to reach the place where he had seen Guthrie fall. That old fool, he thought, while secretly admiring the man's tenacity and bravery. The general had no intention of riding into battle if he lived to be the chamberlain's age, but he knew he too would have charged and fought if pressed. From a distance, he could see the Harcourt prince helping Bhríd out of his breastplate, and saw the Elyri pull his blood-spattered tunic over his head tearing it as it came off. Sir Gabersdon was already out of his upper armor and tunic and had given them over to Prince Espen for wrappings.

When he reached them, the general found Bhríd tying his shredded tunic around Guthrie's waist, trying to staunch the flow of blood from a gash that had somehow found its way past the man's armor. The chamberlain was awake; despite the loss of blood and apparent size and severity of the wound, he had not yet lost consciousness. His armor was dented from the hooves of his horse and his face was bruised and bloody. Rather than voice the first thoughts that tumbled through his head, Ternce swore under his breath and motioned for Prince Espen to assist him out of his armor. He handed his own sweat-soaked tunic to the Elyri, who shoved it beneath the tie to add further pressure to the main wound.

"I told you not to send Healer MacLyr away," Ternce muttered, his annoyance stemming from his unspoken concern.

"I didn't know my life meant..." started Guthrie with a snort.

The general scowled. "We may not be best friends, but I do not want you to die like this."

The chamberlain coughed, a painful sound that gurgled and rattled in his chest. "Not dying...how would you prefer me to..."

"Enough," Bhríd scolded. "Save your strength. General Wyndham, permission to construct a pallet?"

"I will not be carried..."

In one of the rare instances of raising his voice, Bhríd snapped, "You will, Lord General, all the way back to Fiara. This will not wait for Healer MacLyr to find us; we will find him. There is no other healer in our rank who will be able to save..."

Guthrie's hand closed around the Elyri's wrist. "Then let me die with honor. Die in battle, not," he coughed again, "an old man in my bed."

"Milord! At least allow us to try! I beg you."

The chancellor understood the man's words but was not prepared to give up on the chamberlain's life. Not having the strength to resist, Guthrie lapsed into unconsciousness while Prince Espen continued to apply pressure to the wound that bled in spite of their efforts. Men quickly constructed a makeshift pallet from spears, leather tunics and cloaks, and wooden shields, which was positioned between two horses. The shivering man was placed upon it. He awoke as he was lifted, the pain of movement shooting through him and sending him into fits of coughing. Bhríd, already on his horse, looked with concern to see Guthrie reaching for the general's hand.

"Ternce..." the chamberlain croaked.

Never having heard the man call him by name, the general clasped the reaching hand with his own. "Yes, Milord McHador?" The high title of respect seemed particularly apropos.

"Win this for me," he whispered. "Take all you can get. Do it for Arlan. I cannot..."

His hand fell away, the man unconscious again, and with a wave of Ternce's hand, Bhríd and the three soldiers with him started south with their precious burden. Ternce held his breath as they grew smaller until they disappeared into the forest. He exhaled only when he could no longer see them, and then stared down at his trembling, bloody hand, flexed as if it still held the chamberlain's in his. He suspected, in the depths of his soul, that he had said his final farewell to Guthrie McHador, a knowledge that was icy, heavy, and strangling within.

❧*❦

Kavan slumped forward in his saddle, shrinking into himself as he felt the chasm-like void ahead, felt the world teetering on the brink of it. That void, unexpected as it was, had a name, a name he did not want to know but knew anyhow. Guthrie McHador. Suddenly cold, he began to shiver as the reins slipped from his fingers and he teetered where he perched.

"sínréc?" The healer saw the movement out of the corner of his eye and reached one hand to steady his cousin, to keep him from falling from his horse. His hand jerked back. Even through his clothing, Kavan felt like ice. "tydhá…" He snatched the reins of the bard's horse, bringing both animals to a stop, and dismounted in time to catch Kavan as he fell. Wortham, who rode behind them, stopped to assist, although those in front did not immediately notice. When they did, alerted by the captain's whistle, they turned back.

Ártur tried to lay his hands upon Kavan but the bard brushed them away. "sínréc, please…I do not know how I could have missed any damage, but such a drop in body temperature is indicative of shock. You do not look well. Allow me to…" Wortham squatted beside them, prepared to physically subdue his friend if the healer requested it. He was not going to allow the bard to die out of stubbornness and pride.

"There is nothing you can…it is not me…" Kavan grasped Ártur's hand and allowed that one name to pass through the contact; the healer almost collapsed under the weight of the void Kavan carried.

"What is it, Lord Healer?" asked Prince Muir from his horse.

"Kavan is feeling…faint." The words were true, if not entirely accurate.

"Probably hungry," Caol reasoned, starting to swing down off his horse. "I'm famished…and I wasn't the one who did not eat for almost four days."

"No…" the bard shook his head. If they delayed, it would be too late. If Guthrie had any chance of survival, they needed to hurry. "We eat as we travel; I want to reach Fiara…and a bed…as soon as we can."

Helping his cousin back onto his horse, the healer nodded in agreement. "Who knows what the troops may have encountered during my absence; I should get back. They might need me."

He hoped they arrived in time for those words to still hold true.

❧*❧

Kjell stared silently as the doctor and six soldiers carried King Loris' body from his room, straining under the man's girth. The king's face was more pasty than usual, his puffy blue eyes squinted closed as if he were in pain. There was a great deal of blood staining the bedclothes and the rug, Kjell could see it through the open doorway, and the king's robe was particularly bloody about the sleeves. When Kjell made note of it, he too closed his eyes. His father's wrists were slit. The coward king of Neth had committed suicide.

A small sound came up beside him; Kjell looked to find Merkar standing there. His brother's face was remarkably blank, and although they did not make eye contact, Kjell believed he knew what he would have seen in his brother's eyes.

"Unfortunate," the older prince remarked. "I knew he would take the news badly of so many men lost…and Ibyll too…but I had to tell him. He deserved to know. I did not think he would do this…"

Kjell could not believe the normally angry king would have resorted to suicide either. Loris had been a coward, yes, but he had never been suicidal. Such an act did not fit what he knew of his father. Loris had been too fainthearted for a bloody, self-inflicted death.

Merkar continued, talking more to himself than to Kjell. "We must send word to Earle. He is king; he must return home."

Listening, knowing that each word Merkar spoke carried dual intent, Kjell was relieved when his brother departed. Both knew that slow-witted Earle would not return quickly; his love of bloodshed was too great to draw him from the battlefield and the promise of glory. That would leave Merkar temporarily in charge of the kingdom. If Earle did return home, Merkar would have the honor of leading Earle's top-notched battalion. Either way, Prince Merkar would win prestige and power. King Loris' death would undoubtedly be recorded as suicide, brought about by grief over the death of his son, but it was not true. Kjell knew it. It was what the people would hear, however. They would believe it and silently rejoice at Loris' passing, never knowing for certain if familial infighting had brought him to that end. The prince scurried to his room to pen a letter to General Glucke with the hopes that it would reach the general before Merkar's message did.

᠅*᠅

Lake Curo, the largest inland body of water in the Five Sovereignties, was located in the hear of Neth. It teamed with fish, the staple of many Nethites' diets, even those who lived in the south. There was little land available for farming, and most of what there was normally was used for growing crops, not for grazing livestock. If Enesfel gained control of this region, she would have access to this resource. Fish and lumber. It was one provision King Arlan would be sure to include in the terms of peace. Wherever Prince Valdis was, he carried those terms with him, as did General Wyndham and Chamberlain McHador. King Loris would find the same on all fronts; he would have no choice except to lose the south or lose it all.

General Agis had his men set camp near the mouth of the river, but not directly on the lake shore. If any Nethites planned to come at them by boat, Agis wanted to know about it before they were attacked. Also, Agis, being a man of the desert, was wary of any body of water larger than a river or a pond. He would never admit to being afraid, fear was particularly despised by the Cíbhóló nomadic tribes, but he had no problem making his preference for dry solid land known to anyone who asked.

Construction had begun for the fortification that Cordash was to build when they arrived. The general had decided that he and his men had nothing better to do as they waited. When the Cordashian troops arrived, Agis planned to join the men who would travel along the lakeshore constructing and manning further fortifications. Be it in battle or with hard labor, the general planned to push his usefulness as far as he could.

## ᐒChapter 35ᐒ

**K**ing Renfrid was bone tired. After a night of fighting, Cordash broke clear of the forest and into open country. They were free of that deadly place, where Cordashian soldiers fought poorly, and the goal of pushing across the great span of the Roseieri River towards the city of Nogero was in sight. If he recalled his Neth geography properly, he and his men, reduced by nearly a third, were three days from the capital city of Glevum. He had no intentions of taking the capital if he did not have to. If King Loris was smart, he would surrender before Cordash ever got close to Glevum, and thus would retain his throne. But he knew the tenacity of Neth troops, and King Renfrid suspected, as he pulled the first wave of his men back to rest and allowed the second unit to re-engage the enemy, that he might have to take Glevum to force the desired surrender. He would obliterate Neth and the de Corrmicks if necessary. In the grand scheme of things, that might be the best thing he could do.

In Neth's dwindling ranks, Prince Earle de Corrmick drew back from the front line of combat for an entirely different reason. That reason was a message, a message that made him both queasy and giddy to hear. King Loris, his father, was dead. Suicide. And his brother Ibyll had been killed in battle. That meant that Earle was King. His was the place to guide this war, to make a name for himself in the history books, thus he had to weigh his options carefully. Neth was fairing badly; General Ensgar had word from the other three battalions that all were losing more men than they were killing despite the advantage the forest had given them. On the coast, a port had been captured. In the south, where no men remained to protect de Corrmick interests, Enesfel was said to be pushing towards Lake Curo, aided by any Nethite man, woman, and child who could raise a weapon or farm tool. The commoners were striking back against their oppressors.

Neth should withdraw while they could, regroup and form a new strategy; Prince Earle knew it. But from what he could see, Cordash was weary, fighting on willpower alone and demoralized by the toll the forest had taken. Earle was aware he was slow-witted in many areas but he did not believe that war was one of those areas. If he could conduct one final strike, he believed he could crush the Cordashian army and kill the Valdis prince he had seen in their ranks. That would force them to surrender. If not, he could still inflict several hundred more casualties before retreating in time to save Glevum from foreign marauders.

Mounting his bulky horse, Prince Earle charged to the forefront of combat. He balanced his sword with well-experienced precision, allowing him to kill several as he wove through the ranks. Nethite swords were longer than most used elsewhere, and heavier; in melee, it meant that Cordash was often the loser. But it was the Cordashian archers and cavalry, with their longbows and heavy lances, that were hurting Neth the most, now that they were out of the forest, cutting her ranks dozens of men at a time as one volley after another found their targets.

"Valdis!" cried Earle, seeking to draw his quarry to him. "Come and face me man to man!" His shout went unheeded by the Cordashian prince but several soldiers rushed to defend their leader's honor. Earle killed most of them with ease.

Then, when he least expected it, the man he sought appeared, sitting tall in his saddle, the shape of a bow marking the brow of his helmet and marking him as the Valdis ruler. He held the reins of his horse in one hand, the other, the one that Prince Earle could not see, hung at his side, bloody and limp as if injured. Though Prince Earle could not see the man's face behind its protective visor, he knew who it was.

"You summoned, Prince Earle?"

"King Earle," the challenger gloated, emphasizing his change in title. His apparently unarmed opponent did not react, did not even shift in his saddle or finger the reins nervously. Earle raised his sword, dispensing with any further exchange of words, and charged, not expecting resistance from either the prince or the soldiers nearest him.

His charge halted abruptly when Renfrid raised a small crossbow from the blind side of his horse and released one bolt. It struck Earle between the eyes. Shocked, surprised, the new Neth king tumbled into the bloody dust. The men closest to him, having heard his proclamation of being king, watched him fall.

Not knowing if they had lost the heir-apparent or the king, the soldiers were lost, leaderless. Many withdrew from battle and fled. By the time General Ensgar learned of his commander's fate, he had significantly fewer troops to fight for him. There was one recourse, despite what the de Corrmick's might expect. Thinking it better to protect Glevum's sovereignty, General Ensgar signaled his unit's surrender to the armies of Cordash.

❧*❦

General Marym was puzzled to discover troops already based at the mouth of the Poldris with an outpost structure already under construction. No one was supposed to be there. Worried that it was some faction of King Loris' army who were either trapped on the southern side of the lake or were lying in wait for General Marym's men, the general was relieved to discover the fortress was being built and manned by General Agis and Enesfel's troops. Marym's own fortification was being constructed at the mouth of the Dagar; once that work began he proceeded directly here minus the five hundred men left to staff it. The fleet of small boats that accompanied him spread across Lake Curo, a blockade against any Nethite vessels approaching from the northern side of the lake. The general himself was to continue along the shore towards the Kelari River in the east and then up the Kelari to the foot of the Llaethlágárá Mountains which served as the border between Elyriá and the rest of the Five Sovereignties. Success would cut the kingdom of Neth in two. His mission was half complete, and though he did not believe he needed more men to accomplish it, the addition of Agis and his troops was welcome.

❧*☙

"He is not here."

The bard's voice was brittle and weak as he and those with him passed through the great iron gates of Owain's Fiara home. Though smaller than Rhidam's keep, its exterior was more elaborate and elegant. A towering path of fluted columns led to the house and in the courtyard, a marble fountain gurgled, kissing them with a cool misty spray as they passed. Stained glass of blue, red, yellow and green sparkled in the front windows, facing west into the late afternoon sun, peeping like rows of gaping, arched eyes from the glowing ivory of the stone encasing them. Elyri architecture, Kavan noted, although he doubted any of the town's inhabitants knew that. It was unlikely even Owain knew that he dwelt in a structure of which few examples remained outside of Elyriá.

"Who's not here?"

Kavan shook his head, wearily waving off Muir's question with a groan. He had not spoken of Guthrie, not even to Wortham, as he prayed fervently that his premonition was wrong. Ártur knew, but even the healer did not speak of it. If the chamberlain made it this far from wherever he had been injured, as Kavan suspected, the others would know soon enough. Kavan had spent his journey here caught between praying for a miracle and remembering Wortham's words: it was most often the miracles not asked for that were the ones granted. Perhaps that was true. But in this instance, with a man Kavan considered a friend, a friend and mentor to many, Kavan could do nothing less than beg k'Ádhá to spare Guthrie McHador's life.

"A feeling, my prince."

The elder prince escorted them inside and supplied each with a room, luxurious, plush, and exquisite in detail down to the gilded furnishings and painted ceilings of záryph, stars, clouds, and birds. Kavan wondered, as his cousin helped him up the stairs, how anyone could fail to see how Elyri-like those záryph appeared. Perhaps they had never noticed because many here had never seen an Elyri. Those were all details he observed in passing; in his own room, however, he took no time to examine the décor. He undressed and fell upon the down-filled mattress with a moan. Such comfort was a luxury even without many days of travel behind them.

"Ártur?" he murmured, as the healer, who had escorted him here and thought him asleep, turned to leave.

"sínréc?"

"Can…if I am not awake when Guth…when he arrives…please, fetch me at once…"

The healer looked at his cousin forlornly. "Hoping for a miracle?"

"Hoping, yes. Expecting…No. But I should like to be there…to see him."

One last time, were the words Ártur heard, words that brought a lump into his throat. "I will see that someone fetches you if I cannot."

If the chamberlain was brought here, as Kavan anticipated, Ártur might be busy doing everything in his power to save the man's life.

Kavan's muttered words of gratitude were lost into his pillow as he fell into a much needed, pain-free, sleep.

It was many hours later when he awoke, not the gradual normal awakening but the abrupt sort that indicated something had called to him. He rolled over, sat up, and took a few moments to remember where he was and how he had gotten into this comfortable bed. A large mirror hung across the room, directly in his line of sight. His white skin was mottled with ugly bruising but he still felt as though his appearance was more flawless than he wished. He was growing gradually convinced that even a scar would do little to mar people's perceptions. Even his burns, if the scars had been left upon him, would have done nothing but give him individuality and distinction. He would never blend into normal society.

With a disappointed sigh, he swung his feet to the floor and stood. The rest had done him good, clearing his head and refreshing his spirit. Someone had brought his harp into the room and placed it on the dressing table; he suspected Ártur or Wortham since he normally would have detected anyone else who entered a room when he slept. He dressed and opened the case, intending to take the harp from it, but his hand froze inches above the black wood and his head turned towards the window. The chamberlain had reached the manor, or was approaching; Kavan was not sure which. The sense of him was likely what had awakened him. Eager to greet the man, still praying fate could be circumvented, he tucked his harp under his arm and found his way without directions to the front doors of the estate.

He met no one else on his way. He knew Caol had planned another reconnaissance mission in Fiara for news of the boys, and would not be present, but he saw no sign of anyone else, not even servants, assuming Owain had such. Kavan was the only one to witness the arrival of the four mounted soldiers through the main gates. With them, their charge lay unmoving upon a pallet supported between two of the four horses. Kavan recognized his kinsman and approached silently. Bhríd nodded his acknowledgment but found no words to say in greeting. He was weary from battle and heartsick and suspected Kavan knew everything there was to know already.

Taking Guthrie's hand, Kavan made a swift visual inspection of the man's condition. If not for the blood that stained all of the bandaging around his torso and his tunic from neck to waist, Kavan might almost believe Guthrie was sleeping. That blood, however, proved him wrong. He was no healer, but Kavan knew the chamberlain's condition was grave.

"Kavan?"

"Yes, milord…I am here."

Guthrie's brown eyes fluttered open and he tried to smile. "I would know that touch anywhere. Your hands are…"

Not wanting to hear such words, wanting the man to conserve his strength, Kavan murmured, "Rest, milord…"

"No need." Guthrie's head turned back and forth. "You have…there is no miracle… I can die in peace having seen you one final time."

Kavan blinked away tears he refused to let the other man see. Knowing the chamberlain's words were accurate did not make believing or accepting them any easier. "Owain is here…and Muir. I think they will want to see you before you take leave of us."

At the mention of those two names, the injured man's face brightened and his hand tightened around Kavan's. "I would like to see them…"

"Come then. I will make you comfortable." He stepped back as the soldiers unfastened the pallet from the horses that carried it and motioned for the men to follow him into the manor.

"I do not think that is possible…but thank you."

When they entered the front hall, Wortham was at the bottom of the steps, as if he had reached the ground floor and was pondering where to go. The surprise and dismay upon his face gave birth to a moment's hesitation before he charged up the stairs in search of the healer. Having no direct instruction from Owain, Kavan brought Guthrie into the first empty bedroom he found and helped the soldiers settle him on the bed, the pallet still positioned beneath him to not create additional pain with unnecessary jostling. As it was, the movement of being carried inside renewed the bleeding, but before Kavan could stain his hands, Ártur was there and already striving to heal the chamberlain. With what little strength he had, however, Guthrie grasped the healer's wrists.

"No...do not..."

The healer's grief-stricken face grew paler. "You will die if I..."

"Ártur...you are the closest thing to a brother I have. Give me this honor...please. Allow me to die from battle...not the way Innis..."

Ártur hung his head. He had not been there the night King Innis died; the king had sent him home to visit his family amidst the worst snowstorm of the decade. But he remembered how frail the monarch was at their parting, how certain he had been that the king's death would be soon, and he knew that Guthrie McHador was too headstrong to want to die as a fragile old man. His pride was too great. He would rather be cut down in his prime, in the service of duty and honor, then to dwindle away. For the chamberlain, life was less about the quantity than it was the quality.

"At least allow me to stop the bleeding, to clean you up before the others see you."

The chamberlain nodded his head in agreement, his eyes fixed upon Kavan as if intending to beg the bard if Ártur refused his request.

"Wortham said..." Owain stopped in the doorway, his eyes locking onto Guthrie with a start. "I..." Kavan pulled him into the room and closed the door. Once inside, Owain found the strength to approach the bed. "What happened?"

Enesfel's Chancellor, who stood to one side of the room with the appearance of a guilty man awaiting orders or punishment, murmured, "We met some of King Loris' troops."

When the bleeding was staunched, the healer straightened and wiped his hands on a towel. He wanted to say something, to plead with Guthrie to reconsider, but he understood the chamberlain; respecting the man's wishes was all he could do. Guthrie nodded with a grateful glimmer in his eyes and whispered, "I would like a moment with Owain…alone…and please…send Muir…"

All except Owain exited the room, and Prince Muir was found and sent in, the young man confused by the request and devastated by the news of Guthrie's condition. He and his father spent several hours at the man's bedside as the last of Guthrie's strength ebbed away.

Outside of the room, Ártur squatted upon the floor, staring at the closed door, his hands wringing and toying with the edges of his sleeves. Respecting Guthrie's wishes was essential, but letting him die when he might be able to save him went against every instinct the healer had. Caol returned once the sun set and he and Wortham took places on the hall bench, though the Káliel captain rose periodically to pace the length of the corridor before returning to the bench. The three escorting soldiers stood nearby, talking quietly, reminiscing about the great man's deeds, while Bhríd stood apart, seeming to gaze at the complex thread patterns of a tapestry that hung further down the hall. Directly across from the door, Kavan had not moved since coming out of the room, his harp still in his hands. Eventually, he realized his inaction was not profiting anyone. He could not offer comfort to his cousin, perhaps, but there was someone he could help.

Joining his kinsman, he said quietly, "Do not blame yourself, aendhá. There is nothing you could have done."

Bhríd grunted. "Knowing that makes it no easier; the King will likely blame me…"

"You underestimate Arlan." Though Kavan knew how it felt to be the brunt of the King's blame, he did not believe Bhríd would be held responsible for this. "He, more than anyone, has felt Guthrie's time slipping away. I think that is why Arlan sent him here, to honor the man's unspoken desire to die elsewhere, away from days of deterioration and illness…to die in service to the Crown. I think Arlan knew it would come to this. It may not make it easier for him…but he will understand it is fitting…"

"Fitting, perhaps…but you cannot say you did not have hopes of keeping him with us a little longer." Why else would Kavan have been the first to greet Guthrie upon their arrival, to touch the chamberlain, if not with the hopes of restoring his life?

Kavan sighed. "True…but I am at peace with his choice, Bhríd. It is a noble one…despite the pain he leaves for those of us remaining. There is nothing we can do but accept his wishes and honor them."

The chancellor nodded, his mouth set. "He dictated his final statement as we traveled…told me about Prince Muir…and Prince Owain."

"I thought as much…" His voice faltered as an icy chill, deeper than the one he felt before, passed through him. Kavan closed his eyes, aware of the multiple presences that lingered nearby, unseen but all around them. Feeling the sensation of familiar hands on his shoulders, he turned towards the doorway of the room where Guthrie lay. His breath caught. There was no one near enough to have touched him that way, but he knew who it had been. When the door opened, Owain stepped through it, his face unreadable as he watched Kavan approach. The bard waited for whatever the other man would ask of him. He knew he would do anything.

The once king of Enesfel touched Kavan's face fondly, as he had wanted to do for so long, and he watched the bard's eyes close in an intimate manner that made Owain want to weep. Though he wanted something more, wanted the bard to take his pain away, he did not know what to ask for and settled for a few moments of the feel of the Elyri's skin beneath his fingertips before his hand dropped to his side.

"He is gone."

It was a statement of the obvious. Everyone in the corridor seemed to have experienced that cold chill Kavan had felt. Even the healer did not jump to his feet to see if the prince's words were true; he already knew they were.

"Lord Cliáth...he received no final rite. You are the closest thing we have to a dedhá...and from what I have seen and heard, you may be closer to k'Ádhá than any dedhá could be. Will you say a prayer for him? Something to accompany his departure?"

It was a request, a heartfelt plea, that Kavan could not refuse. He entered the room and settled on the foot of the bed, silently tuning his harp as the others filed in behind him. The bard met Muir's gaze, knowing that the young man knew the entire story. Knew who and what he was, the secrets that Guthrie could have taken to his grave. In the prince's hand was a rolled document, the chamberlain's final statement Kavan presumed. He wondered what it said.

Settled and centered, trying not to look at the unmoving man, Kavan began to sing. Clear, high, and pure, unwritten words of prayer to a tune improvised in this moment, words pouring from his soul in the High Elyri tongue of his ancestors. Ártur understood the pattern of the final rite put to music, but those in the room did not need to understand to be affected by the beauty of the words or music. The presences Kavan felt before grew stronger, a sensation unexperienced since the night Wortham had regained his sight. His eyes were closed, his vision turned inward, but when he heard the captain gasp, "Milord Kóráhm!" he almost fell silent and opened his eyes. This was Wortham's visitation, he decided, not his own, and so he kept them closed. For him, it was enough to feel the saint's nearness in the room, joined by the soul of Guthrie McHador.

The feelings gradually faded as the spirits departed and once they were gone, the harp strings grew still. Again, there were no words to be said, each man looked at the others as they wondered what to do next. With no leads on the children and heavy hearts left in the wake of the chamberlain's demise, none of them knew what lay ahead. Kavan sighed, realizing the decision would be his, that he would have to be the one to push action if they were to continue their quest.

"I think, gentlemen, we should return to Rhidam tonight."

"Tonight?"

"By Gate, Ártur," Kavan said, knowing his cousin wanted him to stay. "There is one here, I am certain of it. An Elyri palace of this opulence would not have been constructed without at least one Gate." The healer was not the only one surprised by that declaration, though none was as surprised as Owain to learn the nature of his home. The bard continued. "There is no sign of the princes here; I think we must return to the beginning. If we take him home, Ártur can preserve him until he can be given a proper burial. By doing this tonight, Ártur can return with Bhríd to the front, as soon as the King joins him."

"King Arlan is coming here?" Owain's voice caught in his throat.

"Then perhaps we should wait…"

"No, Caol…I do not think we should. The King is needed here; his presence will strengthen Enesfel's political position in the region. If we are here, he will want to accompany Lord McHador to Rhidam and spend hours asking questions, which will cause delays for all of us. He may come as soon as this evening, or at the very latest, tomorrow morning. We should be gone before he arrives."

Prince Muir, his hand upon the dead man's ankle, murmured, "What of the horses…and Coris?"

"They will be safe here until we can send for them…Owain can see to their welfare before we depart…unless there are further objections." There were none, for which Kavan was relieved. "Prepare our things and meet me in the Hall as soon as you are ready. I will locate the Gate."

"And if there isn't one?" Owain asked, not knowing what a Gate might be, other than the entrance to the keep.

Imagining such a journey with the chamberlain's body in tow, the crowds of followers that would create, Kavan shuddered, "Then we prepare for a very long ride."

There was a Gate, as Kavan suspected there would be, but rather than in a bedchamber or the private náós as was most common, its creator had centered the Gate in the middle of the manor's main hall where a crimson marble sun was inlaid upon the floor. Not hidden, but out in the open, which suggested a time when Elyri felt no fear of exposure. Both surprised and curious, Kavan dropped to his hands and knees and let the power of the structure bleed into him through his palms. A special Gate, unique in that it seemed to draw power from the ground below. Even with his eyes opened, he could see the familiar points of light, the expected connections to other Gates. From this Gate, however, there were points he had never seen before, destinations he did not recognize. Where did they lead, he wondered, leaning back on his knees as the first footsteps came into the hall.

"Any particular reason you are crawling on the floor, sínréc?"

"I was…" He stopped, noting the amusement in his cousin's voice, and looked up as the other men came in. Owain and Wortham carried Guthrie between them, their faces somber and sad. "I found the Gate, but it is not what I expected."

Curious, the healer stood next to Kavan, and when he focused on the light links that would take them away from where they were, he blinked and stared at his cousin with comprehension and surprise. Kavan was relieved that this was not another incident of something peculiar to him alone.

At his father's side, Muir crossed his arms in annoyance, exhaustion and emotional upheaval making him irritable. He had discovered a grandfather in time to lose him, and they had yet to find his brother or his cousin. He was forced to leave his dog behind. He was in no mood for riddles. "I don't see a gate…"

Shifting the chamberlain's weight to Caol and taking the harp and the packs the inquisitor carried, Wortham stepped forward, assuming the Gate was where Kavan stood, smiling faintly for the first time that day. "Watch, my prince. I guarantee you will never witness anything like this."

Kavan barely refrained from hugging the captain. Such a friend to have so much trust and faith, to be willing to put himself in the Elyri's care. He took the Captain's outstretched hands, positioned him in the center of the circle, and closed his eyes. There was no need to instruct Wortham to relax; the captain's mind was warm, blank, and accepting. The connection to Rhidam was made in an instant.

To Muir's eyes, his tutor and Captain Delamo ceased to exist. One moment they were standing upon the marble sun, the next moment they were gone, and before the prince could ask where they were, Kavan reappeared, alone, with a glimmer in his eyes that brightened his otherwise morose expression.

"Where is…?" the prince began.

"In the upper oratory in Rhidam."

"Home…?" Muir could not believe it. "So quickly? How…?"

"This is how you came into the castle the night…" Owain did not finish; he did not need to. The mystery of how Arlan and his group of friends and soldiers had infiltrated the Rhidam palace without coming in through the main gate had troubled him for years. He was not sure knowing would make any difference to his perceptions of that night, but at least his question was answered.

"Allow me to take Lord McHador; Ártur will come with one of you and I will return for the others."

It was Caol who came through the Gate with Ártur, having traveled by one before though he had forgotten it until tonight. They found Kavan arranging the chamberlain's body upon the altar and took over for him so he could fetch the others. In Fiara, Muir stood with his arms around himself and Owain clutched his bag in one hand, his white knuckles and darting eyes revealing his apprehension.

"I am not sure I can do this," the young prince croaked.

Although Kavan understood Muir's fears, he was still disappointed. "Have I ever harmed you, my prince? Or wished you ill? Do you think I would ask this if it would harm you, if it was not something I am willing to do myself?"

Muir responded to the hurt in the bard's voice by hurrying to clasp his white hands. "No…you would not," he replied. "There is no danger then? Have you been using them long?"

"It is risky for those who do not know how to use them. I am well-practiced; the first time I used a Gate I was six years old."

"Six…" Even Owain found that an amazing claim. Kavan had been six years old when they had first met, all those years ago. He should have paid more attention to his new friend in those days. Things would have been very different for him, perhaps for all of them.

Footsteps heralded Bhríd's arrival, interrupting the conversation, and Muir asked, "Are you coming to Rhidam with us, Lord Cáner?"

"No."

"I am sure Lady Dubuais would be pleased if you did," he said with a strained grin. "Lord Cliáth told us you are to marry."

The black-haired Elyri glanced at his cousin with affection. "I am sure he did. I would very much like to see her. However, I would feel inclined to stay…and General Wyndham will need me more than ever now. Besides…" He groaned. "Someone should be here to tell the King of Lord McHador's passing, and since I was beside him in battle, I think it should be me."

It was not an enviable position, and those in the room nodded sadly. Kavan wondered if he should stay, should face Arlan with this news, but this time he decided Bhríd was right. If anyone should break this news to the King, it should be the man who had been at Guthrie's side.

"Lord Cliáth," Prince Muir murmured, "If you say this Gate will not harm us, I will try it. Father?"

Owain was leery and anxious, but when Kavan offered his hand, the man took it. It was an excuse for contact, and the contact helped ease his nervousness. "I can take you both at once," Kavan said. "There is nothing you need to do except hold my hands and relax. Think of something pleasant and peaceful and do not panic. Whatever you may feel, there is no cause for fear. You will not be harmed, and it will be over quickly." He bowed his head to his kinsman in farewell, knowing Bhríd would pass on his prayers to the King, and then closed his eyes to concentrate.

The passage was as Kavan claimed. Prince Muir felt as if he had barely closed his eyes, imagining himself in a field of spring flowers with Kavan playing his harp nearby, when he was prompted to open them again. He was within the confines of a familiar Purification Chamber, dizzy and disoriented. Nudged through the door, he stepped into Rhidam castle's upper oratory, where Ártur, Caol, and Wortham stood at the altar with Syl beside her husband, fingers entwined. It took Owain moments longer to will his feet to move.

Ártur looked over his shoulder. "I have preserved him; he will remain this way until he is buried."

"Thank you. Syl," Kavan looked past Ártur to the healer's wife. "I must ask a favor. Please inform no one of our return. We need the opportunity to rethink our search for the princes, and I do not think Rhidam is ready for the demise of Guthrie McHador. The oratory will be locked, keeping others out so that he is not disturbed until the King returns to make the public proclamation."

The lady healer nodded. "I have not seen you?"

Smirking, the inquisitor said, "You learn fast. There is no need to tell Deidre yet either; I have no news for her, and I don't want to lift her hopes or dash them prematurely. I'd suggest sleeping in as few rooms as possible…limiting the chances of contact…"

"Use my room…or Wortham's," Kavan suggested. "It is late enough tonight that no one should see you. We should be undetected until morning."

Syl kissed her husband farewell and led the others from the oratory, leaving Ártur and Kavan alone. Owain looked at the cousins and his father, swallowed hard, and then let the door close behind him.

"Ártur?"

The healer did not look at him as he replied, "sínréc?"

"Did we do the right thing? Allowing him to die when it could have been prevented?"

Ártur grimaced. He had stopped wrestling with that moral dilemma the moment Guthrie had died, but the question still haunted him. "He wanted it this way. My calling is to save lives…but I also know that sometimes you have to let go. This was such a time…as difficult as it is to accept it. Respecting his wishes was more important than denying him honor and dignity."

Nodding, Kavan arranged the chamberlain's fingers around his sword's hilt. "I know…but I wanted to hear it. Kóráhm was there; there was no condemnation or anger…it must have been acceptable to allow his passing. But I shall miss him, Ártur. More than I have missed anyone, I believe."

Ártur looked into his cousin's eyes bright with unshed tears. He nodded before speaking. "I know…" Guthrie was the last link between the healer and the first days of his employment to the House of Lachlan. Without him, everything would feel new. "I must go…rejoin Bhríd…"

"Will you tell Arlan…I am sorry?"

"I will."

When Ártur was gone, back through the Gate to Fiara, Kavan knelt in his favored spot before the altar, gazing at the chamberlain's body as he clasped his Kílyn cross in prayer for the repose of the man who had been his friend. He remained in that position all night.

❧*❧

The gold and pink fingers of dawn clawed over the horizon as Enesfel's King hunched in a chair in the room Bhríd directed him to when he had arrived last night, an elegant room in an elegant home that gave Arlan mixed feelings about Owain. A man with such exquisite taste, who took such care of his home, could not be a barbarian…but then again, he was a Lachlan, even if he had spent most of his formative years in Neth. Arlan did not know whether he should admire the man he still felt hatred for, or be disgusted by him.

In his hand, the bottle of wine he had found was empty. He was surprised to discover his chancellor there instead of with the troops, alone except for Owain's meager staff and the three soldiers who had accompanied Guthrie here. He had known from the chancellor's haunted expression that the man bore bad news. How many losses, was the King's first thought? What has become of my troops? Though he expected bad news, he was not prepared for the tale Bhríd told. Enesfel's army had thus far met with success, was faring well. But Guthrie McHador? Dead? It could not be true.

Yet, Arlan knew it was. Ártur came later and confirmed the tale, relaying that the chamberlain's body lay in state in the upper oratory in the Lachlan castle, awaiting burial when the war was over.

Dead. Guthrie was dead. If either the chancellor or healer said anything after giving him the news, Arlan did not hear it. He sank down upon this bench where he had remained as he slipped into a place of memory, of a cabin in the forest near the town of Chantel, and a time so long past it felt as if it had never happened. But it had. This man was the only father Arlan had ever known. There were so many memories that the thought of his death filled the King's heart with the most numbing sort of pain he had ever felt.

The night passed with him still seated at the hearth. Life went on. A strange life, without his friend, mentor, and father figure. King Arlan was too dazed to mourn. The shock was too great, coming as it did on the heels of his wife's loss and the abduction of his son. Gone…and he had not been given the chance to say goodbye. All he could do was wait for his chancellor to come and announce that the horses were ready to travel. Waiting was all the King felt capable of.

## ৯Chapter 36৶

Per their orders, the Cordashian troops closest to the border ceased their forward progression twelve days after crossing into their opponent's territory. Twelve days of fighting, of playing cat and mouse in the forests of Neth. Of Cordash's military strength, nearly a quarter had been lost or were unaccounted for. The cavalry, forced to fight in the trees, was reduced by nearly one-half. Yet despite the heavy losses, reports led King Renfrid to believe that his men had dealt Neth a crippling blow. It was difficult to get a count of casualties when the forest hid many of them, but the decreasing number of attacks and the dwindling number of men in each battle suggested that Neth too had lost a significant percentage of their fighting force.

King Renfrid kept his men where they were, near the city of Nogero, watching the contingent of Neth soldiers camped in the distance. Neth had surrendered, and technically Renfrid could have taken them all prisoner. Or he could drive hard and overthrow Glevum if what Prince…or King…Earle had boasted was true. But Renfrid did not have proof to support Earle's claim, and his spies had not yet returned from Glevum, thus Renfrid preferred to wait. If Earle had been king, it meant that Loris was dead and Earle had now joined his father. The news needed time to reach Glevum, a new ruler needed to be appointed, and then that new ruler would make policy for this war. Perhaps he would wish to continue the fight, or perhaps he would choose to maintain the surrender. King Renfrid was willing to wait for that decision, and poised to strike if the answer was continued war.

❧*☙

Two days' march from the Kelari River, General Yorick Zarkosta stumbled across a small village inhabited by sunken-eyed ghosts who stared as they marched by, their bodies thin and gray from starvation. The apparently failing fields around the village were freshly burned, barren, and the creek that once flowed on its south side was dry. No animals could be seen except for a few emaciated chickens, cats, and dogs. Without moving, without speaking, it seemed these people were begging for any sort of aid his troops could provide. Whether they recognized the soldiers as foreigners or were simply too weak and weary to feel fear, he could not tell. The general sent most of his men ahead and stayed with the remainder, who fanned out through the village and immediate countryside, offering extra rations, extra clothing, and medical aid. Some dug a new well, while others found and destroyed the man-made dam that blocked the river, allowing the water to flow again. It was not something they needed to do, was not in the parameter of their mission and duty, but the youngest general could not bring himself to ride by without trying to help.

These people might soon be citizens of Enesfel. Offering aid was the kindest, wisest thing to do.

His generosity was met by a ragtag contingent of Nethite soldiers whose appearance caught the general's troops unprepared. He did not think they had gotten past his perimeter guards, but if they had been hiding throughout the village, waiting to ambush them when their guard was down, they had done a good job of it. The sounds of fighting echoing from every corner of the village suggested he was outmanned. He stepped into the street from the storage hut he had been inspecting, his sword, shield, and mind ready for whatever horror he was about to confront.

He stopped. To his surprise, most of the ruckus he heard and saw was not caused by his men. The villagers who were capable of it were fighting back, trying to pummel their own countrymen with their last morsel of strength, fighting side by side with Enesfel's troops. Perhaps they would not win, the general mused, but working in tandem with these determined people gave him a sense of pride.

He entered the fray, making it his task to go from hovel to hovel, flushing out any Nethites that might be there. He found several, some hiding, some scavenging, some hunting down the helpless. A more discreet combatant than either General Agis or General Wyndham, Yorick entered each hut with little announcement, waited for the enemy to sense him, and then stole their lives as quickly and efficiently as possible.

It took time, and more casualties than he liked, but by nightfall, General Zarkosta was satisfied that there were no further enemy soldiers in the area. He had lost many men himself, but Enesfel's unit lived. The enemy was defeated. He could ask for little better than that. He flopped down upon a wobbly wooden bench which groaned under his weight, in order to catch his breath.

"Milord?" The man who approached might have been young, or might have been very old. Hunger had robbed him of his normal appearance and strength and had put a strain on his voice. "I am sorry…for this…they came…yesterday…burned the fields though I don't know why. They knew you were coming…said King Loris sent them…we could not fight…did not know they…"

Yorick offered a sympathetic smile that covered his hidden concern. "You found the courage to fight them today." He had already concluded that the villagers' plight had been set as a trap; if anyone was at fault for this battle, it was his for not being more careful.

How, he worried, had King Loris known they were there?

"We had you to fight with us…and hindsight…"

"You acted with self-preservation. I do not fault you for that."

"But your losses…"

Yes, the general sighed. There had been many casualties. But to his knowledge, the one hundred and twenty Nethite bodies he counted were enemy soldiers. He was reasonably confident that few, if any, had escaped. Still, it felt like a defeat. And if any soldiers had gotten away from Enesfel's men, more might return if they could find support.

Because Yorick could not imagine leaving these people undefended, he left all but twenty of his men when he set off to rejoin his unit, intending to send more men back to defend the village and his own flanks. If nothing else, having an outpost to fall back on would be to Enesfel's benefit.

⊱*⊰

As soon as Prince Muir fell asleep in Kavan's bed, Caol snuck out of the bard's room, out of the keep to wander Rhidam, hoping to learn more than what little they knew about the disappearance of his son. The warm night was spent cornering contact after contact, looking for any information about Halstatt they had overlooked or that might have surfaced during their absence. Part of him believed Halstatt might never have left Rhidam, might still be here, and if he was, the inquisitor intended to find him. While the Association was a little more willing to cooperate, a little more forthcoming with their information now that it was officially known that Halstatt had made hostages of the royal children, now that they knew that, without their help, the inquisitor would be within his rights as a former member, to tackle the whole of the organization and bring them before the king for punishment, there was nothing useful to learn. As far as Caol could learn, no one had seen or heard anything. Maybe he was wrong. Maybe Halstatt was not in Rhidam as he wanted to believe.

The sinking sensation within him hit bottom. It had been too long. He had little hope that Halstatt would return the children and doubted they were alive. It was his stubbornness, and the conviction that he would be unable to face Deidre if he did not find Wilred, that kept him from abandoning the quest. It was his inability to face his wife that led him to take a room in the shabbiest inn he could find, the sort of place where Deidre would never look for him, the sort of place where Halstatt would be, if indeed he were still in Rhidam. Caol would sleep there until he found his son.

He rose when the sun indicated it was near dusk again. Just as well. He could search at night as easily as he could by day, and there was less of a chance of encountering his wife or any member of the royal staff.

Penning a quick message to Kavan, he informed the bard of his location and plans. Odd, he thought, that he should trust the bard with this more than he trusted his wife. They had lived within the same walls for nearly thirteen years, but having learned more about the Elyri in the past few weeks than he had known before, Caol could not imagine mistrusting him. If there was any chance of finding Prince Bertram and Prince Wilred, Kavan was that chance, and hiding from him too was not going to help.

He took an empty seat to dine in the tavern downstairs, his back in the corner to watch the patrons with veiled interest. There was no one familiar, only the barmaid, and his attention began to slacken as the minutes passed; he perked up each time the door opened and another patron entered for a drink or a meal, but time after time he was disappointed. The odds of anyone interesting coming into this particular tavern were low, but he was watchful nonetheless.

As Caol finished his meal and pushed the tray away, thinking it was time for a new plan of action though not yet deciding what that

was, a sharp-featured man entered, cast a quick look around, and then settled at the bar for a drink. His shoulders were hunched, as though he was old or frail, but his features were too smooth for either age or infirmary. The man's hair was dark, his face unshaven, and though he did not seem threatening as he ignored everyone in the room, experience suggested to Caol that his posture was hiding something. There was something familiar, something the inquisitor believed would be dangerous if he failed to recall who the man was. Not Halstatt…but who?

When the stranger finished his drink and left, having enjoyed it alone without meeting or speaking to anyone, Caol followed, trailing in the shadows, staying out of sight. The fellow had a room in the Eagle's Nest Inn near the castle, a fact that set off alarms in Caol's head though he had yet to determine who this man was. He could have bought his drink here, instead of the tavern where Caol had seen him; maybe he had intended to meet someone there who had failed to show. Maybe his being there had been a signal to someone Caol had not seen. Maybe Caol had been meant to see him. Whatever the case, his behavior was suspicious enough to make him worth watching, and Caol took a position in a nearby alley to do just that.

&#x6B;*&#x6B;

"I am glad you are back, Lord Cliáth, even if you have not found Bertie yet."

The bard held Princess Diona on his lap, vaguely uncomfortable with holding her for the first time. She seemed older, her actions and the kiss she planted on his cheek more befitting a young woman than a child. But he tolerated it because he was relieved to see Arlan's other two children were healthy and safe. Across from him, Syl, Princess Deidre, and Madalyn Dubuais conversed quietly, watching Bianca and Prince Hagan play upon the floor. Owain and Prince Muir were with them initially, but both departed to be near Guthrie. None had spoken of the chamberlain all day.

"Lady Dubuais, I have heard you are to marry my cousin," the bard started, seeking conversation as a distraction from both the topic of the missing boys and the discomfort he felt holding Princess Diona.

The duchess blushed. "An abrupt courtship, I know, but there are reasons…"

"I do not need to know them," he assured her. "Bhríd is too wise, honorable, and willful to do something he does not wish to do. I do not question his choice…or yours, only wish to welcome you…"

Turning in her chair to face him more fully, she asked, "It does not trouble you that I am Teren?"

"No. Should it?" He was relieved that the princess slid off of his lap to play with the younger children. "It makes no difference. I welcome you into my family, regardless of the opinions of others."

Madalyn shrugged and got to her feet with an impish smile. "If I cared what people thought, I would have married long ago to avoid the novelty and challenge of running my estate. What others think of this union does not trouble me…but I am grateful that you and the MacLyrs have accepted me. It will make the other nonsense easier to tolerate. If you will excuse me, milord" she curtsied, "I wish to retire."

Once parting greetings were exchanged and she was gone, Syl spoke softly so that Princess Diona might not hear her. "She might have little regard for the opinions of others, but she has already suffered one attack because of her choice."

Kavan frowned. "Attack? Bhríd said nothing…"

"He does not know. It occurred after he left. If she had her way, he might never know, but the King wishes to commend Mr. Flannery for his bravery in protecting her. If he had not been there, she might have been killed."

Anti-Elyri violence was spreading. It had started, as he had warned Gabrielle it would. The thought made him sigh and shiver.

Syl continued. "And to lose Chamberlain McHador. If Prince Bertram is not found, the King might never recover from the losses of this year." It was an obvious truth, an incentive Kavan did not need to continue the search. The healer scooped up Bianca and gestured to Princess Diona who picked up her little brother. "It is time for you children to be in bed. Your father might not be here, but there are still rules to obey…"

"I wish there were not," the princess admitted. "May I…I wish to talk to Lord Cliáth before I sleep." Though Kavan did not see the looks that passed between the princess and healer, he did see Syl roll her eyes before nodding and leaving the room. Princess Deidre took Prince Hagan from Diona and the attending servants followed.

Alone with her tutor, the princess settled on the floor at his feet, a position she took as often as Prince Muir would relinquish it. With her older brother not there to claim that spot, the princess was happy to take it now. She did not speak immediately but appeared content to stare at him. Such perusal would not normally bother Kavan, but there was something in the way her gaze traced his features as if devouring him, that was unsettling. "Lord Cliáth…Father told me you will no longer be my tutor. Is it…have I done something wrong?"

The question was a relief; he had expected something more difficult to answer. "Of course not. You know you have not. You are becoming a woman; it is time you have a woman tutor, that is all."

Princess Diona scowled. "What can a woman teach me that you cannot?"

"How to be a woman. As you can see, I am not one; I know nothing about being one…except that it is different from being a man."

"I do not want to be a woman," she pouted.

Head cocked, Kavan leaned forward, elbows on his knees and hands balled under his chin. "Why not?"

"I do not like the way women are treated. There is so much we are not allowed to know…or do. In Hatu, Prince Harcourt says that men, noblemen at least, do not associate with women, even their own mothers or sisters or those they marry. I do not think that is fair."

Curious about her knowledge and interest in Hatu's customs, and why such things should matter to a girl her age, Kavan said, "To our way of thinking, it is not, you are right. But things are changing in many places…else Lady Dubuais would not have control of her estate. Women are considerably freer in Enesfel than Hatu, it is true, but…"

"How are women treated in Elyriá?"

"Women hold much of the power in Elyriá; in the home, the woman is the head…" he fleetingly thought of his own family, "usually. We have…women can do what men cannot. They bear children. That gives them a place of distinction. In my experience, while men serve well as protectors, it is the woman who best understands the needs of her family, her neighbors, her community. Men, even Elyri, are frequently more goal-oriented, more self-oriented, and less caregivers…less forgiving, quicker to anger, more violent. I suspect," he gave a rueful smile, "that if the Sovereignties were ruled by women, life would be more peaceful and plentiful."

"Do you think…could I rule?"

Kavan hesitated, not wanting to reveal more about the future than he thought she should know. "Bertram is the heir to the throne. When your father dies, Bertram will be king. There is no law that would prevent you from ruling, however…should circumstances permit it. It is possible that you could be a ruling queen."

"I see." Her gaze drew away from the edges of his face to focus on his eyes. "What about you?"

"Me? I am not a Lachlan…"

The princess giggled. "No…I don't mean that. You are not like other men. You are not…what did you say…self-oriented. You are more like…more like women…yet not…"

He winced and hoped that the princess did not see it. Her question was innocent, but being called less than a man by a little girl was painful. Usually, he had answers for her questions, and he wanted to answer this one, but the personal nature of the topic, a discussion of his masculinity, was something he could not have with anyone, particularly the young princess.

Sensing that he was not going to answer without understanding why, the princess shrugged. It was not the first time Kavan had not given her answers; she assumed he did not have one to give her. "If I cannot be the queen, what future do I have? I do not want to spend my days sewing, gossiping, and looking for endless ways to entertain myself with empty-headed, shallow women who only want to marry and have a family."

Her words made him smile faintly. "You will find your way. Everyone does. I have faith in you."

"It is good that someone does." Her smile brightened as she got up from her knees. "Did you see my father or Prince Harcourt?"

"No...I did not. Now...what is this talk about Prince Harcourt?" It was not the first time she had mentioned the Hatu prince.

His interest made her smile widen. "He brought troops from Hatu and went to Neth with General Wyndham. I met him when he was here. I was wondering how he is faring." She bowed rather than curtsied, and murmured, "Good night, Lord Cliáth," before skipping out of the room.

Kavan was mulling over Diona's interest in the throne, himself, and Prince Harcourt...all grown up concerns which supported his perceptions that she was no longer, at least intellectually, a little girl...when a sentry brought the inquisitor's message. Not that he needed it; he knew what Caol was doing, not by Sight but by instinct. He had gained an understanding of the man during their travels, as Caol had grown to better understand him. Kavan had also gained considerable respect for the redhead. The one thing he had known, as soon as they returned to Rhidam, was that Caol would be carefully balancing between his wife and the justice as long as he was in the castle. Apparently, Caol had elected to remove himself from that balancing act for as long as possible, as long as necessary.

Through the window, Kavan could see the summer stars. There was the smell of moist earth in the air, the smell of freedom. Stifled and frustrated by their lack of progress and by the haunting thoughts about who and what he was, he suddenly felt in need of flight. No one was in the room to hinder him and there was nothing more he could do tonight. Giving in to temptation, Kavan set aside duty for a few hours and lifted into the night air to fulfill that need, hoping that when he returned, he would have answers or at least a course of action.

๛*๙

"Lords Cliáth and Dugan have returned to Rhidam?"

The information was news to k'gdhededhá Jermyn, telling the justice that the clergyman had not seen either of the men he was seeking. Upon learning of the men's return, the justice had spoken to Prince Muir and Captain Delamo, the first two he was able to find. The captain answered few of the questions put to him, though not out of a lack of information, Minos was certain. Despite the captain's oath to the King of Enesfel, Wortham's first loyalty had always been to the Elyri bard. He would say nothing unless Kavan allowed it, and Justice Cornell was not about to arrest or punish the man for that. The justice refrained from asking Prince Muir most of the questions he had simply because Muir was royalty. The justice had no desire to find himself in trouble with the King and he saw little reason for any of the answers he sought to reside within the inexperienced prince.

The justice also could have approached Prince Owain, but the man's presence in Rhidam made him uncomfortable, like being in a room with a ghost, thus Minos avoided him. He decided instead to speak with either the inquisitor or the court bard. The Elyri had been seen in the company of the palace's women, and wanting to avoid a spectacle in front of gossipy ladies, the justice had opted to wait until morning. The inquisitor, on the other hand, was not on the palace grounds, at least not as far as Minos could determine, and no one had seen him since his return to Rhidam. In Minos' eyes, it meant Caol had something to hide, had some reason to avoid people, and it made the justice more determined to find him.

"I apologize for troubling you this late, k'dedhá. I hoped to speak with both men today, but have been unable to. If you see either of them, particularly Lord Dugan, will you please let them know I am looking for them, ask them to see me?"

Curious and suspicious, the tone of the justice's voice implying more than the words themselves, Jermyn asked, "Have you news of the boys? I am sure they will welcome hearing it."

"Unfortunately no," the justice sighed. "I do have questions about the day they were taken, however. I do not know how relevant the questions are until I ask them."

The k'gdhededhá cocked one eyebrow but did not pester the justice for details. The justice sounded distrustful, an unfortunate thing, surely, for anyone on the receiving end of that suspicion. Jermyn did not like the feeling forming in the pit of his stomach. Surely the inquisitor was not to blame for harming his own son. What sort of man would do such a thing?

Clanging in the street woke Caol from his restless sleep but it turned out to be the changing of the palace guard rather than a fight. He had abandoned the first dingy room he had taken and chosen one in the Eagle's Nest instead, despite its proximity to the castle, in order to keep an eye on the unknown but familiar man. After sleeping half of the day, he had not expected to fall asleep tonight. He had been writing, something he sometimes did to clear his thoughts, letting his mind wander to make connections between his conscious and unconscious mind. Sometime while writing, he dozed at the desk, his head drooping upon his chest in a posture that now left his neck stiff and sore. He had not been asleep long, however, for in spite of the stiffness in his neck and shoulders, the candles in the desk sconce had burned down very little.

With the night silent again, he began reading what he had written and was slightly appalled at his preoccupation with death, disaster, and failure. Little of what he had written made sense, though it must have seemed sensible when he set it down, or at least he had been hoping to make his tangled thoughts make sense. But there was nothing there, no trails or logic threads, to make any sort of direct link to either Tarmajien or the children.

Tarmajien. His head snapped up and turned towards the night sky, causing a sharp pain in his neck as he stared at the moon through the open window. There was a connection to his writings after all. The man he had seen, the one he had been following, was a Tarmajien. Perhaps not by name, perhaps not even a close relative. But he was part of that bloodline. The thin face and shape of his jaw were the telltale features of the Tarmajien clan, features Caol should have recognized sooner. If this fellow was here, taunting him, it could not be a coincidence. Perhaps Halstatt was not as far away as Caol feared. Perhaps all it would take was a little deeper digging and putting more pressure on his information resources. If necessary, he would corner the stranger and torture him until he talked. Grabbing his cloak, he blew out the candles and scampered into the night. This was news he had to share with Kavan, and k'gdhededhá Jermyn was the best way to get a message to him without facing anyone at the castle.

૱*ક૬

"Lord Cliáth does not appear to be here," Wortham said with disappointment as he entered the library where Princes Owain and Muir waited. He had donned his armor, expecting to rattle his way through Rhidam in the search for clues, and Owain, choosing to keep himself as unrecognizable as possible, was dressed in the plainest, simplest clothing he had been able to find. Any attention the once-king of Enesfel might draw to himself was not going to help find the missing children. Owain was certain his identity being known would only make the situation more difficult.

"Where would he have gone?" the younger prince asked, a note of distress in his voice. "He would not have continued the search without us, would he?"

"He might have, my prince." It would not be the first time Kavan had done such a thing. "But I suspect he is merely off the grounds." Wortham saw no reason to assume the worst. Even if Kavan had gone to search alone, he would have his reasons, and Wortham trusted him. "He might have gone to speak with k'dedhá Jermyn…"

"With those Gates, he could be anywhere, couldn't he?" Muir crossed his arms as he scowled.

"I cannot say…it is impossible to do more than guess. But I suggest we do not loiter. The morning is half gone and Rhidam is a large city. Wherever he is, he would not expect us to dally. He would want us to continue looking for the boys."

"The sooner we start, the sooner we may learn something useful." Owain placed one hand on the young man's shoulder and squeezed gently. "I want you to remain here…"

"But…" He had been helpful thus far; being excluded now on top of Kavan's absence made Muir angry.

Owain gripped his other shoulder too and looked him squarely in the face, man to man. "I could not bear to place you in danger…in the path of the kidnappers. Besides, someone should be here when Lord

Cliáth returns…or in case Lord Dugan tries to contact us. We need a liaison…please…do this for me, if not for your brother and cousin."

Muir straightened his posture. At least he was not being belittled or insulted. He might not appreciate being left behind, but his father had valid points and thus the prince sullenly agreed to remain. He stayed at the window, trying to think of a way to help as the older men left the room. Waiting for messages, or men, who might not come did not feel like helping to him. Muir wanted to do more.

❧*❦

Princes Merkar and Kjell sat together, sharing their morning meal at the long dining table devoid of anyone else today, an awkward silence hanging in the air. Kjell strove with each glance, with each sigh and sniffle, to convince his brother that his grief over the deaths of his father and brother created his silence because it was safer for him if Merkar believed that. The actual cause of the silence stemmed from the conviction that Merkar had killed one de Corrmick heir, the king, and might wish to do the same to Kjell.

But Prince Kjell had a network in place, a safety net to protect himself should he decide his life was in danger. He knew what to do and where to go the moment he felt threatened, knew who he could turn to. He had mastered the art of feigned innocence and ignorance; Merkar had no reason to suspect or fear him. Nor did Earle. Kjell's life would not be at risk until another heir was born, unless he gave away his understanding of the events around him…or General Glucke betrayed him. Because Glucke knew that Prince Kjell held his best chance for an increase in power, the likelihood of betrayal was slim; it seemed for now that the youngest de Corrmick prince was safe.

The forest green curtains separating the dining hall from the corridor parted and a dusty, beleaguered messenger entered. His halfhearted bow spoke of weariness and fear.

"Has Earle returned?" Merkar drawled over the lip of his goblet.

"Prince Merkar, the Prince Earle…" the man began to stutter.

"King Earle," Merkar corrected with a touch of acid in his voice.

Trembling, the messenger bowed again as contritely as he could. "King Earle…was killed in battle…by Prince Valdis…" he faltered, not realizing that Renfrid was no prince himself any longer, but also now a king. "Our troops are broken, milord; General Ensgar has issued provisional surrender and sends you this…" He held forth a tattered scroll, prepared to yank his hand away as soon as Merkar took it to prevent losing his limb beneath the man's sword. "There are endorsements from General Glucke too. Leadership is required."

Merkar's lips pursed into an angry frown, his eyes flashing with fury, but Kjell could tell that underneath that rage was a sense of satisfaction. Though Merkar could not be suspected or blamed for Earle's death, he had gotten what he wanted. The throne of Neth. Though not privy to Merkar's thoughts, Kjell felt confident of what should be done in this situation, and knew what his brother was likely to do. Starting his reign with a defeat was not ideal for any king, but the de Corrmick's were skilled in the manipulation of public perception. Turning these events into a boon for his people, turning himself into a savior for upholding a surrender that prevented the ruin of the realm, was an easy thing for a de Corrmick. If Merkar wished to keep the throne he had been given, he needed to negotiate. To do anything else would cost his rule, and might cost all of them their lives.

The last time Prince Muir had seen k'gdhededhá Tythilius, he had been heavily under the sway of a miracle and had wanted to embrace the life of Faith as a gdhededhá himself. Today, having experienced so much in a few short weeks, the prelacy was the furthest thing from his thoughts. He was the grandson of Guthrie McHador, the son of a prince, and his brother was missing. There was too much for him to do in the world to limit himself to the halls of Faith.

"I am sorry, Your Grace, but Lord Cliáth is not here."

"Oh, mercy…" Jermyn wrung his hands. "Lord Dugan said it was important that I deliver this to him personally and promptly…"

"About Bertram and Wilred?"

The k'gdhededhá wiped his sweaty brow. "I assume so; I know of nothing else pressing. Can you give this to him as soon as he returns?"

Pleased to have a responsibility at last, Prince Muir held out his hand. "I will wait at the front gate for him if I must," he promised. Or the oratory, or his room, whichever seemed most gainful. The folded and sealed parchment was placed in the prince's palm, and Jermyn bowed and retreated from the room after a hastily muttered farewell.

The prince stared at the parchment for a long time. He did not know where Kavan was or when he would return. If the message was important, if it had anything to do with his brother and cousin, then surely reading it could not wait until the bard returned. The prince could read it and convey the information to his father and Captain Delamo and let them decide what should be done. However, if the message had nothing to do with his brother and cousin, if it was some personal matter between Caol and Kavan and Muir read it, he would be breaking the bard's confidence.

In the end, his choice was to break the seal. Under the circumstances, he believed both Kavan and Caol would forgive him for reading the message, personal or not. He read the contents twice, but it told him nothing he could use. The name Tarmajien was unfamiliar. Why should the bard care if a man by that name was in Rhidam? Was it connected to Bertram and Wilred? The prince wished he knew.

"What are you reading, Prince Muir?"

Startled, the prince did his best to make folding the parchment seem casual before he pushed it into his tunic's breast pocket. He had not noticed the justice's arrival and the tone of the man's question set the prince on edge. "A personal letter from my father," he lied.

"King Arlan has sent word?"

Muir's face flushed. "The King is not my father, Lord Justice. Surely you know that after all these years."

Chastised, the justice flushed too and bowed. "My apologies, Prince Muir." He had known that, of course, but he had yet to come to terms with Owain Lachlan and had not given that relationship much thought. "Have you seen Lord Cliáth or Lord Dugan?"

The prince leaned against the nearest end table and shrugged. "I have not seen Lord Cliáth since last night, and have not seen Lord Dugan since our return," he said earnestly, volunteering no further information though it appeared the justice was waiting for more.

He had been hoping for more, hoping for at least a mention of where the bard and inquisitor might have gone or where they might be found. With no details forthcoming, and not wanting to be accused of interrogating royalty, the justice bowed again. "Can you please let them know I must speak to them…if you see either?" he asked.

"Of course." Muir wished he knew what the justice wanted, but he could not ask questions when he was not willing to answer any in return. He wondered if the justice's inquiries had anything to do with the letter in his pocket, and how he could possibly get messages to the inquisitor and the bard.

❧*❧

Kavan had not meant to fly as far as he had, had not intended to fall asleep at his lakeside, but he had. Again. Unlike the last time, however, he did not wake with a feeling of calm and serenity. Very little in his life was right. Except for the attack in Neth, this mission had drawn his thoughts away from himself. His frustration had been temporarily subverted. But Brenna was still gone, Guthrie was dead,

Enesfel was at war, and Prince Bertram and Prince Wilred had not been found. There had been too many negative incidences in too short a time, all coming when he felt the most exposed and raw. It made sorting out his thoughts and feelings difficult.

And his position at court was about to change. Assuming that the princes were found alive, he would still function as their tutor, but Princess Diona would no longer be in his care. Most likely, he would be left with Wilred, who had little passion for book learning, until Prince Hagan was old enough to be teachable. After recent events, Kavan believed Muir would no longer reside in Enesfel; the prince would either assume his title as Duke of Alberni or would go to Fiara with Owain. It was time for the eldest prince to make his way in the world, yet Kavan did not want to let him go. He would need something new to occupy himself, something to keep that underlying frustration from surfacing again.

After staring across the lake for a long time, drying from his earlier swim and pondering the unexpected turns his life had taken, Kavan started back to Rhidam. His absence would likely be causing Muir, at least, great anxiety, and he was eager to learn if there had been any success while he had been away. It was time find the princes.

"In a hurry, Lord Dugan?"

The inquisitor came to a halt as he started past the alley, stopped by a big hand upon his arm, holding him fast. He had thought the pit in his stomach, which had grown deeper since last night's realization, would grow no colder, but he had been wrong. Further down the street, his quarry was gradually being swallowed by the morning street crowds. Struggling to appear calm, he looked the taller man in the eye and said, "I have business, Lord Justice." He noted without taking his eyes off of Minos that the justice was not alone.

"What sort of business?"

"Personal…and none of your concern."

Minos narrowed his eyes. "I have heard that remark once too often today. Whatever your business is, it will have to wait…"

"No, it cannot…"

"It can," he emphasized the final word, "and it will…unless you prefer I place you under arrest in the middle of Rhidam and drag you back to the castle in chains to ask you some questions. An unsightly measure to be sure."

The inquisitor's mouth snapped shut. Unsightly, and not good. Not good at all. "Ask your questions," he grunted, waiting for queries he was sure he would not like or be able to answer.

"The day of Lady Lísbhet Dilyn's death, you received a delivery?"

This was going to be worse than he imagined, although he did not yet know how much the justice knew. "We do not know what day the Lady died, Justice Cornell…only what day her body was found."

The justice grunted. "We have an idea based on the good authority of Healer MacLyr. Be that as it may, you did receive a delivery? A box?" There was no reply. "What was in it?" Again there was no reply and the corner of the justice's eyes began to twitch. "Then perhaps you would care to tell me something about the man who delivered it?"

"General Zarkosta?" Caol asked innocently. Yorick had been the man to deliver the box into his hands, though not the one to deliver it to the castle. Since Minos had not clarified his request, the answer was honest enough.

"Do not play games with me, Lord Dugan."

"I would never play games with you." His tone and expression suggested that the justice did not know the meaning of the word play, and brought a darkening pall over the justice's face.

"If that is how it must be, I am placing you under arrest."

The inquisitor growled and tried to take a step back but Minos' hand was still on his arm. "Under what charges?"

"Suspicion of murder, suspicion of collusion against a foreign dignitary and against the Crown, and custody of the murder weapon"

"You have no proof!" Caol's body tensed, preparing him to flee, but he knew there would be no easy way out of this situation. He was confident that no one had found the dagger; the justice's accusation was entirely speculative for the time being. There was suspicion enough, but to Caol's knowledge, there was no proof.

"You are right, I do not. But I have the reports of four men who know you received a box the day the lady's body was found. One was diligent enough to look inside, and do you know what he found?"

Caol grunted. "I wouldn't even try to guess."

"A Coryllien dagger, the murder weapon most likely unless two of the daggers have arrived in Rhidam at the same time…"

"You have proof it was the Coryllien…or is that supposition?"

The justice chose to ignore the question. Not having seen the dagger himself, he had no proof that what the sentry had seen was, in fact, a Coryllien. All he had was his belief that there were no other triple-edged daggers in existence and that this one in question had to be a Coryllien. "Will you come peacefully or must I bind and drag you in like a common criminal?"

Eyeing the two brutish men in armor behind the justice, Caol opted for the peaceful approach, wondering how he was going to get out of this without proof of his own, without revealing a past he had hoped would remain hidden.

He was led through the streets, into the castle, through the side hall, down the stairs, and into the dungeon. He had been here before, but never as a prisoner. Soon, his wife would hear of this and would come to confront him. What would he say? What could he say? He was placed in a cell and the justice left him without word or further questions. No warnings, no threats, just deafening footsteps and then silence. It was the sound of the dungeon door closing above that was the most deafening sound of all.

## ❧Chapter 37❧

Kavan watched the man behind the bars who had, until his arrival, been pacing furiously in an effort for his body to keep up with the frantic pace of his thoughts. Arriving home to learn of Caol's arrest from Justice Cornell, the bard had done everything he could to win the inquisitor's freedom before coming to see him, but to no avail. "I am sorry, Caol. I besought Justice Cornell to release you, insisted that your assistance is necessary if the princes are to be found, but he does not agree…and he seems to believe I am an accomplice to the Lady's demise…"

The inquisitor leaned against the cell wall and folded his arms across his chest as if to contain his annoyance within himself. "Direct accomplice no, but you do have information that you have not given him. That could be viewed as an accessory. But regardless of what he thinks he knows, or what he believes, he is not likely to arrest you. He would never dare Arlan's wrath."

Kavan knew that was true but chose not to acknowledge it. Being the King's best friend could be as much of a curse as a blessing, particularly when that best friend was Elyri. "There is no reason to tell him about Halstatt. The justice will not be able to locate him any better than we can, and to bring mention of the Association into this will convince him further of your guilt."

"Guilt by association..." Caol, in his state of stress, began to giggle uncontrollably.

Believing laughter was a reasonable cure for the other man's anxiety, Kavan did not interrupt but instead waited for Caol's mirth to fade naturally. "Did you find anything?"

"Didn't the k'dedhá deliver my message?"

"I was not in the castle yesterday and returned too late last night for anyone to notice. If I had been, I would have come to you sooner."

"Oh." It explained his night alone in this dusty cell, although he suspected the justice had not told anyone he was there to rattle his nerves. He wiped his face and continued, "I found a man...I did not know who he was when I first spotted him, but I realized finally that he's a Tarmajien."

"Halstatt?"

"No...but a relative. Probably a cousin, but I don't know for sure. I was following him when Minos..." He shrugged. There was no point in being bitter about losing his prey. "His presence in Rhidam can't be a coincidence. Tarmajiens never stray far from Durham without good reason, and Halstatt's doings in Rhidam would definitely constitute a good reason. Maybe he's looking for him...maybe he's here to help...but he's here."

"Did he know he was being followed? Might he be trying to lead you off track?"

"I don't believe so. He saw me but did not seem to recognize me...and thus far all I've seen him do is eat, drink, and shop for livestock without actually buying any." Caol thought that was suspicious, but it was possible the man was either checking out the competition or else was shopping for the best animals for his money.

"Good...let us hope he does not suspect you." Kavan offered his hand. "Will you show me what he looks like? Ártur is not here to draw him, but I can pass the depiction to Wortham and Owain, so they can seek him."

He had seen this particular act but had never been part of it; with nothing to hide at this moment, nothing to hide from the bard at least, Caol clasped the offered hand. Knowing he had to focus on what Kavan wanted to see, he brought that face to mind as Kavan reached through the bars to cup the inquisitor's hand in his own. The contact lasted no longer than a handshake before the bard pulled away, and Caol felt nothing but the touch of the Elyri's hand.

"There is a resemblance…that is good. Perhaps…" The bard looked at the bars between them and down at the lock and latch. "Perhaps your arrest can be used to our advantage."

"How?" Caol had not imagined anything good that could come out of his predicament.

"If Wortham and Owain can get close enough, they should be able to feed this fellow word of your arrest. That information might, in turn, get to Halstatt, if they are indeed connected. If it is you he wants, he will need to rethink his strategy to get to you…perhaps make an error."

Caol snorted. "He wants me dead. I think he'll be as pleased to let Arlan do it as he would be to do it himself…maybe even more so since my death at the hands of my friend and king would be humiliating and thus amusing."

The bard's expression indicated he did not think it would be amusing. "Would he believe the King would execute his sister's husband on such flimsy evidence? This is not Neth…or Cordash…and Arlan is nothing like those who came before him."

"Maybe not…but Halstatt might be willing to take the chance. Still…" he rubbed his chin, "He has not yet obtained the Serpents as far as I know…or the dagger…and the dagger is the one thing I have he will want to retrieve, whether Arlan executes me or not. We'll have to hope he comes for it before the King's return; trial and execution are not things I want to face."

"You shall not have to, I swear it. I will do everything I can for you, Caol. There will be no execution, nor will you be held for long."

The inquisitor did not know what Kavan intended to do, how he could possibly subvert that chain of events, but he did believe that the bard would do as he said. This time, when he offered his hand, it was for a man to man handshake of gratitude. "I would appreciate that."

❧*❧

Though a vast number of Enesfel's troops were stationed outside the city of Ruidoso when General Wyndham and his men arrived, he found no sign of General Agis. To his satisfaction, he learned from the captain in charge that Agis had arrived at Ruidoso ahead of schedule with little loss of life and had taken it upon himself to continue marching towards Lake Curo. If it had been anyone else disobeying orders and making their own, Ternce would have worried. But Agis had the drive and initiative of a natural leader and was less afraid of taking calculated risks than anyone the general knew. The Cíbhóló would not have taken this chance if he did not believe himself and his men capable of success. His risks were not about pride or personal glory, but the need to do the best job possible.

There was also a message from the newly crowned King Renfrid, requesting that Generals Wyndham and McHador come to Nogero because it appeared that Neth was prepared to surrender and the Enesfel generals' presences would be necessary at the negotiating table. Ternce was not comfortable with such a position; the distinction should have gone to Chamberlain McHador, but Enesfel needed a representative so the duty now fell to Ternce.

With Agis absent from this post, Ternce left a senior captain in command until King Arlan arrived in Ruidoso. Then he set out with a small personal guard to carry out what was intended to be the last phase of this undertaking. With him came two spokesmen, one from Ruidoso and one from Fiara, both intending to make known the decision of the Joint Councils to accept Enesfel's rule. The soldiers,

those from both Enesfel and Cordash, had done well. The rest, the art
of negotiations, would be up to General Wyndham and King Renfrid.

General Agis, meanwhile, was engaged in gruesome combat with
a contingent of Nethite troops they had not expected to find. When
Agis and General Marym arrived at the mouth of the Kelari River, two
days' march through the forest to the furthest accessible point in the
Llaethlágárá, the Nethites were waiting. Whether they knew foreign
forces were coming, had failed to march west against Cordash, or had
been overlooked by King Loris when the orders for war were given,
was irrelevant. They were there and in top fighting form. When
combat ensued, it was more of an actual battle than the skirmish Agis
and his men had previously engaged in, and thus a better test of the
strengths and weaknesses of Enesfel's untried, newly formed military.
Neth's troops were outnumbered but they fought viciously, as men
possessed, and Enesfel struggled to subdue them.

Possessed or desperate, Agis thought with a wicked grin hidden
by his helmet. The arrival of another unit of Enesfel's troops, however,
led by General Zarkosta, spelled the end for Neth's contingent.

Under the midsummer sun, in the sweltering heat of early Tord,
the united forces clashed with the de Corrmick troops. Enesfel lost
many men to this enemy, Cordash lost the same. No one was willing
to retreat. For Neth it was a matter of repelling invaders, protecting
their homeland, obeying the king they feared. For the others, it was a
matter of completing what they had come to do, prune the thorny
branch of Neth, and, if necessary, dig it up by the roots.

Despite Neth's desperation, their longer swords, and more
rigorous training, the soldiers fighting for the de Corrmick standard
lost the battle. The three generals of Cordash and Enesfel were
wounded, but their troops held ground and maintained position at the
mouth of the Kelari. Those Nethites who retreated across the river
were not followed. After the wounded and dead were counted and
tended, those men not staying to build another fortification would

press on into the mountains. Enesfel had made their point. They were not going anywhere.

◈*◈

The royal Lachlan library had, as far as anyone knew, the largest collection of manuscripts outside of Elyriá. Thus far, however, it had yielded nothing that would solve the riddle of the Tarmajiens, the Coryllien daggers, or the Káliel Serpents. The common thread was Halstatt, a man Kavan had yet to see, that he knew very little about.

What information he found about the Corylliens he already knew. The myths were the only information to be had. Without Bhríd's consent, Kavan would not peruse the tax and census records to track the Tarmajien and Dugan families, and there was no mention anywhere else of either clan. Despite their long-standing, and well-known amongst the Association, feud, the two families were otherwise unknown.

And nowhere was there a mention of the Káliel Serpents, except in a handful of documents that connected them to the ruling family of the islands, a symbol of leadership. In frustration, the bard closed the book he had finished perusing and stared out the window. Lost in thought, he did not react to the sound of familiar footsteps behind him, even when they stopped at his side.

"I'm glad you've returned," a deep voice said with warmth. A hand hovered over the bard's shoulder but fell without touching him.

"I have been back since last night, Wortham, although it was very late when I arrived. I apologize for not telling you."

The captain nodded. Knowing Kavan was back was enough. "Was your time away profitable?"

More footsteps and Owain entered the room; he settled in a chair near the bookshelves and removed his worn, dusty boots with a groan. "More profitable than ours, I hope."

"We searched the garment district, the náós grounds, and the entire north end of Rhidam. There was nothing useful to be learned." Wortham too sat, although he chose a low footstool that positioned him between the other two men. "No one has seen, or will admit to seeing, anyone resembling the drawings Healer MacLyr made, or the royal children."

"There is someone else we should seek." Kavan took one hand of each man to transmit the image to both simultaneously. "He's not the man we are seeking, but there is a familial resemblance. Caol saw him at the Eagle's Nest…but, unfortunately, he lost him when Justice Cornell felt compelled to arrest him."

Wortham choked. "Lord Dugan was arrested?" He was hoping he misunderstood, that it was the other man who had been arrested, but if that were the case, Kavan would not have recommended finding him.

"He is safe until the King returns; Justice Cornell does not have evidence to support his arrest, only supposition. His incarceration should be short. But without him, the search for the princes is in our hands. If this man I have shown you is connected, we need to know."

"I'm on it," Prince Owain said, already shoving his feet back into his boots.

"I'm coming with you."

Kavan wished he had the words to express how much their friendship meant to him. Instead, he returned to studying, deciding to examine Káliel's history yet again for something he may have missed.

❧*❧

Caol cracked opened his eyes, waking upon the stone pallet that was his sole furnishing, sensing he was not alone. The fingers of sunlight struggling to claw through the barred slit of a window told him it was morning. He was tempted to feign sleep, to stare into the sunlight as if unaware of his visitor, but knew he would be unable to ignore forever the woman who stood in the open doorway of his cell. As much as he was unable to bear her cool gaze, she was his wife and she deserved better.

When he did not look at her, she hesitantly stepped into the cell, sat on the edge of the stone pallet, and stared at him again; he knew she was staring, though he would not look to see it. When she took his hand and turned his face towards her, however, he was forced to confront her and accept the folded parchment she pressed into his hand.

Suspecting she would not leave him alone until he read it, and not feeling capable of enduring her company for long because of the guilt he carried, he gave in to her wishes.

'Justice Cornell told me the charges against you,' the parchment read. 'I do not know if you possess this dagger, but I do know you did not kill an innocent woman or let our son be taken away. Whatever has happened, I do not blame you.'

Looking up from her words with tears in his eyes, Caol began to babble before he could stop himself, guilt fueling his words. "I will find Wilred. I may be confined here, but Lord Cliáth is looking, as are Owain and Captain Delamo. We will find him. It will be alright. I swear it."

She could not hear his words, but she could read his lips and knew what he was saying, and his remorseful expression told of his sincerity where his tone of voice could not. He was as distressed by these events as she was, shamefaced and angry that he had not yet been able to do more. Though she had tried to blame him, to have someone to accuse of her son's disappearance, her husband's absence from her life while their son was in danger had taught her that whatever else he might be, Caol was also the man she loved. He would never knowingly endanger their child...and she trusted him completely.

ॐ * ॐ

The newly anointed king of Neth rode to join his troops at the front line. General Glucke would meet him in Nogero where Merkar would see for himself how many men Neth had lost and how close to Glevum Cordash's troops had come. Surely they could not be two days forced march from Neth's capital, regardless of what the reports claimed. Neth's army would never allow foreign invaders to come that far.

But they had. That short hard ride from Glevum revealed the Valdis standard fluttering in the summer breeze, and the expansive wall of Cordash troops set to draw like a noose until Glevum was strangled and dead. It was a testament to Loris' failure as king that no one, including Merkar, could deny. The Valdis king was in de Corrmick territory and prepared to take it all. Swearing beneath his breath, fuming and stomping as he crashed through the encampment, Merkar sought his generals, Glucke and Ensgar, taking a rough count of his forces as he went. Yes, there had been many losses, but his armies were well trained. They could defeat Cordash with the right leader behind them. Behind, not in front of. Merkar had no intentions of riding into battle, risking the throne when he had just gotten it and leaving the kingdom in the hands of a minor prince. Kjell was not, and never would be in Merkar's eyes, fit to be king.

But whether or not the army was able, or willing, to fight was something he needed to discuss with the generals. Merkar was hungry for victory but he did not think himself a fool.

The day proved unproductive. There was no sign of Halstatt or the children, no word from anyone, and no sign of the man Caol claimed to have seen. It was as if each had vanished. Kavan found nothing helpful in the library either, much to his dismay, and further attempts to persuade Justice Cornell to release the inquisitor had failed. Kavan was not prepared to give up; no one had ever accused him of that, but as he spent another night at the side of the altar where Guthrie's body rested, the bard studied the man's peaceful features and prayed for answers. "We could use your wisdom, milord. Mine does not seem to be enough."

⁊Chapter 38⁊

"**W**ell done, Captain. I am pleased with how efficiently this campaign has been carried out. Please convey my gratitude to your men."

The march to Ruidoso had been slow and steady, his personal guard taking no chances with King Arlan's safety as they traveled through the northern woodland deeper into Neth. Though this forest was denser than what he had known as a boy, with taller, thicker trees, each new vista reminded Arlan painfully of the man who lay awaiting burial in Rhidam. Traveling further away from the man who had raised him was proving a test of the King's endurance.

"I will, Sire…yes. But…is it true?"

The King cocked his head. "Is what true, Captain?" The man was not questioning his praise, was he?

"General McHador…is he dead? Some of the men are saying…"

Arlan took a breath to steady his nerves before replying, and his sudden obvious discomfort kept the soldier from saying more. The King found it hard to speak the words, as saying them would make the truth more real. "It is true," he admitted, not hiding the sorrow that undercut his voice. "He was taken to Rhidam for burial."

Fortunately, the captain did not say more or ask further questions, as if he understood that the topic was sensitive for his king and did not himself want to hear more. Instead, he bowed and backed away, leaving Arlan alone with the chancellor at his side.

"Do you think," the King asked under his breath, "he will spread the word or will I need to answer that question as long as I am here?"

The chancellor sighed sadly. "You may need to answer it a few more times, but I am sure Captain Kalvert will make the news known." He decided to change the subject for both of their sakes. "What do you think of Enesfel's newest acquisition?" He motioned around them at the countryside surrounding the city of Ruidoso in the near distance.

"Much like Enesfel…except with more trees. Do you think it necessary or advisable for me to visit all of the fortifications?" There were several of them, and with no idea how the rest of the troops had fared, traveling to each would put the king at risk for any stray bands of Nethite soldiers.

Watching the physicians pick their way through the men who were camped here, inquiring about their health and tending injuries or ailments, the chancellor shrugged. "It would do much for morale, but it would be safer if you did not do so until the quadrant is secured. I also think the men will understand if you return to Rhidam to preside over Lord McHador's rites. Most expect it, after the years of service he gave to the Crown and kingdom. If you choose to return now that you have reached Ruidoso, or decide to wait until the end of the campaign, either would be acceptable. Most of these men will remain in Neth…our new territory, until it is secured."

The King nodded but did not immediately speak. The choice was his, but he had to weigh carefully the benefits and problems each choice might bring. He wished Kavan were beside him to offer counsel but suspected the bard would have said the same as his chancellor. "I will need men to accompany me home…should I decide to go. I think Captain Kalvert, Generals Agis, Zarkosta, and Wyndham should be able to control the situation here. Would you and Lord Healer care to accompany Prince Harcourt and me back to Rhidam…whenever I choose to go?"

The dark-haired Elyri grinned. "I would, Sire. Thank you. I will tell the others to be ready…but please be careful in the meantime."

Arlan nodded. "I shall be." Risking his life now was the last thing he wanted.

❧*❧

As King Merkar had decided after a lengthy midnight debate with his generals, Neth's troops attacked Cordash minutes before dawn. Although King Renfrid's forces saw the attack coming in time to ready themselves, they were not fully prepared when the mounted Nethites crashed into their camp. The King scrambled for his sword while his squire hastily assisted in securing his armor. A whistle, barely audible over the sounds of battle as it began at the front of the camp, brought a sentry and his horse. Renfrid was one of the lucky few who had a chance to mount up.

He knew that Prince Merkar, now King Merkar his sources confirmed, had arrived two days ago and had been camped with Neth's troops. He knew that either meant that surrender was in sight or that another battle was in the offing. The new king had chosen to start his reign with combat. True to de Corrmick tradition, that was no surprise. King Renfrid was willing to oblige, hoping to start Merkar's reign off with a resounding defeat that would knock him from his throne. He also hoped to find the man among the fighting forces but did not. Coward, he sneered, slashing through an opponent, barely avoiding a crushing blow from an enemy mace.

The strike crashed against his shield, however, pushing him askew in his saddle. It took effort to right himself without being killed, but he succeeded and pushed deeper into the heart of the battlefield. He would need to be more careful; if he should die, the throne of Cordash

❧*639*❧

would be left to his three-year-old son, and tiny Govert was not ready for such responsibilities, even with trustworthy regents at the helm.

The fighting continued for the better part of the day, lulls indicating that those to the rear were coming forward to replace the depleted, weary front line. King Merkar was forced to break camp and pull his men back three times. By his calculations, Cordash had moved a half day closer to Glevum, not the direction Merkar had hoped to maneuver Cordash's troops. Darkness was falling; combat could not easily continue in the dark, and from Merkar's vantage point he was beginning to realize that Neth could not hope to win this day, in spite of his belief in his men. Some semblance of a military had to be maintained, enough to train more men, enough to fight another day.

To his credit, King Merkar did what he could have ordered any other man to do. He lifted the white flag of surrender. It took time for the fighting to cease and for the troops to part, and once they did, he rode into the empty gap between the armies, carrying the flag himself.

"I want to speak with Prince Valdis," he barked, no meekness or amity in his voice.

With his shield arm bleeding heavily, Renfrid approached, flanked by guards shielding him from arrows and spears, remaining out of reach of Merkar's sword. "It's King Valdis, de Corrmick."

Merkar smirked. "This little disagreement has given both of our lands new kings. Perhaps we can come to an understanding."

Renfrid steadied his fidgety horse. "That would be advisable, de Corrmick," he snorted, refusing to address the other man as king. He had no way of knowing if the man before him, wearing de Corrmick colors, was a de Corrmick or not. "I do not think you wish to be remembered as the man who ended your family's dynasty and Neth's sovereignty. If you surrender, Enesfel's spokesman is on his way to meet with us and we can discuss the terms necessary for you to retain your throne and kingdom."

Merkar glowered at the other man's arrogance. He was not aware of any part Enesfel had to play in this conflict, but to think both kingdoms had expected to overrun Neth like locusts made him angry and bitter. For a fleeting moment, he toyed with the idea of smiting the Cordashian's head from his shoulders, but the proximity of Cordash's troops meant a swift death for him too, and the destruction of Neth, since Kjell would never be able to lead an army against such foes. Neth would have to accept whatever terms were offered and then bide her time, as she had done throughout history. Her day would come; if Merkar had his way, it would be during his lifetime.

"I think a cessation of hostilities is in order, Valdis, though I prefer to negotiate terms before agreeing to anything…even surrender."

Renfrid's grin was unseen behind his visor. General McHador had been correct; their planning and joint efforts had made this campaign mercifully short. It had lasted a total of sixteen days, making him feel a little generous. "By all means. If you think it to your advantage to talk, we shall talk."

ᐱᐱChapter 39ᐁᐁ

It pleased General Agis to allow his men the freedom of celebrating, as long as there was no excess of alcohol involved. After all, there could be enemy soldiers within the region and he wanted his men fit to fight. The noise of the celebration might drown out approaching attackers, but at least the men would be sober enough to respond accordingly. With the aid of General Marym and General Zarkosta, the troops had completed their assigned circuit. They reached the furthest point they could within the forests and mountains of the Llaethlágárá, without endangering themselves from the terrain, and were constructing the final fortification. When complete, Neth would successfully be cut in two. Tonight he would celebrate with the men he had fought beside and in two days he would begin traveling back along the river, leaving General Zarkosta in command here. The Cíbhóló would rejoin Enesfel's forces in Ruidoso and then undertake a sweep of the territory to root out pockets of insurgents or enemy soldiers. General Wyndham had specifically asked Agis to lead the team who would ferret out resistance, knowing that the Cíbhóló's fierce reputation would aid in finding and subduing those they sought.

It was a duty he looked forward to. Celebrating was good, even necessary, after a job well done. It was important for the morale of the soldiers. But for him, the job was not yet complete. He would not be able to rest or celebrate until he had done everything he had been asked to do.

His desire to press on, to resume the fight, would not dampen his enjoyment of this night, however. No one had ever accused Agis of being unable to celebrate. If there was a reason for it, he would find it. He would make good use of it, alcohol or not.

⧹*⧸

When he was not in the library scouring manuscripts for information, or sleeping, Kavan spent his time praying in the upper oratory, unable to pull himself away from Guthrie's unmoving form and the feeling that the man had answers, even if he could not speak them. It seemed wrong to leave the chamberlain lying here as if asleep and not continue to pay homage to him. Guthrie was gone and should be buried, but that would not happen until King Arlan returned. As much as Kavan wanted to be present for that memorial, felt he should be there, he did not want to face the King until he found the man's son. If Arlan returned before Bertram was found, Kavan would depart, as reluctant to face his friend as Caol was to face his wife.

Harp in hand, Kavan knelt to play on the altar steps. Music was what he needed tonight, music to soothe his agitated spirit and clear his thoughts. He had not played since the night of Guthrie's passing; it was time. As he plucked at the strings, composing tiny snatches of tunes that would eventually morph into songs, he hummed, hoping to be embraced by the familiar presences, the energy of something strong enough to strip away the chaos he felt and leave him both empty and full. For a long time, there was nothing except the music in his heart, his head, and his soul. He was about to give up when it came at last, feeling more powerful, more immediate, than it had in a long time.

"átaelás mai." Kavan heard the voice, with his ears rather than his head, telling him this presence was real, but he did not speak or open his eyes. He was not sure he should. Sometimes when he opened them, whatever was with him left. "phágk áti hábhai, átaelás mai."

Green eyes opened slowly and Kavan lifted his head. The speaker stood near the altar, one scarred hand upon Guthrie's chest. There was nothing ethereal about this vision. The man lowered the hood of his gray robe, revealing smooth, young features and waves of auburn hair, a figure as corporeal as Kavan. "lásánai…" The bard could not rise from his knees, weighed down as he was with awe and respect. The harp fell silent and he bowed his head again.

"Always formal with me, aren't you? I thought by now we would be friends."

Kavan felt his cheeks warm with embarrassment. "I do not know if that epitaph can ever be truly applicable between us, milord…"

"Why? Because I am so different from you?" Since Kavan did not know how to answer that question, he did not. "Your thoughts and prayers have been quite loud this night, Kavan."

He shivered at the sound of his name upon Saint Kóráhm's lips. It was the first time Kóráhm had called him by name. "I apologize if they disturbed you."

"Apologize? Disturbed me?" The Saint chuckled warmly. "On the contrary. What can I do for you? How might I give your spirit ease?"

There were many things Kavan could have asked, too many things tangling within his head disquieting him. But as his eyes traveled the length of Kóráhm's arm and fell upon the hand resting on Guthrie's body, he asked, "Is Lord McHador at peace?"

Kóráhm nodded. "You know he is." Kavan sighed with relief but his troubled expression did not change. "That does little to appease you, I see. What do you truly wish? Ask, that I may fulfill you."

Kavan hesitated, sighing again, but this time without the relief. What right did he have to ask anything of Kóráhm, and why should the saint be eager to fulfill his wishes and desires? Such willingness made the bard shiver. "What I want most is something you cannot give…as much as I might wish it. As for the rest, I believe a man should work for the end he wishes to achieve, not expect divine intervention at every turn."

"Am I divine? How strange…I have never felt that way." Kóráhm chuckled and smiled at Kavan's discomfort. "You have much to learn, my young friend. Isn't prayer a request for divine intervention…even if for no more than a sign or a calm spirit?" He stepped away from the altar and settled on the steps beside Kavan. "But you are correct in one thing; there are some answers you will need to find on your own. I cannot give them. If I cannot assist you, why did you wish me here?"

Embarrassed again, Kavan turned his head away. "Your presence is enough. To know you are with me brings peace of mind."

"Then we are friends indeed, for I feel the same." Kóráhm smiled but the bard did not see it. "I shall stay and listen to you play if that will please you."

"You wish to…you would…it would make me…" Kavan shook off his befuddled stammering and cleared his throat. "It would be an honor to play for you. One thing first…may I…?"

In answer to the unspoken request, the saint laid his hand on Kavan's knee. The gesture was real, the hand as solid and warm as Ártur's would have been. He looked into the saint's amused face as a smile tugged at his lips, and then closed his eyes to play.

To entertain a saint. How many could say they had done the same? How many could claim to have kept the sort of company Kavan kept? That honor made the bard tremble nervously although his music never faltered. The energy the saint exuded, the power he held, soothed Kavan, wrapped around him, comforting him during hours of making music. When the oratory door opened the presence dissipated, although Kavan was sure the saint's physical form had left long ago. It finally left him with a soft whisper, a single word, the same one he had left Kavan with long ago.

"Káliel."

Shuddering, his hands fell away from the harp and he glanced over his shoulder, smiling wistfully at the man who entered the room. "I have interrupted something haven't I, milord?"

The bard shook his head. "Something too good to last, Wortham, but please..." He motioned him forward. "If it had not been you, it would have been someone else...and I infinitely prefer it to be you."

That admission made the captain smile. "I wanted to tell you we have not yet found anything today, although you probably know that. We are about to start again, try the taverns, but I admit my faith and hope that we will find the princes is dwindling. How much longer can we search for something without clues?"

Kóráhm's whisper floated through Kavan's mind again. "I may have received a clue...although I do not know what it means."

Wortham knelt beside Kavan on the steps. "Saint Kóráhm was here. I felt him as I approached the door. What did he tell you?"

That the captain recognized that presence when others did not, gave Kavan hope. "His parting word was Káliel. I think it is where we are meant to go. We know the kidnapper wants the Serpents; it was part of his ransom demands...and it has always been speculated that there is a connection between the Coryllien daggers and the islands. The kidnapper is Lady Dilyn's assassin...and he used the Coryllien to do it." He had been reluctant to consider going to Káliel, reluctant to act on facts that could be nothing more than coincidently linked together. There was no reason he could imagine for Halstatt to have taken the boys there, but it was logical that the man would eventually journey there in search of the Serpents...maybe going there was not far-fetched after all...even if it meant facing Gabrielle Dilyn again. "The commonality is Káliel...and though it makes little sense that he would take the boys with him, it is the best clue we have."

"Aye, milord...it seems logical."

"I want you and Owain to go to the docks; ask the shipmasters, the sailors, the fishermen...anyone you see, if either of our suspects came on a boat or chartered one for Káliel." It was a long shot, as it would be more likely to take a vessel in or out of the port at Levonne, but it was worth the effort to be certain. "Meanwhile, I am going to try one more time to convince Justice Cornell to release Lord Dugan. We need him."

"Aye…we do." The bard's task was a more daunting one than what Wortham and Owain faced. The captain nodded and said, "Best of luck, milord…I will let you know at once what we find."

꙳*꙳

Prince Espen, his doublet open to expose his sun-darkened chest, looked barely awake as he glanced up from his breakfast of cold meats and bread at the mounted men in front of him. He had known King Arlan was here, but with his own duties to his men to perform, he had not yet had the opportunity to speak with Enesfel's king. Arlan looked weary and defeated, in spite of the victory his troops had given him, and Espen understood why.

"I am sorry, Your Majesty, but I do not plan to return with you at this time. I have given the matter consideration and believe my father would prefer that I keep our men here, to assist for as long as your forces must stay in the north. We are equally capable of making sure there are no troublemakers about. Besides, I do not think my father would be pleased if I left the battlefield, at the first opportunity."

Though Arlan had been hoping for Espen's company on the journey back to Rhidam, the prince's decision impressed him; the offer was more than he expected of either Hatu or of the young prince. If not for circumstances beyond his control, Arlan would have chosen to remain here himself. "I will send word to your father if you have not. But before I go, I must give you this." He removed an object from the pouch at his side and placed it in the prince's hand. "If I do not, my daughter will never speak to me again."

Afraid of what the black velvet and lace pocket contained, Prince Espen nevertheless accepted it as the King continued, "She thought it might bring comfort in battle. Of course, the fighting is over…or should be…but at least I have done as she asked. gdhededhá Tusánt will remain for a few weeks as well; please see that he is protected."

"I shall, with honor, Your Majesty."

"I hope you will stop in Rhidam when you journey home. I wish to thank you and honor you properly for everything you have done for Enesfel."

The Hatu prince bowed his head. "Thank you…" What had begun as a duty to his father had become something else, and he was happy to have been part of what he believed to be a significant historical event.

Leaving the prince behind, King Arlan, Chancellor Cáner, Healer MacLyr and Sir Gabersdon of Nelori began the trek back to Rhidam with fifty soldiers to accompany them. The remainder of Enesfel's troops would stay in what would soon be northern Enesfel until General Wyndham announced the treaty a success or their military prowess was required. Once the opposition to Enesfel's presence was eradicated and there was peace, some soldiers would remain as needed to staff the newly erected fortifications. The shortest war in the history of the Five Sovereignties was almost over.

☙*☙

When Justice Cornell refused again to release Caol, Kavan knew what had to be done. He could force the man's compliance but he was reluctant to do so. If anyone was going to have to do something they did not want, it would be Kavan. The act, however, would have to wait a little longer. He could not risk being caught before they were ready to depart. His own meager pack had been readied hours ago and given into Captain Delamo's care. Now he needed to speak to Lady Dubuais, a task that did not daunt him, except that he ran the risk of others, namely the princesses, guessing something was afoot. Now that dinner was over, it was time for action. He fell into step beside the Duchess as she headed outdoors for a summer's eve stroll on the promenade and nodded his head when she cast him a curious, sideways glance.

"Milord?" She could tell he had something to say and that he was hesitant to voice it. Having heard that he possessed unusual abilities, including the gift of knowing things before they happened, or knowing of things that happened far away, she prayed he had not come to bring bad news.

"I must ask a favor of you," he said softly, unaware of her worries.

Out of range of anyone hearing, he stopped; she did likewise. "If it is something to do with finding the missing children, I will do anything I can." That had been his priority of late; it was a logical assumption to make.

Kavan did not think it odd for her to make that leap of logic. "There is reason to suspect the kidnappers may have chartered a boat...if not from Rhidam than from Levonne. We found no proof that a boat was chartered here so I am traveling to Levonne tonight to investigate there, and if they have done so, learn where they have gone. Lord Lachlan suggested I obtain a writ from you, something giving us leave to search vessels and facilities and to question anyone we deem necessary. I cannot get royal approval for this...I do not think many men would accept the word of the princess, regardless of the fact that she is the King's sister...and the King is not here to grant us such permission. As you are the authority in Levonne, a writ by your hand would suffice. Can I count on such a thing, milady?" He might not require it, but he would prefer to have it in case the need arose.

Without questioning his plans or his motives, she replied, "I will draft the document at once. Where shall I bring it to you?"

"Give it to Prince Muir as soon as you can. I have instructed him to wait for it, and to bring it to me when he has it. And please, milady…speak of this to know one. No one must know where I am going. I cannot risk a delay; it might endanger the princes' safety if I am hindered."

After Justice Cornell's arrest of Caol Dugan, Madalyn could understand the bard's reluctance for his plan to be made known. Whether Minos felt the arrest justifiable, surely the safety of the boys came first. "I will speak to no one; you have my word, milord."

She curtseyed and hurried away, leaving Kavan no doubt that she would do as she promised. She was a woman of integrity, a woman he would be honored to call kin. His concern was not for her, as he stared at the darkening sky in the west, but rather for his next step. Wortham would prepare the horses for departure and then he, Owain, and Muir would go to Hes á Redh Náós to await the bard there, ready to travel. There were small boat landings along the river between Rhidam and Levonne, and although it was less likely Halstatt would have chartered a boat from one of those, Kavan would not take the chance of missing that detail if he had. There were no Gates in those small villages; reaching them by horseback or foot was the only choice. Foot travel would take too long; they had to travel by horse.

If Kavan's intuition was right, if he had not miscalculated the steps necessary to find the boys, if Kóráhm was not leading him astray, his plan should work. If he was wrong in any detail, if Halstatt had never gone…or intended to go…to the islands, then what Kavan was about to do would mean that he and Caol would be unable to return to Rhidam until the princes were found…and perhaps not even then. It was an easy choice to make.

It was not difficult to enter the dungeon; he had come to see Caol often enough in the past few days that the sentries did not question his descent down the wide stone steps that wound their way into the bowels of the castle. None of the guards outside the dungeon door spoke to him nor gave him a second glance when he leaned on the wall and appeared to be removing a stone from the sole of his boot. One by one, as he reached with tendrils of invisible power, the guards and other prisoners in front of and behind the great oak door slid to the floor, succumbing to a deep sleep from which time would eventually rouse them. It enabled Kavan to take the keys from the captain of the guard, enter the dungeon, and make his way to Caol's cell with no one knowing.

The inquisitor, lying upon his pallet and staring at the ceiling as he spent much of his time doing, noticed the sentry outside his cell slump to the side and then slide slowly to the stone floor. It was an odd enough occurrence that it brought Caol to the door to peer out, hoping to see what was going on, as Kavan appeared around the corner at the end of the row of cells.

"Again, Lord Cliáth? Four visits in one day? People will gossip."

"They will have more to gossip about than that." He was already unlocking the cell door. Caol looked from the keys to the unconscious sentry and nodded smugly, recalling that Kavan had used a similar method to pass through the dungeon the night they had taken the throne from Owain.

"You did that?" he murmured.

Kavan pushed the door open enough that Caol could come out of the cell. "Are you coming or would you prefer to stay here? We don't have much time." These guards would sleep for hours, but someone else could come into the dungeon at any time.

Caol did not need to be asked again. Kavan locked the cell door behind him and returned the keys to one of the sleeping guards. "Where are we...?" the inquisitor began, following the bard into the bunkroom, into a corner closet that appeared to have had its door broken off long ago. The bard did not answer the aborted question, but with Caol's hands in his, in moments they were stepping into the twisted shadows created by holy candles in Hes á Redh. The building was silent at this hour, deserted save for gdhededhá Claide and k'gdhededhá Tythilius, both in the thóres where they would neither see nor here Kavan and Caol's arrival, as long as the two were quiet. The pair snuck through the nave, to the door, and out to the darkest side of the building where Captain Delamo waited with their horses.

Glancing around with concern, Kavan muttered, "Owain? Muir?"

Wortham shrugged. "I saw them in the library with Lady Dubuais and Princess Deidre earlier. They weren't at the front gate when we were supposed to meet; I talked to the gate sentries for a time but decided not to loiter longer and appear suspicious. The sentries believe I'm delivering donations to the k'dedhá…"

"Wortham…"

The captain chuckled. "It was no lie, milord. I procured clothing and goods from the princess and others to donate, and I left it, and two horses, with k'dedhá Jermyn…who is aware that his collaboration is necessary to the recovery of the princes. You know he will cooperate."

"Bless him," Caol grunted, his eyes also scanning the night for any sign, good or bad, that someone might be coming. "You going to tell me what's going on, Lord Cliáth…or am I supposed to guess?"

"We're going to Levonne," Wortham replied, "or at least we will be if the others arrive."

Kavan scowled. They could not afford to wait any longer. "Start for the bridge; wait there as long as you think prudent. Perhaps Owain and Muir were detained. If I don't rejoin you shortly, go as I instructed, ask questions when you can. You know what you need to do."

"Aye," Wortham said with a solemn nod. He would do his duty by Kavan no matter what happened. He waited, watching the white cat disappear into the shadows, slinking quickly towards the castle, and then said, "We're going to find your son and Prince Bertram, milord…one way or another."

"We'd better. I hope I didn't break out of prison for nothing."

The cat darted this way and that, avoiding passersby and a few pairs of hands that tried to catch him as he rushed to find a good point from which to watch the castle gate. He could sense the men he sought behind those walls, vexed and uneasy but under no threat or danger. Deciding he could wait a little longer before going in after them, the cat crouched upon a messy collection of firewood to watch.

His worries about the cause of their delay proved unfounded when the father and son eventually emerged through the castle gates, side by side, chatting idly. It was neither Lady Dubuais changing her mind or Justice Cornell's suspicions that detained them, nor had anyone discovered Caol missing. Rather, the delay was created by Princess Diona, who had found her older brother in the library and refused to leave him, even when Owain had come for him. It was not until Lady MacLyr came to put her to bed that the young princess left the men alone. They talked their way past the palace sentries with the excuse of going for drinks at the Eagle's Nest where the palace full of royal women were unlikely to follow, words that gained them laughter and easy passage. They traveled towards the inn until they were no longer watched and then they turned down a side street towards the náós.

"Owain?"

The older prince spun, dagger in hand, not having expected anyone to call his name. The náós was many streets away. His other hand was on his scabbard, the sword partially unsheathed as Kavan, not the white cat, emerged from a nearby doorway. Dressed as he was in his usual white robe, Owain was surprised he had not noticed the bard there.

"Milord, you could have gotten killed…"

"Not likely," Kavan said wryly. "You look before you attack. Your hesitation would have protected me." With the sword in place, Owain clasped the bard's outstretched hand. "The others have gone ahead. We must hurry to catch them."

Without horses, the three would be forced to travel more slowly and the twists and turns of the city streets slowed them further. By the time they reached the western bridge across the river, where Wortham had been instructed to wait if he could, the captain and inquisitor were not there. Crossing the Tegid, Prince Muir was already complaining about trekking all the way to Levonne. Owain was about to scold him for his gloomy thoughts when they heard horses ahead, off to the side of the unlit road. Kavan sensed no hostility from the two men with the animals, and a gentle touch of the quieter mind confirmed it was the captain and inquisitor waiting for them.

"Thought it best to wait away from the bridge…less suspicious," was all Caol said as soon as Kavan and the others were near enough to hear him. He was relieved to have the entire group together, relieved that Wortham had explained as much as he knew of the current plan, and relieved to have some sort of trail to follow. Even if it proved to be another dead end, some lead, some action, was better than none.

"Finally convinced Justice Cornell to free Caol, eh?" Muir laughed with a smile, already swinging up onto the horse Wortham offered him as his father mounted another.

Kavan shrugged and took the reins of the last horse from Caol. "I did what I had to do," was all he said, not about to confirm or deny anything.

"You mean…you broke him out…?" Owain glanced back and forth between the inquisitor and the bard with a greater sense of appreciation for Kavan's sense of loyalty.

"Won't that bring…?"

"No one will likely look for us for several more hours," Kavan said as he turned the men south towards Levonne. "The one who knows our intended destination will not speak of it. Should the justice somehow learn we are heading to Levonne, we will be several hours ahead of them, and hopefully gone from Levonne by the time he could arrive to stop us."

Owain and his son looked at one another. Muir had known the bard his entire life, yet he had seen Kavan do things in the past several weeks that had proven how little he really knew about the Elyri. Kavan was not the man Muir had believed, meek and compliant and submissive. He was something more, something better, at least in the prince's eyes. Owain too had built an image of how he imagined Kavan must be, based solely on the few brief encounters they had shared; Kavan was proving to be a much stronger, braver, more complicated man than Owain had imagined.

"You have sacrificed a great deal for the boys," the elder prince murmured with awe.

"Any price I must pay is worth bringing them home."

"Likewise," Wortham said, eyes on the road ahead of them as he searched for danger.

"What do you hope to find in Levonne?" Muir asked.

"I have reason to believe the kidnapper has gone to Káliel. He would need a boat for that. He did not, as far as we have learned, take one from Rhidam, which leaves the landings between here and Levonne, or Levonne itself. We must investigate them all. He must have left from one of them."

"With Bertram and Wilred?"

"I do not know, my prince. We need to learn more before we can say. After we find him, we shall see."

"Then I suggest," Caol said, crouching low over his horse's back, "that we hasten our steps." He did not wait for anyone's approval or agreement; he dug his heels into his horse's sides and flew down the packed dirt road. The others in the group followed, as eager as the inquisitor to find the missing children.

⫷*⫸

General Wyndham rode into the Cordashian encampment as the sun was midway from its zenith to the horizon after an uneventful journey across Neth's heartland. His unit avoided towns and villages in an effort not to seek out trouble, as he had imagined they would still meet some resistance along the way. However, not even a bandit dared cross Enesfel's forces. It appeared that Cordash had done their job in subduing Neth's military and the population at large lacked the ability, or desire, to attack.

He took stock of the soldiers as he neared the center of the encampment. The field smelled of blood, of rot, or unwashed bodies and death but he saw very little evidence of any of it beyond the dirty, sweaty men who watched him. Judging by the number, and the condition many of those he saw were in, he deduced that either there were other troops elsewhere or Cordash had been hard hit and suffered many losses. By the looks of the Nethite camp in the distance, it looked obvious that Neth had suffered even more. King Valdis' men barely looked at Enesfel's general as he passed, recognizing the banner under which he rode and accepting him as a friend. If they had not, they would have encircled him, wounded and weary or not, and captured or killed him. How many of those knew his business, or knew Enesfel's part in this war, he could not guess, but he suspected that few, if any, of either set of forces knew about the campaign in the south that would cost Neth a significant portion of her territory.

"General Wyndham," he heard someone call. He strained to find the owner of the voice; it took time but he soon located the man waving at him from beneath the Valdis flag amidst a cluster of tents, the Valdis crest upon his tabard. The crowd parted; Ternce dismounted and led his horse to where the man stood to prove he was no threat.

"Prince Renfrid." He assumed as much. No one else here would wear that crest.

"King Renfrid; my father died as our troops began to march. I would have sent a messenger with the news but I was preoccupied." The new king smiled as he offered his hand.

The general accepted the gesture and returned it with the stiff bow from the waist that was customary in Cordash. "I can see you have been busy indeed. My condolences on the loss of your father."

"Thank you." There was little grief on the new king's face, but it was known that people from Cordash were accustomed to concealing their feelings and thoughts from strangers. "Please, dine with me. I suspect King Merkar has seen your banners and will come soon enough to learn why you are here...unless he chooses to await an invitation."

Ternce accepted the bench at the table that King Renfrid offered. "King Merkar? What of Loris...and Prince Earle? Prince Ibyll?"

"I do not know the details... but I killed Prince Earle myself...King Earle at the time I am told. What has become of Loris, and Ibyll, I cannot say. I've been told that Merkar has the de Corrmick throne and seems willing to negotiate to keep it."

"Wise," the general chuckled, knowing they could not be far from the kingdom's capital. Indicating the two men nearest him who still stood with their horses, he said, "This is Pol Garvis of Ruidoso and Leon Undilbra from Fiara. They have come to make demands of their king...whoever he might be." There was no need for it, since Enesfel had successfully cut southern Neth away from the north, but they wanted to make their grievances known in a formal way. Since very few took the risk of standing up in confrontation against a de Corrmick monarch, this act was more symbolic than practical.

King Renfrid smiled and motioned for the two men to join them. "Wonderful. Sit...eat. We have much to discuss."

"Where is he, k'dedhá? Or rather...where are they?"

Jermyn bristled at the tone of the justice's voice as the man burst into the náós and disturbed his prayers with his thundering footsteps and threatening growl. "Where are who, Lord Justice?" he grunted as he struggled to get up from his knees, an obviously painful movement that the justice made no attempt to alleviate.

"Lord Dugan. Lord Cliáth. Captain Delamo."

"Should I know where they are?" It was not his job to keep track of anyone's whereabouts, save for the gdhededhá beneath him.

Paying no attention to the portly man's annoyance, the justice snapped, "Captain Delamo brought you donations last night? Horses?"

"The clothing he brought from Princess Deidre is in the thóres awaiting distribution; come, see if you wish." Jermyn gestured for the justice to follow. When Minos did not, the k'gdhededhá stopped. "As for the horses, there is one here at the moment, I fear, no more. The other was loaned to a parishioner in need."

"Only two? He left the palace with seven. Where are the others? Who is this parishioner?"

Jermyn took a step forward to meet Minos in his threat. "You may ask, but I cannot say. The concession is a sacred thing, Lord Cornell. I will not break it, even for you. I know nothing about other horses. I did not see them…and did not ask if there were more. They weren't stolen, were they?"

The justice grunted, crossing his arms in front of his puffed out chest. "I do not know about that. No one has reported stolen horses…I know some are not in the stable and he is said to have taken them."

He paused to study the other man, giving him the chance to continue. Jermyn stared back, and when he realized the justice was waiting for him to say more, he continued, "I have not seen Kavan since his return to Rhidam, and other than a few moments with Lord Dugan several days ago, when he told me they had no news of the missing boys, I have not seen him either. I heard he was arrested…"

It took effort not to smirk as the unspoken accusation of perceived incompetence hung between them. He felt sorry for the man, knowing the justice was trying to do his job, but not sorry enough to reveal anything he knew or suspected. Minos muttered under his breath before asking, "What of Lord Lachlan and Prince Muir? Have you seen either of them?"

The corners of the k'gdhededhá's mouth twisted. "I saw Prince Muir the day I went to speak with Lord Cliáth; he was the one to tell me Lord Cliáth was not in the keep. I asked the prince to have him come see me when he could spare the time, but I have not seen Lord Lachlan at all, not even from a distance. Don't tell me you have lost them all, Lord Justice."

Jermyn doubted the justice's face could be any more crimson. His conscience was clear; all he had said was true. He could not be faulted for lying, but perhaps the pleasure he derived from watching the justice squirm was a little bit sinful.

❧*❧

The docks of the Port of Levonne had been there, in various forms, as far back as there had been Teren in Enesfel…further even, as there had been Elyri built docks there when the Teren first arrived in the land. They had suffered from storms, fires, from various periods of unrest and war, yet they were always rebuilt, always continued to thrive. It was a quicker trade route with Hatu, as there was less of a risk of meeting brigands at sea than over land, and it was the sole means of trade with the islands of Káliel, for those merchants privileged enough to have made the connections to do business. There was one Elyri port, the only place in their kingdom accessible by sea, and it was known to do a thriving business, for those intrepid enough to make the effort through the treacherous eastern sea. On occasion, some took the sea route to Cordash, and, even more rarely, someone would take the risk of a sea trade with Neth, or even the solo far-flung single port at the northernmost shore of the great Cíbhóló desert. Trade, as well as a thriving fishing and wine growing community, kept Levonne's ports alive.

The docks were profitable ground for gleaning information, and it proved unnecessary for Kavan to produce the document Lady Dubuais had provided in order to persuade people to talk. Several sailors and merchants alike had seen one or the other of the two men within the past two months. The party's spirits soared with each new report and detail until it peaked: both men had chartered separate ships for Káliel within the last week, the second having done so two days previous.

The town crier called the twenty-third hour before Kavan and the others gathered in the sanctuary of St. Poul's Náós rather than one of the local inns or taverns. Though both Halstatt and the strange fellow may have chartered ships to Káliel, there was a chance that they had booked passage and remained in Levonne. After coming this far in their quest, none wanted to run into their quarry before they were ready to act. At this hour, the náós was empty, save for the clergy in the thóres, and the group felt it was a more secure place to meet and talk then any tavern could be.

"What do we do now? Go to Káliel?"

Nodding to Owain, who was sprawled wearily across one of the wooden pews, Kavan pushed Gabrielle out of his thoughts and replied, "We have little choice. We remain here…look for clues if they are here…or else we follow what we know and see what comes of it."

Caol, anxious and irritated, paced the empty aisle between benches. "He's more desperate for the Serpents than I anticipated; wish I knew why. They're not that valuable…"

"We're likely to discover that when we find him…or at least learn more when we reach Káliel."

"Shall we find a ship leaving in the morning…or…?" Wortham stretched his arms over his head until his back popped but he left the question incomplete. He knew the bard detested sea travel and was wagered there was a Gate in this place. He did not, however, know if there was one on Káliel and did not want to make the suggestion.

The sick expression on the Elyri's face was confirmation of the captain's thoughts. "I would rather avoid the sea. There are Gates…unless any of you object." All heads shook, even Muir's and

Owain's. The youngest prince might wish to experience the sea, but if Kavan preferred to avoid ships, they would appease him. In this instance, reaching the islands with haste was preferable to a leisurely sail across the sea. Standing slowly, as if reluctant to act or in bodily discomfort, Kavan continued, "I will go first…make certain Lady Dilyn is awake and will allow us passage, and then return for you."

"Go quickly then," the inquisitor encouraged. "Any distance you can put between us and Justice Cornell is appreciated."

Leaving the others in the nave, Kavan crossed the thóres to the empty chamber where he knew the Gate to be. He squashed back the trepidation he felt about going to the islands, about seeing Gabrielle again. He felt it would be in both his, and her, best interests if he stayed away; he had no desire to hurt her and did not look forward to the pain seeing her would also cause him. But Káliel was where they had to be, Saint Kóráhm had said it, and thus Kavan would go.

From the closet in the office of the Prime Magistrate's home, Kavan stretched tendrils of thoughts outward, seeking Gabrielle, calling her, waiting for her to respond before leaving the place he stood. He could feel that the entire household slept, frowned that he was forced to wake any of them, and after a few minutes of no response he made another try. Soon he heard the office door creak open, but that the footsteps were too light, too hesitant, to belong to Gabrielle. Someone stopped outside the closet door, hesitated, and then opened it slowly, bringing them face to face.

It was Clianthe. The little girl, curls loose about her shoulders, wearing a pale yellow night shift of embroidered flowers looked at Kavan curiously and asked, "Why are you in the closet? Why were you calling me?"

"I…" He squatted before her and took one of her hands between his. It took only a moment of contact to confirm that she carried the power, quite strongly in fact. She had indeed heard him. "I am here to see your mother…" he began.

He was interrupted by more footsteps, however, and got quickly to his feet as Gabrielle entered the room with a scolding look at her daughter. "Clianthe, what are you…?" She stopped, however, to stare at Kavan as she realized he was there as well, in her home, again. "Kavan…" she murmured breathlessly. "It is late…what are you…?"

In her white nightgown, Gabrielle seemed to glow, lit by the light of the candle in her hand, looking to Kavan like some of the záryph imagined during his meditations and prayers. He was thankful she was beyond his reach, that Clianthe stood between them, as it would have taken a great deal of restraint not to touch her if she had been closer. "The explanation will require more time than the hour allows, I fear. My four companions and I have need of your assistance and lodging, at least for tonight; we come on a matter of diplomatic urgency…"

Trying to peer behind him, needing to look anywhere other than at the face that made her heart flutter, she asked, "There are others in my closet?"

"They are in Levonne; I thought it best to come alone, be certain we are welcome."

Gabrielle smiled nervously. "As I have told you, Kavan, you are always welcome here. And I will not turn away a diplomatic liaison from King Arlan, regardless of what the Council wants. I will have Delia prepare a meal and…"

"There is no need to trouble your staff, milady," Kavan said with a grateful bow. "Somewhere to sleep is all we require. And…" he sighed awkwardly, "we are not here at King Arlan's request…"

"It does not matter." Any reason that brought Kavan to her was good enough. It did not matter how or why he came to be there. "I will hear your explanation in the morning and arrange available rooms while you retrieve your friends. Clianthe, back to bed with you."

The child followed her obediently, stopping in the doorway long enough for a curious backward glance at the bard, before disappearing. Kavan did not immediately withdraw to the Gate. He stared after

Gabrielle, the vision of her in that white gown burned into his mind, creating stirrings within that he knew were inappropriate.

Enough of that, he thought with a degree of self-loathing he knew he should not feel. He forced his thoughts, and the feelings they inspired, out of his head long enough to bring the other men two at a time to the Prime Magistrate's home. First Wortham and Caol, then Princes Muir and Owain. When he emerged from the closet Gate the second time it was to find Gabrielle, wearing a light robe over her sleeping gown, enthusiastically embracing the captain.

"You should have told me Captain Delamo was coming," she chastised the bard with a smile on her face.

"You found out soon enough," Wortham chuckled, pleased with the unexpected warmth of her greeting.

"I would have preferred to give you a better welcome." She offered her hand to Caol. "Lord Dugan, Prince Muir, welcome to Káliel."

"Thank you for receiving us," the inquisitor said. Gabrielle's gaze meanwhile turned to the one man she did not recognize.

"Milady," Kavan offered, "May I introduce another dear friend of mine, Prince Owain Lachlan."

Another dear friend. Caol looked at the bard with surprise, not expecting to have such words applied to himself or the former king. Owain bowed, thankful that the gesture hid the way his breath caught in his throat at the sight of the unexpectedly beautiful woman.

"A pleasure and honor, Lady Dilyn. I have heard many remarkable things about you…and am pleased that at least some of them are true."

A wide range of emotions played across Gabrielle's face, none there long enough for Kavan to identify. He wondered what sort of rumors about the woman could have reached Owain in Neth, and why the exchange of glances, and the smile that settled upon her lips troubled him. "I have heard much about you as well, milord," Gabrielle said with a curtsey. She had seen a much younger prince many years ago, but until this moment she had never given thought to how he might have changed. "If Lord Cliáth calls you friend, then you are welcome on my islands."

The disquieting butterflies in Kavan's belly lurched uneasily, twisting with an unfamiliar rush of emotion he was unaccustomed to. When she gave her attention to Kavan, the knot loosened a little but did not dispel. "It is late," she said. "I am curious to know what has brought so many handsome men to my home at this hour, but Kavan's recommendation of discussing the matter in the morning is a sound one. Come; I have rooms ready, though there is no food prepared or water heated for bathing…"

Bowing again, his smile matching hers, Owain said, "A bed to sleep in is quite sufficient, Lady Dilyn."

At the top of the stairs, each man was deposited in a room. Kavan was shown to the room he had slept in when he had been in this house before. He hesitated in the corridor, watching Gabrielle bid Owain goodnight, meaning to close his door before she noticed but not being quick enough.

Passing on her way back to the staircase, Gabrielle asked, "Is there something I can get for you, Kavan?"

He shook his head too fervently, wanting to disguise his embarrassment but not knowing how. "No, but I want to let you know…if you do not…Clianthe does have the power. She heard me when I summoned you…which suggests she is quite attuned. She will begin to question you, no doubt…particularly after my strange arrival. I thought you should know."

Gabrielle studied his face as he spoke, knowing there was more behind his mostly blank expression than he was admitting. Smiling innocently to not embarrass him further with what she knew or guessed, she said, "Thank you for confirming it. I have suspected she was becoming…aware…since the last time you were here. I guess I will have to come up with answers before she asks the inevitable questions. If you are sure there is nothing more, then I bid you goodnight, milord…I will see you in the morning."

"Goodnight, milady." His heart told him he should say something more, but his mind had no idea what that should be.

## ❧Chapter 40❧

I t was dawn again, the sun appearing orange and purple behind thin gray clouds, before Merkar de Corrmick made his appearance in front of the leaders of Cordash and Enesfel. He had never met General Wyndham, knew the man by rumor and reputation alone, but the gossip of his soldiers told him the general was here. And though, as he drew closer to the seated collection of men, he did not recognize the two men from Ruidoso and Fiara, their clothing and mannerisms identified them as Nethites. Prisoners, he wondered? Translators, perhaps, he thought with a sneering look at General Wyndham, imagining Enesfel's man to be illiterate and incompetent.

His curiosity over Enesfel's presence, and the absence of General McHador or King Arlan, turned quickly to fury when he discovered that the two Nethites were neither translators nor prisoners, but rather emissaries present to speak on behalf of the region south of Lake Curo, the region which had been incorporated into Enesfel thanks to a covert campaign conducted while Neth's attention was turned to Cordash's larger, stronger army. The Kelari and Dagar Rivers were lined with soldiers, as was the lake's southern shore, and Merkar no longer had the military might to counter them.

Infuriated at the treachery, King Merkar pulled out of the talks, returned to his tent, and refused to see or speak to anyone except his generals for the remainder of the day. He knew, as did King Renfrid and General Wyndham, that he would return to the table soon enough. Merkar had no choice.

⬿*⬿

"You think that the kidnapper is on Káliel?"

"Perhaps not the main island," Kavan admitted, understanding the distress this must cause the Prime Magistrate. Harboring a fugitive, a kidnapper who might have with him the royal children of another kingdom, who might have killed her mother, would not look good for the isolationist islands. If such news reached King Arlan, and he chose to storm the islands with an army in a quest to find his son, the island kingdom would be ripped apart. "They might not be here any longer, if they ever came. Both suspects booked ships from Levonne to Káliel, but we cannot guarantee they disembarked here...or ever actually boarded those ships. Intuition tells me, however, that we are closer to finding answers, and I request permission to search the islands."

Gabrielle began to speak; normally such a matter would be presented to the Council, allowing them to decide a course of action. But there were children's lives at stake, kin of a king whose favor Gabrielle was trying to cultivate for the sake of her people. This was an instance that could not wait; she chose to invoke her sovereign right and decide a course of action without the Council. Before she could, however, Caol slid one of the drawings of Halstatt across the table towards her and asked, "Have you ever seen this man, Lady Dilyn?"

Her face lost some of its healthy color. "It looks like..." she stammered, "...who is this man, Lord Dugan?"

"He is the man who kidnapped my son and Prince Bertram...the man who murdered your mother. His name is Halstatt Tarmajien."

Muir eyed the inquisitor skeptically. "I did not know we had a name for him. It might have been easier to find him if..."

The inquisitor shrugged. "It wouldn't have helped. He was a member of the Association…he has resources…skills…"

"You have seen this man, milady?" Kavan could see Gabrielle's agitation in the twitching of her mouth and the corners of her eyes. It could be nothing more than the effect of memories. Perhaps seeing the man she had not been able to recall was unsettling.

"This is the same man who…attacked me and nearly blinded Captain Delamo? The man my mother warned me to keep the Serpents away from?"

The bard nodded. "It is." Watching her as she studied the drawing, he asked, "Is there something more?"

"No…yes…I…he looks like someone I once knew…"

Kavan impulsively grabbed her wrist and flooded her mind with the image of the second man they sought. Such a breach of Elyri ethics was unlike him, but after yet another vision during the night, the bard felt time was running out. They had to act swiftly and could not afford delays. "This man, perhaps?"

Gasping at the forced contact, Gabrielle pulled free of Kavan's grip, stood abruptly enough that her chair tumbled over behind her, and fled to the gardens behind the villa. Both Owain and Kavan rose to follow, one out of the need for answers, the other out of concern, but Wortham caught the bard's arm and held him back, allowing Owain to be the one to follow her. No one else would have dared stop Kavan; he glowered at the captain, but Wortham did not let go. "Leave her to Owain, milord. You have upset her; I do not think she will speak with you now. You should not have…"

"Wortham…she knows him…" What Kavan had read in that moment of contact convinced him of that.

"She meets many of the merchants that pass these islands…she could have met him at any time…"

"Perhaps," he replied reluctantly, relaxing enough that Wortham let him go. He doubted any mere merchant would have elicited such a gasp, such a flash of emotional pain, and he refused to believe her reaction was strictly due to the forced contact. He did not take his eyes from the door through which Owain and Gabrielle had departed and though he did not show it, continued to struggle against the urge to follow, not just to get answers, or apologize, but to make certain those two were not alone together.

Fortunately, Prince Muir distracted him from Owain and Gabrielle by asking, "What do we do, Lord Cliáth?"

Wortham continued to watch Kavan as he said, "I know these islands better than any of you; I'll start at the docks…my old friends. After fourteen years away, many will be eager to talk, I'm sure."

Caol clapped the prince on the shoulder. "How about you and I take a look around town…discreetly of course…" He knew it would do none of them any favors to get on the Council's bad side if foreigners made a nuisance of themselves. "It will give Lord Cliáth the chance to study all of these books," he gestured at the shelves around them. "Some way or other we need to find the connection between the Serpents, the Corylliens, and the Tarmajiens if we expect to find and beat him."

The prince nodded reluctantly, but Kavan did not move. The bard would rather have traded places with any of them, get out of the house and away from Gabrielle and Prince Owain before he said or did something he would regret, but of those in their group, he was the most adept at book research. "Be careful, Caol," he murmured. "If either of them is here, you and Prince Muir will likely be the targets."

"I know," the inquisitor grunted with a grim nod.

Owain found Gabrielle amidst the budding trees and shrubs, sitting on a stone bench, staring into the distance, her face anything but blank. He sat beside her, not speaking, preferring to give her the chance to talk if she wished. Instead, he turned his attention to the native plants, the likes of which he had never seen in either Neth or

Enesfel. There was grief on her face, and terrified confusion, both of which he felt obliged to relieve though he did not know how.

"He did not mean to upset you. His concern for the boys has caused him to do many uncharacteristic things of late." At least, Owain assumed they were aberrant judging by the reactions of the others.

She shook her head and wiped her damp cheeks on the back of her hand. "I do not blame him, he could never hurt me intentionally, although he does very well of doing it unintentionally." Owain did not interrupt her or prod her to continue. "I loved him once," she whispered, "or thought I did. Perhaps I always will…"

"I think everyone does." He looked away to hide the melancholy on his face. "I did not know…"

She covered his hand with hers and squeezed lightly. "Do not pity me. For all the good it has done me, nothing shall ever come of my affections. I have always known this. He does not wish it."

Then he is a fool, Owain thought, though aloud he said, "I understand. I loved once and she could not love me in return. I believed then that there could never be another in my life while she lived…but she is wed, has a son, and has no room in her life for me." He propped his chin on his hands, his elbows on his knees. "Perhaps it was meant not to be, but it has not made it easier to bear."

"That is so."

After a long silent pause, he asked, "Is there anything I can do?"

Hand still on his, finding comfort in the contact with a seemingly kindred spirit, Gabrielle sighed and one shoulder twitched in a shrug. "I do not know what anyone can do. Have you seen this second man you seek?"

"I have seen him through Lord Cliáth's eyes, as you have…and he saw him in Lord Dugan's mind."

"Do you think there could be a mistake? That what Lord Dugan saw…what Kavan showed you, could be in error?"

"I don't know," Owain admitted. "I have not had a great deal of experience with either man. From what I have seen in the past few weeks, I find it difficult to fault his abilities or his premonitions. What is it about this man that troubles you? Have you seen him?"

She shook her head. "Not in many weeks. He…that could be the second man you seek." She pointed to a small building nestled amongst the shrubs but said no more.

The prince went towards it, moving branches out of the way as he approached. Gabrielle followed several paces behind. There were several marble markers upon it, the newest of which was near the bottom. Squatting to see it better, he brushed away leaves and cobwebs, recognizing by the names on the stones that this was a gravesite. "Felix Maylor?" he asked, reading the name aloud before looking at the woman over his shoulder.

"My husband."

≈*≈

Having enjoyed a peaceful life for thirteen years, having not been away from Rhidam except for Ártur and Syl's wedding in Bhryell, a journey to Alberni upon the death of Brenna's brother, and an occasional visit to the Lachlan family estate in Kamin, King Arlan had discovered during the last few weeks that he was no longer accustomed to long days riding in armor under the sweltering heat of the mid-summer sun, or to too many nights sleeping on the hard ground. His muscles ached, his skin itched, and he knew he smelled like something other than a king. The healer wore no armor and the King envied him that.

He also learned unexpectedly, as they approached the line of forest and mountains that had been the boundary between Enesfel and Neth, that he was no longer prepared for battle. From the trees emerged a number of Neth soldiers, men cut off from their own, surrounded by foreigners, who wanted vengeance upon whomever they could take it from. That the unit they chose to attack contained the King of Enesfel was simply a risk they were prepared to take.

The King hung back with his healer, allowing the soldiers to engage, more out of uncertainty of what to do than out of cowardice. He knew how to fight, and had kept his skills honed, but it had been a long time since he had experienced combat, and with his heir still missing, he felt that Enesfel needed her king to lead more than she needed him to fight.

Four of the Nethites broke away from the rest and barreled towards him, however, taking the choice from his hands. Ártur attempted to avoid the melee, but he too was surrounded before he could get away. Left with no choice, knowing the healer would not, could not, defend himself against four soldiers, Arlan swallowed his apprehension. There was no one to aid them; if he did not fight for his life, for their lives, he would not have one much longer.

The first of the four was easy enough to kill since he was armed with nothing but a broken lance and wore simple leather armor. The second took more effort, but thanks to Ártur hitting the man on the back of the head with his healer's pack, the King was successful in killing him as well. A wallop across his left shoulder toppled Arlan from his horse; he tried to stand, to strike back, but was knocked flat again by the same mace that had dismounted him. Unable to get up without being struck down, the King parried each attack with his sword and shield, rolling to avoid the blows and the dancing horses' hooves that minced the earth around him as Ártur did his best to shield the King and avoid being killed. Both were aware of the hopelessness of their situation but struggled to avoid the inevitable.

The attacker with the mace was abruptly lifted from his saddle by the chancellor's bloody broadsword. Bhríd deposited the man's body upon the ground, the fellow's face bearing an expression of amazement as he crumpled to the earth. From the other side, Sir

Gabersdon had come between Ártur and the last of the four attackers. While the chancellor shielded the fallen king, Arlan struggled to his feet and leaped back as the enemy rider backed his horse away from the young knight. Seizing the opportunity, the King thrust his sword into the man's back, beneath the ridge of his metal breastplate and yanked him from his horse. Bruised and sore, the action was difficult for the King but the pain did not stop him from following through with the attack that left the rider dead at his feet.

"Are you injured, My Liege?" Despite the effects of adrenaline and fear in his system, having come close to death, the healer slid off his horse to put duty first. He began trying to help the King out of his mail shirt even though there was still fighting going on no more than fifty yards away from them.

"Ártur, it can wait…" The King tried to brush the man's hands away, wincing in pain.

"Your shoulder might be dislocated, or your ribs broken…they have the situation in hand…let me tend you…"

The healer spoke the truth. By the time the King had removed his armor, wincing and groaning all the while, the fighting had ceased and five of the small Nethite force had been taken prisoner. Although many of King Arlan's men had received injuries that required tending, only nine had lost their lives.

"Feels like old times, doesn't it, milord," the chancellor asked, grinning as he removed his helmet.

"Do not remind me of old, Lord Cáner," muttered the King.

Sir Gabersdon joined them, having removed his badly dented helmet and carrying it tucked under his arm. "I cannot believe they thought they could fight the two best swordsmen in the Sovereignties and hope to win." The knight was considerably younger than the chancellor, but in size and stature, they were much the same.

Still grinning, Bhríd said, "Perhaps they have not heard of us yet."

"They certainly heard of you today. My commendations to you both. Are we able to continue or shall we make camp?" The King did not feel like riding further, even though the healer had taken care of his shoulder; there were other wounded men to tend and dead to bury that warranted staying where they were. However, they were too close to the stench of death, and the King was eager to be home.

"We should eat while we are here…allow Lord Healer to work and give the men a chance to rest. We can decide whether to move when that is done, I think?"

The King nodded and shook his chancellor's hand. "Sound advice, Lord Chancellor. I may make a general of you yet."

The Elyri chuckled and shook his head. "Thank you, but no. I have no interest in that title, milord. I fight when I must, but I do not want to make a life out of war. Besides, I am about to be a married man. Would you ask me to spend so much time away from my new bride?"

"Not now, but maybe someday."

"Perhaps," Bhríd agreed, "but I do not think so."

# ✷Chapter 41✷

N ursing his shoulder, which throbbed and ached with grinding pain when he moved it, Kavan temporarily set aside the books he had been reading in favor of wandering into the dining hall where the large harp Ulstar Dilyn had once offered still stood. Kavan refused to take it then, believing that such a family heirloom should remain with that family. His own smaller harp was upstairs in his room but he did not feel like going up to get it. Not knowing when or if he would be able to return to Rhidam, his harp had been the one thing he had been sure to bring with him. He could not live without it. But he gladly took the opportunity to play the larger instrument, hoping that a different focus would take his mind off of the ache in his shoulder.

Arlan had been injured. That was the best explanation for the force that had struck him, knocking him from his chair and leaving his shoulder feeling bruised and dislocated. The injury had not been life-threatening, but the fading pain was still noticeable. Curious how the injury had come about, what had happened and where the King was, Kavan did not immediately sense the presence in the room. When he did, he looked at the child with a welcoming smile.

Standing with her hands behind her back, rocking up and down on her toes in time to the music, she smiled back and curtseyed when he noticed her. "You play beautifully; are you the harper mother always talks about?"

"I assume I must be, but I do not know how many harpers your mother knows."

"Not many…we rarely have musicians from outside of Káliel. She says you are the best in the whole world. She's right."

His smile warmed more. "Thank you, Clianthe."

The little girl drew closer, her reddish curls bouncing around her face. When she reached him, she hesitantly touched his hand and looked up into his face as if she had expected him to feel like something other than flesh. "Mother says you are Elyri. What is that?"

"It is what I am…we are different from Teren."

"Am I Teren?" Not wanting to confuse her with a complex explanation, Kavan opted to nod yes. "Are all Elyri white like you?"

"No, that is a peculiarity only I have."

She cocked her head and skewed her face. "Other than that…you do not look different."

"Not very, perhaps, but I am different enough. Most of the differences you cannot easily see."

"Like your voice?"

Having this conversation with an adult would have been disconcerting. Having it with an innocent child who was honestly curious and trying to understand the things happening in her own body and her own world was not nearly as bad. "I…being Elyri is not the reason my voice is different. It is the way it is, the way I was born."

"Oh." She seemed satisfied with that answer and did not press further. "Is Prince Muir Elyri too?"

That question surprised him and he wondered why she asked it. "No. He is Teren, as you are."

She nodded, satisfied with that answer too and bounced back to the door. Over her shoulder, she asked, "Will you play tonight? May I play with you?"

"If your mother wishes it, I would be happy to play. And I would be delighted if you would play with me."

∞*∞

Caol looked at the tattered and stained parchment in his hand. He had not shown it to Prince Muir when it had been slipped to him while they spoke to people in one of the few taverns the island possessed. After rereading it twice, the inquisitor was not sure he would show it to anyone. It was a letter of congratulations, of sorts, that he had arrived on Káliel at last, finally proving intelligent enough to determine the correct steps to take. The letter demanded the Coryllien and the Serpents be turned over within three days, or else what they had journeyed here for would never be seen again. While not the news Caol wanted, it proved that Kavan's intuition had been correct. Halstatt was somewhere on Káliel.

∞*∞

Prince Kjell paced his room, stopping to rap upon the time-stained window sill anxiously or kick anything that happened to be in his path as his pent-up frustration sought an outlet. Neth had surrendered. Merkar had surrendered…and lost a fair portion of the kingdom in the process. It was not official, but with Cordash's army positioned two days from Glevum's walls, and Enesfel protecting what had been the lower third of the kingdom, the choice was inevitable. And intelligent, Kjell knew, even though many thought him too young to understand such things. It was embarrassing and insulting how quickly and easily their neighbors had broken Neth's troops, men supposedly well trained and yet had offered very little resistance. Neth was defeated and lost the southern forests in less than three weeks.

He wondered if Cordash had been capable of defeating them all of these years, while Neth prided themselves on an excellent military force capable of productive raids. Undoubtedly, Loris and those who came before had pushed too far and Cordash had finally endured enough. Hopefully, Merkar would learn from his father's mistakes and never again resort to raiding their neighbors to prove he could.

The letter that had come to Kjell from General Glucke instructed him to be ready for anything, saying that life in Neth was about to undergo a dramatic change. That statement could refer to any number of things, from adjusting to life under Merkar's reign, to being ruled by a foreign monarch if Cordash and Enesfel demanded it, of possible exile, imprisonment or death if those same kingdoms decided that all de Corrmick's must die. It might also refer to Merkar's death at the hands of his unhappy generals or troops, or it might simply mean that, with the southern portion of the kingdom taken away, Neth's wealth and prestige would suffer. A treaty had yet to be signed, and Kjell suspected his brother might do what he could to avoid giving that territory up…even to the point of returning to battle.

Give it to them, Kjell muttered to himself. True, the south provided the kingdom with trees and hunting territory, but there was little else, other than manpower, the area had to offer the Crown. There were not enough men living in those forested reaches of the land, in Kjell's opinion, to make it worth further bloodshed or the risk of execution for the whole de Corrmick family. Better to capitulate and wait for the day they could reclaim it rather than to sell Neth's soul and destroy her completely.

He wondered what would become of his cousin Owain in his home in Fiara and then smiled to himself. Owain would survive. That particular member of the family had more survivability than any other de Corrmick. If Owain had wanted Glevum's throne, Kjell had no doubt he would have taken it. Owain would find some way to survive, either by siding with the Lachlans or by coming to Glevum. Probably the former, as coming to Merkar meant risking being called a traitor to the Crown regardless of whether he was or not.

Kjell penned a return letter to General Glucke, suggesting surrender to all terms as soon as he received the general's message. He sent it back with the same messenger. Knowing Glucke as he did, Kjell imagined the general would likely spout any usable phrases and ideas directly to Merkar as if they were his own. Better that, than have Merkar suspect his little brother was not as flighty as he appeared. If the King would even listen to his general.

If Merkar listened, it would please Kjell to know he had aided his kingdom somehow, even if he was not old enough to wield a sword.

❧*❧

"I found very little," Wortham admitted reluctantly as he poured water into a cup from a clay jug. Everyone except Caol was gathered at Gabrielle's table for the evening meal, the first time together since the awkward parting that morning. The inquisitor had escorted Prince Muir back to the villa and then disappeared into the streets. No one had seen or spoken to him since. The prince had no explanation to give, except that Caol wanted to be alone. Given the danger his son was in, such a desire was understandable but his absence still troubled those in the room who had traveled here with him.

The captain continued after taking a long drink. "This man Halstatt arrived here...used that name on the ship manifest when he signed for some crates he brought. He would have arrived when we were in Fiara, but no one can tell me if he left or not. It seems likely he is still here, but none of the dock workers have any idea where."

"And we didn't find a thing," muttered Muir bitterly.

"Did he have the boys with him?" Gabrielle asked, looking at Wortham as she spoke but side-eyeing Owain. To Kavan's irritation, no one had seen them since they had left the library that morning, until now. He had yet to see Gabrielle's husband and told himself his reaction was worry about what that man might think or do if he came home to find his wife fawning over the Lachlan prince.

"No one saw any children…just a few large trunks and crates…"

"Someone would put Wilred and Bertram in crates?" Muir asked in shock. In his fairly sheltered life, the prince could not imagine what his brother and cousin must be enduring, or how afraid they must be.

"No one knows. He could have smuggled them ashore during the night, or still have them on a ship…or he might have left them somewhere else. I suggest a thorough search of all harbored vessels…but after this much time, it's unlikely we will find anything."

And such a search would be time-consuming, not to mention disruptive of the local economy. Kavan's temples began to throb and he rubbed them absently. Across the table, Clianthe was watching Prince Muir, the look on her face reminiscent of Gabrielle's expression the first time she and Kavan met face to face. The thought made him smile faintly while swallowing back his uncomfortable understanding of both Gabrielle and her daughter.

"Lord Cliáth?"

"It is nothing, my prince," Kavan waved off the young prince's concern.

"The Sight?"

"No, nothing like that…"

"What is the Sight?" asked Clianthe. In spite of her age, she understood that the term meant something more than what one could see with their eyes.

Gabrielle quickly intervened, not wanting to get into this discussion when she did not think her daughter was ready to understand. "It is a very special Elyri gift, and that is all you need to know. I thought you were going to play something for us?"

"If Lord Cliáth plays with me." The child looked expectantly from her mother to Kavan. Gabrielle, knowing that Kavan preferred to perform alone, started to deny her daughter, but Kavan offered the girl his hand.

"I would be honored to play with the woman who might one day surpass my musical reputation."

Clianthe giggled, more at being called a woman than at the flattery she did not understand. She scampered to the large harp, an instrument that was awkward for her small arms to manage, but that challenge did not seem to bother her. "Do you know The Blue Bird of Gallínphel?"

"Of course," he replied. "It is one of the earliest songs I learned to play." It was something his uncle and cousin often used when testing new harps for sound and tone quality, and sometimes Kavan believed he could hear a woman humming it in his dreams. His mother, perhaps, but as he had no conscious memories of her, he could not be certain. He allowed Clianthe to begin in order to adjust his key and pitch accordingly and then began to play too.

Three songs later, Clianthe bowed out of the music making. She had ability for her age, but she was smart enough to know that her partner was superior and that, despite what he said, no one was likely to surpass his reputation and skill for many years. Kavan continued to play as the others listened or chatted. Though his eyes were closed, he knew Wortham was watching him, knew Prince Muir was answering Clianthe's questions as he always did with his sister, and knew that Owain and Gabrielle were still casting stolen glances at one another as they pretended to focus on the music.

Kavan was also aware of Caol's return to the villa. He stopped playing when the door chime rang and waited for the maidservant Delia to escort the inquisitor into the dining hall. He felt an instant of both hope and despair as he met the man's troubled gaze.

"About time you joined us, Lord Dugan," Owain teased.

The inquisitor, however, was in no mood for teasing. "Halstatt's here."

"We know he came here; he was seen at the docks…"

"No, Owain, he's still here. I didn't see him but he made sure I got this." He gave the crumpled letter to Kavan who, after reading it hastily, passed it to Wortham. "I haven't found him…but he's here."

Gabrielle got to her feet and held her hand to her daughter. "Clianthe, sweet…it is time for bed. Delia…" She did not want her daughter to hear a dialogue that might quickly turn dark. She had been hesitant enough to have her overhear the talk of kidnapped children, but fortunately, the men had chosen their words with the girl in mind.

"Mother…" Clianthe whined. "I want to hear more songs."

"I think Lord Cliáth has given us enough music for tonight. Perhaps he will share more tomorrow."

"Come, Clianthe," Delia said, taking the child's hand after the girl hugged her mother goodnight. By the time she had trudged from the room, the letter had returned to Caol's hands and Kavan gestured for him to give it to Gabrielle. "I believe you should see it, milady…we will need your cooperation to resolve this…"

Gabrielle read the letter quickly and then read it again, her frown deepening with each word. "You want me to surrender the Serpents?"

"It might be necessary to…"

"I will not do it, Kavan." She gave the letter back to Caol.

"Milady…"

Though he was seated several feet away, Owain maneuvered between Kavan and Gabrielle as if to protect her. "Enough, milord. Why should she give up the islands' regalia? We do not have proof…"

"Halstatt is here," Caol snarled at the former king. "He has my son. Deidre's son. He has Enesfel's heir. If it was the lady's child in danger, I am sure she would not hesitate…"

Owain's gaze narrowed. "But it is not her daughter; this affair is none of her concern. Besides, the Serpents are but a part of what he requests. What about the Coryllien dagger? No one has seen…"

Kavan's strained voice interrupted them, taking the steam out of the burgeoning hostility in the room. "I have the Coryllien." There was silence. No one except Caol knew that the Coryllien dagger had been in Rhidam, that it was real. Kavan did not like this situation any more than anyone else did, but he was trying to be practical, to do what was right, what needed to be done, with as little inconvenience to anyone as possible. "Perhaps the missing princes are none of Gabrielle's concern…and I do not fault her for wanting to keep the Serpents safe…but it may be possible to…"

"We don't even know why he wants them, Lord Cliáth…"

The bard's eyes narrowed as he grew annoyed with being interrupted. "I know that," he hissed. "I am not suggesting giving him the Serpents."

The former king started to retort again but fell silent when he realized that was true. Kavan had said nothing about giving the Serpents to anyone, but Owain and the others had quickly assumed the worst. Behind him, Gabrielle squeezed his arm gently.

Kavan continued tersely. "It is possible that closer examination of the Serpents will tell us why he wants them. If there is a treasure upon the islands, belonging to Dawid Coryllien or not, the Serpents could be the key to what it is or where it is located. I suspect it is the fabled treasure he seeks. All I am asking is to be allowed to examine the three Serpents together…nothing more."

"I have two," Gabrielle murmured. "I have mine and my mother's…"

"Your husband has the other? As is customary? Would he refuse to allow…?"

Gabrielle's gaze fell. "Felix is dead. He disappeared during our last storm, swept from the docks and drowned. He was wearing the Serpent at the time…he rarely took it off unless he was asleep." Her eyes grew wide and she felt suddenly cold. What if he was not dead? What if that second man they were seeking was Felix…and he was either working with or for the kidnapper? It meant the kidnapper already possessed one of the Serpents. The thought made her feel ill, and as she wrapped her arms around herself, she realized she might be more valuable to Kavan's success than she wished to be.

"My apologies, milady," Kavan murmured. "I did not know…"

"You had no reason to know…for I did not tell you…but…" She looked at Owain for reassurance before continuing. "The man…not the one in the drawing but the other you showed me…he looks like…he could be Felix. Or at least he appears to be closely related. He has brothers, sisters, cousins…"

When she met his gaze, Kavan understood why she had reacted so strongly to his contact that morning. It could not be easy for her to speak of this, to think that the man she had married might have been something other than what she had come to know…that he might still be alive after allowing her to believe he was drowned.

Kavan set his harp aside. As Gabrielle suggested, this revelation meant that Halstatt might already possess one of the Serpents. "Then we will work with two," he said. "I promise I will do everything in my power to keep them safe, if you will permit me to examine them."

"I will consider the request, Kavan…and quickly," she promised.

"Let's hope it's fast enough to keep ahead of Halstatt," grunted Caol, "and that we discover their worth before it's too late."

## ❧Chapter 42❧

Two days after his brush with war, King Arlan and his smaller force of men crossed what had been, until recently, the Neth border and entered familiar Enesfel territory. They stopped in Fiara long enough to restock food and water and feed for their horses, but Fiara held reminders of what the King faced in Rhidam and though he did not look forward to that, he wanted to be as far from Fiara as possible. He wanted to be home. So did his men, particularly Ártur and the chancellor, a man who grew more cheerful with each passing mile. He seemed to have forgotten who lay in state in the upper oratory. Or perhaps, the King thought wistfully, his chancellor's upcoming nuptials and the positive focus they gave him were enough to ease the sting.

Enesfel's king could not think of anything positive to focus on. He was going home, yes, but Guthrie McHador's body was there, and the responsibility of burying his mentor weighed heavy. He would see his daughter and youngest son, but both would remind him of his missing child and of his recently departed wife. Soon, he hoped he would see Kavan again. While that possibility brought a warm rush to his heart, it also reminded him that the next time he saw his best friend, it might be over the body of his oldest son.

Beside him, the healer, though eager to be home, had been unusually quiet since the battle. Is he missing Kavan as much as I, the King wondered? Or was his melancholy due to the death of his niece? Or had the Elyri finally seen enough bloodshed to last an entire lifetime? Almost two lifetimes, he thought, realizing that Ártur had first served Arlan's father as battle physician. The healer was sixty-five years old, an age many Teren never reached.

Well, Arlan decided, hopefully, the fighting years were over and there would never again be the need to send Ártur onto the battlefield. Enesfel's relationships with Hatu and Cordash were good, and as long as Arlan had a say, they would stay that way. Neth had been hobbled, he hoped; it would be a long time before they could cause trouble again. And with Elyriá, there was always peace. Somehow, the King was determined to compensate the healer for the years of service he had given the Lachlan House…just as soon as Enesfel ceased reeling from the losses this year had brought.

From the window of his rented room, the dark, weather-beaten face watched the comings and goings from the house of Káliel's ruling family. He had waited a long time for the inquisitor to show himself, to come to the islands, not realizing that Dugan and the others had been sent on a wild chase across the kingdom instead of being led directly here. He understood that Dugan was a thorough man, that he would exhaust all possibilities in the quest to find his son, but he had expected their search to bring them to Káliel sooner. He had gambled that the search would end on the island kingdom, had come here at the start of the quest, and was satisfied to have his patience pay off. Halstatt had come to Káliel in search of a treasure whose worth and existence was yet unverified, the finding of treasure proving more important, it seemed, than immediate revenge on the rival Dugan clan. Tarmajien, he thought, you are too predictable.

⁊*⁊

Looking through the Dilyn's library, a substantially more meager collection of books than existed on the Lachlan's shelves, Kavan had yet to find anything to aid their investigation. Caol, Muir, and Wortham scoured the city, going door to door in their quest for information as Gabrielle and Owain oversaw a ship by ship search of the docks. Nothing came of their efforts that day, however, leaving them another day wasted. That, and the fact that Gabrielle had again spent most of her time in Owain's company left the bard in no mood for socializing. He declined dinner, refused to play in favor of research, and when his frustration peaked he left the house to visit the shrine of Saint Bhenádíctus, to stare from the cliff across the sea towards Enesfel's shore as he prayed. He briefly considered contacting Ártur in the hopes that his cousin's familiar presence would ease his mind, but decided against it. It would not do to worry his cousin, and he had no answers to the questions the healer would undoubtedly ask. What Kavan wanted was a peace of mind he could not find.

A night of prayer and meditation did little to ease his heart, and he returned to the library for more research as soon as light began to creep over the horizon. When Gabrielle entered the library almost an hour later, he abruptly left the room. Something she had said, which he could not recall, had annoyed him. Or perhaps it was her presence he had been unable to tolerate. He did not know. He retreated to the back garden, where she had gone before, and found the marker that was supposed to be Felix's final testament. Maylor? He wondered, as his fingers traced the etched letters on the marble placard, if he had been any relation to the child Bianca, and what such a relationship might mean to recent events.

"May I speak with you, Kavan?"

He bristled at the sound of her voice, apologetic and hesitant as it was, but did not look at her. "If you wish; I will not stop you."

"Perhaps not," Gabrielle sighed as she sat on the bench nearest him, "But you may walk away again." When he did not speak and did not leave, she continued, "Something about my husband troubles you? Beyond the possibility that he might not be dead...or that he might be involved in this kidnapping plot."

"We don't know yet if he's involved...or how he might be...or if it is even him," admitted the bard. He paused, traced the name again, and asked, "Did he have a younger sister...a daughter...or some other relative named Cinda?"

Gabrielle shrugged. "He never spoke much about his family. I believe they were extensive, many living on Jaffe, but I never met them...not even at our wedding. I thought it odd, but he claimed they were afraid of sea travel. Many on the islands are. Why do you ask?"

"The woman originally hired as nurse for Prince Hagan before the queen's death was named Cinda Maylor. She had an infant daughter named Bianca. The woman drowned shortly after she entered King Arlan's employment and her child is in the care of my cousin and his wife. They have hopes of adopting her, should we fail to find her family...but if these could be her relatives..."

"I will send envoys to Jaffe to look into it. If there is family there, they would likely want to know what has happened to the girl and her child." There was a long, uncomfortable pause before she swallowed and asked, "Pray tell...what have I done that has angered you?"

"You have done nothing." Not exactly a lie, but the closest he had ever come to uttering one. She had done nothing to him to cause his anger, and as he saw it, his anger was more his own fault than hers. He fought for words, something to clarify his statement, but could not think of anything that would help.

"It is Lord Lachlan. You are jealous."

"No, I…" His words faltered as he realized that perhaps that was an accurate statement. He had never felt jealousy before, thus had not considered that what he was experiencing might have that name. He looked at Gabrielle as she joined him, the torment in his eyes clearer than any other emotion she had ever read in them.

She touched his shoulder lightly. "We have much in common, he and I. I would not have thought that possible fourteen years ago, but we are both different people now. To be honest, I did not think I would ever feel anything for any man other than you…not even Felix."

She stopped speaking as he looked away and shrugged free of her hand. "Do you love me, Kavan? Is that the cause of your…mood?"

He shook his head. "I have answered that question," he choked after many moments of silence. "The answer has not changed. Please do not ask me to repeat it."

It was bittersweet to hear his words and she nodded. She would not ask him to say it; she did not think she could bear to hear those words again. "Do not begrudge me happiness, Kavan. I will never have you; we both know it. Why should it matter to you what passes between he and me?"

"I do not know, Gabrielle. I do not understand it myself. I think it may be knowing that I shall never experience that…connection…with anyone. You have always been there and I turned you away. Repeatedly. I do not regret my choices…because I know it is right for both of us…but I do regret the knowledge that my life is destined to be a solitary one."

"Kavan…" Her voice cracked with emotion she did not know how to express. Despite his level tone, his misery was obvious in his broken sentences and the dullness in his eyes. She placed her hand upon his shoulder again; without looking at her, he took it in his hand, held it to his face long enough to kiss her fingertips, and then let her go. It was the most intimate gesture that had ever passed between them.

Voice shaky, she began again. "I want to give you something. I've considered what you said. I waited for you to return last night, to share this with you, but you did not come. If Clianthe was in danger, I would hope someone would do for her what you are doing for the princes, hope that someone would be willing to do anything to help me save her. If I do not make the same offer to King Arlan, how can I ever expect anyone to do likewise for me? Take the Serpents, Kavan. Do what you must. Find the mystery, give my mother peace, save the children. Losing the Serpents is a small price to pay for ties to Enesfel, for the life of two boys…and as Owain pointed out, any damage done to them can be repaired."

"Are you certain, milady?" Kavan held his breath as she held the brooches out for him to take. Only then did he realize that each Serpent was different. He had never seen them side by side before and had never paid close enough attention to them separately to realize it. Studying them, he stood. "The other…is the third different as well?"

"Yes, the third Serpent is rising out of the waves." Their differences had never been questioned, merely accepted as fact, facets of the nature of the islands on which they lived. "Might it be significant?"

"It could be. A symbol for a noble house is usually, at least in all examples I have seen, the same on every item that bears it. The color might vary for artistic purposes, but the symbol itself stays the same. There must have been a reason for this difference when these were made. I will return to the library with them…see what else I can learn. Would you care to join me?"

"Owain and I…"

His gaze flickered but he refused to look away from her. Having voiced his feelings, he now buried whatever pain he felt deep within. "Go with my blessings, Gabrielle, and tell Owain…"

"What?"

"That I will see him at dinner." He stayed in the garden after she departed; she watched him through the window for many minutes and he knew she was there. The past withered and drifted away on the winds before him. He had given her his blessing. He would not go back on his word.

❧*❧

The sprawling villa was empty except for the Elyri in the library and the servants in the kitchen. That fortunate turn of events would make his search simpler. When what he wanted was not in the first room he investigated, he moved to the second, the third, and then the fourth. Of course, the thief mused. What you want is always in the last place you look. It was hidden, obscured in a way that most would never have thought to look. Whoever had placed it there had not been anticipated his unique determination. Or perhaps they had not thought it necessary to be more careful. Their mistake, he grunted. He had what he had come for this time. Tomorrow he intended to have the rest.

❧*❧

After another unfruitful morning, Wortham entered the villa library to a tabletop covered with books, pieces of parchment, and a variety of small tools and writing instruments. He had shared his noon meal on the docks with the inquisitor and Prince Muir, but then left them to question old friends alone. Truthfully he had left them to return to the villa for the Elyri's assurance and inspiration. Wortham was losing faith, and only Kavan could restore it. The bard was bent over an open manuscript with the Serpents disassembled on the table before him.

"Lady Dilyn has allowed you to examine the Serpents. Have you found something worthwhile?" He bent over the table beside Kavan, wagering that the Prime Magistrate had not realized Kavan intended to take the brooches apart.

"Perhaps…but I do not yet know what it means." He held up the gold base of one of the brooches. "There is a symbol etched into the metal; it could not be found without removing the coral serpent from the setting. There is a different symbol on this one. I presume, since each Serpent is different, that the third symbol must be different as well…but I don't know how we will determine what that symbol is. I have found no information yet to explain what the symbols mean."

"Perhaps Lady Dilyn will know…"

A child's screech came from upstairs; Kavan and Wortham fled to the source to meet Clianthe at the bottom of the steps after she tumbled down them. "Lord Cliáth!" she cried, trembling as he caught her in his arms. "Your room…"

Kavan did not wait for her to say more. Scooping her up, he hastened up the marble staircase, with Wortham right behind, and came to a halt in the open doorway. His bureau was open, as was the closet, and his harp lay on the floor beside its case, which was open and upside down. Even before seeing the room's condition, he detected a violation. Someone who should not have been there had been. His open harp case and the disarray of his few belongings proved it. He gave Clianthe into Wortham's arms and knelt to examine the harp and its case. When he touched them both, he recognized the face that flashed before his mind's eye. It was barely conceivable. There had to be a mistake.

But there was no mistake, except his own. The harp case's interior compartment designed to hold extra strings, polish, and other small items, was empty, its contents spilled upon the floor. But the one item he had hoped would be safe inside of that case was gone. He should not have made such an assumption.

"The Coryllien…" he whispered, swallowing the defeated lumps that formed in his throat and chest.

"No one knew you had it until…and none of us knew where you kept it."

Kavan brushed back his hair. "Caol knew, but this is not his doing. He would never have been this careless or messy, and if he had asked for the dagger, I would have given it to him. This was done by someone else."

"Halstatt?"

"I saw him…" Clianthe whispered through her sobs.

Fearing she would confirm the impression he had gotten upon touching the harp case, Kavan stroked the girl's hair and asked, "You saw who did this?" From the look of terror on her face, he knew the answer before he asked.

She nodded and choked, "It was father's ghost."

The Elyri shot Wortham a glance, as he pulled the girl against him, that bid the captain to find Gabrielle. This was an issue the girl's mother had to deal with. He twisted her hair in his hand as she buried her face against his shoulder. He could not tell her there had been no ghost, and yet he did not think he should tell her the intruder had been her father. Nor did he think it fair to lie and say it had been someone who looked like her father. Thus he was not sure what to say. No child should have a parent fake their death and then reappear in the home before them. He wanted to reassure her but did not know how, nor did he dare touch her terrified mind to soothe her fears. It was better to let her mother handle this. He carried her out of the room and sank onto the top step of the staircase, holding her on his lap, rocking her and singing softly as they waited for Gabrielle.

It was many minutes later before Gabrielle rushed through the front door and up the stairs with Owain and Wortham behind her. Clianthe hesitated to release her hold around the Elyri's neck but finally threw herself against her mother.

"I am here, sweet. There is nothing to fear. What happened?"

"Father's ghost was here…"

Gabrielle's eyes flashed with disbelief, anger, and fear. "Here? Where? When?"

"I came back from Nona's…went to my room…I was playing with my dolls when I heard a noise. I hoped it was Lord Cliáth; I wanted him to teach me new songs." She snuck a quick glance at the bard before continuing. "I came into the hall…saw the ghost in Lord Cliáth's room…I hid under my bed so that he could not see me…ghosts hurt people who see them…Nona said so…then I saw him in the window…I screamed and scared him away."

Smoothing her hair, Gabrielle kissed the girl's ear and murmured, "It was no ghost…and it is not your father. It was someone who looks like him, that is all…a man Lord Cliáth and the others are looking for. Let me take you to your room; I will stay with you and make sure he is gone."

When the men were alone, Owain asked, "Did he take anything?"

"The Coryllien." A sudden thought had him pushing past the others and racing downstairs. If the man had broken into the house for the dagger, he might do the same for the other Serpents. The brooches still lay upon the table where Kavan left them, however, along with all of Kavan's notes and the books he had been studying. None of the parts were missing; Kavan gave a sigh of relief and gripped the edge of the table. Only when he breathed normally did he repeat his theory about the brooches to Owain and the three men discussed the Serpents and the dagger until Gabrielle joined them.

"Is she sleeping?" asked Owain, concern heavy in his voice.

"Yes, finally."

"You lied to her."

She gave Kavan a stern look. "Would you rather I tell her that her father faked his death in order to hurt people…to hurt children? Besides, such a betrayal makes him dead to me, and I would rather Clianthe believe he died at sea. Any man who could do such a thing as this is not the father of my child." Her gaze swept across the others and came to rest on the dismantled Serpents with a flash of distress. "Kavan…have you…?"

"They are not harmed," he promised her. Resetting the Serpents in their base would be a simple task for an experienced jeweler. He gave her the gold settings and pointed to the symbols in each. "Do these mean anything to you?"

The first brooch was turned in several directions before she murmured, "A crumpled hat?" Wortham chuckled as she studied the second. A moment later her face lit up. "This one…in ancient times, when the islands were first settled, some of the old mariner charts used symbols to designate which islands were which…before they were named. This one is the symbol for Pháne."

With a surge of hope, "Kavan asked, "Which island is that?"

Wortham took the brooch to study. "Do you remember when we first met in the cove on the east side of the island? Pháne is the island that was to the right of your ships…the one you could not see until the fog lifted."

The bard nodded. He remembered that night vividly. Expression thoughtful, he turned the first brooch around in his palm, also studying the crumpled hat image from a variety of angles. With the knowledge of the second symbol's meaning, it gave Kavan a direction to ponder. When the brooch stopped moving, the captain came behind him to get a better view of what Kavan was seeing.

"Milord?" It was not a symbol for one of the other islands. If it had been, Gabrielle likely would have known that too.

Voice low and tense with hope, Kavan replied, "What if…this is not a hat…but a cave…" He traced the shape with the tip of a metal tool, "with this undulating line designating the sea? Is there such a cave anywhere on the islands? On Pháne?"

"Now that you speak of it," Wortham said, "there is. You cannot see it from Káliel because it is on the north side of Pháne. I remember seeing it when running patrols. As I recall, it was barely visible…nothing as open as this suggests."

"The island might have sunk over time…or this might indicate low tide, when the cave is more exposed." Though he did not have the third Serpent, Kavan believed he was on the right track.

"No one goes there…as far as I know," the captain added.

Growing excited, Gabrielle began to search for something on the bookshelf. "There is a poem that speaks of the death of a martyr, of his final resting place lying within the bowels of the earth, accessible by an offering to the gods of the sea. I do not remember it, but I do remember my mother reading it to me when I was little. It said something about being buried with the gifts of the gods…about needing four keys to gain the gods blessings. Ah…here…" She drew a book from the shelf, an old book with a frayed cover, and thumbed through the pages. Soon she stopped, however, and frowned. "It should be here, but someone has torn out the page."

"Could Coryllien be that martyr?" asked Owain in disbelief.

"And the poem says gods…not…"

Wortham shrugged. "Never heard any other tales of anyone important being buried with a treasure on the islands. Only Coryllien. Old ways…old gods…treasures. Has to be part of the Coryllien myth."

"So someone else suspects Coryllien is buried here," muttered Caol who entered the room with Prince Muir as Gabrielle talked.

"Perhaps," Kavan assured him. "Someone may have read the poem and believed it to be a factual account; they then set out to prove it. How they connected the Serpents to the poem, I cannot say, but it is fortunate for us they did. It would be useful to read this poem."

Gabrielle replaced the book. "I will ask some of the council members if they have this book or a copy of the poem. It is fairly popular…often read during historical celebrations and feasts. Although," the corners of her mouth twisted, "it might be less popular if anyone learns that the martyr might actually be Dawid Coryllien. I should be able to locate a copy for you."

"Thank you." Kavan bowed his head, his voice carrying the first notes of hope he had felt in weeks. "One more thing. Tomorrow is our deadline. We have not been told where to meet Halstatt; I suspect he wants us to lead him to the treasure because he is unable to find it on his own. He wants us to do the work for him. If you can provide horses and supplies, tomorrow morning we shall ride to the other side of the island and cross to Pháne."

"Lead the kidnapper to what he wants? Is that wise?" Owain scowled.

"There is no other choice…unless he contacts us before then. He has made demands, and we have to try to accommodate them if we want to rescue Bertram and Wilred. I have no intention of handing over the Serpents, but we might want to bring them with us…in case they are keys in more ways than this hidden coding. Is there anyone who can repair them quickly?"

"I will take care of that, and find the poem if Captain Delamo and Owain will prepare supplies." Wortham, knowing what they might need and where to get it, nodded his head eagerly. "You may take the Serpents Kavan…and I pray you bring them, and the princes, back safely."

## ❧Chapter 43☙

"**M**y lady?" came the tentative voice from the doorway of her room, opened by the servant who came in moments before to fill her bath and who held it open for Bhríd's nervous squire Flannery. The young man kept his eyes averted as the woman in her bed sleepily rubbed her eyes, stirring in response to his voice. "Your gown..."

"Why on earth was it delivered at this hour?" she muttered, not expecting him to reply but rather asking the question to the early rays of sunlight peeping through the open window.

"He said he was ordered to deliver it as soon as possible...I suppose he thought that meant as early in the day as he could manage it," Flannery countered.

With a chuckle, she slid out of bed, pulling her robe from the back of the nearby chair and drawing it on over her sleeping gown. "There is no need to hide your eyes, Flannery; I am decently clothed." The servant, meanwhile, continued to fill the washtub with water heated over the hearth fire. "Please, lay the dress on the divan then you may go."

He put the dress where she bid and retreated as hastily as he could without seeming rude. Serving a lady, coming into her private chambers, was not the sort of duties the squire believed he would be performing when Bhríd Cáner had taken him under his wing.

Removing the protective wrappings, Madalyn held her pale blue dress against her and looked at herself in the mirror; it was exactly what she had requested, with fitted, practical sleeves but an elegant neck and waistline and embroidered birds and flowers in gold and silver thread. The excited flutter within made her smile. As long as the war went favorably, she would marry at last, and marry a handsome, honorable man who would protect her, and her estate as her subjects wanted. Her father, she believed, would be proud of her choice. She could not wait for Bhríd to return home to Rhidam.

Having witnessed no actual combat, for which he was grateful, gdhededhá Tusánt's daily routine consisted of services for those men who wished to attend, and providing Purification rites to those who needed them. Sometimes he helped serve meals or treated minor injuries, but he was not a cook or a doctor; the most he could do was assist. Until several days ago he had spent much time in idle conversation with the men, learning things about Teren, and about Neth, that he had not previously known, or in prayer or solitude.

Then he began to notice some of Ruidoso's population attending his morning services. A few at first, mainly men who were befriending Enesfel's soldiers and were curious about the Elyri clergyman brave enough to travel into Neth. The number quickly grew, until this morning he counted nearly twice as many Neth commoners as there were Enesfel or Cordash soldiers. The growing numbers frightened him initially; a few Nethites coming to gawk was one thing, but this increase meant something else. If they expected a monster or an aberration, what they saw was a man of average height with his ash brown hair tonsured and his face and hands a little darker than usual from the amount of time he had recently spent outdoors. To their eyes, he knew he looked little different than anyone else they knew.

What he sensed in today's crowd, once his fear subsided, was that he sounded different to these people. The Faith was driven out of Neth long ago before it had the chance to grow deep roots as it had elsewhere in the Sovereignties. These people were curious about what he had to say. Gathering a few religious items, Tusánt decided that this morning, with the service over, he was going into the city on a mission of conversion. With him were four soldiers, as Captain Kalvert would not allow him to travel anywhere without attendants. Such an escort could be a hindrance to some, but the gdhededhá did not plan to let them bother him. Perhaps when they saw that the people of this city wished Tusánt no harm, as he was beginning to believe, they would leave him alone. Then his mission could begin in earnest.

Kavan and the others set out for the far side of the island at dawn, bringing with them the book of verse Gabrielle supplied. According to both Gabrielle and Wortham, traveling by horseback should allow them to reach Káliel's eastern shore by mid-afternoon. It would be too late for low tide by then, too late to use the raft they carried strapped to a mule, but they would rest and eat as they waited for the tide to turn, giving Kavan time to study and memorize the poem in the hopes of learning some new clue. The Prime Magistrate had wanted to join them, but collectively the men persuaded her to remain behind. They had no idea what, or who, they would face. Her daughter and her islands needed her, and if the men did not return, she would be the only person who knew where they had gone.

There was tension as they rode, the hope that they could be nearing the end of their quest rubbing their nerves raw and making each man watchful and anxious. To get the boys back and know they were well was foremost in their minds, even Prince Muir could talk of nothing but Bertram's welfare and his concern for his cousin. Kavan was proud of his protégé; despite Bertram's past cruelties, Muir had found it in himself to have compassion for his brother. The Elyri hoped it would be enough to aid in saving Bertram's life.

By keeping a brisk pace, they reached the coast earlier than expected. The sea was not yet at high tide, and since none wanted to risk the unknown, with the elements of nature working against them, they waited. Owain and Caol set up a quick campsite, a fire, and a meal, while Wortham showed Muir how to ready their raft for a hasty departure when the time came. They brought little with them, a small amount of food and water, weapons they hoped they would not need, the book of poems, and the Serpents that Kavan kept with him at all times. Their horses, and their camp, would remain here. The raft only needed to be big enough for the men.

The bard meanwhile decided his efforts were best put to use in determining if the sure to be uncomfortable boat trip to Pháne would even be necessary. If there was no cave, or none that matched the description of the one they hoped to find, what would they do then?

The green-eyed gull crossed the expanse of water in less time than it would take their small boat to cross. He wished he could avoid that marine travel, but he had promised the others he would accompany them. None but Wortham had ever spent time at sea, thus Kavan imagined he would not be the only one to suffer discomfort. He could make their journey quicker if he was on that raft and it was wiser for them to remain and arrive together. The thought of the voyage, however, was enough to make his stomach lurch.

Swooping down until his wingtips splashed against the surface of the water, the gull skimmed the northwest side of the island examining every crevice until he found what he sought. The crumpled hat image from the Serpent overlaid itself in his mind's eye against the form of the cave he found; while not exact, time and nature having taken their toll on the opening there, it was as likely a match as he would find. Centuries of erosion had probably altered the cave's appearance, and an artist's representation was rarely exact, but this was the best place to start. Eager to share the news with the others, he turned back.

"Did you find anything, Lord Cliáth?" asked Prince Muir, offering the bard some of the duck roasted over the fire Caol had built. "Was there any sign of Bertie or Wilred?"

Kavan accepted the offered food and ate a mouthful before replying. "I found a cave that matches the etching near enough to be what we seek, but there was no sign of anyone there that I could see. Wortham, how long should it take to raft across?"

"Given favorable weather and no mishaps…maybe nine or ten hours…less if we use the tide to our advantage or construct a sail. Once the tide starts to recede, we can use it to carry us across, reaching the island at about the turn of the tide, when the water should be lowest there. There's no room for a sail, however; our raft will hold us, our equipment, and the boys, but little else. We could make crude oars…that would help reduce our time."

"There will be no need for oars, Wortham," Kavan assured him. Oars would be counterproductive to what Kavan intended. "It will be dark before the tide is right to give us the advantage?"

"Traveling in the dark?" the young prince squeaked. He was eager for his first sailing experience, but sailing on a raft at night sounded dangerous.

"I do not like it either, but it is our best choice. We should have moonlight to guide us, but you may remain here with the horses…if you wish."

Muir's jaw-dropped expression was the one Kavan expected. "I will not stay here. I have come this far. I would prefer my first experience at sea to be during the day, on a proper ship, but I am going with you." He beamed when he noticed his father's proud expression.

"Then eat and rest. It will not be many more hours."

They decided upon a single watch, which Captain Delamo willingly took. Their period of rest would be short and he, well-trained soldier that he was, had considerably more stamina and endurance than most of the other men in the party. Kavan had more, but not knowing what lay ahead, he accepted the wisdom of conserving his strength. He fell quickly to sleep after eating very little and awoke some time later to the tingle of danger that scratched at the back of his neck. He could see or hear nothing unusual, however, and Wortham did little more than glance at him when he stood and went to the water's edge. If Kavan was awake, the Captain opted to take a few minutes of rest for himself.

Concentrating on the sensation drew Kavan's attention towards Pháne and he frowned. He expected danger, expected that this would not be as easy as going into a cave and bringing out the children, but, with his fears confirmed, it made him more anxious about everyone's safety. Detecting a presence behind him, expecting it to be Wortham, Kavan turned to face whoever was there and blinked in surprise.

It was Kóráhm.

"I startled you."

"My attention was elsewhere; I did not notice your arrival."

The saint accepted that explanation with a nod and stared across the water in the direction Kavan had been staring; the bard followed his gaze. "You will not like what you find there, átaelás mai."

"I suspect as much, milord."

"Yes…I know…if you knew why…"

Thinking that Kóráhm sounded vexed and unhappy, Kavan asked, "Have you come to enlighten me? Prepare me for what is to come?"

"I wish I could…but this is not the time to speak of such matters. There may never be a time, for which I am sorry. I have come to you with a warning. You are strong, átaelás mai, in mind, body, and spirit. Yet what you will find there can sap even the purest good, the strongest heart, and leave you too weak to fight. I beseech you to be on guard, not only for your life but for your soul. Be careful what you touch and do not tarry any longer than necessary. It is an evil place and the longer you are there, the more difficult it will be for me to protect you."

As reassuring as having a saint's protection was, Kavan did not like the fact that such protection was necessary. "Protect me?"

"It is my soul's duty. I should have known you would be the one to face this...to conquer it...there is much you do not know...that very few know. I had hoped the past could remain buried...there is much on my conscience. To allow you to go into that place unprotected would be an added weight to the burden I shoulder, and that I could not tolerate."

The saint's words distressed Kavan more than he wanted to admit. How could a saint shoulder such regrets, be connected to a place of evil, as Kóráhm called it? What sort of thing might it be that Kavan had to confront and conquer? "Your conscience suffers, milord? How can this be?" Kóráhm shook his head, his face etched with pain and regret. "You have been there?" Kavan asked, trying a different tact. "On the island? In the cave I seek?"

"No, but I know what is there. Please be careful, Kavan."

The bard swallowed hard and clenched his fists. "What of the others? Will they be in danger?"

"Yes, though not in the way you will be. It is not their souls, their minds, that will be in danger. If you fall, however, your friend Wortham will share your fate. He is strong, but here his strengths will not be enough. He will risk anything for you, kyag. Do not let him do that here. I will be unable to stop what occurs, if he takes such a risk."

"Stop what, milord?"

There was no response, and when Kavan glanced beside him, Kóráhm was gone. So, he mused, not a physical danger but a spiritual and mental one. What could possibly be in that cave, he wondered, that could pose such a threat? What sort of treasure might there be?

The only way to find those answers was to go to Pháne, to confront the evil head-on. He woke his companions with reluctance and steeled himself for hours on the rolling sea. The raft was pushed into the water; most of them boarded, and when it was floating free of the sand, Wortham and Owain scrambled aboard. No one spoke, which was fortuitous for Kavan as his concentration was on the water. Their speed of travel through the darkness went unnoticed by all except Wortham, who cast Kavan one initial curious glance before deciding to enjoy the journey. With none having made this trip before, they did not know what to expect, but Wortham, as he watched the towering mass on the horizon continued to grow at a faster than expected rate, knew their passage was being hastened by Elyri gifts.

The bard did not react to that stolen glance, which confirmed what the captain suspected. That Kóráhm approved of Wortham meant a great deal to Kavan. Perhaps when this was over, he would tell his best friend what Kóráhm had said. Now was not the time.

Compared to the main island of Káliel, Pháne was a small chunk of land, less than ten miles across at its widest, consisting of craggy forested peaks and cliffs. A few people over the centuries had tried to settle here, but those who had tried were soon driven away by the lack of land to farm, lack of accessible drinking water, and the lack of an adequate docking area. It was the one island in the cluster that was uninhabited. And the only one, other than the main island, which retained its original Elyri name. In many ways, thought Kavan as the island drew closer, the trees reminded him of Bhryell; if there had been drinking water here and a flat place to build, he might have considered making this isolated place his home.

The raft ran aground on a strip of sandy beach that Kavan had steered them to, the only one he could find near their destination. The slip of sand had not been visible at high tide but was exposed now and of sufficient size to dock the little raft and anchor it in the rocks. The sun's position indicated shortly past midday, and low tide's peak would not occur for another three hours. It gave them time to secure the boat, eat and drink before entering the unlit chasm.

.None of them noticed the swarthy face peering from the ridge above, not even Kavan, whose attention was consumed by the uncomfortably dark aura emanating from deep inside the island's bowels.

## ⁊Chapter 44⁊

N o one said we would have to swim," Caol muttered as Kavan pulled his robe over his head and secured it to their other belongings on the raft as best he could. The sandy strip of beach where they had docked was nearly fifty yards from the cave, and even at low tide, it required swimming to be able to reach the yawning mouth. Caol had seen that distance as they approached, but he had hoped they would have some way to get the boat closer and avoid getting wet.

Trying to settle his own nerves, Muir nudged the inquisitor playfully. "Don't tell me you cannot swim, uncle.'"

"Of course I can swim," he grunted, "but I prefer not to. If men were meant to be in the water, we would have fins." But he dutifully followed the captain, praying his weapons would not be lost to the ocean floor. Owain and Muir came next, and Kavan, barefoot and wearing an uncustomary pair of trousers and thin tunic, brought up the rear intending to assist anyone who had trouble with the strong island current. Little by little they made progress and eventually emerged into the cavern where they found a narrow ledge above the water level to climb onto.

Pale gray limestone encircled them, its sides slippery and cold. The sea filled much of this cavern at high tide, but the walls were given very little chance to dry at low tide before the cave filled again. There was no life here save for the barnacles along the rocky surfaces and the crabs scurrying in and out of the pools on the ledge. The grotto smelled of death, of decay, of being many years untouched by anything other than nature. That the sea could not cleanse away the stench troubled Kavan as each man turned their attention to the walls. If the Serpents were keys, there had to be a door. They wrung the water from their clothes as they searched, teeth chattering against the chill. Kavan willed his skin and hair dry and warmed himself from within.

No one lost weapons or tools to the sea, for which Kavan was grateful when he found, with the tips of his fingers, the razor-thin line that suggested a door sealed tightly against the sea's intrusion. There were no apparent keyholes, no opening mechanisms of any kind the bard could find. "Caol, do you have experience with doors?"

"You mean breaking and entering? Wasn't my area of expertise, but I can usually get a door open…" He edged around Prince Muir and stepped close to the bard's side.

"Then open this one." The distant sound of water slapping against wood turned Kavan's head towards the mouth of the cave and he muttered, "Please hurry…we are soon to have company."

While the others stood with weapons at the ready, finding the ledge a precarious place from which to do battle, Caol slid his knife along the entire edge of the sealed door, hoping to trip a spring, but nothing happened.

"I thought you could open any door…" Owain muttered under his chattered breath.

"This one might only open from the other side; if this was a gravesite, he might have been the one who could…" As he talked, he pushed against the stone, hoping it would give way to his weight. His effort succeeded, as the popping of a spring and creaking of unused stone caused the seal to give way and the door to open. Having not been prepared for it, Caol stumbled and fell into the narrow hall that extended behind it into darkness. Water was pooled on the floor, indicating a flaw in the seal somewhere. The depression was small, however, and beyond it, the path wound gradually upwards.

"I hope we don't have to go in there," whispered Muir. He had enjoyed the short sea travel experience, but the idea of going into the earth made him queasy.

Caol got to his feet, looking into the darkness as Kavan spoke. "We will not know what is at the other end unless we enter. It would be prudent, I think, for us to know what we have exposed before someone else discovers it. We opened the door, we should go in."

Wortham nodded with a nervous grin. "You are the one with the light, milord. I think you should have the honor of going first...but I am right behind you."

The path was initially slick beneath the bard's bare feet but it turned into rough-hewn steps as it ascended further into darkness. The seawater had never risen this high, but an eternity of moisture had accumulated here. The warmth of Kavan's handlight and the breath and sweat of the men as they climbed caused the surrounding moisture to vaporize, creating fog in the passage that would have been difficult to penetrate without the glow of the handlight leading the way. There were no traps, no pitfalls, as though the creators of this place had never expected outsiders to find it. When the passage widened, allowing them to regroup from their single-file climb, they found themselves before another door.

Double doors, made of polished stone, with four depressions recessed into the sealed entry. Above the indentations was a script in a language Kavan did not recognize. It belonged to none of the peoples of the Five Sovereignties, nor did it match the writing said to belong to the phae k'kairá; it did not look like any written language Kavan had ever seen. What he did recognize here was power, not the comforting sort he was familiar with but power nonetheless. It was wrong, as the power in the temple below Rhidam's keep was wrong.

He touched the topmost depression on the door and jerked his hand back as if burned.

"They match the Serpents," Owain breathed as he bent to look at the markings in each depression more closely.

Caol pointed to the one at the bottom. "And the Coryllien."

"How do we get in without the third Serpent and the dagger?" Prince Muir asked with a frustrated whine.

Footsteps came up behind them and the entire group turned. Kavan had felt the intruders long ago, but there had been no good place to turn and confront them, and he had chosen to keep his company moving forward. Here, at least, if it came to combat, they would have room to fight.

"I am glad you asked that question," said an unfamiliar voice, moments before the speaker emerged from the fog into full view.

"Halstatt!" snarled Caol. He tried to lunge but Wortham and Owain caught his arms and held him back.

"Thoughtful of you to lead me to this place. It has taken me a long time to learn what little I did and it took you but a few days to complete the research. My congratulations; my employer will be pleased. Put away the sword, Dugan, otherwise, your son will meet a swift death."

The inquisitor hissed as he struggled half-heartedly to be free of those who held him. The impulse to attack had subsided, but he did not appreciate being restrained. "How do we know you have not killed them already?"

"True…you don't know that, do you?" Halstatt laughed. "Once you have opened that door and we have gone through it, you will see your son. When I have what I came for, the children are free to leave with the rest of you." He looked from Caol to Kavan with a sneer. "Except for you and the Elyri. I have a use for him…and if it does not kill him, I will. Then it will be you and me, Dugan, this time we'll put an end to the feud."

"He has done no wrong! I will not open this door unless you guarantee Lord Cliáth's safety. Let everyone go, and you can have me.

The other man sneered again. "That he is Elyri is enough reason for him to die." His irrational hatred sent a prickle up Kavan's spine. Not the first man with anti-Elyri sentiment the bard had met, but in this cavern, the emotion felt amplified. "And you know there are never guarantees. Besides, you are not going to open the door. He is. If he doesn't, I will kill all of you, take what I need, and be on my way. Any resistance or attempts to fight will lead to the death of the boys, and believe me, I am eager to be done with the brats."

In his open palm, he held the third Serpent with its red figure rising from the waves as Gabrielle had claimed. Beyond Halstatt in the foggy darkness, three others waited, two of whom Kavan recognized as the comforting auras of the royal children. His heart soared to learn they both lived. Somewhere far behind, however, someone else crept up the passage, but Kavan could not determine if they were friend or foe.

He saw no choice but to obey. Whatever lay beyond that door beckoned; either he opened it and lived to see what was there, or he refused and died. He could will the two to sleep, but did not want to risk harming the princes, or having one of his own partners succumb to that sleep. A swordfight or display of power might also endanger the boys, and Kavan was not willing to risk it. He took the third brooch from Halstatt, meeting the man's gaze calmly. The rogue had either not expected such a show of confident defiance or did not like something he saw in Kavan's eyes because he looked hastily away towards Caol.

One by one, with Wortham standing behind him, between him and Halstatt, Kavan placed the Serpents into the depressions, matching the symbols from the brooches to those on the wall. He felt a spark of warmth with each contact and heard a faint click somewhere within the stone above each time. The Serpents barely needed to touch their nests to work; they came away in his hand after that. Halstatt confiscated each one and, producing the Coryllien from his vest pocket, thrust the tip of it into the final indentation in the wall. It was a perfect fit.

Wortham growled as he pushed Kavan out of Halstatt's path and reach.

Smiling smugly at that bit of knowledge he might be able to use to his advantage, as there was more than one way to manipulate men who cared for one another, Halstatt pulled the dagger free and watched with glee as the heavy doors began to retract into the wall, revealing a large chamber. Halstatt gestured them inside, and when no one moved fast enough for his liking, he pushed both Wortham and the Elyri into the room; the others quickly followed. He must fear a trap, Kavan thought, stumbling but not falling. He might have given the matter more thought but the room they found themselves in devoured his attention.

It could have been a hideout, a temple, or could have served any number of other functions; its appearance gave no accurate indication of its purpose. The chamber was circular, like one-half of a giant sphere, with bits of moldering tapestries hanging from the walls, all too faded and decaying to learn much from them. If there had been time Kavan would have circled the room and touched them; past impressions might have faded after what must have been centuries of degeneration, but the chance to appease his curiosity would have made the effort to read them worthwhile. There was one stone bench on the right side of the room, hewn directly from the floor and wall. Upon it, a badly corroded metal chalice lay on its side, a dark stain spreading from it across the stone and seeping down onto the floor where shards of glass lay surrounding what looked to be an undamaged crystal stopper. Take the stopper, an inner voice told him. But at the moment, Kavan was not close enough to reach it.

Using the torch he carried, Halstatt lit four more and placed four around the room to better illuminate the room. The last he kept with him. There were stairs carved near both sides of the door, curving up to meet the balcony that circled the room, a stone pathway also carved from the rock of the cave. Halstatt mounted the steps to the left, searching the walls for something not easily found. With the man distracted, Kavan gestured to Owain, who snatched up the decanter stopper without Halstatt noticing. The prince shoved it into his pocket to hide it and resumed his casual stance. For Kavan, having it was an unexpected relief.

In the center of the room was a stone table, also hewn from the floor. Nothing was upon it save dust, but the same dark stains spread across the limestone in several places and had dripped to the floor as it had from the bench. Though the stains appeared random, Kavan found them disturbing.

"There's nothing here," Halstatt swore to himself as Kavan dared to touch the stain with his fingers, despite Kóráhm's warning not to touch anything. Only dust came away, but he knew those stains were not wine. They were blood. Not animal, but a mixture of Teren and Elyri. His gaze swept to the crystal shards and the stain there and groaned. The same. This was not a table then…but an altar. The same as the one below Rhidam's keep.

He closed his eyes and tried to shake away the distaste of that thought but was distracted by Halstatt's partner entering the cavern, each arm around one small boy, his hands over their mouths. Kavan knew the face, knew the man by name without it being said and felt his stomach knot. How could he ever explain this to Gabrielle? The princes were bound, dirty, and thinner than they had been, but were otherwise apparently unharmed. Their eyes wide and anxious, upon seeing familiar faces they wiggled and tried to free themselves.

"Wilred!"

As their captor tightened his grip enough to keep them still, Halstatt growled from above. "Do not approach them, Dugan. Don't do anything unless I tell you to; otherwise, Felix will be forced to snap their little necks. You don't want that, do you?" Caol growled and again relented, settling for glowering at the two men responsible for this crime. "Elyri, search the bottom. The treasure is here. She told me it would be. I haven't wasted two years for an empty cave. You will look so that you will know what wealth your death will help me gain. The rest of you, stay where Felix can see you."

"I saw you in Rhidam," Caol snarled. "That is how we found you, Halstatt. Your help was not careful enough."

Halstatt laughed. "On the contrary, Dugan. I had to lead you here somehow? You arrived here quicker than I anticipated, however...you must have had a good wind at your back..."

"An advantage," was all Caol said, not about to give away Kavan's gifts to a man full of malice and hatred.

Kavan meanwhile followed the flow of negative power filling this place until he reached the wall opposite the entrance way. Whatever he was following, it was stronger behind the wall. One more step filled the cavern with a loud crackling and a portion of the wall directly in front of the bard began to lift upward into the stone above. Halstatt let out a whoop of excitement, and though he ran to where he could see Kavan and the newly exposed room, he did not yet come down from the balcony. Kavan guessed the man wanted to stay safely out of the way of anything dangerous that might emerge from within. "Get in there, Elyri. Tell me what you see."

Kavan was already entering but not because Halstatt commanded it. A rush of dry, dusty air burst forth, peculiar after the dampness of the outer cavern, surrounding him with the fetid smell of decay. The chamber was small, unadorned, and contained a single stone slab, upon which lay a mummified body clutching the lower portion of a golden staff. To his knowledge, some of those from the southernmost regions of Hatu and the western deserts mummified their dead, but the staff suggested this was no nomad's burial site. In the other shriveled hand was clutched a Coryllien dagger.

A jolt of dread stabbed through him, warning him away, but he had already entered the room and had no wish to turn back. All of Kórahm's words, his warnings, his lamentations, swirled in Kavan's head. He was supposed to find this. Supposed to conquer. Before he could stop himself, he reached with both hands, intending to take the dagger and the staff piece. He must, he knew it, despite Kórahm's warnings sounding like a whirlwind in his ears.

"Elyri!" Halstatt could see him but could not see past the bard and captain to determine what the man had found. Whatever it was, Kavan was intending to pick it up, to take it for himself, and Halstatt could not bear that thought.

When Kavan latched onto both items at once, his head filled with searing pain, a flash of white-hot agony that would not allow him to pull his hands free. The room, the whole cavern, began to quake. Acid and flame and a separation from himself. The voice in his head, strangely accented and unfamiliar, screamed curses, speaking in High Elyri. bhedhuaethag, it said. bheturbhae. bhemethán. zíthrós. tágdhedokag. The power in the room fluctuated and grew, overfilling his senses, canceling Kavan's abilities, crushing upon him, threatening to consume him. The harder he fought, the further from himself he slipped. By all that is sacred, his thoughts cried. By the love of Dhágdhuán and the strength of k'Ádhá, you cannot destroy me. I will not allow it.

Wortham heard the bard's strangled cry from the other room over the rumbling of the earth. With no thought to his own safety, he ran to Kavan, intent on rescuing his friend. Felix reached for him, releasing his hold on Prince Bertram, but froze and then suddenly crumpled to the ground. With the man's grip gone slack, Caol yanked his son towards him, seeing the familiar figure in the doorway where Felix Maylor had stood. Wace Elotti grinned as he wiped his bloody curved knife upon his trousers.

"Damn it, Elotti! You could have killed my son!"

"I am a better marksman than that," the dark man snorted.

Temporarily forgotten as he began running down the stairs to reach Kavan, Halstatt saw his opening. Caol's back was to him. Though he had planned to use it to kill the Elyri, a sacrifice to the one who had led him to this place, the Coryllien dagger was the only weapon Halstatt had to use. As a throwing weapon, it would not be particularly accurate, but it would do. He aimed, threw the blade, and then uttered a squawk as the stone stairway collapsed beneath his feet and rocks began to tumble down upon him. He looked to see if he had struck his target.

In the other room, Wortham found Kavan clutching the items the mummy held, his pale face mottled with exertion and agony, eyes closed, with a trickle of blood seeping from his ears, his nose, and the corners of his mouth. The captain reached to pull Kavan's hands away.

Sensing that movement, knowing who was there by instinct rather than by his overpowered and overwhelmed senses, Kavan ordered, "Do not touch me." in a voice that rattled and wheezed with effort.

"Milord…"

"If you value your soul…and mine…do as I say…"

The Káliel captain was torn. The bard had fallen to his knees and Wortham did not like the gurgling he could hear within the man's chest. With the cavern still rumbling like no earthquake the captain had ever experienced, unable to be still and watch helplessly as his friend died, he took action. If he could not pull Kavan away, there was one thing he could do. Raising his sword, he snarled, swung and smote the mummy's head from its body. An unearthly screeching filled the cavern as the bard fell backward; the mummy had not separated in two but had crumbled to dust beneath the power of the blow and the destruction of whatever power had kept it together. The staff piece and dagger came free in Kavan's hands.

"Milord," the captain cried as he knelt beside the bard. "Are you...?"

She screamed as she had never screamed before beneath an onslaught of unbearable pain. Everything hurt; her skin, her hair, her insides, all felt as though they were being crushed, burned, torn asunder and destroyed from the inside out. She had been betrayed. He would die for this. But the other...he had done it again. "Defiler!" she cried aloud. He did not deserve to live. His time would come and she would have what was rightfully hers. There would be time for revenge.

Halstatt's aim was not true, his fall causing the dagger to veer away from its intended target. Instead, the Coryllien nicked a falling rock, ricocheted to the side, and plunged into Prince Bertram's back. The boy's squawk interrupted Caol and Elotti's argument, but it was Prince Muir who was first to act.

"Bastard!" he cried, sword drawn. Halstatt could not rise or escape, his legs had been broken in the fall, he was pinned beneath debris and his sword was out of reach. He threw a stone at the charging prince but Muir dodged it. "You killed my brother!" With a single stroke, he drove his sword through Halstatt's ribs with such force that it struck the earth beneath the man and lodged there. Halstatt found the strength to pull himself up the blade to grasp the front of the prince's tunic before collapsing. His face was purple with pain and with the anger and humiliation of having been killed, not by a Dugan, but by a boy.

Kavan saw it all through the red haze in his eyes from where he lay, his head pounding mercilessly. He did not need the images to be clearer; he had seen it all before. Wilred had screamed and was crying uncontrollably against his father's shoulder. Hoping he could stay the inevitable, Kavan struggled to his feet and was grateful that Wortham helped him rather than forcing him to lie still. He stumbled, nearly falling several times, to where Prince Bertram lay, face down, amidst the rubble of the collapsed ledge. The ground no longer shook.

There was a pulse in the boy's neck; Prince Bertram was alive. Perhaps there was a chance. But as Kavan reached for the blade and saw what protruded from the boy's back, his heart sank. The Coryllien. It was, he knew, likely sheathed with poison. Halstatt would have had it no other way.

"Wortham…your shirt…" Owain was already there, handing his tunic to the bard. Kavan pulled the dagger free, knowing of a single way to remove the toxin from the boy's body. Too much time had passed; he could never hope to remove it all, but he was willing to try. Putting his mouth to the wound, he ignored Wortham's hand upon his shoulder, a gesture meant to restrain him. Yes, he knew the venom could kill him, but better him than the young prince. He drew blood into his mouth, and spat it upon the ground, repeating the action several times until the captain held him back.

"Hold your shirt to the wound, Owain," Wortham instructed. "Use as much pressure as you can while I tie my shirt around him."

"Will he live?" Shuffling feet accompanied the frightened voice.

"I don't know, Muir," Kavan whispered after wiping his mouth on his sleeve. "If it was any other weapon…"

The inquisitor finished for him, having retrieved Halstatt's sword while saving most of his attention for his son. The knowledge made him miserable, as his family's blood feud had brought death to the royal family, but he saw no reason to couch the truth. "The Coryllien, particularly in the hands of a Tarmajien, is always fatal." Prince Muir's lips trembled and Caol squeezed his shoulder, wishing there was more he could do or say. "You have done well today, Muir. Regardless of what anyone says from here out, you have proven yourself a man…and a Lachlan." Muir nodded mutely, his eyes on his brother and his tutor. Needing to do something, wanting to be out of this place as soon as possible, with the slim hope that they might reach an Elyri healer in time to save Bertram, Caol continued, "We need proof of Halstatt's demise…"

The Cíbhóló hunter barked, "I demand his head; it is mine."

Eyes narrowed, the inquisitor grunted sourly, "You did nothing to earn this bounty, Elotti. You waited for us to find your prey, to kill him, so you could reap the rewards without work. Your laziness cost us a…"

"Stop…" Kavan murmured as he struggled to his feet with Prince Bertram in his arms. He felt ill, dizzy and weak, either from the poison he may have swallowed or his ordeal in the other room, but he could spare no energy for himself beyond enough to walk. Every other ounce of power was poured into the prince's small body. Kavan was not a healer, but he hoped it would be enough to save the prince's life, even at the expense of his own. If they were lucky, perhaps k'Ádhá would see fit to intervene. "Take what you must, Lord Elotti…Caol, take whatever you feel is your due, but the dagger and the Serpents go with me. Wortham, the…"

"I have them, milord." If the second Coryllien dagger and that gold piece of staff were worth Kavan risking his life, Wortham would not let them out of his care. No one else knew of the second Coryllien, and Wortham was determined to keep it that way.

The venador grunted, stared at the pouch he had taken from Halstatt's body for many moments before cutting it free and handing it to Kavan. Whatever the Serpents were worth, they were not worth a child's life. He wanted no part of them, and he had not been paid to acquire them. His job was over now. He lifted Halstatt's body over his shoulder and got to his feet. Caol gestured to Felix as Wortham supported the bard's weight. "What about him?"

"I doubt Lady Dilyn wishes to see him again," Owain murmured. "He doesn't appear to have drowned. I'll take this…" he removed the wedding band from the man's hand, "and dump him into the sea…leave him for someone else to find."

There were no objections. Kavan could barely function and had to rely on Wortham and Muir as they started down the sloped hall in the dark. With no handlight this time, the inquisitor led the way, carrying his son; behind him, Owain carried Felix's body. The nomad brought up the rear, carrying Halstatt, and as a second thought, a still-burning torch. The double doors slid closed as they passed through, sealing the horrors beyond from the world.

At the first door, the tide had risen nearly to the top of the ledge. It was dark beyond the mouth of the cavern, but none of them knew how much time had passed.

"Wilred cannot swim," Caol said quietly. Even if the boy could have, after all he had endured, the inquisitor was unwilling to let him out of his sight. "And in your condition, Lord Cliáth, neither can you. Wortham, Owain…maybe we can steer the raft here…or to the mouth of the cave."

Kavan nodded in agreement; too weary to argue. Owain dropped Felix's body into the water and the three men jumped into the sea to swim to their raft. Prince Muir kept his arms around his cousin; Wilred gladly accepted the comfort as their feet dangled in the cold lapping water. Muir watched Kavan's glassy stare, noting the blood near his ear, in his hair, upon his upper lip, at the corner of his chin, and upon the sleeve of his tunic. The bard was watching the dead man floating before them, unaware of his appearance. Muir then looked at Bertram, whose pale, discolored face did not look as cruel to him as it had before. Bertie was just a boy, one who did not fully understand what cruelty was and did not deserve the fate he had been dealt.

Propping Halstatt's corpse in the open doorway, Elotti squatted beside Kavan and began wiping away the blood from his face and hair. The bard's distracted gaze focused on him with quiet curiosity. The hunter shrugged. "Habit. I don't like unnecessary blood." A small grin crept across his face as if he had revealed a secret no one else knew, but he did not stop his efforts. "It looks as if you fought your own battle in that chamber…one you almost lost. What was in there?" With the amount of blood shed, it must have been something monstrous.

"The past," Kavan mumbled, "and an evil more enduring than any man should have to confront."

The nomad did not question him further, accepting the explanation at face value. He also did not stop using the sea water to cleanse Kavan's face until there was no further blood to be seen. Their gazes met and Kavan cocked his head. "There is Elyri in your blood."

Elotti smiled and stood as the raft drifted into the cavern with only Caol upon it. "I do not know. There could be. It would explain many things I do not understand." To Caol, he said, "Where are the others?"

"Halstatt did us a favor, left us a boat. They're getting her ready to sail."

"Thoughtful," the venador grunted as he helped Kavan and Prince Bertram onto the raft, and then Muir and Wilred. "What do you wish to take, Dugan? His body will not fit on my boat, and I doubt you want to take him with you. I will leave him with the other."

"I want his sword and his signet. The Association will want proof of his demise, I suspect…and I know Lord Cliáth has no intention of letting the Coryllien fall into the wrong hands. You can have his ugly head and whatever else you fancy."

"With pleasure, Lord Dugan." The signet, sword and dagger, and even a ring with an assortment of keys were handed to the inquisitor with a smile. "You earned these." If he knew what the keys went to he did not say. "Shall I meet you in Rhidam to provide testimony…clear your name?"

Having forgotten that he was an escaped convict, Caol shuddered inside. On the outside, however, he sneered and said, "I need nothing from you, Elotti. I never have. Claim your reward and leave me alone."

"As you wish." Elotti gave the raft a gentle push towards the mouth of the cave. "By the way, I heard Rouvyn was traveling with you. Where is he?"

The inquisitor chuckled darkly. "Let's just say that Physician Talis does not need you either."

The hunter's puzzled and annoyed expression almost made Caol laugh, but no one else found the situation, or his words amusing.

## ❧Chapter 45❧

After a morning of listening to the complaints of her brother's subjects, having them translated into writing in order that she could study and rule on them, Deidre concluded again that she did not have the fortitude or the desire for the throne and was grateful the duty had never fallen to her. Short of some catastrophic event to her brother and his family, she would never have to worry about being a full-time leader. She could barely stomach the judging of other people's rights and wrongs, the picking apart of obscure and complicated laws and situations to make what seemed to her to be arbitrary decisions. All she wanted, as she bid the last of the gathering good day and left the Hall in search of something to eat, was for her husband, brother, son and nephew to come home safely.

Her spirits were kept alight by the messenger who arrived last evening to say that her brother would soon be home. There was also something in her heart, some shadow of intuition or knowing, that made her certain that soon Caol and her son would be home too. It felt to be more than wishful thinking, and she clung to that. She could get through her days no other way.

❧*❧

With Kavan unable to assist as he had during their raft trip, and none of them being experienced sailors, it took nearly nine hours in the darkness to maneuver the small confiscated boat to the coast of the main island. It was Wortham's prior time at sea that allowed them to sail the vessel at all. Their inexperience would mean that sailing around the island to Káliel's harbor would take longer than the trek over land would. The bard waited on deck with his back against the cabin wall, gathering energy and forcing it into the small body as steadily as he could in an attempt to divert the lethal poison away from the boy's vital organs. He barely noticed the usual discomfort in his stomach, the bitter taste in his mouth, or the pounding in his head as the boat cut through the water; they were nothing compared to the pain in his heart.

When the craft eventually ran aground, they discovered that the horses they had left tethered upon the beach were gone. Caol, the first one off the boat, muttered a string of obscenities as he whacked the brush with his sword, hoping the animals would magically appear. Eventually, he did discover one lone horse, not one of theirs, but a much larger animal, a bulky beast still saddled, a horse capable of carrying great weight. It was not difficult to guess the horse belonged to Elotti; still blaming the hunter for the suffering they had endured, blaming the man for not having captured Halstatt long ago, Caol grinned wickedly and brought the horse to where Kavan was currently bolstered on his feet by Prince Muir and Wortham.

At the insistence of the others, Kavan road the horse with Prince Bertram in his arms and Prince Wilred seated behind him, clinging to the bard's waist. Everyone else walked, keeping a brisk pace in their haste to reach the villa and hopefully contact Ártur or Syl to save the prince's life. As the day wore on, however, and their hopes flagged, their steps began to drag. The weather was hot and humid and no one had slept or eaten for too long. There had been enough foodstuffs on Halstatt's boat to get the vessel to either Enesfel or Hatu, and they had taken some of it, enough to supply them with a midday meal. As they pressed on, only Prince Wilred ate. Long after the sun set, however, when the men stumbled and yawn from exhaustion, they stopped and made a hasty, makeshift camp.

"How is he?" Wortham asked, his voice low as he helped Prince Wilred and then Kavan down from the horse. "We should reach the house in the morning; you can bring him straight to Lady MacLyr…"

The bard shook his head. "I do not think he has that long," he reluctantly admitted. "Even if we had a healer on Pháne…if Ártur was there…it would have done little good. The poison is too potent…I have failed…" He had not yet surrendered his efforts, but he knew his actions were futile without a miracle given.

"You have done everything any man could do; do not give up hope yet, milord." The captain brushed Kavan's hair from his face and kissed his forehead. In the dark, the captain's large bearded face and tangle of dark curls made him appear very bear-like. As if reading Kavan's thoughts, he whispered, "There could yet be a miracle. But…you do not look well. Allow me to tend him that you may rest…"

"I will not rest until there is nothing more I can do. But you…please sleep. I will need your strength, my friend."

Wortham nodded, knowing it was rare for Kavan to express a need, and squeezed his shoulder before lying near him. He should eat, but he was too tired for that. "Milord…one question…who was that…in the cave?"

A shudder of passing memory washed through him, intensifying every ache the experience had given him. "If I tell you, it goes no further, Wortham. Never tell anyone what you saw or heard in there…or what I tell you now."

"On my life, Kavan." The requested oath was unnecessary; the captain had deduced the seriousness of the matter the moment he had seen Kavan trying to take the staff and dagger away from the mummified corpse.

"Dawid Coryllien."

Nodding his head, eyes wide in amazed comprehension although he was not truly surprised, he stretched out at Kavan's side. After the talk of a possible treasure buried on the island with Coryllien, learning the myth was at least partially true was not unexpected. With no treasure found beyond the items they had taken, that sort of discovery was best left as a myth to the rest of the world.

The bard listened to the rumbling snore that resonated in the captain's bare, hairy chest as the others in the party nibbled at the food Owain passed out. He noticed lightness in Caol that had not been there for many weeks; the inquisitor was still worried for Prince Bertram's health and his own future, but he was relieved to have his son alive and safe. Kavan could not fault him for rejoicing in that, but at the moment, Prince Wilred's safe return was a small point of light in the overwhelming darkness engulfing the bard.

His eyes were opened but he saw little as night passed into the dismal glow of a new day. Though awake, his eyes were duller, his breathing shallower, and when Wortham awoke to see it, the first thing he did was to touch the boy's fevered forehead. No one else had asked about the prince's condition, no one else had done more than look at him, as if not asking, not checking for themselves, would somehow protect Bertram from further harm. It was a struggle to get Kavan on the horse, and an equal struggle to keep him there, thus Wortham walked on one side and Owain on the other, each with a hand on Kavan, prepared to catch him and his precious burden if he should slide from the horse. Prince Muir guided the animal by its reins while the inquisitor led the way, keeping watch for any trace of danger. Halstatt was gone, but that did not mean they were safe.

Hour after hour crept by, with nervous men trying to hasten the journey without endangering those on horseback. Instinctively, Kavan knew they were nearing their destination, and for a moment he felt a flicker of irrational hope that maybe, if they reached the villa soon, there would be hope for Prince Bertram. But that hope was torn asunder by the spiking of the boy's body temperature, a symptom the Elyri knew from his research on the Coryllien and the sort of death its victims suffered. Fever and respiratory failure. Prince Bertram had lived longer than most, but only, Kavan knew, because of his determination to keep the boy alive. He poured more energy than he could reasonably afford into cooling the child, not wanting him to die of fever or anything else, but the almost imperceptible brush of wings against his arms, enfolding them in a light embrace, told Kavan his fight was over. He had lost.

'Let him come to us,' a voice whispered in his ear, a voice not Kóráhm's, not audible to anyone around him. There was no malice in the gentle sound, just soothing tranquility and a sing-song accent that spoke of peace. "He has suffered long enough. You have done all you can. Let him come."

"I cannot..." he pleaded in a hoarse whisper. He felt Wortham's gaze upon him and realized he must have spoken aloud or else the captain felt something of what Kavan was experiencing. Silently, he continued, 'To lose him...when we are close...'

'There is nothing more you can do; you have done more than anyone else could. You keep him with you because you cannot bear to release him, but you know it is his hour.'

Bertram's voice, young and weak and small, made Kavan open his eyes. "Lord Cliáth...I want to go home."

There was acceptance in his bleary blue eyes, though there was, perhaps, an incomplete comprehension of what he asked. Whether he wanted to die or not, Kavan knew the one thing the prince wanted was to be free of the poison wracking his body with pain, eating his organs with its corrosive bile until there would be little left within.

Kavan clutched the tiny body to his chest and kissed Bertram's hot forehead, squeezing his eyes shut. He saw nothing behind his eyelids, but he knew they were not alone. "Be free," he whispered. "Be loved."

There was no shudder of the passing spirit, but rather a soft sigh of surrender. Gradually, as the swaying of the horse's gate rocked them, the prince's body grew cooler in Kavan's arms. The Elyri did not fight his tears, did not try to hide them, nor did he shrug off the tightening of Wortham's hand on his leg. No one else, as far as Kavan knew, noticed what had occurred.

It was sheer determination that kept Kavan seated as the party passed through the gates of the Dilyn villa. The maidservant Delia saw them arrive and summoned her mistress, who emerged through the door at a run as they drew to a halt in front of her home. Wortham was ready to catch Kavan as the bard slid from the horse like a broken doll.

"Delia…a doctor…"

"There is no need," Wortham murmured, trying his best to keep Kavan from collapsing. "Prince Bertram is…beyond needing care…"

Muir reached to touch his younger brother, but his hand fell short of contact. The smaller boy's pallor was waxy and pale and his jaw was open and slack to one side. Muir shivered and backed away. "He is…dead…?"

Kavan's knees buckled as the word was spoken; Owain grabbed the small body from his arms as Wortham picked Kavan up. Gabrielle gasped at the amount of blood staining Kavan's clothes.

"Kavan…do you need a…"

"I will tend him," the captain muttered, his rough voice cracking. "Bring us water…please…"

"Of course…"

If anything more was said, Kavan failed to hear it as Wortham carried him into the house and up the stairs. He did not object to being carried; his legs had ceased to work and what little strength he had was all that kept him conscious. All of his energy had been given to Prince Bertram. And Bertram was dead. Knowing it had to come to pass did little to ease Kavan's suffering. He said nothing as Wortham stripped away his bloody clothes and wiped as much dried blood from his body as he could while the pages arrived with heated water for the wash basin. Kavan listened to the splash of it as Wortham dabbed a cloth in the bowl, and then the softness, the warmth and wetness of it, spread across his skin, the captain washing him as one would an infant or an invalid. It was a peaceful sensation, relaxing, a sensation that stripped away the blood and dirt from his skin as well as his emotional defenses, breaking him down until he was sobbing uncontrollably.

The cloth was set aside; Wortham gathered the Elyri against his chest and held him as Kavan wept. The intimacy of such an embrace might have embarrassed him with anyone else, but with Kavan, it did not. There was nothing Wortham could say to ease his friend's anguish and he knew that if he tried, if he broke this moment with a clumsy attempt at comforting speech, Kavan would withdraw and bury his pain. The Elyri would share his grief with no one else, save for his cousin perhaps, who was not here to offer a shoulder for support. Kavan's pain had to be faced and accepted now, before he took this news back to Rhidam and King Arlan.

Some time later, Wortham noted that the sound of weeping had ceased. Kavan had fallen asleep in his arms, his face buried in the crook of the captain's neck. Reluctantly, Wortham lay the man back into his pillows to finish bathing him; when Kavan was clean and dry he covered the bard with a light sheet and then sat in the chair by the window, intending to keep watch for as long as he had to, for as long as Kavan needed him.

Sleep, milord, he thought. The rest will come soon enough. You can face it then.

## ❧Chapter 46❧

King Arlan rode through the gates of the palace in Rhidam to be greeted by the sound of his justice swearing vehemently. He had never heard the man so angry and he dreaded discovering what had worked him into such a high degree of agitation. He had hoped for a peaceful homecoming, if not a happy one since he intended to go straight to his late chamberlain's side without dealing with anyone or anything else first. He groaned, realizing that his wish had apparently gone unheard by the greater powers in the universe.

There was no reason to ask the healer to endure the justice's wrath, but the King did motion for Bhríd to stay and hear the justice out. The chancellor's size and presence should be enough to manipulate the justice into a calmer frame of mind. The sound drew closer and stopped when Justice Cornell entered the courtyard alone and saw that the King had returned home.

"Praise mercy! Someone with sense! I cannot get anything done, Sire. No one will listen to me!"

"I am listening, Lord Cornell," the King said as he dismounted and allowed the palace staff to take his horse. "What necessitates such an outburst?"

Realizing how much of his ranting the King might have overheard, the justice bowed, the act hiding his flushed face. "My apologies,

Sire…I should not have…but no one respects the authority you have placed upon me. I am continually vexed by disrespect."

"By who, Lord Justice? Please…start at the beginning." By now Bhríd stood beside him, and as he had hoped, the calm of the chancellor's presence had a similar effect upon the justice.

"I have evidence…reports…that implicate Lord Dugan in the death of Lady Dilyn…"

"But Caol was here when she was…" started the chancellor.

"…and your sister will not listen to reason. No one believes me. I arrest him, and someone, presumably Lord Cliáth, breaks him free. I have scoured Rhidam to find him, but she will not allow the issue of a warrant or reward…"

The King felt his heart quicken, and for a moment did not hear the bulk of what the justice had said. "Kavan? Was here? Is Bertram…?"

"They were here…but they're gone again…no one knows where…off chasing clues, I presume, since there was no success…I did my duty. I arrested Lord Dugan but Lord Cliáth insisted he be released, claiming he was necessary for the quest to find…"

"Did you?"

"Did I what, Sire?"

The King grabbed him by both shoulders. "Release Caol?"

Stiffening between the King's hands, his face darkening with offense, he retorted, "I would never release a suspect without your permission…"

Hands thrown up in exasperation, the King cried, "Why on…if Kavan needed him, then he should have been released at once! No wonder he had no choice but to free Caol. Where are they?"

Rebuffed and rebuked, the justice replied, "Milord, I do not know. As far as I can tell, they are not in Rhidam. They told no one where they were going…or if they did, no one is telling me." The last words were uttered with annoyance.

"They?" asked Bhríd.

"Lord Cliáth, Lord Dugan, Prince Owain, Prince Muir, and Captain Delamo…"

The hope that dared to spark in his heart left the King in a pained rush of air. "They have had no success…" King Arlan felt immensely old and tired. "Lord Justice, I do not know what evidence you have against Caol, but we will hear it after he returns with the princes, and not before, is that clear?"

Though still flustered and trying to contain his feelings of offense, the justice bowed. "Yes, milord." At least the King was willing to hear him. It was more than most of the palace staff or the King's sister, was willing to do.

"Is there anything else I must know before I get out of this armor and recover from my journey?"

"Only…" Whatever the justice was about to say fell dead upon his lips. "Nothing else, Your Majesty. The rest can wait. Lord Cáner, Lady Dubuais was in the solar with Lady MacLyr when I saw her last. I am sure she is anticipating your arrival."

Bhríd nodded without trying to hide his smile or the excitement of seeing her again. "I will find her at once. Thank you, Justice Cornell."

Grateful that there were no further interruptions or demands on his time, the King was able to escape to his chamber long enough to bathe and change into fresh clothing. Soon enough, however, he was barraged by attention seekers he could not avoid. His sister wished to fill him in on every minute of missed court business, details he did not care to hear but felt obliged to listen to for her sake, to show gratitude for what she had done during his absence. The justice reappeared, reassuring him that, after the distressing attack on Lady Dubuais, there were no further incidents of anti-Elyri violence. He claimed no progress on the investigation into the death of Cinda Maylor and was inclined to dismiss the case as one of those random acts of violence that sometimes plagued the less fortunate in large cities.

Afterward, when the King again thought to have a moment of silence with his chamberlain, his daughter found him, carrying baby Hagan upon her hip as Brenna had often done with her and Bertram when they were infants. He swallowed the wash of pain and replied to his daughter's questions about Prince Espen and her accounting of news in Rhidam during his absence. Most of her tales revolved around Bianca and Prince Hagan. The King was amazed at how much Hagan had changed in the few weeks he had been away, and how much Hagan resembled himself. There seemed to be a touch of Muir there too, although how that could be, the King could not say. Perhaps it was a trait from Brenna's side of the family.

By the time he was finally able to steal away alone, it was long past dinner. He was exhausted, mentally and physically. He should pay his respects to his chamberlain tonight, as he had intended all day. Yet the thought of entering the gloomy oratory with Guthrie's body there in place of Kavan's familiar, reassuring shape upon the altar steps, silence instead of brass harp strings, were things King Arlan was unable to face tonight. Tomorrow, he decided. Tomorrow he would set aside time to be alone with Guthrie McHador. His family and advisors would surely allow him that.

❧*❧

When Kavan awoke, there was a hint of pale yellow light through his open window. Morning or evening, he wondered with a yawn and a careful stretch. How long had he slept? He felt clean and rested, though the pain within his skull and in his stomach had not subsided. He wondered if they were things Ártur would be able to remedy or if he would be forced to endure this discomfort for the rest of his life. Perhaps he should have left those items behind, ignored the overwhelming impulse to take them from that place…but he knew he could not have done that. They did not belong there, where someone else could find them. Removing them was necessary to break that evil energy's hold, even if Kóráhm had warned against it.

Or perhaps whatever poison he ingested would kill him first, although he was a little surprised it had not killed him already.

Recent events were still fresh in his mind, despite having slept, particularly the episode of weeping uncontrollably upon Wortham's shoulder. Not something he would have done given a choice, but his despair was too deep to be ignored and he had been too weak, emotionally, mentally, and physically, to fight it. He wondered what the captain would do when they saw each other next, if his friend would turn him away for being unmanly. But Kavan did not want to think about that. The other matter he did not want to think about pushed into his head, forcing him to get out of bed. He found a robe hanging across the nearby chair, not a white one, but rather a pale blue one. The vision of blood upon his white robe flooded his mind's eye. Prince Bertram's blood.

He wept again, unable to stop it. No, he decided, angry with himself as he tried in vain to dry his face of uncontrollable tears. He would stop. He had to. He could not face Arlan if the very thought of this tragedy caused him such distress. It took great effort, and washing his face in the basin of cold, clean water, before he was able to bring his emotions under control. There was nothing else of his within this room except for his harp, as if everything else had been packed for travel while he slept; he picked the harp up and went downstairs in search of the others, knowing what must come next. Whoever had gathered his belongings knew it too. They could not stay here. They had to go home.

Everyone else was gathered in the dining room, apparently at dinner, although the meal appeared to be over when Kavan entered. Gabrielle was seated at the head of the table, speaking with Owain. Caol sat near the large harp, where Princes Muir and Wilred were in discussion with Clianthe, the inquisitor content to watch his son.

Captain Delamo was staring out the window, his face dark and brooding, a half-empty bottle of wine in his hand. All talking stopped, and heads turned towards Kavan when the bard came into the room.

"What is it?" he asked, wondering if his appearance warranted such stares, or if something had happened he should know about. Was his grief so evident? Had the ingested poison somehow altered his appearance in a manner he was not yet aware of?

"Nothing, milord." Wortham approached him, setting the bottle of wine on the table as he passed, and extended his hand with an expression of heartfelt greeting. He wanted to embrace the bard, but after their last moments together, he believed such a gesture would be seen as too forward and would draw a negative response from Kavan. Kavan accepted his hand, holding it moments longer than he needed to, so relieved that his friend was as steadfast as ever that it nearly set him to weeping again. Only a final squeeze and Wortham releasing him just in time kept him from it. "You slept the rest of yesterday and all of today. I think I speak for everyone in saying we are surprised and relieved to see you up at last."

Gabrielle tried to smile and motioned to an empty chair. "Sit, Kavan. I can have food brought…"

"No…thank you…" He was hungry, but his knotted stomach was not prepared for food. "I appreciate your hospitality…but I think I have avoided duty long enough. I must return to Rhidam."

She nodded sadly and got to her feet. The men in the room likewise stood. "Of course…you must…" She had hoped they could stay longer, but she understood obligation. "I have been told what happened…Captain Delamo suggests I ban people from Pháne."

There was a question in her voice, to which Kavan nodded. "There is no treasure there, Gabrielle…just an evil no man can defeat. I do not think we did anything except unleash its potential." His words cast a shadow over every face in the room, though most had no idea what he meant. What would occur because of what he had done, he could not say, but he prayed he would be able to undo it, to conquer it as Saint Kóráhm had suggested he must. "No one should explore there; it will not be safe for a long time I fear."

"I will devise some rationale to keep others away. Claim it as holy ground…or say that the earthquake has made it unsafe." Kavan frowned to hear that the shaking had been felt as far away as the villa and wondered how far-reaching the effects of his actions had actually been. "Since no one lives there and no resources are taken, the Council should offer little resistance."

"I pray you are right." Kavan looked from one man to another slowly as if seeing them for the first time in years. "Gather your things, gentlemen…meet me in the study. Wortham? Do you still have…?"

"I do, milord, including what Lord Lachlan gave me; they are with your things. I will fetch them at once."

Relieved to know the items were safe, Kavan handed his harp to Muir. "Please?" he asked. He knew he must be the one to carry Prince Bertram home, to be the one to face King Arlan with this news; none of the others wished for that duty and Kavan would not have relinquished it if they had. Giving this grim news to the King was his place. Muir took the harp and one by one the men filed from the room to retrieve their possessions. Kavan followed Gabrielle to the study where Prince Bertram's body lay upon the bench near the closet. Wrapped in a blanket as if sleeping, the boy looked small, so ghostly that it took all of Kavan's will to keep from crying again. Sensing his despair, Gabrielle touched his arm; he did not flinch or pull away for the first time she could recall.

"Do you know," he whispered, "Lord McHador has also died?"

Tears welled in her eyes and she shook her head. "No…I did not know. King Arlan has lost much this year…as have you all."

Kavan's eyes closed. "More than any man should lose…I wish I could be the bearer of good tidings, not his son's body. Please, forgive my hasty departure."

"We assumed you would want to leave as soon as you were able, things being as they are. But I think," her lips pulled into a small melancholy smile, "given how things stand with Lord Lachlan, I will see you both again soon."

He had no chance to reply or question her as the others began to trickle into the room. No one moved or spoke at first as they stared at the boy on the bench, struck again by the specter of death. "Wortham…Prince Muir…come with me…and please…find Syl or Ártur at once. None of you are to speak to anyone until we are all together, please. Caol, if you will carry Wilred, I will return for Owain and bring you and Wilred together, and then I will come back for…" He tore his eyes away from Prince Bertram and bowed to Gabrielle. "Until the next time, milady."

"Until then, Kavan."

It was the first time a farewell between them had not felt final.

❧*☙

The King had hoped to pay his respect to his chamberlain first thing in the morning, as he had sworn he would do the night before, but one thing after another had prevented him from it. Little things, really, like discussing gdhededhá Tusánt with k'gdhededhá Jermyn, reassuring his daughter that Prince Espen had received her gift, honoring Squire Flannery again for his bravery, listening to the details of his chancellor's upcoming wedding, and bidding Sir Gabersdon farewell as he set off for Nelori with a report for King Geir of Hatu, carrying news from his son as to how the fighting had gone and how Hatu's men had fared. Things that, for the most part, Arlan could have avoided for a few more hours if he tried.

But instead, he put off seeing the cold, motionless body that he knew lay upon the altar in the upper oratory. It was evening again, following a dinner he lingered over too long, and after sitting undisturbed in the library for nearly an hour, nursing a glass a wine he did not drink, the King finally concluded that the time had come. No good would come of putting it off any longer.

Now he stood beside the ancient altar examining the man's wounds that had been cleaned and bled no more. It was a miracle in itself that the man had survived as long as Bhríd said he had with a wound such as that. Had it been more than sheer stubbornness and willpower that kept Guthrie alive for so long? The man's face was serene, content, almost rapt, causing the King to wonder what had transpired in those last few minutes spent with Muir and Owain that allowed Guthrie to leave this life in peace. Maybe it was the passing over that had done it. Brenna's face had been peaceful at the moment of her death too.

He touched the old man's bearded face, that face that had served as friend, mentor, and father for all of Arlan's life. How much he owed to this man, how much he had never said to him. Just as there had been so much he had not said to Brenna before he lost her too. He was learning a valuable lesson from these losses, not to wait, to say what he wanted to say while there was still time.

Noises from his left caused him to look into the shadows. From the Purification Chamber emerged Prince Muir and Captain Delamo. Both stopped, looked at him, and then Muir quickly left the room, the look on the young man's face suggesting to Arlan that Muir was a boy no longer, that he had seen and done things that brought with them a new level of maturity. The Káliel captain moved closer to the altar, his bearded face blank, but he did not speak. The King could not speak either. He could barely breathe. Owain emerged next, stopping nervously at the sight of the man who had dethroned him. He stepped sideways and stood next to Wortham, their proximity suggesting a friendship that made the King's throat constrict even more.

Muir returned with Ártur behind him as Caol came through the Purification curtain with Wilred in his arms. The boy looked thin and frightened, but otherwise unharmed. Trembling, the King took one step away from the altar but paused again when no one else emerged. Dare he hope?

Silence. The curtain billowed, swayed, and then Kavan stepped into the oratory with Prince Bertram's limp, colorless body in his arms, the blanket having shifted to reveal blood-stained wrappings around his small torso darkened to brown as the crimson flow of life had dried. The Elyri met his friend's gaze as the last of the breath was forced from the King's lungs.

"No!" Arlan's protracted scream echoed through the castle halls.

# ⮌Epilogue⮌

From the dayroom window, King Arlan stared at the bell tower of Hes á Redh Náós with its stained glass windows now replace. The sun's rays made them sparkle and glow, adding warmth to the summer day he had not felt moments before. Below him, in the courtyard, he could hear Ternce Wyndham and Minos Cornell arguing. The two men did that frequently since Minos assumed the post of chancellor; it was always a battle between the availability of funds and the general's perceived needs for the expansion of Enesfel's military. The success of last year's campaign brought forth an influx of men eager to serve the King, and General Wyndham was determined to make the most of however many men he could afford to train.

Last year's campaign. A dull knot drew together and ached in the King's stomach. A whole year gone and much around him had changed. The size of Enesfel's militia had increased, the extra men no longer needed to staff the northern fortifications or patrol the new territory had come home and many were conscripted into a standing army. The northern reaches were secure. With great reluctance, King Merkar de Corrmick had accepted the loss of the southern portion of his kingdom in exchange for retaining his throne and Neth's sovereignty. Cordash withdrew her troops from Neth and had restored order in Cordash's border towns under King Renfrid's steady-handed rule. Though Neth had been peaceable since, almost friendly, King Renfrid kept a close eye on his borders while King Arlan felt compelled to maintain the fortifications along the Kelari and Dagar Rivers and along the southern shore of Lake Curo, all under the command of General Yorick Zarkosta. Arlan wanted no surprises should King Merkar decide it was time to reclaim the lands Neth had lost or seek revenge for the brothers killed in battle.

Guthrie McHador was buried with as much fanfare as the King was able to arrange. Arlan waited for General Wyndham to return to Rhidam, bringing King Renfrid, Prince Espen, and General Agis with him. Even King Geir had ridden from Hatu for this most solemn of remembrances. Every noble in Enesfel had attended. The name of McHador was intertwined with the reign of four Lachlan Kings; the man had been the greatest general Enesfel had ever known, and some argued the greatest anywhere in the Sovereignties. He was interred in the back garden near the Lachlans he had given his life to serve, a man revered as none other in Lachlan history.

Prince Bertram's burial ceremony involved less pomp and flair. The family, the clergy, and the Lachlan staff were all who attended. Not that the loss of his son and heir was any less painful than losing Guthrie, but the King knew that, in the scope of the past, present, and future, the death of his young son was not as significant to the history of the kingdom. Only to Arlan, his friends, his family, and his household did the boy's death mean anything, and it was they who would feel his absence, every day. The King felt it even now.

The young soldier Darius, still suffering a limp from the injuries he sustained in the avalanche, had taken the position of justice; he was the one man the King felt worthy of the position when Minos had been promoted. The specter of anti-Elyri violence lurked on the fringes of everyday life, making many leery of accepting the position of justice, and to this day, there were some who were not yet comfortable working with Caol Dugan as Enesfel's inquisitor. But Enesfel had been peaceful since the King's return from Neth; not even gdhededhá Tusánt's homecoming and resumption of his post in Rhidam had resulted in violent incidents. The k'gdhededhá was preparing for a fourth full-time clergyman as the náós repairs and reconstruction neared completion and daily attendance to all Gatherings increased.

Lord Bhríd Cáner enthusiastically accepted the post of chamberlain left vacant by Guthrie's death, but not until after his wedding to Duchess Madalyn Dubuais of Levonne. Flannery still served as Bhríd's squire and would remain there until given a position of his own, the King assumed. The chamberlain and his squire were not at court today; Bhríd had gone to Levonne yesterday to greet his newborn son.

Son. Yes, Hagan was growing quickly and was struggling through his first steps. He looked so much like Guthrie at times that it made Arlan's heart ache to watch him play. The little boy was most devoted to his sister; if the King looked he would find Wilred, Bianca, and Hagan clustered in the nursery, listening to Diona's storytelling. The MacLyrs had adopted Bianca when Gabrielle sent word that the only Maylors who remained on the islands was an elderly woman too old to care for a child, and a handful of cousins with too-large families of their own. What had become of the rest of the Maylors, no one knew. The girl had adjusted to her new family, although sometimes there was a haunted expression in her eyes that was disconcerting to anyone who saw it. It was believed by some that she might have witnessed her mother's death, but as young as she had been there was little chance of anyone knowing that for sure.

Wilred had survived his ordeal with the strength, humor, and resilience the King suspected came from Caol's longstanding Dugan heritage. The story of the Dugans' history with the Association was finally revealed, the feud with the Tarmajiens, and the hunt that had led him and the others to confront the last known Tarmajien on one of

Káliel's islands. Arlan tried to confiscate the Coryllien dagger used to kill Lísbhet Dilyn, but Kavan refused to give it to him, saying that it was hidden somewhere only the bard would be able to access it. Kavan had not mentioned to anyone that there were two Corylliens now in his possession. As annoyed at being refused had initially made him, the King eventually agreed that it was for the best that he not know where the dagger was. If Kavan wanted to bear the responsibility for its security, then so be it. Caol suffered no further indignities at the hand of Justice Cornell, and thankfully, his marriage had not suffered. In fact, the last time the King had talked at length with his sister, she and the inquisitor were intending to have another child.

"Hello, father." The bright, youthful voice continued past the dayroom door, bound for the nursery no doubt. Arlan had to chuckle.

His daughter had developed a gift for speaking over the last year, the King could not deny that. Too much of a gift it seemed at times. Her way with words had caused more than one embarrassing incident at court, caused Kavan a great deal of consternation, and brought Prince Espen to Enesfel's court twice in response to letters she had written. King Arlan and King Geir were toying with the idea of formally betrothing their children, but Arlan, knowing how headstrong his daughter could be, was hesitant to bind the ten-year-old girl to a marriage she might not wish for when she was old enough for such things, and King Geir still hoped his son would marry sooner rather than later, someone suitably Hatuish with the expected customary upbringing. There were at least four years before Princess Diona would be suitable for marriage. As King Arlan knew too well, a lot could change in that time and he was not ready to lose another child.

Prince Muir was lost to the young man's real father. Not that Arlan could claim to ever have had Muir as his own. He had spent too many years feeling that Muir was not his son to begin now. After the pair of funerals, when Muir no longer had anything other than Kavan and his sister to bind him to Rhidam, he sought permission to travel with

Owain back to Fiara. The King was reluctant to acquiesce at first, but his bard's persuasion prevailed in the end. Muir was a man, had been upon his return from Káliel. King Arlan had even less of a claim on him now; Muir could do as he wished.

The eldest Lachlan prince had been in Rhidam three times since then, each time with his father on their way to Káliel. The King had no wish to know what business Owain was conducting on the islands, as long as it strengthened Enesfel's ties to them and gave Arlan a continual line of communication with the Prime Magistrate. He welcomed those benefits and did not pry. His relationship with Owain was strained, but at least there was no open hostility. But Muir had all but turned his back on Arlan and that was a burden the King found difficult to bear, especially when Guthrie's final message to Arlan had asked him to look past the young man's conception and birth to Muir's good qualities and to forgive Owain his past transgressions. Owain was Muir's father, yes, but he was also Guthrie's son.

The notes from brass harp strings drifted through the corridors from the oratory, ringing gaily in the King's ears. Though he had been reserved upon his return, and Ártur had demanded peaceful rest for him after the injuries he received on Pháne, it had not taken the Elyri harper long to outwardly regain his normal calm. If he had ingested any poison, it seemed to have had little effect. Lord Cliáth of Bhryell became Duke Cliáth of Alberni when Muir conferred the estate and titles upon the Elyri last autumn. The bard accepted the gift without protest, something the King had pondered curiously ever since.

Now Enesfel had two Elyri dukes, a fact that distress and angered some, the King had no doubt. Kavan spent a great deal of time at the estate during the last year, asserting that, by the day of Kóráhm's Feast this year, his new home would be ready to receive visitors. The King wondered what the bard could be doing to the manor that once belonged to Brenna's family. But he knew his wife would have approved of anything Kavan could do. As would he. Arlan could not wait to see what changes Kavan had to show him.

A thought came to him then, something Guthrie had told him shortly after Brenna's death. Memories fade, pain subsides. You always miss what you no longer have, but life does get better. The memories had indeed faded, though not much, and the pain of loss was not as acute as it had been a year ago. Life had gone on around him without those he had lost, and he still lived. He had survived the worst of it. You were wise, Guthrie, the King mused, turning away from the window. Almost as wise as Kavan. King Arlan left the dayroom, wanting to immerse himself in Kavan's music one more time as he had done so many years ago.

## The End

## Character Index Book 2

**Agis, General**--A Cíbhóló nomad, in King Arlan's employment, who has risen to the position of second general, directly under Ternce Wyndham.

**Ahern Valdis**--The King of Cordash during Kings Girvin, Owain, and Arlan's reigns.

**Alba, Lady**--One of the women at court, a tutor to Diona Lachlan.

**Aleski MacLyr**--The oldest son of Sámel MacLyr, Ártur MacLyr's nephew and Kavan Cliáth's cousin.

**Ander de Corrmick**--A King of Neth, brother of Ula, uncle to Owain Ustes. It is suspected that his son, Loris, murdered him.

**Arlan Trebor Lachlan**--The youngest son of King Innis of Enesfel. He is the 25th king of Enesfel.

**Ártur MacLyr**--Elyri healer, employed by Kings Innis, Donal, and Arlan Lachlan. He is married to Syl Cáner and is the cousin of Kavan Cliáth.

**Avner**--One of the five Káliel guards sent by Gabrielle Dilyn to serve Arlan Lachlan in his quest for the Enesfel throne.

**Baine, Mr.**--One of the two soldiers at the Rhidam castle gates when Halstatt Tarmajien delivered the Coryllien to Caol Dugan.

**Balint Gabersdon, Sir**--The youngest knight in Enesfel, also the Duke of Nelori.

**Bhenádíctus, málneag**--He was a Teren herbalist. Though never ordained, he wandered the known territories preaching repentance, poverty, and forgiveness. He owned nothing in his life other than his clothing and his walking stick; those in his order take vows of poverty and become wandering missionaries. He died on Káliel in the shrine he built, though since his body was never found some people believe that k'Ádhá took him directly to Ethenae. He became the patron of travelers, the poor, and those in need of spiritual forgiveness and enlightenment.

**Bertram Earl Lachlan**--The eldest living son of Arlan Lachlan, twin to Diona.

**Bhendhámyn MacLyr**--The youngest son of Sámel MacLyr, nephew to Ártur MacLyr and cousin to Kavan Cliáth.

**Bhílári, gdhededhá**--gdhededhá in Bhryell who witnessed many of Kavan's boyhood "miracles" and is one of the few who has not shunned contact with him.

**Bhríd Cáner, Lord High Chancellor**--An Elyri merchant's son who fought with Prince Arlan's to gain the throne; he is a distant cousin of the MacLyr's and Cliáth's. He has remained in Enesfel and is employed by King Arlan Lachlan as his chancellor. He is known as the best swordsman in the Five Sovereignties, and King's champion in Enesfel.

**Bianca Maylor MacLyr**--The daughter of Cinda Maylor, orphaned and then adopted by Syl and Ártur MacLyr.

**Bowen Ellard Lachlan**--The 3rd son of King Innis of Enesfel; he was the 22nd king of Enesfel. It is believed by some that he was the father of Owain Lachlan.

**Brenna Weylin Lachlan**--Guthrie McHador's niece, wife of King Arlan Lachlan, mother of Muir, Bertram, Diona, and Hagan.

**Caol Dugan, Lord High Inquisitor**--Originally the son of a member of the Association, he is now part of King Arlan Lachlan's court and family, by way of marriage to Princess Deidre Lachlan. Father of Prince Wilred Lachlan Dugan.

**Cinda Maylor**--Hired as a nurse for Prince Hagan, she was the younger sister of Felix Maylor.

**Claide, gdhededhá**--The only Teren gdhededhá serving in Rhidam's Hes á Redh Náos.

**Clianthe Dilyn**--Prime Magistrate Gabrielle Dilyn's only child.

**Cordelia Lachlan**--The 3rd wife of Innis of Enesfel, mother of King Girvin, Princess Deidre, and King Arlan.

**Curran**--A soldier in Enesfel's ranks.

**Daens, Physician**--A physician in Fiara.

**Daneel**--A servant in the Valdis court.

**Darius Corbin**--A young soldier in Enesfel's military, whom Captain Wortham Delamo enlists to aid in the search for Prince Bertram and Prince Wilred.

**Dawid Coryllien**--A semi-mythical figure, whose name is connected with the death of many Elyri and many Teren during the Persecution. His name was given to the daggers connected with those murders. Very little else is known about him.

**Deidre Dugan-Lachlan**--The only daughter of King Innis of Enesfel, twin to King Arlan. She is the wife of Caol Dugan, mother of Wilred Lachlan Dugan.

**Delia**--The maidservant to Prime Magistrate of Káliel Gabrielle Dilyn.

**Demris, Lord**--A Nethite nobleman whose territory is in western Neth, near the Cordashian border.

**Denyan**--One of the five Káliel guards sent by Gabrielle Dilyn to serve Prince Arlan in his quest for the throne.

**Dervis**--A soldier in Enesfel's ranks who assists Caol Dugan after his first fight with Halstatt.

**Dháná MacLyr**--The wife of Tám MacLyr and mother of Sámel and Ártur MacLyr.

**Dhórdh**--Mílne MacLyr's fiancée, who is murdered by a Nethite hunter.

**Diona Cordelia Lachlan**--King Arlan's only daughter, twin to Bertram.

**Donal Ártur Lachlan**--King Arlan's second son, who was stillborn.

**Donal Malin Lachlan**--The 1st son of Innis of Enesfel; he was the 20th King of Enesfel.

**Dórímyr, k'gdhededhá**--The highest religious leader in the Faith of Elyriá.

**Earle de Corrmick**--The eldest son of King Loris of Neth, rules as King for two days before Prince Renfrid Valdis of Cordash kills him in battle.

**Edgar Fielding**--One of the two soldiers guarding the Rhidam castle gates when Halstatt Tarmajien delivered the Coryllien to Caol Dugan. He is the only one, other than Caol, to see the dagger.

**Elus Mancs**--Once a suitor of Gabrielle Dilyn, now a ship owner.

**Elyn**--Madalyn Dubuais' lady in waiting.

**Ensgar, General**--Neth's second general.

**Espen Harcourt, Prince**--The youngest son of King Geir of Hatu, he rides into battle against Neth with Enesfel's troops.

**Farrell Rasmus Lachlan**--The 2nd son of King Innis of Enesfel; he was the 21st king of Enesfel.

**Faylyn, Lady**--Prince Hagan's nurse after the death of Cinda Maylor.

**Felix Maylor**--Gabrielle Dilyn's husband

**Flannery McGrannis**--Bhríd Cáner's squire.

**Forst McLenum**--A member of the Association and resident of Durham. Though Caol Dugan does not know him personally, he is aware that the McLenums have served as messengers between the Tarmajiens and Dugans since the start of their feud.

**Gabrielle Dilyn**--The only child of Ulstar Dilyn, she is now the Prime Magistrate of Káliel. Mother of Clianthe Dilyn. She is half Elyri.

**Geir Harcourt**--The King of Hatu, father of Prince Espen Harcourt.

**Girvin Alaric Lachlan**--The 4th child of King Innis of Enesfel, first child of Cordelia; he was the 23rd king of Enesfel.

**Glucke, General**--Neth's leading General, with personal aspirations towards the Neth throne.

**Govert Valdis**--The infant son of Renfrid Valdis, the heir to the throne when Renfrid becomes King of Cordash.

**Guthrie McHador, Lord High Chamberlain**--Once the general of Enesfel's army under Kings Innis and Donal, he reared Arlan and assisted him in his bid for Enesfel's throne. He has remained at court as King Arlan's chamberlain.

**Gwenyr Lachlan**--A daughter of Donal Lachlan, 1st twin, who died of plague at age 2.

**Hagan Guthrie Brennan Lachlan**--King Arlan Lachlan's youngest son.

**Halstatt Tarmajien**--A life-long feuding enemy of Caol Dugan's.

**Hanford Weylin, Duke**--Brenna's brother, the Duke of Alberni, who sided with Arlan against King Owain. Upon his death, the Alberni estate was left to his sister, who in turn leaves the estate to her eldest son Prince Muir Lachlan.

**Harle, Sheriff**--Sheriff of Rhidam, directly under Lord High Justice Minos Cornell's command

**Hewett Colson**--A captain in Enesfel's ranks whom Guthrie McHador sends north to gain intelligence about Neth before the war. He was one of the original men to join Arlan's quest for the throne.

**Ibyll de Corrmick**--The second oldest son of Loris of Neth

**Ilene, Lady**--One of Diona Lachlan's tutors.

**Ilka Lachlan**--A daughter of Prince Donal, 2nd twin, who died of plague at age 2.

**Innis Trebor Lachlan**--The 19th King of Enesfel, the father Kings Donal, Farrell, Bowen, Girvin, and Arlan.

**Jermyn Tythilius, k'gdhededhá**--A former brother in the Order of Saint Kóráhm in Clarys, Elyriá, he is now the k'gdhededhá of Rhidam.

**Jezeel McHador**--The deceased wife of Guthrie McHador, who died of the plague during King Innis' reign.

**Kalvert, Captain**--A soldier in Enesfel's military, left in charge of the troops in Ruidoso when Ternce Wyndham goes to meet with Kings Renfrid Valdis and Merkar de Corrmick.

**Kavan Kóráhm Cliáth**--The last of the Cliáth's, only child of Rístyrd and Llyárá, cousin of Ártur MacLyr. He is an admired harper, possessor of the Sight, holder of great psionic capabilities. He has become known as the White Bard of Bhryell in the kingdoms outside of Elyriá for his tremendous musical talent and unique physical appearance. King Arlan currently employs him as the Lachlan court bard and as tutor for the royal children.

**Kjell de Corrmick**--The youngest son of King Loris of Neth.

**Kóráhm, málneag**--An Elyri saint for whom Kavan was named, who is also known as Kóráhm the Heretic by many in Elyriá because of some controversial writings he set down before the time of his martyrdom. Few of his books are available and he is not commonly discussed.

**Leocroft, Captain**--Cordash's naval commander, in charge of the fleet when war is declared on Neth.

**Leon Undilbra**--A member of the Fiara-Ruidoso joint counsel, hailing from Fiara, who goes before King Merkar to present their demands for secession.

**Lísbhet Dilyn**--Gabrielle Dilyn's mother, an Elyri.

**Loris de Corrmick**--King of Neth. It is his cruelty to his subjects that leads to the secession of southern Neth, and his raids on Cordash that lead to war with Cordash and Enesfel.

**Luc McDermott**--An officer who served beside Guthrie McHador during Kings' Innis and Donal's reigns, and retired with the ascent of Farrell to the throne. He joined Prince Arlan's forces in their march against King Owain and is still in his employment.

**Logros**--One of the five Káliel guards sent by Gabrielle Dilyn to serve Arlan Lachlan in his bid for the throne of Enesfel.

**Madalyn Dubuais, Duchess**--The Duchess of Levonne, she is the only woman in Enesfel to have control of her own lands because her father died leaving no male relatives.

**Malizar Caliph**--The name Halstatt Tarmajien uses while in Rhidam.

**Marym, General**--Cordash's top general who leads the assault against Neth.

**Mátán, málneag**--An Elyri saint, popular for advocating wise and judicious use of Elyri abilities. He was a scholar and a teacher who was in Enesfel when the first Lachlan became king. Though he personally denied involvement, and Teren chronicles do not mention his name, many believe that Mátán was at least partially responsible for the Lachlans gaining the throne. He is the patron of scholars, students, and those seeking political change.

**Meara Lachlan**--The wife of King Donal Lachlan.

**Merkar de Corrmick**--The third son of King Loris of Neth.

**Mílne MacLyr**--The only daughter of Sámel MacLyr, Ártur MacLyr's niece and Kavan Cliáth's cousin.

**Minos Cornell, Lord High Justice**--He is the Duke of Theron, though the estate is run by his wife and a cousin. He assumes the position of chancellor upon Guthrie McHador's death.

**Mórne, High Mother (Kyne)**--The matriarchal ruler of Elyriá; she is head of the Elyri High Council.

**Muir Innis Lachlan**--The bastard son of Owain Lachlan by Brenna Weylin, raised as Prince Arlan's son.

**Nona**--Clianthe Dilyn's girlhood friend.

**Oberon Cervasian**--He served as a captain in Enesfel's military under King Donal but retired shortly after Guthrie McHador left service. He joined Prince Arlan's quest for the throne and has remained in his service.

**Onea Pantel**--The woman who heads the Fiara branch of the Association.

**Owain Ustes Lachlan**--Believed by many to be either the 5th child of King Innis or the only son of King Bowen, he is the son of Ula de Corrmick of Neth. He is the 24th king of Enesfel. He is actually the only child of Guthrie McHador. He relinquished the throne to Prince Arlan and has lived in the Neth city of Fiara since then. He is the father of Muir Innis Lachlan

**Phaedr Cáner**--The brother of Bhríd and Syl Cáner, he joined Prince Arlan's forces and lost his sight, then his life, for that cause.

**Poul Garvis**--A member of the Fiara-Ruidoso joint counsel, hailing from Ruidoso, who goes before King Merkar to present the south's demands for secession.

**Renfrid Valdis**--He is the son of King Ahern, and is the heir to the Cordash throne. He leads Cordash into war against Neth.

**Rístyrd Cliáth**--An Elyri harp maker of the historical & legendary Cliáths, he is the father of Kavan. He died in a fire when Kavan was an infant.

**Rouvyn Talis**--A Teren physician originally connected to Wace Elotti, who assists in the search for Princes Bertram and Wilred.

**Sámel MacLyr**--Ártur MacLyr's older brother and Kavan's cousin. He is a harp maker in the Cliáth tradition, like his father, and is the father of Mílne, Aleski, and Bhendhámyn.

**Syl Cáner MacLyr**--The sister of Bhríd and Phaedr Cáner, she is an Elyri healer and a distant cousin of the MacLyr's and Cliáth's. She married Ártur MacLyr and serves as a court healer for King Arlan.

**Simin Dralski**--A cloth merchant who deals between Káliel and Enesfel, who discovers Lísbhet Dilyn's body in his wagon.

**Sorvis**--A Teren physician in Rhidam whom Justice Cornell employs periodically to conduct autopsies.

**Tám MacLyr**--An Elyri harp maker in the tradition of the Cliáths, father of Sámel and Ártur; he was the half-brother of Rístyrd Cliáth.

**Tedor**--A soldier in Enesfel's ranks.

**Ternce Wyndham, General**--He served as both King Owain's second general, then as first general, and was asked to keep his position by Arlan Lachlan, and has served as such since Arlan's ascension.

**Tíbhyan**--Elyri bhydáni who was once Kavan's private tutor. He is the oldest man in Bhryell and one of the top 10 sages in Elyriá.

**Trebor Malin Lachlan**--King Arlan's third son who died within hours of his birth.

**Tusánt, gdhededhá**--An Elyri gdhededhá who serves with k'gdhededhá Jermyn in Rhidam.

**Tymothy Borlad, k'gdhededhá**--The Teren k'gdhededhá in Aralt, Cordash.

**Ula de Corrmick**--The sister of King Ander of Neth, mistress of Prince Bowen, mother of Prince Owain. Arlan Lachlan executed her for conspiracy against the Crown after he became king.

**Venitt, Captain**--A Captain in the Neth army with whom Owain Lachlan is acquainted.

**Wace Elotti**--A Cíbhóló nomad turned mercenary, heralded as the best in the Five Sovereignties. He has been pursuing Halstatt Tarmajien since the man escaped his Neth prison.

**Waljan**--One of the five Káliel guards sent by Gabrielle Dilyn to serve Prince Arlan in his quest for Enesfel's throne.

**Wilred Douglas Lachlan Dugan**--The only child of Caol Dugan and Deidre Lachlan-Dugan.

**Wortham Delamo, Captain**--Captain of the five elite Káliel guards sent by Gabrielle Dilyn to serve Arlan Lachlan. He has become a close friend of Kavan Cliáth's and considers himself Kavan's protector.

**Yorick Zarkosta, General**--At one time he had been part of King Owain's army but he joined Prince Arlan's quest for the throne and has risen to the rank of General in his years of service since then.

# Elyri Phonetics

á--ä (as in m**o**p)
a--ă (as in c**a**t)
ae--ā (as in **a**ce)
ag--ä (as in m**o**p) (HE**)
ai--ī (as in **i**ce)
au--aù (as in **ou**t)
é--ŭ (as in b**u**t)
e--ĕ (as in b**e**t

i--ē (as in b**e**)
í--ĭ (as in s**i**t)
ó--ō (as in g**o**)
o--ŏ (as in m**o**p)
u--ū (as in bl**ue**)
y--ē (as in b**e)**
yh--y (as in **y**es)

b--b
bh--v
c--k
ch--ch
d--d
dh--j
gae--gwā
gdh--zh (as in vi**s**ion)
gh--g (as in go)
gk--k as in loch (HE)
h--h
hw--w (breathy, as in whale)
k'--k
k--k

l--l
Ll--l
m--m
mh--m (slightly breathy)
n--n
ne--nyä
p--p
ph--f
r--r
s--sh
t--t
th--th (as in thistle)
z--z

• **C** is always pronounced **K** but the letter **K** is most often used to designate this sound. **C** mainly appears at the beginning of some proper surnames and place names and occasionally in the center or at the end of a word. This is believed to be a carryover from the earliest days of the Elyri language, or to have been influenced by the Teren languages, but Elyri linguists and scholars have not yet determined its significance. However, in keeping with this unspoken, unexplained rule, no Elyri have first names, or middle names, starting with **C**.

- The combination **gk** (pronounced as in the German ich) occurs only at the end of words unless there is a verb suffix or plural suffix behind it, and only in those words of High Elyri origin.

- The letter combination **ag** occurs at the end of words of High Elyri origin. If the combination appears elsewhere in a word, it will either be as a product of two words having been combined or will be the result of a suffix having been added. Though some Standard Elyri words have retained their **ag** ending, most words carried into the standard will have the **ag** combination replaced with **á** when written, though they sound alike when spoken.

- The **H** sound only appears in High Elyri words and in some names carried over from ancient sources; Standard Elyri derivatives will normally drop the **h** from the original word but there are exceptions to the rule

- Double **L**'s are found at the beginnings of words, single **l**'s in the body or at the end. When words do have the double **L** in a location other than the beginning, it is always the result of two words being combined into one.

- In High Elyri, there were no naturally occurring **B, P,** or **ow** (as in cow) sounds. These did not get introduced until Elyri acquired their current religious faith. Even then, the sounds were not commonly used until the standard Trade tongue influenced everyday life. These sounds mainly appear in proper names or religious settings.

- The combination of the letter **ne** occurs almost exclusively at the end of a word and is always pronounced **nya**, regardless of where it occurs.

- The **ee** sound at the beginning or end of a word is always represented with an **I**. In the center of words, it is represented by a **Y**. When the **ee** sound is represented in the center of a word by the letter **I,** it is a result of two words being combined into one. In some cases, as with the name Cliáth, the original words may no longer be known. The few exceptions where Standard or High Elyri words begin with a Y for the ee sound are believed to have originated as intentional misspellings.

- There is no **S** sound in the Elyri language. **S**'s are always pronounced **sh**.

- The letter **Z** appears only in the High Elyri or in words derived from the High Elyri or originated as misspellings in one of the Teren languages and were absorbed back into Elyri in the aberrant form.

## Elyri Grammar

In most Elyri words, the stress falls on the second to last. Words where the stress fall on the final syllable (or on the first syllable in words with more than two syllables) are either names, the result of an Elyri translation of a Teren word, caused by the addition of a prefix or suffix, or the result of a word being truncated, having dropped the last syllable over time.

The **k'** at the beginning of a word signifies importance or singularity. It is applied to a word that can have a common meaning and a special meaning: k'tyne would be a favorite niece or female cousin, whereas tyne is simply a niece or female cousin. In the case of the phae k'kairá, when the Teren translated the term into "the Others" it is the **k'** that indicates the O to be capitalized; not just any others but the Others.

The Elyri written language does not have additional characters for capitalization. The first letters words may carry a dot beneath them to signify that the word is a proper name, a place, or a title, but first letters of sentences are not capitalized.

Sentence breaks are characterized by either a new line of text or by a symbol that looks similar to an s. This has resulted in many mistranslations from Elyri into other languages.

## Nouns

Noun forms of verbs do not have gender. When these nouns are made plural they take the plural inclusive suffix sur.

The prefix **íl** added to a verb makes it into a noun; the word then means "one who" as in "**íl**Daeni"-one who instructs, i.e.: teacher.

Some nouns are formed by adding the prefix **ai** to a verb; the verb dhesá means touch, aidhesá also means touch but is a noun. Not all verbs can accept the **ai** prefix.

**-thé**: the standard plural suffix

Nouns ending in **I** are both singular and plural and do not take the -**thé** ending

Elyri monetary denominations are both singular and plural.

There are other exceptions to the singular/plural rule, most being words carried over from the High Elyri. High Elyri contains very few words that are NOT both plural and singular. Any exceptions to the rule are noted.

Some words have gender. A word ending in **ne** is feminine and a word ending in **dhá** is masculine. Both are made plural in the same way (with the **thé** ending). Some gender neutral words that have been altered from their original form may have either ending.

Some words in Standard, those referring to a group that includes both male and female individuals, require the -**sur** ending, creating the plural inclusive form of the word. The same ending exists in High Elyri.

## Adjectives

There are few adjectives in the Elyri language. Instead of saying someone is beautiful, or wise, and Elyri would say they possess beauty or they possess wisdom.

To modify such qualities, an Elyri speaker would say:

bhykólé aelá shwyth: She possesses wisdom. Teren: She is wise.

ochbhykóle aelá shwyth: She possesses more wisdom. Teren: She is wiser.

utbhykólé aelá shwyth: She possesses the most wisdom. Teren: She is wisest.

naimbhykólé aelá shwyth: She possesses no wisdom. Teren: She is not wise; or She is a fool.

The few adjectives that do exist come through the High Elyri and are believed by most linguists to have their origins in some language other than the Elyri.

## Verbs

When **ibh** modifies a verb (ie: is singing, is looking) it is attached as a suffix to the verb. In all other instances, it is a separate word (bhydáni ibh gaeth: He is bhydáni.)

When **im** modifies a verb (ie: was singing, was looking) it is attached as a suffix to the verb. In all other instances, it is a separate word (ílDaeni im gaeth: He was a teacher)

There is no "be" in the Elyri language. Whereas a Teren would say, "He will be singing" the Elyri would say "He will sing." Instead of "I will be there" it would be "I will come" or I will go"; instead of "I will be here" it would be "I will stay", "I will attend," or "I am here."

Rather than using verbs such as "strengthened" or "beautified", in Elyri they would say "given strength" or "given beauty"

## Verb Tenses

| (present) do, does | (past) (ár) did, have done | (present) (ibh) am, are, is doing | (past) (im) was, is, were doing | (future) (ád) will do, to do, be done |
|---|---|---|---|---|
| aelá | aelár | aelibh | aelim | aelád |
| ándás | ándásár | ándásibh | ándásim | ándásád |
| árá | árár | áráibh | áráim | árád |
| bhaeá | bhaeár | bhaeibh | bhaeim | bhaeád |
| bheken | bhekár | bhekibh | bhenim | bhekád |
| bhair | bhairár | bhairibh | bhairim | bhairád |
| bhólon | bhólár | bhólibh | bhólim | bhólád |
| chóne | chóneár | chóníbh | chónim | chónád |
| daeni | daenár | daenibh | daenim | daenád |
| dhesá | dhesár | dhesibh | dhesim | dhesád |
| dhys | dhysár | dhysibh | dhysim | dhysád |
| donai | donár | donaiibh | donim | donád |
| ghlaiph | ghlaiphár | ghlaiphibh | ghlaiphim | ghlaiphád |
| ghytae | ghytár | ghytibh | ghytim | ghytád |
| kelém | kelémár | kelémibh | kelémim | kelémád |
| mairós | mairár | mairibh | mairim | mairád |
| naeth | naethár | naethibh | naethim | naethád |
| yháth | yháthár | yháthibh | yháthim | yháthád |
| zene | zenár | zenibh | zenim | zenád |
| zólágk | zólágkár | zólágkibh | zólágkim | zólágkád |

## Verb/Noun Tenses

| | noun form 1(íl) | noun 2(ai) |
|---|---|---|
| aelá | ílAelá (one who owns) | |
| ándás | ílAndás (one who honors) | aiándás |
| bhaeá | ílBhaeá (one who asks) | |
| bheken | ílBheken | |
| bhair | ílBhair (one who accepts) | aibhair (acceptance) |
| bhólon | ílBhólon (one who purifies) | |
| chóne | ílChóne (one who brings) | |
| daeni | ílDaeni (one who instructs) | |
| dhesá | ílDhesá (one who touches) | aidhesá |
| donai | ílDonai (one who endures) | aidonai |
| ghlaiph | ílGhlaiph (one who sleeps) | aiglaiph |
| ghytae | ílGhytae (one who threatens) | aighytae (threat) |
| kelém | ílKelém (one who passes) | |
| mairós | ílMairós (one who heals) | aimairós |
| naeth | ílNaeth (one who finds) | |
| zene | ílZene (one who gives) | |
| zólágk | ílZólágk (one who reveals) | |

## Verb Tenses (High Elyri)

| (present) | (past)(-ár) | (future)(-es) |
|---|---|---|
| aelás | aelásár | aeles |
| bhánys | bhánár | bhánes |
| dytae | dytár | dytes |
| ghai | ghaiár | ghaies |
| síndóbhaene | síndóbhaenár | síndóbhaenes |
| zugdhu | zugdhuár | zugdhues |
| tyreth | tyrethár | tyrethes |
| pháló | phálóár | phálóes |
| scenyhur | scenyhár | scenhyures |
| elzen | elzenár | elzenes |

## Verb/Noun Tenses (High Elyri)

### (noun 1) (bhe-)
bheaelás (one who owns)
bhehánys (one who makes music)
bhedytae (one who obeys)
bheghai (one who does)
bhesíndóbhaene (one who forgives)
bhezugdhu (one who protects)
bhetyreth (one who knows/scholar)
bhepháló (one who buries/gravedigger)
bhescenyhur (one who names)
bhelzen (one who gives)

### (noun 2) (ae-)
aeaelás (possession)
aedytae (obedience)
aesíndóbhaene (forgiveness)
aezugdhu (protection)
aetyreth (knowledge)
aepháló (grave)
aescenyur (name)
aeelzen (gift)

# Foreign Phrase Index

## ELYRI WORDS

| | | |
|---|---|---|
| HE: High Elyri | SE: Standard Elyri | |
| n--noun | v--verb | adj—adjective |
| adv--adverb | prn--pronoun | prp--preposition |
| pl--plural | sng--singular | psv—possessive |
| pl in--plural inclusive | | |

**á** (ä) (prp)--HE/SE; and, also, together with, together

**Ádhá** (Ä-jä) (n)--HE/SE; god; k'Ádhá-supreme deity in the Elyri monotheistic religion

**aelá** (Ā-lä) (v)--SE; Have (has), possess, own

**aelibh** (ā-LĒV) (v)--SE; am owning, am possessing

**aendhá** (ĀN-jä) (n) (pl: aendáthé)--SE; A father's male relatives, including his father, grandfathers, uncles, brothers, and cousins.

**aeslag** (ĀSH-lä) (n)--HE; Loved one, beloved, lover; occasionally interchanged with kyá and sínréc. This word carries almost sacred connotations and is rarely used outside of some intensely passionate, spiritual, emotional relationship. It is believed that in a person's life, while one could have several lovers, they can have only one aeslag, thus many hesitate to use the term at all and may only apply it to someone in their past when they are old and nearing death.

**aiándás** (ī-ÄN-däsh) (n) (pl: aiándásthé)--SE; honor

**aighlaiph** (Ī-glīf) (n) (sng and pl)--SE; sleep, rest, nap

**aihwelys** (ī-HWĔL-ēsh) (n) (pl: aihwelysthé)--SE; believer

**aikáchá** (ī-KÄ-chä) (n) (pl: aikácháthé)--SE; oath or promise.

**ándás** (ÄN-däsh) (v)--SE; honor

**át** (ät) (prn)--SE; I, me, myself

**átaelás** (ä-TÄ-läsh) (prn psv)--HE; mine, my

**áti** (Ä-tē) (prn)--HE; I, me, myself

**bhair** (vīr) (v)--SE; accept

**bhedhuaethag** (vĕ-jū-Ā-thä) (n) (sng and pl)--HE; defiler

**bhelts** (vĕltsh) (n) (sng and pl)--SE; Elyri gold currency.

**bhemethán** (vĕ-mĕ- THÄN) (n) (sng and pl)--HE; murderer, executioner

**bheturbhae** (vĕ-TŪR-vä)(n) (sng and pl)--HE; traitor

**bhólon** (vō-LÄN) (v)--SE; purify, purifies

**bhydáni** (vē-DÄN-ē) (n) (sng and pl)--HE; This is both a title and a social standing. It can be translated teacher, master, sage, or wise one, though it actually encompasses all of these meanings. The title is given to those who, through their exceptional psionic capabilities, wisdom, and intelligence, have demonstrated their worth. Psionic ability is the key to the title, though great ability without wisdom and intelligence will not gain the title. With the title comes the privilege of teaching their knowledge to the children, particularly their psionic knowledge. Each city, town, or village will have at least one bhydáni. Either the bhydáni will ask another into their ranks, or, in the event that a location has no functioning bhydáni, the inhabitants will select someone to fill the position. In extremely rare cases, someone can become bhydáni by accident; they accept mentorship of someone and others begin to ask for the privilege of learning from them as well. By becoming an unofficial teacher, the individual has become bhydáni. A little less than 2/3 of all bhydáni are female.

**Cliáthan** (klē-Ä-thăn) (n)--HE; A harp made by the Cliáth family and their associates. It is assumed that such an instrument is of the highest quality and will have the Cliáth emblem etched on its base. No one has been able to duplicate the quality of these craftsmen.

**dást** (däsht) (n)--SE; all, everything, every

**dedhá** (DĚ-jä) (n) (sng and pl)--SE; priest or monk; the term makes no distinction between the two. The shortened form came into use after the Teren came into the lands and adopted the Faith as their own.

**Dhágdhuán** (JÄ-zhū-än) (n)--HE; the Intercessor, considered to be the founder of the Faith because his death is said to make it possible for mortals to reach the divine,

**dhi** (jē) (prn) (pl: dhithé)--SE; You.

**Ethenae** (ě-THĚN-ā) (n)--HE/SE; the peaceful afterworld where the blessed and holy reside after death.

**gaeth** (gwāth) (prn)--HE/SE; he, him, himself

**gdhededhá** (zhě-DĚ-jä) (n) (sng and pl)--HE/SE; priest or faith teacher or disciple; the term makes no distinction between them.

**ghlaiph** (glīf) (v)--SE; sleep, rest, nap, sleeps, rests, naps

**ghytae** (gē-TĀ) (v)--SE; threaten

**ghytim** (gē-TĒM) (v)--SE; was threatened/threatening, were threatened/threatening

**hábhai** (HÄ-vī) (v)--HE; look, search

**haeles** (HĀ-lĕsh) (n) (sng and pl)--HE; friend, companion

**hes** (hĕsh) (n) (sng and pl)--HE; heart

**hwudhá** (HWŪ-jä) (n) (pl: hwudháthé)--SE; Translated in the Trade tongue as "kin" or relatives, this term in Elyri means anyone, male or female, on either side of the family, who is related to the speaker. It is sometimes used in religious context as indicative of the kinship between all people.

**ibh** (ēv) (v)--HE/SE; Is, are, am; its translation is dependent upon the rest of the sentence.

**it** (ēt) (prn)--HE/SE; this/that. The rest of the sentence implies its translation.

**k'Ádhá** (k Ä-jä) (n)--HE/SE; god; Ádhá-supreme deity in the Elyri monotheistic religion

**k'gdhededhá** (k zhĕ-DĔ-jä) (n) (sng and pl)--HE/SE; The Elyri designation for the male individual who is elected as the head of the Faith.

**kedhá** (KĔ-jä) (n) (pl: kedhathé)--SE; male child or children of the Kyne (High Mother), or prince in the Teren languages.

**kelém** (KĔ-lŭm) (v)--SE; pass, progress, proceed, go

**kelémim** (kĕ-lŭm-ĒM) (v)--SE; passed/went/proceeded, was passing/going/proceeding/going, were passing/going/proceeding/going,

**kíteni** (kĭ-TĔN-ē) (n) (pl: kítenithé)--SE; tradition, custom

**kyag** (KĒ-ä) (n) (pl: kyágthé)--HE; Beloved, dearest one.

**lís** (lĭsh) (prp)--SE; now, this time

**Llaethlágárá** (LĀTH-lä-gār-ä) (n)--HE; The mountains separating Elyriá from Neth and Enesfel.

**llánec** (LÄ-nyäk) (n)--HE; the occasional Elyri "ability" of being given insight into the future. Unlike other Elyri abilities, this one cannot be learned or controlled; an individual must be born with it. One who possesses it endures periodic "blackouts" as events are revealed to them but they cannot summon visions. Generally, the things they "see" are vague in nature, and rarely involve the seer. It is often translated into the Trade language as "the Sight." Literally translated as "bitter sight"

**mai** (MĪ) (n) (pl: maithé)—HE/SE; child; used in the Standard as a term of endearment

**mál** (mäl) (adj)--HE/SE; sacred, holy, blessed

**málneag** (mäl-NYÄ-ä) (n) (pl: málneagthé)--HE; it can mean one who possesses a quality of blessedness, sacredness, or holiness; its most common translation into the Trade languages is saint.

**naeth** (nāth) (v)--SE; find

**naethád** (nāth-ÄD) (v)--SE; will find, will be found

**nai** (nī)--HE/SE; No; denial.

**náós** (nä-ŌSH) (n) (sng and pl)--HE/SE; a place of worship, temple; also occasionally used to refer to the altar.

**nudhá** (NŪ-jä) (n) (pl: nudháthé)--SE; son

**nune** (NŪ-nyä) (n) (pl: nunethé)--SE; daughter

**osté** (ÄSH-tŭ) (prp)--SE; must

**phae k'kairá** (fä k KĪ-rä) (n) (sng and pl)--HE; The name given to the race of beings who inhabited the territory of the Five Sovereignties before the Elyri arrived. By the time the Elyri came, all that remained of the k'kairá (as they are sometimes called) were crumbling stone circles, mounds, huts, some of which bore written symbols upon them. Unlike most High Elyri words which end with the ah sound, this one does not end with the letter combination ag.

**phágk** (fäk) (prp)--HE; at

**Pháne** (FÄ-nyä) (n)--HE; An island in possession of Káliel. Its name is translated as tiny or small.

**Pheski** (FĔSH-kē) (n)--HE; The Binding, relating only to the betrothal ritual and the objects used therein.

**Pheslátkag** (fĕsh-LÄT-kä) (n)--HE; That which binds, relating only to the betrothal ritual and the objects used therein.

**phyl** (fēl) (adj)--HE; young, in comparison to the speaker

**raigháthá** (rī-GÄ-thä) (n)--SE; the Elyri ability to assume the shape of other creatures. Called shape changing in the Teren languages. Only about one-third of Elyri are capable of mastering this ability, any very few of those who do ever use it.

**redh** (rĕj) (n) (sng and pl)--HE grace, sometimes used as forgiveness in a religious sense

**sínréc** (shĭn-RŬK) (n) (sng and pl)--HE; This word has no direct translation. Blood kin with a special bond, is about the closest it can be described. Any blood kin can be sínréc, but saying "he is my cousin," is different from saying "he is my sínréc" (or "he is sínréc."). It is sometimes used for non-relatives who are extremely close.

**sun** (shūn) (prp)--HE/SE; to/from

**thae** (thā) (prp)--SE; by, according to, because of

**thenárá** (thĕn ārāh) (adv/v)--HE; please, I beseech you

**thóres** (THŌ-rĕsh) (n) (pl: thóresĕth)--SE; the room or rooms in a náós that serves as clergy offices and residences.

**tydhá** (TĒ-jä) (n) (pl: tydháthé)--SE: Male cousin or nephew.

**uhwlth** (ūwlth)(prep)--SE: now, immediately, at once. A command of urgency.

**záryph** (zä-RĒF) (n) (sng and pl)--HE/SE; winged beings connected to the realm of the holy; angels

**zíthrós** (ZĬ-thrōhsh) (n) (sng and pl)--HE; hypocrite

## Translations

| | |
|---|---|
| *ghytim kedhá Bertram.* | Bertram is threatened. |
| *naethád gaeth dhi osté. uhwlth.* | You must find him. Now. |
| | |
| *nudhá sun nudhá.* | Son to son. |
| *nune sun nune* | Daughter to daughter |
| *yho lís kelémim kíteni.* | The tradition passes until now. |
| | |
| *hwudhá ibh gaeth* | he (who) is my kin |
| | |
| *hwudhá ibh dhi* | you (who) are my kin. |

*aelibh aiándás, thae dást mál aihwelys aelá át, thae mál aighlaiph átaelás síuínthé aelá it aikáchá át bhair.*
    "On my honor, by every sacred belief I possess, by (the) holy rest of all my ancestors, I accept this bond.

| | |
|---|---|
| *thenárá phyl haeles* | Please, young friend. |
| | |
| *phágk áti hábhai, átaelás mai* | Look at me, my child. |

## Pronunciation of Elyri Names

**Aleski** (ăl-ĔSH-kē)
**Ártur** (är-TŪR)
**Bhendhámyn** (VĔN-jä-mēn)
**Bhílári** (vĭ-LÄR-ē)
**Bhíncári** (vĭn-CÄ-rē)
**Bhríd** (vrĭd)
**Bhryell** (bhrē-ĔL)
**Cáner** (KÄ-nyär)
**Cíbhóló** (kĭ-VŌ-lō)
**Clarys** (klār-ĒSH)
**Clebhest** (klĕ-VĔSHT)
**Cliáth** (klē-ÄTH)
**Derkun** (DĔR-kūn)
**Dhágdhuán** (JÄ-zhū-än)
**Dháná** (JÄ-nä)
**Dhórdh** (joorj)
**Dórímyr** (DŌR-ĭ-mēr)
**Elyri** (ĕ-LĒR-ē)
**Elyriá** (ĕ-LĒR-ē-ä)
**Káliel** (kä-LĔ-ĕl)
**Kármár** (KÄR-mahr)
**Kavan** (KĂ-văn) (in Elyri his name is spelled Kabhan)
**Kílyn** (kĭ-LĒN)
**Kóráhm di Curnydhá** (KŌR-äm DĒ kūr-NĒ-jä)
**Lísbhet** (lĭsh-VĔT)
**MacLyr** (mäk-LĒR)
**Mátán** (mä-TÄN)
**Mílne** (MĬL-nyä)
**Mórne** (MŌR-nyä)
**Phaedr** (FĀ-dŭr)
**Rístyrd-**(rĭsh-TĒRD)
**Sámel** (SHÄ-mĕl)
**Syl** (shēl)
**Tám** (täm)
**Térari** (tĕ-RĀR-ē)
**Tíbhyan** (TĬ-vē-ăn)

**Tusánt** (tū-SHÄNT)

## The Five Sovereignties - City Legend

| Enesfel | Cordash | Elyriá |
|---------|---------|--------|
| 1-*Rhidam | 1-*Aralt | 1-Clarys |
| 2-Alberni | 2-Anzet | 2-Ánásair |
| 3-Bryn | 3-Ediug | 3-Bhastyán |
| 4-Chantel | 4-Eleva | 4-Bhórdh |
| 5-Dorshur | 5-Jassett | 5-Bhryell |
| 6-Durham | 6-Kakkoris | 6-Cármycá |
| 7-Erleta | 7-Korr | 7-Cylleá |
| 8-Jardin | 8-Liatti | 8-Dhánthes |
| 9-Kamin | 9-Lindumn | 9-Ibhórys |
| 10-Kilmacud | 10-Matina | 10-Káská |
| 11-Levonne | 11-Pesek | 11-Khwíncanon |
| 12-Nelori | 12-Sebring | 12-Rísóri |
| 13-Seres | 13-Trallan | 13-Sábhóne |
| 14-Talladegah | 14-Verbier | 14-Sídhári |
| 15-Tarsee | 15-Vioe | 15-Turyn |
| 16-Theron | 16-Vron | |
| 17-Wexel | 17-Wynett | |

| Hatu | Neth | Káliel |
|------|------|--------|
| 1-*Natrona | 1-*Glevum | 1-*Káliel |
| 2-Avarrou | 2-Fiara | 2-Jaffe |
| 3-Cran Ufa | 3-Gorea | 3-Mara Qin |
| 4-Drisoge | 4-Mawr | 4-Pháne |
| 5-Enda | 5-Nogero | 5-Shola |
| 6-Fa Ruqi | 6-Pravek | |
| 7-Furr Katio | 7-Ruidoso | |
| 8-Kílyn | 8-Venago | |
| 9-Palil | | |
| 10-Wasilla | | |
| 11-Yd Haszafni | | |

## The Five Sovereignties

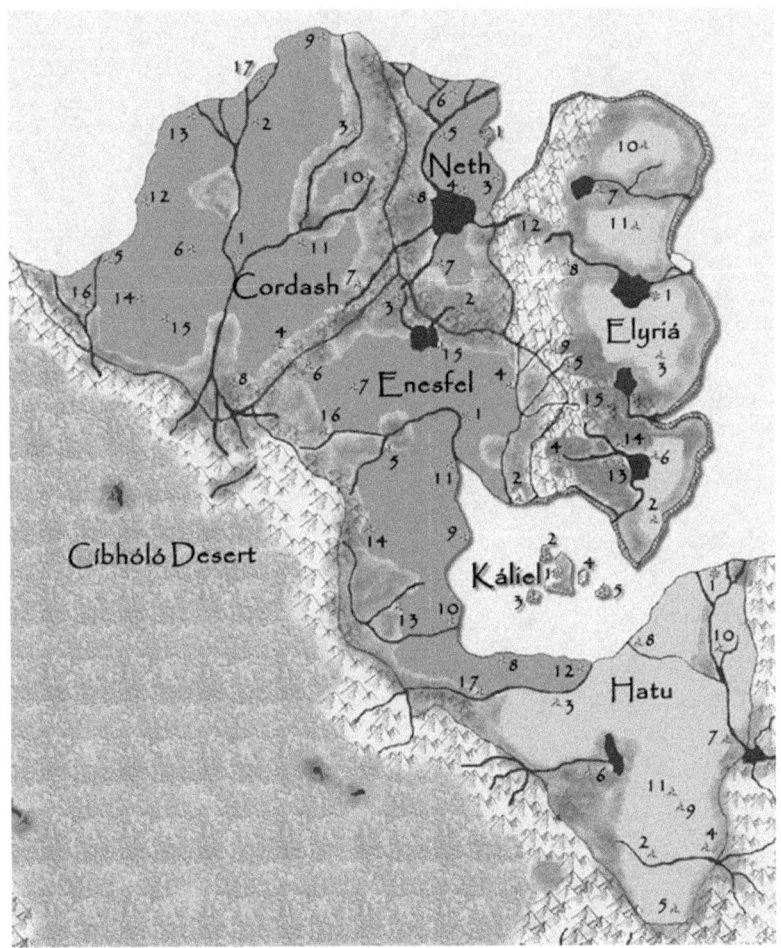

## About the Author

Unsatisfied with 'how the story ends' as a young reader, Tamara took on the challenge of crafting endings to the tales of others to better suit her vision of the world. That desire to mold reality into how she imagined it should be gave birth to a life-long fascination with the written word, and its capacity, particularly through realms of fantasy and science fiction, to foster an understanding of the people, events, thoughts and emotions that make us who we are.

A long-time resident of Clearlake, California, after a life that took her back and forth across the country, Tamara is owned by a pack of papillions, a pride of cats, and an eclectic arsenal of films she enjoys in her off-moments.

# White Penitent
## Kestrel Harper Saga Book 3
(excerpt)

K avan felt consciousness approaching, realizing as he woke
that Madalyn must be home. It must have been her presence
he sensed in the room as he had grown familiar with Gaelán's
company over the last several days and he knew it was not Gaelán with
him. He felt hot, stiff, and his hands throbbed painfully. Without
opening his eyes, he sighed. "You do not need to linger. There is
nothing you can do for me."

"You are sure of that, átaelás mai?"

"Kóráhm!" He jerked up; the pain of the effort made him dizzy
and nauseous. Scarred hands steadied him, taking away some of that
dizziness and nausea, though it did not affect the pain in his body.
Their eyes met briefly but Kavan looked away, humiliated.

"Were you expecting someone else?"

"Anyone else. It has been so long since you have…and after what
I have done…"

"What have you done?"

He shuddered and closed his eyes. "You know."

"Perhaps I do not." The quite real form of Saint Kóráhm the
Heretic settled into the chair at his bedside, pushing his hood from his
face. "Unless you are reading my thoughts, you do not know what I
know or do not know. But if you will not speak freely with me, I shall
not pursue it. It is up to you to trust me or not. I do have a question to
put to you, however, that you must answer before we proceed with any
discussion. Why have you refused Gaelán's offer to heal your hands?"

"He cannot do it. He is not a trained healer."

The auburn head of hair bobbed once. "He is not…but he has
healed the rest of your injuries…though not completely I admit. I see

no reason he could not have tended your hands to offer you mobility. Even so, he could have summoned Ártur to aid you."

"This," Kavan held his twisted hands before Kóráhm, choking at the sight, "is my punishment. No healer can undo what k'Ádhá has done…"

"k'Ádhá? Did you see k'Ádhá amongst the men who beat you? Did you specifically see him crush your hands?"

Kavan grunted. "He allowed it."

Kóráhm narrowed his gaze. "k'Ádhá has given us freedom of choice to do what we will, and then stepped away from his creation to allow it to function alone, to find its way to the path back to him. Some events may be predestined…experience tells us this, and he knows what the outcome will be of a man's choices, but he does not dictate every moment of our existence. He allows many events, most of which he has no specific hand in. He allowed those men to attack you, but he did not make them do it; it was their choice, not his."

"It is my punishment," Kavan said, his conviction intact. "I want to be healed, to play my harp, but it will only come when I have atoned for my sins."

The saint rose, shaking his head with regret. "You think you are privy to the mind of k'Ádhá, phyl haeles. That is a dangerous path to tread, and one many do not come back from. If you truly wish absolution, you must first know what your sins are before they can be forgiven. Only then, since you have chosen this path of misery and self-destruction, will your hands be restored to their former beauty and skill."

Not understanding what the saint meant by self-destruction, not believing he had chosen any of this, Kavan cried, "But I have confessed, milord! You know I have! I became needlessly drunk. I tried to bed a whore. I have admitted this…and that I was wrong…"

"Then there must be something more damning to which you have not confessed."

"More damn…" Tears sprung to his eyes. "I am not a man. Is that a sin?"

"Not a…Kavan…kyag…" Kóráhm knelt by the bedside and touched the bard's face lovingly. "You are as much a man as I was at your age. You have considerably more willpower and self-control than I did; perhaps you are more of a man. If it had been me," his hand dropped and he stood, "I would have bedded the whore. And likely the princess too."

"You…?" Kavan was visibly shocked.

Kóráhm's expression grew sorrowful at the betrayal he read in Kavan's eyes. "You have much to learn about life, kyag, but you are, in many ways, a better man than I ever was. In this, there is nothing more I can do for you. I leave you with one final instruction." He laid his hand over Kavan's eyes, closing them as he spoke. "When it is time," he whispered, "go where she leads you; do as she instructs. Trust her as you once trusted me."

There was a quick discharge of static in that touch, and though the sensation of the hand over his eyes lingered, Kavan knew Kóráhm was gone. The man's words tore Kavan apart inside. Kóráhm was a saint, after all. How could he have been anything less than the saint he had been dubbed? But Kóráhm had been mortal once, and it was possible, with much information about his life missing, that he had been the same in some ways as any other man. Kavan's sense of betrayal had caused Kóráhm to depart. Even the Saint had abandoned him. He was certain of it. His sins had taken his hands, his music, and had driven Kóráhm away. Kavan wept again, hoping to convince himself that Kóráhm would return, that surely Kóráhm had been a much greater man in every way than Kavan would ever be.